The

HUNTED

ALSO BY L.A. BANKS

Minion
The Awakening

The HUNTED

A VAMPIRE HUNTRESS LEGEND

L.A. BANKS

 ST. MARTIN'S GRIFFIN ❦ NEW YORK

www.stmartins.com

Library of Congress Cataloging-in-Publication Data

Banks, L.A.
    The hunted : a vampire huntress legend / by L.A. Banks.—1st U.S. ed.
        p. cm.
    ISBN 0-312-32030-2
    EAN 978-0312-32030-0
    1. Richards, Damali (Fictitious character)—Fiction. 2. Women in the performing arts—Fiction. 3. African American women—Fiction. 4. Women martial artists—Fiction. 5. Vampires—Fiction. 6. Brazil—Fiction. I. Title.

PS3602.A64H86 2004
813'.6—dc22   2003069723

10 9 8 7 6 5

DEDICATION AND *SPECIAL* ACKNOWLEDGMENTS

THIS BOOK is dedicated to my support system, those individuals who have always had my back and helped me through the exciting process of writing an ongoing saga. Everyone, even my series heroine (the Neteru), needs a squad, backup, and in that regard I'm truly blessed. Those who have helped me (in both seen and unseen methods) are many . . . and they are loving, patient, and bring boundless encouragement in ways too numerous to list. So, this book and this series are dedicated to my husband and children, my sisters and parents, my sister-authors, and the many book clubs and readers groups that keep me so thoroughly engaged in developing the next installment.

Special acknowledgments go to "the engine" of people who are also dear friends who consistently fuel me: my agent, Manie Barron, who created the opportunity—THANK YOU; my editor, Monique Patterson, who is a visionary, a pure joy to work with, and a consummate professional whom I consider a true friend; Monica Peters of GritsNCheese, who is tireless in her publicizing and diligent promotion of this body of work; Penny Makras, who always hits the mark and is a ray of sunshine; Harriet Seltzer, for her invaluable help in setting up venues for our Huntress; Christopher Bonelli, my webmaster of unparalleled talent; Vince Natale, the cover artist for this series— Vince, your images blow my mind and are awesome!; Michael Storrings, whose cover designs are brilliant; my alumni brother and homeboy, Ray Jones, who makes sure my science is tight and my head is right for each incarnation of Carlos and Damali—*bless you*; Sean, Kelly, and Angela of ArtNoir for their fabulous launches; Professors Tukufu Zuberi and Guthrie Ramsey, for their solid friendship, encouragement, and belief in my work; Lorene Cary, my sister-author friend who makes me stretch and grow and step out on faith; Jeff Hart from my Art Sanctuary family, who uplifts my spirit with his constant support; Rick White, my brother-friend and earth angel of inspiration; Dr. Erle Leichty at the University of Pennsylvania Museum of Archeology and Anthropology, for his assistance with ancient languages; William Hanson, another alumni brother and architect extraordinaire, for his brilliant research help; Isabelle Smith, who goes all the way back; Derrick Ward of RBG, for spittin' the sick beats; and the supportive authors who generously agreed to read my work and offer positive blurbs . . . thank you all!

$\mathcal{P}$ROLOGUE

On the outskirts of Rio de Janeiro, Brazil. Present day

THE AMERICAN embassy official turned away from the grisly sight, bent over, dry heaved twice, then lost his lunch. Two American CIA investigators posing as embassy military police mopped their brows in the dense humidity, the smell of old, rotting flesh and new vomit making their skin go pale. The stench was so thick that it practically blurred the vision of those assembled. The befouled air could almost be seen rising on translucent waves of heat. The villagers kept their distance, and even the Brazilian police were slow to move too close to the carnage.

Four bodies lay in a mangled heap. Three men, one woman—their throats and limbs missing, their abdominal cavities gutted, with huge hunks of torn flesh—were scattered across the ground. Within the heat-liquefied slurry, there was a mass of flies buzzing, larva writhing, and beetles skittering for cover in the three-day-old flesh. Disturbed buzzards waited their turn to feast again from their patient posts in the trees. Twenty local farmers that had found the dead shook their heads and made the sign of the cross over their chests, while murmuring, *"Cuidado, por favor! Diablo—Exu."* The crowd was growing behind the police barricade.

"This wasn't the damn Devil," a CIA operative muttered. "Although I can see the locals' point. These folks definitely died a helluva awful death."

The embassy official only nodded, still trying to regain his composure.

Investigators stared at the khaki safari clothing torn away at the chest down to the abdomen on each body, making the fabric dark, muddy brown, and stiff. Removed entrails torn from the gaping abdominal cavities had been snatched away so brutally that bits of splintered ribs littered the ground next to each victim. Dead hands paralyzed with rigor mortis still clasped hunting knives, while cameras and other equipment scattered the area. Mouths were still frozen open in silent screams, gums and tongues picked away by wretched scavenger beaks. Only one skull still had eyes left in it, which were open and glassy and stared at the sepia-stained earth.

"The buzzards missed one," the other CIA man said and then glanced away toward the trees. His pale face had gone ashen even under the blaring sun, and his blond hair was matted and stained dark by sweat not generated from the heat but pure fear. He tried to summon calm as he straightened his red-and-blue rep tie, and loosened his white button-down Oxford shirt at the collar, opening the top button, then wiped his hands on the pockets of his navy blue suit. "Rebels sure have a helluva way to make a point to mark off drug territories."

"This was not rebels," the coroner finally said with conviction. "This is not an international incident. Don't make it one, either."

Slowly pushing himself up from his stooped position, the American embassy official nodded, blotting his mouth with a handkerchief then with his forearm. "I know," he said, trying not to breathe too deeply. The air smelled like blood and rotting flesh. His eyes watered from the stench.

The two CIA men stood there in navy suits and white shirts, their grim expressions partially masked behind dark aviator sunglasses. They looked almost identical, save one had brown hair, one was blond, but their just-the-facts façade was blown by the way their once-crisp white shirts clung to their bodies, sweat staining them, making them limp. Heat wasn't the only culprit. Their silent fear was palpable. All the officials and authorities present shared the same quiet terror with the locals.

"Looks like our National Geographic science team was attacked by some kind of animal. No slicing with a knife could have dismembered these bodies like this. All their expensive equipment and cameras are still here," one of the CIA men said after a moment. He raked his fingers through his perspiration-soaked brown hair. "Even the local boys didn't disturb the site by moving in to fleece the bodies of valuables, which would have made for more paperwork. So we can at least thank superstition." He walked around the remains, glancing at the carcasses. "No shell casings, there wasn't even time for them to defend themselves."

"Then, Señor, make sure that this is what is said in your media. This was no crime—just an unfortunate animal attack." The Brazilian police captain wiped at the trickle of sweat running from his temple with his forearm.

"Problem is, there's hardly anything left to ship home," the other CIA man said, shaking his head at the remains. "That *will* make the news. If we don't tell it, one of the family members will."

"As long as it doesn't put a negative slant on our country," the Brazilian police captain said anxiously. "Tourism is down and only coming back very slowly, Señor, especially with the Americanos. Tourism is big—"

"This was a freak situation," the embassy official assured the nervous officer, while ignoring the terror-stricken expressions on the villagers' faces. "The incidents in the regions of Belem, Manaus, Para, Salvador, and Maranhao were all locals who were deep in the jungle where most of our wildlife live and tourists generally don't go there. The fact that this American team was attacked in the hillside areas near Rio de Janeiro—"

"Should not be made into an international incident. Yeah, we got it," the senior CIA official said impatiently. "Bag the bodies, inform the families, and we'll handle the media. Case closed."

Los Angeles, California

Detective Berkfield studied the Internet report with care as he slowly sipped his morning coffee and stared at his laptop. Nothing had even hit the US news. Weird. He could smell a coverup a mile away, and had it not been for his relentless search into obscure news for all things strange, he might have missed it. Ever since his encounter with Carlos Rivera, every bit of information he'd gleaned from Rivera's tips had sent him to search those regions for anything out of the ordinary, particularly bizarre murders, accidents, and deaths.

His gaze darted nervously around the slightly modern suburban kitchen, wondering if it was time to have a priest come in and bless his house. Somehow the gun he wore just didn't seem to bring much comfort, especially not when reading this type of news. It reminded him too much of what he'd seen in an alley not too long ago, and he thought that was all behind him. The world was going from bad to worse. He was still having nightmares, and this crap didn't make him feel any closer to making them stop.

"Do you believe this shit . . ." he whispered in the vacant kitchen and read the tiny, almost insignificant article again. "Happened over a week ago, and we're just hearing about it?" His mind wrestled with what could have kept something like this hidden in the middle columns of the papers, out of the headlines of the Brazilian press, and away from major news sources in the States. There was only one plausible answer; it had to be much more than what was reported, if someone had gone to such lengths to bury a story.

The hairs on the back of his neck stood up. He'd seen shit similar to this before, right in his own backyard. Kids with their throats ripped out and chests torn open, bodies mysteriously disappearing from the morgue . . . The article said mutilated. What did that mean? It was what the paper didn't say that disturbed him. He'd seen plenty of madness that he still couldn't explain to a soul, much less himself. Question was, where was one Carlos Rivera?

Maybe he'd have to go ask the only person that might know—an always very hard to locate Damali Richards.

You've got a piece of my soul buried within you.
Why you gotta take us both through pure hell?
—Damali Richards, "Piece of my Soul"

CHAPTER ONE

Los Angeles, California. Present day

VAMPIRES HAD a vibe, and right now it was thick. She could feel them on her skin, making her flesh crawl beneath it. Oh, yeah. Tonight it was on! Damali glanced around the club, all her extrasensory instincts humming. The electric blues, fluorescent greens, and flaming orange stabbed into her brain as the insistent reggae tempo seeped into her blood and created a second pulse within her. She could feel the rhythm of her walk becoming smoother, longer in stride as the music filled her up. It beat inside her, mingling with the grief and rage that had been her companions for the past month.

Lingering cigarette and spliff smoke burned her eyes. The stifling, club-sweat heat of bodies dancing, pressing, grinding, nearly smothered her as she shoved her way through the crowd to get close to the bar. Screw what Marlene and the guardian team had to say about her venturing out alone at night. She was a full-blown Neteru now—a vampire huntress . . . and the vamp empire had killed her man. A Corona was in order . . . no, perhaps a Red Stripe beer. Fuck it. Make it Jack Daniels.

"Whatchu having, pretty sis?"

How about every vampire's head on a silver platter? she wanted to say. Ever since that cop, Berkfield, had rolled up on her earlier today asking about Carlos, grilling her about his Jamaican territory, and wanting to know where he was, she'd seen red. She'd clean out every lower-level vamp left in Nuit's old vamp zones while the cops chased drug dealers till the end of time. That's all she had left to cling to—revenge, the old-fashioned way . . . just like Carlos would have done for her, if the shoe was on the other foot.

The bartender leaned in and smiled. "Having trouble making up your mind? I'm not g'wan card you, baby. Dis your first time out?"

The comment grated her. Yeah, she'd cut out his heart, too. Then she checked herself. Okay, so the bartender wasn't a vamp, but the hair was standing up on her arms.

"A Red Stripe," she told him instead of ordering a Jack. When in Rome . . . and it wasn't about getting totaled if she was gonna kick some serious ass.

The bartender nodded and turned away to fill her order, but the sideline glance he'd cast to the other end of the bar forced Damali's gaze to follow.

Bingo.

The moment her eyes locked with the dark stranger's seated twenty-five feet away, Damali opened herself up and her internal radar kicked up a notch. Yeah. Vamps were in da house. Cool.

She accepted the beer, declined a glass, paid for her drink, and took a healthy swig from the bottle. She allowed her peripheral vision to scope out a potential rush. She could now sense at least four of them, and knew they could smell her. Good.

Damali watched the condensation trickle down the side of the cold bottle in her hand as she waited for the approach that she knew was imminent. A fucking pretender to the throne . . . She hated lower, third-generation vamps—always trying to push up on a sister. But that was all there was left to battle. The vamp empire had wiped out all rebel second-generations, and what the civil war didn't claim, she had dusted or they'd gone into deep hiding. Weak bastards.

"Lovely lady, what brings you out on a night like this . . . to a place like this?"

She didn't turn around as the smooth island lilt penetrated her ear and stroked it with sensual precision. She glanced down to where the dark stranger had been sitting and sighed at the empty seat, knowing that he was behind her and just inches from her jugular. Damali sipped her beer.

"Was looking for some action. Got bored home alone," she said in a weary tone, then casually took another swig of her beer. "There are no more masters of the game left in LA, or didn't you hear?"

The stranger laughed, slow and easy, just like the music.

She finally turned to look him up and down. She smiled. Brother was fine. Shame. Long, black, shoulder-length locks, height judged to be about six two, *built*, nice chest, perfect abs, the color of semi-sweet chocolate beneath an opened, burnt-gold silk shirt and black leather pants . . . flawless complexion, dark, lazy eyes—and *very* white teeth.

She took another swig. Such a waste, and she'd have to dust his ass. But at least some mother's child would go home safely tonight.

For a moment, they simply stared at each other. His smile was one of challenge, hers of warning.

"So, you came out looking for something different, tonight— something unusual?"

"Yeah," she snapped, growing annoyed that he was playing with her.

She could feel his hot gaze rove over her as it caressed her throat, fondled her bare breasts beneath her black belly shirt, then licked at her exposed navel, and began to trail down to that precious place beneath her boot-cut black jeans. Her muscles tensed at the psychic violation, and the Isis dagger stashed in her right boot began to feel warm against her calf.

"Chill," she said, her tone attitudinal enough to brush off the vampiric invasion. "You don't know me like that, yet."

"My bad," he crooned. "But the operative word is *yet*."

"Can a sister at least finish her brew?" Damali let her breath out with impatience. "Or you could buy her a drink—since you gettin' all familiar."

"Name your poison," he murmured, stepping closer to her than advisable.

"Blood."

He stared at her for a moment, and then a slow smile spread across his face, giving her a glint of fang. She shook her head. The lower generations were so much less cool than the seconds or masters. In a public fucking club, this bastard wanted her so bad he was giving her fang? Pullease.

"Carlos made you? Before his unfortunate—"

"We were close," she said, the venom in her voice cutting off his statement. "He and I went to Hell and back together. Shit happens. Let's leave it at that." She didn't even want to think about it.

The dark stranger rubbed his palm over his chin and glanced at his four henchmen in the crowd. "Damn . . . I thought for sure I was sensing Neteru. And, if so, then Carlos is the only one who could have turned her."

Damali followed his gaze, monitoring the reactions of the vamps with him. Good, she was talking to their leader, which meant his backup was a generation below him. Four brothers, each a serious specimen of Jamaican male in a delicious range of hues from cinnamon to ebony, serving silk and leather, muscle shirts and kid glove–supple pants, skin and sculpted fineness, brilliant smiles set in fine faces, all nodded at her.

"We are what we are," she finally said, her tone now becoming amused. "Can't take everything from a girl in one night."

The leader nodded, stepped closer, and ran a thumb over her jugular. "Sorry to hear 'bout what happened to your man . . . but, as they say, it's all good. You're still here, got to live your life now. Right?"

"Yeah," she repeated, her tone once again icy. "It's all good." Damali set down her beer hard on the bar. "Can't sleep during the day anymore, though. You feel me?"

"I feel you . . ." he murmured, low and sexy. "Wanna get out of here?"

"Yeah," she said. "And bring your friends. Miss Rivera already." She let the truth dangle as bait, knowing they'd sense authenticity in what she'd said. But the truth cut her to the bone.

He hesitated, stared at her, confused, and then chuckled. "That's five of us, you know."

Damali cocked her head to the side and smiled. "And?"

"Damn, sis . . . aw'ight. That's cool."

"I was made by a master. What did you expect?"

The vampire before her shook his head. "I'd heard about master-made second-level females, but I confess I didn't know it was like that."

"Follow me. Watch and learn . . . since this is your first time with a sister like me." She didn't even wait for his response as she strode through the crowd toward the off-limits section at the back of the club, elbowing people out of her way.

She could feel the five eager vamps behind her, knew they were intrigued and off-guard. Half of her questioned her own judgment; the other half of her just wanted to get it on. What was there to live for, really? If she went down, she'd go out swinging. If she lived, so be it. Either way, all these potential victims in the house got another night of reprieve.

As she passed club-goers, she glanced at the silver crosses some of them wore, and other religious objects embedded in their jewelry, disheartened by the fact that none of it would ward off an attack if the wearer of the object didn't believe. Most didn't.

The narrow hallway she'd entered that led to the back alley made her claustrophobic. It was too reminiscent of the corridors of Hell she and Carlos had battled in together. Everything reminded her of him, especially the thick, palpable desire emanating from the vampires that followed her in the dark.

She threw her weight against the heavy, metal door and was greeted by fresh air. The evening was unseasonably cool, and she welcomed the rush of breeze against her face. She closed her eyes and leaned her head back for a moment, preparing for the inevitable. A pair of chilly hands rested on her shoulders. Icy breath filled her ear.

"You have any preference about which one of us goes first?" a deep male voice intoned.

"No. Do you?" she murmured, shrugging out of his hold and bending over so she could reach the pant leg zipper, concealing her stashed dagger.

"Damn," one of the henchmen whispered. "I don't care, man. Just as long as I'm in the lineup."

"Good," she said, chuckling as she glanced up at the four weaker vamps hanging back in the shadows. A hard erection poked at her behind in a sultry grind. Hands were on her hips now, caressing them, stroking her backside, and making the beaded triangle sarong that was tied against them shake. "I'm not choosy about which one of you goes first, either."

"Pull down your jeans, baby. We'll work it out."

"Okay. But first lemme show you what *I'm* working with," she said with a dangerous half smile, peering up at him over her shoulder.

In one deft move, she unzipped her pant leg, snatched her dagger, spun, and plunged it into the chest of the vampire that had been on her ass. His eyes opened almost as wide as his mouth. His fangs exploded from his gums and he made a choking, gasping sound as he tried to speak. His face was still frozen in shock as his skin turned to ash and crumbled away to red glowing bones, which then disintegrated.

"Oh, shit! A fucking black widow!"

Damali wiped her blade on her thigh, ignoring the comment as the four remaining vamps took battle stances. Adrenaline shot through her as she watched their size bulk up, their once deep brown eyes turn fiery red, and their sensual smiles gave way to full-fanged snarls.

"Only two inches of fang, gentlemen? Rivera gave a girl six to eight, when provoked. Is this the best you can do?" She shook her head and studied her fingernails. "Guess there really is a difference between masters and wannabe lower levels. Size does really matter after all."

She sensed them go airborne before she'd even looked up, and quickly dodged the first one's grasp as the others came down in a circle around her. She moved counterclockwise to their movements, their snarls and growls making them sound like rabid pit bulls. Her senses heightened, she waited for them to attack again.

The one behind her was the first to strike—and was the first to get his throat slashed as she spun and kick boxed a second one away from her. As soon as the second fell back, another was on her, only to find her Isis blade deeply imbedded in his chest. Another pile of ash crumbled at her feet, and she sidestepped the burning, putrid heap, assessing the placement of the last two vamps in the alley.

They stared at her then glanced at each other.

"Later, bitch!" one of them said.

"Bring it now, punk," she spat back.

"Later," the other repeated.

Then they were gone.

"Can't even get a good whup-ass on out here!" she screamed into the nothingness.

Pure frustration claimed her. Two of them had gotten away. "Damn!"

Club music and street traffic filtered into the dark alley. Damali kicked the Dumpsters as she passed them, hoping the vamps might have changed their minds and been lying in wait for her, or at least might have gone somewhere to bring back a fresh crew for her to mix it up with. What was wrong in the world? Couldn't even get a good beat-down these days. Her hands were shaking, not from fear but from total rage. Anything left from Nuit's line had her name on it— tattooed to its skull like a bull's-eye. That was the least she could do. She felt hot moisture rise in her eyes, and she blinked it away. Fuck it. Whatever. If this was her life, so be it.

A sudden motion made her go still. She watched a male form approach her from the shadows, coming from the direction of the street just beyond the alley. She listened to its footfalls and clenched her dagger in her fist more tightly. Heavy. Too heavy. She sniffed the air. Sweat. It was human. She relaxed.

"Can't get a good alley fight on? Is that what I heard you yelling, young lady?"

Detective Berkfield shook his head as he stepped closer to Damali, holding up his shield, his expression of confusion now clearly visible under the dim alley lights.

"What the hell is a female rap star doing out, alone, at night, with no security, in the freakin' Jamaican badlands?" He glanced at her hand. "Clearly looking for a fight."

"I'm a hip hop, spoken-word artist—not a rap star. And for your information, my songs are neo-soul."

"Whatever," the detective said, pocketing his badge. "If you're looking for trouble, this is a place to find it. What's the deal? What're you doin' in an alley by yourself, hon?"

Damali looked at the pudgy, balding white man in the rumpled raincoat. He was still huffing just from the mere exertion of walking fast. She let her breath out hard and bent to sheath her blade in her boot.

"An expensive, flashy entourage ain't my style, and I only came out here for some air," she grumbled. "Some punks thought because I'm a fairly successful hip hop artist, I was soft, okay? What's it to you? They're gone and I didn't stab anybody. I was protecting myself and wouldn't recognize them again if I saw 'em."

She stood and folded her arms over her chest, defying him with her glare.

Berkfield nodded. "Okay, okay. But, lemme ask you this. Why is it that after *you've* been somewhere, there's always these mysterious piles of ash left in a goddamned alley, huh? What is it with you and Rivera?" He glanced at the ashy heaps and then stared at her harder.

"You really don't want to know. Trust me."

"Try me." He held her gaze, thinking about the last contact Carlos had made with him—an envelope with all the Jamaican territory laid out . . . this club listed as a source of trouble. And there was something in her eyes, the unsaid, that made him realize she had to know that Rivera wasn't the average Joe, Carlos's drug-dealing history notwithstanding.

Locked in a standoff, for a moment all he could do was stare at her.

This kid was so wrong when she'd just said that he wouldn't want to know. It had been the very question that had kept him up at night for months. Yet he didn't want to sound crazy, even to himself, by broaching the subject. He couldn't explain any of what he'd witnessed to another living soul. The unfathomable possibility of what Carlos might be had forever changed his life, his perspective, and it was now possibly threatening his sanity. He'd almost been able to chalk it up to the trauma of being double-crossed by a trusted partner and nearly shot in the process. That had somehow been a comforting rationalization—until the Brazil thing had gone down. The carnage there just reminded him too much of the unsolved cases that would always haunt him.

The detective searched the young woman's face with his eyes. He had to know if he'd seen what he'd seen in that alley in LA . . . had to know if there was something else on this planet that wasn't human.

Berkfield practically held his breath as he continued to eye the angry young woman before him. If she were somehow Carlos's woman, Rivera wouldn't have been able to stay away from her. Every instinct in him as a cop and a man told him that much. *That's* what he trusted.

"Look," Berkfield finally said more gently. "I'm not after him for something he did . . . I'm just trying to get a bead on something that went down. It struck me as odd. That's all I can say about it now, but when me and Rivera met in an alley, one time a while back, I saw some things . . . some shit I still can't totally comprehend. He saved my ass that night and—"

"If he saved your ass, you'd have to ask him," she said coolly.

"That's why I came looking for you—to find him," the detective said. There was no anger in his voice, just the urgent need to know. He could see her studying him, deciding, but every instinct he had as a cop told him she knew—had seen it—just like he had. *"I don't care about the Jamaican territory,"* he said quickly, coming in close to her and holding her by both arms.

She appraised his hold with cool disdain, but didn't move. All she did was look at his hands and then narrow her gaze at him. "Then why did you ask me about it, huh? Why'd you roll up on me in the street while I was out grabbing some lunch and start poking around in the subject? Now you're sweatin' me, following me and shit? You keep talking about the Jamai—"

"That was the last contact we had with him," Berkfield said, his tone becoming more panicked as he watched her mentally retreat. But what the hell was he doing, telling an unknown risk about his info source—giving up his inside man like that? He either needed more stress counseling, or it was too late and he'd already lost his mind.

"Berkfield, I'm warning you. There are some things in life you just don't wanna know."

He quickly dropped his hands away from the young woman before him, now becoming terror-stricken as he stepped back. That's *exactly* what Rivera had told him. What if she was one of those things like Rivera? He was alone in an alley with no backup. The reality sent a chill down his spine.

Berkfield crossed himself as she simply stared at him. "All I want to do is ask him a personal question so I can sleep at night." His request came out as a plea. Heaven help him if he'd stumbled upon a female monster.

"Too late," Damali said softly, looking off into the distance.

"And why's that?" His voice caught in his throat as he glanced around. The darkness was now suffocating him, and he nearly pulled his gun on her, then remembered what Rivera had done to his partner—sent the bullet right back through the man's chest.

She didn't even look at the detective as she began walking away. "Because Carlos Rivera is dead."

CHAPTER TWO

DAMALI RESTED her forehead on the steering wheel of her black Hummer. Berkfield's questions, the constant monitoring from the team, and now she was being followed to clubs? It was bad enough that Berkfield had rolled up on her in the streets, and had opened a horrible wound, a gash that wouldn't close—then poured Drano in it. But the look in the man's eyes was the last straw. He was afraid of her.

She could feel moisture build beneath her shut lids, and she sniffed hard, tasting salty tears. Damn, damn, damn! It was not supposed to go down like this. Carlos had saved a cop. *A cop.* Had saved her entire team, *and her.* Not to mention, however many people by dusting Nuit. The man had even saved her from a lecherous old bastard back when she had been in foster care . . . he'd done so much good; why wouldn't the light give a brother a break? It just wasn't right.

Damali pushed herself off the steering wheel and turned the key in the ignition. She reached for the radio and put on the loudest music she could find, 50 Cent worked, and she pulled away from the curb. Motion. She needed motion. She had to keep moving. What was done was done. Big Mike had told her about some of his experiences in 'Nam . . . that sometimes the good died young and that it always hurt when it was one of yours. Truth.

She wasn't really paying attention to where she was going; she was just driving. It wasn't about going back to the compound, back to the state pen. That's the last thing she wanted to do and the last place she wanted to be—where there were eyes.

Eyes.

She was constantly dealing with eyes. Had to deal with eyes that held pity and worry and a hint of fear for her state of mind. Eyes were everywhere. People stared at her onstage, prying when she went certain places. Eyes wanted things from her, a little siphon of fame.

Cop eyes had just stared at her like she was one of the monsters. Terror-filled eyes that didn't know shit about who she was. Eyes that had judged her. If Berkfield only knew. He was probably standing in the safest spot on the planet—right next to a fully matured Neteru. A fucking huntress! Eyes of the teammates *watched* for signs of weakness, signs that she might break down. Eyes had kept careful watch to be sure she didn't go to Carlos when he needed her . . . Carlos who had the most intense, wonderful, deep brown eyes before the vampires had turned him . . . but even after he had been turned they had been awesome. She would never forgive the vamps for taking him from her. She wanted blood.

Swallowing hard, Damali wiped angrily at the building moisture in her eyes. She needed someone who knew her before she became what she was—a rising star, the huntress, the savior of the freakin' world! She needed friendly eyes. Laughing eyes. Tender eyes. Nonjudgmental eyes. Marlene's eyes always saw too much. She needed girlfriend eyes. Eyes that didn't see monsters around every corner.

A bitter sob threatened to break though she held it tightly in check.

Damali jerked her wheel swiftly to the left and stepped on the gas, veering away from the beach. She had to get out of there, get away from the old 'hood. What had she been thinking to come there? It was like walking over a grave.

She blew through the red light. She couldn't stop, sit, wait. She'd done that all her life, and for what? The road was blurry anyway. Apartment buildings and houses all melted together as the tears began to form and threatened to slip down her cheeks. She would *not* cry. Never again. She'd done that all the way home from the *Raise the Dead* concert. Had done that for a month in her room alone. Tears did not bring back the dead, neither did prayers.

Finally sitting quietly at a curb, she allowed the bone-jarring music to stamp out all thoughts. She let the heavy bass line become her pulse. Right now she was so numb it was like the only one she had. Breathing deeply, she calmed her too-fast heartbeat. What was death like, she wondered. Had to be better than this. Yeah, being a Neteru was no way to live.

Then she laughed. It was a hollow, brittle, sad sound that bounced off the walls inside the vehicle, bonding with the music. She should have let Carlos just fucking bite her. The light didn't have shit to fight with, compared to the forces of darkness.

What did she have? A blade. A rag-tag team of old warriors and a few priests. All she was really was a sistah who hadn't even had a chance to fully live. This was their squad? Pitiful. The light needed to take a walk down to Hell with her next time and really see what was in the dark, then maybe they'd send in some serious reinforcement—Special Forces, not some crazy Neteru. This was bullshit. Matter of fact, Hell was topside, didn't they know? Could've just asked her, because she was living it.

Oh, God, you let the man die . . .

She covered her face with her hands and ignored the teenagers gathered on street corners and hanging on her girlfriends' apartment-building steps. Tinted windows were her only salvation while she struggled for composure as curious glances scoured her souped-up Hummer. She had to get it together. As soon as she stepped out, the neighborhood kids would make her—she was their star.

They'd rush her worse than vamps, seeking autographs, wanting her attention, just to touch a little bit of fame off her, to get close to what they considered a sister with serious bling bling . . . they'd want her to let the magic of new stardom run off her fingertips and onto their palms, hoping for instant discovery. They'd never understand that it just didn't work that way, you had to earn it, and even then there was no guarantee. Fame was a crapshoot, and all that glittered wasn't gold.

And she couldn't go up to Inez's joint all broke up, crying and wailing and sobbing her heart out about how her man had turned into something terrible. Another brittle chuckle escaped Damali's lips and flushed her hands hot with sudden breath. Her best girlfriend. The only one who'd had her back in foster care, and she couldn't even tell Inez about the worst heartbreak of her life.

But Inez would have kind eyes, a soft hug, some chips, some wine, a video, some laughs. *That* was sanctuary. The compound was just a hard reminder of what she really was—trapped.

Sucking in a deep breath, Damali let it out slowly, sat back, and checked her reflection in the rearview mirror. She touched up her light eyeliner, just using the pads of her thumbs to wipe away the damage the tears had done, and threw her locks over her shoulders. It was a performance. That's what she had to tell herself as she braced her nerves to open the door and prepared for the onslaught of kids.

"Yo," she shouted, jumping down from the Hummer and walking up to the building.

Recognition was instantaneous, and just as soon as she'd taken ten paces, she was mobbed.

"Hey, D! You back in the old neighborhood?"

"You got CDs with you? Can we ride in your Hummer?"

"That's bangin', gurl—go 'head wit your bad self!"

"Daaayum . . . will you look at the rims on that sweet bitch. Aw, man, with the fog lights up top."

"Your last concert was *all that*—the video is off da chain, sis!"

"Off da heezy fo' sheezy. Tight."

"Who you know up in here? Dey wit your band?"

"I got dis tape, sis, I want you to hear—hol' up, I'ma go get it and be right back. Cool?"

She smiled, she nodded, she signed T-shirts and bare arms. She gave the right answers and passed the huddle slowly, giving encouragement, good wishes, laughing with them, but she kept walking. Her goal was singular. *Make it to sanctuary. Get to Inez's door. Don't cry. This is a performance. This is what all those young eyes want to see. She was reaching icon status. Keep the light and hold up your torch.* As soon as the inner words hit her, it reminded her of what Carlos had said: "Raise your Isis, baby."

Keep walking. Don't you dare cry, gurl. Not here. Not now. Not in front of the crowd. Keep walking. Keep smiling. Keep from dropping to your knees weeping. Ring the bell. Don't look too long at that young boy with the dark eyes, leaning on your car talking about "Yo, que pasa?" *Inez, be home, please, girl, don't do me like this. Open the door, now!*

"Damali!"

She didn't even see Inez's face as she barreled into her arms, hugging her tightly, tears now flowing freely, almost hiccuping sobs that she made sound like laughter. Forcing a smile, she allowed Inez to hold her back from her, and then squeeze her hard again.

"Y'all go 'head, now. This is *my* girl, and I haven't seen her in a minute," Inez said, laughing and shooing the neighborhood away as she shut the door behind them.

Damali's hands were shaking as she wiped away the tears and took deep breaths.

"Look at us," Inez said, wiping her eyes, too. "Crying and laughing and snottin' and shit. This don't make no sense. It hasn't been *that* long."

Damali swallowed hard, making herself chuckle, and a part of it was no act. It was release laughter. She'd made it to a sanctuary that had not changed. Inez was her girl. As she looked at the deep brown eyes set in a dark walnut face framed by beautiful braids, and her best friend in the whole wide world standing there in a yellow sundress like old times, hands on thick hips, saucy pout, she lost it.

Next thing Damali knew, her arms were around Inez again, just rocking her almost off her feet, laughing to keep from screaming.

"Oh, gurl, I missed you!" That was the truth, as well as the only thing she could say to cover what was really wrong.

It seemed like holding Inez this way was sucking every unshed tear up and out of her. She could almost feel her skin siphoning comfort out of Inez's warm, plump frame. So much had happened, where did one begin? But she'd never put her girl in harm's way by disclosing any of that. Not here, not ever, no matter what.

"Whew," Damali said, as she finally let Inez go and got herself together, still chuckling as she wiped her eyes.

"Girl, get yourself in here and tell me what's been going on," Inez said, looping her arm around Damali's waist and guiding Damali into the kitchen.

All Damali could do was shake her head as she passed through the small, well-kept little apartment. She dropped into a plastic kitchen chair with all her weight, closed her eyes, and leaned her head against the wall. *Sanctuary*. "Oh, girl, I hate the road. You just don't know."

Inez went right for the wine in the fridge, and went up on her toes to fetch down some chips. The blare of the television was balm to her tattered nerves, just like Inez's voice was. Peace, was the small TV on the counter, street traffic, loud music, kids hollering at each other outside. Peace. Normalcy. Damali could hear her girlfriend working to play hostess, knew exactly what she was doing even with her eyes closed as Inez rooted through her cabinets. More tears slipped down her cheeks.

Here her friend was of such humble means, and the kitchen of her ultra-modern, totally fortified guardian compound could swallow Inez's entire apartment whole by ten times, but Inez was giving to her. The tragic part of it all was, she couldn't even invite her best friend to her place. What, show Inez around the weapons room; show her rocket-propelled grenade launchers? Hook her up with one of her sharpshooter big brothers, all so her girl could be vamp bait and go out like Dee Dee had? No, it would never happen.

Damali's chest was so tight that she almost couldn't breathe as Inez came back to the table, excitement glittering in her eyes, and made the most gracious offering from what little she had.

"Here, sweetie. You know I ain't got much, but *mi casa es su casa,* always. I know this isn't the good stuff," she said, unscrewing the bottle of wine. Her voice held a bit of shame in its timbre, "If I knew you were coming . . . but if I've got fifty cents, you'll always have a quarter."

Damali smiled brightly, breathed in deep, and accepted the glass of wine that had been presented in a Dollar Store glass. Didn't Inez know that to her it was Waterford crystal? The cheap wine poured by Inez was better than Cristal, any day. "Girl, you know the same holds true, and I'm not like that. I haven't changed."

Then Inez messed around and put a kiss on Damali's forehead. "That's why I love you so much, and why I'm so proud of you. We all are. You're real, and you haven't changed at all."

"If you ever need anything," Damali whispered, her throat too raw to speak louder. Oh, God, if Inez only knew how much she had. "Just—"

"No, girl. I ain't tryin' to be in your pocket. That's not what our friendship has ever been about." Inez sat down, her eyes holding Damali's the whole time. "Right? We go waaaay back. You made it out. You're living the life we always talked about." Inez clasped Damali's hand across the table. "The demons didn't get you, girl. You made it."

Damali immediately stiffened, then forced herself to relax. "Demons?" Shit. She had almost drawn her blade. If some fucking demons had sniffed out her girl, it was on!

"Chile," Inez laughed. "The *entertainment industry* demons. You ain't still that superstitious, are you?" Inez laughed harder. "Remember when we were kids and you would swear you always saw some guy in an alley with glowing eyes as we'd pass by? You so crazy, that's why I love you, with your paranoid self."

Making herself laugh along with Inez, Damali sipped her wine. "They almost did get me, though, gurl. I've had some close calls. I went right down into the belly of the beast—you have no idea." It was the truth, but not a comprehended confession. However, just saying it, and letting a bit of her life out, felt like an anvil was being lifted from her shoulders. "Tell me what's been going on, catch me up."

"The neighborhood ain't changed since you left, except it's gotten worse. But my life is an easy read. I go to work, I type and answer the phone for a nasty old bastard called my boss, and stay one step ahead of bill collectors. Then I go pick up my daughter from day care, come home, make dinner, clean up, put her to bed, and crash and burn to do it all over again. Girl, don't you let no man talk you into having his baby—I love my daughter, don't get me wrong. But she's going through the terrible twos, money gets funny, and life is one long drama trying to get my baby's daddy's trifling ass to act right. We broke up, but that was bound to happen. The relationship was hell. I'm over it."

Damali could only nod and sip her wine. Hell was a matter of perspective.

Inez sighed, her voice going soft as she looked over Damali's shoulder toward the bedroom that she and her daughter shared. "I'll let you peek in on her, but you don't want to wake up that little monster. Her bad ass is possessed, but I love her to death." She brought her gaze back to Damali. "Nothing in the world like having kids. But," she added, taking a liberal sip of her wine, "I'm being selfish, and just want you all to myself for a little while."

Damali reached across the table and covered Inez's hand. "I hear you," she murmured, but wanted so badly to tell Inez not to call her child a monster, not to say that the child was possessed. Words had power. Didn't her girlfriend know?

"All right, *chica*. I just took you on a brief tour of single-mother hell. Boooring. Now, pleeaaase tell me the latest of diva-hell." She laughed warmly and richly, making Damali join in. "Unlike my story, I know the men are fine! Start there, and work your way out."

Damali sat back in her chair and shook her head, and began munching on chips. "All demons," she said, then laughed hard at the truth in her statement. "Fine and demons. That's all I've met on the road. What can I say?"

"But I know they're rich as shit," Inez said, leaning in. "Gurrrlll . . . talk to me."

"Wealthy enough to make a sistah act stupid. Crazy, *ridiculous* amounts of money—spent on pure bullshit. Decadent, girl. I swear to you." Damali laughed, battling not to cry, and slurped her wine. The truth, even a half-truth hidden behind double entendre and the known lack of comprehension of her friend, felt so good. She had to get some of it out, so she chose her words with care.

"Girl, I've seen some mansions that would make the hair stand up on your arms. Chile, please . . . seen some brothers so fine they could talk your drawers off from across the room. But, you know me, right? Had to drive a stake in one motherfucker's heart. Poof," she said, flicking her fingers in the air. "His ass was dust. What can I say?"

Inez put her head down on the table and screamed, then sat, laughing hard with Damali, and slapped her a high five. "Oh, my God, Damali, what did you do to the man—and tell me *all* about him."

"In truth . . . he was tall, like six somethin', had jet black wavy hair, looked like a tall version of Prince . . . gurl, had it all, even a *panther* in his house—"

"Shut. Up!"

"Yup. Crazy. A security entourage that was not to be messed with . . . the brother was fine. I'll give him that. Old New Orleans money." Damali shook her head. "Uhmmph, ummmph, ummph. I almost went down for the brother."

Inez's eyes sparkled. She let her voice drop to a low whisper, looked around the kitchen like there might be someone listening, and giggled. "Fifty-million-dollar question. Did you give him any?"

Damali leaned her head back on the wall and laughed, and shut her eyes. "You know me better than that." She sat up and winked at Inez. "He almost took the draws—I'm not gonna lie. But, I wasn't having it."

Inez folded her arms over her chest. "Gurl, I could never figure your ass out. If it had been me—shit. Especially if he was all that."

She was laughing, but it was a weak chuckle. What her friend said made her blood run cold for a moment. Yeah, if Inez had been there, Nuit would have, no doubt about it—then her girl would have been dinner. Time to change the subject.

"All right. So, that one was a bastard. But, I know there's got to be somebody special on the horizon by now . . . *fine* as you are? So, who's the latest?"

The question made Damali pause and become very, very still as she sipped her wine more carefully. "You know me. Working all the time, getting ready for gigs. Working on new cuts . . . there's, well, there's just never time for that. I have to stay focused. Got a lotta people depending on me."

The frown on Inez's face wasn't one of disappointment; it was one of concern. "Girl, seriously, all work and no play will make you snap."

"Yeah, I know. I take breaks, go to the clubs, hang out and stuff and—"

"All them fine men around you, when's the last time you had some?"

Damali just stared at her girlfriend and then at the table. A loose piece of linoleum captured her interest and made her pick at it. "I haven't . . . I mean . . . I don't go there, don't take myself through changes like that over no man. My work is . . . girl . . . you know me."

A pair of wide eyes stared at her as Inez put her hand over her heart and stood up fast, almost toppling the chair behind her. "You mean you still haven't . . . Damali, stop lying!"

"I'm into my music, my work, you know . . . when the right person, or situation . . . girl, it ain't no thang."

Damali watched her girlfriend's eyes fill as Inez backed up to the kitchen sink.

"Oh, my God," Inez whispered. "You never got over it, did you?"

"No, I—that's not the reason I haven't found anybody . . ." Damali's gaze locked with her girlfriend's as Inez's tears began to fall.

For a brief moment, neither woman spoke. All the noise, and even the blare of the small kitchen television on the counter sounded like silence. It was only the two of them, breathing, staring, remembering, and holding the secret. Then suddenly Inez broke down in tears.

"It's all my fault!"

Damali was on her feet in seconds and had Inez in her arms, stroking her hair.

"No, it's not," she said, her voice mellow, healing, trying to chase away Inez's pain.

The foul image immediately slithered into her mind despite her efforts to banish it. She was in a basement, bent over the washing machine. She was jamming to her music, hadn't even heard him come up behind her. Something male and strong and reeking with liquor held her like an anchor around the waist. She pivoted instantly and saw a pair of reddened, bloodshot eyes. He smiled. He was so tall, so much bigger, and he loomed over her tiny frame.

Her mind had processed the threat in milliseconds as his grip tightened and his sweaty hands pulled her closer, sealing the gap between them. Terror zinged to her shoulder, lifted her arm, and wrenched her waist into another hard pivot. Her elbow connected with his Adam's apple. In an instant, a lead pipe from the shelf was in her hands. From some unknown reservoir of survival instinct, she went for his jaw, swinging the pipe like a baseball bat when he stumbled backward, pipe connecting with bone and shattering it, then she'd gone for the forearm that had extended with rage. Blood from his mouth splattered the floor, and she ran. Basements, lairs, bloodshot eyes, gleaming eyes, massive strength against the smaller female form, human jaws, vampire incisors, they were one and the same.

Damali shut her eyes for a moment, remembering the terror that had coursed through her as a girl, and what she'd experienced in Hell. Something tall and huge and deadly and aroused, with a steel jaw and red eyes had come up behind her in tight, subterranean confines . . . only she didn't try to hurt the one that had fangs—even with a blade in her hand. All she'd try to do was reason with him and get away.

She rubbed Inez's back harder and held her closer. No, this wasn't Inez's fault at all.

But Inez broke Damali's hold and went to a far side of the kitchen with her arms wrapped around her waist. "I should have told you how my uncle was," she murmured, her voice rising with hysteria through mucous and tears in her throat. "But I couldn't tell even Momma. She'd left me there with my aunt and uncle until she could get enough money to come to the States and get me. She had a good job in Rio, but . . . after Poppi left her, she needed time to get the money. I will never forgive myself—if I had just told."

"I know, I know," Damali said, but not going to her friend. She understood space. "Inez, baby, we've been over it a hundred times, if once. You *don't* owe me. And I never told anybody what he did to you before I came . . . how long it went on."

"My uncle was a demon, a nasty, perverted, sick bastard who beat my aunt, so she was afraid, and I was there all alone for months until you came. I swear I didn't want anything to happen to anyone else like what was happening to me. He wanted to make money on foster care, and my aunt was so afraid of him, they didn't have kids . . . and Momma thought—" Inez drew a shaky breath. "She thought I was safer, had better schools, more chances here. He had a good job. They were respectable people. If it weren't for you . . . he would have kept doing what he did to me."

"Baby, listen, it was *not* your fault. You were just a kid, like me. Stop blaming yourself."

Inez closed her eyes and turned away from Damali. "As soon as you came, two weeks, that was it. I could see him plotting, trying to bide his time—but it kept him off of me." Inez spun around. "I am *so* sorry."

Her voice was so quiet that Damali almost couldn't hear her. "He got to you, didn't he? That's why you're messed up—don't trust any of them. You were younger than me."

With that Inez crossed herself and fetched more wine, took a swig of it out of the bottle, and then set it down hard on the counter. "I should have been protecting you. I was too scared, though. In a new country. Momma had said behave, I didn't want to let her down . . . I thought I did it, made him act like that. And I saw how he beat my aunt. He was strong, but God forgive me. I couldn't warn you."

"Listen to me, Inez," Damali said very carefully, coming to her slowly and extracting the bottle of wine from her grip. She lifted Inez's chin with her finger to force her friend to look her in the eyes. "You were sixteen. I was fifteen. The man was as strong as an ox. That was your family. I was in foster care. Nobody had your back. He didn't get to me. I kicked his ass and ran. Remember?"

She folded Inez into her arms, hugged her tight, and whispered to her like a mother would speak to a hurt child. "I should have never left you in there. I should have killed the bastard. Period. But I ran, and I vowed to never run from a fight like that again, or to leave my own behind in danger. I'm sorry I didn't get there for you earlier, Inez. Trust me."

For a long while they just stood there like that, holding each other and allowing the memories to wash over them while their tears washed away the grit, horror, and hurt they'd shared. Yeah, there were demons and predators in the world—inhumane humans as well as the living dead. Wasn't much difference between the two entities. Both stole lives, shattered futures, broke spirits, and twisted healthy minds.

"You had to live on the street for a month, until Momma could come get me. She asks about you all the time." Inez's voice was a ragged whisper, and she sniffed and wiped her nose with the back of her hand. "Damn, this shit takes me back. We were supposed to be laughing and having fun tonight. I don't know why I went there."

"I was all right," Damali said. "This conversation was probably good for both of us." She pulled back from Inez, and wiped her girlfriend's tears. "I kicked his ass good, though. Left his ass jacked up and in the hospital so he couldn't mess with you while you waited for your mom. Right? You got out, I got out. We survived. It's all good."

"You saved my life, D," Inez murmured, her gaze tender with gratitude. "And your crazy ass had the balls to call my momma long distance, using his stolen credit card, and you told her everything. Just confessed." Inez shook her head. "And then told *everybody* about him coming for you—even called foster care on the run, and charged his plastic until it melted."

Damali smiled sadly and took Inez by the arm and brought her to the table to sit down. "It was reparations," she said quietly. "Fair exchange is no robbery." She then retrieved the wine and poured two new glasses for them both, and plopped into a chair across from Inez. "Girl, you know me. I'd been in foster care all my life. I knew how to survive—so, by rights, I was really older than you, experience-wise. Gotta let it go. I ain't mad at you, never was. If we never talk again, for whatever crazy reason—'cause life ain't promised, please, Inez, you gotta believe that."

"You're scaring me, girl. Don't even say we might never talk again. I've seen so many of us from the old neighborhood die young . . ." Inez shook her head. "Don't even say it; words have power." Then she shivered and looked at Damali hard. "Not my girl. You cannot die on me, hear?"

She held Inez's gaze. "I have a sixth sense about when bastards are plottin' on a sister. It's always in the eyes. That's why I don't have anybody yet. Until I can look a man in his eyes and see his soul—see no malice of intent . . ." Damali shook her head. "Nah. I ain't going out like that. Neither one of us are. It's settled."

She took a sip of her wine and allowed her gaze to travel out the window once Inez had squeezed her hand in agreement.

"Girl, you pray this house up good, hear? Like your momma taught you, she's a good woman," Damali murmured. "Your uncle tricked her into thinking he was cool, and your poor aunt, bless her soul, was trapped. So, you put down some salt and sage and incense and shit around you and your baby girl. There's all types of demons in the world. Predators. Fucking vampires. Goddamned werewolves. Snakes in the motherfucking grass, sis. Trust me. And I don't want you going out like that, either." She looked at Inez hard. "I have seen them. Ask me how I know."

Her girlfriend only nodded. "I hear ya."

Damali nodded, and looked out the window again. Inez had heard her, but hadn't heard the pure truth.

"Well," Inez sighed, "I guess if you made it a month on Rivera's mom's sofa without anything happening to you, then you're gonna be all right. The music industry ain't got nothin' on that. You were always a fighter, D."

"That was so crazy," Damali said, chuckling as the bittersweet memory threaded through her on another sip of wine. She couldn't fight it, had to relive just a little of it within the safe haven of Inez's kitchen. Memories locked so deep inside her began to surface, coming out of hiding in the sunshine of Inez's sad smile. Marlene couldn't even help them escape. The more she battled to keep from speaking, the more the memories fought with her, making her soul ache until she gave in.

"Inez, girl . . . feels like it was yesterday that I was standing under that bridge, all amped, a pipe in my hand, looking crazy and wild in the eye, clothes half ripped off, then these guys rolled up on me and were hollering out a car window and were probably about to gangbang me . . ." Damali's voice trailed off as a red, souped-up Chevy came into her mind's eye. She swallowed hard. A street knight in shining armor, damn. She shook her head and chuckled again quietly to herself, her gaze going to the floor.

Inez looked at her and smiled, but said nothing. She was glad that her friend allowed a reverent moment of silence. She needed the time to just wrap that warm part of the memory around herself like a much-needed hug. It was so long ago and yet felt like it had happened yesterday. He'd jumped out of his car wearing a black muscle shirt, black jeans, a red bandanna wrapped around his head, pointing a huge silver Glock toward a pack of wolves. Her very unlikely hero had seemed insane.

It was the way he did it, and the wild look in his eyes. Crazy . . . crazy for her. She'd seen that look not so long ago. That I'll-take-a-bullet-for-her stare of ready-to-die-with-honor expression . . . the muscles in his outstretched arm corded so tightly the weapon in his hand shook with sudden fury. Then his arm had snapped back and he'd motioned for her to come to him with a nod. It had been reflex; she knew which way to run—toward him. And he'd gotten back into his gleaming red car on a leisurely stroll as the danger disbanded and drove off. He'd moved with casual authority, unafraid. His eyes were on the road, the muscles in his jaw pulsing, and once deep inside his territory where the music changed and the language on the corners was native to him, he'd pulled over, stopped, and looked at her hard.

Damali tried to keep the tears from rising beneath her lids as her mind refused to come back to Inez's kitchen. She'd been so afraid of him, then, too. But he reached out and touched her hair to move it off her shoulders. He'd fingered her micro-braids and cocked his head to the side with a lazy smile. She remembered flinching, her breath catching in her throat, wary of a possible new predator . . . but he wasn't one at all. Not when he dropped his voice to a tender murmur and said, "Don't. I won't bite you. What's your name . . . where's your momma's house?" Oh, God, he'd been so sweet to her . . . she had even kept his bandanna after all these years.

Seeing it in her mind's eye, secretly stashed in her dresser, she opened her eyes and tried to act like none of it mattered. She made her voice falsely upbeat as she spoke to Inez. There was no reason to allow her girl to see her bleeding to death on her kitchen floor.

" 'Nez, I was totally outnumbered, and would have gotten my ass kicked for sure. Then Rivera happened to roll up 'cause he was making a delivery and patrolling his territory; he jumped out his car, went off, cussed them out in Spanish, and pulled a nine." She covered her eyes with her forearm and leaned her head back against the wall and laughed hard to keep from sobbing. "Crazy, Latino, wild man. Oh, man, I miss his ass, girl."

"I thought for sure you two were gonna hook up," Inez said in a faraway voice. "Damn shame he got caught up in the life, and they got him."

"Yeah," Damali said, her tone flat as she dropped her arm and poured more wine. This was definitely a get-fucked-up-and-sleep-on-your-girl's-couch kinda night.

"My mom was hysterical after she got your call," Inez said quietly, her voice sounding even further away. "Sent a bunch of cousins over to my auntie's house to protect me and her, and to visit my uncle after he got out of the hospital," Inez added with a slow smirk. "He left the house mysteriously until my mother got there, and could get her own place with her sister. Never came back, fancy that. Reparations, I suppose?" Then Inez's face went serious. "Why didn't you come back with us till—"

"I couldn't walk back into that house," Damali said fast, standing. She just needed to move. Why was Inez going here tonight? They'd been over a lot of this stuff before.

"But you were lucky. It was dangerous where you were. Once Momma got to LA, it was okay to come back. My uncle was gone. I know you told me, but I never really understood that. I kept thinking it was because, down deep, you never really forgave me." Inez's eyes searched Damali's face now, looking for forgiveness that wasn't required.

"Girl, it wasn't you. I didn't forgive you," Damali said firmly, "because there was nothing to forgive. You didn't do anything wrong!"

Pacing in the small confines, Damali gestured with her hands as she spoke. "You're my girl, my tight. And, yeah, Mrs. Rivera had a lot of crazy shit happening in her house, but, oddly, I felt safe there—like I was supposed to be there, even if for just a short time." She ran her hands through her locks.

"The poor woman and her mother prayed day and night, worked like *dogs,* Inez. Her crazy-assed sons had taken over the house, were distributing right from it . . . had all kinds of foot traffic, if you know what I mean. But, shit, as long as Carlos was around, wasn't nooooobody messing with me—not even Alejandro, with his wild, off da hook self."

Inez chuckled. "You mean with his *fine,* off da hook self. Them Rivera boys was fine, chile. And their cousins wasn't no slouches, either. Guess if I had my choice of where to be . . ."

"It wasn't even like that, girl," Damali said, chuckling, but frustrated by the reality that Inez might never understand. "His sister gave me a lot of rags to wear, was cool, but strung out like a mug. None of her shit didn't fit her; she'd gotten so skinny. His mom, at first, was like, 'You ain't bringing no *Negro punta* to my house, *Carlos*. You *loco*? Oh no, we don't live like dat.'" Damali put her hands on her hips, approximating the older Latina, designed to make Inez laugh. Designed to make herself laugh.

"Said it to my face, gurl. I was standing right there, my shit all ripped up, dirty, bruised, looking crazy—I wouldn'ta let my son drag nobody home to my house like that, either. Then it was on. They went into this flurry of arguments I couldn't understand, and whatnot. All I could do was stand in the corner and watch. Brother didn't even know me, but dragged me by the arm, pushed me up in his momma's face and said, 'Her foster father tried to molest her, Momma. You gonna go to church and tell the priest in confession that you turned away a child—she's fifteen. Talk to me!' Then he swung his arm around and pointed to a statue of the Blessed Mary and said, 'What the fuck, Momma? You a believer, or what?'"

Damali threw her head back and laughed with Inez and wrapped her arms around her waist tight. Hers was a brittle sound next to Inez's warm melodic tone. She needed to laugh to keep from crying, just as much as she needed to relive the past like a wake. Thinking about Carlos made her whole body hurt.

"I knew I was in, Inez, when the woman started fussing and walked away, grabbed a pile of clothes and a pillow and threw it in my face."

"That's deep, D, for real. We been gurls a long time, and I know you crashed there, but I thought Carlos took you in 'cause, well . . . and that you didn't really wanna say, 'cause . . ."

"Noooo," Damali said, her laughter sliding away as new tears formed and fell against her will. "Went against his mom for me, stood up. Then his mom went into this thing about nobody was screwing under her roof, blah, blah, blah—drugs were cool, right, but not screwing."

Damali suddenly chuckled again, and sucked up the tears with an angry sniff, wiping her nose hard with the back of her hand. She walked to the sink and snatched down a paper towel, forcefully blew her nose, and crumpled up the damp paper, then took a deep breath as she cast it into the trash. "That was revenue that Mom Riv turned a blind eye to and just prayed would convert into legitimacy, I guess. Whateva. But her son was not gonna screw no *Negro* tramp in her house."

Damali slapped her forehead and closed her eyes as she stood in the middle of the kitchen floor. "Heaven help me, it was crazy. She made him *actually* swear he wouldn't touch me in her house as a condition of me being there—*on the Bible*—okaaay. And that fool did it—for me."

"Stop lying, D," Inez said, shaking her head and chuckling. "Carlos Rivera put his hand on the Bible, for you? Gurl . . . you never told me that!"

"At first, I was like, yeah, whateva. That'll hold up for twenty-four hours, till his mom went to work." Damali smiled sadly and let the memory run through her like clean rain. "I thought he'd done it just to get the old bat out of his face. But the more I came to see how he rolled, and how much he cared about his mom . . . and how truly a sweet lady she was, I knew he wasn't playing. Gave her his word, so that was that."

"D . . . for real, now. We go way, way back. Brother never tried you?"

Damali just shook her head. "Not over there," she whispered, then found her voice again and spoke louder, but her tone was introspective as she really thought back. The magnitude of what he'd truly sacrificed as a matter of honor, and just for her, hitting her hard.

"I slept on the sofa in my clothes for a month, Inez, and when Alejandro pushed up on me, like he always did any of Carlos's territory, Carlos gave me a nine and said, 'Shoot the bastard if he gets in your face while I'm out handling my business.' Oh . . . shit . . . Inez. I have lived a wild life! I cleaned that woman's house from stem to stern every day to keep her off my back and a roof over my head—when she walked in from work, I practically fucking genuflected and brought her a lemonade."

Damali bent over and forced an even harder chuckle as Inez's laughter collided with hers. The floor became blurry and she sucked back new tears along with what was fast becoming hysteria. *Oh, shit . . . they'd killed him.* He mighta been a lot of bad things, but he didn't deserve to go out like that.

After a moment, she stood. "Girl . . . your mother saved my life.

Debt cleared, even though there never was no debt between us." Her gaze held Inez's tenderly. "She didn't go to the police, didn't tell where I was."

"Momma understood immigration issues," Inez said, smiling. "She came from Mexico, but Poppi was from Rio—*Portuguese,* that's why she was there. She got stuck there after he left her." Inez's expression became serious. "Momma understood about being a young woman stuck somewhere with a man, somewhere you might not want to be, but had to stay until you could make your break." Inez sighed hard, the weight of it filling the room. "She hated the authorities, still does, so as long as you said you were okay, she was good with that. Knew if you weren't, you'd tell the world." Inez chuckled softly. "I'm glad you came back to her—us, though, after she got her apartment."

"Me, too," Damali said quietly.

"Glad Mrs. Rivera didn't tell on you."

Damali smirked. "She got to like having a maid, and wasn't about to bring any authorities to her house. Plus, the way I kicked your uncle's ass, they would have tried to pin it on one of her sons. It was all good. It was only a month—but it was a great month." Damali sighed and walked to the tiny window and looked out. "I had so much fun. His sister and her friends were so cool . . . so nice to me. And even if his boys woulda been game if I was, they chilled and became like a bunch of big brothers, ya know?"

Her voice became very far away as she spoke, suddenly realizing that if she hadn't lived with Carlos briefly, she might not have ever agreed to go into a community-living situation with the guardians. The sheer irony of it made her weary. "I learned a little bit of Spanish, watched the fellas race." She shrugged. "Carlos even taught me how to shoot a nine. Deep. When you think back, it's amazing the things you remember."

"Yeah, girl."

She could tell Inez was going back to the past, too. Inez stood and came by her side so they could both peer out the window together. She had crazy-good things to look back on, things to warm her soul when life got cold and real; her girlfriend didn't. In an odd way, despite all the trauma, she felt blessed. Damali said a silent prayer that Inez's future would make up for everything stolen from her girlfriend's childhood.

"How about if I peek at your princess?" Damali said. "I know she's more beautiful than her pictures."

"She is," Inez said, and then she slung her arm over Damali's shoulder.

They walked the short distance through the kitchen and living room, going down the hallway, and Damali took in all the things that made Inez's apartment a real home. A crooked picture on the wall. Dirt smudges from sticky little fingers marring the ivory-hued paint. A light blue carpet that needed vacuuming. An overflowing laundry basket. A faucet that dripped. Sanctuary. Just like Mrs. Rivera's house had been.

Not perfect, but filled with family, love . . . Crazy sons, wild activities, drugged-out daughter, but laughs. A full house, a superstitious grandma that finally relented and gave her the a-okay from a vision. Damali smiled just thinking about the old dolls. It had a lot of things the compound had, as well as a lot of things it didn't.

Dinners that were a noisy gathering of people eating from plates while standing up because they had things to do, business to handle, all crammed in the kitchen, tossing beers to each other, talking shit, laughing, and laughing, and cussing each other out, coming home the next day after catting around . . . women falling by and sitting on the sofa to wait for some man like sparrows on a telephone wire, guarding their territory over whichever fine brother they were trying to hook up with. The kitchens were the same, in that way, but the living room was devoid of outsiders—a closed environment. Even though all of it was insane, part of her knew that she'd do it again any day. By comparison, Mrs. Rivera's house wasn't all that bad.

Inez pushed open the bedroom door, and in the middle of her queen-sized bed slept an angel. Damali covered her mouth to keep from gasping. She went to the side of the bed and knelt, watching the tiny body shudder with peaceful inhales and exhales. Unable to stop herself, she traced the soft, caramel cheek, and brushed back the fuzzy, thick plaits twisted with multicolored, plastic barrettes. "Oh, God, Inez, she's so gorgeous."

There was no way to stop the new tears from forming in her eyes as she glanced up at her girlfriend who was beaming with pride.

"Job well done," Damali said, kissing the toddler's butter-soft cheek. "Well done." Then she stood, allowing her fingers to linger in the dark brown nest of cottony textured hair, and then tiptoed out of the room with her friend.

"I know you didn't like his lifestyle," Inez murmured as they walked down the hall with Inez's arm around Damali, "but you should have had one for Carlos. Mighta changed him a little?"

Damali felt her back stiffen. "You know how I feel about that," she said, trying to find the line between preaching and not offending her girl.

"Yeah, you're right," Inez said as they reentered the kitchen. "His lifestyle was dangerous, especially when he moved out and got his own place and moved up. Then, with your career . . ." She shrugged.

It hurt her soul that her girlfriend had so completely missed the point. You didn't *have* a baby *for someone*. Lord help her. A baby didn't change a man, nor did it seal a relationship, and that was the *last* reason you had one. A child wasn't a hostage, or a choker chain. New, innocent life wasn't supposed to be created for those reasons. Only the spirit could bind a person to another, and the mind had to clearly sort that all out in the flesh.

Damali suddenly felt tired. There were so many things she wanted to tell Inez's deaf ears. But tonight was not the night for that old debate. "He lived a dangerous life," was all she could say to terminate the discussion. Again, salt in the wound.

"It's a shame, though, that y'all never got a chance to hook up," Inez said with a yawn, glancing at the near-empty bottle. "Then, all his boyz got shot up bad, and then his brothers and cousins—man, the guys who assassinated them did them ritual-style. Wasn't right, closed casket funerals . . . their moms didn't even get to see them good before saying good-bye. I don't know whose money they jacked, but dayum. And they still can't find Carlos to bury him. That's messed up. Think he's—"

"He's dead. They all made a deal with the Devil," Damali said flatly, and kept her gaze on the television. "A lotta fine men went to waste."

She had to tune Inez out for a moment. Mentally retracing a path to the Rivera house one last time, she remembered how she stayed tight with Carlos and his people even after she'd moved back to stay with Inez for a little while. That part of it all really hurt. She'd watched Carlos climb the street-money ladder almost to the top, and then fall—hard.

If it hadn't been for Marlene tracking her down, hearing about what happened with Inez's uncle from the word on the streets, she would have lived with Inez as her sister till they were grown. If she hadn't told on her foster father, if he hadn't reached for her and drawn back a nub . . . if she hadn't been so outraged that she called everyone she knew in Inez's family to protect Inez by telling the truth, bringing the light to that dark, scary, secret shit going on over there, the guardians might not have found her. Not being found maybe wouldn't have been so bad. Maybe then she could have stayed with Inez and lived a normal life.

But then again, by being there, Damali also knew that, if vampires were looking for her, Inez and her whole family might have been turned. The universe had a perverse sense of humor. Damali poured the last of the wine into her glass as the television droned on and she and Inez sat hypnotized, watching nothing.

All of it was a closed circle, now she understood why. Inez's mom told all her people in Rio, and the male cousins mounted a revenge posse, stateside. Marlene's friends from overseas had heard about it . . . bullshit traveled all the way from South America to LA by the grapevine. One of Shabazz's old boys knew who was in the hit squad, and told him. Then one night while she was free-styling on an open mic, Marlene had walked up, gave her a business card, and a supposed record deal—if she would come and live with her, and get groomed while laying down tracks in her studio. Inez's mom had relented, because Marlene had credibility and money. Full circle. Yes, the universe was a trip.

Crazy . . . just like Carlos, Damali had to admit that she'd been seduced into a new lifestyle by the lure of the brass ring. Had left the safety of Inez's people's home to go on an adventure, and now it had become a roller-coaster ride she couldn't get off.

Suddenly she just wanted to go home.

Damali stood, totally sober. She embraced her friend who was like a sister.

"I have to go home and handle some business. You kiss your daughter for me, and tell her Auntie Damali is gonna send her something soon . . . and kiss your mom for me, hear?"

Inez nodded and hugged her tighter.

"I'll visit soon, and you know I always write."

"Stop sending money, girl. Hear?" Inez said, stroking her back. "You gonna be all right getting home safe this late?"

"I'll call you when I get in—but tonight is not the night anybody wants to start some shit with me."

"Damali, the world has gotten worse since we were kids and hanging out. I'm just worried. Don't start no shit with anybody tonight. 'Kay?"

She kissed Inez on the cheek. "Lock the door and say your prayers. You know me. I got this."

In the darkness of her lair she watched through her inner vision. Her eyes narrowed to cruel, green-glowing slits. Pure jealousy sent her own claws into her palms. If she were free to move about . . . were she not shackled to a region . . . just one false step, just one mistake, and she'd have the young Neteru's head on a pike.

It wasn't fair; she'd been robbed. They didn't make Neterus like they used to. This one, from this era, was weak, had no sense of purpose. This one cried. This one believed she had the right to bear the Isis. This one had challenged two very eligible master vampires, and due to a fluke in cosmic law, won. That's why this lucky little bitch had to be dealt with soon. This one would not be allowed to ruin her plans!

CHAPTER THREE

MARLENE STOOD very still in the compound kitchen in silent meditation. She held onto the sink breathing slowly, watching the steel grates lift by timer just as dawn broke. She kept her eyes on the new rose-orange-hued horizon, and didn't turn when she felt a massive male presence at her back cast a shadow in the doorway.

Then she closed her eyes and waited. A pair of male feet would hit the hallway soon. She could feel the weight of the heavy heart coming toward her. The air got denser, literally thickened around her before she heard the first footfall. There was only one guardian in the house that she knew held such private pain. He had a black box around his emotions that was so hidden even she couldn't reach into it.

"Good morning, Rider," she murmured over a sip of mint tea without opening her eyes.

"Yeah," he grumbled and plopped down in a chair.

"You want some coffee?"

She didn't wait for the response as she heard the flask hit the table. Marlene simply went to the counter, and brought back a steaming mug as she came back to sit with Rider. She appraised the cloudy colors around him, noting that his aura had a roiling anger tingeing it. His normal turquoise and light earth tones were dark, smoldering, swirling furiously, and growing, unlike Mike's tight gray line. All of the guardians had gray in their auras now.

Rider's white T-shirt was so crummy and so raggedy that it might as well have been the same color as his beat-up, cut-off shorts—gray. Marlene let out a long, weary sigh.

He gave her a sheepish glance and unscrewed his flask. "Tryin' ta bite the snake that bit me," he said, pouring a healthy jigger into his mug, nearly overflowing it. He leaned over and slurped down the coffee and Jack Daniel's concoction without lifting the mug.

"Oh, shit, Mar," Rider said, taking another sip, making a noise like he was clearing his sinuses while he shut his eyes tightly, then he abandoned the mug and went straight for the flask. He turned it up to his mouth and winced when he pulled it away, swallowing hard. "Getting too old for this."

"I know, baby." Marlene covered his hand, then patted it before drawing it back to reach for her teacup.

"My boy, Jose, is all messed up. Got a newbie, Dan, that's totally battle-freaked—I mean, the kid's real first time out was in Hell . . . c'mon, Mar. Kid's got nightmares like he's been to 'Nam. The prep time to get these kids ready is spinning by us fast like an out-of-control top. Now, Damali? Our Neteru gets her heart ripped out in Hell? It ain't fair, Marlene, I'm telling you."

"I know. But she'll have to work through the anger and the grief on her own—just like everything else. We can't help her with that, all we can do is support and guide her, now that she's grown. Good people die every day. That's why we do what we do, to trim those numbers back."

"She's not going to get over this, Marlene." He looked at Marlene hard. "This ain't like when we lost the others."

"I know."

"That's all you can say, 'I know'?" Rider stood up and walked over to the sink to lean on it. "Big Mike's hearing is off, and the poor bastard doesn't even want to eat. He ain't about chasing tail with me . . . I couldn't even tempt him with a little day trip to New Orleans." Rider sighed hard and rubbed the gray-and-blond stubble on his jaw. "I tried to get Jose to ride with me, like old times, go watch a few ladies dance the poles . . ." He shook his head. "Young buck wouldn't even take the bait. Sits by Damali like a hurt puppy until she gets up and leaves, then waits till she gets back. It ain't healthy. Dan's scared to even leave the compound. That boy is young, he needs to get out before he snaps."

"I know."

"And Damali ain't far behind him. She comes in here every morning smelling like sulfur and demon innards—not like she's been out having fun." Rider pointed to his nose and glared at Marlene. "I may be old, and my nose may be off, but if she'd found a diversion, I'da smelled him on her. This shit ain't healthy. But she's probably afraid to risk being with an innocent, if there's still master vamps out there hunting her down. The child might as well be living in a convent, Marlene! And, who knows, after losing Rivera, she just might do that."

"I know."

"Will you stop with the 'I know,' Madame seer? What're we gonna do?"

"I don't know."

Rider took another chug from his flask. "Marlene, you are making me nuts this morning. I swear I don't know how Shabazz deals with it."

"I know," she said, chuckling. "Give everybody some time. We lost a guardian down there," she said, her voice growing quiet. "That's a hard loss. But she'll come around."

"No, Mar," Rider said, wiping his mouth with his forearm. "We lost our Neteru's soul mate. That's not a loss, that's a cosmic catastrophe."

"I know," she said very calmly, but very carefully. "How's your nose? You said it was off."

"Fucked up."

Marlene nodded. "And Mike's hearing?"

"Jacked." Rider pushed off the sink. "Jose's nose is, too. Dan can't shoot the broadside off a barn—his tactical senses are fried. JL, and I could always count on JL, but our little brother got caught counting cards and almost got iced at the casinos in Vegas . . . if JL can't do mental sleight of hand, then . . ."

"I know. Shabazz ain't exactly right, either—"

"But I bet *his* ass sleeps at night!"

Rider walked a hot path between the sink and the door, took a hard swallow of liquor, and glared at Marlene. She just stared at him, keeping her voice a murmur as she spoke to him, trying to heal him while not addressing what he'd said about Shabazz. It was the truth, and it suddenly disturbed her. She and Shabazz had been the first ones to shake off the grief, and she'd chalked it up to the fact that they were the elder guardians in the group.

But as she studied Rider's very personal reaction to Damali's inner pain, she wondered why. Something didn't jive. Rider had been in battles before; they'd lost crew before. All of them loved Damali like a daughter or a sister, except Jose, who perhaps felt something more. And they'd all seen Damali bounce back, too. But that Rider's head was so twisted about the incident, horrible though it was, gave her pause.

"Rider," she said, her voice as gentle as she could make it, "my third eye is nearly blind. All I get is impressions, no sharp images. We've *all* got a lot on our minds. As long as the masthead of the ship is broken, we have no way to raise sails. We're dead in the water until her aura lifts, the gray goes out of it. We're all connected, Rider, that's why I keep saying, 'I know.'"

Marlene sighed when he didn't respond but took another drink from his flask, glowering at her. "If you take the fellas to a hangout, go find some entertainment, bring back lighter energy . . . who knows? You have to shake the horrible images you saw down in the pit, maybe it will help her?" She had to give him something constructive to do. Rider had no patience, never did.

Rider looked out the window. "It wasn't the horrible images that we saw that are messing us up, Mar. It's the beautiful ones that are a bitch."

She studied his back. "Talk to me." A shiver ran down her spine.

"You're the seer of this group, and if you didn't see it, then your senses must really be off big-time . . . I guess I can't be mad at you for being so blind. Third eye or not, you have no frame of reference and like all of us, you're human." His tone became gentler, resigned, as though beaten down by sudden fatigue. "My bad, Mar. I'm just rambling. We all take everybody's skills for granted, and we've just gotten used to you being the all-seeing Marlene with the answers. I'm sorry. That's not fair. I'm going to bed."

She stood and came to him, resting her hand on his shoulder so he wouldn't leave. "Rider?"

"You wouldn't understand—you have Shabazz." He looked at her; his voice was gravelly but held no judgment or sarcasm in it. "You and Shabazz are the only guardians on the team that have paired up. We saw it in Hell."

"What are you talking about?" Her hand left his shoulder and her arms went around her waist. He was scaring her. "We fought just as hard as anyone down there. You think because he and I are paired that we would have let any of you get harmed without a fight, would have saved ourselves and let you fellas die?" She was incredulous.

Tears filled her eyes. Rider's accusation had hurt her to the bone. She flinched away from him when he reached to cup her cheek.

"No, Mar. You read me wrong."

She began to slowly relax, watching his pained expression and the quick moisture that had formed in his eyes. The way he looked at her made her nervous to hear the raw truth for the first time since the team had come together. That terrible seesaw of emotion was further eclipsing her ability to read him. She practically held her breath as she waited for him to explain.

"There comes a point in every man's life, Mar, where he wakes up and doesn't want a gorgeous thing that dances the pole beside him. It ain't enough. Feeds the body, but doesn't feed the soul." His eyes held hers and he kept his voice gentle as he pushed a stray lock over her shoulder and sighed. "Comes a point where you just don't want an easily interchangeable somebody, you want a woman who you'll call by name . . . who you'll, as a man, walk through the fire for . . . will lay down your life for, if you have to."

He shook his head and walked away from her, raking his fingers through his tousseld hair. "Mike saw it, and the big guy is done with New Orleans's finest. Jose saw it, and . . . he's messed up. He came close to having that with Dee Dee, even though I suspect she was never the real McCoy—but at least the boy had hope. Dan saw it, and knows that at his age, living like this, he can't bring anybody home and set up housekeeping. JL saw it, and wigged." He eyed Marlene carefully, but there was no malice in his expression. "JL headed right for the casinos. And, if I were a bettin' man, I'd say he took a month's salary to the blackjack table to double-down on a way out."

"What . . ." Marlene's voice caught in her throat on a horrified whisper.

"Yep. Was probably trying to figure out how to win enough to finance then set up a small safe house with every piece of electronic-surveillance and high-tech weapons-launching gizmos available, so if he did find somebody—"

"Oh, no . . ." Marlene closed her eyes. "I thought he was just letting off steam, like you guys always do after a battle."

Rider shook his head. "Why you think JL got in trouble, couldn't concentrate, when of all the guardians, save you and Shabazz, JL has laser focus? That's why he's our equipment man, our weapons' room expert. Have you seen him tinkering with his gadgets and computers lately?" He paused and waited for Marlene's nonverbal response. "My point, exactly. He just takes his post, stares at the monitors, looking right through them, and then goes to bed at daybreak." Rider took a slow swallow of Jack Daniels and then let his breath out hard. "The only brother that's straight in here is Shabazz."

Marlene felt for the side of the sink and found it so she could lean against it to keep herself from falling down. It was all so clear, and she'd been so blind. It wasn't just Damali who was grieving, or the team just grieving for her . . .

Rider nodded, his lopsided smile holding hollow triumph. "You following me? These guys are all reevaluating their entire lives. It wasn't the demons they saw and killed. It wasn't Damali's battery going down from grief. They are grieving their choice to become guardians, because after the adrenaline subsided, and they had time to think, their reality is fucking them up. Won't be no wife and kids. Won't be no regular life. Nobody special, and unless she comes packing with ammo, she's shark bait—and they know it. They also know, for the first time, having visited Hell, just how helpless they are to protect a regular woman, especially after coming so close to losing a Neteru on their watch. The whole thing spooked 'em, and fucked them around good."

He looked away from Marlene, studying the sun. "I've accepted my fate . . . did when Tara turned. I don't even take myself there anymore—which is why I watch the ladies dance the poles, indulge myself stupid, and numb any useless thought when I start going down memory lane."

"Rider, you've gotta stop drinking . . . and if the guys are looking for real life-mates, they won't find them in the clubs or hoochie bars, brother." She wasn't scolding him. Her voice was filled with so much hurt for him and the others that it was hard to speak.

He chuckled and kept his gaze on the horizon. "Solves a short-term male problem. But the fact that that's getting old . . . hey. The long-term solution is very complicated. My boys and I are caught between a rock and a hard place," he said, his chuckle hollow and waning. "Literally. And this shit is gonna go on for the next twenty-five years. Might as well tell these boys to join up with Father Pat's Covenant. They've accepted their fate, too, for different reasons. But, hey, a monk is a monk."

She was going to walk toward him, but thought better of it. He needed space. So, instead, she spoke softly, trying to dispense hope and healing with her words. "Somebody will come along for each guardian . . . I mean . . ." Her own lack of confidence in what she was saying just made the sentence trail off. What could she say?

"You got a vision, a bead on this, Mar? A gut hunch? Or are you just trying to make this old warrior feel better?"

It took her too long to answer him. They both knew she wouldn't lie straight to his face. All she could do was shake her head. "My visions have been off . . . I haven't specifically seen . . . but that doesn't mean—in the future, it may not have materialized yet, but—"

"Ain't your fault. Even you can't conjure up what's not out there." He took another swig and winced. "I already found my somebody once and lost her to a vampire turn. That was it for me. Had a name I used to call, don't want the heartbreak of losing another one. I know what the girl is going through, Mar. But Damali never even got to . . ."

Rider took another fast sip, but his hand was shaking as he brought the flask away from his mouth.

"I'm done. But a lotta guys in here aren't. They still want that. And, Mar, you've got a whole team of young bucks about to be all screwed up like Damali is now. Me and Mike, we're older, and can hang. We've crossed the line and ain't sitting up at night thinking about a future wife and kids and shit."

"Oh . . . Rider . . . but, you said in Hell . . . in the battle . . . why would being there—"

He chuckled sadly. "In all the places in the universe, where you'd least expect to see it—I'da lost that bet, if you'da told me. It's a man thing, and Marlene, you *definitely* wouldn't understand."

"Try me," she whispered, her voice tense with worry. "Because, Rider, I really need to know how to heal this team, if possible."

"You can't fix this, Marlene. That's what we all know, and what's fucking up every man in here." He began slowly pacing, raking his fingers through his hair, looking at the floor, his voice so thick with emotion that she almost couldn't hear him.

"All right. Here we are, Mar, strapped to the nines, standing in the middle of a battle. Shells flying, fucking demons everywhere, green gook exploding, all-out mortal combat . . . a damned master vampire in our midst, serious battle hazard close by, adrenaline kickin' like a mo'fo, everybody in there ready to go down, knowing any of us could at any time . . . the priest's squad is getting slaughtered, we had to do some of our own to keep them from turning, got a Neteru going through changes . . . dragging bloody wounded that's drawing Hell sharks, almost out of ammo. Rivera had a firestorm coming his way, was hungry, exhausted, and should have used all twelve of us that were left standing to feed." Rider looked up at her. "We were in Hell, Marlene. Right? We weren't in Kansas, Dorothy."

She could only nod and stare back at him.

"If he'd snapped our necks, tranced her out, and fed well, he would have had enough energy to transport her out of there and start a damned empire." Rider paused, letting the silence in the kitchen envelop them. "But he didn't, did he?"

Rider pulled a hair out of his head fast with two fingers and thrust it toward Marlene. "The line of choice made within seconds was as thin as this," he said, gesturing with his hand, "and could have gotten snatched in the wrong direction as fast as I just pulled this hair out of my head, Mar. And the one who had the fragile balance of choice was a damned guardian that had turned. *A male vampire.* Not just our Neteru. If the dude had decided differently . . ."

Rider sucked in a shaky breath. "I done seen a lot of battle, Mar, but even for me, that was deep. In *seconds* he could have done us and saved himself, *and* took a bride."

"Oh . . . Shit . . ."

"Right." Rider flicked away the hair and crossed his arms over his chest, biceps bulging as his body tensed. He looked down at the flask he was clasping with disdain.

"Rivera *begged* her to leave him, *made us* pull her out while she was ovulating, turned around and watched our backs—not just hers, but the whole family, just because we mattered to her. Fought on low fuel, and got fucked by whatever was coming through the tunnels. *Just* for *her.* Even if he wanted her away from the battle zone, he could have snatched one of us to feed on just to even his odds and perhaps save his own ass—but he didn't."

Rider held Marlene's gaze captive, his expression grave. "We all saw love transcend *Hell,* Marlene. Saw the most advanced predator in the demon food chain give up a prize that he'd battled another master for, and won . . . just so the girl could live a normal life topside. That shit right there would give any man pause . . . will make you reevaluate your entire existence. And, if you're a believer, it'll make you have a loooong conversation with the man upstairs about all the shit you've done wrong."

He nodded and took another swig from his flask when Marlene closed her eyes.

"Will make you argue with Him about justice, too," Rider said, re-newed rage at the unfairness of it all keeping his voice a low rumble. "Rivera was one of ours, wasn't supposed to turn—definitely wasn't supposed to go out like that. And we had to leave him, just because of what he was. But judging by the way the man fought . . . yeah, he was one of ours. By rights, who knows, maybe we shoulda stayed? That's part of what's tumbling around in that girl's brain, just like it's tum-bling around in all of ours, causing survivor's guilt, too." Rider saluted Marlene with his flask. "Respect. He went out with honor. Just like a guardian. This is man-type shit, Marlene. Don't try to figure it out or heal it. This conversation stays A and B."

He glanced at her again as he moved to the kitchen door. "Shabazz got a second chance to get out of prison and find somebody, I got a second chance not to die . . . Mike got a second chance not to die—we all did, so did you. That's why we're here."

"I know, but Rider, the kids have time."

"The young bucks on the team never even got a shot off," he said, pure frustration in his voice that turned into bitter defeat. "Where's Rivera's get-out-of-jail-free redemption pass, huh? Where's Damali's? Where the fuck is Jose's? Dan and JL ain't even smelled love, let alone felt it—and in here, under these circumstances, they probably won't. Our entire younger level will not replace itself, won't heal. This shit is not right, Mar, and that's why the team's not right. The trinity of en-ergy is the masthead that broke, Mar, when this crap broke our girl's back and we had to watch it. We won the battle down there, but the dark side is winning the war—our spirits ain't right. Everybody is los-ing faith. Hope . . . shit, that's history. Love," he said, shaking his head, "is really fucked up for almost everybody around here. Not even a possibility. If we saw those two connect, woulda gave the rest of us hope, renewed faith, and maybe a little encouragement to keep looking for *the one*."

"Rider," she said, her voice as gentle as she could make it, "in time . . . with patience . . ."

"Whatever. All I know is, I'ma kill Rivera for dying on my watch in front of my team. Every man, not just guardians, I mean regular average Joes, are searching for his own Neteru, Mar, even though we're human." He looked at her, his eyes hard. "Every man is looking for the one that will make him walk through fire."

Marlene closed her eyes and continued to lean against the sink. What was there to tell the man? Shabazz wouldn't even talk about it. Now she understood why. Double survivor's guilt . . . he'd made it out alive, and still had a life mate. As a blessed man, he was grieving his heart out for his brothers, knowing they didn't have what he did, but he couldn't fix it. Shabazz always had profound philosophy, wisdom to impart. But, this time, there were no words he could offer. They'd isolated him from their grief, he couldn't share their pain over a beer—it would be like a wealthy man telling a homeless person he understood his pain, not credible . . . salt in the wound.

Her soul was so heavy that she couldn't even cry. It took another male to explain what even a mother-seer couldn't see. And damn it, it all made so much sense now why her lover wouldn't come to bed with her at night, or touch her in the compound with the other guardians still home. It was beyond worry for Damali. It was beyond post-battle trauma or introspection. The family was disintegrating around them.

Her voice was just a slow whisper as she formed words to respond to Rider's truth. Didn't matter that it was. Rider was already gone. So she spoke to the empty kitchen.

"Oh, God, it isn't fair. I know."

CHAPTER FOUR

Tijuana, 45 miles into the Mexican desert, right after the battle in Hell

CARLOS LAY motionless against the cool earth. Only a whisper of existence flickered within him as his disoriented mind replayed the outcome of the vampire civil war. A travesty. A variable. Destiny was laughing. He could only hope that Fate's cruel sense of humor had spared his woman. At twenty-one years old, Damali Richards didn't deserve to go out like that. Yet, who would have thought he'd be made into a vampire at twenty-three? Way before Damali learned that she was a vampire huntress she'd been right; there were worse things than death.

He had heard his own bones snapping and flesh ripping, his cries echoing in the caverns of Hell as he fought off the attack. His body had suffered carnage, but it had also temporarily kept the Minion forces at bay. With all that he had to give her, he'd put himself between his kind and her humanity. That he had been turned into a creature of the night was moot; she was made of living, mortal flesh, and still had a soul. It was the last gift he could give her: protection, and a chance to escape.

It was a foolish concept that he nursed as he lay dying. Protection. For minutes, hours, days until they tracked her down again? His kind was relentless and had all the time in the world to go after her once they regrouped. That he killed many of them in the combat was of little consequence. His efforts would barely make a dent in the numbers that hunted her. He'd come to understand that as the tunnels of Hell had filled and they'd rushed him.

Even for a master vampire like him, there had been too many of them. Rogue vampires had descended upon him with their allied demon forces, however his objective had been singular: keep them away from the Neteru, away from Damali and her guardian team. Were it not for his alliance with the Vampire Council of old, he would have immediately perished. But, then, that might have been a more merciful fate.

Agony from his wounds stripped the breath from his lungs as his mind struggled to hold onto consciousness. Bone cut through his skin like jagged, bloody, white knives, leaving his leg a distorted wreck. His jaw had been shattered, neutering him, leaving him no vampire defense. His left arm was almost amputated, hanging by a bloody mass of muscle at what had been his shoulder. Sections of his rib cage protruded from beneath ripped flesh and had dug into the ground when they'd dropped him, almost trapping him against the sand until he could bring himself to roll over onto his right side. He couldn't even groan when he did. Pain had seized his vocal cords and impaled him.

His chest rose and fell with intermittent shudders for air. He trained his mind on the distorted faces that had attacked him. In the chaos of battle, he'd avoided being beheaded, and something he couldn't fathom had made it impossible for one of Fallon Nuit's master vampires to drive a stake through his heart. Odd. A strange arc of energy had spared his chest and had given his attackers pause. The split-second advantage allowed him to take out his immediate opponent, but it had not kept him from being badly mangled in the blood struggle with the others. Were he not in so much pain, he would have questioned what spared him, and then laughed at the irony of it all.

"Pride goeth before a fall," his mother had always said when he was still human. She, too, was right. What good were expensive suits on a dead man? He thought about how he'd once put so much emphasis on being well-groomed, the perfection of his haircut, his material possessions, all that he owned. No wonder he was damned. He'd never put a value on his soul, and now his once-athletic body was ripped to shreds and of no use.

His right eye was almost sealed shut. Multiple blows to his face had left a gaping hole that remained from where a claw took out his left eye and a part of his cheek. An attacker from behind had gotten to his one arm in mid-swing—that was now precariously dangling from filleted cartilage and ligaments, no longer in the shoulder socket that once housed it. When he'd fallen from the impact, like vultures they'd gone for his legs, his mobility, leaving one leg stripped of muscle and flesh down to the bone over a multiple compound fracture, and his ribs on one side had been crushed. There had been just too many of them that descended upon him like rabid wolves. Now his immortality was a curse, keeping him locked within a pain-riddled carcass.

His entire existence flashed through his mind in snapshots. Everything in his short lifespan was measured before the vampire turning point, and after it. B.V., before vampirism, and A.V., after vampirism. Before he had been turned, he'd squandered his talents for business by investing in the drug world and had been king of his hill. He was a real predator—and had been preyed upon by his own kind. Vampiri. A mournful howl entered his chest and escaped from the confines of his broken jaw. *What had he done?*

When the Vampire Council's forces had rushed the tunnel in search of him and his Neteru cargo, it had created a distraction for Nuit's army—but not before the rogues had angrily jettisoned him to the topside, earth. Their demons had made haste to lay him in the open desert two hundred yards away from a cave entrance before returning to the underworld civil war . . . two hundred yards away from the safety of a sunshield with dawn approaching. No mercy. That was the way of his world.

Badly wounded, and unable to hunt to feed himself in order to regenerate, he knew his fate was sealed. He didn't even have enough telepathic energy to mentally project himself to a safe place beyond the sun's reach; he could barely lift his head. He just laid there in the dark awaiting dawn.

Yet an eerie calm befell him, like that of a man who has finally accepted his demise. Soon daylight would incinerate him. It would burn away what remained of his flesh and turn it to a pile of ash, but it would also release his embattled soul. The pain of sunlight would pass in minutes, and would be nothing in comparison to the suffering that tortured him now.

Carlos stopped struggling against the hard, rock-strewn ground. The desert night air was cool. Coyotes howled, and he could sense them coming nearer to him; he was carrion. What did it matter? He had already been ripped to shreds, and his heart had no beat, no blood flowed through his veins. The Covenant of Light had been wrong. There was no second chance. In life, he had been a predator, feeding on the weak and dying as a drug lord, luring them and seducing them with his product. Now the carrion feeders were about to fill their bellies with his dying remains. Yes, only fitting. Karma.

Besides, there was no going back to a human existence, not with two significant mob factions looking for him, as well as the FBI.

There was no joining the Minion, Fallon Nuit's rogues, even after conquering Nuit, their attack made that clear. The old vampires posed no option, either. They wanted him to hunt down the only source of light in his life and bring her to them—and he'd never give them Damali.

So, Carlos waited. He could feel his body being nudged and sniffed by the jackal-like creatures of the desert. Out of pure reflex, he snarled, having no real energy to do more to defend himself. But the animals yelped and backed up in confusion. He could feel their terror and see them retreat with his inner mind's eye, at least. But eventually Damali's image eclipsed even that. *God, please let her have made it out alive.* He fully closed his half-shut eye. Profound. Near death, and with her name in his skull, he could call the name that used to scorch his brain.

Seeing her inside his head, the last still frame of her as she turned to him once, her eyes filled with tears, her voice strong but trembling, begging him to come with them. She'd seen him in full vampire mode, knew what he was, had watched him transform, but foolishly insisted that he come away with her and her guardians. Carlos allowed the sweet balm of her belief in him to enter his bones. It dulled the excruciating pain. As long as he could see Damali's face, her eyes, her Isis sword raised above her head . . . her eyes closing as tears for him ran down her face . . .

They had taken his soul, but they could never take his memory of her. The warmth within her being blanketed him. He remembered her touch, her kiss, her smile, her passionate spoken words, her music. His undamaged hand clawed the sandy earth as he remembered the softness of her bronze skin, the smell of shoulder-length locks, the way her black pupils eclipsed the color of dark brown irises when she looked deeply into his mind. All five-foot-seven inches of her lithe, athletic frame had fused to his in a desperate hug. She had not given up on him, refused to let him go, even when she saw the beast within him. And both vampire nations had wanted him to turn over such a precious vessel to them to pollute her with their demonic seed . . . to turn her untouched womb into a sanctuary for daywalker fetuses? Never! Not even as a dead man.

His foot pushed against the stones and gravel. One hand clawed and grappled at it to drag his battered form forward. His inner radar drew him to where it was dark and cool as the planet slowly began to heat with approaching dawn. Pain riddled him as he slithered along the ground millimeter by millimeter, tearing open flesh wounds against his abdomen and torso.

Exhaustion and agony claimed him, filling his pores with profound torture until he stopped his struggle. His skin began to feel hot, prickly. A cold shiver washed through him. He knew he was going into shock. Sweat ran down his face and covered his back and chest, the salt of it igniting new shards of pain as it entered his gaping wounds. It wouldn't be long before the night lifted and gave way. He'd loved Damali so much; didn't she know if he could reverse the hands of time, he would have? But that was beyond even a master vampire's powers—just like he was beyond redemption. The situation was what it was; he was what he was, and soon the sun would cook that away.

Damali's voice entered his skull, the last stanza of her concert song, the one she'd composed as a secret message to him . . . the refrain that he'd so arrogantly ignored, *"Remember, baby, how it used to be? When we were just kids, and so free."*

Yes, baby, I remember . . . It was all he had left.

Three nights later . . .

"Father Patrick, are you sure you should get so close to the beast? It is not yet full daylight, it's wounded and could attack." The younger cleric placed a trembling hand on the old man's shoulder, trying to get him to heed caution as he glanced around the dark cavern, a torch and flashlights their only source of illumination. He made the sign of the cross over his heart as soon as one of the lights glinted off a set of fangs. *"Madre de Dios . . ."* His voice was a strangled whisper.

The gruesome remains of a vampire were the last thing he'd expected to ever see when he entered the clergy and became a priest. He'd heard about myths and legends like this that were rampant among his people in the countryside, but never in his life had he believed. These were superstitions, the rationalizations of simplistic people left over from a time gone by. In fact, he didn't even believe in exorcisms. The church itself was very, very skeptical about even discussing such things. But now he was out in the middle of nowhere in the desert, in a cave, *at night,* with three old men claiming to be clerical warriors, who were advancing, without fear, toward something unfathomable? Until he spied the thing they spoke of, he had simply not believed.

Padre Manuel Lopez swallowed hard and wanted to look away, but could not. Fear gripped him and kept his gaze firmly on the thing that bore fangs and had only half a face.

"Padre Lopez . . . Manuel, there are only three of us left from the original twelve in the Covenant," the senior cleric replied after selecting a place for the others to set down a huge, silver chest. "My friends, Asula, Lin, and me." The Moor and the Buddhist nodded. "You are new, and do not understand *this* beast like we do." He let out a long, patient breath.

"My visions have led us here. The only reason you are here, Padre, is because your parish is near and we don't know this region. We needed an anointed man of faith to be our guide, or we would have spared you this grisly sight. On your insistence, you have entered this cave. We tried to warn you, but you would not heed our advice. So, please do not interrupt our mission."

"Patrick is right. He is a knight of Templar from the highest order, and the seer of our Covenant of the twelve major faiths in the world. The others were lost in the battle to protect our Neteru. Her team made it out, but ours all but perished. So many of us died with that honor. Those who made it out alive, died soon after from the wounds they'd sustained," Asula said quietly. "This beast saved our lives. Saved our Neteru. That is what matters here."

"How can that be?" Manuel's eyes darted between the three older men and the heavy silver trunk they had set down only yards away from the creature.

"He placed himself between our teams and those who attacked us," Lin answered, folding his arms over his chest. "The adversary showed no mercy."

"You think it's too late?" Asula stared at Father Patrick, worry lacing his question.

"I don't know," he said, his tone carrying the same grave concern. "Three nights is an eternity for a vampire who has been wounded and cannot feed himself."

Manuel looked stricken. "I thought we came to kill it, not revive it with witchcraft!"

"Calm yourself," Lin warned as they flipped open the trunk. "This is no witchcraft—it's donated blood from our order."

"Since when does the church authorize—"

"This did not go through normal channels," Father Patrick said, cutting him off.

"Obviously not!"

Father Patrick sighed. "Think of it this way. If we were the government, this would be considered a necessary black ops mission. But we work for the highest realms, and this is a white light mission of salvation. Therefore it's a very discreet white ops mission." He studied the young man for a moment, and then went back to the task at hand.

"How so?" the young priest whispered, taking a cautious step backward. "You come with bags of blood to revive a creature of the night . . . our church does not know about this . . . You have the gall to carry it in a Vatican silver chest with the holy crucifix on it—"

"Enough. We do this because the warrior angels wrested this creature's soul from the pit, and it is now in Purgatory," Asula said calmly, lifting out a bag of blood and tossing it to land near the vampire's face. "The dark side violated supernatural law, took him too early in accordance with the three-day laws of transformation. He was immediately turned, and his choice was stolen from him. This entity did not willingly give his soul—he was deceived. And now he is on our side."

"As long as his soul is in Purgatory," Father Patrick said, "Carlos Rivera still has a choice, has time. He has not fed from an innocent human victim, yet. Our job is to see that he doesn't."

Lin cut the top off a container and threw it toward the vampire's ravaged body, splashing his face with its contents. "But I fear we're too late. If he were stronger, he would have awakened to attack us, smelling our blood, or the blood we carry." He then looked at Father Patrick, ignoring the alarmed young clergyman. "If the blood doesn't revive him . . ."

Father Patrick and Imam Asula nodded and spoke in unison. "Then we're too late."

"The merciful thing to do would be to behead him," Monk Lin said upon a whisper.

The smell. Obviously he was hallucinating. Carlos inhaled the sweet elixir of life and licked his parched lips. A series of sharp pains about his mouth made him tentative about exploring the pungent scent further. It *had* to be a starvation-induced hallucination, anyway. Why waste the energy or endure the agony?

He was so close to extinction that he could feel warm bodies close by and hear the clamor of men debating in low tones. He stuck his tongue out and lapped at the sticky, cool fluid on his face, unable to resist the survival reflex to seek blood. The salty, thick liquid burned the open wounds on his face. Blood should be warm, not cold.

Another cold splash hit his face, and a smooth pouch landed against his clenched fist. Plastic blood bombs from above? Carlos laughed inside his mind. Yeah, right . . . But the taste and the smell of life were all around him. He opened one puffed, battered eye and squinted.

The young priest stared in horror as the creature before him opened one glowing red eye that intermittently flashed gold. "You have awakened the beast! Now kill it, before it's too late!"

"No!" Asula argued, and flung another bag of blood toward Carlos. "We told you! This one was once a guardian, and was destined to be paired with the Neteru—"

At the mention of Damali, Carlos struggled to push himself up. All the men before him drew back, weapons raised, dead silence enveloping them. He could hear their hearts beating loudly within their chests, their pulses racing, their lungs slowly expanding and contracting with small, terrified sips of air. *Be afraid,* he warned within his mind. *Be very afraid.* Even a few swallows had revived him enough to imperil a human. He reached his hand toward the scent of blood and snatched it, splashing the cold substance against his fist and on the ground with his tight grasp, then sucked as much as he could from the bag. His body began to heal itself.

He snatched another bag in one deft motion as it hurled toward him. He tossed the drained bag away in frustration, narrowing his gaze on the four warm bodies before him. Yes . . . be very afraid.

"Carlos," a familiar voice said, "we have come to help you. Here is more. Regenerate quickly. Heal yourself. We have less than an hour to get you to a lair." Another bag hit Carlos in the chest.

Carlos caught the bag before it dropped to the ground, snarled, and drank down the contents, feeling a surge of energy as some of the pain abated.

"He'll need all of it," another voice said, "if he is to completely heal."

"And, if that's not enough? What then?"

That voice was younger, higher. He gave off the delicious scent of fear.

"Then, you'll be the first to go," Carlos said in a low warning.

"No," the older familiar voice said firmly. "He is an innocent. A cleric. Kill him, and my warriors end this while you're still wounded."

The familiarity of the voice, talk of innocents, and clerics . . . It forced Carlos to focus, to strain to see the blurry shapes around him as he drank. Templars? Still not sated, but much improved, he held onto his near-amputated arm with his good hand and leaned against a column of rock.

The electric blue robes worn by the human with the familiar voice held his attention, and he studied the strange crucifix that had a bleeding heart surrounded by thorns in the center of it. The white-haired cleric slowly lowered his sword, and the glint of the silver in the dim light brought it all back for him. Father Patrick, the blue knight of the Covenant. The seer who had told him of his fate and fought side-by-side with Damali and the guardians against his predecessor, his nemesis, Fallon Nuit.

"You recognize me, don't you?" the man said in a steady, confident voice.

"Its eyes have gone from red to gold, Patrick," a tall, strapping African-looking cleric swathed in all white said. "That is a good sign. He's normalizing and is not in attack mode." He continued to hold his machete in a readiness position, but his stance seemed relaxed.

"Yes. His face is nearly healed, save the empty socket," another of them said. He was an Asian man in dark brown clothes, who also bore a familiar voice.

The only man that looked positively terror stricken was a young priest without a weapon, dressed in a black Catholic habit.

"There were more of you," Carlos finally said, his voice raspy. "You were with us in the tunnels, right?"

"Yes, and we saw you fight with honor," the Moor replied. "We also know you nearly died before we evacuated."

"And Damali?" Pain sent a seizure through Carlos as his partially severed arm locked back into its socket, and he bent, letting out an awful cry of agony. He could feel his ribs reconstruct under the skin, and he grabbed his face as a lightning strike of torture made the raw flesh where his missing eye had been feel like a knife had been gouged into it.

Dropping to both hands, he panted as his ruptured kidneys realigned and healed and the compound fracture in his leg reset. His arms trembled, forcing him to drop to the dank cave floor. Skin from undamaged sections of his body stretched and multiplied to cover areas that had been stripped of flesh to conceal skeleton and ragged muscle that knit itself together like steel cable.

"Throw him another bag," Father Patrick ordered.

Almost too sick to ingest it, Carlos grappled with the bag that had been flung toward him, slitting it with a fang and practically inhaling the dark, thick liquid. As his body temperature heated up, he pulled the shreds of his shirt off, sweat running down his chest, his back, coating his arms. Panting, he lay there for a while, allowing the last of the shudders of pain to abate. He felt stronger, whole, but was tender as all hell. His entire body felt like he'd been punched and then run over by a Mack truck. The parts of him that had not been previously injured now stung from the process of splitting and cloning more tissue for the wounded organs. But at least he could see. At least he was alive, or more correctly stated, still existed.

"Damali?" he wheezed, trying to stand too soon, but wobbled and fell. "I have to get to her."

"You would let a vampire near the precious vessel?" Manuel crossed himself again and glanced nervously at the other men of the cloth.

"He is the only one who can help her at present," Father Patrick said. "Our Neteru's light diminishes daily."

"What happened to her?" Carlos was on his feet now, pacing. His fist connected with a section of the cave wall, leaving a crumble of rock where it had landed. He tried to think of her, to lock in on her present location, but all his mind would offer was glimpses of the past. He stared at the old seer.

"I cannot locate her, either, my friend. She's blind."

"What do you mean, blind?" Carlos stared at the man, thinking of how his own eye had been ripped from his skull in the fight. The thought of that happening to his woman made the air stop moving in and out of his lungs. Her beautiful face . . . even her name meant *beautiful vision*, to have that maimed, with no way to regenerate—all the plastic surgery in the human world couldn't repair her. Anger burned in his stomach, forcing bile up to his throat. He swallowed it back down along with unshed tears.

"She couldn't withstand the thought of your turning . . . or what she saw in the tunnels." The older man's voice was calm, sad, almost soothing. "Our huntress has shut down her third eye."

"But she's vulnerable without her second sight," Carlos murmured, his gaze holding the blue knight's. "You have to make her see again."

The clerics all nodded, as the one in blue rubbed his hand over his jaw in contemplation. "She still possesses the other gifts . . . superior strength, heightened senses of scent, taste, and hearing, she can feel with profound enlightenment. But her third eye is extremely vulnerable. It is what helps her see into souls, thoughts . . . and before long, if it doesn't come back, her other senses will begin to erode."

"I know," Carlos said quickly, "but why is she blind? I still don't understand. She was fine when she left the tunnels. Why now?"

"She had others she cared for at her side . . . it is in her nature to protect her own," the elder cleric said in a quiet tone. "But once the immediate danger had passed, her heart sealed with total despair and the loss of hope. She saw you ripped apart and die—at least she believes you died in those tunnels. Her third eye took those images into her mind and she watched it all. She loved you and your brutal death broke her heart the way nothing else has. Up until that moment she still had hope that you would turn to the side of light and come with the guardians. That hope was so deep and strong that the loss of it is eating away at her soul like a cancer."

"The loss of this hope—of you—makes her imminently more vulnerable to the Vampire Council, Carlos," the Moor added in a quiet, worried tone. "They will eventually sense this and will relentlessly pursue her." He paused. "And she may very well surrender. Once she does, they will not relinquish her until her next fertility, and once again the threat of daywalkers will be upon us." Asula hesitated. "You know we cannot allow this . . . even if we must ultimately take the Neteru out of the equation for her own good."

Carlos snarled, and flexed his hands. They had actually threatened her in his presence? Were they mad?

"That was never our intention," Monk Lin assured him.

"Do her guardians know about this?" Carlos's tone was even and lethal.

"Their gifts are ebbing, too, with a significant loss of hope, shaken faith, and . . . other issues clouding their judgment." Father Patrick looked at him squarely. "The Neteru compound is in jeopardy. The family is fracturing, and were it not for the civil war within the vampire realms, it would have been under siege as we speak."

"The compound is a fortress!" Carlos shouted. "I saw it, it's nearly impenetrable."

"Nearly," the large cleric named Asula said in a calm voice. "Nearly. But you got in—through her. *She* had them lower the barricades for *you*. One day, perhaps for the same reason, another shrewd master vampire will get in, too, but with very different intentions and horrific outcomes." He paused and stared at Carlos hard, but there was no anger in his eyes, just urgency.

Fury roiled within Carlos, but it was also mixed with something else now—fear.

"There's an old Ghanaian proverb that says, 'The ruin of a nation begins in the homes of its people.' " Asula's voice was unwavering and held authority, just like his gaze. "The Neteru compound is representative of nations. The guardians are all from every faith and group of people, merged as one family—as it should be on earth. Her home, her family unit, must be strong. There's not enough technology in the world to keep out evil . . . and we know that religious amulets are playthings, if there is not strong faith to back them up. Break the family and the second line of defense at the compound fails. We, the Covenant, her first line of defense, have all but been broken . . . we lost two-thirds of our number down in Hell."

Father Patrick nodded as Carlos backed away from Asula and relaxed.

"This is why we need your help. She doesn't even have uplifting music in her heart—which is the core of her gift. Without her spoken word, without her ability to touch others through this medium . . . her spirit will further wither."

"And what am I supposed to do?" Carlos gave them his back to consider in frustration as he walked a few paces deeper into the cave. "She hates all that I am, all that I stood for in life—and hates what I am now. No wonder she went blind."

Profound guilt claimed him and tore at him like a fresh wound. "I can't even trust myself in her presence." Carlos found his vision blurring once more as he kept his face turned away from the misguided clerics. "I never want to see that look in her eyes again," he finally said, his voice dropping to a broken whisper. "Never."

"Our ranks are thinning," Asula said. "Hers are battered, exhausted, a few may be on the run trying to reestablish another safe house. The vibrations Father Pat has picked up say the group is splintering, looking to go their separate ways."

"Where is she now?"

"When the Neteru and her guardians came up from the tunnels, they immediately sought hallowed ground," Lin replied.

"They've been moving from those places in a crisscross pattern through LA, trying to get back to the compound for the last few days," Father Patrick said in a quiet voice. "The first night after the concert, the streets were crawling. They had to seek immediate shelter in the cathedral closest to the stadium. The next morning, human vampire helpers worked through the police to have them briefly detained for questioning after the concert on the ruse of needing information about the young people that had been victimized at the events. This ate up precious daylight for them to move within. But a man named Berkfield worked behind the scenes to have them quickly released before nightfall."

Carlos stared at Father Patrick.

"You know this man?" the older cleric asked, stepping forward.

"I did him a favor, guess he did me one without even knowing it. Yeah . . . I know him. He's marked by me as off-limits."

All the clerics glanced at each other. Shoulders relaxed. Weary expressions gave way to what Carlos could only interpret as hope.

"They were released and had to find a safe place to wait out the second night," Father Patrick said, his voice now more urgent. "On this third night, we've lost her trail, because she went completely blind. Her team seer is nearly blind. The guardians have broken the cord to the Light, and even I can't get a clear vision on them, the loss of hope in them is so great. That is the other reason we sought you."

Carlos sucked in a deep breath and let it out slowly. "What was the first reason? And *how* did you find me?"

"There is still the unresolved matter of your redemption," Father Patrick said wearily. "I am a seer, and I was led by the same thing that saved you from being staked. Hope. Faith. It was my only beacon to find you. Your hope for her was bright; hers for you is so dim, I cannot sense it to locate her. When you, a vampire, asked God to spare her—you called on the Almighty, then I could clearly see you." He nodded toward the young cleric, Padre Lopez. "He also helped immensely. For some reason, he, even more so than I, could get a direct lock on you—and he knew the region."

Carlos turned around and folded his arms over his chest, closely watching his odd benefactors. "My possible parole, which you call redemption, saved my life in the tunnels?"

All of the clerics except the young one shook their heads no. The one named Manuel just stood there with his mouth slightly agape.

"The Neteru's brand saved you," Father Patrick stated, nodding at Carlos's chest. "See for yourself. You owe her."

Carlos looked down at his bare chest. A full-scale imprint of a woman's fist with a dagger clutched in it, and part of a slender forearm was now a slightly darker bronzed-tone, a raised keloid burn scar that covered his heart. He reverently touched the strange marking on his flesh with the tips of his fingers.

"From when you carried her in the silver suit she wore in the tunnels," the older man stated calmly.

In snatches of memory Carlos remembered holding Damali in his arms. He'd cradled her against him like a baby, and it had nearly torched him. Yes, he remembered the smell of her hair, even while his own skin slowly burned. No question he remembered the scent of her ripening, and he'd never forget the way his desire for her had blunted even the pain of silver searing against his flesh.

"When Nuit's forces attacked you, her brand kept their stakes from entering what she'd sealed. She even prayed in your arms in the middle of Hell—as a fully ripened Neteru—which you didn't violate." The old priest shook his head and addressed his colleagues. "You are very much harder to kill now. As long as the Neteru's seal is upon you, you cannot perish from the stake. She covers your heart. But you can still be beheaded . . . Think fully with your heart on this situation—not just your mind."

Deep. Carlos laughed. "Are you serious?"

"Deadly serious." The old priest arched an eyebrow. "Help us find her. Our Covenant trackers perished, my sight is useless. No one is answering the phones at the compound. She doesn't want to be found. My two colleagues are hearing and tactile sensors, but they are out of range. Help us find her and restore her hope. Time is of the essence."

Carlos shook his head. "You're men of the cloth; you must have words of strength, prayers for her. But if not, I can find her . . . dead or alive."

The clerics looked at each other and then at Carlos. For a moment no one said a word.

"Then replenish yourself with the rest of what's in the trunk," Father Patrick finally said. "We have a safe house just over the border in the Santa Monica Mountains. Project yourself there. We will need a day to fly in the traditional way via airlines to subsequently meet you. The lair is protected by prayers. Don't worry," he said when he saw Carlos stiffen. "You will be able to pass through them. The refrigerators are well-stocked with donated blood. Your chambers are the lower level. We hope you'll find it comfortable. A reinforced steel door locks it from the inside. The place is also externally fortified against intrusion."

For a while Carlos leaned against the cave wall and looked off into the distance, thinking. "I don't know if I have enough energy to project myself that far and the tunnels are too dangerous. I might have to travel with you all tonight."

"So be it. We cannot wait here another night, but we can possibly do this like it was once done in the old days . . . as unsavory as that may be to you."

"The old days?"

"In Dracula's era, a master vampire was couriered during daylight inside a coffin surrounded by the earth of his lair."

"No way!" Carlos pushed himself away from the wall. "I'll stay here for a night or so, get stronger, then leave on my own."

"Your choice. But every night you stay here alone, you run the risk of your enemies picking up your trail. Our prayers at the safe house will keep you hidden from them. We have opened the boundaries to you only."

That reality gave Carlos pause, and he let his breath out hard in frustration. He was not going out like that again. Yet the last thing he wanted to risk was an airport search where some stupid security guard might open his coffin and fry him in broad daylight.

The elder cleric nodded. "You'll have to trust us. No one will open the coffin if priests are accompanying it. There are some protocols afforded our calling."

"Seems you guys have thought of everything," Carlos said slowly, still not fully trusting them. "How do I know it's not a trap?"

Father Patrick stepped dangerously close to Carlos. "I give you permission to use your telepathy to see the location and to sense through me whether or not there is a trap."

Carlos studied him carefully. "You got a lotta faith, Father. Might be foolish. You know, I could reach out and snap your neck. I'd get a real kick from the adrenaline rushing through your blood. The bagged stuff is much weaker and it takes more to produce a buzz, feel me?" Carlos smiled a half smile as the other men bristled. But he had to respect the old dude when he didn't even flinch.

"That's not what you're going to do, however."

"Why not?" Carlos asked, seriously mulling over the possibility.

"Because you still have a chance to save your soul, which is something you now want almost as much as you want Damali back in your arms."

The response gave him pause.

"I opened my mind," Father Patrick said, "and to read me, you have to open yours. We both know how a mind lock works, and are too wise for games. Fair exchange is no robbery, Carlos. I believe that is a favorite saying where you're from."

"This is bullshit."

"Is it?"

"I'm out."

"You know, redemption requires a period of atonement." The priest casually studied his nails as Carlos moved even closer to him. "I'm old," he added. "I've lived my life, done what I was supposed to do. Kill me and I ascend and will have nothing more to do with this foul earth. But, you, my friend, have a long road before you. You might want some guidance along the way. But, again, as always, it's your choice."

Carlos frowned. He felt trapped, and hated it. "I find her for you, secretly guard her while you—"

"No secrets," the old man said evenly. "We have four men here—"

"Four?" Padre Lopez's glance shot around the small cavern. "I am not—"

"We pleaded with you to stay outside the cave," Asula said, cutting him off.

"Can you go back to pretending that incarnate evil does not exist, now?" Monk Lin asked, staring at him hard.

"Once you have seen this, life as you've known it has ceased to exist. This is why we gave you a choice, Padre. Now you have just been inducted into the Covenant."

"Seems like homeboy just got jacked, if you ask me," Carlos said, shaking his head. "He could pose a risk."

"All of us pose a risk." Father Patrick sighed. "We all have free will. Padre Lopez can go back to his parish and tend weddings and funerals, and do what a good shepherd does. Or, he can be a part of something larger. It will always be his choice. But that can be decided later."

"Get back to the part about this protection squad," Carlos said, tiring of the conversation. He wanted to get to Damali. He needed to see her, even if he couldn't be near her. He needed to know what was expected of him, and what his atonement sentence was all about. The approaching dawn was also a threat, and he needed rest and to feed some more.

"Damali Richards and her team make eight additional members, added with our four, less one, to bring the total to eleven . . . we are missing one for the holy number of twelve. It is Canon Law—twelve. Always twelve." The cleric pointed at Carlos. "You're number twelve."

"You must be high." Carlos brushed past the four men and headed toward the cave's entrance. He'd project himself far away from all of this madness even if it took the last of his strength. "Join a human team to fight vampires and demons? Plus, your math is off! You said you're four—less one?"

"Me. I'm the one who cannot go on the last leg on this mission," Father Patrick said.

"Why not?" Carlos stared at the man hard. "You a punk, now, or something?"

"Hardly. But I am a seer and this is not my destiny. I would only add an additional risk."

The concept disturbed him. He'd seen the old cleric fight valiantly, with honor. Had to give credit where credit was due. Plus, he'd just saved his life. Aw'ight, he'd let his argument rest. "Okay, respect. My bad. But since y'all are into this destiny vibe, then what's my destiny?"

"You were supposed to be a guardian," the old man coolly remarked. "You strayed from the path and caused much heartache and destruction in the world, even before you became a vampire. The law of our realm requires guardian service. Think of it like community service, in exchange for this misused time. Seven years. You began hard dealing and took a life at sixteen—you were turned at twenty-three, we want your seven dark years back . . . and you'd better be thankful that threefold the time was not exacted. By rights, we could have asked for twenty-one years, but your atonement time has been reduced, given the nature of your assignment, and the lives you saved when it counted most. And . . . it may be seven years, but it will feel like twenty-one when you're done. Trust me."

"Fuck that!" Carlos said angrily. "Seven years of being a guardian, seven years of going into battle like the one I just narrowly escaped?"

"Protecting the Neteru, yes." Father Patrick folded his arms over his chest. "For every person you killed, you must save three. For every life you altered by your negative energies, you must restore threefold. For every family you hurt by the sale of drugs, you must restore three. Our sentence is light. You've already been to Hell and have seen the alternative."

Carlos closed his eyes and felt his shoulders slump in defeat. Seven years of invisibly moving throughout the earth to save lives, seven years of being a spiritual cop . . . seven years to possibly watch his woman fall in love with a human male, make love, live life, possibly marry and have kids . . . seven years to walk the planet as a shadow, her shadow, loving her like he did from inside a prison without bars . . . and never able to be with her, because when she ripened to Neteru fertility again, together they could start a line of daywalkers—and if she had a man and children, those she loved would be at risk.

It was too much to ask; nothing on the planet could stop a master vampire from going for a fertile Neteru. He'd kill whatever was in his path to get to her, even these kindhearted, misguided clerics. He'd learned that much about himself while in Hell. Yeah, just as he was finishing his sentence, the way his luck was running, she'd ripen and they'd smoke him. But that was the future and right now she was at risk from his kind.

There were four other master vampires topside, one for each point on the council pentagram, and Nuit had just been dusted. Carlos studied the odds. Those guys were probably too busy defending their borders right now, and wouldn't immediately risk coming into Nuit's old zones. They wouldn't cross borders, anyway, without council sanction. But soon one of them might get bold and try a power grab.

Carlos closed his eyes for a moment, seeing the world map from Hell's perspective. The sixth point was for the crest—the council—the sixth continent where they drew their food down from transporter bats. The seventh continent was laid fallow in wait for the coming Armageddon. The bullshit was supposed to go down right in the old Biblical lands. Oh, yeah, the priest was right. They were coming for his baby—one side or the other—eager topside masters or council. That was unacceptable.

"My mom, and my grandmom . . . Juanita . . . will be safe?" Carlos asked, distracting himself from torturous thoughts.

"They have been put in the federal witness protection program, courtesy of the police officer you saved and gave information to regarding your former drug connections. They live well, Carlos. He's a man of his word—honorable," Monk Lin said with compassion. "Your assets have been liquidated and transferred to them. Our prayers also protect them."

Carlos could only nod. Everything the blue-robed priest said made sense. Even in his former life, the deal was a body for a body. It went down like that in the vampire nations, too. As above, so below. He owed, big time. He'd been given a second chance, something many a dying man would covet. But why did it feel like such a hollow bargain? Here he was a man that had lost his whole world and had to seek shelter in a coffin in order to get on a flight to LAX. This situation was beyond fucked up.

"Aw'ight." Carlos sighed. "But only on one condition."

"You're not in a position to cut any further deals, Carlos," Father Patrick said in warning. "Have you any idea what intercessory prayers had to be heard to even get this case plea bargained at the highest realms? Do you know what we each have put on the line if this mission fails? And have you any idea how all of us are in the same proverbial boat should you kill an innocent? We have stepped out on pure faith for you. We put your case to the highest levels of mercy, and were given the message of atonement I gave you. Do not trifle with this opportunity—or I will exterminate you myself. That is also my job."

The two men stared at each other for a moment. Carlos nodded. The old man relaxed.

"If I were to hear your appeal, however," the priest said, "what would that one condition be?"

Again Carlos's gaze sought a distant place within the cave's blackness. "I don't want her to see me, if it can be avoided. I'll find her, will protect her, but don't want her to see me . . . at least until I know I can take it."

The small group of clerics shared concerned glances.

"If it can be avoided . . . That's fair. It doesn't violate any of the rules of engagement—but she must know of your existence. We will not have secrets, or risk her team inadvertently taking aim at you as a predator. Unless you become one." The old man looked at Carlos hard, but his eyes also held empathy. "The first assignment is an anathema to us, and we need a full team. There have been a strange series of deaths in the mountains in Brazil—none resemble vampire bites, or demon possessions. We don't know what it is."

"Let me investigate it alone," Carlos said fast. "I don't want her or her team near it—forget that full team shit. Damali almost got wasted, and if one of her family gets snuffed, there'll be no way for any of us to help her deal with that." He looked at the clerics hard. "*That* is non-negotiable."

To his surprise, the clerics simply nodded and didn't argue. He relaxed a bit.

"Then let's do this clean and simple," Carlos muttered, waving his hand to fully clothe himself with the illusion of a black tailored suit, white silk shirt with a bandit collar, closed by an onyx stud that matched his cuff links. He looked down and willed a pair of black leather slip-ons, and straightened a hint of white handkerchief in his breast pocket.

With a glance, his nails buffed and any traces of dirt and blood vanished from his being. He wiped his face with his hands to remove the shadow of stubble that had begun to sprout on his jaw, and ran his fingers through his hair to instantly bring about the well-groomed image, then ran his tongue over his incisors until they retracted. He didn't care about the stunned expressions of his wardens. If he was gonna go out in a black box, then let it be with style. Some dignity.

"Where's the casket?"

Her head jerked up. She drew in a deep inhale. Erotic reflex to the scent slowly lowered her lids. *They'd found him.*

A quiet ache of anticipation traveled through her. The low purr emanating from her chest echoed off the lair walls. She had to go to him, but how? Frustration became an angry roar, muscles tensing. She walked out to the lair's narrow ledge.

If he only knew how long she'd waited for him. Just one male Master had been made for this region—then fate conspired to bring an embarrassment of riches to her territory. There had been *two* of them. And because of one foolish little girl, they had both perished on the same night. It had been a travesty. An obscene waste of valuable resources. This Neteru had to die a swift and awful death for the offense.

No one could ever fathom how the loss of hope had nearly strangled her, because who knew when the vampires would begin to repopulate the region properly? With a civil war going on, it could have been decades.

But, then again, survival of the fittest has been the way of the world since the dawn of time. She chuckled low in her throat and stopped pacing on the narrow ledge. The street rogue, not the bourgeois, had survived. Perhaps the young girl had actually assisted her in discovering which male was the more worthy mate? Ironic.

She cautioned herself not to be hasty. Capturing prey was a combination of stealth, strength, skill, but most essentially, patience. To be truly effective, one had to get in the right position and wait for the open opportunity to pounce.

Maybe this girl was useful as bait? The Neteru had mobility, could lure him . . . It didn't matter, as long as he came to the right territory. From that point, nature—basic vampiric instinct—would finish the transaction. Promiscuity was the foundation of their nature.

However, there was one thing for sure: even injured, he exuded a level of charismatic power unmatched by his predecessor. It was the rough edge and raw strength that she loved best, the bit of male animal just under the surface blended with his sense of swift justice . . . as well as his affinity for strategic vengeance. The fact that he was an extraordinary physical specimen was an added attribute that could not be denied.

She let out a long, satisfied sigh, then breathed him in again. She had to hand it to the council. Their craftsmanship was superb when it came to developing empire builders. He was perfect.

CHAPTER FIVE

SHE'D SLEPT as long as she could, but then had to get up. The visit with Inez had made restful sleep impossible, but she wasn't sleeping that much these days anyway.

Damali glanced around her bedroom. What was the point in trying to keep the illusion going that there was a way to make oneself safe? As long as the world was at war, there was no place to hide.

They'd done the best they could to gild her cage: wonderful private bathroom within the suite of her private sanctuary, her bedroom, that had been practically turned into a lush replica of the Garden of Eden with plants everywhere, Moroccan tiles on the shower wall, and a gorgeous slate-framed Jacuzzi. In fact, each room within the guardian compound, except the weapons room, was like a veritable museum, filled with comfortable appointments and beauty all around, designed to take the sting out of spending so much time behind its walls. But just like comfy chairs and art couldn't totally take the sterility out of a hospital, art and a game room and whatnot sure didn't make the compound feel like any less of a fortress.

Sitting up slowly, Damali pulled herself out of bed and hurried through a shower. She snatched on her jeans and a top with purpose, not even taking the time to really labor over whether the combination matched. She had things to do.

"Yo," she said on a yawn as she entered the kitchen and saw Rider, Jose, and Big Mike. She didn't wait for a response as she bent and began rummaging in the refrigerator.

A series of disgruntled "Good mornings" followed her greeting. That always bothered her. Hunting vamps and demons had put them on the predators' schedule. They got up out of bed late, like shift workers, and went to bed at dawn, just like vampires. Crazy. In the process of her mental battle, she spotted just what she wanted. A beer.

Damali stood and shut the door, and saluted Rider with the brew when he gave her a concerned glance. "Just trying to bite the snake that bit me."

"Which one would that be?" Rider asked, his gravelly voice holding tension as he watched her screw off the cap and take a healthy swig.

"Cheap wine after a Red Stripe."

Rider shivered, made a face, and smiled. "Will do it every time."

"They serving cheap wine in the vamp clubs these days, D?" Jose's detective-like question had come out quietly as he took a slow sip of coffee.

"No. Can call the vamps a lotta things," she said, amused as she took another sip, "but tacky isn't one of them." She knew Jose was trying to get all up in her business about where she'd been. He was right, too, about the wine. She wouldn't have bought cheap wine at a club. His intense eyes followed her around the room as she sat down across from Big Mike.

"Don't you think you need to have breakfast, first?"

She glanced at Big Mike, then leaned across the table and pecked his cheek. "Got cereal in a bottle, just like Rider showed me." She chuckled and turned the beer around and read the label. "It has hops and barley . . . hmmm . . . probably sugar—"

"Rider, I told you about your ways," Big Mike thundered, not amused. "After y'all eat, we need a weapons room meeting. Got a bunch of shit to get off my chest."

The threesome sat quietly peering at Big Mike's back as he stormed out of the kitchen. Damali glanced down at her beer and then up at Rider.

"Damn," she whispered to Rider. "A beer could do all that? What's his problem?"

Jose stood fast, glared at Damali, abandoned his coffee cup, and followed Mike out of the room.

Rider shrugged and clinked his spiked coffee mug against her beer bottle. "Guess it's just us two heathens for breakfast this morning, kiddo."

"I've had enough," Big Mike argued, his gaze holding each member in the weapons room for a moment before he spoke again. "For three days after the concert, we were on the run like we've never been—and

I never said a word. Held my peace while we went underground to re-group, hiding in churches, mosques, temples, synagogues—any hal-lowed ground we could find." He stared at Damali. "Then, I haven't said a word for the last month, but I'm not going to sit here and watch my little sister self-destruct."

Damali let her breath out hard in frustration. "I'm not self-destructing, I'm polishing my skills." She looked at Big Mike who was leaned against the door frame, then over at JL and Dan by the moni-tors for support. Finding none in their eyes, she bypassed Shabazz and Marlene who were sitting on stools on opposite sides of the room studying the floor, then over to Jose. His arms were folded as he sat on the sofa. Her gaze sought Rider for an ally as she plopped down hard on a stool and took another swig of her beer.

"Listen, people," Damali said carefully, setting down her brew on the edge of the table next to her Isis long blade. "We all got battle-freaked after doing Hell, right?" No one answered, so she pressed on. "If I'm supposed to be your so-called Neteru, then it's important for me to get back in the hunt. I had to know that I could hang, could still bring it, still had some juice after that bullsh—"

"Your language," Marlene said in a fast snap, cutting her off. "Everybody's language," she said, standing and walking toward the table that held an array of ammo. Marlene took the half-empty bottle off the table and walked back to a nearby waste can and dumped it. "Your attitude. Everybody's attitude," Marlene warned. "True, it is important for you to get back into the hunt. But it's *how* you get back into the game that's important."

"Mike's point, exactly," Shabazz said, his voice even, authoritative, and no-nonsense. "Marlene's point. We may have physically re-grouped, but we're a long way from being straight—as a team. The vibe ain't right." He looked at each team member, then again held Damali's eyes with his own. "You feel me?"

"Yeah, I feel you, 'Bazz," Damali said, her voice tight. "That's why it's time to get back on the road."

"What?!" Rider was off the sofa and now walking back and forth between the equipment table and the monitors. "Why in the hell would we—"

"Because we have to pay some bills, Rider," Damali said fast. When he stopped pacing and the others didn't jump in to debate her, she continued. "You all know how much the electric bill is in here, not to mention the maintenance on a fleet of Jeeps and a Hum-V, the artillery, and what it costs to constantly develop new weapons systems. That doesn't count what we normally spend on food, travel, your gig gear, or what have you. We need a few international venues now that we've done the *Raise the Dead* concert to keep the momentum going. I can feel it in my bones. Gotta make sure our CD goes platinum so we'll have royalties long after we've stopped gigging . . . we also need the soft-drink commercials, anything that will repeatedly play our music and send in checks. Maybe even land a film deal, something that keeps us mad-paid. I'm not overreacting."

Vindicated by their silence, Damali folded her arms over her chest. "Yeah, I've had a lot on my mind. Look around this joint and tell me our other sources of income? It ain't just the battle that's got a sistah stressed—it's the reality that, if for some reason the money gets funny, I have to know we can stay alive with or without all the electronics and the barricades." Her gazed raked Shabazz hard. "Now, do *you* feel me?"

"I may be the only non-musician in the group," Dan said after a moment, ending the standoff, "but Damali is right." He glanced around nervously toward the elder guardians in the group. "I do promotions. We can't afford to let this thing cool down, no matter what we've been through. While we were getting our heads together, I've been keeping the media wolves at bay." He sighed. "I told them that we were on a temporary hiatus so we could work on breaking out some new sounds, told them that the mysterious phenomenon called Damali was working on new cuts . . . it was bait for *Entertainment Tonight, Rolling Stone, People* magazine. The phones have been jumping, and I've tried my best to—"

"See," Damali said, opening her arms. "Stress!" She looked at Dan. "Thank you, *Dan,* for making my point. Of all people in here, the newest guardian understands what time it is." She watched him glance away, flattered but a little embarrassed by the compliment. "Book us wherever you can, tell the lesser venues we're gearing up for a world tour. I don't know where I want to go, but put some feelers out, Dan. I just can't sit around this compound much longer. I'll go nuts."

"Done," Dan said quickly, but his glance shot around the room.

Marlene nodded. "The utility companies don't wanna hear a long story about how we saved the world and that's why their checks are late."

"I know this was the last thing you expected after your bar mitzvah, Dan," Rider said, his glare sweeping to Dan, then back to Damali. "Just for the record, none of us *signed up* to be a guardian. We got the short straw in the grand cosmic equation. Dig? But, I'm ready to roll, if that's what we've gotta do to keep the lights on."

"I want—"

"Damn what *you* want, Damali!" Shabazz shot up from his seat and swung his arm toward Marlene and pointed at her. "I've got a bad vibe. *We* can feel it." He snatched his arm back and folded both of them over his chest. "I'm traveling with precious cargo. You're grown now, and need to dig it." Then just as suddenly as he'd spoken, he fell silent and walked back to his stool, sat heavily, stared at the floor and rubbed his jaw as though he'd said too much.

She felt the entire team bristle, and Marlene hadn't said a word. Big Mike and Rider had looked away. What the hell was going on?

"Eventually, I want a concert in every continent," she said again, taking her time to speak firmly. "I want us to hit every place that we know there's a topside master vampire still running shit. We're supposed to clean out master lairs, one by one, vamp territory by territory, taking down second levels and thirds after we hit the mast—"

"Are you nuts?" Jose shook his head and stood up to leave. "I'm not taking you anywhere to get yourself killed. Let's stay in the States for a while, since we know Nuit is history."

For a moment, the whole group stared at him. It was something about the way he'd said what he did, had personalized it a little too much. Damali shook off the uncomfortable feeling. Yeah, after losing Dee Dee, it made sense that Jose wouldn't want to take his little sister anywhere that might be crazy. That had been the main reason she wouldn't let him hang out with her. If he saw where she had been going, what she was doing every night, he would flip.

"Jose," she said more gently, "sooner or later, we have to go after the rest of them. The longer we wait, the more time the vamps have to regroup and get stronger. Just like with the music, we have to keep the momentum going."

"Yeah, D, but, we don't have to rush headlong into danger all the time. We're all only human, and need a break . . . need some time to just live life a little." Jose's eyes held a request in them that she couldn't comprehend, even though his words made total sense. "Damali, sometimes—"

"—A man needs to pick the right time to drop something on a sistah," Shabazz said quickly. The tension in the room was so thick now that you could cut it with a knife. Shabazz's comment sliced right through it. "Now ain't the time, little brother," he said, his tone even but gentle. "I ain't trying to risk nobody in here, either."

Damali looked at Shabazz, and noted that Marlene remained conspicuously silent. All right. She could appreciate Jose trying to stick up for the older couple, who, of all the members of the team, had the most to lose—namely each other. She could *definitely* appreciate that now. Damali nodded, ran her fingers through her locks, and sat back down.

"It's instinct," she said, her tone no longer holding the edge of rage. "You all said fighting evil was in my blood, and, yeah, it's personal." She let her gaze go to each team member and linger there. "Should be for everybody in here, truth be told." She didn't mention the name that no one had uttered for the last month, Carlos. Then she glanced away and studied her blade.

Damali picked up her Isis. "I'm tired of running, tired of wasting time fighting lower-level vamps . . . I won't be right till I go big game hunting." She stared at Madame Isis, getting lost in the beauty of its jeweled handle.

Seven stones, each a different color of the metaphysical chakra system: ruby at the base of the handle, followed by golden topaz, emerald at the heart level, sapphire, blue topaz, amethyst, and crowned by a large diamond, spaced perfectly to fit her hand. The beauty of the weapon, an instrument of sure vampire death, mesmerized her. It always did, and she kept it close to her like a security blanket. The warrior, Isis, fought a demon serpent intricately inlaid with gold and silver at the head beneath the jewels. She wondered if the ancient warrior had won. The blade was magnificent. Damali ran her finger down one of the blood grooves imbedded in the three blades that came to a sharp point on the end, capable of opening a wound in a vampire's heart shaped like a crucifix.

Deep contemplation overtook her as the team remained silent, watching her. She wondered how something like this had come into her possession along with the fate to bear something so majestic. But the weight of the responsibility that came from owning it was no joke. This was no way to live. She also didn't want to be psychoanalyzed anymore. Her first ripening had passed. She wasn't afraid, just tired. She was sick of all the team histrionics about what could happen. The worst already had, as far as she was concerned. She'd already been hurt to the bone by the underworld—Carlos was dead.

Damali finally looked up. Her gaze went to the group's mother-seer. "Put some new feelers out for where we can gig, Dan," she said, no room for negotiation in her tone. "Can you handle it?" She waited for his slow nod then stood. "Anybody who doesn't want to go doesn't have to. But I'm out."

No one moved, except Jose.

"Wherever you wanna go, D . . . I'm down," he said quietly. "Wanna go get some real dinner 'round the way?"

"Yeah, Jose," she murmured, coming up to him and slinging her arm over his shoulder. "Let's get outta here."

Humans were always so very careless, she mused, savoring the bitter taste of black blood on her mouth. How ironic that a simple chalice filled with a seemingly dead substance could render unfathomable power.

The night felt like a missed lover, the freedom of being topside beyond comprehension, especially under this particular moon. The taste of succulent human flesh, the thrill of the hunt, while exhilarating, bore no comparison to the rush that power offered.

She stretched her long legs, loping toward a tall tree, and in two feline strides ascended to a high branch. She narrowed her gaze on the blue-black terrain, laughing to herself as she thought of the expressions on the faces of the humans she'd gored in the mountains. This was her land, her territory, all poachers beware. She opened her mind to sense for danger, her instincts as sharp as her fangs. Then she felt him.

As promised, his power was unprecedented . . . sultry, seductive, a force of animal nature that ran all through her. Primal to his very core. Oh, yes, this was so perfect. She closed her eyes, a low purr rumbling inside her chest. *Baby, come to me . . . just tell me where you are.*

That he resisted her call, left it unanswered, amused her. Another dominant female had his attention at present . . . ah, logistics. But he had indeed paused, had swept his mind through his region, intrigued, sensing for the mystery of what could have stabbed into his libido so viciously. It was a curious thing, however. Prayer lines barricaded him? How so? Mild panic arrested her amusement. She didn't sense that he was endangered, only that there was a barrier. His location was indefinable. No matter. The point was, he existed, had not perished, and had been promised to her.

If his presence held that much charge while cloaked to the night, that far away, then an encounter would surely be worth unraveling the shadows around him.

"Carlos," she whispered. "It's only a matter of time until I find you." She laughed low, and deep, and sexy. "Come out, come out, wherever you are."

No answer.

Frustration would not lay claim to her; she willed it away, but sent a very graphic representation of her skills into the night air with a desirous growl. She smiled as she again sensed him pause. *Yes, think about that tonight . . . and do not ignore me again.*

With a sigh of exasperation, she dismounted in one fluid flex of her spine and landed on the ground on all fours. Her attention went to the nearby village. Her shape shifted into human female form. Flimsy doors, half-hearted prayers, open windows, adulterous men in the streets. Humans were so very careless.

Carlos closed his eyes and inhaled deeply. She was walking, her long, confident strides fluid beneath her faded jeans. He loved the way every toned muscle beneath her gorgeous, bronzed skin worked as she moved. His mind seized upon the small tattoo at the base of her spine and caressed it. He could almost feel the soft texture of the fabric of her lemon-yellow tank top. He remembered her mouth, her kiss, her smile . . . One of her guardians was with her, making her laugh. He could literally taste the taco as she bit into it.

"You've been monitoring her telepathically for a month, Carlos."

Father Patrick's comment made the vision evaporate. Angered by the sudden loss, Carlos set his jaw hard and kept staring out the window.

"We're also no closer to finding out what is going on in South

America," he pressed on. "My visions reveal the deaths themselves, but not what caused them. Is it vampire? Maybe some of the hybrid things left over from before?"

Carlos kept his back to the priest he'd come to call Father Pat. As his gaze remained fixed on the full September moon, harvest season ran through his mind. He sent a glare over his shoulder, and watched them bristle. Only Father Pat seemed cool.

"I've told you a hundred times, if once, since I got here. This ain't my kind—we don't eat flesh." He returned his gaze to the moon. "We're purists. Only do blood."

"The hybrids from Nuit's colony left sloppy signatures—real brutal bites that tore out organs," Father Patrick countered.

Carlos thought about it hard. The twisted bastards Nuit made had kept human body parts and meat hanging in their lair refrigerators . . . he was just glad he wasn't one of them and had been made by council. His mind went to the young girl Nuit had gutted for his brothers to feed on. His kind was capable, but that was the new regime, not the old one. Something about this wasn't right; he could feel that it wasn't from the empire. "Those victims in Brazil didn't get back up and turn," he said after a moment, trying to convince himself that it wasn't possible for vampires to be involved—like whether the victims turned or not really made a difference. He knew better than that. These were feed kills.

But this was so damned boring. Carlos folded his arms over his chest. Just one night out . . . "Demons possess—so they're careful about what they do to the bodies they plan on inhabiting. I told you that! They go in before the body is declared dead, or known to be dead by the living. That way, they can walk around undetected, and they can cast illusion to keep the living from seeing the decay—that's why they smell the way they do. They're fucking parasites." He turned and looked at them hard. "I don't think it was vamps, but I need to get out of here to really investigate. I need to employ all my senses to—"

"No," Padre Lopez said, fast. "That's not part of the deal. You must avoid proximate occasions of sin until your willpower is stronger."

"Fuck it, then," Carlos said, his tone a low grumble as he turned back to look at the moon. "Have it your way." He closed his eyes. Good food and a good woman—that was what was in order.

But he could feel the team at his back grow tense with his silence. Each one of them possessed a sensory gift, and if they were picking up half of what was on his mind, then they had every right to be concerned. Just the thought of a hunt was making his gums thicken, and thinking about Damali was having the same effect on his groin.

Fully healed and well fed, he was out. But he had to play this cool and not get staked because he hadn't been strategic. At night, Asula, Lin, and Father Lopez were always a little standoffish when he was awake and moving about in their section of the cabin quarters. He could dig it. He made them nervous, rightfully so. He could feel it as they continued to stare at his back, waiting for him to say something.

"She's still partially blind," Carlos said softly. "I wanted to give it time to wear off . . . thought maybe it was temporary shock. That way, I wouldn't have to go to her in person. She didn't even move her compound like we thought she would. I don't understand."

"This is what we feared," Father Patrick said sadly, allowing Carlos to change the subject without resistance. "She doesn't care about her own safety anymore."

"No . . . knowing Damali, she's taken a stand. She's even trying to book concerts all over the place. She's thinking about working on a new CD. She's just stronger, and not afraid anymore." Carlos rubbed his jaw and let out a hard breath. "My baby is all grown up. I was the one who taught her to stand her ground, to claim her territory, and not be moved. Guess I was good for something."

He walked away from the window and then back toward it. The night was calling him, like a siren. He couldn't stand being cooped up like this, or having to always roll with a cleric, lest he lose himself to temptation and have dinner in the streets. Watching Damali from afar had been Hell on earth.

"Have you eaten yet tonight?" the monk named Lin asked in an apologetic, but nervous tone.

"I'm not hungry, yet," Carlos said with a lopsided smile, tilting his head and appraising the cleric in a way that he knew would engender fear.

"*Compadre,* you should, uh, go to the refrigerator . . . there's been new shipments."

Padre Lopez's comment made his smile broaden. It was twisted, but he enjoyed fucking with these guys. He wasn't sure why, but maybe it was lingering resentment over being so powerful a creature, held hostage by the legal technicalities of supernatural law. Seven years living with monks was definitely incarceration. Seven years of Damali living only a few miles away, but never being able to touch her, was working on the wrong side of his brain. He decided not to bear fangs, though. That always caused them to sweat and go into defense mode. Tonight a whiff of their adrenaline-soaked blood might push him over the edge.

"I need to go out for a few hours," he said, studying them all hard for their reactions.

"You know that isn't advisable, or allowed in your current frame of mind."

"Yeah. I know. Can't blame a man for trying, though," Carlos muttered in disgust, returning his gaze to the window. To vaporize and turn into mist . . . to feel the night enter his pores and to become one with it once again, was such a seductive pull that it made him close his eyes. He could feel his incisors thickening and threatening to rip through his gums again. In the distance, wolves howled, and it was all he could do not to answer their baleful call with one of his own.

Oh, shit, they had no idea what this was like. It wasn't that bad while he was rehabilitating, getting his head together, and coming to terms with his existence. But now . . . How did a man ignore his basic instincts, divorce himself from his nature? To hunt was in his very DNA. It had always been there, even before he became a vampire. The clerics even told him he was designated by fate to be a tracker guardian, once an olfactory sensor. Her scent was so close . . .

Before he had been turned, he'd had a heightened sense of smell— it had helped in his former business. But they didn't understand that that ability had been further heightened through his new vampire status. The scent of their blood, sweat, everything in his environment was beating against his brain with its call, *especially* Damali's scent. And she was out hunting again, tonight, the song of her blood filling the air. *Shit.*

"In the zoo," Carlos murmured, "sometimes the lions don't eat because the kill is brought to them like canned dog food. They'd rather bring down a kill themselves . . . get a good run on. I watched them, as a kid, and never understood it until now. After a while, even the kings of the jungle just lie there, defeated. You can see it in their eyes." He turned and looked at the men around him who he knew had no concept of what he was talking about. They had never been on a blood hunt, or probably never had a woman. "Have you ever looked in a lion's eyes, or a panther's, for that matter?"

Each of them immediately averted their eyes, and he let his breath out hard. He would have showed them what it felt like—all of it, even what being with a woman was like—if they hadn't turned away. He was getting stronger by the moment, by each night that his true master vampire status took root within him. Things that he never knew before had finally lodged into his awareness. Power like he'd never felt was threading through his system. Even his vocabulary was changing, making him multilingual.

He could speak *Dananu*—power, or as humans called it, *Vampyre*, now, as well as serve Old World, if necessary. Plus he would always have the language of the streets, and the one his parents gave him. His vision was more precise. He could now actually see blue-white bands of light within each cleric's aura, especially when they stood next to each other. It was like a filament that bound them in a prayer chain. A similar barrier barred the doors and the windows. When he'd first been turned, he had only felt it as a dangerous heat, now he could actually see it like a lit electric fence. Yet, for all this new power he was dying. He just wanted to try some of this new stuff out, but was trapped. Seven years, then what?

Father Lopez glanced up. Carlos smiled. There was something about Lopez that drew him. Within his young aura, the glowing blue-white band linking him to the others held a hint of red . . . just a thin thread, but enough to break the line. He followed that thread into a dark space within the man's heart. A lie was a sin, so was deception, Padre . . . Interesting.

Carlos's attention went back to the red within Lopez's aura. The line was so fragile, that it was almost inconsequential. But from everything he'd learned from taking a brief seat in a power throne, nothing in the vampire world was insignificant.

A theory developed in his mind, as willful defiance escalated within him. If Lopez's will could be breached, he owned him.

Carlos glanced at the others, but their auras were too bright and their wills too strong. He went back to the youngest cleric, studied him hard. Then he reached out and forced him to give up his secrets.

The *priests* had lied to him. They had known where Damali was the whole time, ever since the concert. Fury coiled within Carlos. Some strange killings were going on down in Brazil and from the MO they suspected it was of the paranormal influence. So they'd planned to use Damali as bait to get him to figure out what was going on down there. Just wanted him to go as insurance protection—because they knew *she'd* most likely go there. These bastards had actually raised him from near extinction to use him, redemption notwithstanding? All right . . . then let the games begin.

"Curiosity killed the cat, Padre," Carlos said seductively, holding the younger man's stare. Then he violated the man's mind and sent the rest of his message telepathically. *I haven't been out hunting in a long time. Wanna go with me? You know you do. It's in your blood. You can taste it. I can have a female at your side in seconds. Boyz' night out—*

"Stop it, Carlos!" the elder priest warned. "Lopez—look away! Recite a psalm to mentally block his words!"

But it was too late. From his peripheral vision Carlos watched the three clerics arm themselves around the dazed Father Lopez. His smile broadened as the mental hold he had on the junior priest tightened. "She's beautiful," Carlos whispered, "and feels so damned good against you. You're a sensory tracker, too . . . thought you might appreciate my predicament. Her skin is like butter, and her—"

"Enough!" Asula shouted.

Carlos ignored the burly Moor. He watched, amused, as two clerics rushed to the young priest's side and began shaking him. Father Pat had stepped between Carlos and Father Lopez, trying to stop the vision to no avail. Carlos trapped the young, curious mind within his own, sending image after image to it, bludgeoning it with sensations of power, exquisite lust, and the pure carnal knowledge of lying with a woman.

He gave Lopez a nude taste of one of his old flames, Juanita. Damali was off-limits, even as a ploy. Juanita was fine, arched hard under his hands, her breasts smooth and full . . . yeah he remembered her. Nice ass. Gave good head. Sweet personality—just like Lopez would want. Carlos chuckled and cocked his head to the side, watching Lopez mentally drown as he focused on Juanita, deep and wet. "It's good, *hombre*. We should go out . . . she lives right near my mom's. Just drop the line by the door so I can cross, and me and you can—"

"Taking an innocent by psychic possession will increase your sentence, Rivera! I demand that you stop this invasion now!"

"He wanted to know. He mentally opened the door by asking the question in his mind," Carlos murmured in a sensuous voice. A slow smirk crossed his face as he sighed with a shrug. "It's not my fault that he wanted to know what was pulling me into the night. All men want to know. Need to know. It's instinct." That was no lie, and no matter what Father Patrick said, tonight, he was out.

Carlos inhaled sharply and sent the last of his thoughts full force to Lopez. He watched with great satisfaction as the young cleric writhed and fought against a desire he'd never known until now. Beads of perspiration had formed on the young cleric's forehead and Lopez was taking in shallow breaths. *Uh-huh, it's just like that.* Carlos smiled when the junior cleric shuddered, allowing his thoughts to descend even further. From memory and the simple reflex of thinking about making love, he accidentally conjured Damali's scent and released it into the air. *Sweet, isn't it?* he thought, chuckling to himself. *Bittersweet when denied.* Yeah, maybe it was time to stop; his own game was messing him up.

Lopez closed his eyes, leaned his head back, and groaned, as Father Patrick tried to break Carlos's hold. *"Compasion, por favor."*

"All I'm asking for is a little mercy, too."

The sound of Carlos's voice made Father Lopez look at him, despite the futile attempts of his brethren.

Tears were glittering in Lopez's eyes. "Take these vile things from my mind!"

"You ain't never really had none, have you? Fucking pity . . . and you got yourself locked in here with me jonesing? A virgin? Shit, I will rock your world." Carlos laughed, his voice bitter. "Mercy is in order, all the way around." The other clerics looked at him hard. "I'll let him go if you let me go. Damn, man, why you let them put a collar on the poor bastard before he got his run out?" Carlos shook his head. These old bastards knew no mercy. "Me and Lopez both need a night—"

"No," Father Patrick said, his tone lethal. "Under no circumstances—"

"None?" Carlos leaned against the window, looking out. He then closed his eyes and sent Lopez a full-blast sensation of what it was like to be midstroke, hard-thrusting, going for broke, sweat running down your back, can't get enough air, deep plunging, all the way to the hilt, and a woman's voice fracturing the night.

Lopez dropped to his knees.

"Same reaction I had outside her compound that night, bro, when I was calling her and the guardians blocked me, then when we were together outside of Nuit's lair—"

"I said stop!"

"Will bring a grown man to his knees." Yeah, it was definitely time to stop. Carlos scowled at Father Patrick and relaxed his mental grip on Father Lopez. The line between the older clerics burned brighter and the band thickened, now shielding Lopez with it. Just seeing it made Carlos angrier.

"You stop fucking with me, and I'll stop fucking with him!" Carlos punched the wall, but was careful not to put his fist through it. Who knew where those crazy old bastards had prayed? It wasn't about drawing back a nub that couldn't regenerate.

He could hear Lopez breathing hard, trying to recover his dignity as he stood. This was beyond bullshit. If he didn't know better, he'd swear Lopez had vamp traces somewhere in his lineage. The way he had been able to get a lock on him, his gut-deep reaction to the images, didn't make sense.

Carlos watched the young priest closely from across the room. The man had lost it at the end when the vision of Juanita fused with Damali's scent, almost as though he could detect Neteru. The fragrance had felled him like it would have blown away a male vampire . . . Now he knew he was tripping! The invasion was fucking with him just as badly. That had to be it—he had to see it, feel it, and envision it to send it. That's the only reason he'd relented. He had to get out of there.

"Before he judges me again, I thought it might help him, as a young man, to walk a mile in my shoes. None of you know what this is like." Carlos turned back toward the window to ignore them all. The old men might be beyond remembering a woman, but the young blood sure wasn't. Lopez was the weak link in their chain, and one night, he'd break him. It was only a matter of time. And it served Lopez right for acting like he was so above him.

Carlos snarled when they hastened to sit Father Lopez down and bring him a glass of water. "Sonofabitch needs a cold shower, not a glass of water, gentlemen. Unless I'm losing my touch."

Watching them try to restore order and help the disoriented Lopez, while issuing nasty glances over their shoulders in his direction, truly got on his nerves. Carlos paced, hating how they flinched at his every move. "All right, all right. My bad. I'll chill."

"This is going to be a long seven years for all of us, Carlos, if you keep this nonsense up," Father Patrick snapped.

As soon as the priest reminded him of the length of his sentence, he reached out toward the door, ripping it from its hinges from where he stood across the room. Wood and metal splintered and bent as it came to a hard crash against the floor. Seven years, fuck that. Seven more minutes was a stretch. The fact that everybody was on their feet was of little consequence. Yeah, he was getting stronger—they needed to know that, too. So were the urges that came with the increased power he owned.

A thick, blue-white band surrounded the house from the threshold out a hundred yards and heat rushed through the door as though he'd opened a furnace. He'd never make it across without torching himself. Carlos waved his arm in frustration and immediately repaired the door and then paced from the door to the window.

"You fucking lied to me. That's a sin! Fucking clerics and you lied? You brought my coffin over that shit out there . . . and . . . and—that shit ain't right! Don't tell me about being a master of deception! All you want is for me to go to Brazil with Damali—track her, protect her, go hunt down and kill whatever is over there—just fucking work for your asses like a mule! Deliver the package, untouched, right? But I'm not allowing her to get in harm's way. You think I'm crazy? Stupid?"

"No," Father Patrick said calmly. "You're not crazy. We did conceal the full purpose of our mission."

"What!" The sofa hit the wall and three lamps blew out. "You admit that shit to my face?"

"Yes," Father Patrick said with a sly smile. "We had an agenda. No sense lying about it now." He glanced at the others who had weapons firmly in their grip in the darkened room. "Carlos knows this is how business is done. Fair exchange. We work on saving his soul, all the stuff he wants . . . well, almost all, and he works on what we want."

All sarcasm and amusement went out of Father Patrick's tone as his glare narrowed on Carlos in the dark. "We want the Neteru safe at all times, just like you do. We want whatever is causing chaos to be eliminated—just like your vampire world probably doesn't want anything harvesting humans from their territories, we don't either. We have the same end goal in mind, but for different reasons."

Begrudgingly, Carlos righted the furniture and repaired the lamps.

"You're getting stronger," Father Patrick said.

"Yeah. Goes with the new territory—literally," Carlos muttered as he sulked and paced away.

"Power concentrating from Nuit's old areas?"

"Yeah. What's it to you?"

"If you're strong, that's a good thing," Father Patrick said carefully. "A heck of a thing for us to cope with in here, but something you'll need where you're probably going."

"If you had any sense, you'd let me talk her out of getting herself in harm's way . . . and just let me go over there and dust whatever's lurking . . . if that would shorten my sentence." Carlos stared at the old man, trying to keep a plea out of his tone.

"You know that tonight wouldn't be a good time for you to talk to her. Let us focus on the Brazilian problem instead."

Carlos sighed and found a stationary post by the window. "Yeah, I know the deal. We can do this the hard way, or the smooth way."

"Correct," Asula said in a harsh tone.

"No more attacks on our junior member, understood?" Lin said evenly. "He's young, and it's not a fair match!"

"Tell me, what about any of this is fair?" Carlos didn't look at them as he asked the rhetorical question. This shit was royally pissing him off. "What if I made Lopez feel it every time I did? Made him lose his goddamned mind like you're trying to make me lose mine . . . for seven years?" Carlos glanced at the young priest, considered just taking him there on general principle, then decided not to for the sake of his own sanity. "Shit," he said, going back to the window. "Don't mess with me, tonight, about what's fair. I am *not* in the mood."

"You have not answered my question about the mountain killings,"

Father Patrick said with a glare of disapproval blazing in his eyes as he tried to wrest back Carlos's focus.

"Yeah, well . . . whatever. Probably not vampires." Carlos sighed. This was really getting on his nerves. He ran his fingers through his hair and stared into the darkness, wishing he were an invisible part of it. "Those bodies were mauled, found, and pronounced dead—with no signs of a ritual near them. The hybrids from Nuit's camp have probably been hunted down and killed by the Vampire Council's squad by now."

Carlos placed both hands on the windowpane, as if trying to touch the moon through the glass. "These guys fell in some pretty remote locations—by the time the search parties found them, whatever was out there in the wild had gotten a piece of them as well. Wasn't like they dropped in a city park. Dumb bastards were out in the freakin' Amazon and dickin' around on some nature jaunt. One thing I've learned is, if you ain't where you're supposed to be, you'll get fucked up—and do not mess with Mother Nature. Heads probably rolled when a predator went for their throats. Motherfuckers should stay out of the jungle. Period, end of story."

Carlos smiled as he studied the clerics' drained expressions. "You know how delicate the human throat is . . . how very few bones keep it attached to the shoulders? Something eating or attacking could easily decapitate a victim without even trying that hard." When Father Lopez looked away, it was all he could do not to chuckle.

"Are you sure?" Father Patrick said, his tone firm, sending a quiet warning to stop scaring the young priest.

"Yeah, I'm sure," Carlos muttered, defiance claiming him.

They nodded, and he enjoyed the worry on their faces.

"I cover North America, South America, and the Caribbean because Nuit took South America topside and ceded it to me for bringing him Damali. That's history. But the attacker wasn't one of mine. If there was vamp tracer on a body, from either one of my diluted line or a poacher, I would have known. If those humans that fell were inhabited by a demon, I would have picked up the sulfur trail right away. Nothing goes down in my territory by another vamp without it transmitting to me. But I do need to get out, all bullshit aside, to properly track it."

"You wouldn't feed from any people . . . or human remains while you were out there, would you?" Padre Lopez brought his hand up to his cross and began nervously toying with it. "You'd only take a deer, like you promised us before, right?"

He was pleased that the young cleric's resolve was wavering. After a mental blast like that, he'd be shocked if the man hadn't responded.

"I don't eat carrion," Carlos said, indignant. "The victims were already dead for a coupla days when they were found and were too far for me to even think about getting to—*if* I was so inclined, and *I'm not*." He hated that a collective sigh of relief from the clerics greeted his statement. What did they think he was? A bottom feeder? Only lowlife demons ate dead meat. He was a *master* vampire!

"Gentlemen. I'm the only male master in this region, on two continents. I've got all the lower-level males who had not allied with Nuit, and therefore, haven't been dusted by council, pushing up on my business enterprises, jockeying for position. They can only assume I'm out there, somewhere, but must be too badly injured to respond or that the council has me detained in the Sea of Perpetual Agony for some offense. That leaves major sectors of my territory wide open. I need to get with that and address the flagrant violation of my authority!"

"Okay," Father Patrick said, growing weary. "We understand that you have ego-based concerns that have to be addressed in the vampire world to keep up your ruse—"

"You *do not* understand what I'm telling you," Carlos yelled. "It's *not ego*, it's primal. It's the fiber of what a master vampire is!" Four sets of widened eyes stared back at him as the color drained from the clerics' faces when his fangs inadvertently slid down from beneath his gums. Carlos ran his tongue over his teeth to send them back—but the shit felt good. Had been a while.

"I want you to imagine where I am right now," he said quietly. "And I'm not going to screw with your minds—this is just the facts." He waited until the group's seer, Father Patrick, nodded before he continued. "Gentlemen, I have vamp females out there who are sending out probes to sense for the strongest male in the territory, and even though I'm blocked behind your prayer wall, I can hear them— since you left a breach for me to detect what you needed me to. And the shit they send to lure a male master . . . you have no idea. I'm just glad Damali's isn't transmitting, too . . . but she doesn't know I'm alive."

He drummed his fingers on the edge of the window frame. "The females of our kind are designed for two purposes. Primary—take the stake, the daylight, the arrow, whatever, in the event that a master's lair is breached. When we make one, or acquire one, it's in her cellular code: be a body shield. We always travel with five points of the pentagram, therefore at least five females; the sixth element is the crest, the centerpiece is the strongest male. Same formation with peripheral, male bodyguards. So, the five strongest females in the regions will compete using telepathy until they lock with a male master, then they'll leave the weaker males and come to me. They know the registers haven't run blood with the death of a second master . . . they are calling me by name . . . no, you have no idea."

Just confessing was making his hands begin to shake. He put them behind his back and walked toward the kitchen to go find blood. "As above, so below. They have the same instincts as female lions, that's the way we're set up. They'll even hunt for you, if you ask, and feed you from their veins if you're injured or too lazy to break a sweat."

"Carlos . . . we didn't know—"

"No, Father. You don't understand my world *at all*." He glared at the elderly man, and then allowed his gaze to sweep the others in a hard rake. "When one of us gets injured, it's in their code to track us, find us, and take us to shelter and bring blood. Preservation of the line at all times." Carlos wiped his face with both hands, truly feeling the call of the night in multiple female timbres.

"They can sense me near, but haven't been able to locate me for a month because of the damned prayer lines blocking them. It's driving them crazy, and me with them, because they know I was injured and in danger of the sun. The more frenzied and panicked their calls become, the harder it is for me to stay in here." He chuckled and looked out the window.

"Carlos, you're going to get through this difficult transition," Monk Lin said, his voice an attempt to soothe. "You died with a prayer in your heart, which is why you can hear the name of the Almighty, even say it, and because you still have a piece of a soul."

"Ultimately, you are moving toward the light each night that you purge yourself of your old ways," Asula said, his voice dropped to a calm timbre. "Our goal is not to torture you. This is not a period of punishment in the atonement process, but rather a reversal of your perspective."

Carlos chuckled, the tone in it brittle. "Torture? This is the fucking Inquisition, fellas." All he understood right now was what they were dangling over his head, but what he couldn't have. Freedom. He knew from his old life how to give a man a taste of something he craved, just a taste of it, then how to dangle it over his head to keep him in line. He used to do it all the time.

"We didn't want to deceive you," Father Lopez said in a quiet voice. "We wanted to illustrate your options in a safe environment . . . so you could make informed decisions."

"Informed decisions? I wasn't *informed* that you wanted me to hunt down a predator on my turf. The last thing you said was help the Neteru get her sight back so she could hunt and stay safe—and *investigate* what was out there. I was down with that. No problem. I wanted baby girl safe, too."

"We also need you to restore her hope, by giving her some of yours. We wanted to rejuvenate your spirit, as much as we wanted your body repaired."

Carlos stared at Father Patrick hard. "Hope? You all definitely came to the wrong place for that . . . and I *know* you don't want me to work on her body." He shook his head and laughed. "If I remember from my old catechism classes, evil is everywhere and will ride the airwaves until the big war, Armageddon, or until the good guys go up in the Rapture. Right? I cannot mind lock with her on a two-way. No. Thought I could hang, but I can't."

"Why not?" Father Lopez glanced from one cleric to the other and then looked at Carlos nervously. "You just did it to me, sent me the wrong thing, but . . . you could send her—"

"*Hombre,* just squash it." The young man was so foolish it was making Carlos pace.

"The Lord works in mysterious ways," Father Patrick said with confidence. "If a person goes through their whole life without a break, hope can die and our Neteru is losing the battle with—"

"Spare me!" Carlos whirled around and held up his hand.

"We did," Father Patrick said, his eyes not holding anger, but something close to amusement.

"I'm not hearing this bullshit. Okay, ironically, the prayer lines have been taking some of the cut out of that blade in my skull . . . but shit . . ." Carlos leaned against the wall, his gaze toward the clerics unwavering. "Don't ask me to do a two-way lock with Damali, ever. Especially not with the female vamps sending and open for my telepathy signal . . . their secondary purpose is beyond your comprehension, fellas. A couple of nights ago, I almost went there and blew my cover. The only reason I didn't is that I wanted to be sure I was back to full power, all my wounds were thoroughly healed, and that I could battle another male, which is always inevitable if you go out. Self preservation is always first, but after that . . ."

"Your will is strong enough to—"

"Father Patrick, get real. The whole job of a female vamp is to keep you sated, in lair, and out of danger, only coming out to feed and hunt when absolutely necessary . . . patrolling your borders with caution. They'll gorge on fresh, adrenaline-pumped kill, bring it to you *hot* . . . for a double-plunge siphon . . . aw, man, you just do not know . . ."

He walked by the coffee table and kicked it to stave off the shiver just knowing had sent through him. It was of little comfort that his misguided jailers had compassion in their eyes, because their wills were still tightly bound on keeping him in tonight.

"Neteru scent works the same way—it locks around *all* your senses, and fucking drags you into the street, five lair kittens notwithstanding, it beats their call . . . which ain't no joke." He pointed to the window, his arm extending in a hard snap. "You have me trapped in here with Neteru pumping adrenaline in nightly blood hunts, singing her heart out . . . some sad shit about losing her soul in Hell, five strong females calling my name with bait like you wouldn't believe, goddamned competitors eating up my territory, and you want me to do this sentence cold turkey, and don't even have a blunt on you?" He was incredulous when they didn't flinch. "You can't hear it, but I can."

His gaze was drawn to the window like a magnet. He faced the night and listened to her siren call to him. She was wearing pitch black, and she was serving stars like diamonds. Nothin' but da rocks—night was all iced up. He focused on the stars. The moon cast a bluish tint on the tall redwoods and pines surrounding the cabin. The colors moving against the tree leaves had the allure of a silk scarf floating gently on the breeze against a woman's throat. The night was one sexy bitch . . .

"Carlos, son, evil creates plagues and disasters, violence. You're right. These things have been unleashed to inhabit the planet. But each time an individual goes against evil, whether in a small personal battle with themselves, or within their family, or whether it is a group that conquers evil with peace, harmony, beauty, love . . . or the sword of truth, we win. Just like when we see people rush to help people they don't even know . . . you've seen average individuals do heroic things, risk everything in their lives and rush to aid someone in a fire, or something equally as tragic. That action also affects those less courageous, gives them hope. Perhaps it helps a mother hug her child tighter, or makes a man give up a vice—nothing is ever wasted in the battle, not even you. Our side uses disasters, that we did not create and that evil did, to bring out the best in mankind."

"It is akin to spiritual judo," Monk Lin said softly. "We use the enemy's aggression against itself, and use its weight to flip it. Such a cry goes up to Heaven when people see things that are so terribly unjust that it gives them pause. Even the worst of men, generally, have a limit."

"You must battle—"

"I am *losing* the battle tonight and I have reached my limit," Carlos said, pure honesty in his tone. "Now at full strength, I can't take these calls—while injured, yeah, but not tonight." Carlos slapped the center of his chest and then went to the refrigerator and slung the door opened so hard that it came off the hinges. "And all you got in here is cold blood?" With total disgust, he repaired the refrigerator. "I need something to bring me down . . . a damned Valium or something." Carlos raked his fingers through his hair.

"The only thing that's keeping me sane is the fact that Damali's third eye is half blind, she hasn't sent a mental lock my way . . . 'Cause if girlfriend ever wakes up and calls me . . . I'll fucking torch myself trying to breach that line out there." His voice dropped to a low threat. "But not before gorging well like I need to." He eyed each one of his captors, his resolve to keep his soul in Purgatory wavering. "Some shit, gentlemen, is just nature." He allowed his words to come out slowly, one at a time, to make his point. "Let. Me. Out. Very soon. I can't hang indefinitely."

Father Patrick's grip tightened on his weapon, as did the others around him. "Before we can do that, we need to be sure that—"

"You need to *respect* our cultural differences," Carlos muttered, finally opting for a cold plastic bag, and taking a swig from it before he totally lost it. His gaze went to the window again as another urgent call split his senses and ate into his brain. "Every man has his limits. Tonight, I just found mine."

CHAPTER SIX

⸺ ⸻ ⸺

FREEDOM. PRECIOUS freedom. Carlos stood in the dense woods where he had first been made and breathed in the scents of the night. Things were so different now that there was no fear. The cicadas' call merged with that of the night frogs. The leathery sounds of bats' wings flapping echoed through him with the lonely hoot of a hunting owl. But the call of his female kind, now that he was beyond the barriers, was so visceral that he shuddered. But he couldn't blow his cover. The empire needed to think he was still somewhere injured.

As a mental diversion to sure temptation, he became mist, then indulged himself to transform into a large, black panther stalking nothing and everything until the cry of wolves seduced him to change again and become one of them, howling until they went still from known terror.

Yes! Every sensation was heightened as he took his own form again, his peripheral vision casing the landscape, his night vision capable of detecting the slightest movement within the tall redwoods. From afar he looked up at an insect burrowing into the bark of a high branch. It seemed so close that he could reach it with his hands. The pleasure of being outdoors at night sent another shudder of sudden arousal through him that was stronger than had been anticipated. What a rush . . .

Standing there breathing in the night, he realized just how much his vampire nature had been repressed. Out here, all alone, yeah, the clerics had reason to worry. He needed to hunt so badly that his fangs suddenly lowered without his permission. The erection that came with it felt like a lead pipe straining against his leather pants.

Perspiration wet his brow as he thought of the human throat, what the veins looked like under the skin, how the blood sounded as it pulsed life through a body, and he trembled. He was for sure gonna drop a body tonight . . . go check out the ladies, establish a lair. Fuck going back into captivity. It was a wise choice for them to let him out tonight, probably for their own safety, but it was also the stupidest thing they could have ever done. Letting a master vampire out that hadn't been fed right in a month?

Carlos began walking, trying to decide what part of LA to dine in. Then he stopped. Oh, shit . . . He was like a virgin. He laughed and shook his head.

His amusement soon dissipated as the harsh truth entered him. He'd only tasted blood from another vampire's veins. Had only fed on the carrion Raven left behind—an already dead, half-drained security guard. Disgust filled him. Damn. He'd only taken a drink from the tap and bottled blood within the Dominican don's vampire lair, and now was being sustained by monks. Their blood was as devoid of adrenaline as grain-fed beef. It was laughable. It was pitiful. It was a waste of sheer power. He was a disgrace as a master vampire. He was a virgin, after all. "Kiss my natural ass . . ."

Gathering self-control, Carlos smoothed out the arms of his suit jacket. He couldn't afford to psyche himself out. The erection would go down, just like the urge to sink fangs into a fragile throat would. Hopefully. He had business to attend to. Couldn't go back into his territory and clean out poachers without having his shit straight. Not. And as badly as he also wanted to get laid at the moment, it was not about screwing himself for a little bit of tail. He'd never allowed pussy to come before business, not even while alive—no matter how raw it was. Not hardly. *Hombre* was many things, but foolish was not one of them.

Carlos focused his energy and siphoned more from the life energy around him within the night. The smell of death entered his nose. It tasted like metal at the back of his throat. Good. The messengers were on their way. 'Bout time.

The trees looked liked they'd split cells and doubled as four hooded entities stepped out of the shadows, their red eyes glowing in faceless black holes within their dark robes. Carlos smiled.

Brandishing scythes, one moved forward, pointing a skeletal finger in Carlos's direction. "You called us."

"Yeah, man. *Que pasa?* I need to get word to the Vampire Council."

Carlos waited, knowing that there was an inspection to pass.

"He is clean," one of the others said without advancing. "He still bears the council's mark. It is Rivera."

"We were concerned," two said in unison. "You did not report in after the battle in the tunnels. The slayer was lost for three days. You left no trail."

Carlos put his hands behind his back and let his gaze settle on each entity one by one before speaking. "I was to bring her to the council, and also hit Nuit. I did that—hit Nuit. But I ran into a roadblock."

"Continue," the lead messenger said. "We have registered that kill, as well as many others by your hand. Of that, the Vampire Council is pleased."

"Aw'ight, then chill. I had her in my arms, trying to get her through the tunnels, when I was ambushed. You know that, because your squads got there *late*." Carlos allowed his fangs to come down in a mock show of sudden rage. "I was calling for backup, and you slow motherfuckers left me out there hanging, *hombre*. I got half my face ripped off, my shit jacked, you feel me? The best I could do was put my body between Nuit's forces and the Neteru to ensure the cargo didn't get damaged."

All four entities nodded. They blinked, the red orbs in their eye sockets disappearing.

"This is a statement of truth," the lead messenger said.

"Damn straight it's the truth. Now I have a message—"

"Wait," the entity said, holding up his hand. "How did you regenerate? They left you for dead in the desert. We tortured one of theirs and learned that much before eliminating the captured—"

"Long story," Carlos scoffed. "Suffice to say, I feared failing the Vampire Council more than the sun. So I crawled my mauled ass into a cave as far as I could. Some carrion feeders came to eat from what they thought was dead meat—and lemme just say that all I needed was for one coyote to get within my reach. You dig?"

The messengers all nodded.

"There was a pack of them," Carlos went on, knowing the messengers were blocked to his mind unless he gave them permission to see certain images. Enjoying the game, he embellished the story to make it gruesome enough to pass their test. "Desert dogs, however, only gave me enough strength to repair the basics . . . but later, there was this quaint little Mexican town nearby . . . filled with innocents. Until I fed, I didn't even have telepathy or projection capability. Had to take them down one by one the old-fashioned way. It was regrettably messy, but effective."

He could feel palpable excitement run through the eerie foursome like an electric current. "Come, smell," he offered, knowing that the donated monk blood reeked of innocence and had no adrenaline trail to it. That alone would be enough to convince the messengers that he'd fed on a school yard of children.

The leader leaned in close to Carlos, its decaying scent stinging the insides of Carlos's nostrils. But the thing came away from him with no glowing orbs showing. It hissed, and released a sigh that was the things' version of ecstasy.

"Ohhh . . . yeeesss . . . the Vampire Council will be pleased with this transmission." The entity shuddered and opened its eyes, which had gone from red to dark green then red again as it spoke. "They are pleasured beyond your scope of understanding, as am I, your messenger, Master Rivera."

Another of the entities approached the lead messenger and touched its shoulder, sending a collective shudder through the group. "It is almost as good as when he had ripening Neteru in his nose. You must tell us of this town where the blood runs so pure."

Carlos nodded, not about to send a pack of vampires to descend upon a defenseless country town. "Later. Back to the point, so we don't piss off the council with delayed info."

The messengers all nodded, apparently aware of the extent of the Vampire Council's potential wrath.

"After I recovered," Carlos said, resuming his story, "I got back on point and tracked down the Neteru. She'll let me in—she thinks I saved her and her team's lives."

"Brilliant," the leader said. He cocked his head, as if listening to some inner voice, then said, "The Vampire Council has monitored and heard this conversation, and would like a word with you—*personally*."

"Oh, no," Carlos said fast, putting up both hands and walking backward. Maybe the blood scent thing was over the top. "I don't do the tunnels *ever* again in life—or death, you know what I'm saying. Been there, seen it, and don't ever want to do it again."

"While we can appreciate your trepidation, Mr. Rivera, the Vampire

Council's word is final. That is why they sent four of us to escort you to their chambers."

This was mad-crazy bullshit. A meeting below would eat up precious night. He still had to feed, and had other things he wanted to do. All he was trying to accomplish was to keep council off his ass and at bay—not go downstairs for some corporate conversation. Shit! "I'm done with subterranean meetings, man."

The lead messenger conferred with the other hooded creatures behind it for a moment, and their eyes disappeared in their hoods. Carlos waited until their transmission was sent, and when their eyes opened again, he eagerly anticipated the determination.

Shaking its head no, the lead messenger pulled out a scythe. "The Vampire Council says the conditions on all levels above six are inconsequential and they will assure your safety through the realms on your descent to chambers."

"Inconsequential?" Carlos walked in a wide circle. "Tar pits, and black maggot-covered stagnant ponds, it even fuckin' rains maggots and whatnot on the levels above ours down there—plus it stinks like the worst garbage day you can imagine, and I need to establish a lair. I have been rehabbing for a full month, trying not to burn excess energy or draw poachers from other territories to me who might be following a female's trail to me, which means I was out there solo, without—"

"They understand your delicate master vampire sensibilities, and say that passage will be brief. On level four, the Amanthras are engaged in a civil war, as their supreme council has sent legions after the rogues that dared band with Fallon Nuit's vampires to form the Minion. That side of the equation guarantees our quick passage—and topside, we have hunted down and eliminated all of Nuit's remaining lair supporters. The Minion has been broken. Even our human consultants have eradicated his dens of human helpers."

"Can't it wait till tomorrow night, man? Can't you just let them know—"

The lead messenger shook his head slowly. "The Vampire Council will not wait, and they demand a word. It is done."

The messenger lowered his scythe to the ground and violated the earth—just as he had when Carlos had been first summoned. But this time, Carlos had no fear in his heart, nor did the phenomenal speed suck the air from his lungs as the earth opened, uprooting trees, forming a giant pit that pulled him down into the blackness. He changed into something more appropriate to wear while hurtling downward. Old World conservative.

He looked on with pure disinterest as the four messengers used their blades to hack at demon hands and tentacles that grabbed for their cargo, him. He might as well have been riding the subway, watching the dark columns go by, watching the freaks come out at night. But when he passed level five, a slight shudder ran through him. It was an erotic pull, not a frightening one. Hmmm . . . later. Level five was the black forest where the things that could only temporarily hold their human shape lived—were-demons. He returned his focus to the matter at hand. You didn't fuck around with the Vampire Council.

"You know the procedure," the lead messenger said, pointing down the long corridor of blackened stalactites and stalagmites when they landed in a swirl of charcoal smoke.

Carlos brushed the splinters of tree branches, tiny rocks, and earth from his tailored black suit, and willed his shirt white again, then smoothed his hair. They needed to figure out a much less dramatic way to roll, he noted, stepping over rotting bodies as he made his way toward the chamber.

This time the stinging smell of bat urine in the damp cavern didn't make him wretch, it was just mildly annoying—they also needed to do something about their messenger service. He heard the titter of laughter coming from the high, vermin-covered ceiling. Bats huddled and winked at him with red, glowing eyes, and treacherous fangs.

But one could never be quite ready for crossing the moat around the Vampire Council's chambers. Carlos looked down into the orange-red lava, the inferno of the bubbling pool created translucent heat waves just above its surface. He had to cover his ears to the shrieks and cries coming from the Sea of Perpetual Agony. *Poor bastards,* he thought to himself, as he crossed the narrow, slippery strip of rock-bridge. Coulda been him. Hell, if he didn't play his cards right, that would be him.

Using his energy as a magnet, he hurried across to the other side and stood before the huge, black marble doors that bore golden knockers with fangs. This time, though, he knew not to grab them. They would bite. Instead, he pounded on the massive double doors with his fist and waited for the left side to eerily creak open. Shit, they had his scent and could do the security check a little smoother.

There was no period of disorientation, and the denser air didn't make his lungs struggle to absorb it. He walked through the double doors, his shiny Bali slip-on loafers echoing against the black marble as he strode toward the pentagram-shaped table and bowed slightly in deference to the four-seated council members. He noted that there was still an empty, tall black throne positioned at one of the table's star points. Yet, the table still held power, its red blood veins flowing through the black marble and keeping each council member's gold goblet filled with the ruby power liquid. Blood.

Carlos assessed the elderly entities, who did not bother to waste illusion energy to make themselves look more appealing. Things seemed in order. The walls still bore torches in huge iron holders, black tallow dripped from the candles mounted in heavy iron floor candelabras. Above the table still swirled the screeching, black funnel cloud of smoke that carried messengers and served as his transport out of there. But this time, he could read what had been strange hieroglyphics that covered the room's arches, graced each throne, and surrounded the huge, fanged gold crest in the middle of the table. It was the history of each of the five original vampire lines on the five continents, with the history of the empire's founder in the center of the crest. Deep.

Now if he could only read the expressionless faces that studied him. Their pale grayish-blue skin showed the black blood flowing through their veins. That it was moving slow was a good sign. When excited, he remembered, or angered, you could see their blood pulsing faster beneath their pale skins. Everybody's eyes were glowing gold. Cool. Nobody was in the red zone. Nobody's claws were growing, and all fangs were at the normal two-inch, non-hostile level. Civility was in order. Carlos bowed again. The Vampire Council nodded.

"Mr. Chairman, Mr. Counselor, members of the council, I report per your request."

"We are extremely pleased with your efforts," the chairman said, adjusting his high black hat that resembled a pontiff's cap. "We understand the difficulty you've experienced, as well as your period of incommunicado. Your plan to restore our cargo, Mr. Rivera—now that she knows you are a master vampire?"

"Since there is no need for pretense, normal seduction should work. . . . I've held her in my arms, been inside her head, and she clung to me in the tunnels. I can get to her. I have seven years, correct?"

The council members passed a nervous glance between them.

"We would like to know that she is *fully* compromised of her own free will well before the next ripening window. While we appreciate your efforts, seven years is—"

"A blink in the eye of time," Carlos said fast, chancing the break in protocol by cutting off the chairman. He instantly regretted the move, but kept steady.

The chairman replied with an even glare, his tone distant, and very cool. "We have other plans for you. There is an empty throne, which you have already experienced. Its power is unparalleled. One so valuable as you should not be lost to minor topside battles. You are a general, not a foot solider. Now that we know the slayer's whereabouts, we can most assuredly break her spirit with another, insignificant human male. One from our compromised human pool. We wouldn't send a vampire on such an easy assignment—that would be a waste. This would achieve our aim, and seven years from now, we'll send our best, nonmasters to collect her for the planting ritual."

Carlos remained very still—but that was not going to happen. He listened to the chairman but wasn't hearing him. He didn't care what the old man was talking about. Human or not, nobody but him was breaking Damali in, and after that, fuck it. They could stake him, but he wasn't letting another male near her—unless he heard her say she wanted it that way . . . even then . . . sheeit.

"As you know, the effect that a Neteru has on master vampires, when she's in cycle, is too strong a temptation . . . she's like a drug, Carlos. We need you clean and in a stable frame of mind," the chairman pressed on, trying to persuade Carlos of what was in his supposed own best interest. "Plus, we have already lost many of our top generals in the battle with Nuit. We cannot send a master of value for the collection—we have come to understand . . . only third- or fourth-level lieutenants that pose no threat to our goal can bring her in without tampering with our vessel."

"Even second levels hold aspirations. We would have to take harsh measures while you were not yourself, while you were under the influence. Too risky," the counselor said, shaking his head. "We have fortunately retrieved you, and would never dream of imperiling one of our rising stars again. You stay down here with us until your territory is realigned and cleaned out of any potential rebel forces."

This was not a part of his plan, and Carlos watched in dread as the attorney slid the eternal contract across the table toward him.

"Sign," the attorney hissed. "The last time you left our chambers without a signature. This is a policy breach. But, as men of our word, we all kept our bargains. Good faith had been demonstrated on both sides, therefore let us seal this in the appropriate manner."

Desperate for a diversion, Carlos clung to the only information he had that would make them hesitate. No vampire in his right mind would refuse a throne of all power and knowledge. To do so would blow his cover and end his game—and start a very long period of torture. Carlos glanced around. He was so far down in the pit that no sources of light would be able to evacuate him. The Vampire Council knew it; he knew it. There was only one option. Go for the jugular.

"I'm not signing shit under these circumstances. This is a bullshit deal, and you know it! First of all, Damali Richards was my hit," he said in a defensive tone, his eyes roving over the group with an expression of frustration. "I was the one who was supposed to bring her in, and I want my name going down in the history as the one who brought in the millennium slayer. Let's start my complaint there, Mr. Counselor."

The chairman smiled. "Raw, unadulterated ambition. Passion. This is why he is such wonderful new blood for our council table. He reminds me so much of myself in my younger days." The chairman sat back and watched the brewing debate, his fanged smile widening.

The attorney paused and begrudgingly nodded toward the others. "That minor amendment can be made in the documents—however, he still needs to sign the eternal contracts."

"Why?" Carlos shot back. "I thought that practice was passé, and did any other council member have to sign? Oh, so because I'm a young blood, right, and a brother . . ."

They didn't answer, but the attorney's eyes narrowed.

"By the way . . . where's my soul? On what level is it? One of the transport messengers said y'all were looking for it. I wanna be sure it doesn't wind up lost on level four with the Amanthras." Carlos folded his arms over his chest as the full council responded with silent, stricken expressions. "Now, I have been gone a full calendar month, putting my limbs back together and slowly restoring my power off of coyote blood, then nonadrenaline-spiked innocents and damned highway roadkill—before I sign anything, fair exchange is no robbery. Where's my damned soul? It needs to be in the right hands, or the contract is void anyway." Checkmate.

"We can assure you that our vigilant search continues, and that our alliance with the old Amanthra Supreme Council—"

"You know what," Carlos said evenly, taking the risk to show fangs for theatrical measure, "this is bullshit!" He walked to the table and slammed his fist down, causing the blood within its marble veins to spill over the edges.

"I infiltrate the Minion, alone, risk going after a rogue master with Neteru in my nose, *and his,* literally castrate the bastard—then I off several of his top-ranking, second-level rebel generals; single handedly get inside the Neteru compound to keep a lock on her, then carry her while she's wearing silver, no less, through demon-infested tunnels—and you guys send my backup late! Your boys *were late.* I almost died on this mission. Now, you promise me the throne, but I have to sign some shit to show *my* good faith? And let's not forget about the matter of my lost soul. Down in your own territories? Fuck you. I finish this mission the way we agreed—*I* bring in the Neteru, *then* I sign the papers and the throne is mine. In fact, I shouldn't even have to sign that shit for the power in it to be ceded to me, since I was the one who hit Nuit! You need to give me a seat just on general principle."

The chairman nodded, the blood within his transparent veins not even quickening. "Hmmm . . . hatred, pure rage . . . intelligence, strategy. Absolute ruthless ambition—and balls enough to challenge a seated councilman? No fear—*down here?*" He suddenly laughed. "You're going to bring much to this council. So be it. We'll discuss the possibility in the near future." Without looking up, the Chairman waved his hand. "Gentlemen, on to the next item on the agenda."

Carlos stood there for a moment dumbfounded. He'd expected more of a fight. In truth, the other council members seemed shocked, especially the attorney.

"Uh . . . Mr. Chairman," the counselor said in a slow, cautious tone. "We do need that signature."

"Mr. Rivera has shown more loyalty than some of our current council members," the chairman snarled. "In fact, Mr. Counselor, he has also demonstrated greater effectiveness than our member responsible for corridor containment." The blood sped up in the chairman's veins under his skin as he looked down the table at a nervous council member at the far end. "Please do not provoke me to explore this discussion any further tonight. Mr. Rivera has slayer scent in his system, and asks the small favor of this council to allow him to bring her in before she ripens. It is done. This is the way we used to do business in the old days—when a man's word was his bond, his actions were his oath. I am satisfied."

"I have a question, though," Carlos pressed after a moment, testing his luck. "There have been mountain climbers killed on topside . . . and when I passed level five—"

"That is out of your jurisdiction," the counselor cut in.

"I only asked because I want to know everything that's going on that could endanger the Neteru while she's topside. If I'm protecting the package, hey." Carlos shrugged and began to walk away.

Again the chairman nodded and waved his hand. Another council member from a far point of the star-shaped table spoke in a hushed tone, making Carlos turn around slowly.

"There's been a breach on level five. We do not know the extent— as it is, again, in the most insidious of the demon provinces. Our fight was with the Amanthras on level four, and we can ill afford to scatter our energies to contest a breach on the formidable level five were-demon realms. If not for our civil war, we would have dealt with it swiftly."

"Well how did some whack shit like that happen?" Carlos was appalled. These old boys weren't handlin' their business.

The counselor narrowed his gaze and hissed. "Apparently, Nuit's international *Raise the Dead* concert opened several portals to demon energies on our five continents, but not all the portals have been resealed. We quickly sent forces to North America, Europe, Asia, Australia, and Africa, which includes our guarded Middle East provinces that are being held fallow for the Armageddon—places where commerce interruption would be highly visible and problematic for our financial arrangements. A few nagging elements escaped topside, but nothing to trouble oneself about. It shall be rectified."

"Why didn't you send anybody to check out South America? That's a major piece of real estate in my territory that should have been on lockdown while I was rehabbing. See, here again, y'all haven't had my back proper and—"

"South America was illegally ceded to you by Nuit. He was only to cover the US and Canada, North America, and he assassinated the South American ambassador to annex that area, and to pick up the Caribbean. It caused major alignment issues, because we must keep the Biblical city for level seven—with three of the most powerful world religions battling over it. We must have a continent to feed from, as council. We had to elevate a second-level vampire in Australia to keep the balance, so that we had five continents covered, with two to match the realms that never venture topside. Do not quibble with this council over your land distribution issues."

"Quibble? What?" Carlos was leaning forward across the table glaring at Counselor Vlak. "Motherfucker," he yelled, pointing at Vlak, "your ass may be council, but I tore North America and South America out of Nuit's ass. Matter fact, he'd ceded the Islands and South America before we even came to blows—just from a hit of Neteru." Carlos pushed away from the table; this time the rage was no act. "You keep sending me through changes about shit that is by right mine . . . sign this, leave the package and let some other bastard unwrap it. Now you're taking my land? Oh Hell no!"

"I will kill this young bastard with my bare hands!" The counselor said, standing quickly, about to reach for Carlos's chest, but his arm was immediately slapped away by a mere glance from the chairman.

The chairman smiled. "Vlak, sit, and do not be hasty." The chairman looked at Carlos. "Young man, have a seat in the throne and calm yourself, get a power surge from it. Your nerves are frayed to the limit. You haven't established a lair yet, nor responded to the insistent female calls in your region, given your rehabilitation . . . and that has made you volatile. I understand . . . the counselor understands, don't you, Counselor? Let's see what we can siphon from his seat. If he does well, I might be so moved to give it to him."

The chairman's smile went to a chuckle as he glanced at Counselor Vlak. "Indulge me this once, gentlemen. He delights me. He hasn't fed well for a month, hasn't sated himself with a harem . . . but he came to us, first, to handle his land issues." The chairman made a tent before his lips with his gnarled fingers. "This is a *real* businessman. You want him to sign trivial documents, when his ambition is a palpable lust?" He looked at Carlos and he dropped his voice to a seductive murmur. "Young man, sit in the chair. Please."

With trepidation, Carlos sat slowly, hoping like hell that whatever was there wasn't strong enough to break the black box Father Patrick had around his thoughts. He watched the old vampires close their eyes and touch the table gently, caressing it with the tips of their clawed fingers. A current ran through his producing a rush like he'd never felt before, along with it a power hit that made him shut his eyes and arch his back away from the chair. *Damn* . . . He gripped the throne's arms with trembling hands. He almost couldn't take it all in. The first time they let him sit there, he'd absorbed centuries of knowledge, this time absolute carnal pleasure ran through him, along with the knowledge of how to deliver it with a bite.

"Oh, shit," Carlos murmured, tears brimming beneath his lids. "It's almost as good as pure Neteru."

"You feel that?" the chairman whispered to the other seated vampires. "You feel how much he wants her . . . but he came here about business, first. You feel that pent-up desire . . . sheer aggression, but with willpower enough to resist the call of five strong females in the most seductive regions of his territories, but he came here, *first.*" The chairman closed his eyes. "This man hasn't even been on a proper blood hunt. He was made at twenty-three years old, and the stamina in that body . . . the virility . . . but to have the presence of mind to be strategic—I'm awed."

The chairman sat back, his hand trembling slightly as he released the table, causing the others to break the trance. "Give this young man his fucking South American territory *and* a throne, Vlak. He won it, earned it, winner takes all. Trim back another master's continent, if necessary—but I haven't felt a power erection like that in years." The chairman dabbed at his brow and let his breath out in a slow, controlled stream. "Damn. He was practically one of us before he'd turned. All predator."

The old men chuckled, and the councilman in charge of alignments smiled. "Makes you want a cigarette afterward, doesn't it, Mr. Chairman?" He shot his gaze at Counselor Vlak. "Give the young blood his territory, cede him a throne, and stop this bullshit. You've been on his ass since he got down here. We've got other business to address tonight . . . and after that, I might go topside myself." He shook his head and laughed, gaining nods from the others around the table.

"His South American provinces are not safe—if he is so valuable," the counselor shot back, fury making his eyes glow red. "Our amusement with what he brings to these chambers notwithstanding."

"What are you talking about?" Carlos mumbled fast, now sitting forward and trying to get ten inches of battle-length fangs to go back up into his gums with much effort. The hard-on had left a wet spot in his pants. It was ridiculous what they'd done—embarrassing. He could hardly speak around his fangs. Shit. He hadn't even gone there while fighting Nuit, that battle only produced six to eight inches. He watched them laugh harder as he used both thumbs to send his incisors up and into his jaw. "What's not safe in my turf?"

The chairman released a weary sigh. "We closed everything we could, but one portal remains partially opened, and we can only fathom that there were human forces leveraging the event. Nuit's cursed concert. For all we know, humans at one of the concert points might have performed a ritual. But we don't know what it was, or what it was designed to release. They could have then gone behind the concert and reopened one of the places we had shut down. Simple logic dictates that the site we cannot totally close has to be the primary ritual site, because the other portals were easier for us to reseal. Our vampire forces of topside sniffers have been erstwhile diverted to tracking down any remaining Nuit Minions. That's our issue. The civil war has been a tremendous resource drain on the empire, and we do not have enough information, at this juncture, to immediately ferret out and cope with this minor breach."

The counselor glanced at the council members and then settled his line of vision on Carlos. "It's not the Amanthras. As we said, they are embroiled in their own subterranean civil war, at present."

"Where was the first breach?" Carlos asked carefully. "I need to keep the Neteru from that region—it's in her nature to go after it, though. She's already talking about doing concerts again."

The chairman nodded. "Brazil."

"I'll try my best to persuade her not to go there," Carlos said quietly, their combined voices mentally entering his head. "But, you're right. She is stubborn."

The chairman and the council simply nodded in unison.

"Do what you have to do to protect the package," the chairman said, dismissing him.

While it felt good to be topside again, and he'd narrowly missed getting off-ed at the Vampire Council's meeting by Vlak, worry consumed him as he loped through the woods back to the cabin. Eyes were everywhere, watching, waiting, and he'd have to figure out a way to communicate to Father Pat . . . maybe just before dawn, when the dark eyes of his world couldn't see. Once he got inside the monk's safe house, he was cool. Their protective barriers sealed out the dark forces' sight.

But he couldn't be detected entering or exiting a fortress of monks—at least not without a good story, which even he couldn't come up with to address that unlikely match. That meant he'd have to hang out in the woods all night, and couldn't get near his blood supply after using so much energy. If he did, it wouldn't be enough anyway. Sitting in that throne had literally been a bitch.

The monks would be at risk, then his soul would be in Vlak's claw. And after experiencing those old bastards again, he definitely knew he had to protect Damali.

If he went to her like this, he'd open up their package for sure—and the council would smoke him. If he went to any of the known lairs in his regions, five strong females would instantly gravitate there, and he'd definitely do 'em . . . there'd be no choice about it. But they'd also be a threat to Damali. They'd smell her as soon as he fantasized about her—shit, he could smell her right now, his brain was working overtime on just the thought of it. The old clerics were crazy. He had willpower; sure he loved her, but shit . . . Block the shot without taking a human body? Madness. If that young blood in her compound, Jose, got in her face, or one of the human helpers was already on her trail and couldn't pull up off it, his soul was history.

This was definitely being between a rock and a damned hard place.

Fatigue and hunger clawed at his gut, yet he was also filled with a new level of strength. He was breathing hard just from walking. Slow awareness entered him. Yes. Each time he went down he got stronger, more knowledgeable, darker. A doe lifted her head and froze. The scent of fear filled his nose, lowering his fangs. *Run, sweet thing,* his mind whispered. *Run.*

The night air felt awesome against her damp body as she reveled in the freedom of standing in the open air— alone. Her crew needed to chill. After the big argument, going out for a bite to eat with Jose had been good, but she'd brought him home to try to get everyone else to understand. They all needed to go out and do what they loved. She'd tried to convince Shabazz to go check out some jazz. Tried to get Rider to go get his Jack Daniels on with a good card game—him and JL and Jose were some gambling fools. She'd even tried to coax Big Mike to find a barbecue joint and to turn Dan on to some *real* soul food. Marlene's crazy ass wouldn't even budge to go check out a flick, her favorite pastime. Their loss. She'd tried. And she was out again!

Perspiration damped her skin, her T-shirt clung to her, and her leather pants were now vacuum-sealed to her thighs and butt. Clubbing was da bomb. Dancing put the music back into her veins, her heart was thumping. Yeah, it was all good.

Damali looked down the street. North Hollywood was alive at night. Neon lights flashed, horns blared, people dressed as outrageously as they could, waiting and hoping to be granted access into whatever happening spot. Pullease. All the freaks were out tonight and people were looking for get-high or a drag race. Yeah, the night was alive. So was she.

Danger was all around, certain eyes flickered gold beneath brown irises but didn't approach her. They betta act like they know. Betta recognize. She laughed as third- and fourth-generation vamps steered clear of her like she was their predator. She walked to her Hummer without a care in the world. Yeah, they were gonna get back in the game, start touring, shake the fear and frustration—would kick some more vampire ass. That was all she needed to focus on.

But then she stopped and listened. The night air stirred behind her.

Something familiar caught her nose . . . a deep, male, sensually musty scent—then was gone. She was tripping. Probably an average, run-of-the-mill vamp trying to push up on her. Demons always left a sulfur trail. Despite the warm night, the sensation had made gooseflesh come out on her arms. The erotic pull this one left was ridiculous, almost made her wet her panties. What was that all about? Adrenaline had shot through her, not fear. Damali put her palm on the handle of Madame Isis, slowly closing her fist around it. A deep ache almost swallowed her as her hand relaxed and the sensation eased.

God, she missed Carlos.

He just needed to go to the graveyard before going back in. The club was nearly a disaster. What had been on his mind? Human bodies, vamps present, and Damali glistening with sweat. Just seeing her had messed him up, bad.

Yeah, he'd eaten, but not what or how he'd wanted to. But this visit was destined to bring him down, make him think, help put things into perspective. It would have the same effect as Valium, no doubt. That was important before going back to the safe house just before dawn.

He drifted like vapor over the markers, watching disembodied spirits float by, dazed. Poor bastards were locked topside and didn't have a clue, couldn't feel, were just a waste of ectoplasm.

As he neared his brother's headstone, he materialized and walked toward it, stopping to touch the name. "You were too young, *hombre,*" he whispered. A dull ache in the center of his chest wiped away all the hungers that had been competing for his attention. He glanced over at the others that had been buried side-by-side by request.

Shit, as young men they had all told their people, "If I go down, put me on my boy's flank." And so the families had honored those requests. All of them. His entire territory stretched out in a long, military-like row of men under twenty-five. The only marker that was missing was his. His body had not been found, didn't make it to a morgue to be tagged. Even though his brothers got up and walked, they were known by humans to be dead, so a memorial service had been conducted.

He studied each headstone. They were all *so young* . . . It hit him now, finally, after going down to council again and having a seat. The throne had centuries of wisdom emanating from it. Twenty-something years on the planet was nothing. If he'd only known. And Father Pat had been right about one thing. He and his boys, as bad as they were, he seen shit that gave them pause.

Carlos closed his eyes, fully seeing how Alejandro was turned. He should have ripped Raven's heart out himself. No man deserved to go out like that. He could also remember his dead posse sitting around just kicking it. They'd watch the news together sometimes while laughing and drinking, or would read something in the paper, and despite their own proclivities to violent solutions, they'd been taken aback by some things they'd seen.

Yeah, every man had a limit. Bombs that went off and took out innocent bystanders were off limits. Molesting children was waaay off limits. Shooting up women and kids in a sloppy drive-by was off limits in his territory while alive. People's moms and elderly family had always been off limits. He and his boys would debate the craziness and become outraged that some things just weren't done. Even for them. Deep.

Shit . . . until he'd turned, he didn't think God gave a rat's ass about a little spec of blue planet in his universe. Before he'd seen what he had, he'd assumed that the Almighty didn't care and was too busy to be worried about things like that. But, if what everybody from both sides kept telling him was true, as above, so below, then territory was territory. If anybody moved on even the smallest bit of his, he knew he'd have that foolish individual seen . . . so why not the Almighty? He wouldn't brook the disrespect, neither.

Carlos slid his hands across the cool marble and spoke to his brother softly. "Damn, man, if I had known. Didn't think He put his eye on the projects, or anything going on in the barrios. Moms told us, right, though. I had no idea of how much one soul was worth to both sides—serious product, *hombre,* worth a lotta weight. Hope you understand why I had to dust you . . . was just trying put it back in the right territory."

Had he known that it wasn't all superstition, he might not have ever picked up a gun or sold product to finance himself out of Hell on earth. They'd all been deceived. Was messed up that he had to die to find out how much truth there was to the rumor about this thing called Heaven and Hell. And here he was, a lost soul trying to get his shit back together, and they wanted him to talk to Damali about hope . . . in a mind lock? With cold blood in his belly because the microwave would make the shit clot, they had expected him to just go in and chat with her.

Didn't they understand? He glanced down the row of graves. They shared too much. Both had sustained heavy losses. It was beyond the physical with her. This shit between him and Damali went *way* back, before he'd turned and she'd ripened into mature Neteru. It was volatile. Her music was like the language of ancient Babylon, it bent wills, morphed as she gained new experiences. It was the light's secret weapon. Her voice touched millions. Was as strong as anything he could bring. Yeah, they were too much alike, just on opposite sides of the fence, and ironically, she was all that he had left from his old life, topside.

Sudden tears blurred his vision as he drew back his hand from a headstone and looked up at the sky. Dawn would chase him home soon, and he needed to go check on his mother and grandmother . . . Juanita, too, just to make sure his markers had held. But as he concentrated on them, he couldn't even detect them. Only a searing heat entered his brain and made him back away from the thought.

He let his breath out slowly, the tears now coming down his face. He wiped them away quickly, and blinked new ones back. All right. They were safe. At least the light had done their part to make sure his people had a solid prayer ring around them that even he couldn't cross, if he got tempted to feed from home. If that failed, he'd marked them as off limits within his zones. *It was cool,* he told himself. *It was all good.* He wasn't gonna cry like no punk just 'cause he couldn't see his moms and grandma no more. Fuck it. The DEA had taken his club, liquidated the rest of his shit, moved them to safekeeping under the Witness Protection Program. Human drug lords he'd bested probably wouldn't find them. Vamps wouldn't violate them; the Covenant had surrounded them with light. *It was all good,* he repeated to himself as he wiped his face hard and swallowed down a sob. He'd watch their backs at night if they ever took a vacation outside his territory—but that cop bastard Berkfield had better have given his mother a maid!

Damn straight. Carlos began walking and then turned back to look at his row of homeboys. "I dusted your asses so you could go to the right place, motherfuckers. You best be looking in on my peeps as guardian angels. You owe me." His voice became gentler as he vaporized to nothingness. "Just do that much for me."

"I don't like it! The Covenant can't just call us and ask us to deal with a nuclear time-bomb like that!" Rider yelled. "Carlos is back—that part is cool, but the other half of the deal the Covenant is trying to work is some seriously risky shit."

"Damn, though, Mar," Big Mike said slowly, giving Rider a nod. "If brotherman can't go down with a stake—"

"You're saying the only one that can plant a sword in his chest is our Damali?" Shabazz, who was normally cool, was on his feet now, pacing with Rider. "If boss comes into this compound again, and loses control like he did on her before . . . you feel me?"

"Yeah," JL said nodding. "Remember what happened last time? He waltzed right in here on her invitation, which I don't think she's ever rescinded, and faked out our alarms, blew our generators, cut the power, held back the sprinklers—and that was after he'd *just* turned. Dude has been one of them for a while, at this point. He might have given that old Templar the wrong vision, might have compromised his judgment, ya know?"

"And if he presses up on our little sister like he did before," Big Mike said, growing more tense, "if we gotta put him down, the situation could get real ugly real fast. I agree with Rider. Too risky, Mar. For real, for real."

"But, guys, Carlos saved my ass when he was already a vamp, remember?" Dan stood and kicked a metal stool. "He kept me from getting eaten alive in a parking lot by Raven."

All eyes went to Marlene at the mention of her turned daughter's name. None of the team wanted to ever mention the incident that had broken Marlene's heart when Damali had to do Raven, but the facts were the facts.

"I know," Marlene said quietly. "But the last remaining members of the Covenant are strong, and they've been accurate so far. Plus, the choice is hers."

All eyes went to Jose who had been quiet. It was as though they were straining to hear the opinion of the one person in the group who knew what it was like to experience the loss of a lover. The team didn't move as they waited for him to speak.

"If I had the chance to see Dee Dee again . . . and learned that there was hope for her salvation . . . that there was a tiny window of light that she could grasp onto—I'd never forgive you guys for not having the faith to try it. I'd be done with you all until the end of time, if you didn't tell me." Jose sighed and closed his eyes, wiping his face with his palms. "Maybe if she really sees what he is and plants the Isis herself, it'll be over, once and for all, and she can live a normal life with a regular guy—once Rivera's soul rests in peace. Don't ask me to lie to her, though."

"Jose, do you know what they want him to do?" Rider used his hands to speak as he talked excitedly. "They want him to block the shot, dude! What part aren't you getting? These fucking crazy monks want a vampire to keep a normal human guy from coming near her by keeping her hope and attention on him!"

"It's fucking nuts," Shabazz said, shaking his head.

"What are you talking about, man?" Jose was off his stool, pacing.

"They think, rightfully so, that a regular guy—any guy, who is an innocent, who gets near her in the next seven years will be vamp bait." Marlene nodded and pursed her lips for a moment. Then she looked at Jose hard. "And, he will be. All heroics aside." She ran her fingers through her locks and looked out the window. "We could lose a lot of good, well-intentioned men that way. Conversely, if a vampire helper in the music industry gets to her, initially starts helping her career, sweet talks her, gets inside her head and then burns her, she'll become jaded. It'll come right out in her music."

"She'll have a strong façade," Mike said, his voice mellow. "The young lady has class, Jose, a tough exterior, but her heart, man . . . her heart. Another good man dies on her watch, or a snake burns her . . . So, the Covenant wants Carlos to cut a deal with the vamps to be the primary one to watch her, and to block the shot."

"Are they crazy?" Jose was nearly stuttering. "They want us to go along with that? And what if they just track him and snatch her, then what, people?"

"His name is stripped from their tracking capacity until his atonement period is over," Marlene said, trying to make her statement sound logical amid the bizarre facts. "The dark side can't register him, or track him, other than through crude methods because they don't have a hold on his soul. He still has a margin of choice. The Covenant has boyfriend under heavy prayer—"

"This is too crazy, Marlene," JL said. "But I hear you," he added, glancing at Jose, who was speechless. "If she was to hook up with somebody, have a kid, and the vamps went after it, she'd flip. Right now she's half blind and impulsive—just imagine if somebody else she cares about like that goes down."

Dan nodded. "If she can't see all the way, then she can't see into a man's soul, a human, to truly know a good one from a bad one. The vamps can manipulate things to happen to screw her career, too, and to leave her exposed without capital. Bad press. Shift in popularity. Fans swayed to lower sales. Blocked from hot venues. You can break a star in less than six months, fellas. I've seen it happen. We all have."

"That's what Father Pat was saying, Dan," Marlene added. "That's when they'll send in the vamp human-helper to be her lover. He'll be their conduit. Yep, I can see it: He'll be the one sent to enter her mind when her spirit is weary, when her own human needs are at their worst—when she ripens the next time."

Dan let his breath out hard. "I'm not trying to be negative, but she's human. Like, he's probably hovering around her now in the industry, we just haven't seen him yet?"

Marlene just nodded along with Shabazz. Rider had closed his eyes and Big Mike was slumped in his chair staring at the wall.

JL looked at Jose. "Man, I'd rather take a chance on Rivera than having some human-helper devastate her, or see a regular good guy get jacked." The two younger guardians stared at each other until Jose looked away. "Rivera needs to be the one to block the shot—I'd say, let's take the risk. He's already dead. Go with the clerics on this one, man."

"Right," Dan said quickly, his gaze going to the other guardians. "We should do this. Step out on faith. Rivera is strong, fast, has fangs like the other vamps . . . knows how to spot 'em, can even see marked human-helpers. Plus, he's street smart. Got enough resources to keep harm at bay. And we can't ice a human, bad or otherwise. Rivera might not be able to, either, if his soul is hanging in the balance, but I bet homeboy's got enough juice to draw her from some mere human. Shit . . ."

JL agreed emphatically, but didn't look at Jose, trying to get the others to listen to him and Dan. "Last time I saw what brother was bringing, hey. Besides, the risk ain't all that much. She can't turn if he does slip and bite her, and we know he won't take her underground, because he doesn't trust the tunnels . . . he laid his life down for her, too, to keep her from all the vamps—whatever side they were on. Saved all our asses in the mix."

"Yeah. We owe him," Jose said grudgingly, and then walked out of the room. "Whatever will keep Damali safe. Fuck it. Do it."

Rider slapped his forehead. Shabazz found a stool and sat down hard, and began cleaning Sleeping Beauty. Dan smiled. Marlene closed her eyes and leaned on her wooden walking stick. JL picked up a set of wooden crossbow stakes, threw them to the side, and began rooting around on the table for silver arrow tips to attach to them. Big Mike just shook his head.

Carlos stood across the street from the diner as pure mist, watching the rose-orange light filter through the clouds. He only had a few moments, but would not miss the sight of her in near daylight even for personal safety. It was the eeriest thing, but he knew he was okay, would be all right. The clerics told him they had a gift for him, if he'd promise on his honor to come back without incident, no bodies, no vamp females, no escapes . . . and he'd immediately known what carrot they dangled. A little bit of light.

Damali stepped out of the diner, turned her face to the not-yet full sun, leaned her head back, breathed in the surf, closed her eyes, and smiled. Her blood-red, spaghetti-strap tank top clung to her torso, proving her nakedness beneath it, and her black leather pants fit her like a second layer of skin. Dawn glinted off her Isis blade. Fans thought it was just a prop for Damali; the press, interestingly, found it funky and eccentric. If they only knew.

It was hard for him to inhale as he watched her simple joy. He wasn't sure if it was the dawn weakening him, thickening the air with slivers of light, or just the sight of her. The way the cresting sun played with the colors of her cocoa-bronze skin paralyzed him. Her lush mouth looked so soft, were it not so close to the hour of bright danger he would have made himself breeze to kiss it. And what that red cloth covering her breasts did to him . . . He could see her hardened nipples beneath the shirt, the tiny dark caramel pebbles of them pouting, straining to be tasted.

With his last ounce of discipline, he projected himself far away, back to his mountainside prison with the monks.

"It's done," Carlos announced, kicking open the flimsy steel cabin door.

Immediately four sleepy clerics scrambled to stand, brandish weapons, and gather their wits.

"We were worried!" Father Patrick fussed. "You were only supposed to be gone for two hours. Where have you been all night?"

"To Hell and back," Carlos grumbled. "The Vampire Council took my offer. I'm her cargo transport. I came back as promised, so dawn didn't burn me. A deal is a deal. I'm tired, and I need to sleep. Good new night."

"Wait," Asula said. Carlos stopped and looked at him. "You haven't fed—"

"I ate take-out," Carlos said, his lips curling. "Venison. Again."

Asula continued to eye him. Padre Lopez had gone white. Monk Lin raised an eyebrow. Father Patrick simply shook his head.

"How do we know that's true?" Padre Lopez stammered.

"You don't," Carlos warned. "Look, I am really not in a good mood, so I suggest you get out of my way and let me go downstairs in peace."

Father Patrick quietly chuckled and lowered his weapon. "Oh, yeah . . . he ate in the woods, and has not breached his promises to the Covenant."

Carlos gave the seer cleric a hard look and brushed past the others that had blocked his lair entrance. Once the door slammed shut, the stunned clerics gathered around Father Patrick.

"How can we be sure? He may have—"

The old seer held up his hand, cutting off Asula's question. "He is angry, surly, very agitated."

"Yes, and—"

"Lin . . . a man who has just feasted well, and sated his other desires, is generally not in such a bad mood."

Lin bowed with a wide grin. Asula nodded, chuckled, and walked away. Father Patrick sat down heavily in an overstuffed armchair and closed his eyes. Padre Lopez's gaze shot around the room.

"But . . . I don't understand?"

"Just stay out of his way."

"But—"

"Son, unlike the rest of us," the old priest sighed, "you took the vow very early . . . You will never totally understand his agony. Be thankful. You are blessed."

CHAPTER SEVEN

"HOLD UP, everybody," JL said, his tone cautious. He glanced around the team, and everyone just nodded. "Got four monks, or priests . . . but they're warm bodies incoming. Think it's our old crew from the tunnel battle."

Marlene just stood and nonchalantly went to the door. But her expression was beyond concerned; it was pained. She turned to Damali and shrugged. "The Covenant."

"What's the Covenant doing here? I don't like it." Damali looked at Marlene hard, then toward the computer screens for a moment. It was them, sure enough. The old guy in blue Templar knight robes who reminded her of a lean, silver-haired version of Rider, was with Big Mike's practical double, save the Muslim white garb and machete, plus Monk Lin was with them, donning his traditional brown robes that looked like burlap . . . and they had a new, young, Latino priest with them who could be mistaken for a teenager. "We're tight with them and everything, but generally they call first. What do you think they want?"

"They want to bring a word."

"A word?"

"Oh, boy! Here we go!" Rider shook his head.

"Rider, shut up," Marlene said with a weary tone.

Big Mike nodded at Shabazz, who passed the nod to JL and Jose. Dan shook his head.

"Crossbows and weapons up, gentlemen," Mike intoned in his drawl.

"Roger that," JL replied. "Got a cold body reading on screen one, though."

"Mar, JL's got a cold body reading, and you all are just sitting there? Open the freakin' door, let the clerics in, and man your battle stations, people!"

She almost had a heart attack when JL hit the lights, and her crew nonchalantly stood, weapons in hand, but with relaxed stances. Marlene had flung the door open wide like it was a summer day, and was passing out hugs to the four guys who entered. Beyond flipping out, Damali watched her team exchange male hug-back-slaps with the Covenant team, and noticed that all UV in the weapons room were doused.

"All clear?" JL asked the oldest-looking cleric who wore blue robes.

The Templar knight glanced around. "Yes. I believe so."

"Okay, okay," Damali said, walking in a circle around the oddly assembled team. "Father Patrick, Imam Asula, Monk Lin, and Padre . . . I'm sorry but—"

"Oh, Damali, this is Padre Lopez. He's new to our team."

The shy, young cleric smiled and fingered the sword that he was obviously very unused to handling. "Hi."

This was mind-boggling. Her team had picked up a cold body reading, but had hit the lights before the clerics were safely inside— were they nuts? And that they even hit the lights made no sense. Her team was slipping, *big time,* and they were worried about *her?* Part of her wanted to laugh, another part of her wanted to shriek from the craziness of it. Steadying herself, Damali began again more slowly.

"It is good to see you all again, and we appreciate your stopping by, but somebody wanna tell me why you all registered a fifth body, a cold one, when you came through our door—that no one but me seems to be concerned about, and would somebody explain to me *what the he*—I mean, heck, is going on? JL, get the lights up in this freakin' place, would ya? You're bugging me out."

Marlene glanced around the group then shot a nervous glance at Father Patrick. "I told you she wasn't ready. Her senses registered nothing. She's using the technology, not sensory awareness."

Damali wanted to scream. Why were they talking about her like she wasn't standing right there? Damali's gaze tore around the team, noticing how their shoulders sagged, and their expressions held a level of empathy. Tears were now clearly visible in Marlene's eyes, and she didn't bother to blink them away.

Big Mike seemed like he'd just lost his best friend. "Our baby girl is a sitting duck. She's blind, y'all. She can't even sense it."

"It was the final test before we stood down," Rider said, sitting hard on a stool. "Damn!"

Shabazz walked away and slapped JL and Jose on the shoulders. "Happens to the best of 'em. We did all we can do."

"I didn't think it was that bad, though," Dan murmured. "I just didn't understand."

"What the *hell* are you all talking about?" Damali yelled. She hadn't meant to swear in front of the clerics, or to totally lose it, but her team was tripping, and people were all talking in code about her, in front of her. It was too rude, and it was pissing her off royally.

"They're right, baby," a deep, familiar male voice said as a figure stepped out from behind Father Patrick, as if materializing from thin air. "You never picked me up, never saw me coming, and if I was any other master, you'd be dinner by now."

Reflex had brought Damali's hand to her blade, Madame Isis was drawn, but her mind was having difficulty accepting the image. Her breath caught in her throat. She stared at this predator that had on a black soft-structured linen suit, black T-shirt, dressed to the nines . . . Dear God it was Carlos. A thousand emotions ran through her at once. Then as she stared at this being, rage began to fill her, heating her insides, causing her blood to pump hard and fast. Carlos was dead, and something had inhabited his form. Stolen him. Polluted his body. Her arm trembled as she gripped the Isis tighter, and she knew within her heart that split second of hesitation would have cost her a jugular. The arrogant creature before her had been right.

Damali stood speechless, her eyes never leaving this entity claiming to be Carlos as he rounded the clerics and walked toward Dan. She poised herself to take a clear swing, but had to wait to get into position so she wouldn't hurt her teammate. Her mind screamed at the others to take aim, to get into the correct stance. Even Marlene seemed deaf to her silent battle stations' commands. What was wrong with them?

Slack-jawed, she watched in horror as the two men exchanged a careful hug. She kept panic at bay, however, knowing that this entity had come for her—so be it. She'd lay in the cut, wouldn't make a false move to make it snap the neck of one of her brothers . . . oh, but when she got in range—it would be on.

Rider nervously backed up a little to give the Carlos look-alike room. Had her entire team been seduced? It couldn't be Carlos . . . could it? And that was just the problem. She wasn't sure. But one thing she did know for sure, master vamps moved like lightning, could kill a man with his bare hands within seconds and this thing was messing with her, staying out of range. She shuddered with rage. It smiled. *Oh no, motherfucker, not in my house.*

"Yo, dog, how's it hanging?" Carlos grinned, and pounded Dan's fist.

"I'm . . . uh, I'm cool," Dan stammered.

"You lived through Hell, guess you all right."

Dan nodded. "Thanks, man. I owe you."

Carlos laughed. "Never tell a master vamp you owe him. Not even me." Carlos shook his head and looked at Shabazz with a half-smile. "You need to school the newbie, *hombre*. Don't want him ass-out when it counts."

"I feel you," Shabazz said with a slow, sly grin. "We got his back. He don't go out alone yet."

"Good. It's all good," Carlos said, pounding Shabazz's fist. "You cool, Big Mike?"

"Yeah. I'm cool. Sounds crazy, but part of me's glad to see you, brotherman."

Again, Carlos nodded, understanding. "Thanks for chillin' with the lights till I got in, JL." He looked at Jose and smiled. "*Ese* . . . whassup? Know it took a lot of self-discipline not to freak at the last minute."

JL and Jose just nodded as Carlos scanned the room. Rider was still jumpy, though. He gripped the pump shotgun Carlos knew was loaded with hallowed earth shells. He could smell it. "Yo, dude. You all right?"

"No fist pounds, definitely no close hugs, Rivera. I appreciate what you did for us down in the tunnels, and even kinda like your style . . . However, you will excuse me if I give in to a nervous twitch." Rider lowered his weapon, but didn't break the barrel back.

"Sho' you right," Big Mike said. "We being real in here. You cool and all, but we just being real."

"No problem," Carlos replied, letting his breath out slowly. He'd tried to keep Damali only in his peripheral vision. Looking at her directly would mess him up for sure. Her pulse was already making his ears ring.

Marlene studied him for the slightest incorrect movement, and he could feel every sensor in the room locked on him. "Marlene, thanks for allowing this ten minutes. The point was made, and you all know what you've gotta do. Keep her safe. I'm out."

Marlene nodded. "Thank you."

"We cool, Mar. You're good people. Always were."

"I'll catch you, later, baby." He briefly looked at Damali, wrestling himself from her, and keeping near the clerics. "I wanna talk you, honest I do, but now is not a good time. Aw'ight? We'll pick it up later."

He had to get out of there. The look of shock, relief, disappointment, and rage on Damali's face was working every cell in his body. Plus it had only been a month since her first ripening and the mild, but wondrous scent of Neteru still lingered. She hadn't said a word, just circled him, staring, her blade held low, moving counterclockwise to him like she'd lunge at any moment. Her team was not his greatest danger. Nor was the Covenant team. She was. He needed to roll.

"JL, hit the exteriors, all right?"

JL nodded, but Damali held up her hand. Everyone stood still, waiting. The room crackled electric with quiet. No one even dared to breathe. The hum of air-conditioner compressors created a low sump-pump sound in the background. A stereo was on somewhere in the compound. The humans had enough adrenaline oozing from their bodies to give him a contact. He could see their eyes blink in slow motion as they stared at him and Damali while they continued to circle each other. The pores on their faces enlarged within his peripheral vision. He could detect the moment a bead of sweat slipped down their skin. His tongue glided over his lips and he tasted salt. The tension in their muscles increased, joints locked so tight that with the slightest movement, they threatened to pop. He felt the air, sensing for a weapon release. He smelled their blood, twelve nervous humans with hearts beating a rhythm out of their chests.

"I have to go," Carlos said, his gaze steady on Damali.

She shook her head slowly no. It was a millimeter of movement. Her locks swayed ever so much. The adornments in her hair and her earrings chimed. Lion's teeth, a tiny silver charm . . . Ahnk fertility symbols created natural music at a nearly imperceptible timbre. Her pupils had eclipsed her irises. Shea butter, almond oil, the scent of her was an intoxicating blend with something else she emitted . . . something different than Neteru. He'd smelled it on her before, but couldn't place it. Her face and arms glistened. The muscles beneath her smooth skin were a network of taut, steel-like cable. He could hear the blood pumping through her veins as she stalked him. She was gorgeous, poetry in motion. The crocheted white dress had holes that showed skin. As she moved, the dress moved with her body, barely concealing it. The fluorescent lights glinted off of the Isis and sent shards of illumination against patches of warm, damp flesh.

He allowed his gaze to rove over her in a slow undressing. "I have to go," he repeated more firmly, his voice dropping an octave. He had meant it as a statement, but even to his own ears, it had come out as a plea.

"You talk to me," she whispered through her teeth and stopped circling.

"Oh, shit . . ." Rider backed up a few paces and leveled his shotgun.

"Shut up, Rider," Marlene snapped.

Damali's eyes never left Carlos's. All she did was hold up her hand and her team went still once more.

"We should leave," the eldest cleric said quietly. "Before somebody gets hurt."

"Oh, what the fuck," Rider threw Big Mike a crossbow, and he caught it, nodding. Rider glanced at the clerics. "I thought you had an understanding with dude?"

"We do, and it's time to leave," Father Patrick insisted. "If it's not too late."

The Covenant team backed up, cautiously rounded Damali and Carlos, standing the line on the side of the guardians with weapons raised. JL had armed himself with a battle-ax, even Dan and Jose now had silver-tipped stakes in their hands. Shabazz had pulled Sleeping Beauty out of her holster.

Marlene folded her arms and leaned against the weapons table. "Steady, gentlemen. Nobody get an itchy trigger finger. Stay cool. Have faith."

"Have faith? Mar—"

"Shabazz, we know how this has to go down."

Damali tuned out the other voices, her goal singular, her mind focused. There was no shred of trust in her as she looked at the master vampire that had made her taste fear. She had to remember what he was, not allow the illusion to take her. This liar had fooled trusting clerics. Carlos was dead. This was something else. And this entity possessing a familiar body, had shape-shifted to trick her team, had rolled up on her in a battle-station ready compound, and dissected her while she was blind. The worst part of it all was, he'd been right. If it had been Fallon Nuit, she would have been dead . . . or worse. What did this thing want?

"Speak to me!"

"It's me, Damali—Carlos. Use your third eye!"

"You're a liar! Carlos is dead!"

She circled, moving with him. She was indeed more dangerous to him than sunlight at present.

"I can't get a mind lock," Carlos told Marlene and Father Patrick. "She's in a mental black box."

"Don't screw with my team! They don't have telepathic capacity that can break my will, I don't care what illusions you throw at them—"

"No, Damali," Marlene said, her voice urgent and strained. "Listen—"

"No! They sent this one as a decoy. I heard Carlos die—I saw it! Vamps are the masters of deception." Damali narrowed her gaze on the entity before her. "How dare you assume his shape . . . I will kill you." She seethed, her grip tightening on the Isis.

"Then plant the Isis," Carlos said, his voice escalating with emotion. "If that's what you need to do so you can see, then plant it right in the brand." In one deft motion he tore his black T-shirt from his chest, exposing his scar. Hot tears of frustration stood in his eyes. "Remember this, huh, Damali? Ask the damned men who pulled me out of a cave in the desert! Ask them how they found me. I suffered for three days in a cave in the fucking Mexican desert before they could get me stateside."

Carlos slapped the center of his chest. "I got this carrying you, baby," he said, his voice low and strained. "You're the only one that can smoke me in this room."

He closed his eyes, stretched out his arms, and leaned his head back. Her legs moved beneath her, hurling her toward the thing claiming to be Carlos, sword raised. She heard Marlene scream, "No!" She heard

Rider cry out her name; she heard the Covenant gasp; could feel her team move forward as though to stop her, and the tip of Madame Isis came to a sudden rest against bare skin. Her blade arm trembled; her intended target didn't open his eyes or flinch. The tip of Madame Isis never even smoldered. She dropped her blade and wept. It was him.

And then her mind pried open.

Horrific images poured into her brain as she stepped back from Carlos. The battle in the tunnel; his wounds riddled her body, contorting her, making her cry out with his invisible pain. Starvation claimed her, and she felt a section of her face get torn away. Her eye was gone, and she regenerated herself in agony; cold blood splashed against her cheek, strength entered her body, and she weaved, and held onto the weapons table for support. Marlene backed her team away from her, shouting that she had to do this herself.

Confined, she couldn't breathe, she was in a casket. Dirt was under her fingernails. Locked, trapped, she yearned for the night. Messengers brought her to Hell, and she stood in terror before an evil council. She could smell their old, rotting forms, and then black smoke choked her and deposited her topside. A deer stood frozen in the forest—"Run!" she screamed.

She took flight, branches breaking against her body, becoming primal, hunting to bring down fresh kill. Sated, she was mist, and she saw herself through Carlos's eyes. Felt his desire, so close but yet so far. Her mind was burning need. Her head jerked back as she took a hit of Neteru, experienced the thing that drove him insane, and felt it wash through her system in an erotic wave. *Damn* . . . She was breathing hard. Carlos glanced away. Her team looked confused. She had to get out of his mind. She struggled to open her eyes, but when she did, the visions still wouldn't stop.

The images kept hurling through her brain. Pain, not physical, sobs of deep regret. "Please, baby, believe in me . . . just one more time." Her voice was foreign to her own ears. She covered them, squeezed her eyes shut. Cried hard. "I'm sorry!" She couldn't catch her breath. She was afraid because she was hungry.

Panting, she stood up, wiped at her eyes, and looked at the stone-faced exterior of the man before her. The muscle in his jaw pulsed. She ran her tongue over her teeth. She could feel her gums nearly splitting. She sucked in a huge breath. Her gaze darted to the other humans. "I have to go," she said, the words coming from inside her head. "I can't take it anymore."

Carlos closed his eyes. "Her sight is back," he said. His voice escalated, becoming more urgent. "I did what I was supposed to do. Now shut down the exterior lights and let me the fuck out!"

Damali stared at Carlos. He was frantic, his breathing was ragged, and she could barely catch her own breath. He turned away. "I saw it all. I'm not afraid," she told him.

When he slowly turned around to look at her, her team again raised their weapons. Not even Rider said a word as a collective gasp passed through the team. A pair of red glowing orbs had replaced Carlos's intense, dark eyes. His incisors had come down, two inches and had not stopped lowering, and his shoulders had increased in bulk.

Something strange was happening to her. She was not afraid as her gaze traveled down his solid chest, studying the brand over his heart, then the tight bricks of his torso, and allowing it to slide over his belly, dipping into his navel, clinging to the silky black wisps of hair that disappeared under his belt. His nostrils flared at the image in her mind that stripped him bare. She registered his anger at her blatant hunger in front of the team, and checked herself. It wasn't her fault; she wasn't playing games; it was pure reflex. Dayum, she'd never felt it like this.

"I told you to let me out of here," he said coolly, quietly, his even tone belying his rage and desire. The need to be with her was so thick in his tone that the statement had come out as an open warning.

"Shut down the lights, JL," Marlene ordered. "Now!"

"No," Damali said in a too-calm voice, walking toward Carlos. "I'm going with him. We need to talk."

The look Carlos gave her was pure electric current, one thousand volts.

"Damali, not a good idea!" Rider said with a frown and worry clear in his voice.

"Li'l sis, he ain't himself. You'll make us have to shoot him." Big Mike spoke in an easy tone, his gaze steady as he dropped the crossbow in exchange for pointing the barrel of his shoulder cannon at Carlos.

"You'll get hurt, or someone on the team hurt, if you try to attack him," Father Patrick warned.

"Everybody stay cool, let the man out, and everything will remain chill," Shabazz said, raising Sleeping Beauty's barrel above Damali's shoulder line.

"Dan, talk to your boy," Jose said fast, his tone urgent. He couldn't get a clear crossbow aim because Damali blocked his shot. "Talk to him, before we have to do him."

"Let her out of the trance, Carlos," Dan begged, clutching a holy-water grenade. "Don't do this, man."

"She's not in a trance," Marlene said in a quiet voice. "Stand down. She's made a choice."

"What!" Shabazz turned toward Marlene, but she shrugged away.

The room again went still, the tension in the atmosphere was so tight that the walls threatened to bleed.

"I saw it all," Damali told Carlos. She moved toward him, following him, until he backed up to the cinder block wall. She continued to come closer until there was only a breath of space between their two bodies. "And you will not hurt me."

This woman had no idea. He closed his eyes as her hand found the center of his chest. "There's so much about this that you don't understand."

"Then, talk to me," she said quietly as she laid her head over his heart. "I thought you were gone forever."

He cringed and pushed her away. "There's no heartbeat, for starters."

She noticed his eyes had gone from red to gold. He was coming down. "What else?"

"There's no future," he said in a low tone, his fangs retracting.

She could feel relief sweep through the teams.

"What else?" Her voice was slow and gentle, the way you would talk to a wounded animal.

"I'm trapped . . . and I did it to myself." Carlos swallowed hard. "And I'm so sorry for all the things I did to get here. More than you'll ever know." He headed for the door.

Damali nodded. "JL, *now* you can shut down the exterior lights."

Carlos turned and looked at Damali as she walked up behind him. Carlos shook his head no, and repaired his ripped shirt as he did so.

"Where are you going?" He was beat, mentally wrung out, hungry. He couldn't take any more tonight.

"With you." She folded her arms over her chest, and ignored the stricken sounds of disapproval coming from both teams. "A lot went down. We need to talk—alone."

"Not advisable," Carlos said, truly meaning it.

"You heard the man," Rider said. "He's being honest, so let's not—"

Damali held up her hand. "That's why we need to talk alone. No sidebar commentary. No third-party advice. Me and you."

"You're serious?" Carlos laughed wearily. His gaze shot to her team. "Tell her again, people. It is *not* in her best interest."

"I'm going," Damali stated plainly. She didn't raise her voice, just walked over to where she'd dropped her sword and calmly picked it up. "You won't kill me, or rip out my throat. That's not what you have on your mind. I can see again, remember?"

Carlos nodded as a shudder of anticipation ran through him. "Then you'd better bring the blade . . . if all you want to do is talk."

Their gazes met, and she smiled a slow smile, and carefully abandoned Madame Isis on the weapons table, never taking her eyes from his.

"Oh, no, no, no, no, no, no no!" Rider fussed. "Hell no! You are not rolling out of here without *your blade!* Are you crazy?"

Damali nodded.

"Let it go, Rider," Marlene said in a weary voice. "Man, for once, just let it go."

"Listen, D, there are watchers everywhere, especially at night," Carlos warned, scanning the terrain outside the cabin safe house.

"If they saw you leave your compound," Father Patrick said, "and get into the Jeep with us . . ." His gaze darted toward Carlos. "Carlos can then enter the building at will after us—but the watchers will assume that we have taken you to higher ground, that you're on the move, and it won't blow his cover . . . understood? It has to always appear that he's deceiving us, had found a way in through a weak line—but it can never appear that he's colluding with us."

She nodded. She needed to get out of the Jeep, away from these well-intentioned, but babbling men, and into Carlos's arms so badly she thought she would scream. Carlos wouldn't even look at her. She could feel him pick up the thought and knew what it had done to him. She tried to retract the sensation, issuing a mental apology as they sat in brief silence. His hands were almost trembling and he stared out the window at nothing.

Truth was, there was no need for him to travel by Jeep, but he hadn't left her side since she'd walked out the front door of the compound with him. They were both messed up—had been that way for years.

"You should eat first," the cleric named Asula warned, glancing at Carlos with concern. "You've always been trustworthy in this . . . and our assumption is that the Neteru is sacrosanct with you as well. Therefore, we will have to muster faith that this conversation to purge old wounds and emotions between the two of you will be worthy of such continued trust and faith. Correct?"

"You ask a lot of a dead man," Carlos said, his gaze remaining fixed on the darkness beyond the passenger-side window.

Damali watched Father Patrick's body language. He was tense, but he wasn't nervous.

"Perhaps a better plan would be for our team to take up our post outside the safe house, to guard it for any possible breach by these sniffers you told us about?" The older man smiled. He glanced at the other older priests who smiled and looked away with a nod.

"Yes, this would be best so you may talk and also develop a strategy," Father Patrick pressed on, glancing at Father Lopez who seemed stunned.

"Padre," the older priest said. "Calm yourself and have faith. This is about safety. Our detection systems are not as sophisticated as the Neteru's compound, and I would have felt better if she brought her sword. On my honor, I pledged to her seer guardian that we would return her unharmed. Damali, you should have brought your sword."

"She brought me," Carlos said, his voice a low rumble. "You think I would let anything hurt her?"

The old cleric smiled and shook his head. "I suppose not."

Remember, baby, how it used to be?
When we were just kids and so free.
"Remember Baby" by Damali Richards

CHAPTER EIGHT

CARLOS WATCHED her walk around the clerics' spartan quarters, noting the way she took everything in. He kept his distance, just to be on the safe side. She had a totally destabilizing effect on him, one that he enjoyed and yet feared. This was not the place, and there was too much heat between them—had always been that way . . . but not here. He owed the old priests that much respect. But damn she was fine . . . and he'd missed her so much.

"You wanted to talk," he said quietly. "We need to do that, fast, and get you back where you belong."

She didn't answer him, but went toward the refrigerators. "You need to eat."

He shook his head. "Don't. I don't want you to ever see me do that."

Her hand fell from the door, and her eyes held so much sadness that he had to look away. He folded his arms over his chest, leaned on the door frame, then studied the floor.

"No, don't," she said.

He couldn't take it. She was standing there pitying him, knowing what he was, but still not afraid.

"Say what it is that you couldn't say in front of the others . . . please. Let's not drag this out."

"Then look at me, so I can," she whispered.

Couldn't she understand that just watching her move in that dress was painful, knowing he couldn't have her . . . shouldn't. He continued to look away, remembering he was in a clerical safe house, and tried to tell her things that were off the too-hot subject. The situation was beyond ludicrous. He still had shaky borders, and to whisk her away to a lair would put them both at risk to other males until he reestablished his line authority.

"You scared me, girl," he said quietly, his words absolute truth.

"When I came out from behind the clerics in your compound, if I was someone else, I'd have used them as body shields before you could even throw your weight behind your Isis. While you were trying to pull your blade out of an innocent's chest, you wouldn't have had swing time to come at me again. That's why you have to focus through the pain . . . even when there's a hard loss, baby. You, *of all people,* cannot afford to ever go blind. Not doing what you do."

"I know, but I . . . Going temporarily blind isn't the worst thing that's ever happened to me."

He sighed, his gaze now riveted to her. "Yes it is. Ask me how I know." He found a neutral point on the wall that was safe to stare at. "I've put down my own boys . . . even *my brother,* D. Buried so many friends . . . But even while I was still alive, my territory was danger-ous, and I couldn't lose focus. It'll change you, no doubt. But that's the only way you can survive this shit. Going blind ain't an option, D."

Her pull was greater than he'd imagined, as she made him look at her again. "I know," he said gently. "We've both lost a part of our hearts to the graves along the way. Regardless. Don't let *anybody* take you there—not even me."

He shoved away from the place he was leaning and walked deeper into the dining area, just to put more space between them.

"There are so many things we need to discuss, Carlos. If you'll just listen, and stop pushing me away because of what I am."

He let his breath out slowly. She was so naïve and still so damned blind it wasn't funny. She didn't even have her Isis on her.

"I'm not blind, anymore," she said quietly, openly reading his thoughts. "I didn't walk through this door naïvely either. I left my blade for a reason. You're the one that's blind tonight, Carlos. Always have been. That's what's made you vulnerable. Now look at me."

He honored the request against his better judgment, glancing up slowly to allow her gaze to capture his. "Talk to me," he said in a low voice, nervous as hell that she might take him somewhere he couldn't come back from.

Her mouth didn't move. He felt her mind grip his. It wasn't right what she was doing, probing the most erogenous part of him, getting all up in his head until images of laughter and good times created flashes of sensation within him. He was forced to close his eyes. He felt himself smiling as he saw her dancing, dropping a bandanna to start a drag race. "I remember that souped-up Chevy." He laughed as she nodded. "Oh, girl . . . I miss those times." His voice had become far away and gentle. *Please stop.*

"I still have it," she murmured. "Kept that old red rag since you gave it to me."

Her admission pleased him beyond measure, then she rocked him with the memory of an argument that entered his mind, stealing the joy, sending a rush of defensive anger through him that was quelled with the touch of her hand on his jaw. He hadn't heard her move toward him. He opened his eyes and saw that she was still across the room. She'd sent the gentle caress from her memory, touching him with her mind—not fair. He nodded. Yeah it was fair, they'd argued from day one about his life, and she'd told him where it would lead . . . if only he'd listened. Hindsight. Perfect vision.

Carlos sighed. He couldn't argue with her now. It was the truth. Tough, but gentle, that's what she'd always been. Tears filled her eyes as he stared at this woman standing across the room, a vision he couldn't have because of what he was, what he'd become.

But she had mercy in her mind. He heard the beach, waves pounding the shore; smelled salt air chase away the burning rubber and exhaust fumes from the drag race; he saw the sunlight catch her cheek and fire it bronze, red, gold; his finger traced it in the air. Yeah, he remembered that day . . . when a small thing like a button on her blouse drew his attention. The mental collage she sent was so beautiful, then she put music to it. The last refrain of her slow song from the concert . . . *Remember, baby.* His lids slid closed. No, he'd been right. What she was doing to him wasn't fair. This was an outright seduction, and he couldn't do shit about it.

Carlos opened his eyes and looked at her. She moved toward him and stopped so close to him that he could feel the heat rising from her skin.

"When I thought you were gone, I kept those memories of you tucked away to keep me whole," she whispered. "I was so angry at you for allowing yourself to—"

He put a finger to her lips, his mind weeping, trying to let her know that he understood, and no one regretted his path more than he. Picking up the end of the last vision she'd sent, his mind sent her his hopes . . . the dreams that could never come true. He was standing in a church watching her walk down the aisle toward him, then they were in a house, laughing, wearing T-shirts in bed—he rubbed her tight, round belly as the life they'd created kicked inside it.

"You're right. I was the one who was so blind for so long, Damali. Forgive me. I'm so sorry, baby . . . you just don't know."

His mouth found hers, and she tenderly returned his soft sweep against her lips. She covered his hands as they trembled against the sides of her face. He backed up an inch, his fingers touching her hair, his eyes searching hers for forgiveness, acceptance.

"I don't ever want to hurt you," he whispered, "and I have already."

"I'm immune," she said, sending a double message with the brief statement. "You can't." Then he watched her take out the silver earrings from her ears and let them fall to the floor. He stared at them, understanding what that meant, but almost not believing.

His hands found her shoulders. He glanced out the window, then he shook his head no.

"I'm not afraid," she said quietly, reading the conflict in his mind.

"I know . . . that's why I am."

She sealed the small space between them, tilting her chin up to him. The action caused near-delirium. Her skin made his catch fire. The scent of her flooded him and drowned the rational side of his brain. His grip on her shoulders slid to her upper arms and tightened. This was not how it was supposed to go down. This was not how he'd ever envisioned being with her. Not like this, not under heavy guard . . . not . . .

Damali put her finger to his lips. "Shush . . ."

The rush of her voice fractured his resolve as he lowered his head and found her mouth. The sweetness within it drew his hunger, and his tongue found hers, dancing in an urgent duel. His tongue plundered those hidden places, pulling a moan from her, which he swallowed, making him move against her as the sound lit him up inside.

When his hands found her back, he let them revel in the feel of her skin. Delicate knit allowed baby soft flesh to tease his fingers in intermittent patterns. Each vertebra he revered as his hand slid down to her round backside and her shudder of desire entered his body, shaking him to his bones. He had to let her go.

He pulled back. "Baby—"

Her mouth sought his again, harder this time, halting his protest. Her hands found the sides of his face and held him firm until he surrendered. He grabbed her wrists, intent on sending her home, but soon his palms covered her knuckles, his fingers twined with hers, making him lower her arms to guide them to his waist. She felt so good; his hands couldn't touch enough of her. He filled his fists with velvet soft locks, every texture she owned summoning a new wave of need.

He'd known hunger, but tonight she'd driven him to ravenous. What she offered was all-consuming, beyond mere flesh. She offered her mind and her spirit along with her body, and demanded the same in return . . . He'd never experienced anything so profound. There was no way to resist when her mind opened wide and trapped his with the truth . . . *Carlos, just once. For my first time, I always dreamed it would be you.*

There was no decision to be made. All of a sudden she was in his arms and with the speed of thought, he'd taken her down into the lair. He locked the steel door and he'd set her down easy on the hard, clerical cot.

She stared up at him with her big, brown doe eyes, but this was no passive prey. It was innocence with a burn beneath it, seeking. He could feel her desire hunting him as her chest rose and fell with shallow sips of air. She was past the point of guessing what could happen, just like he was. He looked around the room of what had been his prison cell. No, this was not how it was supposed to be with his woman . . . she deserved way better than this.

He waved his hand and instantly transformed the space around her. She sank into a lush, king-sized bed that became the centerpiece of the room. White silk just for her. Much better. He snapped his fingers, adding appointments; the walls went marble, candles lit, a torch flared by the bed, a gentle breeze blew, and an instrumental version of her song came on. If only he had his own lair, he'd give her cliffs and make the moon her spotlight. He sealed the room's exterior with silence. The clerics didn't need to hear this.

Carlos slowly took off his jacket. "You're sure?" His eyes never left hers. She had no idea what she was getting herself into. He'd waited for this moment for years.

She glanced around the transformed lair then looked back up at him and nodded. "I knew you were a master . . . had heard about . . . but didn't know you could do stuff like this . . ."

He didn't answer her as he dropped his jacket and came to her. She had no concept of what he could do, if she'd let him. Trying to decide where to begin, he garnered patience. She deserved all the pleasure he could give her. He'd stop time until she begged him to let her go.

He nuzzled the hair away from her neck, and she tensed. He planted a gentle kiss against it. Her mind began to close him away. "Don't . . . I won't bite you." His whisper drew a gasp from her, and he chuckled low in his throat.

She wasn't sure if it was a vamp line, right now she didn't care. He'd said that to her when they'd first met, and right now it meant the world. There was no resistance, any fear had been replaced by something that went way beyond that.

It wasn't a line. Didn't she know what the feel of her skin was doing to him? It was an aphrodisiac, just like her scent. Biting her was the last thing he was thinking about, she'd already taken him back to that first encounter when they'd met—blowing his mind. He rubbed his face against her shoulder, and with that their clothes vanished. She had wandered into a master vampire's lair . . . an innocent . . . in a priest's house. Shame on it all, but he was already damned. Natural law superseded any other laws they could levy. He'd tried to warn her . . . he wouldn't bite her. *At least not yet . . . not till you beg me to.*

"I might," she whispered. Shit . . . what was she saying?

Yeah, she would. But not yet.

He became dull heat, blanketing her, sending pleasure through every cell of her, licking away the sudden smolder he'd put onto her skin followed by a kiss that made it burn hotter. The arch of her neck was gasoline on his open flame. He lowered his mouth to it, like lowering a torch, and let the inferno consume him, then drew back to study her throat and willed himself to save the best for last. Not yet . . .

Kissing along her collarbone, finding the delicate tips of her breasts, suckling the tight dark pebbles, making her moan and lift her hips until her fingernails dug into his shoulders, he took his time. He knew . . . soon. Yeah, he felt it all, too. *Baby, be patient . . . you'll want this to last.*

Abandoning the soft mounds of flesh to explore each tender underside, his tongue trailed down her belly drawing a slow hiss of air from her as she arched again. *I know.* The sound of her voice made his hands splay under her rising backside, drawing a harsh gasp from her with each gentle pull of skin, the smell of her unleashing bands of color behind his lids, every shudder almost making him forget this was her first time and that his mouth needed to take her, tease her, totally spend her.

He buried his nose in a downy forest of curls where a stream of pure want spilled from her plump slit. Oh . . . man . . . she was so wet it was dissolving his control. And she smelled so damned good, was so swollen, he could hear her pulse between her legs. His moan traveled inside her, quaking her womb, causing her to grab the silk sheets in another hard arch.

It made him mentally tell her the truth. *Baby, you don't know how long I've waited for this.* Ever since he'd let her sleep untouched on his mother's sofa. *You know how many nights I went to bed jonesin' for you, la amante? Losing my mind in my own mother's house . . .*

Gentle caresses sent the message, he opened her with deep kisses, letting her feel the softness of his mouth against the soft slickness of her, preparing her to soon receive the opposite of that. Her fingers raked through his hair, holding him to her, a deep guttural moan aching within him as it pushed its way up her abdomen. He caressed her hips with his palms flat, tracing them, while his tongue drizzled pleasure into sweet folds and flicked at her bud. He let it find the deep cavity that had a throbbing rim, circling it, intensifying the ache, making it flutter with contractions, sending her voice through the roof as he probed gently at the thin skin that was partially blocking him easy entry— refusing to stop until the passageway became newly flooded. Then he drove in his tongue for real, claiming her sweet territory.

She called his name in her mind and it instantly came up from her throat low and deep. *That* was the sound he'd been waiting to hear. She'd called his name, repeating it like the refrain of a song that soon lost its beat and measure, drawn out on a spasm that choked before it died on a breathless gasp.

Tears filled her eyes and spilled from the corners of them down the sides of her pretty face. He could taste the salt in each fast-running drop the moment they hit the air. When he lifted his head to witness his handiwork in her expression, a sheen of fresh orgasm-perspiration made her skin glisten. He felt her total surrender, saw it glittering in her irises, the torch fire making it dance as her hands again found his shoulders and she slowly closed her lids, tilted back her head to expose her throat. He ran his tongue against his teeth—not this time. Not her first time. No. He'd be gentle.

But it was her ragged breathing that was messing him up, just like her urgent arch had . . . just like her racing pulse did. He slid his hand down her inner thigh, opening her wider, the rapid thud in her femoral artery a magnet. He was trying so hard to simply love her like a man, and not like what he truly was. She had given herself freely without him having to employ any powers of seduction from the dark side of his being, and that gift deserved to be cherished with the best he could give in return. Pure pleasure.

He studied her face, the tilt of her chin, and allowed his eyes to slide down her throat, her deep breaths burning him. He watched her chest rise and fall, lungs expanding and contracting like she couldn't get enough air—because of him. She was in his bed—his lair. She had gone against family, just for him. She had crossed a prayer line and left a fortress—*just for him.* He hadn't even called into the night for her, and she knew what he was, but yet she came to him on her own, re-gardless. And she was writhing beneath him—warm . . . wet . . . suf-fering with a need he understood all too well.

It messed up his reason, her sweet seduction had, and now it was threading its way through the dark crevices of his mind . . . that place within him that had wanted her like this for so long. He had to honor that request, as well as his own nature. The night was young, and he owned it.

He slid against her like they shared the same skin, swept his cheek hard against the side of her neck, making her shudder, then captured her earlobe with his lips, suckling it, drawing the same pleasure into it that he'd just visited upon the delicate bud between her legs. He could feel her open her eyes with the gasp she'd released, shocked. Yeah, *hombre,* do her right. The night was young, and so was she. She'd never been with a man before. Don't break the seal on this package too fast—be all-pro. Give her the best.

Her grip tightened on his shoulders as he left her earlobe just before she climaxed, and he breathed a command into the canal of it. "When I call you, come to me. Hear?"

She nodded and shut her eyes tight, her body moving beneath him, trying to capture him within it, but he shook his head no. Not yet. Her response was a series of short pants that he stopped with his mouth, his kiss deep and feral as his tongue scored the roof of hers and concentrated on a single point.

In his mind he could see that agonized strobe of tender flesh within her canal. It hid just behind her cervix, deep, like a glowing ember that had never been properly stoked. He copied its throb into her mouth, using the tip of his tongue to make the transfer, then deepened the French kiss until she almost choked on her own spit when she came hard.

He abandoned her mouth, but not the sensation it carried, depositing points of pleasure along her jugular. Damn right, the road to Hell was paved with good intentions. He wanted every kiss to claim her, every brush of her earlobe to devastate her. He wanted to be able to glance across a crowded room at her and take her over the edge. He demanded an imprint like a maker's mark. A permanent bond. She was his, and he'd rewire her body's circuitry until she only responded for him.

While kissing her shoulder he went into her mind with purpose, a hard-thrust thought, like he was planning to do to the rest of her later, only to be so rewarded by her fantasies that he almost wept and busted a nut himself. Entering her thoughts so fast had felt like he'd just plunged into her up to the hilt. It took him a moment to steady himself through a shudder and her diaphragm-sent moan. Her smooth hands were running up and down his back, sending shivers with them as they slid with his sweat and her legs wrapped around his, then slipped over his hips to anchor around his waist.

No, it wasn't over yet. Sweet torture was divine, didn't she know? He gently pushed at her knees until she released his waist. He chuckled low in his throat as she shook her head to tell him no more, not again, that the pleasure was unbearable. He savored the fact that she was beyond words, even telepathically. Stop? Not hardly. He wasn't finished leaving his brand.

He gathered up everything she'd forbidden herself on a hard inhale, letting the tension in those secret places build like slow thunder, moving down her torso, trailing her belly with his tongue again, collecting and stroking each time she'd whimpered alone in her bed, connecting to every time her hand had cautiously slid down her stomach searching for release alone but denied, years of pent-up want straining to hold out and do the right thing, her pillow her lover. Six years of agony, of night sweats and wet dreams . . . years of brutal intensity unanswered, her delicate hand a poor substitute for him. *Oh, baby, you suffered . . . want me to kiss it and make it better?*

When she nodded quickly, tears streaming down her face, he let it all go with a deep plunge of his tongue, finding her unspoiled opening once more. He sent all of her denied release as a spiral of sudden climaxes bound to shock waves of pleasure, answering each unquenched night he'd endured in the pulse of his tongue.

In a subtle fusion he made both his pent-up agony and hers collide on his deepening kiss and offered her the threat of spontaneous heart failure lick by lick . . . six years was a long time to want somebody this badly . . . didn't she know he had the power to make her feel it all at once, in one incredible flash-fire moment? Love her like a mere man, impossible now. She was more than a woman; she was his Neteru. *You ready?*

This time she released his name in the key of G, perfect pitch, then riffed the scale with one shrill word— *"Yes."*

Oh . . . yeah . . . the night was young, and he was night itself. He was gonna put his thing down hard so she'd never question him again, or tell him no.

Yet her seizure had almost made him forget that it was indeed night, just like her voice had . . . and her sobs . . . *damn* . . . he had to remember to breathe. She had scorched him like daylight; her burning response left him near ash. He nipped her inner thigh, but didn't break the skin, determined to finish the brand with authority. But she grabbed his hair, her spine a snap-flex that had her almost sitting up to make him look up at her.

"Oh, fuck it—stop playing, Carlos," she whispered, tears washing her face, her voice coming out fast, harsh, so urgent that it made him shudder.

The expression in her eyes stunned him for a moment, so had the husky demand. It had instantly caused a groin contraction that filled his shaft with hot fluid pressure. He could feel it pearling at the tip and oozing from it in a thin, clear line down to the sheets. She'd made him want to slide inside her so badly his vision was blurring. Damn, he was gonna lose control if she kept talking to him like that. But not to-night. He'd brand her with pleasure, just like she'd branded him with her Isis—a slow, sizzling burn. He would molten-bronze cast that shit before he was finished with her. Make her *banish* the word no.

He came to her fast, covered her in a hot slide against her, and kissed her hard, then broke from her mouth and held the sides of her head, but didn't enter her. He made her look into his eyes as his fingers tan-gled through her hair. "I don't want you to bleed, not there." He heard her mind shriek that she didn't care as her pelvis gyrated beneath him. Fuck it, he did. "Uh, uh, I don't want you to ever associate pain with me, not there, baby. You don't want it like that. Neither do I."

Focus. He slid his hand to her back, pressing against it hard to hold her close, giving her a little bit of what she craved, just the tip, and held her pelvis down against the mattress to keep her from moving, to keep himself from moving and in check. He dropped his voice low so she would pay attention. "Let me work it in slow. Trust me."

He had to stare at the wall for a moment to get himself together; her contractions were like a desperate siphon, her voice had unraveled to an agonized wail carrying the word, *"Please."* When a sob of plea-sure ripped through her and she begged him to hurry and put it in hard, he almost did. His breathing was getting ragged, and the point on the wall wasn't working.

Oh . . . shit . . . this woman was fine. She was like a piece of rare, passionate art, needed to be displayed proper in the correct venue, mounted right and handled with care, not ruined. But her voice was blowing the lid off his mental black box. It was taking him places that he knew he didn't need to go . . . not for her first time. But, shit, his possessiveness was loosed, he was a Scorp before he died . . . and she needed to know what she'd been missing from him all these years. Needed to know one voice, one pair of hands, one set of eyes when she closed hers at night—his. *He owned this;* her pussy was claimed. She was his territory. Fuck a pillow—never again, not on his watch. *Tell me it's mine!*

The side of his hot face caught her temple; she arched, nodded, sputtering, sobbing, and answered him righteous.

"Oh, God, yes, *Carlos,* it's yours."

Exactly.

That was probably his undoing . . . Especially when she sobbed and told him it always had been his. True he was a vampire, but he was also a man. Her shudder became his sudden shudder, and his kiss against her throat became more aggressive than intended. He almost dropped fang. She smelled so damned good, and the way she felt around him, her legs constricting his waist, squeezing him in the rhythm she was aching for—hard stroke. But no, if he went there, it would be all over way too fast. She was holding him to her, her nails digging into his skin until he could smell his own blood. *That's what I'm talking about.*

"When I call you like this, *for this,* don't make us both suffer," he said on a ragged breath. Her gasp was his answer. "I don't care what your family's got to say," he whispered hard against her neck. "This is between me and you."

"I will, I swear," she said, weeping under his hold, her voice a knife to his system, slicing it, cutting away his will. "I can't take it."

He cradled her in his arms, and eased against her, slow, steady, then brought one hand to her hip to still her frenzied movements so she wouldn't hurt herself. Then he stopped and kissed her forehead, her eyelids, the bridge of her nose, her mouth. With his heart full he moved against her in small, smooth increments, letting her adjust to his weight, to his penetration of her body. He allowed himself to fill the tightness until his pelvis touched hers. Caressing her cheek, he nuzzled her temple, and stayed away from her throat—lest he forget. But her mind ravaged his as it begged for him to take her that way as well.

She couldn't stand it. The pleasure was so profound it made her nearly insane. She let her voice go. No shame. There was no way to hold it back anyway.

Each touch set a glowing iron of hot want to her skin . . . his mouth, oh God, this man's mouth . . . she never knew. Seconds seemed like hours, and minutes had fused into what felt like days, time had literally stopped as he tasted her ear again while lodged deep inside her not moving, left her writhing, wet, sweaty, dazed, in a fever, and now he wouldn't let her move as he sucked her earlobe and made her feel it in her bud.

Every inch of him that covered her was purely honed strength, and she allowed her hands to travel down his back, dip into the valley of his spine that rose again into his tight ass that clenched on the slow down stroke. Have mercy. Thick muscular thighs pushed against the bed, against her, in a maddening, lazy rhythm designed to spare her, but prolonged the agony of needing immediate release one more time.

Sweet torture, sweet Jesus, this man was finding parts within her, sensitive spots, hidden deep and stroking them with his lazy rhythm, making her beg him to go faster . . . wanting him to hit that spot he found down deep . . . shit, he could bludgeon it, *just hit it.* Her mind pulled him, begged him to keep coming back to that place being kissed by his shaft then gone, returning slowly to pass it again, making her arch, making him hold her hips tighter to slow the pace, the compromise almost shattering his promise to himself that she'd heard through his skin. Hell yeah, she'd come to him for this—*any night—* just call. He owned her. Her eyes were crossing beneath her shut lids. Any night, every night, just don't stop. There was no pride when it came to something like this . . . if she'd only known.

And the feeling . . . the feeling of those muscles moving beneath taunt skin as they contracted in a dance, a slow salsa, good lord . . . he had to stop. Oh, lord, he'd better not. Ribbons of light scored her shut lids, a current of electricity tore through her until her body seized and convulsed and the shudders would not end. She couldn't breathe, forgot how to, his face burned her cheek as his head burrowed into her shoulder. The wondrous release shot up the core of her, shook her womb, entered her spinal cord, and imploded at the top of her skull. She was gonna die from pleasure, have a damned stroke. Her stomach muscles pulled her up hard, his weight on her notwithstanding, jerking her, whiplashing her; she could only ride it out holding his hair and his back with her fists till it ended.

And he lay within her, breathing hard, not opening his eyes. She could feel his jaw packed with sudden steel. Then he left her.

Damali opened her eyes and sat up slowly. She stared at him in stunned disbelief. "What's wrong?"

Why had he stopped—not *now.* The separation from his warmth, especially between her legs, felt like a cold stab up her center that brought her hand to her abdomen to stave off the shiver. His absence left phantom spasms, her rim burning, and her entire canal on fire. Oh yeah, she was beyond shame. What had he done to her? *Come back to bed, shit . . . Carlos.* She needed him so badly, tears were standing in her eyes. "Baby, what's wrong?"

He shook his head, his back to her, and held up his hand, unable to form words. His mind was still open. His thoughts sent another hard shudder through her that made her body clench. She wanted him again, needed him one more time . . . it had been so long, and she'd almost lost him forever.

In her mind she was begging him, trying save some of her dignity by not saying it out loud. Trying not to get on her hands and knees for it. But right now she felt like a junkie craving one more hit. Didn't he know what it was for a woman to wait twenty-one whole years to be with a man . . . him? Had he any concept of what that was like? Agony. They had a second chance.

"No. We don't," he said quickly without turning to look at her.

One time would never be enough. She stared at him, needing his touch so immediately that she almost cried out for it. Didn't he know how many fantasies he'd fueled, then had answered?

"Baby . . . listen . . . I can't. Okay?"

She studied the back that was bronzed in the candlelight and by torches, its every detail quickening her with the need to reach out and touch it. Then she understood. Without the bite, with her, a Neteru, he couldn't finish. The side of her throat throbbed; instant heat seared it and matched the pulse in his shaft. Her hand covered the ache at her jugular and a moan escaped her lips as she stroked it.

"Stop . . ." His voice was a low, urgent warning. "It doesn't matter. Just leave it alone. I'll be cool in a minute."

"I can't." That was the cold-blooded truth. Stop? Was he mad? She couldn't breathe. "Baby, you don't understand."

"Hell, yeah, I do. *You don't understand.* I can't come back to you right now without hurting you. Like I said, gimme a minute." He dropped his head back with his eyes closed tight and pulled in a sharp breath that cut the air. "Oh, shit . . . I'm okay. I'm all right."

Her eyes trailed down his body and she felt his shudder from across the room. Then something strange happened. It began inside of her, as though something dormant woke up. Sudden strength crept through her and made her womb contract. He staggered farther away from her, and she could hear him inhale hard on a strangled gasp. She nearly climaxed again when he did—just seeing him that way, on the border of no control, was like a rush.

"What is the scent?" he murmured, his breaths erratic, pained.

"Me being *really* ready for you . . ." She leaned back on her elbows and mentally dared him to turn around. She needed him to. It was a reflex after what he'd just done to her. Her lids lowered to half-mast, her voice dropped to a sultry, provocative octave free of all fear and inhibitions. "Matured . . . willing . . . Neteru that is not afraid of the bite. Antibodies that ward off a turn. I challenge you. Just once." Then her voice fractured to a whisper. "Baby, please, I really need that now, too."

He turned around and she could tell he was desperately seeking composure. But his eyes flickered gold, then intermittently red.

"I don't want to hurt you."

"You can't." She'd breathed out the plea. This wasn't up for negotiation. He'd turned her ass out, and wasn't gonna leave her hanging like this. Not tonight. "It's no longer my first time." Pride stripped, she didn't care if he was gonna make her beg—just as long as he came back to bed.

Every desire she ever had became directed toward him. Her mind dredged his and locked in on the scent. "This is what was mixed with ripening Neteru outside Nuit's lair. When I really want you, it's something just for you. Come back to bed."

She'd told the man the truth; she'd been so aroused by the fight, the adrenaline, and the primal rush of it all . . . if it weren't for certain death, he could have done her right there. "Tell me you didn't feel it, too, in New Orleans."

He closed his eyes for a moment and breathed in deeply through his nose, his will shattered. "I wanted you so bad that night my hands were shaking, girl."

"They're shaking now," she said with a sly smile. "When I call you like this, don't make us both suffer."

"You sure?"

She nodded, watched him stalk back to the foot of the bed and slowly climb onto it, coming toward her on all fours. His eyes never left hers now; a hint of fang was showing as the last of his suave façade crumbled and he went primal.

"I won't be able to hold back this time . . . you know that? I'm past the point."

She closed her eyes and leaned her head back as he covered her again. "Yeah . . . I'm counting on that," she whispered, then lifted her hips to take him in.

As soon as he entered her she nearly lost her mind. His hold under her backside was more aggressive than she'd expected, but she met his ardent response by immediately wrapping her legs around his waist again. The sound he released as he sank deep within her was so animal that it opened a new channel in her brain. Sound fused with touch and became liquid heat. She arched hard and found herself above him. Holding his jaw, she forced his head to the side and bent quickly to kiss his neck, making his eyes roll to the back of his head as she delivered the first bite.

Everything in her shook as his moan washed through her bloodstream and pleasure reverberated back through her in an endless recycling ecstasy. Her name started in his chest, got trapped in his throat, and escaped on another groan. She could feel him arch, pull her down against him harder. All gentleness gone, she was beneath him in seconds, part of her hanging off the side of the bed, him plundering her so relentlessly that they both fell. She was laughing and crying at the same time, hysterical it felt so good. She banged her head on the floor and opened her eyes. He stopped, the expression on his face intense, and rose above her. No laughter in his eyes, no flicker of gold, he was over the top—solid red. *Yeah, baby, that's more like it.* "Hit it like you need to . . . I can take the bite."

He stopped breathing and closed his eyes slowly, tilted his head, trembling, deciding, as though almost afraid to move. She made the decision for him, arched suddenly, raked his back, and bit him as hard as she could. The breath he'd been holding came out with her name planted in a guttural wail. Beneath her hands every muscle in his shoulders, back, hips, thighs, ass instantly united toward the goal of pure leverage.

On the floor he punished her, trying to cushion her spine with his hands, his arms, unable to stop moving against her. Tears of pleasure were running down his face, his head thrown back, one hand outstretched to save her skull from concussion against cement. His voice was a low rumble, a baritone vibration that she could feel through the floor and her skin, tears and mucous deepening the unintelligible staccato fusion of Spanish and English, stuttering something about *"Don't stop"* as she moved hard with him, split by *"Oh, damn, baby . . ."*

She clung to him, absorbing every deep thrust with searing pleasure, not caring who heard her. He was chanting, "I love you"; she was sobbing the same words. Then her name became *mi corazon* upon another choked fusion of English and *Español,* garbled by paralyzing spasms.

The room soon started losing form and shape as the illusion began to fracture—his concentration singular—total release inside her. She could feel him approaching the edge of sure completion, which only made her tumble over her own, claiming his, merging with it, bonding it with their bodies, their heat, combined chants of release ecstasy, every fiber joined as she heard his gums rip. Her hard contractions sealed him to her, pain at her throat, a blinding strike that turned into a tidal wave of orgasmic pleasure. He threw back his head, breathing hard through his mouth, fangs glistening with blood and saliva.

There was no fear; he was a sculpted work of art that brought nothing but pure Eros. She could see him in the dark, his strength staggering. It was reflex, she bit him as hard as she could once more, and that seemed to make him more aggressive. His jaw collided with hers to forcefully knock her head back, and he took her throat again, then came hard in blinding spasms that he sent into her jugular with the same intensity being unleashed between her legs. His siphon from her throat synchronized with driving rhythm of his hips. She felt herself losing consciousness. He tried to pull out of the bite, but she flattened her palms to his back, and he practically wept at the physical command for him not to stop. She didn't care if she died tonight, as long as she went out like this.

Never in his life . . . *never* . . . What had she done to him . . . Every shudder, every whimper, every moan riddled his system with sensation after sensation of wondrous release. He felt her multiple orgasms at the cellular level, and as he siphoned the sweet, salty fluid from her jugular, her body siphoned seed from him in equal measure.

Adrenaline, passion, unbridled lust, small doses of her fear filled his mouth, his throat, sweet heat coating his insides, drugging him, becoming an erotic hallucinogen of exploding, exponential groin torture. It took him to near blackout, sent needles of pleasure through every inch of his skin. He pulled out of the bite and cried out just to keep from flat-lining her. Never before . . . life from her veins . . . never could he have imagined . . . the myths the other masters had tried to tell him, but he couldn't comprehend such ecstasy . . . and that she loved every minute of it was killing him.

Thick saliva, blood, tears became one inside his mouth, consciousness ebbed and flowed as each hard thrust contracted his body with a violent arch followed by another shuddering release from his groin. The combination hurt so good it made him sob. His mind was putty. Control, what was that? She had to stop arching, let him pull out to save his sanity. *Woman, I can't stand it . . .* Seconds prolonged on a wail transformed into persistent need—he had no choice, had to keep moving inside her, repeating the unbroken rhythm, repeating the bite, taking more of her than he should while giving her all that he had.

His voice was a muffled plea against her neck. "Baby, forgive me . . . I can't stop." Didn't she hear him? He'd hollered he couldn't stand it, told her as loud as he could in his mind that he was nearly insane it felt so good, but stop—impossible. Blood was running down his chin. She should have never taken him there, never opened that channel, dredged his mind, soldered him to her body . . . mentally gave him the scent to her ripened. Never. Shouldn't have made him taste it undiluted on her sweat-slicked skin, in her mouth, riddling her hair, while taking his seed. Oh, shit, she shouldn't have denied him for years, then made him battle for her—not smelling like this in a priest's house.

She was dying in his arms, but he couldn't stop moving against her. Gasping for breath, he, too, was dying from sheer pleasure. His eyes were shut tight, her name had become an agonized chant comingled with a moan on each deep invasion against her womb, sweat and tears ran together and mixed on the bridge of his nose, dripping hot on her face, the sheets, her fingers tangled in his soaked hair, opening his scalp to the coolness of the room till he shivered. *Oh, goddamn, don't stop . . .*

Her body would not relent. Her hips moved against him like liquid fire, scorching his barren skin that had waited for her for so long. And she smelled so damned good, adrenaline competing with natural female, working shea butter, almond oils, blood, and something just her.

Without mercy she continued to invade his mind, echoed back a call and response that made him lose control, he was clay in her hands, whatever she wanted from him was hers. Never in his life, not even in death, had he so completely surrendered in a woman's arms. *Shit . . . yeah, he'd come to her whenever she called.* Yeah, baby, would cross prayer lines and risk a hollow point bullet for this—*just call.* Sweet seduction thy name is Damali. Her first time, correction, it was his. *Baby, take everything I've got—name it. I don't care! It's all yours.*

He was babbling in his mind, yelling, *Yes,* hollering that shit and thinking it all at the same time. Had she any idea what Neteru did to a man, what she did to him? Turned out, done righteous, and he couldn't even catch his breath he was broke down sobbing so hard. If he had only known it could be like this . . .

She pet his trembling shoulders as he tried to push himself up to look at what had overtaken him, this creature, this huntress, who had just stripped his cool to the bone—blown his mind.

But he couldn't remove himself from the tight, rhythmic hold her body had on his. As long as he stayed in her, the shared sensations ricocheted between them with each one of her hard contractions. He had to pull out but couldn't; she had him drooling on himself, blind. He heard his mind beg her to stop, it was so damned good, and as he gathered the strength to look down at her, he saw multiple puncture wounds in her neck, blood oozing from them. She wasn't breathing. Her hands fell away from his hair. His vision blurred as another shudder passed through him and finally bled his scrotum dry.

"Damali!" He tightened his hold on her. Her eyes were open and she wasn't breathing. Panic ripped through him. Reality kicked his ass, brought him down hard. His breath caught in his throat. No, *Por Dios,* not like this! He gathered up her limp body and rocked her against him, still in her. *What had he done . . .*

A sudden gasp, then a huge exhale of air escaped her mouth. The sensation passed through him like a ghost. Tears streamed down his face as she clutched his shoulders and inhaled again hard.

He was beyond words. A sob shattered him as he touched her hair, expecting her to pull away. "Baby, I—"

She reached for his cheek and shook her head, then laughed. He just weakly stared at her.

"Daaaayuuum . . ." she whispered, her voice hoarse. "Carlos, I had no idea." Her hand went to her neck, and her fingers came away with a few drops of blood.

Shame constricted the muscles around his lungs. He hadn't even sealed the wounds when he pulled out—his shit was raggedy, unprofessional, wasn't even smooth, but damn it was good. "Baby . . . I . . . couldn't help it . . . oh, shit . . ."

She licked her fingers and raised one eyebrow. "I'm a couple of pints low. Dang."

When she chuckled again, he finally laughed, but it wasn't funny. "You need to stop," he argued. "I tried to explain . . . but. Girl, for real. Now, look. This bullshit is dangerous."

It almost hurt to pull out of her, she felt so exquisite. But they'd just danced on the edge of disaster, and he couldn't have her go out like this. He stood with effort, then scooped her up and laid her on the bed. Yeah, he had to kill Nuit for this. In an odd way, he now better understood where the brother was coming from.

"If I had known it was your first time," she said in a lazy, sexy voice, stretching on the tangled sheets, "I would have been more gentle with you."

Carlos put his head in his hands and finally laughed, mostly in relief. She was definitely dangerous. What was he doing locked in a lair with a huntress? Girlfriend didn't need her Isis to slay him. He glanced around the plain room, remembering exactly where he was. "I need to get you back home." He dropped his hands and shook his head as he looked at her neck. "You sure you're protected?"

"Just like a man, all late and after the fact," she said with a sly grin, shaking her head. "Wouldn't have come over here, if I wasn't."

"Okay. Cool. It's all good," he said, beginning to pace, not sure why. "Uh, I gotta explain some of this to the monks—damn . . . in their spot. They might have heard us. See, this was raggedy. I don't generally roll like this, D . . . but my circumstances." He raked his fingers through his damp hair and wiped his mouth again with the back of his hand, smelling her sweet scent all over him. He closed his eyes. This woman was definitely a drug. "You gotta go home. It wasn't supposed to go down like this. I tore up your throat, baby . . . I've gotta seal the wounds or Marlene will freak. No, see, you gotta go home."

When she didn't answer him, he just stared at her for a moment. "Does it hurt? I'm really sorry . . . yeah, no, you've gotta go home."

"You sure you're ready for me to go home?"

He opened his mouth and then closed it, not sure what to say. Hell no. But . . .

"Trust me, it didn't hurt," she said, her gaze intense. "I've *never* felt pleasure like that in my life." She brought her hand to cover her neck where he'd bitten her, not touching the surface of her skin, but allowing her palm to hover over the bites. "I could actually feel an org—"

"I'm in prison," he said fast. He didn't need her to remind him. "Got people I have to answer to."

"You need me to put on my dress and go get a few bags from the refrigerator? Figured you burned all that energy . . . and if we have to bar the door, you'll need it. Or, I could just go up there, show 'em my passion mark, tell the old boys to stand down. Explain that I'll be in your lair for a few. I'm over twenty-one and consenting. We're grown. If they see I'm all right, they'll chill." She allowed her smile to broaden and then she tilted her head and pouted. "C'mon, Carlos. I waited a *long* time to get with you. Tighten me up, one more time before I go home?"

She was insane. He loved her. He was the one that was crazy. "That's no passion mark. It's a real bite that might have killed you. Don't get it twisted. Another pint and—"

"Aw, relax. It was just a love bite." She allowed her voice to drop to a low, sexy timbre. "This was only a passion nick, *es verdad*."

Yeah, it was true, but that was not the point. This wasn't supposed to turn into a conjugal visit. He glanced around again, half waiting for the door to break open and a crossbow arrow to find his chest. "You're crazy, and I'm taking you home." She also needed to stop trying to seduce him with language.

"Why? *Por que, mi tesoro?*"

He looked at her hard. "Because you're turning me on. Stop." He couldn't help telling her, it was the truth.

"You sure you want me to stop, baby?" she murmured.

"No." His gaze traveled over her naked body, hovering at her petite breasts, the swell of her hips, and the way they tapered down into long, agile thighs. He looked back up at her intense eyes and the way open desire flickered in them, and for a second, he thought he saw a hint of gold. It did something to him, and he glanced at the steel door. "They'll behead me if I go upstairs, and trust me, I'm in no condition to square off with anybody right now." He lowered his gaze. "And, I broke my word to them."

"No you didn't," she murmured, coming to the edge of the bed.

"I did."

He shook his head. Yeah, she was wild.

"I was the one who seduced you, remember? I never promised them I wouldn't deflower you."

"Girl, please," Carlos said, mildly outraged. "You did not seduce me—or *deflower* me."

"Really?" She issued a lopsided smile. "You went for broke, brother . . . just like I did. Tell the truth. You've never actually punctured a living throat vein, have you?"

He didn't answer her for a moment. Her directness was embarrassing, stung his pride—he'd always been the teacher; she'd always been the student. *He* was the damned master vampire, not her. Now everything was upside down, and it messed with his head. She had been his first, he had the real hunger now . . . and he was faced with going back to cold bags of blood. This was beyond dangerous.

"You made history though, baby." She winked at him.

He cocked his head in question.

"Bet none of the masters ever delivered a bite on a Neteru, the millennium Neteru, at that, and lived to tell about it. And I can guarantee you that they didn't make her sing four-part harmony in the process." She studied her nails, mischief playing around her mouth as she did so. "Hmmm . . . guess you're still da man. You got skillz." She patted the cot and her tone suddenly became serious. "Come back to bed and finish what you started, *por favor*. Like you told me, why make us suffer? I'm bitten now, you already broke the skin . . . so . . ."

For a moment he was speechless. She'd read his mind without using her gift; this thing that she'd just said, he knew came from old-fashioned female knowing. And it further endeared her to him that she would even care about his pride, would be so gentle with the most fragile part of any man—his ego. But he truly loved the way she'd put a grappling hook in his libido just by the tone of her voice and her devastating stare. *Shit*. How was he gonna say no to that?

They both knew they were in trouble—she'd get her ass kicked out of the compound, he'd get a stake in his heart. Whateva. The night was young, and she was so *damned* fine. It was worth the risk, down to the last shiver. Let the chips fall where they may. If they were gonna exterminate him, this was definitely the way to go out.

He walked toward the bed, knowing that was the wrong thing to do. She chuckled, leaned up, and willed him to bend toward her so she could kiss his cheek, and made him laugh. He relaxed and sat down on the edge of the bed, thinking of how long it had been since he'd truly laughed, truly felt joy. She looked so satisfied, so sexy, so positively tempting as she laid back and sprawled out before him in a generous offering so that his body stirred at the sight of her.

"I should take you home before history repeats itself." He sighed and rubbed the nape of his neck, and gave her a sideline glance. "I've already tasted you now, if we go there again, I'll definitely bite you harder. Truth be told, I'm all fucked up, right through here at the moment."

He let his breath out slowly, trying not to let her see him begin to breathe hard again. Oh, man, this woman had almost made him hit the vanishing point by himself. If she kept messing with him, he'd turn her tonight, just so she could go there with him. They had to stop.

"Can you actually turn into mist . . . or anything else?"

He looked at the sly expression on her face and tried to ward off the shudder the question produced. She had no idea what he could do to her. "Don't even go there," he said, his voice low and husky. "If I shape-shift on you, by tomorrow night you'll drop fangs."

She got on her knees and leaned against his chest. "Teach me everything you know," she whispered, her voice like raw silk.

"Can't do that in one night," he murmured with a smile, his finger tracing her cheek. Sheeit . . . he had centuries of knowledge at his disposal. She needed to stop playing with this.

"Then I'll take my lessons in nightly installments." Her gaze raked down his body and lingered where it shouldn't have if they were going to leave. "Why don't we start with what you'd really want me to do to you right now?" She kissed his chest, then nipped his stomach and looked up, eyes smoldering. "Talk me through it, just how you like it—so next time I'll know."

She rubbed her cheek against his lower belly, dragging it up his torso, and slowly pulled one of his nipples into her mouth then bit down gently, grazing it with her teeth before she suckled it hard. "Like that? Right there . . . or lower?" His grip tightened on her shoulders. "Lower?" Her hand slid down his shaft and caressed him in a slow, pumping motion.

She nipped his belly, and darted her tongue into his navel, making him gasp, then looked up at him. "You don't want me to go home, do you?" Her voice was a throaty whisper, as he shook his head no. "Want me to stay to kiss it and make it better?"

He nodded yes, unable to speak for a moment, as her mouth became a wet, hot pulsing sheath around him. His breathing instantly synched up to her rhythm—that's when he knew he was done. She won. Against his better judgment his hand touched her hair and against his capacity to stop himself, his eyes slid shut. Damn she was a quick study. "You ain't fighting fair, D."

"Want me to go upstairs to get you a refill from the fridge?" she asked in a seductive voice, now on her knees on the bed, leaning against his stomach, her breath hot against it. "The night is young, and I figured we could maybe try plenty of stuff together . . . for the first time?"

Why was she taking him there? But he wasn't about to argue. Baby needed to stop talking and go back to what she'd been doing. "Okay . . ." His voice was on autopilot. The ceding of power was one word that came out fast on a hoarse breath. Fuck control. What was that around her, anyway?

"All right. Don't move; I'll be right back." She gathered up the rough cotton sheets and swathed herself in them with a giggle.

The bolt on the door slid back. Instant reflex. Yeah, don't go home. Not yet. The night was young. He sat very still, not moving like she'd told him to, just breathing with his eyes closed, willing her to hurry back, *por favor*. Oh, shit, they were gonna smoke him for sure, if she didn't first.

"How many bags you want?"

"Bring down a case—I don't want to accidentally kill you."

"Uh, Father Patrick," Padre Lopez said, folding his arms against the chilly night air. "It's almost dawn, and uh, do you think we should check on our Neteru? See how the talks are going? She's been in there a long time."

The old seer shook his head. Asula and Lin joined him with a yawn.

"We can only hope that an agreement can be reached by dawn," Monk Lin said.

"I am going to have much to explain to guardian Marlene." Father Patrick sighed.

"I just heard the refrigerator open and close. That must be a good sign," Asula said gently. "He's still taking cold packs."

"She must be all right," Padre Lopez insisted. "If he attacked her, then we would have heard her cry out, *si?*"

"That's just it," the eldest cleric grumbled. "It was too quiet . . . means the lair was soundproofed." He held up his hand when Padre Lopez would have spoken. "Which means the talks are going well."

The young man let his breath out in reluctant relief and sat back down. "Then all is well?"

"Uhmmm-hmmm. And Marlene Stone is gonna kill me."

CHAPTER NINE

❦ "BABY, PLEASE . . . *no mas, por favor.*" Carlos dropped his head to his pillow, his lungs battling for air in the sex-sweetened, post-dawn atmosphere. "What time is it?" He groaned. "I have to get some sleep."

Damali laughed and glanced around the barren room that was still sealed shut. There were no windows, clocks, or anything that would give her a sense of time, and there were no mirrors so she could see how disheveled she knew she had to be.

"I dunno," she shrugged, "but okay." Pouting, she stood up to look for her dress and panties. "I promise to be careful when I open the door. I'll just crack it and slip out."

"Uh, huh," Carlos said, still breathing hard, his eyes closed, losing consciousness fast.

"But you have to throw the bolt—you did that with kinetic energy, and I don't think I can move it. Last night you had it sealed so tight SWAT couldn't get in here."

"It's open," he wheezed. "The sound barrier . . . the lock . . . anything I materialized reversed well before the sun came up, woman. Please, I'm begging you. Just a few hours of sleep."

She laughed and covered her mouth for a second. "No, tell me the sound barrier stayed intact."

"I tried . . ." He couldn't even muster the balance of his response.

"The monks! Are you crazy?"

A low, lazy chuckle rumbled up from Carlos's chest. "Yeah . . . I know."

"Father Patrick, it's almost noon!" Padre Lopez walked in a circle, wringing his hands. "I have heard of the Neteru's legendary stamina, but she's been battling a master vampire *all night,* and even into the day. He should have lost strength, should have been vanquished by now. He must have had the advantage, if she wasn't able to escape his lair. It sounded like they were killing each other—now I don't hear either of them! This was a very bad idea, we have much to explain to her guardian team!"

"I know." Father Patrick sighed, glancing at the other seasoned spiritual warriors who had manned a post outside all night. "But calm yourself, Padre Lopez."

"Calm myself?" The youngest cleric was incredulous. "But . . . but . . . he was murdering her! Torturing her! I don't even hear her cries to the Almighty anymore!"

"Yes," Father Patrick said in a weary tone, standing with effort, using his sword to assist him, "and she killed him, too. The storm has passed."

The young cleric's panic-stricken gaze bounced from one snoozing elder to another. "But we have to reclaim her body. We cannot let the Neteru's body be desecrated!"

"Too late," Monk Lin said on a yawn. "Think I should check the blood supply?"

"That would be advisable," Asula replied, stretching. "Better make an emergency run. He's probably near extinction."

Father Patrick nodded.

"You would again revive the beast that—"

The appearance of Damali halted Padre Lopez's argument. The four men watched her slowly open the cabin door, adjust the strap of her dress on her shoulder, smooth the front of it, and rake her fingers through her locks. She squinted hard at the sun, and glanced away with a sheepish smile.

"Uh . . . gentlemen . . . can I get a lift home?"

"Neteru! Oh, thank God!" Padre Lopez rushed to her, grabbed her by the arms and held her back, inspecting her throat. "She's been wounded!" He looked at his brethren for support, and they only lowered their eyes and smiled.

"Yeah," Damali murmured, weaving a bit. She covered the wound on her neck with her hand. "You guys have any more blood in the fridge?"

"She needs a transfusion. We should get her to a hospital!"

Damali chuckled, and pecked Padre Lopez on the cheek. "Naw, I'm good, but Carlos could use a case or two."

The Neteru, bitten? Willingly? Interesting. The darkness of her lair gave the darkness in her mind room to breathe and expand. The huntress was on the move, out in the open, yet she could smell the stench of clerics all around her . . . just as she could detect the unmistakable scent of sex on her. Very, very intriguing.

A sudden smile graced her mouth. *No wonder the master didn't answer my call.* She cocked her head to the side. How had he gotten beyond what were obvious prayer barriers, laid down by seasoned warriors, to corner such worthy prey? The thrill of that conquest might have been more of a seduction than any vampire could have resisted, but it still annoyed her that the young Neteru had such pull.

Yet, in a very odd way, it increased the level of anticipation within her. If Master Rivera could accomplish such a wanton feat, then he was indeed worthy of all she had to bargain with.

Again, she surveyed the wounded Neteru. The huntress's throat had been ravaged, her own self-protection in shreds . . . and her telepathy was down, no barrier to a scan in effect, and her focus was still singular—Carlos. She laughed out loud and dropped her scan of the Neteru to preserve her energy for the coming night.

They had been wrong. This man was obviously so much more than a mere vehicle to amass limitless territory; he was a consummate professional. This morning he'd gained her respect.

She raked her fingers through her hair and shook her head at the dilemma. She might have to find a way to keep him without killing him—at least for a little while.

"It's past noon, Marlene!" Shabazz shouted. He paced back and forth within the weapons room, intermittently pounding his fist on the table. "The man is a *master* vampire, and nature is nature, Mar! Fuck all this philosophical rhetoric about him not killing Damali! You hear me! Bottom line, he's still a vampire! He'll flat line her."

"That's right, Mar. I told you we should have done the sonofabitch when we had him in the compound," Rider added, going over to stand by Shabazz.

"Yeah, Mar," Big Mike argued. "Noon? We need to be real. She's toast. Our baby went outta here without her blade . . ." Tears stood in Big Mike's eyes. "He done killed our baby girl . . . and I'ma kill him up good for this!"

"Aw . . . man . . . I never thought he'd do her," Dan murmured. "I never thought—"

"*Never do her?* You saw the way he looked at her!" Jose was on his feet, walking a hot path of rage between the doorway and the equipment table. "But you guys had me convinced that he was on our side, was the only one who could really protect her with that block-the-shot bullshit y'all came up with!" He spun on the group and pointed hard at the elder guardians. "I must have been out of my mind going along with allowing a master vampire to guard her against another master vampire. Are we crazy?"

"That's right," JL said. "We all saw the way he looked at her. Were we nuts, or what?"

"Marlene, if he was a third or fourth generation, I wouldn't be as worried . . ." Rider's words trailed off as he gazed out the window. "Love will make you do some crazy shit, and I think this time we messed up, getting all sentimental, hoping against hope. Aw . . . shit, Mar, tell me you've got something to shock her system and purge it, if we find her body . . . that is, if she's still breathing."

"Are you gentlemen finished?" Marlene said, yawning.

"Finished? Finished!" Rider spat. "We haven't even gotten started, Mar." He grabbed a round of artillery, as did the others. "We hunt this motherfucker down and stake his ass in broad daylight, if she's not breathing."

"Word," Shabazz said, picking up a handful of holy water grenades along with his Glock nine. "Might even have four dead monks out there in the woods. Last night, Father Pat said the shit was cool out there. In fact, I was cool until ten o'clock this morning. If Marlene hadn't been arguing about not being hasty, I would have been out. Now we ain't heard from nobody in hours. What's that shit about? Huh, Mar? How do we know that Rivera didn't answer the phone last night and throw the clerics' voices, or something? What if they were probably dead on arrival last night—fuckin' DOA when we called! But, no, I couldn't tell you jack—you said, 'Oh, Shabazz, have faith.' You crazy? I'm a man. I know what I'm talking about!"

"I just want her body back," Big Mike said, trying to keep his emotions in check. "Gotta drive a stake in her heart and bury her ashes on hallowed ground . . . that's the least we can do."

"Yeah . . ." Jose agreed, wiping his eyes. "We never leave our own."

"Uhmmph, uhmmph, uhmmmph," Marlene said in a blasé tone, glancing at the monitors before the reading even came up. "You got incoming, JL. Man your station. Five warm bodies approaching."

Ignoring protocols, the team rushed the compound doors, weapons in hand, leveling artillery and fanning out in battle stances.

Ohhh . . . boy . . . she was in trouble. Damali glanced at the clerics when their Jeep came to a stop in her compound driveway. "Uh, look . . . uhmmm . . . it's gonna be a little tense with my family when I go in there, so, how about if you guys go back, make sure Carlos is all right, and uh, I'll get back to you later?"

Father Patrick glanced out of the window and nodded. "You will give Marlene my best?"

Damali smiled. She could dig it. If she could send word by third party herself, she would have opted for that, too. "Yup. Will do," she said, opening the door slowly to avoid any sudden motion that would start bullets flying. "Thanks for the lift . . . and uh, the evening."

Without looking back, she watched her team visibly relax as the Jeep made a SWAT turn in the driveway and took off. Carefully strolling toward them, she opened both arms and turned around in a full circle, allowing the sun to speak for her. "Can I come in and get some breakfast and a shower?" she asked, trying not to laugh.

Only when Big Mike lowered his shoulder cannon, did she approach. Marlene was standing in the door shaking her head. Shabazz took his time, but ultimately put Sleeping Beauty back in its holster. Rider spat on the ground, and lowered his crossbow, while JL, Jose, and Dan mopped their brows and went inside.

Have mercy . . . it didn't have to be all of this. But she knew she had to face the music in order to stop a lynching. Taking the lead, she walked past her team and went into the living room. Right now, the last place she wanted to go was into the weapons room. God how she hated this.

"Okay, y'all," she said, yawning, feeling every deliciously placed bruise on her body. "I'm fine, sorry that I worried you, and I—"

"Sorry you worried us?" Shabazz looked like he wanted to slap her.

"Try stopping our hearts," Big Mike muttered, giving her a glare of disapproval.

"So'd you kill the bastard, or what?" Rider asked. "Tell me you killed him, so we don't have to." He rubbed his hands over his face and punched the wall. "Look at her throat." He leveled his gaze at her, then sent the hot glare to Shabazz and Big Mike. "A master did that? Let her come home raggedy and torn up like she'd been in an alley attack! Is it me, or am I insane? No respect, whatsoever, to send the girl home like that!" His line of vision returned to Damali with fury. "Tell me you killed him—broke a wooden table leg off and gored that sonofabitch!"

She couldn't help it, but a lopsided grin found its way to her face. "Yeah . . . I think I killed him. Several times."

She watched their shoulders slump, bodies dropped in sudden relief onto chairs and the large sectional sofa. JL laughed with a nervous burst, while the muscle in Jose's jaw pulsed. Tears streamed down Dan's face as he shut his eyes and silently wept for his friend, not comprehending. Marlene leaned against the wall with one eyebrow raised.

"You could've called," Marlene said casually. "Not that we're in your business, and we know you're grown, but even at my age, if I'm going to be out all night, I do leave the team a message so nobody freaks."

"Yeah, you're right, Mar . . . but, uh . . ."

"Yeah, I know," Marlene said calmly walking toward her.

"Okay, Mar, I know we were all worried, but, 'You could've called'?" Rider glanced at the other guardians who also shared his confusion.

Marlene swallowed away a smile and took Damali's chin, moving her head to the side. "Quite a bite you got there . . . couple of 'em, in fact. Gonna need a scarf and some makeup—"

"A bite? A bite! And all you got for the girl is a scarf and some makeup? You lost your mind, Marlene? When I got bit—oh, shit . . . you lose your magic, Mom? Not now!" Big Mike was hysterical, and rushed over to Damali before she could push him away. He'd swept her up in his arms like a baby and was pacing toward the hallway. "Get an ambulance—a holy water douse! Lord, Jesus . . . a bite and

Mar's magic is shot! That's why she didn't call, she's dying and we ain't got no antidote!"

Struggling and laughing, Damali wrested herself from Big Mike's arms, kissed his cheek quickly, and hopped down.

"Guys . . . I am really, really tired. I need a couple hours and a shower. Mar, we got anything in the fridge? I'm starved."

She watched with amusement as her team backed up. Marlene chuckled and shook her head.

"I can rustle up some breakfast. You look about a few pints low."

"Yeah. Oh, Marlene, try a half gallon."

"She's gonna turn, ain't she?" A sob caught in Big Mike's throat.

Shabazz looked away. Rider inhaled sharply and faced the window to hide his emotions. Dan hung his head and Jose slung an arm over his shoulder like he was holding them both up. JL covered his face with his hands and breathed in deeply.

Marlene winked at Damali. "Go get a shower, and let me break it to the fellas gently, hon. I know you're a vegetarian . . . but this morning, you need some steak and eggs."

It felt like the worst hangover he'd ever experienced. Carlos sat up slowly, feeling as if he'd taken several body blows, then smiled. Oh, yeah . . .

He ran his palm over his jaw, noting the prickly stubble. He didn't even have the energy to shave. With effort he stood, groaning from the exertion, found his pants, and tried to sense time . . . Eleven o'clock at night? *Man.*

His legs felt like jelly, even the muscles in his ass were sore, but hunger pulled him through the lair door, up the steps, holding onto the wall for support. Four pairs of worried eyes greeted him as he entered the main section of the cabin safe house on the way to the refrigerator.

"Yo, *que pasa?*" he muttered on a yawn.

For a moment, none of the clerics replied. Whatever.

"Are you all right?" Father Patrick asked.

"Just need a few pints. I'll be cool." Carlos stumbled toward the refrigerator, and grabbed two bags, slit them, and downed the cold liquid they contained and grimaced. Cold. Shit. He hated leftovers. He let out his breath and took out two more. The blood was slow to hit his system, and definitely didn't have the same kick as hers. He glanced up at the nervous clerics and shrugged off the temptation they presented. "I'm cool, y'all," he murmured when their faces blanched.

Father Patrick stood and approached him with caution. "We need to have a conversation . . . about the, uh, events of last night."

Carlos closed his eyes and leaned against the counter. He was in no mood for this bull right now. His body hurt, he was still tired. Needed a shot of adrenaline . . . needed a shot of Damali. He let his breath out slowly. "Talk to me."

"There are a number of issues," Father Patrick said, his tone firm as he tried to find a delicate way to begin. He glanced at his team who remained mute. "We were all concerned."

"I didn't hurt her," Carlos grumbled, too embarrassed for words.

"True, but, uh . . ."

"Look, I need to get out of here for a couple of hours."

Father Patrick glanced at his team for support. "That's not a good idea."

"Why not?" They were pissing him off, and he could feel Damali waking up. Her pull was distracting. The monks needed to talk fast.

"You're in a compromised state."

Carlos stared at the cleric, then chuckled. "You're telling me."

"No, I'm serious, Carlos. You need to regenerate more, first."

"Pulleease, spare me."

"That's what I'm trying to do."

Carlos shook his head. These old boys had no idea. If he had to die like this, then so be it.

"You have to stay away from her . . . uh . . . No more *talks,* that is."

His gaze narrowed on the old seer. "Then you might as well drive a stake through my heart right now. What do mean, stay away from her?"

Carlos brushed past them, heading for the door.

"Right now, try to use your energy to change what you're wearing," Father Patrick said quickly.

Carlos turned and studied the man. Impatient, he let the thought enter his mind and fuse with kinetic energy. But nothing happened. Panic coursed through him. Satisfaction registered in Father Patrick's eyes.

"Sit down," he told Carlos. "And grab a few more pints while you're at it."

Damali stood before the refrigerator weighing her options. She felt more alive than she'd ever felt in her life. But she was still hungry as hell. Dang, they never kept the fridge stocked right. The guys always ate everything that wasn't nailed down. Sensing the entire team gathering behind her in the kitchen, she let her breath out hard, slammed the door, and turned to face them.

"Aw'ight. What now?" she asked, folding her arms over her chest.

"You can't go over there tonight," Marlene said with a sigh. She turned to the rest of the team when Damali bristled. "Gentlemen, would you give us some space? This is a woman-to-woman thing."

Begrudgingly, the male members of the team filed out of the kitchen, and Damali bided her time until they were gone before she launched into an argument with Marlene. What did she mean, "You can't go out?" She was grown, last time she checked!

"Mar—"

"Listen," Marlene urged, cutting her off. "Just hear me out, then you can do what you want."

"Fine," Damali muttered, too through for words. Carlos's call was pulling her, making it hard to tolerate the delay.

"Father Patrick called . . ."

Damali closed her eyes and groaned. Oh, shit . . . Yeah, the old dudes had a right to have their feathers ruffled, if they heard half of what had gone on. Humiliation singed her—but she was going out. Had to.

"He said that Carlos isn't himself—"

"What's wrong? Is he hurt? The daylight? Oh, God . . ." Damali put her hand over her chest.

"No," Marlene smiled. "Daylight didn't get into the lair, but his ass is burned out. Fried."

She released her breath and closed her eyes in relief.

"I don't even want to venture a guess what you did to that poor man," Marlene said with a wry grin, "but uh . . . it was his first time out, you understand?"

Damali just looked at Marlene for a moment, and then burst out laughing.

"No, this is serious, D," Marlene said, trying not to laugh. "He's in a seriously weakened condition, which is dangerous for a master vampire."

Now Marlene had her attention.

"That's right, girl," Marlene pressed on. "If he goes out with you before he fully regenerates—which you didn't allow because the Covenant said you had that man hollering past daybreak, okaaaay— any weaker vampires in the territory will pick up the scent of a compromised master and try to rush him for his turf. Not good, since, ironically, he's on our side."

"Oh, shit."

"Now, you get the picture." Marlene folded her arms over her chest, a look of triumph blazing in her knowing eyes. "You have to be responsible, Damali. You've opened that brother's nose so wide he can't see. Father Patrick said the man couldn't even muster projection, or change his damned clothes."

The two women stared at each other for a moment, then suddenly burst out laughing.

"Damn, girl," Marlene sucked her teeth and shook her head. "In a priests' compound?"

Damali had to cover her face and laugh harder.

"He took his virgin bite from a virgin Neteru, *pure Neteru*—nearly an overdose, from the looks of things, and your blood is full of antibodies that are designed to kill off the vampire virus. That part ain't funny. Endorphins rushing through both your systems are probably the only things that kept him standing. Neteru hits their brains like dopamine, blocks out all pain until they start coming down. He's probably not feeling too good at the moment, now that he can feel the virus you gave him in his system."

The words slammed into Damali's brain, instantly cutting the mirth, making her hands fall away from her face as she stared at a very serious Marlene without blinking.

"They tried to revive him with an *entire case* from the monks' donations, and when he still couldn't get himself together to bear fangs, me and the fellas had to each give a pint."

"Oh, shit."

"Yeah, girl," Marlene said on a heavy rush of breath, shaking her head, chuckling. "Brotherman was strung out. But our team had enough adrenaline still running through their veins to shock his system back to normal. For him, normal human blood with adrenaline or terror running through it is like methadone. You are pure crack. You understand?" Marlene shook her head. "Problem is, y'all are both strung out. It'll take a full day and night for your system to purge the vamp trace in it. Until then, you're gonna feel it."

"Oh, my God, Mar."

"Yeah, sweetie, that's how it goes. Your temper, your passion, your appetite, your draw to the night is gonna make you bounce off the walls. Right now, we've got four innocent clerics over there trying to contain a master vamp who's jonesing for you so bad he's howling—and looking at them with a very hungry stare. The blood packs just aren't doing it for him anymore. Not after you. The fellas are concerned."

Damali nodded. "You don't think Carlos would . . ."

"That's the variable," Marlene said flatly. "We don't know how much he ingested, truth be told. That's why you and I are standing in this kitchen. How bad was it, D? Not to get in your business, but we need to know."

Damali turned and faced the sink and closed her eyes. She had no idea . . . "It was bad, Mar," she finally admitted, unable to look at Marlene.

"How many bites?"

"Six . . . maybe seven, and then I lost count."

"Oh, my God . . . past daylight?"

"Yeah, I blacked out a couple of times after that. That last time was just before noon."

"Noon! Noon? You kept a master vampire awake feeding and . . . and . . . *past noon?* Oh, Lord have mercy!"

Marlene's silence made her turn around. Her stricken expression drew Damali's hand to her own throat. It was healed, but she then looked at her wrists, and the insides of her elbows, and closed her eyes, not even wanting to think about the bites that had landed on her inner thighs. But damn . . . it was *so* good.

"Don't even think it," Marlene said quietly, chuckling despite herself. "Oh, girl." She covered her mouth and then laughed. "Pretty soon we're going to have to get you sunglasses and a transfusion."

Damali wrapped her arms around herself trying to stave off the tremor the memory produced.

"Look at you," Marlene added, shaking her head. "Your eyes are flickering gold . . . pretty soon, you won't have a reflection."

Pure alarm raced through Damali and she ran to the refrigerator and stared at herself in the shiny stainless steel surface of it. "Oh, Mar . . . shit. My eyes!" She whirled on Marlene who was now chuckling with her hand over her mouth. "I won't turn, will I?"

"No, but you wore his ass out," Marlene said, wiping tears of laughter from her eyes. "Damali, listen, okay? He can't get you pregnant, so you're cool. He can't pass any human disease—if he had any—because everything that could have killed him died when he became a vamp. In that regard, you're safe. His vamp virus only has a temporary effect. But *you* can hurt *him,* so you have to cool it. Plus, he now has a full tank of Neteru in his system. It'll draw other male vampires to him like flies, looking for you, then they'll fight him. But, he doesn't have the strength, tonight, to ward them off. Dig?"

Marlene walked over to her and placed a hand on her shoulder. "You've gotta let him recover, and let the team's blood thin out and dilute what he's ingested. By tomorrow evening, he'll be fine. He just needs to chill."

She nodded, and let Marlene put her arms around her. Marlene stroked her hair and kissed her temple.

"This is going to be a rough night, baby," Marlene warned. "Hold onto your seat and get ready for the ride."

"What am I gonna do?"

"I don't know, baby. The choice is yours," Marlene chuckled. "But tonight, you're gonna walk a mile in that man's shoes."

Four armed clerics barred the door, and his gaze shot around the room for a way out. Turning over a table and a sofa, Carlos snarled, "I have to go to her!"

Father Patrick remained calm. "If you don't have the energy to take us, or to project yourself past simple steel and wood, you're staying until tomorrow night. Then there's the not so small matter of our prayer line, Carlos." He sighed. "Why don't you watch some television?"

Asula cringed as the television lifted and smashed against the cabin wall, then he let out a weary breath. "I was going to watch the foot-ball game, Carlos. This is ridiculous."

Even Padre Lopez sat down as Carlos paced. Monk Lin fished in his robes and pulled out a deck of cards.

"Poker, anyone?"

She couldn't sit still. The room was closing in on her as the team worked on weapons, talked about general goings on, idly chatted about everything and nothing. They were getting on her nerves. In fact, she had no nerves left. She stood before the large picture win-dow, willing her mind to see beyond the steel grate. The moon was si-phoning her, calling her. Carlos.

The image of him immediately sent a shudder through her. Five-o'clock stubble covered his jaw, darkening it. The tips of her fingers tingled, remembering what it felt like first thing in the morning. She saw him stop pacing in the monk's cabin, close his eyes, and run his hand over his cheek. *Yeah, baby, I miss you, too.* It was agony.

She saw him go to the window and place his hand on it, splaying his fingers, then drop his head in defeat. It drew her to the window, and she rested her palm on it slowly, splaying her fingers to match his distant handprint. Sudden warmth filled her, and she felt his knees buckle. Phantom thrusts entered her, sending a tremor to wash through her. She stifled a gasp. Torture. She could hear the silent plea from four miles away echo into the night. Wolves howled outside—not all of them wolves . . . some third-generation vamps. Fuck it. She was out.

"Look, fellas," she said, turning from the window abruptly. "I'm just gonna—"

Marlene shook her head. Rider stood up. Shabazz stopped cleaning his gun, and the muscles in his jaw tensed. Big Mike folded his arms over his chest. JL let his breath out hard as Jose and Dan passed a ner-vous glance between them. Humiliation claimed Damali. Damn, she was a junkie.

She stared at her team, but another image in her head eclipsed her physical sight. An erotic touch ran down her arms, and a deep, sensual kiss covered the side of her neck. She struggled for composure as the sensation created goose bumps on her arms. Her nipples stung with need and she felt herself get wet.

"Is it me, or am I the one who is crazy?" Rider said flippantly. "Give girlfriend a mirror."

"Uh, D," Big Mike said slowly, "baby, your eyes are going gold again."

"Two minutes from now she'll be bearing fangs, if she doesn't sit her ass down and chill," Shabazz fussed.

Rider folded his arms. "You're creepin' us out, Damali. You gotta let this shit wear off. Play some music; watch some TV. Damn I need a drink!"

"You still got that bottle of Jack Daniel's?" JL said, standing and heading toward the kitchen to look for it.

"Bring a coupla glasses," Dan shouted behind him.

"Hell, why stand on ceremony?" Jose added. "Get the cards out and just pass the bottle around. It's gonna be a long night."

There were no words. Never before had she felt so exposed, and so thoroughly out of control. Her business was all in the street; the team was all up in it. Her man was locked up. And her body was talking to her. How in the *hell* was she supposed to fight this?

"Mar, can I talk to you alone, for a minute?" Damali searched Marlene's face and found a patient but weary expression in it.

"Yeah, hon. In your room."

Relief swept through Damali as she picked up her sword and paced quickly down the hall, listening to Marlene's slow footfalls behind her. As soon as Marlene shut the door, she cast the Isis blade on the bed and began walking in a tight circle, talking fast.

"Mar, I'm losing my mind. What part of this is normal?" She was now breathing hard, trying to collect herself, beyond shame.

"About seventy-five percent of it," Marlene said with a smile, taking a seat on the bed as she studied Damali.

"Okay, okay, okay." Damali continued pacing. "That's a good thing, right?"

"Yeah," Marlene chuckled. "I remember those days . . . the pull was just as strong as a vampire's bite. Uhmmph, uhmmph, uhmmph."

"Well, how do you shake it, get it out of your system?" Damali fought off another shudder and briefly closed her eyes, drew a deep breath, and looked at Marlene for an answer.

"Turned you out, didn't he? Uhmmph." Marlene shook her head.

"It's not funny, Mar. Stop laughing. Don't you have an antidote for this shit?"

"Nope."

"For real? Aw, man . . ."

"Nope."

"It hasn't been twenty-four hours!"

"Nope. And it's gonna get worse before it gets better," Marlene said, swallowing away another chuckle. "That part didn't have jack to do with him being a vampire."

"Oh, man . . ."

"Yup."

"But, Mar . . . if I just go out one more—"

"Nope."

"But—"

"Deal with it, honey."

Damali grabbed the sides of her skull. "He's in my head, Mar. My full vision is back, and . . . oh, man . . . listen . . . Mar . . . for real, for real . . . I gotta go out."

"You wanna kill him?"

"No," Damali said on a pitiful wail. "No. I do not want him to be hurt."

"Then stay put."

"But—"

"Remember how he kept trying to tell you?" Marlene's question made Damali open her eyes and look at her. "Remember the night he came in here to deliver the information about the tunnels to the team?"

Damali nodded but didn't speak.

"Remember at the concert when you were walking around him and he kept telling you to be still, stop stirring the very air around him?"

"Yeah," Damali finally said on a quiet breath.

"Remember the look on his face when he had to carry you . . . and the sound of his voice when he let you go in that last battle in order to save your life?"

Remember? Was Marlene crazy? It was a tattoo in the middle of her brain. "Yeah," Damali whispered.

"Well, then now you know how hard it was for him to do that."

Damali nodded. Tears of frustration filled her eyes.

"It was just as hard for him to back off when he wanted you like this, even before he was turned. The brother loves you. Always has. He had the will power not to try to bring you into his life at a time when you were vulnerable . . . at a time when he knew you couldn't hang, and his life would have been dangerous for you—gotta respect that much about him."

"I do," Damali said quietly, sitting down hard on a bedroom chair. She leaned over, placing her elbows on her knees and stared at the floor. "Always did."

"Can you image how difficult it must have been for him to know how much you wanted him, how willing you were to be with him, all new to the game, filled with passion just ready to explode for him— and he had to push you away for your own good?"

Damali closed her eyes. Marlene's words shredded her conscience.

"Tonight, you gotta do that for him."

"Oh, Mar. I thought I knew, but damn . . . Now I really know."

"Pure agony."

"In a word, yes."

"It'll pass."

"I hope so."

"It will."

"It has to."

"It will."

"Oh, Mar."

"I know."

"Get some rest."

"Yeah, right!"

The two women sat in companionable silence for a moment, then suddenly Damali jerked her head up. Her heart was beating fast, and she was on her feet. "Got a cold-body reading on monitor one."

JL burst through the bedroom door, the full team behind him. "Got a cold-body reading on monitor one!"

"So we gathered," Marlene stated in a blasé tone.

"What do we do, Mar?" JL said nervously.

"Hit the lights . . . and let Carlos in."

"Are the monks okay?" Damali ignored the disgruntled team that flopped onto stools and chairs behind her. She couldn't keep her eyes off him. However, she was glad that the guardians had lowered their weapons.

"Yeah," Carlos said slowly. "But they have to repair the south wall before morning." He smiled, appraising her from head to toe.

"Awww, maaaan." Rider just shook his head.

"About that Jack Daniel's," Shabazz said in a disgusted tone, standing and leaving the room.

"Wanna go out?" Carlos murmured, moving one of Damali's stray locks over her shoulder with his finger.

"Maybe just for a little while," she whispered.

"Card game, anybody?" Marlene said, leaving the room with the team slowly filing out behind her.

"Wanna go to a club?"

Damali shook her head. The sight of Carlos was practically paralyzing as he ran his hand up and down her arm.

"If you're hungry, I can take you to dinner, or a movie, maybe we could just take a walk on the beach . . . or whatever you want to do, just name it," he murmured, stepping in closer to her.

His scent filled her as she inhaled him deeply. "It's too dangerous for you right now outside. You shouldn't have risked coming out. They explained everything to you, right?"

He nodded, tracing her collarbone and slipping the edge of her T-shirt off her shoulder with his finger. "I love you in red," he said, his eyes burning her, igniting an internal fire. "Noticed you've been wearing that color a lot lately."

She swallowed hard. "Baby . . . uh, listen. You've gotta go back home."

"So early?"

"Yeah, like right now, okay," she stammered, closing her eyes as his nose trailed across her shoulder, past her neck, and his lips captured her earlobe.

"I missed you . . ."

"I missed you, too," she breathed. "But not here. Not in this compound with my whole family here. Some things are just not done."

He chuckled low in his throat. "You're right."

"I know I'm right," she whispered, melting against him as his arms enfolded her.

"Then you wanna get your blade and go somewhere?"

"Aw, Carlos . . ."

"Please."

"Well . . . maybe. Just for a little while."

CHAPTER TEN

DAMALI PUSHED open the compound door, then locked it, and staggered down the hall. She couldn't even hold her blade steady, and she dragged Madame Isis behind her, scraping the tip of it along the concrete floor. She swayed in the doorway as her team yawned and looked up, and then dropped to her knees. Marlene held up her hand to stop the guardians—who had summarily abandoned their card game—to keep them from rushing toward her.

On her hands and knees from fatigue, Damali pushed herself up and slowly stood, picking up the heavy sword, weaving where she finally righted herself. "I woulda called," she said in a weary tone. "But—"

"We know, we know," Rider snapped. "Something *literally* came up."

JL hadn't even checked the monitors when she'd approached.

"Don't look at me, fellas," Marlene said, studying her cards. "We ain't got a single weapon in the house for this—and no, I do not have a cure."

Damali yawned as the steel gates began to lift to let in the sunlight. Out of reflex, she raised her forearm to shield her face from the rose-colored glare.

"Damn. Reminds me of New Orleans," Big Mike chuckled, glancing at Damali, and then shaking his head, slapped down a card. "Relax, y'all. The girl is going out. You know you can't do nuthin' 'bout mojo. It's the most powerful shit in the world."

"Don't go there, Mike," Shabazz said, slapping down a card over his. "This shit ain't funny. The girl's probably a quart low."

"Relax," Marlene said with a weary sigh. "She's protected and grown. I ain't got nothin' to say."

Rider tossed Damali his pair of sunglasses from his vest pocket. Too uncoordinated to catch them, they hit the floor with a clatter.

"Pitiful," Rider said, looking at the now-chipped glasses. "Reflexes are all off . . . just outrageous. I paid seventy-five bucks for those."

"And, how's our boy?" Marlene said, unperturbed.

"He went home," Damali said through another yawn, and headed toward the kitchen. Damn . . . what a night.

"This is a full-scale crash and burn," Father Patrick said, shaking his head.

"You do know, Father, that the monastery has asked if we're harboring more than one illegal vampire. They are becoming concerned about the donations . . . after all, we cannot continue to feed him at this rate, if, well, if his present *activity level* continues." Monk Lin's nervous glance darted around the group that studied the body in the middle of the cabin floor.

"I know," Father Patrick admitted, glancing at his team, then down at the floor. He stooped where Carlos had fallen through the door to touch his shoulder, noting the fingernail marks that had scored his skin and where his T-shirt was ripped. "We'll figure it out later. Right now, just get him down into his lair."

"He'll be in no condition to deal with Brazil."

Father Patrick nodded at Padre Lopez's comment.

"Okay, that's it," Marlene said, her hands on her hips. "Enough! We've got work to do on this concert tour you've had Dan try to set up—and you haven't even been home or awake long enough to decide on which contracts you want him to sign, what venues you want to do first . . . chile, I swear! You're in no condition to travel anywhere to fight anything, and haven't worked on a single routine in over ten days."

Guilt swept through Damali, but she was still going out. Okay, so she'd taken ten days to block out the world and to claim a little happiness for herself, and yeah, she wasn't on point, wasn't on the job. But she was only human, and this thing with her and Carlos was new and white-hot.

However, Marlene's glare wasn't one of judgment, just defeat. It slowly made her think about all the things she'd promised herself after she left Inez's. Plus, there was something else in Marlene's eyes that she couldn't put her finger on.

Conflicting emotions battled within her. Marlene was right. True, the world needed a champion. But, *damn,* did it have to be tonight?

Marlene looked away and ran her fingers through her locks, then glanced up at the ceiling. *So help me Father, I wanna slap her.* She drew in a steadying breath and closed her eyes, then focused on the threat that Damali was still oblivious to. All right, she wouldn't slap the child's face with that information, and would give her a few more days of peace to get it together. No more innocents would be killed until the next full moon. Had to be demons, vamps had to feed nightly. But it was patently clear that, if Damali was so scattered, she had to pull her thing together on her own in order to be in mental condition to fight. "The fellas are worried, if we're going to a foreign country somewhere to do battle. Everybody's head has to be on straight."

"Yeah, but we've laid down all the new CD cuts, and wherever we finally sign for venues will be cool," Damali said quietly, hoping that Marlene wouldn't make her feel worst than she already did. What was Mar so worried about, anyway? She wouldn't turn, Carlos was fine . . . it was all good.

Damali tried to steady her hand as she put on her lip gloss in the bathroom mirror, mentally fending off Marlene's words. Just a few more nights, Lord . . . that's all she needed. Marlene just didn't understand. There was no such thing as the word "no" when it came to this Carlos-thing that gripped her.

"There's nothing I can say to get through to you, is there?" Marlene sighed. The poor chile was still so blind. Something was blocking her third eye—love. All she could see was Carlos, and was seriously off her job. But having been there, too, there was no judgment, just sheer frustration.

Damali set her lip gloss down and looked at Marlene.

"I'm crazy about him, Mar."

Marlene sighed again and leaned against the door frame. "I know. Heaven help me, but I know." Please, Heaven, let this child wake up.

"We haven't been attacked."

"Yet." Lord, don't make me have to go in there and have another argument with Shabazz.

"I know. We're being careful, though."

Marlene just stared at her for a moment. She'd have to take this mess to the pillow with Shabazz. The man was gonna be off the hook, if she went in there and told him another night had passed and Damali was still not tuned in to Brazil.

"You two have been lucky, that's all. And even thought your sight is *partially* back, it's totally focused on *one thing*. And that's not good. My poor overtaxed brain won't even go near you guys to monitor for safety. There are some things I just don't need to see. Do you know that even Father Patrick's second sight is blanking on him, because of the images you two left in a monastery safe house!"

"Oh, man, that wasn't supposed to happen, and we both apologized for that. It was that first night, things got carried away, but we never went back there again. Swear we didn't." And what did Marlene mean by her sight being partially back? She could see just fine. She always heard Carlos in her head loud and clear, that was for sure.

"Regardless. You're out in the streets till all hours, and neither of you has your guard up. You're both blind, and can't see beyond each other, or the stars in each other's eyes." Marlene stared at Damali hard. "Plus, one night, that brother is gonna scare the mess out of you." Marlene paused and sighed. "You're gonna find out how strong he really is, gonna see him come out of a bag that's going to freak . . . you . . . out." Marlene ran her fingers through her locks and closed her eyes. "Don't ask me how I know."

For a moment neither woman spoke. Marlene silently prayed for patience and a healthy dose of discernment. There was no competing with a new lover, especially as a mom. But if Damali didn't snap out of it, before the next full moon came near . . .

"He won't hurt me, Marlene. We've been through that."

"I don't doubt his heart. It's his nature that concerns me, sweetie." Marlene smiled sadly. "He is what he is, and he won't mean to, but one day, you're going to push a button, girl . . ." Marlene sighed hard again and looked at the floor. "You are *so* on the edge and don't even *know* it. But, we all have to see for ourselves. I did, too, so I ain't talking bad about you."

"No, seriously, Mar. Okay, I admit that a couple of third-generations tried to push up on him a few times, but you know, when both of us stood side-by-side and stared them down, it was cool. Most of the second-generations were wiped out on his order after the Nuit thing went down. It's cool. Really." Even to her own ears, her words sounded contrived, despite the truth in them. Besides, Marlene didn't know anything about something like this. Marlene's look of total disdain didn't help matters, so she pressed on. "He's been hunting at night to replenish—"

Marlene gasped.

"No, no, no, not like that. Deer. We found this cool little place in the woods that—"

"I don't want to hear any more," Marlene said quickly, holding up both hands.

"Oh, Mar, but he's *wonderful*." Damali sighed and leaned against the sink. She needed a good girlfriend right now so badly to share her experience with, and while Marlene was part girlfriend, she was also part mother. That mother part stood in the way of a total confession. And God knows Inez wouldn't understand. She allowed her gaze to go toward the steel-covered windows.

"We talk about *everything*," she said in a distant voice. "What it feels like to be the only one of your kind . . . growing up, knowing what it was like to be different. What made us each choose our different paths." She looked at Marlene in the eye. "He's changed so much, has seen so many things. All he needs is a second chance."

Marlene nodded. "I know, baby . . . you love him." She sighed with final defeat lacing her breath. "Be careful when you go out and have a good time, while it lasts."

Without another word of protest, Marlene turned, left the bathroom, and was gone.

"He's fully immersed in the Neteru, Mr. Chairman," the counselor said, pacing before the Vampire Council. "He's not rational! We have sent the edict to our families topside that there will be no attacks, but my concern is Rivera's ability to complete the Neteru-delivery mission when it is time. He is compromised, and he will not be able to part with her."

"Are you blind? Surely this is part of his strategy, Counselor Vlak, to totally seduce her, gain her trust, throw off her team's guard . . . He enters their compound at will, escorts her openly, even in front of the Covenant team that cannot contain him. He grows strong, not weak!" The chairman's fist landed on the table and came away with blood, momentarily stopping the argument. "We are watching vampire history in the making!"

The counselor spun on the chairman and folded his arms over his chest. "But he has not properly fed! He will be in no condition to address the Brazilian breach! Right now, given our heavy collateral damage from the civil war and the Amanthra incursion—fighting two major battles on two fronts simultaneously, Carlos Rivera is the strongest master vampire we've got topside, and he's . . . he's . . . The man has been decimated!"

For a moment, silence crackled in the room. Soon the murmur of dissent filtered among the seated council members. The chairman's eyes narrowed on the counselor.

"Could it be," the chairman offered in a lethal tone, his voice escalating with every word as he slowly stood, "that he is not feeding because he's been filled with Neteru?" The chairman knocked over his goblet and sent blood splashing to the floor. "Would you drink from mere human if you could have that as a nightly option?"

"He eats venison in the woods like a damned werewolf. A disgrace!"

Seething, the chairman reached out a bony hand, his claws extending as the fury swept the counselor close enough to him to snatch out his heart. Breathing heavily from the sudden burst of rage, he petted the terror-stricken counselor's chest. His voice became a sinister whisper. "In front of her to gain her trust. He cannot risk her believing an innocent died at his hands to inspire doubt in her. And he guards her every night from the moment the sun goes down, until dawn . . . when would he have time to bring down a kill?"

The chairman pushed the counselor away, and in relief, the counselor covered his heart with his hand.

"Rivera seduces her every night, at his own risk," the chairman said. "Her blood is a toxin to his system when not ripe—and he hasn't even flushed it with a human feed. He did this for *the empire*. A true blood sacrifice of merit."

Garnering calm, he walked behind the table, rounded it, and came to stand before the counselor, bearing fangs. He allowed his voice to dip to a threatening whisper followed by a hiss. "Now you find his soul, and you never speak ill of the master vampire who is so shrewd I wish he were my own son. Are we clear?"

"Wow," she said, laughing as she walked past the compound light barrier up the road to Carlos's car. "I thought you sold it years ago, and traded it in for the black Mercedes?"

"Yeah, well, what can I say? I sorta resurrected her from memory. I shoulda kept her and never got the sedan. I don't know what I was thinking."

He tried to seem casual, as though Damali's words didn't affect him. He watched her with sudden pride while she walked around the blood-red Chevy that used to be his heart. Although Damali had replaced his once-favorite girl on four wheels, he still had a warm spot for his old speed demon. Yeah . . . but the old girl couldn't hold a candle to his boo.

Damali was standing there all-fine, matching his car, in a red halter top that had rips in it like claw tears, her smooth belly exposed. Her long, gorgeous legs were sliding out from beneath a black leather mini, with her baby Isis dagger peeking out at the thigh as though her legs were flashing a hint of fang. Girlfriend was working a pair of strappy black stilettos to the bone that tied up her calf. He let his gaze travel up her legs. Damn, every time he saw her, she did something to him.

She had her hair swept up off her neck just like he liked it. Tonight she wore ruby teardrop earrings, had lost the silver and had gone to platinum settings just for him. Blood-red nails, toes, and have mercy, her mouth. She'd done something different with her eyes, too. They had a real smoky charcoal effect that made her look all-vamp.

It would have been nice to be able to pick Damali up at the door, but her guardians were just not having it. He smiled. Just like old times. Beep twice. Meet me. This was nuts.

"She's *beautiful*," Damali said, as she ran her hand gently down the door, but careful not to mess up the brilliant wax job. "Would'ja look at the rims on her . . . twenty-twos, wires, damn, Carlos. She's *all* that."

Damali looked at him with a wide, mischievous smile. He had to laugh.

"But how do you see over the engine to drive this thing? You got chrome coming out of the hood sittin' up higher than the driver, brother." She laughed and bent over to peer down, which gave him a nice view. "And the exhaust pipes look like they belong on Rider's Harley."

"You shouldn't make fun of a man's car, girl. It ain't right. And I don't need to see over the engine." He gave her a sexy smile and winked. "I drive her like—"

She held up her hand, laughing harder. "Do *not* say it."

He smiled broadly and shrugged. "I don't know what you're talking about. I wasn't gonna say, 'I drive her like I drive you.' D, all I was gonna say was, 'I sense the road—got skillz. Can drive her with my eyes closed.'"

"Uhmmm, hmmm. Yeah, aw'ight," she said, going around the vehicle one more time with a bright smile. "She is pretty. I love this car," she said, her hand trailing over the black leather seats as she walked around the convertible. "I'm not making fun of it." Then she laughed and shook her head. "Of course I like it. Always did."

She liked the car, but was also fucking with him. She knew the sound of her voice, and the way she allowed her fingers to trail over the chrome grille as she went by, the way she let her fingers hover over the custom, iridescent crimson paint job, was giving him a hard-on. But he was glad she liked the car. He should have thought of it earlier, would have been the perfect place to take her . . . he'd fantasized so much about it when he was a kid.

She glanced at him. "So, you wanna take her for a whirl?"

"Rhetorical question, right?" He smiled and opened the door, watching how she slid against the leather, the friction hiking up her skirt to expose more thigh and blade. Damn.

"Where are we going?"

That question made him get serious and focus. "Need to take you 'round the way for a bit. Then we can chill. Cool?"

"All right," she said, but her smile faded.

He could see the wheels in her mind turning as she gazed at the horizon. He revved the motor without needing to turn the ignition key. He put on "Choppa Style," loud, letting the bass throb through him so he didn't have to talk to her just yet. He bopped with the refrain in the music. Oh, yeah, *it was on now . . . and we ready.*

This was something that she would never understand. Before he went to Brazil solo, he had to get a few things straight, handle some business. A week ago, a couple of lower-level males had pushed up on him, in the fucking street, when he was with his woman, no less. The only reason they'd backed down is because he *and* Damali had stood united. *That* could never happen again. Motherfuckers betta recognize, and she shouldn't even need to grip her blade when she was with him. The fact that she did, still didn't sit right with him. He was her weapon—and if that wasn't clearly established, she wasn't going anywhere on tour. Period. He was just glad she hadn't siphoned that info from his brain . . . and he was too glad that she hadn't picked up anything in the news yet.

Yeah, he had to make a run, then deal with Brazil before girlfriend found out. The Covenant and Marlene had given their word that they'd let him handle whatever was over there alone. The fact that she hadn't gotten hip was evidence enough that she wasn't completely back . . . then again, he did have to admit he'd had a role in keeping her a little blind. He didn't feel guilty in the least about that bit of sleight of hand while her mind was wide open; he was not allowing his woman to go on some damned hunt. That was out. Her crazy hunting days were over. If something needed to be iced, that was his job. She just needed to stay safe.

Not to mention, it was bad enough that the council had put an off-limits marker on him, as though he needed their protection like some weak vamp human-helper. They'd even put a temporary one on Damali, like *he* couldn't protect her! Vlak probably loved that shit . . .

Carlos kept his gaze fastened to the road, allowing the Chevy's speed to kick up with his rage. "Get Low" came on, building his confidence as the music got louder, the bass got stronger, words said what he needed to hear, *All skit skit, mo'fucker, Aw skit skit got-damn.* The music became his pulse. Lil' Jon and the East Side Boyz' lyrics were his theme. The bastard who stole his club was his.

Over in Brazil, whatever he was tracking might not honor that council mark. Most likely it wouldn't. He needed to know that if something jumped off, he could handle it. This was personal and very primal. The kinda shit women didn't understand. Even lower levels over there were off da chain, just like in the human realms. You didn't fuck with the South American dealers without serious heat and a squad.

Yeah, he was coming into his own, as power from the throne continued to take hold of him, but it bothered him to no end that it had taken this long to build up some immunity to Damali's blood. If he was a lower level, and wasn't getting a nightly dose, who knows? But it was working in his system the way the antidote to snake bite did. Needed a little venom in the cure.

Each time he bit her, he could actually feel his system absorb all of her passion, then take a jolt from the light within her as it threaded through his system and battled with it in his veins, temporarily weakening him, almost burning his insides—only to make him stronger when he came out of the bite. She woulda scorched the insides of a second-generation brother, slow heat implosion. Damn, she was awesome. Everything about the way she'd been designed was a lethal weapon . . . her eyes, her scent, the feel of her skin, her voice —even her blood, and it was designed to lure a master and slay him. And the Covenant and the council said ease up. Let his system regulate. Were they nuts? How?

With power came certain privileges. The thought almost made him smile. He glimpsed her from the corner of his eye. Hopefully her system was building a tolerance, too, because he damned sure needed to bite her every night at this point.

Carlos let his breath out hard and tried to push the nagging concerns to the back of his mind. He pumped the volume till he couldn't even hear the traffic around him. "Damn," by Bonecrusher, worked.

Vibrations from the speakers nearly rocked the Chevy off the road. It didn't make sense that first night. He had been so blitzed that he couldn't even seal her wounds as he pulled out. Had sent the girl home all raggedy in the throat. He shook his head. That was some un-smooth, virgin vamp bullshit that still embarrassed him. Her people did not need to see that. He didn't blame them for the way they were acting. If it was his daughter . . . perish the thought. He changed the cut and blasted Nellie. *Who you came wit? Yeah . . . shake your tail feather.*

As a master vampire, as soon as the tip of the incisor was out, the punctures in her neck should have vanished. But messing with a Neteru, it took three freaking nights to master that nearly impossible level of concentration with her in his arms. Now he was about to go do something really crazy. But no leftover, second-generation wannabe from before Nuit took this region was gonna take his club! Oh, hell no. Bastard bought that shit from the DEA on auction, and had renamed it? Without asking him? No respect.

Protocol demanded that when a new master stepped up, everything got realigned, and if you wanted something you had to earn it and get it ceded. But this motherfucker, Nitro, just did a power grab? Carlos could feel the wind rushing by them, and Damali's body become tense. He needed to make a visit to New York, Miami, Jamaica, St. Lucia, Toronto, Peru, and Brazil. Hot spots. Had to get his main jaun, LA, on lock. Do a couple of shakedowns, then word would be out. Control would be reestablished.

"Baby, aren't you going a little fast?" Damali said, her tone strident and loud to compete with the bass thumping from the speakers.

Carlos looked down at the dashboard and read the speedometer: 110 mph. This was nothing. "I'm cool."

"Uh . . . baby? What's on your mind?"

He shrugged, bopping to the music while he kept his eyes straight ahead. "Nothing. Just wanna get a drink. See a few people. Then, we can go somewhere alone." He wasn't looking at her as he yelled over the music. He could feel her clutching her seat belt and the blood draining from her knuckles. "Where we're going," he said slowly as the Chevy sped up and bounced when it hit a seam in the road, "you gotta follow my lead to the letter."

She reached out and turned down the volume.

"Carlos, where are we going? For real."

He glanced at her, taking his eyes off the road to study her thighs. He smiled when she gripped the dashboard and almost shrieked. The mild terror the ride produced within her, plus the adrenaline, and his own rage, not to mention the way she looked and the way she smelled was making him crazy, not just a little irrational. The speed was exhilarating. The night was perfect. Maybe, later, he could convince her to sit on his lap while he did 220? He chuckled.

"All right. I'll slow down. Just wanna go see my old club. Brings back memories."

Damali glared at him. "Your old club was seized by the DEA, and I don't think it's a good idea for folks to know you're alive . . . I mean, you know, around."

Her concern for him warmed his heart, but she just didn't understand. "Yeah, true. But they sold it at auction. Heard a guy in my territory picked it up, and—"

"Is it a vamp club, Carlos?" She sat back in her seat as the wind whipped her face. She pushed a loose lock back up into her ponytail, then crossed her arms over her chest.

"Baby, don't act like this. It's about power. Absolute control of my zones so that no matter where you are, there won't be no shit. Feel me?" He looked at her hard, and then looked back at the road, dodging slower-moving vehicles. There was a motorcycle cop up ahead. Carlos blinded them to his eyes as they blew past him. "When you go on tour, when you're out in the street, I don't want no bullshit. If lower levels are trying me, I need to get this locked down, *now*."

The fact that she didn't answer him, grated him. On one hand, he was glad that she wasn't being her normally stubborn self. But if she didn't challenge his need to make a stand, then her gut instinct was registering something he didn't like. Her confidence in his ability to protect her was not as firm as it should be. That, also, could *never* happen again.

When he pulled up to the curb, he yanked a pair of black shades out of his leather suit breast pocket and put them on. He smoothed down his burnt-gold silk shirt, tucking it firmly into his pants, and steadied himself for the inevitable—drama when he walked in with the Neteru. He studied the change to his marquis. Club Vengeance was now Club Eternity . . . Yeah, we'll see, when I smoke that motherfucker who owns it.

Carlos, don't start nothing in here. Please. Damali noted the tension in his body as he put his arm around her waist, and pulled her in tight. This mess was prehistoric! She watched male vampires in line puff up a little as they took a step forward, then thought better of it, ran a testosterone sensory check over Carlos, backed up, nodded, then let him through, bypassing the long line outside.

Lower-level, third- and fourth-generation females snarled under their breaths at her, but gave Carlos seductive smiles that she did *not* appreciate. Cleavage was everywhere, some of it real, some of it plastic. Some of her stage outfits weren't as daring as what some of these women were wearing. Damali almost felt dowdy in comparison.

But an eerie defensiveness entered her as Carlos escorted her to the bar, his gaze roving over what was once his. She could feel his rage building the deeper they walked into the club. Every nuance, every change within his environment sent a jolt through him. His grip tightened on her waist as he glanced up at the VIP booth and what had once been his office.

She could feel it in her bones, like a summer rain coming. Her man was outnumbered, and all she had on her was the baby Isis, her short blade.

As soon as the thought crossed her mind, his head jerked around and he pinned her with a hard stare. His gaze was so intense that it nearly burned her. She could see red flickering behind his dark shades. The warning in his eyes was implicit—*Don't ever doubt me like that! Not here!* He pulled away from her and offered her a seat, running his tongue over his incisors and breathing slowly through his nose.

She touched his arm gently. He looked down at her hand and nodded. She let her breath out very slowly. Okay, she had to learn the nuances of vampire culture fast and on her feet. But, then again, it wasn't all that different from life as she knew it on the streets. Primal. Alpha males in full force. Any hint of weakness was quickly sniffed out, any sign of disrespect swiftly dealt with. She sighed. She'd rather be making love.

"Later," he muttered, his gaze slowly going around the club.

Damali opened her mouth and closed it. Okay, he was definitely getting stronger, because she hadn't even mind locked with him that time.

"Chivas, just a hint of color," he told the bartender, "top shelf. How old is it?"

"Two days," the bartender said, smiling, bringing him a bottle to inspect. "Got same day if you want it?"

Carlos stared at him. "I asked you for top shelf, didn't I?"

"My bad," the bartender said, holding up his hand, and removing the offending bottle. "For the lady?"

"Dom—no color," Carlos said, not even looking at her.

Damali's gaze shot between Carlos and the bartender. Carlos's gaze was constantly sweeping the terrain, but the bartender was totally focused on Carlos.

"No color? In here?" the bartender said after a moment, and then shook his head. "You a bold mo'fucker." He pulled down a short rocks glass and a black bottle from the top shelf, along with a bottle of Chivas Regal, and blended the blood and liquor before Carlos. He then got a clear champagne glass and poured Dom Perignon for Damali, hesitating as he gave it to her. "Remember, I'm just the bartender . . . I just work here, if anything jumps off."

Carlos swirled the drink around in his glass, threw the murky concoction into the back of his throat, swallowed fast, and then winced as he set down the empty glass hard. He handed the bartender a C-note. "You tell your boss that the old owner is here, and that he's a bold motherfucker, too."

Carlos stared at the paralyzed vampire. His dark brown eyes glittered with fear and what little color was in his thin face drained away. "Now would be a good time for you to hit that panic button by the register," Carlos said in a low, even tone. "You don't want to make me go up to my old office to get him."

She knew this was a bad idea . . . She should have listened to Marlene! Now she was in Hell's kitchen, surrounded by vamps, and a mortal combat was about to jump off. Oh my G—

Not in here!

"My bad," she whispered. She could see the vamps in the midsection of the dance floor area discreetly realign themselves. Females gravitated ever so subtly to certain males. Certain males grouped together, bulking slightly—not too much, but like they were on standby. Humans quickly exited, on the excuse of needing a smoke, whatever, but even human helpers knew that their markers were no protection when two dominant males squared off.

Carlos hadn't even moved. He was sipping a second drink, appearing casual with his back to the staircase that led to the owner's office. Part of her was indignant; she could understand how he felt. They'd changed the paint to a sick purple. Had switched out his once beautiful black marble and mahogany bar, and put some crazy Lucite in there. The music was all right, but the lights were giving her a headache. The place had been classy before. Now it was so . . . tacky, it didn't make sense. She looked at Carlos as his biceps flexed.

Damali could feel his rage building as he was forced to wait for the new owner to grace him with his presence.

Suddenly Carlos stood up, looked at her, and nodded. "You're right, baby. It is tacky."

She opened her eyes wide. "Don't do it," she whispered. "Not—"

Damali closed her eyes and shook her head, knowing it was already done. When she opened them again, the old décor was in place, Carlos was smiling, six inches of fang showing, his brows knitted as he studied his old establishment.

"Much better."

The twenty vamps in the room immediately went into battle stances, but parted as a tall, very angry second-level vampire stormed down the stairs from the offices. She watched, numb, as a lanky, built brother with locks came barreling down the stairs, eyes solid red.

"Out of order!" he said, pointing at Carlos.

"No, motherfucker—*you* are *way* out of order." Carlos hadn't raised his voice, but the crowd stepped back.

She watched Carlos stand, turn slowly, and take off his shades. He was eye-to-eye with the male who faced him. The brother backed up, his long locks swinging. The competitor brandished gold-capped fangs with diamonds in them, and his eyes glowed the same color red as his silk shirt. His territory crest medallion moved with his cinder block chest as he took in and released air hard. When he recognized Carlos, he snarled.

"They said you were dead."

"You know in our world, hearsay is dangerous, and doesn't hold up in council."

She watched a half smile cross Carlos's face. She tensed when she picked up motion in her peripheral vision. Five females had slowly gathered behind the new club owner, but when Carlos had spoken, they took a deep breath and hung back, their positions now in the middle of the two potential combatants without a clear choice being displayed. Deep.

"I'ma give you a choice," Carlos said, his voice low and lethal. "Since you didn't know I was around, as you claim, you can get your shit and your bitches out of my club—now, or die." Carlos walked to the center of the dance floor, putting space between him and Damali. "What will it be? And tell me my lair in Beverly Hills hasn't been opened. If you breached my lair, motherfucker, there will be no saving your ass. I'll pull a bone out of it."

She couldn't believe what she was watching. The five females walked over to Carlos and stood behind him as the other male bulked but he still didn't make a move.

"Like I said, man. I didn't know," the club owner said.

"Knowledge is power," Carlos said in a deep rumble that made the females come nearer to him, tilt their heads, close their eyes, and inhale his scent.

"Oh, Carlos . . . We had been looking for you, baby. Where you been?" one tall, voluptuous, female said, her island lilt pouring over him.

"Later," Carlos said. "Back up off me while I'm handling my business."

Later? Damali bristled as she watched the vamp flash her man a hint of fang, her breasts practically falling out of her red halter dress as she smiled and backed away. Damn hoochie had her double-D tits up in his face, and the Latina chick with the black patent leather bondage gear was gonna make her slap her if she tossed that long, silky ponytail seductively one more time. Yeah, that blonde had betta recognize, too.

"How'd you feed?" the new club owner asked.

"That's my business," Carlos said, his tone icy. He gave the other vampire a stare that practically turned him to stone. "We understand each other?"

"You fed from her?" The blond female asked, her glare narrowing on Damali.

"Respect," Carlos said calmly, nodding toward Damali. "Don't come into my lair, unless I call you. She brought me back. Chill."

What? Now she was going to air this whole joint out. What did *Unless I call you* mean? Had he lost his mind? And hadn't he told those females to *back off*?

She watched them move away from Carlos, confusion crossing their faces. Then they glared at her. The venom in their glares felt like daggers piercing her body. That was cool, too. She would gladly handle them.

But, then, just as the storm was about to pass, the club owner breathed in deeply and looked at her. Damn it, her rage had spiked the air, and now he was looking at her with a little too much interest.

"You was gone a long time, Rivera. Heard they fucked you up bad in the tunnels. Month or so of rehab . . . word is, you ain't eating right. None of your lairs are sealed. Ain't answering no calls. Makes people wonder if you mighta gone soft. Dragging a human female around, and shit. Council mighta marked you, but anything goes topside. Accidents can happen." Then he looked at Damali. "He taking care of you, baby? If—"

"Yeah, he takes care of me," Damali said through her teeth. "Back off."

"Accidents do happen in the strangest places . . . like clubs. Happens every night," Carlos said evenly. "Believing your own hype is a dangerous thing. So is pushing up on my woman right in my face."

"Hey . . ." The new owner opened his arms and smiled. "If a man's got the skills to pull her, just like a man's got the skills to move up and take this club . . . what can I say?"

Damali braced herself for the lunge, but was shocked when Carlos just smiled.

"Wanna test your skills the old-fashioned way? Brute strength, I got you. I'm talking about who can finesse the best—since you're talking shit about my woman. Let's take it to the master level, since you wanna be one so bad."

The second-level male glanced around the room as the females again hovered between the two would-be combatants.

"I'm not gonna mess up my club," Carlos said casually. "And I'm not really trying to dust any more vamps in my territory—lost too many in the civil war. But if you think you can take me on a skills challenge, then let's go. Winner takes all."

The second-generation vamp laughed. "Your punk ass is so soft, you ain't even trying to fight. Pitiful."

Again the females shifted. The second-level vamp was focused on Damali, but kept Carlos in his line of vision.

However, the room went still when Carlos closed his eyes, and opened them. Pure red-glowing fury was in them when he did so. Eight inches of battle-fangs had dropped, his shoulders had bulked by three inches. He opened his hand and shock spread across the vamp's face as he started to move across the floor toward Carlos, obviously against his will.

"There is no fight, because it isn't worth it. Ripping out your punk heart will just mess up my suit and put me in a very bad mood, and I'm with my lady tonight." He body slammed him against the bar, hurling him across the room to collide with it, and looked down at where he'd fallen on the floor.

"Get up. Find your car keys. We do this the old-fashioned way,"

Carlos ordered. He glanced around the bar. "If he lives to tell about it, he can keep this club. If I smoke him, all my lairs get resealed, and you let the regions know I'm back and I ain't bullshitting. Don't make me go lair to lair, kicking in doors to make it known—I ain't got that kinda time, but I will if I have to."

Visibly shaken, the challenger stood up. But it was clear that the scent of adrenaline-spiked Neteru was making him foolish and cocky.

"Aw'ight, man. A skills test. You ain't been a master that long. Before Nuit, an old master had this region, and even Nuit had years on you—"

"And Nuit got his ass neutered by this hand," Carlos said, his glare narrowing as he flexed his fist. "Bet you heard that, too."

The females smiled and nodded. "We did," one of them breathed.

"What's the challenge?" the Caribbean chick said, boldly going to Carlos and leaning against him.

"My Chevy against your Hummer. Twenty miles. Dematerializing, materializing grand prix—open highway, then through streets. No human body count, no property or collateral damage. Smooth as silk, dead as night, no witnesses. Winner takes all." Carlos spoke directly to the challenger and extricated himself from the female's embrace.

"That's not fair," the second-level vamp said, trying to save face and back out. "Your car is lighter, has less weight, and—"

"What, punk? You scared?" Carlos chuckled and studied his nails. "Tell you what. I'll weigh my car down with a human female. Complicated cargo, especially when it gets hyped, tense, screaming, adrenaline-kicking, Neteru in full effect, distracting as shit. You don't have to take a human-helper with you, to keep it fair. Cool? Takes a lot of skill to jettison vamp bodies and illusion-matter at high speeds, switch frequencies, and bring human cellular structure through solid matter and then come out on the other side without losing velocity. Need skills like that to hit V-point, too—ask the ladies. That's why I'm a master, and you're not. So, either your out-of-order ass goes for the ride, or I can just smoke you here. I'm giving you a chance to do what you should have done when I walked through that door." Carlos smiled. *"Run."*

Damali couldn't catch her breath. Carlos was out of his mind. She was not getting in that car! She glanced around quickly as the five females draped themselves on him. She watched in horror as the other males in the room gave him a nod of respect, reduced bulk, and pounded fists. She watched the second-level vampire shakily produce his car keys in his hands and nod without a word. She watched her man nod at her. Was he mad?

Carlos stared at her. Damali stared at him.

Two females were at his side, nuzzling his neck.

"Carlos, baby, if you pull this off, call me, hear? Tonight."

He stroked the bondage-gear-wearing babe's hair, and gently pushed her away.

"If she lives through it," Carlos said seductively, "I gotta save it for her. You know that, right, *mami*?"

Damali's jaw went slack.

"But, baby, she can't deliver a double plunge bite or hit V-point with you," the babe from the Caribbean said, running her hand down Carlos's chest. "When you take this human bitch home, come back to Beverly Hills before dawn, lover. I know it's been a while since you had it like a master needs it."

"I'll see," he murmured, looking at Damali. *Come to me, now. Don't front. Not here.*

"Just nip me before you go, baby," the blonde murmured against his throat. "This is the wildest shit I've ever seen. You're turning me on."

The two sisters from around the way had book-ended Carlos. It was like an out-of-body experience as she watched this madness go down. Damali didn't know which vampire to stab first—Carlos, or one of the babes up in his face. And even though common sense told her to leave, something purely female had her rooted to the floor.

"Baby, that weak punk is gonna spin out on the first turn." They both looked at Damali. "Why don't you bring her back to the lair, and we can all eat in the Jacuzzi. Bet she'll be pumping enough adrenaline to knock everybody's head back."

Come to me now!

Carlos held Damali's gaze with his unwavering line of vision. The other males were slapping each other high-fives, laughing, talking about the pending race. Vampires were placing wagers and yelling about how awesome this whack shit was going to be. Damali folded her arms over her chest. *Come to you? Get those bitches out of your face, now!*

When he didn't move and one amorous female vamp grazed his

earlobe with her fang, Damali started walking forward, her hand sliding up the side of her skirt toward her dagger.

"Do not make me come over there," she whispered, making the room go still.

Then Carlos chuckled. "See, that's why I'm crazy about her. She's nuts." But he untangled himself from the females' hold and got out of Damali's swing range. "C'mon, baby. We do this like old times—only you don't drop the bandanna. You ride shotgun. Cool?"

CHAPTER ELEVEN

DAMALI JUST glared at Carlos and walked ahead of him toward the parking lot. She was so angry it felt like smoke was coming out of her ears. Yeah, yeah, yeah, she understood now that he had to show that he was back and in full effect. Yeah, okay, she got it why he had to give them something that probably no other male in the territory could do. And, fine, his point was made about how he had to be sure he was respected when he went anywhere with her. But he had unnecessarily dragged her into pure craziness! What if he couldn't do it? She'd be road pizza, or maybe some poor, unsuspecting bystander would. And those hoes!

Couldn't leave you behind with them, he said in a quiet transmission as they neared the cars. *Not until total control was established. They'd try you just to try me, and you don't have Madame Isis on you. My concentration would be jacked during the race, worrying about you back there. That's the only reason I did it. This is for us.*

Yeah, whateva.

You see how bad it is out here, right? They took my Beverly Hills lair, my club, have to get my authority reestablished, without council assistance.

What-the-fuck-eva, Carlos.

A punk second-level just pushed up on me. I couldn't allow—

Five vamp bitches just pushed up on you, and I couldn't allow—

Had to play the game, baby . . . come on. You know me better than that. How would I look as a male master turning down free tail like I couldn't hang? Some things are just not done in public.

What's the double-plunge? And what the hell is V-point?

Later. I gotta concentrate. He looked at her hard as he opened the passenger-side door for her to get in. *For real, D. While we're riding— don't make me lose focus.*

Anger immediately ebbed away from her as she sensed nervous energy thread through Carlos. He'd jumped over the door and slid into his seat. The other driver was looking straight ahead, his black Hummer rumbling, the engine a dull roar. The kit on the Hummer made the other driver's vehicle look like it had silver fangs on the front of it. What was she doing? And he didn't want her to pray? Carlos glanced at her once with a warning glare and gunned his engine.

A sexy female vampire with long brown hair, wearing a hot orange tank top and an orange patent leather skirt, tipped on stiletto heels between the two racers. She pulled a hundred dollar bill out from her ample cleavage, leaned over, and brushed Carlos's mouth, and tucked the bill under his belt, then stroked his groin. Damali set her jaw hard but refused to do anything that would jeopardize her own life. Later. Yeah. Like Carlos said. Me and you, bitch.

"Just for good luck, and 'cause I'm betting on you, suga," the female vamp said, her New Orleans accent thick and husky. "I'm left over from Nuit's reign, plantation days before he got Amanthra in his system, and I heard all about you. I'll be dropping the bandanna tonight . . . later, when you win, you can drop fang on me." She looked at Damali. "Let her hit a wall, but do come back to us in one piece tonight. You'll still be the best. You never had anything to prove to me."

Then she sashayed away, blew Carlos an air kiss, took off her top, and stood half nude before both drivers. Were it not for the significant matter of life and limb, Damali would have jumped over the door and kicked her ass. She smiled at Damali, issuing a provocative dare, then put one hand up to her ear, extending her thumb and pinky with her other fingers folded in to resemble a telephone receiver, closed her eyes and mouthed the words, "Call me," toward Carlos.

The only thing saving her was the fact that Carlos wasn't even watching her huge breasts jiggle as she raised her arm. His focus was on her top, and when she released it, the orange flag fell in slow motion. That's when the world became a blur.

Centrifugal force sucked the air right out of Damali's lungs. Her back slammed against the seat. Oh, shit, they were gonna die!

Sparks flew as the doors of both cars scored each other. They were madmen, trying to run each other off the road at a speed that didn't even register on the speedometer. Red lights from highway traffic made her nails dig into her palms, waiting for the impact. A tractor trailer's bumper came right through the windshield, shattering it, making her cover her face and shriek at a decibel she never knew was possible. She was instantly wind; the Chevy reconstructed, bounced hard, spiraled over the highway guardrail side-by-side with the Hummer, eating up expressway, upside down. She shut her eyes, tears flying from the corners of them as she tried to gulp air, her heart rising to her throat, then they were right-side up again, streets blurring by so fast that she couldn't tell where they were. The front bumper collided with a warehouse wall, crumbled in toward her, briefly trapping her knees, then releasing them, papers flying everywhere as they exited the building whole.

She almost wet herself as they took out a chain-link fence—it reconstructed behind them—the cars zigzagged, making a space widen between them before the Hummer slammed Carlos's door again hard. Their car spun, hit a pole that went right through it between their seats, carving the Chevy in half, each part flipping over three times in opposite directions, and then reconnected in a hard snap.

Sweat poured down her temple, her tears blinding her. Her feet were pressed hard to the floor, applying phantom passenger breaks, her hands covering her face as they whooshed through parked cars, and were heading for a church. They were playing chicken, dragging black smoke down the street toward a sanctuary. Cliffs and beach were behind the building. They'd run out of road. Vampires were on the sidelines, their excited faces blurred by the speed. Final destination, she felt it. That's when she screamed in earnest. If they hit the church, all magic and illusion was gone. Both males would be smoked, and she'd be a bloodstain.

It came out on reflex. A shrill, garbled call, "Oh my God!"

Carlos pulled the Chevy onto two wheels just before the church gate, rolling the Chevy over in a crashing flip that kept skidding on its side beyond the church property gates, sending sparks down the street, momentum carrying them into dirt, onto rocks. An explosion sounded behind them. Shards of stained glass, wood, and brick followed them over the edge of the cliffs, hurling their car down an embankment. Then two arms caught her and set her on her feet.

"What a fucking rush!"

She dropped to her knees, could hear people cheering. Carlos was laughing. She could smell a fire. Hear sirens in the distance. She dry-heaved but was so shaken that nothing came up. A pair of strong hands lifted her under her arms. She stared at the jubilant face and slapped it.

"You're nuts! Get away from me!" She pulled out of Carlos's hold, and staggered to a tree and held onto it.

"Oh, man, Rivera! History again! Daaaayum," a male voice behind her shouted.

"You's one baaad motherfucker, dude. You know humans always freak at the last minute—but you held your concentration through her prayer?" A male vamp pounded Carlos's fist. "I saw that shit with my own eyes, boss. She screamed the word we don't say, the other brother cringed, didn't pull up in time, smoked his ass—went right through the church front door. It was lovely, man. Why don't you and your lady come back to the club, we'll treat you righteous, feel me?"

"Naw, man," Carlos said, breathing hard, and raking his fingers through his hair. "I need to walk this off." He bent over and sucked in a huge gulp of air.

"I can dig it," another male said. "Give yourself a minute, man. That was some near-extinction type shit, if I ever saw it." He nodded to the gathering of female vampires on the curb. "We told 'em not to rush you. After a display like that, a brother needed some space. Needed to be able to pick and choose." Then he winked at Carlos as he stood. "You got 'em in a lather, man. But, uh, this Neteru is off da hook . . . kicking—no disrespect. Contact is in the air like a mug. When she slapped you, man, I thought I was gonna pass out."

"Yeah, me too," Carlos said, chuckling, rubbing his jaw with appreciation. He looked at Damali. "You just don't know."

The other vamp sniffed hard and wiped his nose with the back of his hand. "See why you roll like that. So, since we know what you can do, and all the fellas ain't trying to piss you off, and whatnot . . . uh . . . if you got any lair queens you can spare . . ." He held up his hands in front of his chest. "We asking, you know. Respectful, like. Hoping you might hook a brother up. Ain't trying to jack your shit without permission, though."

Carlos nodded, wiping his nose and still breathing hard. "It's cool, man. Consider it a gift for me coming back from the ashes. Take 'em all. Do 'em right. Seal my lairs, though, and watch my back. No more bullshit while I'm out in the streets with my woman. And don't be sweatin' her, neither, if she's by herself. That's all I ask until I figure out how I'ma realign my shit. I'll let ya'll know who gets what, later."

"That's most cool, man," the male closest to him said. "My name is Yonnie. My posse, we never worked for Nuit—we was made earlier, had to lay low for a few. We're from the old empire, never went rebel. But, shit, man, we got your back."

Carlos just nodded and glanced at Damali, hoping she was taking all of this in. She was leaning against a tree as though it were holding her up. Her eyes were closed, her entire body was damp with sweat. She was breathing so fast that she was going to make herself faint. The sight of her like that was intoxicating. He glanced at the grouping of males and smiled.

"Knock yourselves out," he said, getting his breath regulated and motioning to the female vamps. "That's me right there," he added, pointing toward Damali.

"We can dig it," Yonnie said, shaking his head. "We be out."

Carlos waited until the coast was clear and all the vampires had left before he approached Damali. She was going to go off, he could feel the hysteria brimming under her skin the closer he got to her.

"Baby," he said quietly. But she held up one finger with her eyes still closed and stopped him from saying a word.

So he stood there in the dark on the edge of the cliffs, looking at her, listening to her pulse, so loud it made his ears ring. Terror, adrenaline, rage, you name it, it was fused with Neteru and it saturated the air. His own adrenaline high was still pumping through him. His dick was so hard there were tears in his eyes.

He was about to approach her again when she put her hand up and then pointed toward the church. "Fix it, and take me home!"

Her eyes were filled with gorgeous, glittering fury like he'd never seen before. The sight of her wrath stole his breath.

"Baby," he said again, trying to approach her, needing to be near her. "Okay. I'll fix the church, but then I need to feed. All right?"

She just nodded and closed her eyes as he walked away from her and repaired the damage as best he could. He couldn't do a full reconstruction of the building running this low on fuel. Besides, it was hallowed ground and took way too much energy to try to hold it in his mind safely. His concentration was splintered now, anyway. The angrier she got, the hornier he got. Oh, man, he needed to feed. But at least she had been able to see what he'd been trying to tell her about traveling without some controls in place.

He glanced up toward the hills. "My car is totaled; can't fix it right now. And, uhmm . . . even though things are pretty cool in the territory, I don't think it would be wise to leave you here standing by a tree. Some male might just happen by, get a whiff of what you're trailing, and lose it. Then I'd have to fight without a full tank."

She opened her eyes. The color was still drained from her lovely face, and her hand was over her heart. He hadn't thought about the fact that she could have died of natural causes from something like an aneurysm or a heart attack. Then, again, if she did, he did have a solution, albeit not a perfect one. He smiled.

When she balled up her fist, he laughed and backed away from her. "My bad," he said, laughing harder. "Oh, damn, Damali, that was some crazy shit, girl!"

He leaned his head back and wiped his face with both palms. "I can't believe I did that. Whoooo, shit!" But as he stood there and looked at her, the more rage glittered in her eyes, the more he knew he had to go eat. "Let me take you up there with me," he said, motioning toward the hills as the mirth slipped out of his tone. "I'ma eat, then I'll take you home."

"Fine," she snapped.

He nodded, but was thoroughly disappointed. *Baby, please don't leave me hanging. Not tonight.*

"And I will never forgive you if you go back there and pick up one of those hoochies."

"No, no, no, you got me all wrong. That was just theater . . . a little drama, baby. I'm cool."

She walked up to him and when she slipped her fingers in his pants he shuddered at her touch. She snatched the C-note out of his belt, and flung it in his face. He'd forgotten about it, but her scent almost made him reach out and pull her to him. Hope would do that sorta thing to a brother after a hunt. Even now he had to steel himself against the insistent incoming female vampire calls. They were on fire and lighting up his senses like a Friday night police station switchboard. Red pulses were everywhere in his brain, but there was one . . . one that was so primal, so fantastically alluring that he was almost afraid to even admit it was there. Definitely female, whatever it was. And it definitely was not Damali. It was coming strong from a distance . . . All right. *Focus.*

He led Damali to a densely wooded area where he knew deer were plentiful and placed her by a tree. "I'll be right back. This won't take long, I promise."

She folded her arms and looked up at the moon. He was getting on her nerves so badly, she wanted to scream. It didn't have to be all this. Truly, it didn't. This was the most reckless, dangerous, unnecessary . . . Then she froze.

She watched him walk into the underbrush and disappear, but a long, black velvet tail parted the foliage before it vanished. She took a deep breath. She knew masters and second-generations could shapeshift, but seeing Carlos do it was a whole other story . . . she'd only been teasing when she'd asked him to show her that before. And they were still connected. She could feel the power rushing through him, rushing through her. Oh, no, it had never been like this. Yeah, they'd been hanging pretty tight, but there were areas of his mind that he kept telling her not to wander into. He had a black box around them. This was one of those areas. She knew it the moment his focus wavered. Sometimes it even gave him pause. His blood lust side.

Suddenly she heard branches snapping, a low growl that cut through the night and made the crickets stop singing. She heard a hard thud. He'd brought something big down fast. The desire that ran through him made the hair stand up on her arms. Then she felt it. All the adrenaline, energy, everything that had been coursing through him before, during, and after the race. Yeah, he'd taken her to a safe private glen a few times to make love, and had left her side to go discreetly feed himself from deer. But she'd never experienced the quiet terror of the woods like this, never connected to the lurking predatory power within it. Never understood the true danger hidden in the underbrush.

She glanced around, and felt for her blade. Tonight she needed it. He was on a mission. She'd definitely been playing when she'd asked him to shape-shift. Pure curiosity. Hadn't understood what that

THE HUNTED 🦢 203

meant. And the moment she thought it, two golden eyes appeared in the thicket, and she could feel something huge, were-like, stalking her.

Damali took slow steps, drawing away from the presence until her back hit the tree. But she was forced to hold onto it for support as a rough, catlike tongue licked up her leg, a strong velvet jaw forced them open, and she could feel the rough wetness slide between the crack of her butt, come up her front, opening everything in its wake, then taste her navel, dragging a rough moist trail up her torso.

Her sphincter muscle twitched and contracted at the delicious invasion, but she tensed. Uh, uh, not the back door, when he was like this. No way. She could feel him probe every orifice on her. But the eyes in the bushes hadn't moved, so she knew he hadn't physically touched her. She heard a low constant rumble that sounded oddly like a threatening purr.

Then just as suddenly, the sensation passed, and Carlos stepped out of the bushes. Carlos, the man, that is. He wiped his mouth with the back of his hand, looked at her with longing, then glanced up at the moon. "I have *got* to get you home."

She wasn't about to argue with him as he walked toward her, his motions still fluid like the thing he'd temporarily been. His breaths were ragged, his gaze intense. Something was definitely wrong with his vibe. Vampires were smooth; tonight he was . . .

"Sorry about that," he murmured. "You smell so fucking good, and . . ." He closed his eyes and breathed deeply for a moment. "Like I said," he whispered, opening his eyes slowly and holding her stunned gaze in the moonlight. "There are some things you do not want me to do." Then he smiled, fangs coming down without censure. "Unless you want me to?"

She lifted her skirt and unsheathed baby Isis in response.

"Please, don't do that," he said, his voice a tense plea. He wiped his brow and took a deep breath. "Not while serving a red thong underneath that skirt. Put it away."

The shudder that ran through him made her hands shake as she fumbled with the weapon and tried to sheath it. He closed his eyes and walked away from her while she did, but she could feel the blatant desire wafting around her. In all the times they'd been together, she'd never seen him like this. He was so aroused it was turning her on, and yet, she didn't know why. This was crazy. Curiosity was drugging her, and the lingering urge to mark her own territory was lighting a dangerous fuse within her. She had to know what the female vamps had been talking about. And if there was something they could do for him that she couldn't . . .

"What's the double plunge at V-point?"

He turned around so fast that she backed up two steps.

"Don't ask me that shit right now! Are you crazy?"

"All right," she said softly. "Okay." But the image that slammed into her brain nearly set her on fire. Apparently the double plunge required her to bear fang . . . They were right, she couldn't accommodate him. And it disturbed her, deeply, that they could do something apparently mindblowing for him. But there was also no way she was going to sit at home and watch TV with Marlene, while he prowled the streets in this state. He wasn't going to make it through the night without answering a vamp call.

"Damali, you have to understand that there are some things about my world . . . It won't mean anything." Carlos tilted his head as though listening to something in the distance and breathed out slowly. His voice dropped an octave. "It won't mean what it means when I'm with you. Let me take you home. You don't want me to take you like this."

Furious, she stood tall, pulled out her blade, hiked up her skirt on one side, and cut her thong with it, then let the flimsy red fabric drop to the grass.

The minute the scrap of material hit the ground, she froze. The Isis blade was *not* supposed to be used like that, and she knew it. This thing had passed through the twelve major religions and then had come from the *Vatican*. She closed her eyes and took a deep breath. But she was on a mission. No vamp female was calling her man out into the streets over her. She touched the blade with shaky fingers then cast it to the ground.

She turned away, walked off a few paces, and got down on her hands and knees, then glanced over her shoulder. She could see him trembling where he stood. Knew he'd be on her in seconds. But also knew that tonight, whatever he did, it would be over quick. Ten hard strokes and brother would be done.

"Go for it," she told him, her voice low and sure. "Just don't turn into something that's gonna scare me."

He walked over to her slowly, knelt behind her. His palm caressed her exposed cheek, and he groaned before he melted naked against her tense body. He covered her like a hot seal, drawing a hard gasp from her. She braced for impact when he paused at her still-virgin opening, hovered just outside of it, then wrested himself away from it. She released her breath when he sought refuge where he normally entered her. Oh, this man was close to the edge.

He filled her so hard and so fast that she nearly choked. There was no gentle nuzzle at her neck. He held her by her waist with one arm, and braced himself against the dirt and grass with the other. No foreplay, nothing. No tender words, no whispered endearments. Just deep pants keeping time with his hard strokes, his body hot and sweating, lunging.

She couldn't see him. She peeped at his extended arm through squinted eyes to make sure his form hadn't changed. If he had, she didn't want to see it—not while he was in her . . . But the size of his forearm was nearly twice what it normally was. Veins were standing up beneath the skin on the back of his hand. It was almost as though he was drawing strength right out of the ground. A steel biceps bulged and released his weight near her shoulder, and what was moving inside of her felt like granite.

Her arms and legs were trembling as she tried to hold herself up and take his thrusts. Pleasure and pain became one as the width of his shaft stretched her to near-tearing, but the length hit every glorious place that she needed it to, and then some. She dropped her head forward, breathing with his rhythm, and felt the night air thicken around her when her cries blended with the other noises of the forest.

A long, soulful growl came up from his abdomen with a shudder that made her clutch the earth. The timbre of it was so primal that it shot hunger through every opening she had. It made her throw her head back and dip her spine into a deep sway and release a primal call of her own.

He threw his head back, and shuddered.

"Oh, *shit,* girl . . ."

His voice was deep and hoarse, and he was almost lifting her off the ground as his body convulsed with repeated spasms. The siphon strike at her neck was so powerful that it flattened her instantly, slamming her breastbone to the ground, his knees shoving her legs open wider, his hand at her belly keeping her in rhythm with him without missing a beat. Then his hot face dropped to her back, and she could feel him battling for air as the last of his shudders abated. She was only glad that he'd gone in the right door. Heaven help her if . . .

"I knew better than that," he said between huge breaths, trying to push himself up on trembling arms. "I wouldn't take you like that in this condition."

He rolled her over onto her back so she was beneath him as he crouched above her on all fours. She kept her eyes closed tightly and knew he was studying the wound. Then a rough tongue gently licked the side of her neck, and she could hear a low rumbling purr of satisfaction come up from his chest. A gentle kiss touched her eyelids.

"You can look now," he said, smiling. "I'm good . . . oh, yeah, I'm good, now." He let his breath out on a heavy sigh. "You okay?"

She peeped at him, only opening one eye, and let her breath out slowly, thankful that he'd normalized. "Uh, huh." It took her a moment to process what had just happened. "Where did *that* come from?"

He kissed her softly and chuckled, nipping her earlobe. "What can I say? A good hunt takes me there every time, and I was mad as hell at that bastard." He drew away from her and gave her a sly glance as he dressed, and helped her to stand so she could pull down her skirt.

Her hands were shaking as she went to fetch her blade. She was careful to stoop to retrieve the dagger off the ground. His vibe was still thick and she just hoped that what she'd given him would be enough to send him home cool. Soon her team had to go on the road, and brotherman could not be acting like this around family.

"I'm good," he said, casually, smiling slowly, watching her straighten her clothes. His eyes caught the moonlight, glistened gold, and followed her with feline concentration. "I'm going home. I promise. I'll act right while you're on tour, baby."

She didn't like the sound of his voice or the fact that she could still sense a repressed shape-shift just beneath his surface cool. It grated her. She knew how Carlos operated. Sure, he'd tell her the truth, but the double-meaning context was what was the lie. That old, I'll-act-right-while-you're-on-tour-baby, probably meant he'd promise to act right—real good, with every female in the hemisphere. She wanted to slap him.

She shook her head as she dusted off her top. The whole thing was ridiculous; she didn't even have a purse, had used her blade for some seriously untoward mess, and had sex running down her leg. She could not go back to the compound like this.

Carlos smiled and let his gaze trail down her wet thigh. His eyes glittered gold but were slowly going red. "Come here," he said in a husky tone and began to walk toward her. "I'll get it off of you."

She held up her hand. "Keep your panther tongue in your mouth! I am fine! Just stay on your side of the forest."

"Aw, girl," he murmured, his eyes amused as he watched her walk a wide berth around him. "Don't be like that. Take it as a compliment."

"What?" She was incredulous, but still staying away from him, no matter how good it felt. The experience was deep. Too deep at the moment.

"If you can pull that kind of reaction out of me . . . . You definitely are *the one*." He leaned against a tree and closed his eyes with a satisfied smile.

She would not laugh. This was not funny. Nor would he seduce her again tonight. It was time to go home. She was making a squishing sound as she walked. All she could think of was the noses in her house . . . and if Big Mike heard this. Damali kept her eyes forward staring at nothing. They'd probably blot her name out of the huntress book for this one. None of the tacticals could ever touch the dagger until she died. Oh, the vibe off of that! The clerics couldn't have it, either. This was so over the top. "I'm glad you're cool, and I'm not exactly sure what just went down, but—"

"Wasn't nothing," he said, laughing as he followed behind her, then stretched like a big, lazy cat. "Relax. Every man's got a little animal in him. Don't you know that by now?"

Carlos stood outside the safe house, watching it while leaning against a tree. Choices. Being with her, after he came down, always made him think. He loved that about her as much as he hated it. But now that his body was somewhat satisfied, his mind could go to work.

There was no way to get the old men inside to understand what seductive choices he faced. On the one hand, if he stayed out in the world as a vampire, he'd continue to experience what he'd just felt tonight. Absolute, incredible fucking power. A woman in his arms who drove him to the brink of his own sanity. He closed his eyes and allowed remnants of those sensations to wash through him. Damn, he could still smell her on him.

This is what they didn't understand. They kept telling him about the trinity of gifts from their world: hope, faith, love. Carlos shook his head. From his world the trinity was equally simplistic: feed to gain power—blood for the physical body, knowledge for the mind, human terror for dark spiritual strength; fight—to protect and to gain, absolute power being the relentless goal; and to fuck everything walking—the pleasure principle. Fuck a competitor out of a business deal, fuck a woman, fuck with somebody's head . . . it didn't matter. It was all about power. His kind were accomplished in knowledge about all the arts, history, science, all areas of information, because it allowed them to feed that never-sated power hunger, and fight better, and ohhh . . . yeah . . . fuck anything walking *way* better than the average man.

Problem was, Damali was fucking with *his* trinity, fusing it with hers. There were nights when he just wanted to simply fuck her, but wound up making love to her instead, or wanted to feed from her, but wound up hoping for the redemption of his soul and feeding her his dreams. And there were nights she got on his nerves so bad that he wanted to fight with her about her naive philosophies . . . then she'd tell him to have faith, would saunter up to him, and fuck him hard enough till he lost his mind. Then she'd demand something nowhere in a vampire's nature—monogamy. Yeah, she was confusing, and was messing him up big time.

She'd done that tonight, and had trapped him by her three golden handcuffs . . . shackled him by his hope that she would never leave him, his faith in what they had together, and the fact that he loved her so much he never wanted to hurt her. *That* was absolute power. A novice had done that, had absolutely ruined him! He hadn't allowed a woman to do that to him while alive, and now he was a vampire and had practically ceded all that he was?

It pissed him off. He paced hard just thinking about it. But the fact remained, his ass had come home, just because she'd asked him to, and he had honored her request—as if he were already married. No, uh-uh. There was too much out there in the world yet to see and do. He was young and strong and . . . shit, what was that call?

Carlos tilted his head and listened hard, and then shook it off. He needed to get back to the basics of what he was, because being all confused was a good way for a master to get staked. And that vibe running through his territory needed thorough investigation. For ten damned nights, Damali had kept him from that call—blocking it with her body, her mind, and her all-consuming spirit . . . but whatever was calling him now was definitely coming from the southern hemisphere—the same region where the killings were taking place.

For ten damned nights, ever since he'd completely healed, something out there had been pulling on his level-five capacities, making him almost want to give up human form altogether. Madness. Maybe he needed to go ahead and take that council seat, after all? He was out of control and could feel it, and there was nothing that frightened him more than that.

Then, on the other hand, if he went with the clerics—what? Either way, he was doomed. If he went with their plan, he'd get his soul back and die, probably after his seven years were completed. He'd have to give up every pleasure . . . be a spirit. What they were offering just didn't work for him. Their offer was weak. Because what he wanted more than anything else was a for *real* second chance. That option wasn't even on the table. And if he went with Hell's option, Damali would never come to him again.

Carlos pushed away from a tree and swallowed hard and began walking deeper into the woods. Yeah, they told him to block the shot and watch out for her. He had been crazy to take that bait. For one night, with her, hell yeah . . . But he also knew when he agreed that once with her would never be enough, and it was getting complicated now. Real complicated.

He had messed around and fallen in love with this woman—had years ago. Just being with her sealed it, blew him away. And tonight she took him primal? He shook his head. Now he was really trapped by her spell. He had to do the right thing, or he'd never be able to look her in the eyes. Then again . . . maybe she'd never know? Carlos chuckled and let his breath out hard. That was bullshit, and he knew it. Women always knew—second sight was in their DNA, Neteru or not—especially when it came to another woman, or women, plural. Damn that call tonight was strong . . .

Still, it was easier not to have that complication and not be totally driven by the Neteru drug. Loving her was a whole lot more addictive and problematic. Was dangerous. That shit would make a man crash and burn.

He had longed for her to be able drop fang tonight . . . His heart sped at the thought. But, no, he couldn't make her what he was, just for the pleasure of experiencing everything with her. The passion bites he had been giving her wouldn't turn her. But what about the moment the first gray hair appeared on her head? He'd be tempted to turn her then. What if she got sick? Truth be told, he had no idea what it felt like to give someone eternal life. He couldn't fathom the exchange that would go down if he gave it to Damali . . . He closed his eyes. He had to banish it from his mind; it was too tempting.

If he couldn't bear the thought of her old or sick, was it any wonder that he had been mentally blocking her from finding out about what had gone down in Brazil? He had almost lost her in the vampire civil war and she was currently in no shape to deal with whatever was down there. So, until her powers were at full strength, he was keeping his ear to the ground. If activity flared up again, he'd either approach the guardians or go down there and handle it himself. But Damali was too precious to risk right now.

If he was going to have to handle some serious business in Brazil, then he could no longer avoid the other responsibilities pressing him. He had a council seat to consider, he needed to check the female vamps in his territory, he had borders to secure, and motherfuckers that needed to be organized into productive industry sectors. Sure he could cast temporary illusions to transform a room at will or could put some supernatural topspin on an engine, but he needed money to keep things running. Even vamps weren't above needing good cash flow.

He also had a reputation to establish. He couldn't hold anything if others thought he was dead, or worse . . . a punk. His territories would be in constant chaos and then the Vampire Council would have to step in. And that was unacceptable. So much hinged on him doing what needed to be done. And he couldn't do it, sleeping on a monk's cot.

Carlos put his head in his hands. It seemed that being dead hadn't taken away the necessity of being a good businessman. It remained in the fabric of his soul. So far, every deal he had cut with the darkness had come up golden. But every deal he made pushed him further away from the light as well. A helpless anger filled him and he looked up at the sky and yelled, "What do you want from me?"

He waited. No answer. As expected. They didn't have the answers to the tough questions—just wanted a brother to walk out on faith, no guarantees. Yeah, right. Some deal. Which made him wonder if the Light really made deals with people like him. A monster with only a few scraps of honor left to his name.

And he was a monster. Tonight had proven that. After the power rush he'd just experienced, how was he supposed to do Brazil and fight without a true feeding? If he took down one innocent, *just one*, then all bets were off. Even now he fought not to go into the safe house and do exactly that. Carlos scrambled farther away, found a place to sit on high rocks, and stared up at the stars.

What the Covenant wanted from him was obscene. He was what he was. His belly was full, but the need for human blood was making his hands tremble. And mercy, he'd almost lost it on his baby. If she only knew. His kind craved blood and fear, and when he'd smelled that on Damali, mixed with her heady scent . . . would only be a matter of time before he flat-lined her while fucking her to death. And she'd come to trust that he wouldn't hurt her.

Suddenly he felt the need to move. He jumped rock formations, enjoying the power. That was the problem. The power was getting good to him, had always been good to him. He had loved the power of having her under him, panting. Loved the power of the race, of his control, even up until the moment he had crashed his car. And that scared him. Neteru or not, Damali was flesh and bone and living and irreplaceable. That's what made humans complex—they were one of a kind and fragile.

And in Brazil the power possibilities would be extreme. Clubs with hot bodies, filled with adrenaline, drug-saturated blood, sexual arousal, all the good stuff, times thousands screaming his baby's name if she did a concert there.

Real predators, like you don't see in North America, would be luring him to the jungle to hunt in the dense heat. The night calls alone would seduce him to turn into something very scary that she might not like, but that he'd love, until he dropped her limp and sweaty body and got up off her.

Carlos closed his eyes. If he had to battle whatever was over there, he'd have to feed an army—and they weren't going to do deer. Neither was he. Right there, his number would be up. Besting some local second-level was one thing, but if there was a serious international threat out there, he'd have to feed the way a vampire was supposed to feed.

And the worst part was, Damali would see that part of him that he'd managed to keep from her. His heart squeezed in terror when he thought of the horror that would fill her eyes. She would be disgusted that she had allowed one of the monsters to touch her, lie with her, love her. He had been caught up in her arms and no matter what happened, he would cherish that time with her.

Carlos turned into vapor and began drifting back to the safe house. He and Father Patrick needed to talk. He might have to say good-bye to that old man tonight.

"Well, what a surprise to have you home so early, Carlos," Father Patrick said in a cheery tone. "Want to join us in some poker?"

Carlos shook his head. "No. I need a supply, and then I'm going back out."

The monks looked at him.

"I'm going to Brazil and I need to go subterranean to raise an army, so don't even start."

Father Patrick abandoned his cards and stood, coming to Carlos's side. "Son, it's too dangerous for you to go underground again. You made your deal. Why do you have to go back? And . . . an army?"

"Need to investigate a few things. Need a squad."

"Can't it wait? If you go with other vampires and not our teams . . ."

Carlos shook his head no.

"At least let me contact Damali's team for some stronger donations? We don't have to tell her why."

"No, forget it. It really doesn't matter anyway. Besides, I don't need to get used to the taste of her team's blood. One shot of that was bad enough—got me looking sideways at Big Mike and Shabazz, as it is."

"Hold it. A word. Me and you. In your lair, before you go?"

"Aw'ight." Carlos brushed past the cleric and headed downstairs.

He was sitting on the edge of his cot, staring at the floor, when the cleric entered the room.

"I lived like this when I was a kid," Carlos said in a quiet voice. "Raggedy, old, narrow bed, in a fucked-up, tiny room. I swore to God that as soon as I got old enough, I'd never go out like that again." He looked up at Father Patrick and held his gaze. "I don't expect you to understand because you took a vow of poverty, but I didn't."

The priest nodded. "I think I understand better than you know."

Carlos was on his feet in seconds. "No! You don't!" He snapped his fingers and instantly converted the room. "*This* is what a master vampire's lair looks like."

Father Patrick put his hands behind his back and slowly walked around the converted room. "Impressive. I like the four-poster bed . . . candles add a nice touch . . . Did she like it?"

"Yeah," Carlos said with a scowl, waving away the illusion. He sat on the cot, in frustration.

The cleric shrugged. "So?"

"So . . . so . . . I need to be able to do more. I need more juice in the human world."

The priest just looked at him for a moment. "We get our *juice*, as you call it, from On High. I have the gift of second sight, but I don't have any magical powers to confer, if that's—"

"I know *that*. I wasn't talking about that. Forget it. Stupid for even bringing it up. I wasn't talking about fucking décor!"

Finding a wooden chair in the corner, Father Patrick brought it to the foot of the bed and sat down in front of Carlos.

"Son, talk to me. What's on your mind?"

Carlos took in a deep inhale and shook his head. "I'm dead."

The priest nodded.

Tears welled in Carlos's eyes and he blinked them back in anger.

"I ain't got no future."

The priest said nothing.

"Ruined everything . . . can't marry her, buy her a house, give her a kid, you know? Can't protect her in Brazil like I'll probably need to if she gets a wild vision to go—not without putting innocent people at risk . . . People who got what I want. *Life*. No matter how rich, no matter how poor, they ain't dead. They got kids, and people to care about them if they die, you feel me?" Carlos looked at the wall, rather than at the priest. "I needed to explain some hard shit to her tonight, man. But I couldn't. I haven't told her, yet, what would happen to me if I don't eat right after a battle. And if she saw it, it would break her heart."

He rubbed his jaw. "That's some gruesome shit to tell your woman. I can't look in her face and explain that if I don't take a body, mine will decompose back to the date of my real death."

Carlos sucked in a hard breath, actually absorbing the information himself for the first time. "I can't tell her how every wound I ever sustained in every battle I've fought will manifest, because I'm undead." The wall became blurry. "Man, how do you explain shit like that to your woman, when you've had her in your arms, and she's allowed you the privilege to be in her body?"

His gaze sought the floor, then went to the ceiling as he struggled against the damnable, building tears. "I don't want her to ever look up at me one night, and flip, because she finally gets the fact that she's been sleeping with something that's truthfully supposed to be in Hell. Every time I drop fangs in her presence, I keep waiting for her to scream. I beat the odds, *hombre*. But I am what I am. I hate lying to her, keeping her in the dark, but if I go to Brazil . . . I'ma hafto eat to protect her—which will end your and my deal."

Carlos looked at the priest, then away to the wall and swallowed hard, knowing Father Pat didn't have an answer for this. "I know it's fucked up what I'm saying, but you and I are rational men. So, understand that you and I are cool, and it ain't personal . . . You've been good to me, man. But if it's her or you, you know what I've gotta do. Protect her at all costs, even if it makes her never look at me the same way again . . . even if I have to take a throne. But I will survive to come for her in seven years—whether she wants me to, or not. That's instinct."

Carlos felt a warm hand touch his arm, but didn't shrug it away like he usually did. His chest got tight and his vision blurred again. But he wasn't no punk, wasn't gonna start cryin' like a pussy. Not about some real shit that he had to suck up and take like a man. Fuck it.

He heard Father Patrick swallow and it made him take another shaky breath. Hell no, he refused to have some bullshit take him there.

"It's all right, Carlos. It's just me and you."

"Oh, yeah, right. I forgot. Even carrying a blade, you're still a priest." Carlos forced himself to laugh and wiped his nose with the back of his hand. "But what are you doing sitting in here with me, alone, so close?"

"Talk to me," Father Patrick said, his hand now on Carlos's shoulder. "Get it all out before you go underground and try to cut another deal."

"You know what? I've just decided I'm *not* going to Brazil," Carlos countered all of a sudden, feeling defiant. He refused to look at Father Patrick. "When she finds out that bodies have been dropping over there I'll try to convince her not to go—but you and I both know Damali. So, I'm just gonna go get some info from the streets, give it to her when she finds out, and then I'm out. I'm done. She's almost got all her sight back; she should be fine. If I go with her, I might have to do some things she won't be able to deal with. And, I don't need this bullshit. I don't need a relationship. Don't need to be arguing with no woman—it's bad enough I have to constantly argue with y'all." He folded his arms over his chest. "That's the whole point. I haven't decided what I'ma do, and everybody is trying to rush me to play my hand. I need you *all* to *back* off!"

Father Patrick's hand remained on Carlos's shoulder. "Before you do anything permanent, and we both now know how important choices are, I want you to think about how she really makes you feel, way down deep in your soul. We agreed to let you be the one to break the news about Brazil to her—or to clean it up before she had to think about going . . . but remember that it is her job to keep innocents from harm. You can't protect her from her destiny, no more than she could protect you from yours. So, study your heart long and hard, young man, before—"

"I don't have one, remember? Least not one that beats. It ain't nothing real between us," Carlos argued, now shrugging off the priest's hold, and then standing. "I know you wanted me to block the shot, but, hey . . . It's just a physical thing. It'll pass. Wasn't supposed to get all involved, so I need to let it rest. Ain't worth trippin' about, and definitely ain't worth—"

"You can lie to me, you have already lied to her, but don't *trip*, as you say, on yourself." The old man stared at him hard. "You'd give your life for that woman, already have a couple of times." Father Patrick stood slowly and moved toward the door. "This period of atonement is very hard—we never said it would be easy. But there's nothing wrong with wanting better in life or death, Carlos. It's all in how you go about it. You need to tell her about the bodies in Brazil, before she finds out some other way, and wheels get set in motion."

For a long time, Father Patrick just stood there by the lair exit, as though waiting for something while Carlos stared at the blank wall. How did one explain, especially to a priest, how the tender touch of a woman could transform life itself? How could he describe the sight of sunset in her hair, her scent, or how her laughter ran through his system like a clean, hard rain? When she looked at him in the darkness and traced his face with one finger, she made him feel like he still had a soul.

So how did a man who once had everything, come to a woman, busted, destroyed, and dare love her in return? He had everything she didn't care about . . . money, cars, villas, you name it, but he was destitute when it came to providing everything that ever mattered to her. So how did one tell an old priest that, and make him understand? How did you come to terms with the bitter reality that by chasing everything she never cared about, you'd fucked around and lost everything she'd willingly give her life for? There was no way to explain how helpless and powerless that felt. Especially when your woman deserved so much, had lost so much, had done for so many and all you wanted to do was give her the world in return . . . And her way, time would rob him, and he would most likely die on the spot at the end of seven years of hard time.

Carlos chanced looking at Father Patrick, and was met by a gaze of compassion that held him hostage. This priest was a decent man. But he couldn't understand pain like this, or the rational decisions that needed to be made.

"Every time I hold her, and she rests her head against my chest . . ." The confession got trapped in his throat. Carlos breathed hard and slow. "I pray each time that just once she'll hear my heart beat for her.

But I don't even have that to give her. Like I said, *hombre,* I'm just trippin."

"Stay in tonight," Father Patrick said quietly. "And, in a few nights go with Asula, Lin, and Manuel to Brazil. Don't raise an army from Hell that will sway your path. Take ours. We'll be your backup. I'll prepare your transport and supplies. I'll man the safe house until the four of you get back. We'll ship blood over there for you, Carlos. Like you told me, you and I are rational men . . . You want her more than anything else in the world. Take a few nights to think about that, and don't allow the dark side to rush your decision. Make them wait, just like you're making us wait for your decision. That's a fair compromise. In the meantime, I'll keep the faith for both of us."

"I can't promise—"

"I may be an old man, but I'm also a seer." Father Patrick's eyes held compassion, but not pity, as he stared at Carlos. "The beat of your heart is in your caring for her. She can feel that because it's real."

"It ain't the same."

"No, it's not."

"Then why try? If I mess up over there—"

"Have faith. I think you're ready."

Carlos paused, clearly struggling. Father Pat waited.

"If she calls, I don't . . . I won't speak to her until I'm ready."

"Then don't. Go to Brazil when you can handle it."

After a while Carlos sat down slowly and just nodded.

Hot water from the shower mixed with soap and made her shudder. What had she been thinking? She'd come in, hit the hallway, and hadn't even said hello to anyone in the compound—just went right for the shower. Her short dagger went in the shower with her; it needed to be hosed down, too. Madness, craziness, she had to get this man out of her system and get back on the job.

Annoyed at herself, Damali snatched a towel, paced across the room, and tossed the dagger on the bed. If she ever allowed herself to do anything so foolish again, she'd slit her own wrists with it.

Tugging on a pair of jeans and a white T-shirt, she searched for her Tims and laced them up hard, then looked at the cell phone on her dresser. For ten days she'd been in a trance. For ten hot nights she'd been out of her mind. She'd been caught up so hard in a love jones that she'd been disconnected from the world . . . hadn't even watched the news—and her team had let her. Shit.

She went to the dresser and found a leather thong to tie her wet hair back, and searched for her favorite silver earrings, then sighed. Oh, yeah, she'd flung them across a priest's floor in a moment of passion that first night.

Total shame filled her. She'd been lax, to say the least, and it was more than obvious what she'd been doing every night. Group housing sucked. She reached for her cell phone and turned it on and let out an annoyed breath. Well, the fellas had their nights like this, too . . . so . . .

But the digital display on her telephone stopped her rambling thoughts. Inez had blown up her phone over several days, and her repeated calls had gone unanswered. Damali cringed. Inez never called her like that, unless it was a 911.

Immediately she hit speed dial and waited, her heart racing. The moment Inez's voice came over the receiver, she didn't even say hello before launching into her discussion.

"Girl, I was all tied up," Damali said. "What's wrong? You okay?"

"Damali," Inez said, her voice sounding tense, "have you seen the news?"

"No. What's happened?"

"Put on CNN. I'm scared."

Damali paced to the large unit across the room, too jangled to even bother looking for the remote to turn it on. "A war, girl?"

Inez didn't say anything for a moment. "No, maybe I'm crazy . . . superstitious, but . . . I shouldn't have called for something like this. You're busy, and this is stupid."

Damali watched the crawl on the bottom of the screen. Nothing odd was coming up, just general world chaos. "Talk to me, girl." She closed her eyes and focused on Inez. It had been almost two months since she could bring a person into her focus and actually see them inside her head. She hadn't even dreamt about anyone else but Carlos. When her sight came back, she couldn't even lock with Marlene in the same house, let alone someone miles away . . . all she'd been able to see was Carlos. Under any other circumstance, she'd always been able to pick up a vibe. Guilt stabbed her. She'd been off the job and insanely love-blinded.

The hair stood up on her arms as she quieted her inner being, then she saw Inez clear as day and locked with her. She watched in her head, like a slow-motion reel, as Inez suddenly shot out of her chair and turned the volume up on the television.

"You hear this?" she shrieked, watching the TV. "That happened right outside the town where my mom worked! Oh, my God, D . . . what could have eaten those people like that? We still have family over there!"

Damali opened her eyes, keeping Inez in her mental sight and the television in her normal sight, watching in horror as the media descended upon a sleepy little town, far, far away, circling the bewildered inhabitants like sharks, sucking the lifeblood out of their pain, and presenting it to faceless spectators who could watch from the comfort of their safe homes. This . . . she had been blind to *this*.

She stared in horror, barely hearing the reporter on the television or Inez on the phone. Reality slammed into her like a sledgehammer. She couldn't do this anymore. She couldn't put her head in the sand, couldn't lose herself in a lover's arms, couldn't pretend she wasn't who she was. She was the Neteru.

She thought of Inez's precious little girl, asleep down the hall from her frantic mother. No more.

She closed her eyes and opened them again. It was clear to her now. Carlos had lied, had blocked this from her. Her guardian squad knew—but hadn't trusted her to be ready to fight. The truth stabbed her. They had been right.

"Inez," she said slowly, "I'm going to send you a large check. I want you to put whatever family you have over there on a plane and bring them stateside for a few weeks—on me. Don't argue. I've got their food and hotel; just bring them here. When I get back from tour, I'll come see you. It's gonna be all right."

Fuck all this. It was time to go to Brazil.

In the dark, where you do what you do what you do to me, baby . . .
in the dark . . . blood running through my deep rivers, baby
—"In the Dark," Damali Richards

CHAPTER TWELVE

THE SUN was so bright, Damali squinted as she tried to peer out the plane's window. She gave up and lowered the shade. She blinked and finally closed her eyes, the sun's golden glow permanently affixed to the insides of her eyelids. Carlos hadn't answered her calls. After the incident in the woods, had he just walked? Even when she'd left word with Father Patrick that it was urgent, and had told him that she was heading to Rio on tour, Carlos had actually gone AWOL *knowing* she was going to Brazil—when they both knew that something serious was lurking there?

It was over, big time. She didn't care what Marlene had said about the man being worried for her safety. That was bullshit. Marlene didn't understand that she'd opened herself up fully, had let Carlos into every section of her mind, her being, her very essence. She'd had nothing to hide, no fantasy or secret that she had been ashamed to share with him. But his brain had dark corridors, entire compartments blocked to hers. Now she knew why.

His shutting her out, keeping critical information from her, keeping her from a hunt, maybe even costing a few innocents their lives, was a betrayal to everything she was as a Neteru. Before she'd become his lover, she was the Neteru! Still was, and she'd let the team know how much she seriously didn't appreciate them not pulling her coat. Yeah, Marlene had said that she'd divined that no innocents would be harmed if Damali came to these conclusions before the next full moon. But the simple fact was, all of them still thought of her as a child to be led in baby steps, not as the Neteru who must lead. And the truth was, she had been acting like a child, a silly young girl, blind to everything except the boy she loved. They should have called her on it, as they would have for any other member of the team.

But it was Carlos's lies that hurt the most. Her team had waited for her to wake up and trusted she would do the right thing when she did. Carlos had deliberately kept the knowledge from her, taking advantage of her feelings for him because he *didn't* believe in her abilities as the Neteru. He didn't believe in her ability to handle what was going on in Brazil, and he didn't believe in her ability to handle whatever burdens he was carrying. How could she be with a man like that? Shabazz's philosophical rhetoric about every man having some things better left in the dark had truly pissed her off. The fact that the team's rock had come to her, quietly trying to fix what was too broken to glue back together had unnerved her. Every damned body was all in her business. She was just thankful that Dan had played a hunch and played it right, and had booked this venue first . . . then, again, Dan was probably already hip and following Mar's lead, which really irked her. The most junior member on the squad even had insight for a while that she didn't!

It was time to regain control of her title, her mission, her life, and her private mental sanctuary. That was the only thing Marlene had been right about.

Hurt and anger shared the same space within her. They took up inseparable residence within her soul. No, she didn't care what Father Patrick said about having faith, and it still burned her up that he refused to say more, regardless of his vow to honor any confessions. If he wanted her to have faith, then he needed to tell her where Carlos was, if he knew. Period. She needed closure, needed to tongue-lash that bastard.

Damali willed away the tears. They were useless anyway. She'd never let some man take her there again; she had things to do.

Damali listened distantly to the airplane captain announce their pending arrival into Rio de Janeiro, his Portuguese phrases dipping and turning, being translated into English by a stewardess, while their jumbo jet descended into Aeroporto Santos Dumont.

She opened her eyes and took in the spectacular view of mountains carpeted with lush, emerald green, valleys with inlaid ribbons of white sand beaches, and jewel-toned waters below her. The *cariocas*—what they called the ten million citizens of Rio she'd been told—were right. This was "the marvelous city," the *cidade maravilhosa*. But Carlos would never see it by day, and perhaps never by night. So be it. It didn't have to happen like this.

She had to shake this feeling of dread as the plane touched down. She'd been over it all a thousand times in her mind. He had never come back. He left no message and no trace. Not even Father Patrick knew where he had gone, supposedly. Just like before, Carlos had vanished into the darkness. But this time was different; she didn't care.

Answering only perfunctory questions, she remained quiet as her team disembarked and entered into a hot, not-so-scenic urban chaos that shamed Manhattan in terms of its utter crush of humanity. It was only a matter of minutes before her natural, Egyptian white linen slacks and matching sleeveless duster were clinging to her skin. Her sunglasses kept sliding down the bridge of her nose, and her sleek, gold-toned shoe-boots felt like they were asphyxiating her ankles. She adjusted the spaghetti strap of her white silk camisole and lifted her chin, resigned to the long internment of heightened airport security exit protocols.

Languages from all nations spoken loudly, vibrant colors, pungent body scents, and every hue of skin imaginable filled the teeming airport as people fought to claim luggage and go through customs checkpoints while enduring the heat. But the traffic outside the airport was a scene in and of itself. Even her rugged warrior team seemed skeptical about the prospect of ever driving here.

Brazilian traffic was outrageous! Cars ignored traffic lights, drove at maddening speeds, cut off pedestrians and other drivers. Wild. Instead of braving it, all agreed to have two minibuses ordered for limousine service to collect them. She hated that it reminded her of the vamp drag race, and chastised herself for wishing she was riding with Carlos through the mayhem at night so they could fight side by side. She had to stop going there. Had to get herself in check.

A blur of noise, insane motorists, sandal-wearing pedestrians of all ages swept past the windows of the vehicle while she looked on, mentally removed. She watched an old couple, both had to be past their sixties, leisurely stroll through what looked like downtown New York wearing only the thong-like bathing suits called *tangas*. Rio was definitely deep. She'd never grow old with Carlos. He wouldn't age. He was history. She averted her gaze.

The vans carrying her and the team precariously dodged in and out of traffic along Avenida Beira Mar on the way to the luxury beachfront resort area, Copacabana, carting the team and their equipment to the ritzy Avenida Atlantica. If she weren't so numb, she would have sobbed. Her man should have been here with her. He should have been honest, and they could have fought this new threat together . . . he shouldn't have sided with the vamps against her. He'd succumbed to a call that wasn't hers. Damn . . .

Yet, everything Carlos had told her about this section of his territory had been truth, straight without a chaser. Rio was sensual, wild, seductive. Her erotic music threaded through you the moment one got off the plane. Pan pipes, reed flutes, and birdcalls were infused in the vibrations to combine nature with man–made percussion sounds. The rain forest and jungle permeated Damali like the humid air seeped into her pores carrying the *berimbau*.

In her mind's eye, she could see the instrument's bow and string made of wire, or leather, and hear the twangy sound it issued when tapped with a stick or stone. A perfect weapon for disguise; a proficient archer's delight. Just like the *cuica* box could be alternatively used for defense, as it was covered with a sheet of skin on top, perforated by a small stick that could double as a stake. She could hear the *cuica* instrument wail from somewhere she couldn't detect, imitating the call of a jaguar with reed pipes blended in. This was no way to live, thinking about weapons and battles in this paradise. But she had to.

Damali released a bitter, quiet chuckle and settled back in her seat. Two reasons she had to keep her focus on going to war: one was because she wanted to kick Carlos's ass in the worst way right now, and secondly, because there was something out there dropping bodies. All right, she hadn't totally lost perspective.

Wide mosaic sidewalks, cafes, hundreds of bars, *choperios* issuing spicy exotic smells that made her stomach growl, lounges, vendors walking, hawking, in a city that also never slept. Until now, she'd believed New York held the title, but Rio was something else. Good thing Dan and Marlene had teamed up on her, had signed contracts, and begun promo way before she'd come out of her daze. At least somebody had been handling her business, even if she temporarily hadn't been. Now that was deep . . . she hadn't even known what was going on in the compound all around her. Stupid. How could she have been so wrapped up with Carlos that she didn't even know what venues the group had slated?

She tried to wrest her mind from the clutches of worry. Homeboy would be cool. Maybe something else had gone down, and he was handling things . . . shit, maybe he was out there hurt? She shook it off. She wasn't going to be a really blind fool and begin making excuses for the man. It was what it was, abandonment. Betrayal. She didn't feel danger around him when they parted, just a constant nagging erotic pull.

Her guys were experiencing visual stimulation overload. Every female that walked by looked better than the next, and wore less, and drew their attention. Damali shook her head. Just like Carlos. The guys were gonna get whiplash before it was all over. Rider practically had tears in his eyes he seemed so happy, and Big Mike appeared faint. The two of them held each other upright as devastating beauty after devastating beauty passed them by with a smile. Her boys were done. She overheard Mike say something about this being better than New Orleans. She couldn't even laugh. Yeah, brother . . . Finally she truly knew what that look in a man's eyes meant. Hated it every time she saw it, now.

Shabazz's eyes were hidden behind a pair of dark shades, but she could make out that pulse in his jaw. Yeah, he was into it while trying to maintain some level of cool in front of Mar. Men . . .

But JL and Dan looked like excited puppies—heads turning with no cool or suave whatsoever. However, Jose only glanced at her and looked away as if he were embarassed. Marlene glanced at her and then looked away. Okay, what was that about?

Marlene's eyes sought hers again, and this time they held empathy. Damali thanked her silently for understanding. Yeah, this was not a town for a master vamp who was supposed to be living on rations. Carlos would take a body here for sure, and probably not hers. This was best. She didn't need to have that mess in her face. Plus, she had work to do, she reminded herself.

Damali kept her gaze fastened on the traffic and let out a sigh of relief when the limo pulled up to the hotel. Peace. She could finally get out of the public eye, away from the team, and just chill.

The Copacabana Palace was sumptuous. Damali shook her head in awe. It would most definitely not have been a good idea for her and Carlos to check in here. The joint felt like one of his plush lairs. Luxurious touches of inlaid agate graced the hotel lobby, as did gold leaf, high vaulted ceilings, crystal chandeliers, hand-carved mahogany . . . a place that drew the likes of Ginger Rogers and Fred Astaire, Robert De Niro, Eva Peron, and Princess Di. She had to stop thinking like that; she and Carlos were done. No matter how much she missed him, she wasn't allowing him to touch her again. "Oh, I don't think so," Damali whispered.

"What?" Marlene asked as they assembled to check in.

"Nothing," Damali responded, trying to tuck her private thoughts away.

The scents were driving her nuts, too, as was the music, the very pulse of this place, and it was broad daylight. Her palms went moist, just thinking about him here. She could only imagine his agony of restraint in a paradise of opulent decadence like this.

What would happen at night? The clubs had to be off da freakin' chain! Samba was already etching a permanent tattoo in her soul. Brazilian beer was calling her name. Fresh juices from the kiosks not far away on the beach made her lick her lips, and she could taste *caipirinha* drinks too . . . crushed lime, crushed ice, with potent sugar cane liquor in it—*cachaca*. Her mouth went dry. As soon as they unpacked, she'd be on it. If Carlos had been here, they'd get into something again for sure, and with temptation like this, he'd be in the streets— then it would get really ugly. Not to mention, here, she'd have to see him break ranks with the clerics and lose his soul. The thought gave her pause. What if he already had?

For a moment, she couldn't breathe.

The scent wafting from the hotel's posh restaurant was maddening, and it pulled her away from the sobering concern while they waited for check-in. Spicy, al dente oil-grilled vegetables, coconut milk– sweetened breads, papaya crème puddings topped with a bit of cassis, seasoned smashed white beans, black beans, fried palm hearts . . . but even being vegetarian, the seafood was calling her name—*bacahhau,* cod, and the seafood medley, *sinofonia marittima* . . . Yeah, sin . . . Instant desire slammed her, and she felt consumed by need. Damali briefly closed her eyes, and then just as abruptly stopped fantasizing and glanced around, dazed.

Wait. She didn't know the language, much less any names for the foods or drinks. And where was this—this, desire coming from? Oh, no, not here, and not now. Marlene looked at her hard.

"When we get our room, we need to talk. Cool?"

Damali nodded.

Everything seemed to happen here at a leisurely pace, a no-one-is-in-a-rush-so-chill type of schedule. But eventually she and Marlene were able to shut the door, feigning fatigue, to let the boys off the leash to go play in the bars and at the beach.

"What are you feeling?" Marlene's question was direct, calm, and unwavering as she sank down on the edge of one of the room's soft, queen-sized beds.

Damali went to the terrace. She watched teams of perfect bronzed bodies below play soccer-volleyball using their feet, toddlers run from waves and dig in the sand, lovers openly neck on towels, and older folks put sunscreen on each other, while others read books. It was like staring at a tiny city within a city. She wondered if God looked down at all the ants of humanity, not knowing the individual struggles of the specks He surveyed.

"We're gonna have a harrowing ride for several miles to get to the soccer stadium tomorrow night, Mar. Maracana Stadium is on the other side of the city, but I figured the fellas needed a break so we'd come to this side of Rio, and—"

"Damali," Marlene said gently, "I know the logistics of the concert. That's not what I'm asking you. How's your head?"

This time Damali turned around and faced her friend. "I miss him so bad, Mar . . . and I'm scared. We argued about him going home, he dropped me off and promised he'd go to the Covenant. He only stayed in the cabin with the Covenant for one more night, then lied to them and said he was coming to see me, and was history."

Marlene nodded. "I know. Father Pat said he was pretty messed up, emotionally. He's not sure what he'll do. Said Carlos refused to be shipped here, and the clerics stayed behind at the cabin rather than join us, to wait for him, and hope and pray for his return. Father Pat said they might join us after the concert for the hunt, if Carlos doesn't show. But he's not coming, only Asula, Lin, and Manuel."

"Why not?"

"Some past history went down over here within the Templar situation," Marlene said with a sigh. "Father Pat said that as a guy with an old European bloodline, it might be best not to confuse things . . . plus, he's getting up there in years. His main concern is Carlos. If he shows, they'll be just as worried as if he doesn't."

"Yeah," Damali murmured, and sat heavily on the adjacent bed. She didn't quite follow what Mar was saying about Father Pat's lineage, but it didn't matter. Whatever the old dude's reasons, Carlos and whatever was out there were her main worries at the moment. "This isn't the place for somebody who has to restrain himself."

"No," Marlene agreed. "There's something else I want to talk to you about, too. Several things, in fact. But I wanted to allow things to cool off before I told you about a few of the concerns I've been having."

Damali shrugged without looking at Marlene. "Sure."

"Ever since the tunnels, and the *Raise the Dead* concert . . . your music has changed."

Damali stared at her.

"That's not a bad thing, but it's richer, more . . . frankly, I don't know how to put it, but it's more sensual."

This time, Damali laughed, relieved that Marlene wasn't going to go deeper. "You're talking about that new cut, 'When You Call,' right? And I know that cut, 'In the Dark,' is over the top. But it works for Brazil."

They both laughed.

Marlene rubbed her hands over her face, trying to blot the oil and perspiration away. Despite the air conditioning, the heat from the travel still stuck to them.

"But Damali, you've got three thumpin' cuts that are about kicking evil's butt, then you have one so sad, girl, the guys can barely play it. But, 'When You Call' . . . chile! Uh, you're gonna get an NC-seventeen rating on the CD. That's a bit of a departure from what we've been doing, and will draw a bunch of different energy out. 'In the Dark' is commercial and sexy as hell, and it'll be off the charts, but child!"

Damali shook her head. "Y'all wanted a chart-buster, right?"

"Well," Marlene sighed, resigned, "the concert will be a media magnet, that's for sure. Warriors of Light will have more platinum, but that's not necessarily the point. I just want to be sure the media is the *only* thing we attract. And the things that song is gonna do to men, girl . . ."

Damali didn't formally answer the charge, but chuckled with Marlene knowing exactly what she was talking about. Being called on it, though, made her blush a bit. A couple of those songs went down on paper during the month before she knew Carlos was still alive—or better stated, existed. "Piece of My Soul" was so sad it was practically morbid. And "In the Dark" came after his awakening, so to speak, as they referred to it. Hell, after he'd blown her mind and made love to her like he did, it had been her awakening, too. But "When You Call" . . . shit . . . that came out as reflex. Damali smiled and looked at the floor. "If there's another master in this territory, the new music should draw him." What else could she say? "You always told me to work with my experiences."

Marlene just gave her a knowing smile, but remained silent.

Damali thought of one song's sultry, sad, wailing sound filled with desire. The first song she'd written after they'd made it out of the tunnels entered her bloodstream. She could feel it, and hear the refrain as it drifted through her mind and painted a renewed ache inside her. The words were true: *You've got a piece of my soul buried within you. Why you gotta take us both through pure hell? Would go there again for one more night. Don't leave me hanging. Lost a piece of my soul without you.*

But the other song was totally about the insanity of wanting someone so badly it hurt.

Every time she sang it, thought about it, performed it in the studio, she could see Carlos, newly turned, outside her compound, calling her till he dropped to his knees, aching for her to step beyond the barrier and come to him.

She hadn't been sure she could do "When You Call" for the show, but had to now. Marlene was talking, saying something, but the song had taken over her brain.

When you call, I can't say no. 'Cause when you call, I just gotta let go . . . wanna feel your arms around me . . . Oh! And when your eyes burn into me, I flash fire instantly. 'Cause when you call me, baby—I just come . . . to you . . . Call me, and I'll be there. When you call . . . Call me. I don't care. When you call . . . Anytime, anywhere—

"Uh, yeah," Marlene chuckled, apparently locked in on the lyrics, too.

"I can't help it," Damali easily laughed with her as she shook off the pain. "That's what was in me at the time, and I had to stay true to what I was feeling as an artist, make what I'm going through make some sense."

"Yeah," Marlene countered, "even though you can save that canned sound bite for the press, I have no issues with that—but have you noticed the instruments in your work?"

"I'm not following." Damali was about to flop back on the bed, but she leaned forward instead.

"Close your eyes and listen to 'In the Dark' in your head, and put the music behind it."

She didn't struggle with Marlene, although she struggled with herself. That song always messed her up, and she was wondering how she was going to stand on the stage and give that one all she had without bugging herself out. It was so personal, so close to the bone . . . so reminiscent of the things she shared with Carlos in the dark. Yet, this song also made her feel strong. She could see the performance as she allowed her mind to slip into it.

Brazil, yeah, the Carnaval headdress thing, she'd give them *Carnaval,* baby . . . sheer, peacock-feathered dress with gold running through it, goddess-level head piece—lights black out, then step out onstage into an azure-blue sheath of light from the darkness, and wail a lover's croon of agony . . . Shabazz's heavy bass *kickin',* Rider sensually walking his lead guitar to make the hair stand up on your neck, berimbaus, reed flutes, conga drums, cow bells, chimes, keyboards . . . awwww sookie, sookie, they was gonna rock da house! No . . . she'd save the blue for the other slow song. For this one, she'd wear a sheath of pure blood red. Sheer, with embroidery barely covering where it counted, and she'd step out into a splinter of crimson light. Yeah. Even though her baby wasn't there and hadn't told her what he should have, *that* was his color. She was a performer and would get through this. Just ride it out. That's what you had to do with pain.

Damali leaned her head back and belted out the ballad, husky, low, sensual, like her voice had recently become, unable to keep it inside her head or her heart any longer.

"*In the dark*, where you do what you do what you do to me, baby . . . *In the dark*, blood . . . running through my deep rivers, baby . . . *In the dark* . . . sissss . . . ohhhh . . . in the dark . . . *In the dark*, yeah . . . you feel it with me, baby . . . *In the dark* . . . no shame in begging for what's so good to ya, baby—"

"Ya know what?" Marlene said laughing and standing up. "Do that song like that, and we'll have every freaking vampire in the hemisphere topside."

"Oh, please, Mar. It's not *that* bad. But it does sound good when Shabazz and Big Mike harmonize with me on the parts after I sing the *in the dark* part, right? Have you heard the way Shabazz just jams on his bass on that song, lady? Rider's ax just screams on it, too."

"Yes, I have to admit that this one is *the one*."

"Okay, then, we have no problem. We'll draw whatever came up from Hell and deal with it." Damali flopped back on the bed and let her breath out hard. Dang, she needed a shower.

"Oh, really?" Marlene sat down slowly again, sharing a sly smile. "Oh, with your costume, the stage speaker system blasting that out on however many watts per channel in an *open-air* stadium before a sold-out crowd, sending shock waves subterranean, crooning *like that*, girl—sheeeeit, the old vamps might come up from Hell for this concert! I'm not sure we have enough ammo."

All Damali could do was laugh. But it did give her an idea. Maybe Carlos might hear it? Maybe he'd already heard it? Naahhh . . . She disallowed the thought. His ass didn't need to be in Rio. Besides, it was over. "Okay, so what about the instruments? You asked if I had noticed the instruments."

"You've already incorporated this African-Brazilian sound in the music, well before we got a definite booking for this concert—it's infused in the latest cuts we just laid down for the gig. 'When You Call' has it, 'In the Dark' has it. Fine. But I kept watching your reaction to the environment . . . you blended into it like a chameleon, like you already knew it. You'd put it into your music even while you were still blind. Maybe we need to rethink that; maybe you weren't as blind as we thought? So, what happened in the lobby? The color drained from your face."

All she could do was stare at Marlene. Yeah, she knew Rio blind.

CHAPTER THIRTEEN

DAMALI SOUGHT Marlene's eyes, and all modesty fled as she sat up slowly. "Marlene, I felt Brazil running through my veins. I could taste the food, smell everything, knew the language, knew the landscape, and . . . and I felt myself calling him—*hard*. So much that I felt a presence . . . a highly erotic one, in broad daylight."

She wrapped her arms around her waist, but never lost eye contact with Marlene. "What's freaking me out is, while whatever is out should have been my primary concern, it wasn't. Isn't. Are you hearing me? I shouldn't be thinking about getting with him, not with my girl's family at risk, innocents at risk, my whole team at risk, but I swear Mar, I can't shake this feeling. It's not normal. I'm so ashamed to be acting like this; I don't know what to do with myself. I *hate* being out of control, and I think I am." Damali's voice went to a low murmur and her gaze went to the floor. "Marlene, I don't know what he did to me, and I'm scared."

Her eyes sought Marlene's again for understanding and found it, which gave her the wherewithal to continue the confession. "Plus, he's got strong vibe, but brother ain't that bad that he can cut through equatorial sun. Come on, now."

Marlene nodded. "I don't think it's him," she said quietly.

Damali was on her feet. "And then when we arrived here it felt like I had done some of this before . . . I just knew what was going to happen next, but it wasn't like a premonition. Then I felt this really hard-to-shake sexual presence . . . That's what made me freak. But it was there, and it wasn't playing."

Marlene's voice was quiet and her expression was grave. "I know, because it happened to me, too."

Damali let her breath out in relief. "Glad I'm not trippin' by myself in here. But I'm really worried. I thought I was the only one."

"You're not." Marlene stood and paced to the window. "Have you been watching Jose? He had the opposite reaction—nearly bristled when we walked through the hotel lobby."

For a moment, the two women held each other in a worried stare. Truthfully, she hadn't noticed Jose's reaction. She had been too immersed in her own. "You think he's all right, Mar?"

"Yeah. But he sensed something, too. And the guys are losing perspective here. Shabazz is quietly going nuts . . ." Marlene's gaze slid from hers. "I know him very well, and my man is a tactical. He's usually the team's voice of reason; the rock. He had to get away from me in the lobby and go get a drink—that ain't Shabazz's way. And I watched Rider inhale and go weak in the knees. JL and Dan practically melted down as soon as they crossed the threshold. And Mike . . ." Marlene shook her head. "We've gotta put a short choker chain on him. Boss is ready to nail anything walking, and Mike is usually pretty selective. This environment, for whatever reason, is kicking everybody's ass—even mine. It's making everybody lose focus. But it's also like our whole team has done this before, and we can't get our concentration together."

Marlene looked at Damali, her gaze a stronghold, and nodded. "Yeah, even me, the den mother," she admitted. "None of us should be thinking like that, given all we have to do. The question is, why? Carlos didn't do that to the entire team. Something else is in the equation. So don't be too hard on yourself, for whatever it's worth."

"This whole thing is weird. Not like what we generally do isn't out of the ordinary, but you know what I mean."

Marlene nodded again. "When I heard your song lyrics, I knew what you were going to say before you read them to us in the studio, and not because I was inside your head. I knew the music, the sound beneath it, just like JL was able to pick up the percussion and lay it in—perfectly. Everybody on the team almost knew the same song, all of us were throwing in flava with the sound. Then something jumps off that makes us need to book here for a concert? C'mon, D, you know how this mess goes. You don't cut a CD in a night, in one take—it's not done. Nor do coincidences like all of us vibing on Brazil *just happen*. We were all beginning to get drawn to this region before the bodies dropped. It was in the music, came through before this mess hit the news. Once it did, we were all on lock. But we wanted you to zero in on it on your own. After ten nights, you did. Give yourself a break."

"I know . . ." She walked about the room, raking her fingers through her locks. Marlene's absolution meant a lot, and it took some of the sting out of her wounded pride.

"I didn't put innocents at risk," Marlene said firmly. Wouldn't do that, even for you. Bodies have dropped at distinct moon phases . . . and you and Carlos hooked up when the moon was full, and the relationship ran aground when the moon waned, just like the incidents did. Father Pat and I convened and both came to the conclusion that your telepathy would start to strengthen as the moon waxed over here again. But I think I need to call in some experts on this particular hunch. I know some people who've mixed it up with were-demons and have even been nicked. They would know."

Damali looked at Marlene hard. "All of our guys are solid, right? So are Father Pat's . . . I mean, even if they had a little vamp in them from generations back, it should be diluted enough and they'd passed all the will tests to be able to handle this. Talk to me, Mar."

Marlene nodded. "If what we're dealing with are vampires."

Damali sighed. "The Covenant said some mess went down over here, right? They were trying to talk to Carlos about finding out more about what was happening here when he disappeared."

"Yeah." Marlene folded her arms over her chest. "Said all they knew from their Vatican sources was that in 1500 the pope, unrightfully, gave the Amazon and Brazil to Spain, months before Pedro Alvares Cabral claimed it for Portugal, and he brought a bunch of convicts to settle it. But for about a hundred years, things were fairly cool—the Portuguese harvested the red dye, *basile,* from the Caesalpinia echinata tree, where Brazil gets its name, and—"

"Red . . . The color red . . . I just was thinking about how that needed to go with 'In the Dark.'"

Marlene looked at her. "Right. And, then the Germans came. Ambrosio de Alfinger—beheaded the African-Brazilian Indians, and—"

"Stop!" Damali walked over to Marlene and held her by both arms. "Okay, now listen . . . Didn't the clerics say they couldn't intervene on this one?"

"Yeah," Marlene said.

"Don't you think that's odd?"

"Definitely."

"What if they can't get in it because . . . like Carlos always says, 'fair exchange is no robbery'? A Catholic pope sanctioned—"

· "Oh, my God."

"Right," Damali said quietly. "And, isn't beheading the only way Carlos can be killed, because of my brand?"

Marlene took in small sips of air.

"Mar . . . you should see the way he looks at the color red. Maybe he was scared to death for me to come to Brazil. I thought the red fetish was some vamp blood thing, and the fear of me coming to Brazil was just Carlos being selfish. What if there's more to it that he just didn't tell me? In fact, I know there is, but he's got me blocked now." She sighed. "This is getting complicated. I just wish he would have been honest with me." She rubbed her hands over her face in frustration and let her breath out hard. Secrets, lies, drama, she hated all of it, but needed to figure out this maddening puzzle to keep her team safe while they hunted. Shit!

"Damali," Marlene said slowly, "he told Father Pat that the other portals had been closed, but the vamp empire was still seeing disturbances in his realm coming up in Brazil—"

"Where people have been mauled and beheaded." Damali grabbed Marlene's arms and stopped her words. Two weeks of getting ready, going over battle plans, preparing for the show, doing promo hype for an impromptu venue, and staying away from the subject of one Carlos Rivera, had left a hole in their strategy. Her gaze locked with Marlene's. It was in her mother-seer's eyes. The team had been too concerned about her sense of privacy, not wanting to violate it, needing her to fathom the facts on her own, and had not gone over this essential data . . . all for her. They needed their Neteru to come to her own conclusions on her own terms, and within her own time frame. Marlene just nodded. Fury at her own selfishness claimed her.

But Marlene simply looked at Damali with gentleness in her eyes. "Baby, don't disbelieve everything you saw in him during those ten nights—and yeah, you deserved to have a little respite, a little happiness all your own—not shared with anyone but him. All right?" She waited for Damali to nod. "Recognize that the team was conflicted, too, about not being able to just blurt out what was happening. That was hard, as well as necessary. It was easier when things were black and white, not all these shades of gray. We've all been selfish in our own way—even Shabazz didn't want to come here and do our job . . . because he has a personal issue at stake. That's human."

Damali let Marlene's arms go, and went to lean against the wall. "You guys were right, though; I was still blind . . . and it wasn't all Carlos's fault. I played myself."

"We all do that the first time out," Marlene said quietly. "That's the process, and it's normal . . . it's just that, given your level of responsibilities, you had to come to these conclusions fast and on your own so that your judgment never gets clouded again. We didn't have time to burn—but we all wanted you to have that small window of joy. All of us did, even the clerics. Child, you have a bigger responsibility than any of us know."

"Mar," she said, her voice strong, even though she wasn't completely sure what Marlene meant about a bigger responsibility than known, "all right. I'm over it." She looked at her mother-seer and snapped her focus to the mission. "These deaths are possibly history repeating itself, right? You and Father Pat knew that, didn't you?"

"Yup. What's going down here is just like what the angry mobs did to the Jesuits in Belem, and Para, and Maranhao—because the Jesuits went against papal edicts and were trying to stop the human trafficking. The church was at war with itself. The Jesuits were the only ones against the Amazon slave trade . . . there was an old Vatican letter that Father Pat showed me, it said a cleric had even written a plea . . . 'What is a human soul worth to Satan? There is no market on earth where the Devil can get them more cheaply than right here in our own land—an Indian for a soul.' But even the Jesuits created havoc from the diseases they imported while going out trying to stop the violence. It was a mess. It was all a big mess—the conquistadors were insane barbarians searching for gold and the mythical El Dorado . . . burned people at the stake, even cut up and fed the Indians to the alligators. That's why we're not sure it's vamps running amuck, or what. The moon-phase killings make me say it's the work of demons."

"How much of this did Father Pat tell you, and how much of this did you pick up in visions?"

Marlene sighed. "Half and half. I saw wars, saw mauled bodies, and went to Father Pat . . . he told me I was seeing the conquistador history, and he was ashamed that the highest levels of his particular church at that time had a hand in it. That's why he didn't want to come over here.

He thought he'd dredge up more of this near the team, and was ashamed. Then he confirmed it with the letters and sat me down so we could talk about the history, where a sixth of the native population was murdered. Then we started scavenging as many facts as we could from the Internet and the news sources, and did the astronomy on when the bodies began turning up."

Marlene drew a long breath and shook her head. "Until the lobby thing, I just assumed I was picking up residual vibes from the past in a place that had a lot of bloodshed on its grounds . . . that happens to seers sometimes, so I didn't put a lot of stock in it. Didn't pick up vamps, demons—so, I let it go . . . till you and Jose freaked quietly in the hotel. I was hoping that the music thing, with the sounds of Brazil in it, was just your sensory systems kicking in to feel this location, and groove with it. Truthfully, I was praying that we only had another twisted master vamp to contend with, and that perhaps he'd brought up foul energy with him . . . but, baby, now that I'm here and watching the effect on the team, I know it's way more than that. I just can't put my finger on it, though, because I can't get a lock. That concerns me."

Again, silence passed between them as both women looked at each other, slowly nodding.

"All right," Damali said, holding her hands out, trying to make sense of the jigsaw puzzle that had eluded them for almost two months. "We have seen the killings around that specific region in the Amazon—and near Brazil, which also means red . . . which Carlos has a thing for. Don't ask. But it also makes a metaphor for blood, and red peoples, peoples of color, and war, and he's connected to all of that somehow. Correct?"

She waited until Marlene nodded. "The Catholic cleric of European descent can't get into it, because his line already has blood on their hands, so to speak, past karma on this one . . . and those that weren't directly dealing with it from that perspective, did as much harm from the diseases they brought with their attempts to convert native peoples. It was genocide—a sixth of the people were wiped out here, is what you're saying. So Padre Lopez, of Indian descent, or Asula, of African descent, and even Monk Lin—because his people weren't in it—could have come, but not Father Pat. Deep."

"Yeah, seems so," Marlene said, her voice heavy, matching her heart. "It all went down so long ago, and is in perfect alignment with the stars, too. Remember, right before your birthday, when me and Shabazz saw the trinity in the sky—Mars, war, Venus, love, and Saturn, the planet of big karmic lessons—make a huge triangle in the sky?"

Damali nodded. "How could I forget?"

"Yeah, well, Mars is the *red planet*. Saturn is dealing with lessons and karma . . . and Venus is about powerful female energy, love, plus is the planet of female warriors . . . girlfriend, we just thought it applied to you—but it appears that, wherever there's some mess to be worked out, this alignment is affecting more than just you. And, let's not forget how close Mars is coming to the earth. It's the closest transit in sixty thousand years. Red war."

"I almost can't even wrap my mind around this right before the concert, Mar, for real. The fellas are going to freak. They think they've died and gone to Heaven here. They're not even thinking about chasing evil, they are too distracted chasing tail. I ain't mad at 'em, ain't throwing no stones, believe me—but you hear what I'm saying, right?"

Marlene sighed and nodded.

"Have you told them all of this?"

"Some of it, most of it . . . but it's not sinking in—which is also very strange."

Damali paced in a slow, thought-filled stroll back and forth across the room. The last thing she wanted to do was blow the groove on some hypothetical past yang. And after experiencing what she had with Carlos, she could appreciate the guys' need to break out and have a little fun. However, all stress-relief therapy aside, there was definitely something to go after. But it didn't register like anything she'd ever experienced. It also gave her pause as she thought about Carlos. If this mess was in his territory, and he was vibing on it hard, maybe it had already drawn him here ahead of her? That could not be good. She wiped her face with both hands again. It could be a past life, or a present danger, or a combination. Oh, this shit was complicated. She needed to be angry with him, and to put what was going on into a neat box—but none of it fit. One thing for sure, something was dropping bodies in a very nasty way.

"Maybe we're just feeling what went down before, and it's unearthing everything that should have stayed buried, or something." Damali's tone was hopeful as she stared at Marlene. "Or maybe there's an ancestral link that a few of us on the team are extra sensitive to? Something we've all experienced before, in some way?"

Marlene had a crazed look in her eyes, like she'd just had an eerie epiphany. "Or . . . what if this is reverb from a past life, Damali? What if it isn't so much that we've lived it before, but that each of us fits a role to something that went down before?"

Again, both women just held each other's gaze.

"Whichever scenario is correct—and we'll figure it out—after the church conversions, the conquerors brought in Africans. So you have the same ancestral ethnicities that are represented on our team . . . Spaniards, Africans, Portuguese, with native Indians here, children and women and villages held hostage with men beheaded and ripped apart . . . all for the quest of gold, and sugar, rubber, and—" Marlene stopped herself and slapped her head. "Damali, your eyes! Gold! The flickers of gold! That wasn't a vamp trait from those love bites Carlos laid on you! It wasn't because you temporarily overdosed your system with vamp virus from repeated bites—your body has been giving clues like a road map!"

Marlene had flung herself around the room like a madwoman as she snatched up her mud cloth satchel. "I have to look this up in the *Neteru Temt Tchaas*," she said with a wink. She pulled out her huge, mystical black book, the one that nobody in the compound dared touch or ask her about.

Damali got very, very still. "Mar? When did the first Neteru show up in this neck of the woods?"

Marlene shushed her with a wave of her hand, going through the symbol-covered leather bound book and then sat down very slowly. Then she stared at Damali. "There was no Neteru in this area. Just guardians . . . the one before you came from the Nubian empire in Africa." Then Marlene fell silent, and her body tensed.

"Look it up," Damali said firmly, and then sat by Marlene. She could tell Marlene was holding something back as she peered down at the pages with Marlene, trying to read the symbols and gleaning some phrases that her mentor had taught her.

"Okay," Marlene said on a weary sigh, "I'll look up the guardian history here again. I've been over this section of the book a hundred times, if once, Damali."

"Humor me," Damali said quietly. "Read it to me out loud as you go."

"The *Pedra Pintada* . . . based in the caves, and painted the insides of them at *Monte Alegre*, who used triangular arrowheads like your Madame Isis blade tip—same folks who'd been there over 12,500 years before the conquistadors discovered it." She looked up and closed her book. "President Roosevelt's daughter, Anna Roosevelt, studied them, too, and took *a Brazilian* team with her. These peoples that they found the remains of were skilled navigators, *and artists*, Damali. A woman was the one to find it. Female energy is all in this situation."

"Open the book," Damali said, her eyes glued to it, "and read, Marlene."

"I know what it says," Marlene protested. But she gave in and looked down and read. "All right, in the footnotes it says that when Anna Roosevelt went in, she found mummified bodies that suggested a stratified society of rulers and leaders." She looked at Damali. "These people had it going on, before they were wiped out, and there was a thousand years of calm where they created art and music. They still don't know how to make sense of these people's agricultural techniques that were so advanced. The last of them were massacred during the fifteen hundreds, during the conquistador invasions."

"Talk to me, Mar . . . Follow the thousand years of peace, and read it directly from the text."

Marlene conceded on a tired sigh. "There was major movement upstream of the peoples from the Amazon Basin during 2000 to 3000 BC, from a stretch of river between Santarem and Manaus in modern Brazil." She glanced up at Damali.

"Didn't the newspapers say that there'd been killings centralized near that area, and near those caves? The other similar ones had stopped, but these over here hadn't."

"Yeah, and a thousand years comes up—a Neteru is born every thousand years to create a reign of peace. If a Neteru was born in that span of 2000 to 3000 BC to peoples untouched by outside cultures, then ancestors of that tribe had heavy concentrations of Neteru in them. Maybe enough of the recessive gene to create another actual birth of a Neteru—at least a serious female guardian—that would come to those same peoples, one would think, during the end of their era to help them. But that couldn't happen, because the timing would be off. She'd be born five hundred years too early for what happened with the conquistadors. Plus, she isn't in the book."

Damali froze and kept her gaze locked within Marlene's. "What if for some reason she *was* born, though? Like in the conquistador era?"

Marlene rubbed her chin. "But she's not in the book, even though those conquistador guys invaded paradise. They were running rampant, just running amuck with these old civilizations that had been cool for thousands of years, until they bumped into these two huge jaguar totems at the mouth of the Rio Negro, the black river, which is how it got its name. The newbies to this region renamed everything in their language." Marlene's expression was incredulous as she pointed out the information to Damali with her finger. No matter how many times she read the history of old cultures, the arrogance of men never ceased to amaze her. "Further downstream from that they ran into a tribe of women warriors, otherwise know as—"

"Amazons."

Marlene smiled in triumph. "Guardians. Carvajal, the Spaniard expeditions' chronicler, wrote of ten to twelve women warriors near Monte Alegre, close to Caverna da Pedra Pintada, where there were these gorgeous villages—you know women ran that, right . . . Okay, I digress for editorial comment, but he wrote that the female warriors were out in front of the men, leading the native troops. The Amazons were said to have fought so courageously that the Indian men didn't dare turn back—the sisters killed anyone who turned back, dig? He described them as tall, with braided hair, wearing white, and could each fight like ten men." She looked at Damali.

"Sounds like a female Neteru team to me. Or, at the very least, an all-female guardian team."

"What are you wearing . . . or I should say, what possessed you to put on that outfit?"

Damali looked down at her all-white outfit and then back up at Marlene. "I just wanted to wear this color today for traveling here. You think a Neteru was with them, the Amazons? Sounds suspiciously like the stuff of legends—and they have actual historical accounts of these women, too?"

"No lie, girl. But it's not in the book! All of that last battle Father Pat told me about went down in June 1542 through September 1546, or thereabouts . . . the massacres continued, but the Amazons held their own against the expedition crew that was trying to plunder their villages, after being cool for over twelve thousand years—you following me?"

"The *Raise the Dead* concert happened between those months, just like the subsequent mountain-climber deaths, and within the new millennium same years—right in the middle, 2003." Damali rubbed her hands over her face. "Back then, women were leading the charge, the men followed, it's all in the same area. Shit, Mar . . . but what's come back from the dead—the good guys, or the bad guys? And, how the hell do we tell?"

"After we do this gig, we gotta go north to the spiritual city—Bahia, also known as Salvador . . . to get a bead on this thing before we go in deeper. September here is their spring, and although it's now October, I wanna ask the folks in Bahia if they noticed anything deep when they went through their normal spring fertility rites ceremonies—for us, the third week of September is when fall equinox happens—"

"Mar . . . Carlos and I, uh . . . that third week. Uhmmm. It was a month after my birthday, plus ten nights when we hooked up."

"Harvest . . . The fall harvest rites." Marlene covered her mouth. "Something over here is waxing, as you were waning . . . you were coming out of your ripening, as something here was going *into* its ripening—right before the rainy season of rebirth here. This is female energy, girlfriend. This ain't male—that's why our mostly male team is jacked up. Probably what's messing with Carlos's head, too."

"Now, I'm really scared, Mar." Again her arms went around her waist and Marlene came to her, placing an arm of support about her shoulders.

"All right. Let's not freak ourselves out here. From Bahia, we can fly into Belem, the capital of Para state in Brazil to get close to the first maul citing. From there, we're gonna have to trek down the Amazon the old-fashioned way—by small planes and boat to hit the interior where this stuff has been going on in Santarem and farther west beyond Manaus, near where the Amazon and the Rio Negro meet—female Amazon warrior country. Ya oughta be at home, kiddo, with the same DNA and peoples all running through your veins. You'll be our lead tracker. Always will be since the last major battle."

Massaging her temples, Damali sat slowly on an overstuffed chair, abandoning Marlene's arm. "You remember the *Raise the Dead* concert?"

"How could I forget it?" Marlene scoffed and went to put her book away carefully.

"The energy was to open portals, but also the ritual in the music was to make a Neteru, me at that time, able to merge with male vampire energy—"

"For a mating ritual."

Damali nodded. "A highly sexually charged event. One that happened on the onset of their spring rites of fertility here, too. Now, we know there are energy zones in the world that have—"

"A lot of history," Marlene said, finishing her sentence. "Could it be that the people didn't even know—maybe nobody ever intended . . . but the dates, the times, the cultural norms of what was going on, the stellar constellation, and crazy Fallon Nuit messing with the cosmic order of things . . ."

"Ya think?"

Marlene stood and began pacing. "What if something backfired? It happened before, that's how Fallon Nuit got out of vampire incarceration before to form an alliance."

"Yeah, but I drove a sword through his evil heart myself," Damali protested, still rubbing her temples.

"But what if this doesn't have anything to do with him?" Marlene's question hung in the air. She sat down and looked out the window as she spoke. "Say if the vampires went and closed the seals—and we did too, with our Warriors of Light positive energies . . . but say if the prayers couldn't seal a certain area, because the church had blood on its hands? What if the spring rites held open a seal to something the native peoples didn't even know was opened?"

Damali stopped rubbing her temples. "And what if the old vamps could seal those concert areas, the portals where no additional energy was added this strong by concurrent spring rites that were going on in the hillsides, plus given the history, thus energy charge this ground already holds—"

"The incantations of the evil concert, plus the positive spring fertility rituals, might have crossed, fused, and called up something the vamps and demons couldn't vanquish . . . like an entity peculiar to this region formed by the chaos of this region? A dark one, a female one, twisted by Nuit's ceremony and strengthened by the rites, and jettisoned from a place down deep? Something like that could have easily been made here in an act of desperation by oppressed people, where justice was never served to the native peoples." Marlene closed her eyes. "If that's what came up, if that has been dredged up from the caverns, what are we going to do?"

"Oh, shit!" Walking in a circle, Damali felt her breath getting short. "Mar, Mar, the amount of rage . . . the amount of righteous indignation, the amount of unfinished business . . . or karma. Oh, Lord! No wonder Father Pat didn't want to come over here wearing robes, carrying a conquistador's sword with a bleeding, high-ranking Vatican cross on his chest! Shit! I wouldn't!" She looked at Marlene hard. "There were also two master vampires in Nuit's lair during that concert."

Marlene opened her mouth and then closed it.

"One died, one didn't . . . and one lost his vampire cool on me out in the woods—went near ballistic primal, and   "

"He didn't shape-shift on you, did he?"

Marlene's question felt like a slap, it hit her so hard. The tone of her voice was so panic laden that it made Damali shiver. She swore she'd never tell a soul something so deeply personal. Damali looked away and wrapped her arms around herself again.

"Normally," she said, trying to make herself sound calm, "he is, uh . . . smooth. In control. Yeah, passionate, but uh, brother never just lost it."

"What did he turn into, Damali?" Marlene's voice was firm, like a doctor who was trying to diagnose an ailment.

Damali shut her eyes tight. "He didn't actually change, on me, but, he uh . . ."

"He flipped out and went were, right?" Marlene stood and walked across the room. "What creature, kiddo? It's just me and you; just us girls. So let's be real. I need to know."

It took a moment to answer Marlene, but she found her voice and finally did. "He kept looking up at the moon and went panther."

"Oh, shit . . ." Marlene shut her eyes. "Don't you understand the were-realms? Didn't I explain to you how they roll?"

Damali just nodded.

"Tell me he didn't go all the way, did he?"

"I'm not exactly sure what you mean." Damali glanced up at Marlene and then looked away. "He went far enough, though."

"Did he actually transform and hold the form while with you?"

Marlene's eyes glittered with something she couldn't put her finger on. But the question was so damned personal. She couldn't speak.

"Did the man bring you fresh kill afterward, and drop it at your feet?" Marlene's voice was escalating with renewed panic. "Did he—"

"No!" Damali said, unable to have this conversation with her mother, of all people. "I just felt the animal presence, he didn't actually, I mean . . . oh, shit, Mar. Close, but—"

"Girl." Marlene began pacing, and had stopped speaking for a moment, appearing completely frazzled. "Master vampires detest the were-demons. They only shape-shift to amuse themselves, or to leverage their advantage during a fight, or to use it as a means of escape when cornered and they want to drop a body in a gruesome way as a warning. They'll mist on you in a heartbeat, will vaporize for you in a flash, but they generally prefer the superiority of holding the human form—that's their signature, chile. They *do not* drape that on a woman when seducing her—ever." She stared at Damali until she looked up. "Honey, I told you I was feeling a serious primal undercurrent coming from him. And I told you that something was pushing that man's buttons."

"I know, I know," Damali said quickly. "But I didn't do anything out of the norm . . ." She stopped, and tucked the whole thong incident far in the back of her mind.

"I'm not blaming you. I'm not saying it's your fault. I just felt it coming, but you were so caught up in love . . . plus you know my rule. I don't get into people's heads or envision that aspect of their personal business—so I refused to vibe on it." Marlene stopped and walked over to Damali and put her hand on her arm. "Were sexual energy is very different than male vampire energy. You hearing me?"

She waited until Damali looked up at her again. "It's raw, unshakable, violent. It is touched off by the phases of the moon—something vampires are impervious to. If that's what Carlos is tracking in his territory, then his normal male vampire reflex would be to hunt it down and kill it. He wouldn't allow it to be near his females, or poach his zones, no matter what its gender. If a female vamp called him into the night, the way he feels about you—plus the fact that your Neteru call would block her call—would not have been enough to make him leave you." Marlene's gaze narrowed, not in anger, but in an attempt to gain critical information. "I'm not trying to get into your business, but when he left you, how was he?"

"Still on the hunt, and not for fuel," Damali said quietly. "He never totally chilled out." She couldn't even look at Marlene as her self-confidence fractured.

"Has that ever happened before?" Marlene asked as gently as she could.

"No," Damali admitted, her voice becoming softer.

"All right, baby, listen. This isn't normal—not that anything about any of this is normal, per se, but you know what I mean. A master vampire is smooth enough to leave your side and go find a female vamp without your even knowing it. He wouldn't be blatant about it. So if you saw that he was still . . . well, that lack of suave just ain't done by masters. Period." The older woman sighed and scratched her head. "That mating ritual put some spin on it, maybe . . ."

"That's what's messing me up, Mar. Right in my face! He had the nerve to be trying to tell me some raggedy shit about why he needed to go out. To my face, Mar." Damali let her breath out in a slow, unsteady exhale.

"Uh, uh," Marlene said, shaking her head. "Not done. Out of character. Shit, even alive, Carlos Rivera had more cool than that. Something got his nose open, and it ain't the average vamp female."

"This thing has a lock on him, Mar. Even I can't break it."

Both women held each other's gaze for a moment.

"Damali, male vampires are not attracted to were-demon females. Conversely, were-demons will try to use strength in numbers to rush male vamps to get them out of their limited feeding grounds—since that entity's available time to feed is bound by both the phase of the moon and the location it was turned in. They wouldn't draw a *master*, of all things, right into its feeding zones. But we do know that a male vampire will accommodate and respond to the female he's trying to seduce by becoming what she wants him to be. They are masters of illusion."

Marlene rubbed her chin deep in thought as Damali kept her gaze fastened on her. "That's in their nature, too. So, if Carlos is suddenly taking on these new proclivities, then he's drawing something to him—or being drawn by something that is primal like a were, has form like human female, and a scent that beats Neteru. It's also bound to this region, one that has very funky karma, because that's where the bodies have been dropping. Whatever it is, it eats human flesh. That much we do know." Marlene blew out a long whistle.

"We've never seen an entity like this before, one from the demon realms that has enough power to attract a strong male master vamp. Carlos probably hasn't either." Marlene's gaze softened as she touched Damali's cheek. "You need to fight for him, and not let this thing get ahold of him. D, this ain't a normal male-female vamp pull. Whatever this thing is can jeopardize more than your relationship, it can compromise his soul in Purgatory—if he hasn't already dropped a body to feed her. And, trust me, I would never tell you something like this as a mother figure, or just as a woman, because I normally don't believe in it. But in this case, baby, screw it. Pull out all the stops. Fight for your man."

Marlene let her go and folded her arms over her chest. But suddenly both women's focus went toward the abandoned book on the bed.

"Mar, I smell paper burning."

They both rushed to the bed, and Marlene took the book up slowly. They watched in awe as the pages scorched and realigned, ancient markings entering new information beside it as they gaped.

Marlene's gaze remained riveted to the text. "The book reveals what it wants you to know, only when it is time for you to know it . . . this name was never entered into the pages until I just opened this book in search, or I would have seen it before now—so would the vampires. How is it that none of us knew?"

She had no answer for Marlene, just a wide-eyed stare.

"Baby, something foul had to go down beyond the mere history of this region, to keep her shadowed from the sacred texts. The Amazon in my books was only made five hundred years ago, not a thousand. We knew the light sent you early, child . . . that had to be by design—just like the one now mentioned in there was sent early. Hold it . . . she actually predated Nzinga's reign?" Marlene's eyes were so wide that it made Damali cover her heart with her hand. "Damali," she said reverently, "you know Queen Nzinga lived from 1583 to 1663, and never surrendered, even at eighty years old when she died. Girlfriend battled the Dutch and Portuguese from her base in Africa—she was the only one me and Shabazz had seen on the pages before you."

"You guys knew Nzinga was a Neteru, and that I was born early, but never gave me the dates . . . Why?" So much new information was hitting her, it made her head spin.

"Because if you were, it meant something serious—we had to know what that was to ensure your guidance. Only Shabazz and I know. But that's why she pulls you as a role model, and you admire her headdresses and garb . . . and like we told you, before that, we thought the Isis blade was held in the Nubian empire. If this Amazon fell in the mid 1540s, Nzinga was sent *real* early, too! A *forty-year gap,* not a thousand? *That,* we didn't know. I'd put money on it that the vamps didn't, either. As above, so below . . . Heaven has her mysteries, too. And now that we're standing in Brazil with the *Temt Tchaas* on us, the Amazon is written in? And she'd been fighting the same people . . . same slave trade?"

Marlene shook her head as her fingers reverently touched the new etchings. "Uh, uh. This is scary deep. The *Temt Tchaas* rarely violates itself like that. It took your energy on this soil to make it respond. I've only seen it do that one other time since I've had it." She looked at Damali hard.

"When was that?" Damali whispered, almost afraid of the answer.

Marlene's eyes had never left her face. "When Carlos was named your life-mate guardian, then burned away early. Wasn't supposed to happen like that. I wept as I watched it. You were only fifteen when his drug trade kicked up a notch too far."

Damali's hand slowly covered her mouth but her eyes remained fixed on Marlene's. Her mentor only nodded and quietly closed the book.

"Go get him, and burn him back into the pages, baby. He was one of ours, and whatever's over here can't have him—not like this, just like Hell hasn't been able to hold him. This is big shit going down in the universe. I can't claim to know all, but I've seen enough. You were born *early.* There has to be a reason that you both have all these influences battling over y'all. He's a pivot point to disaster, somehow, too. But you're the only one who can get a lock. Use it, before the wrong side uses him. Do that for me; it's way personal now." She closed the book slowly. "The light has sped up the cosmic timetable. Neteru's are coming fast and hard, and there must be a reason female warrior energy is required for the big one, the Armageddon. This is real personal, even at the levels of Heaven."

For the first time in her life, she saw something in Marlene's eyes that went well beyond being a guardian. There was a shadow, an angry one that spoke of a past experience that couldn't be shared. And for the first time Marlene's focus wasn't solely on the universe's grand plan to save the world, but was also on salvaging a little bit of happiness for one of her own. Within this frank discussion, Marlene wasn't giving her platitudes, cautioning restraint, or telling her to be patient. Marlene's eyes said to go for broke. Claim your territory; mark it. Just do the shit with authority, like you own it, because you do. It was destined to be yours. The book said so.

"Marlene . . . I had a feeling about there being a Neteru in the equation." Damali steadied herself. "That's the DNA link—and why the team is vibing here so hard, linking to female energy. I have a mostly male team, the Neteru before me had a team of Amazon warriors . . . and I had a dark guardian life-mate. Whatever this thing is, it's syncing up and shadowing our team in a one-to-one matchup, and like you said, the mating ritual is giving it additional energy—topspin. It's gotta be the past trying to link to the present, finding cellular matches to draw more energy . . . and Rider and Dan have bloodlines, like Father Pat, that could make them instant targets . . . while the others would-be mates. Either way ain't good. What if—"

"This is definitely personal, then—and all of it, since you began fighting, has centered around mating energies," Marlene said, cutting her off. "It ain't about losing any of the fellas, especially Carlos, because he's the strongest one on the team and has the most to lose . . . and if it's a female vamp that got caught in the vortex, or a demon, who cares? We smoke that bitch." Marlene's eyes held Damali's in a lock. "I know we have innocents to protect, but I also care about you, your joy, your future . . . and I damned sure care about this team, way beyond some grand cosmic plan. Nzinga wouldn't have it; you shouldn't either . . . and if this Amazon couldn't hold onto her reign, or something corrupted it, do her. Yeah, girl, it's personal, now, if that's what's going on. I trust your instincts on this one."

That small but profound statement, *I trust your instincts,* made a huge difference as Damali stood there watching her mother-seer's outrage over something threatening her joy, her future, as well as the team's. For a few moments she could actually feel that, while Marlene grieved the loss of lives out there, it was okay that this was also personal. Something was after her daughter's man, and the lives of their squad, which made it a more visceral mission. It linked them in that very private moment in a way they never had before. Right now, they weren't just mentor and protégée, master and apprentice . . . or even friends. They were something much more than that.

They were peers.

CHAPTER FOURTEEN

HEAT AND music and the sweet, potent flavor of her *caipirinha* drink coated Damali's insides with warmth. She'd craved the lime and sugarcane taste as much as she craved a few moments without worry. Everything that had been said in the room alone with Marlene was so wild that she needed time to regroup. If they were going to fight, they needed to be fresh, ready, with their heads on straight. Her team needed this night out just like she did, Damali thought, as she looked at their happy faces. She shot a knowing glance toward Marlene.

The guys had taken the news of pending doom fairly hard, and as though soldiers about to go off to their last battle, they were in the nightclub going for broke. Knowing what you were hunting, or what was possibly hunting you, was one thing. The not-knowing part was the real monster. It also gave her a certain peace about Carlos. At least there was a reason, perhaps some thin shred of hope to cling to. She was just glad that Marlene had been discreet about the more personal aspects of what she'd shared. The fellas didn't need to know all that.

Damali watched them from the corner of her eye amid the colors of the club strobe lights. Men definitely had a different way of dealing with stress. Her mother-seer had been right about that, too.

It seemed that each one of them was having their last affair with life, and grabbing it with all the gusto they could. She could only silently pray that she and Marlene had been wrong and thus filled with unnecessary anxiety. Maybe it was just strong Amazon vamp female energy fusing with the whack history of the region, and not something worse. But, then, when had their intuitions ever been that wrong?

The four small tables the team had pulled together to make a long row for their group vibrated with the samba. One could actually see tiny ripples inside each glass and mug of beer. Voices, laughter, couples, people searching for a partner; the club was throbbing with other types of energy that made Damali sad. There was so much yet to see in the world, and if she lost anyone on her team, she'd never forgive herself.

"Aw, man. Rider, check it out. Three o'clock over your shoulder, brother." Big Mike's eyes were trained on a tall sister by the bar, and Rider gave him a nod of endorsement.

"She has you written all over her, dude."

"She's serving pure Pam Grier, man, with her tall, fine self." Big Mike stood slowly. "Anybody want a drink?"

Shabazz chuckled and gave Big Mike a warning glance. "Brother, remember what D and Mar said. Be careful. And, just for the record, everybody's glass is already filled, so you need a better excuse than that to go over there."

"But look at her," Big Mike said with a grin, moving away from the table despite the word of caution from Shabazz. "She's gotta be six two, and is built like a brick house."

Shabazz sighed. He glanced at Damali and Marlene. "I ain't feeling a vamp or demon vibe. Let him go."

"Yeah," Rider murmured, distracted by two pretty Brazilian locals who were wearing skin-tight, mini-length halter dresses. The one that smiled at him had long, ebony hair flowing down the center of her back, which stopped just above the round of her behind. Rider's gaze slid down her butt to her slender thighs. He sniffed and then smiled wider. "They check out clean, my man. All red-blooded human female. I'm out. Remember New Orleans," he added, standing, "I had your back then, Mike, got it now, and I'll help you go bring over some more drinks. The one in turquoise there is *killing me.*"

"The one wearing black ain't bad either," Jose murmured in awe, standing slowly and pounding Rider's fist as he inhaled deeply. "Damn, man, this place will definitely get a man killed. But you only live once."

Damali couldn't understand why Jose hesitated and then gave her a glance like he had a bit of an attitude before leaving the table. She watched him straighten his back and walk away tense.

"I hear you," JL said in a distant tone, his line of vision fixed on a bevy of pretty women clustered about a small table at the far end. "Excuse me. Err, I'll catch up with you folks later." Then he was gone.

Marlene and Damali didn't even protest as four of their best men on the squad got up and followed the call of the wild. What was the point? It was impossible to fight nature. They were all practically dog meat anyway, Damali reasoned. But she did catch a vibe going down between Marlene and Shabazz. Damali took a slow sip of her drink and watched Dan out on the floor dancing like a maniac.

Yeah, Shabazz was in hot water with Mar, because even for all of his cool, Mr. Aikido Master was having a visual meltdown. The thought made Damali chuckle. How was a tactile sensor, a guy who could feel everything through his skin, supposed to chill in a place like this? Bad luck that his woman was also a seer, and was probably kicking his rusty butt inside her head right now. Been there, seen it, done it, and it was helping her perspective on Carlos immensely.

"You know, you can't blame the man, Mar," Damali finally said with a sly smirk as she took another swallow from her glass. She'd said the comment low enough that only Marlene heard her and she enjoyed this new aspect of being with Marlene as a peer rather than as a kid to be kept out of harm's way.

"Mind your business, chickie," Marlene snapped peevishly as Shabazz's head swiveled again toward a passing flock of beauties.

"Thought y'all had an open relationship?"

Marlene took a sip of her Brazilian beer and winked at Damali. "We do, but dang."

"I hear you, but you and I both know he ain't going nowhere, Mar. He's just window shopping."

Marlene glanced at Damali and tipped her beer in her direction. But the vibration that Marlene was trying to contain was palpable.

"Why don't you two get out of here?"

Marlene halted bringing the glass up to her lips and stared at Damali for a moment. "And who has your back while we do?" She motioned toward the team with her beer, and used her eyes to signal that each of the guys had been able to pick a lovely lady off from the herd and were now engrossed in a heavy rap.

"I know," Damali said with a weary sigh. Even the loud music wasn't enough of a distraction to ward off her inner thoughts. "But, listen, I've had my ten nights of splendor, believe me. It's unlikely that some mess will go down before the concert—moon won't be full until two or three nights later, and if something jumps off, I'm strapped."

She discreetly glanced at her thigh under the table and pulled her gold-tinted mini up just a tad to give Marlene a glimpse of her Isis dagger. But Jose's vibe was worrying her. He'd gone off with the others, but she could tell he was hanging back a bit. She could understand it, though. The Dee Dee thing was still fresh, just like for her, the Carlos thing was still fresh. Being with somebody else when there was a special person you really needed just wasn't the same. Then an idea came into her mind and she quietly nursed it while talking to Marlene.

"This is a foreign country," Marlene said in a low warning tone, breaking through Damali's thoughts, "and everybody needs to stay alert. Just as important, nobody needs to get locked up for a bar fight. You understand?"

Damali smiled. "Go tend to your man, Mar. I'll be fine, and I'll behave. I'm in a public place right near the hotel. No sulfur is in the air. None of the fellas has sensed vamps in the joint. Look at our noses; they're cool. Plus, neither of us has picked up heavy subterranean presence." The last part of her statement came out on a wistful note, and she sent her gaze into the crowd to double check. No sign of him at all. There wasn't even a third-generation sniffer topside in this club. "Feel it for yourself, Mar," she added with conviction. Then she glanced at Shabazz and smiled. "Your boy is dying over there."

"He is, isn't he?" Marlene chuckled, relaxing back into her chair. Although Shabazz still had his eyes on the dance floor, his arm soon slipped over Marlene's shoulders.

"I'm going to dance. Y'all do whatever." Damali stood and polished off her drink, set it down with precision, and waded through the pulsing throng on the dance floor. Immediately four men approached her, each extending a palm toward her to take. She laughed. A blonde, a Rasta, a geek, and a local. God, Brazil was so much fun! If this was her last night before battle, so be it.

She accepted the outstretched hand of a tall suitor with walnut-brown eyes that were deep and intense. He reminded her of Carlos the way he openly assessed her, and that had been the thing that swayed her decision to choose him above the others. He would work perfectly.

His smile broadened as her hand found his, and she gave a little shrug of apology toward the men she'd declined. With grace, they seemed to take the rebuff well, and simply raised a glass to her as they found another partner. People here were cool, relaxed, open, she noted, but she wasn't prepared for the total invasion of her personal space. Nor was she prepared for her own reaction when the Brazilian brother she'd chosen to dance with swept her into his arms, and ground out the music against her pelvis.

Way too close and personal. This wasn't like LA, or the States. A sister got a minute to get herself together before all of that. But she was feeling the music, the effects of her third drink, and definitely enjoying the local flavor of the club. However, it was still too sensual the way he moved against her, and his natural funk was pungent, drawing her in a strange sorta way as it settled on the back of her palate. She inhaled it, held it in her mind, then smiled. Ignore my call, huh . . . we'll see.

Her dance partner was sporting an open maroon silk shirt, had a nice chest, and was already sweating from dancing. Also he had on skin-tight black pants, and was packing about ten inches in them. Wow. A great testosterone sample. Laughing as he pushed her away and twirled her around, and grabbed her to him again, she couldn't shake the wicked thoughts. Brother had a *real* nice butt, too. She just had to be careful not to get the poor man hurt.

Yeah, her guys had a point: if you were gonna get a beat down, and possibly die, why not live life to the max while you could? Tomorrow wasn't promised. The dancing and music were good morphine to chase away fear and doubt. No wonder tribes had war dances and got blitzed the night before a battle. Made sense. Made just too much sense.

Over her dance partner's shoulder, she saw Big Mike leave with the Pam Grier look-alike on his arm. Rider had long been gone, and Dan was still rapping, trying to get some action. JL had two gorgeous women enthralled—dang! Jose was so smooth she hadn't even seen the brother leave. When she glanced back at the table, it was empty. Guess Marlene took her advice? But when she saw a shy, blond college-looking chick giggle and stand up with Dan, all she could do was shake her head and keep moving.

The brother she was dancing with was now in her ear, telling her something in a language she could barely understand. Since the lobby incident, the ability to translate had faded. Go figure. But one didn't need to be fluent to pick up the message, nor did a woman need to be psychic.

"Como se chama, por favor me de?"

Feeling the full effects of the drink now, she began to relax. Damn his voice was smooth as silk. She laughed. Then she opened her mind to be able to communicate, knowing the effect that might have on the man who'd left her hanging. "My name is Damali . . . but, uh, you need to back up."

"Por que, hoj a noite?" he murmured.

"Why tonight? Because."

He touched her face and made a little clicking sound with his tongue as he dipped his thigh deeper between hers. "You have a man?"

The fact that he just switched up to English so she could better understand what he was saying, tickled her. Oh, so now that you're getting to the fundamental question, homeboy, you want to be sure I'm clear, huh? She laughed again. But the fact that she couldn't readily answer his question quelled her amusement. "Yes. I do."

"Nao lhe entendo, onde e—"

"He's not here, but I do have someone who cares."

"Meu nome e, Javier."

It was evident from the broad smile on his face that he wasn't the least bit fazed by her protest. In fact, it seemed to be driving him to a challenge. She needed to extricate herself from this guy, and the song felt like it would never end. His confidence was working on her, reminding her too much of the man who'd abandoned her in the States. "It's a pleasure to meet you, Javier. But you are going to have to back up off me a little."

"Your man should be here to protect his territory, then," he said grinning. "I would never allow such a flower from my garden to be picked simply because I wasn't tending her garden."

All right, that did it. Damali backed up a pace and shot the man a glare. Her plan was perhaps a bad one. True, Marlene had said pull out all the stops, but, dang, she'd never done this thing before and Marlene was long gone. Where was good guardian advice when a sister needed it?

He smiled with understanding, chuckled, and twirled her around. Were all the men from south of the border like this, she wondered?

Hell, guys she'd met in the Northeast and out West talked as much smack, too. *"Muito obrigado,"* she told him, thanking him for the dance as she bee-bopped away from him to another waiting partner.

Damn, where was Carlos's ass when she needed him?

Carlos sat up in the pitch-blackness of the abandoned Beverly Hills lair. It was still daytime, but darkness couldn't get there fast enough! Another man? *Oh, hell no . . .*

But he steadied himself and tried to ease back down to rest for five more hours until darkness descended over the city. The old Dominican don's lair was a much better alternative to the safe house cabin, and he'd needed time to pull himself together and think. The spoils of war were his. He'd beaten Nuit and could go anyplace Nuit's generals had fallen. It was the law of the jungle. As above, so below. The rules of the vampire world applied, and as the primary topside master vamp, he gladly sought temporary refuge in its luxuries. He was just relieved that the lower-level males had scooped up his harem and put it on lock since the race. That complexity he didn't need right now— a bunch of females sweatin' him. He'd even gotten a bit of a handle on the strong female vamp sending lure from overseas. Until he made his decision, nobody was rushing him to do shit.

Besides, he'd needed to fill himself with the remainder of the privately stocked bottles of blood that had more of a kick than the monk donations, but the main thing was, nobody was stressing him here— except Damali.

For the past two weeks he had been kicking down lair doors all over his region, sending a message, ripping out hearts . . . Miami had been no joke. Fucking New York had almost made him drop a body to feed. Sons-of-bitches in Canada had been neglected so long that they thought they ran the joint. Only saving thing was they had good wild game up there! And down in the Caribbean he'd almost gotten sidetracked. . . . the babes in St. Lucia had almost made him weep after tearing out an opponent's throat. It had barely kept his mind off Damali. And it hadn't been easy.

Initially, her intermittent calls had practically worn a hole in his brain. And though she didn't call him directly today, she'd sent her urgent concern as a vibe that he couldn't ignore. It was like having somebody blow up his cell phone with a hundred 911 calls. But why had she stopped calling after she got into a club filled with human males?

Then the ache that she produced, her desire for what they both wanted so badly from each other, had made him need nearly a gallon of blood to chill him out. Guilt temporarily swept through him, but he let it go. The only reason he'd jetted on the monks after talking to Father Pat was because those old dudes were in danger while he was like this. All jacked up, confused, pissed off, way too hungry, and needing that damnable woman in his arms.

He *had to* get out of there, especially with her gone, before something unnecessary jumped off in the cabin. He'd tried to detox while she was still in the States. Was trying to come down nice and slow before she left, so the days she'd be gone wouldn't make him snap. But with her so close, and the four monks so near, and some strong lure messing with his mind, he'd almost lost it the second night. No doubt, he had to get out of there. They were innocents, and he wasn't. Yeah, he'd needed to focus on his territory and get his head right.

Carlos brought his hands up to his temples and shut his eyes tightly. His brain felt like it was on fire. He had a skull-splitting headache from the interrupted regeneration. Why couldn't Damali just accept that he needed some space? She wasn't in any immediate danger. He knew his limitations. Shit!

His eyes suddenly opened and narrowed. He could smell the bastard, and had felt the tremor run through her. The inside of his thigh had touched the inside of the thigh that had only been supposed to open for him! Sweat. Another man's sweat on her? He could literally taste it in the back of his throat. The awareness lowered his incisors. And *hombre* was talking shit in her car, too, now? Oh yeah, he was going to Brazil!

"I said, take me to the Vampire Council, and stop on level four and five on the way down! You deaf, or something?" Carlos paced back and forth in the woods as the messenger peered at him but didn't move.

"Master Rivera, while I would be glad to take you down to the council's esteemed chambers, I am sure you are aware of the imminent danger of a border breach with the demon realms at this time. Chaos is rampant, and—"

"You want to lose your—"

"No need for threats," the entity hissed. "But as you recall, when you were first made, and I collected you, and on your return to the surface, I have already escorted you on a brief tour of the realms."

"Yeah, yeah, yeah," Carlos muttered, still pacing.

"And you might also recall that we had a mere two minutes on level five before the were-creatures began to move in, and we never even stopped on level four, due to the dangers."

"You gonna take me, or what?"

The entity stared at him for a moment and let out a long hiss of disapproval, but pulled out his scythe from beneath his robe to open the ground. "If you are lost, or abducted, I will report that this was your suicide command, and will tell the council that as a messenger, I had to defer to your rank."

"Do it, then!"

The thing before Carlos sighed. "I will also inform them that this was a command coming from a disoriented master with active Neteru in his nose."

Shrieks and screams that echoed within the hellish terrain had now become so familiar to Carlos that they seemed like the mere background drone of street traffic. He allowed his line of vision to absorb the dim, jungle-like region. Interesting. Level three was a swamp, but level four was dense, humid jungle, the darkness a heavy weight. Things here slithered with serpentine agility. Even the plants moved and writhed to a sultry, seductive snake dance. Dense, yellow sulfur smoke surrounded everything, and the moisture in the air was so oppressive with fumes that Carlos covered his nose with his hand. His eyes watered and stung. Slithering, wet insects were everywhere. Eerie black slugs, slimy beetles and cockroaches, and fat, ambling grubs inched along dense foliage all around him. Too disgusting.

"We are well within the borders of the level-four territories, and should make haste."

Carlos nodded. If he didn't know better, he'd swear that the messenger's scythe was trembling. Definitely interesting. Fetid bodies that were still half alive twisted in agony, groaning and reaching for him as he stepped over them. They were bloody, skinless, half crushed, as though they'd been turned inside out, and their moaning, vile forms made Carlos glance back at the messenger.

"This is the serpentine realm of revenge," it said in a low murmur. "The Amanthra are snake-based creatures of deception, and swallow their victims hole, consume them, and then spit them back up, allowing their venom to do the rest." The messenger pointed on the ground at a nearby torso that was still alive. The arms of the victim reached out and empty eye sockets dripped with a foul, running stream of green jelly clumps. "Where these bodies lie, suggests a feeding nest. We must go."

Again, Carlos nodded, but felt no immediate sense of danger. It was odd, but he actually felt partially safe. "If we're in the middle of a nest, why aren't they attacking?"

His night vision locked on the tangled vines above them, and it became immediately apparent that the branches were huge, muscular reptile bodies. The entire terrain was a mass of teeming, deformed serpents. Some of the entities had the distorted attributes of other animals, giving their snake-based bodies weird limbs, claws, and matted fur in strange places. The more he studied the forms, the more he could begin to differentiate the various species of the Amanthra that could be made out in the darkness.

Many were dragonlike entities with huge talons and large leathery wings giving them the appearance of fierce predator birds. Some were snakelike and bore no limbs, while yet others resembled sphinxes with their marriage of feline, serpent, and dragon. The more advanced levels, Carlos noted. Those had to be the ones Fallon Nuit made an alliance with before he perished.

As soon as the thought entered his mind, multiple glowing green eyes opened and a chorus of hisses followed. He could feel the messenger at his elbow, but was mesmerized by the eerie beauty of the eyes.

"Tarry not, and do not stare into the eyes of the green-eyed monsters."

"Hmmm . . . wise advice," Carlos noted, feeling their hatred, envy, their pure thirst for revenge filter through him, knowing that a significant portion of his soul had resided with these creatures at one time. Maybe some of him was still there.

Oddly, upon the realization, a large serpent lowered its head from a branch, appearing out of the nothingness, its black body shimmering like a cut jewel as it dipped and swayed hypnotically before Carlos.

The head of the creature was the size of a small, compact car. The monster's low-slung coil formed a U shape that was the width of two men's bodies, and its full length was indecipherable; it just kept uncoiling. Opening its jaw slowly, Carlos stood frozen as the massive jawbones unhinged and deadly fangs were revealed, dripping a sulfuric ooze that burned away the dense foliage at Carlos's feet.

"Master, I urge you!"

But Carlos held up his hand, sensing a meeting of the minds. The serpent closed its eyes, sniffed him, and nodded. "You may paaassssss," it said, then studied the messenger with an evil half grin. "You, however . . ."

"He's with me, and we're out," Carlos said fast, grabbing the messenger's robe.

Without needing to be told, the funnel cloud of vampire transport descended upon Carlos and the messenger, but not before he saw how quickly the Amanthras could move if they wanted to. The thing that had been a slow, patient, seething mass of muscle suddenly struck, seizing a half-digested body from the ground so quickly that Carlos didn't have time to blink.

From the smoky ring that encircled him, Carlos watched in disgust as the nearly dead man the Amanthra consumed fought against the beast's throat, trying to push his way out, creating moving lumps beneath the creature's scales as the acidic burn of flesh filled the air. Screams of pure agony echoed above them, and in a last glance, Carlos saw the beast heave, vomit the man up, as hundreds of lightning-fast smaller serpents snapped and hissed, ripping at the now quivering soft tissue left on the ground.

He thought of his brother's death, the way Marlene's turned daughter had done Alejandro. The acid from Raven's fangs had burned away his brother's manhood. The way Fallon Nuit's Minion crudely ate with unhinged jaws, instead of two, cleanly delivered vampire puncture marks, all came together in his mind. No wonder his brother and his boys had been ripped to shreds in the feedings. Carlos tried to banish the image. That was the past. The fact that Nuit had a deadly score to settle with the council, revenge his primary motive, really brought it all together. If a vampire was mixed with these things, adding the vampire's intelligence, and predatory shape-shifting capacity, you'd have hell on your hands, indeed.

He just wanted to see this realm of revenge one more time, because if he went with the council's offer, he needed to know what feeding den his soul might be tortured in before it bottomed out on six. The thought, while revolting, was something he had to consider. Choices.

Carlos rubbed his own jaw, realizing that at times it did unhinge to make room for a powerful bite, and even though he didn't feed like the hybrids, he still carried a little of what Nuit had left from that fateful night in the woods. That was the thing about his kind, whatever bit you left a repository within you. He was just glad that the council's bite had more power and overrode Nuit's shit, but still . . . He wondered if that's what had given him a pass?

Insane that this was what Fallon Nuit had gone into alliance with to create a hybrid race of vampires. No wonder the Vampire Council was buggin'! The messenger just nodded.

"You are still insistent upon visiting level five, Master Rivera . . . after what we just narrowly escaped?"

Carlos smiled. "Where's your sense of adventure?" Curiosity had a stranglehold on him now. He had to know where he could have gone, had his soul not been rescued. And more important, if there was a topside breach, he needed to understand what he might be facing in Brazil. What had slithered up from a hellhole? He studied the messenger with a sideway glance. "I know you can't be a punk, not couriering for the Vampire Council." He strode away from the thin, skeletal entity that remained stricken, still, and quietly enraged.

"You have been deposited to level five," was all the entity would reply.

"I remember this place," Carlos said in a murmur. He narrowed his eyes to adjust for the even darker region. This was the black forest. Unlike the jungle above, it was dry, but the trees had eyes. Multiple, glowing gold eyes of the were-demons. The remnants of bones and skulls underfoot had once made him think he was standing upon rocky gravel.

The last time he'd stopped here with a messenger, in two minutes the creatures had advanced, stalking, about to rush him. Their howls were bloodcurdling, as were the cries of their victims. Pure hatred lived here. Pure rage was its companion. The place that turned men into beasts capable of any atrocity. The primal place of twisted passions and extreme, unnecessary violence.

"This is an uncharted realm," the messenger warned. "Our council has no formal alliance here, and these creatures move quickly. They can take the human form by day, feast upon human flesh, and are very shrewd. It is more dangerous here than in the realm we just visited. Make your survey swift."

Carlos nodded. This was the realm of hunters, warriors, pure predators—and a part of his soul had lived here, too. He could make out the shapes of human forms transforming into wolves, bears, big cats, and his eyes locked with that of a jaguar. A familiar scent filled his nose. Female. He knew it instantly. She was hungry. Twisted . . . and sexy as shit. Her musk entered his nose and held him as she loped toward him. He ignored the messenger who drew back when she growled.

She was near enough now to make a lunge before the smoke could evacuate them—not that he was all that ready to go. Damn, she had an effect that would knock a man's head back. If he didn't know better, he'd swear he'd taken a hit of Neteru. But there was something also very vamp about her. But this was a deeper, mustier, earthier, older scent . . . She reminded him of when he first saw Raven, Nuit's woman, transform into a huge black panther. However, Raven's scent wasn't as strong. This bitch was awesome. A *real* predator. This one, damn . . .

She purred, issuing a low rumble from her throat.

"I urge your haste," the messenger said, backing up. "The females play with their food before consumption, I'm told."

Carlos nodded, trying to stave off the erection she'd given him. "Later," he told the alluring thing with golden eyes that flickered green. She turned, looked over her shoulder once, and sauntered away. Damn . . .

"Yeah, man, uh, take me to the council. Cool?"

"What would possess you to take a risk like that, Rivera?" The chairman was on his feet, walking in a short line between his throne and the counselor's.

"I need an armed messenger transport to Brazil—need a passport, because the Neteru went there, and I hate traveling by day in dirt."

"I beg you to use another courier. Carlos Rivera is a madman. He forced me to take him to level four *and* five, without heavy guard,

Your Eminence, and he was so flagrant, *so arrogant* in his abuse of the demon borders that they did not attack. He is a loose cannon."

The messenger bowed and the Vampire Council immediately went silent.

"You said yourselves that there's been a breach," Carlos said quickly. "Some very weird shit is going down in the demon realms, and our nation hasn't had the manpower to find out why, or exactly where. All we have is a general location. I wanted to test a theory, because the messenger is right—as a master, they should have immediately attacked me. Now, I'm really concerned, *because they didn't.* Seems to me like they might have something real big they're laying for, biding their time, you feel me?"

"I smell Neteru on you so strong that *that* concerns me. Ripening Neteru?" The counselor had rounded his desk and was on Carlos in seconds.

Carlos pulled back. "Don't get it twisted. The only thing that's on me is Neteru, not ripening, and damn straight you should smell that. I'm headed over there to Brazil now to protect our investment—if I can get an underground passport, gentlemen." He brushed past the counselor and approached the table, holding out his wrist for the chairman.

Cautiously lowering his face to Carlos's pulse point, the chairman sniffed, then straightened himself. Trepidation consumed Carlos as he waited for the chairman's assessment. Nobody fucked with the top man, and if any hint of a problem became apparent, the old man would snatch out his heart before he ever saw the claw coming. The chairman's gaze narrowed. Carlos held his breath. Momentary terror caused perspiration to break out on his brow, and he could feel his shirt clinging to the dampness of his body.

"It's only our package in his bloodstream, but his visitation to the demon realms has left a residual trail of sulfur, and the stench of rotting meat. Rectify that before you go topside, Mr. Rivera. As a master, you represent us—and we have a reputation to maintain. This is why I so detest the demon realms. No finesse."

He walked away from Carlos. "That is all I can detect, Mr. Counselor. Obviously we are dealing with a master who has the courage to protect his cargo, and our empire, at all costs, and therefore deserves our gratitude, not suspicion. I have already warned you several times, Mr. Counselor, about my growing impatience with your innuendo.

Were it not for our already strained resources . . . We cannot afford to lose another council throne at this juncture—but do not press your luck."

Carlos nodded and issued a glare toward the counselor, who returned it with a venomous glance of his own. If the old chairman dude couldn't smell what clung to him from level five, then what was up with the attorney? How'd the counselor catch that whiff? Something wasn't right. On the other hand, the counselor was the one who had come from behind the table first, and had gotten up in his face. Maybe by the time he'd approached the table his own sweat had muted the scent? Plus, he was close, but had not made physical contact with the she-jaguar on five. Whatever. But she was definitely something that had a trace of ripening on her . . . and he was definitely tracking that to his South American provinces.

He eyed the counselor. For now, he'd let it ride. Besides, no one had seriously addressed the question of why he wasn't attacked.

"Like the messenger said, they let me through. What's up?" Carlos asked.

"The Amanthra demon forces are diminished on level four, due to the wars, and we have an alliance with their old Supreme Council that was to aid them in routing out their rogue elements," the counselor said impatiently. "You were foolish, but very lucky. You had probably fallen into one of the nests that are within our alliance zone."

"But," the messenger countered, "I wasn't—"

"Silence!" the chairman bellowed. "You fool. I will kill you myself for allowing one of our few remaining topside masters to go into enemy territory without my sanction."

"His rank superseded mine, Your Eminence," the hooded creature said, cowering, its head bowed.

"And, he has also been guarding a Neteru—are you not truly aware of his potentially compromised state? Adrenaline or terror in her sweat or blood can also disorient a master. As a courier, you are a disgrace!"

The entity only bowed and backed away.

"However," the counselor argued, "there is still the question of level five." He narrowed an evil gaze in Carlos's direction. "Could it be that we have a potential traitor in our midst? A master vampire seeking to form his own dark alliance with a stronger level-five empire?"

All beady eyes at the table focused on Carlos, and he slowly folded his arms before him. "If I was that insane, and had such capability to move through their tunnels at will, I would not be standing here asking for an international passport through to Brazil for starters, and I damned sure wouldn't take one of *our* messengers with me, or roll in here after being on level five, if I wasn't on the up-and-up. I'd at least let my suit air out."

Silence met Carlos's logical response, but the tension in the group slowly eased as one by one, council members sat back in their thrones, the chairman took his seat, and the counselor made his way back toward his end of the table. Relief uncoiled in Carlos's system, taking its time to thread through him just like the Amanthra had taken its time to lower itself to feed.

The chairman nodded. "We will call in our troops to take you in, but need the balance of this night to collect our forces from the nether regions. Our international couriers are more suited for the job than our domestics. Get the Neteru away from the unknown breach. Next eve, midnight, your passport is ensured."

The sweet drinks had snuck up on her and had packed a wallop. The heat, the dancing, and over-proof alcohol had taken its full toll. She had called him the old-fashioned way, stirring male jealousy, and he still didn't respond. Damn. Whatever had a hold on him, had a hold on him for serious.

Her confidence thoroughly rocked, Damali got up from her bed with effort and squinted at the clock. It was already noon. She glanced around the empty room. No Marlene. Okay, that was cool—she hoped.

Pacing to the bathroom, she splashed water on her face, and her mind immediately went to her team. It was time for a roll call. She hurried through her bathroom routine and made her way back to the bed, walking in a zigzag pattern before she flopped down. And she was supposed to perform tonight? Yeah, right.

"Yo," she said in a hoarse whisper as Shabazz picked up in his suite. "Everything cool . . . Marlene all right?"

"Yeah," he chuckled. "We woulda called, but something came up."

Damali had to laugh, even though her head hurt. They were never gonna let that mess rest. "Okay, cool. Get some breakfast, huh?

Remember, we've got a show tonight." She seriously needed some of that strong Brazilian *caffezinho* to get it together. Black.

"No problem," Shabazz replied through a yawn. "The rest of the guys cool?"

Now *she* was the den mother? Oh, deep. She would never get on Marlene's case again.

"I'm doing roll call as we speak, 'Bazz, okay?"

"Good, baby . . . uh, we'll see y'all later on. Peace."

Damali stared at the telephone as Shabazz abruptly hung up. This was just too wild. Her team had flipped the script on her, and she was sitting there with a phone receiver in hand, all worried and whatnot, with no one in *her* room. Very deep.

Big Mike was the next person on her list, because that tall sister he strutted out the door with looked like she was definitely Amazon material. But when his sleepy voice filled the receiver, she chuckled. Maybe she and Marlene had just freaked out from the residual vibrations, because the guys were safe and feeling no pain.

"You cool, though, Mike? I don't have to come down there, do I, and check on you myself?"

"Naw, naw, I'm good, li'l sis . . . and, uh, now wouldn't be a really good time."

She heard the telephone fall, a woman giggle, Mike's low rumble of chuckles, and then his voice came back strong in the receiver.

"You okay, D? You don't need me to come down there for any-thing—I mean, everything's cool, right?"

She shook her head. "Uhmmph, uhmmph, uhmmph. Yeah, I'm fine—but you eat something and bite the snake that bit ya last night. Those drinks weren't playing, I still feel it."

"*Yeah* . . ." Mike groaned.

Okay. That was it. She was off the telephone! "Bye," she snapped, peevish, but knew in her heart she couldn't be angry with him. Then she burst out laughing.

The tone of Rider's voice when she connected with him was somewhere between severe agony and annoyance. Ooops. "Bye Rider," she said fast.

"Two more hours, D—that's all I ask." Then he was gone.

She got more or less the same response from JL and Jose, but felt compelled to check on everyone nonetheless. She'd never be able to live with missing one call, or the possible after-the-fact knowledge that a missed call could mean a guardian was laid out somewhere hurt, or worse.

Damali stood and opened the drapes and was met with a bright glare of morning light. It hurt her eyes, but the sun felt good. Hey, it was daytime, and her guys were still at it. All was right with the world.

But when she called Dan's room and the phone simply rang, she panicked. She resisted the urge to just open up her mind to find him, because if he was in a delicate situation, he didn't deserve to be telepathically swept. Damali sat down in a chair hard with the desk phone beside her and counted to ten. That was her and Marlene's house rule—no prying into people's deepest thoughts, no mind locks on their personal business. It took willpower, but after having her own very personal business to guard, she knew better than to go there.

Finally when her fingertips began to tingle, she reached for the telephone and tried Dan again. This time the phone picked up on the first ring, startling her.

"Dan? I was worried."

"I know, I know," he said out of breath, "but, uh, D, can I call ya back? Something, uh, came up, 'kay?"

"All right. You be safe."

"I will, hon. God, I love Brazil!"

Damali could only stare at the phone as the call disconnected. Even Dan? Oh, my goodness . . . a sudden pang of loneliness swept through her that she hadn't anticipated. It got tangled up with her worry for the team as well as for Carlos's safety, and it battled her anger with him for going underground—and she wasn't sure if he'd done so literally or figuratively. Hurt, anger, worry, frustration, and missing him all collided in the center of her chest and remained there like an unmovable stone. Now she knew just how Marlene felt all those nights worrying about her, when she'd sashay in calmly and give Marlene the look that said *don't start*. Damn. Karma. Heavy Saturn lessons for sure. For real, for real.

But, still. Given all of Carlos's issues, and given the vampire nation's factions, he should have left some type of word, or connected with her mind. All because of a stupid argument and some female draw? What the hell was this thing they were tracking?

She'd tried to sense him, just to see if he was alive, but now being so far away, that was impossible. Father Pat couldn't reach him, Marlene couldn't see him, and there might be something terrible out there ready to take his head off his shoulders. And she'd weakened him to the threat, hadn't listened to Marlene's advice—they hadn't been able to keep their hands off each other. What if he'd been jumped by second-level vamps from another region . . . or what if he'd snapped and formally fed from an innocent; killed somebody because of that? Because of her? Or because of this other unnamed thing? She shuddered. And, he'd warned her of his addiction.

Slowly, she moved toward the bed and wrapped the jumble of sheets around her, curling up within them, and drawing them into her arms. What if something terrible had happened to him?

Marlene had said the concert would shake the ground. Her mother-seer said fight, and she would. No doubt about it, she needed to put out a call to him that would be heard.

CHAPTER FIFTEEN

"A COUPLE of issues," Carlos said slowly, putting his hands behind his back. Spending a whole twenty-four hours underground waiting on resources was nearly more than his nerves could stand. Each time he had to come before the table put his survival on the line. But he needed the resources badly enough to withstand the drama. Still, he hated having to rely on others to bestow anything on him.

Following protocol, Carlos waited until receiving the chairman's nod, and he ignored the scowl coming from the counselor at the table. "There are four clerics, that no doubt, you have seen me interact with?"

The chairman smiled and made a tent with his fingers in front of his mouth, only nodding.

"Infidel!"

The chairman held his hand up to the counselor. "Speak."

"These men are how I have an exact location of the huntress. Between my comprise of them," Carlos said quickly, "and of her guardians, I can get to her at will." A half smile appeared on Carlos's face. "One of them, I believe, is a lower gen. An eighth or ninth in my line. How can I use him?"

The chairman sighed. "Insignificant. By that generational level, his effectiveness is so diluted and his status within our ranks is so negligible . . . they're not even what I'd consider true vampires. They're a subclass of a subclass, an actual embarrassment to all we hold dear. After the fourth generation, they can't even produce fangs—totally useless vermin."

"But he's a tracker, and a cleric, and can cross prayer lines. Our Neteru trusts him because he wears a collar. So do the others." Carlos waited, his gaze locking with the chairman's.

The chairman lowered his hands, his smile broadening. His countenance relaxed. "Yes. As always, done with flair, Rivera. But your point?"

"I need them to be off limits . . . if they get rushed, or bitten—"

"No one will flush your hunt and terminate your compromised informants while you are abroad, Mr. Rivera . . . will they, Mr. Counselor?" The chairman shot a warning glance toward the counselor and then looked at Carlos. "I do understand your concern about things going awry in your absence . . . another reason I insisted on this meeting before you left—so that we are all clear." He cast his narrowed gaze around the five points of the pentagram-shaped table, and waited for nods of agreement before speaking. "If you find your travels expand, simply call an exterminator, look into its eyes, and a safe location will be shown to you."

Imperceptibly, Carlos let out his breath. That's all he'd need was to come back to the cabin and find four corpses. Not to mention, the last thing he'd need would be to have Damali's crew wiped out over there. That would freak her out and send her into a spiral of pain that she'd never recover from.

"This is your mission, Mr. Rivera. We are all clear . . . albeit your methods are unorthodox, they have been effective thus far."

"Thank you, Mr. Chairman. I just want to be sure they don't take a body while we're in Brazil. Can't have it. Over there, I call the shots, or send me alone. This part is nonnegotiable."

"Are you mad, Rivera!" The counselor was on his feet, and two of the exterminator bodyguards snarled their discontent at Carlos's statement. "These are highly skilled, trained assassins that *eat well*. We've removed them from our borders, at your request, for this ill-fated mission to collect a girl that will probably get on a flight after shopping! This is valuable vampire power gone to waste, and now you don't want to feed them in one of the adrenaline capitals on the planet? Mr. Chairman," he urged, opening his arms so wide that his black robes swept the table, "we cannot continue to suffer these offenses, these indignities. These methods are of a rank amateur who hasn't—"

"You draw a hotel or stadium police sweep, and get foreigners detained at the airports, you make my job harder," Carlos argued coolly. "Obviously, it's been a while since you've been topside. This is my era, the twenty-first century—it ain't the horse and buggy days."

"I am from the Roman era, when evil was at its apex on the

planet—as was shrewd, duplicitous politics and aggression. The days of *chariots*; not horse and buggies. So don't you dare presume—"

"You make her afraid, or worse, flush her to go hunting, you'll take my cargo deeper into the badlands of the Amazon jungle looking for the source of what ate a few concertgoers. Hurt her team, and she'll never leave Brazil until she finds out what killed some of her guys. That's Neteru nature . . . if you ever had one, you'd know, motherfucker."

Carlos studied his nails as he spoke, and then glanced at his watch. The counselor didn't have an immediate comeback and was silent. The chairman seemed amused. The others at the table appeared anxious for a heart-ripping to take place—and from the looks of their expressions, it was a fifty-fifty split who they were betting on. Whatever. He was wasting time. The concert was probably almost over, and he needed to get to Damali while he was still sure of exactly where she'd be. All he needed was to have to search through the clubs and hangouts all over Rio to find her; some poor innocent might become his dinner.

"There's plenty of drug dealers in the jungle hiding cocaine and heroin plantations that the authorities won't miss, or don't care about, and that the Neteru won't be upset about if you guys get hungry— just make it look clean, like a dispute went down, not a feeding. The boys," he added, motioning toward the exterminators, "will get one helluva adrenaline rush along with a nice hit of coke or reefer. That's a fair compromise. But tourists and locals, if you're going with me, are off limits. Besides, I hear water buffaloes pack a wallop—if you stampede them first."

The robed entities nodded, as did the chairman. The counselor sat slowly, seething, but with no option. The logic of Carlos's argument was rock solid. Yeah, he was definitely getting stronger.

"You are of great value to us, Carlos. Might I suggest that you take a couple of my favorite resources as added insurance . . . something made for special occasions by our Dark Lord on level seven?"

Before Carlos could answer, the chairman dispatched a ceiling transport bat, and Carlos waited for his unspecified resources, trying to stay cool.

A loud commotion beyond the council walls made everyone train their attention towards the sound. Bats screeched in terror, and incessant growls and barks careened through the cavernous space. The front doors flew open, and four super-strength international couriers paired off to restrain the two beasts they held by chains.

Beasts, each with six yellow glowing eyes that ringed the circumference of their huge skulls, stood three feet high at the shoulder, their muscular black chests rippling as they scrabbled against the slippery marble floor to get to Carlos, leaving deep gashes in it as they clawed their way forward. Their jaws were so packed with fangs that they couldn't fully close their mouths, and foamed, slick saliva dripped from them, leaving acid burns in the floor. They flapped their leathery wings, half flying, as they pulled the couriers along the floor, slashing at them with their spaded, double-blade tails.

Almost speechless, Carlos knew he had to rescind the request, "Naw, gentleman. The pit bulls are over the top."

"You don't approve?" The chairman asked with a smile, then sighed. "Next time."

Carlos wasn't sure how to respond. While the offer was generous, this wasn't about a few easily willed creatures that could give him a heads-up with a bark . . . like a coupla security dogs . . . dayum. "Yeah, next time. Thanks, though."

"As I said, Mr. Rivera, it's your mission."

"We all clear?" Carlos waited for heads to nod again.

"Make it happen, and bring our cargo back safely," the chairman said with a sly smile.

But before Carlos could reply, a thunderous rumble made all beings in the room look up at the swirling black messenger cloud that was ever-present in the high, open ceilings of the chamber. Intermittent sound waves sent the swirling mass into a noisy, chaotic screech as domestic couriers in bat form were thrown from the smoky whirlpool, and then reentered it, trying to keep their flight patterns. Red glowing eyes blinked in a frenzy of confusion, as wave after wave of sound shocks disturbed their habitat.

"Oh, shit . . ." Carlos laughed.

"We've been breached at the chamber level!" The chairman stood instantly with the council members. The messengers took battle stances. The hounds raced back into the chamber, flanking the chairman and barking up toward the sound.

Carlos shook his head. "Listen to it. Damn . . . Can't you hear it?"

The other beings shot their gazes to Carlos, but were still on red alert. Carlos closed his eyes. *She's all that* . . . Girlfriend is breaching the breach.

"Explain!" The chairman was in no mood for Carlos's amusement, and snatched the front of Carlos's suit. But confusion loosened his grip as the hounds began to howl.

"All of you, open up on my channel," he murmured. "Your cargo just kicked things up a level."

The Vampire Council came from behind their table, and the armed exterminators formed a ring around them. Carlos extended his hand, placing one on the chairman's shoulder, another on the lead messenger's. He could barely hold his head up as Shabazz's bass line rocked him. He could hear Rider's guitar screaming. A crowd of a hundred thousand was nearly prostrate. He could dig it. The stage was black. Birdcalls and special effects of jaguars roaring had been layered in. Heavy percussion with the bass was breaking the barrier, scattering bats in Hell, a hundred thousand people all jamming, all grooving to the same erotic beat. Drums sounded like thunder. The Vampire Council closed their eyes; the old boys, finally relaxing the hysteria, were catching on.

A sliver of red light hit the stage. Carlos felt the chairman's knees almost give way as the old dude steadied himself against another council member. Then Damali stepped into that crimson splinter, dusted in gold and red glitter. A sheer sheath of blood red netting was all the dress was made of . . . a serpent covering her breasts and her Venus in a barely concealed wrap of embroidery. She wore a high priestess headdress that had coils in it, seeming almost serpentine as the gold and red in it interleaved into an endless spiral.

When she hit the first chord of the song, her voice almost as low as the bass, bats screamed and he shuddered, sending a collective shudder through the assembled group. Moisture came to his eyes. He inhaled deeply. The others did, too, and glanced at each other, stricken by the power of the sensation. Yeah, he remembered. It had only been a few nights.

"God*damn* . . ."

The chairman nodded. The hounds walked in an agitated circle.

Even the counselor shook his head, but the look he issued Carlos cut like a blade inside Carlos's mind.

Unable to dislodge himself from the vision, Carlos listened to the sultry sounds she made. Damali's echoes of lovemaking, a preamble to her lyrics, decimated him. He opened his eyes and his gaze caught the counselor's expression of pure hatred. It was an eerie concoction, Damali's voice juxtaposed with Vlak's venom. Interesting that his hatred competed so virulently with the pull of the Neteru's voice. He didn't know such a thing was possible.

Carlos glanced around at the other men. Each of them, even the chairman, had been thoroughly seduced by her sultry tone. Their eyes were closed, heads slightly leaned back, as though offering their throats for a sure siphon . . . their fangs had lowered, and they seemed to be breathing through their barely parted lips. His line of vision went back to the counselor, who fought against the erotic rush Damali produced, his jaw set hard, and his fangs dropped to battle length, not passion length. Something was wrong.

"Don't you hear me calling . . ." she crooned like he'd never heard her voice before. "Don't you feel me wanting . . . don't you know . . . don't you know . . . ooohhhh, yeaaaah, baby . . . 'cause you know when you do what you do . . . *In the dark* . . . where you do what you do what you do to me, baby . . . Yeeesss . . . I'm calling you, Carlos . . ." she murmured, talking to the cheering crowd, and then resumed her saxophone wail, sliding up and down the octaves with her voice as though it were her hand tracing his spine.

"In the dark . . . blood running through my deep river baby. . . . Sisssss. . . . Ohhhhh. *In the dark,* you feel what you feel when you feel it, baby. . . . Night's not the same without you in me, baby . . ." Then she stepped forward, causing Brazilian police to redouble their efforts, dropped her voice, stretched out her arm, beckoned with one finger, while sliding her other hand in an aching motion down her side. She whispered, the crowd roared, Carlos swallowed hard.

Now she was talking co-modena, cash shit. Was challenging him. Whispering into the mic all sexy, walking to the front of the stage. Carlos shook his head, noting that his council's eyes were slits.

"You know you want this . . . so stop playing with it . . . before it burns you, baby. I can't take it . . . I'm burning up. Need the night to cool it off." She took a deep breath, closed her eyes, leaned her head back and belted out another line full throat. *"In the dark—"*

"I'm out!" Carlos broke from the group. "I told you this package was *da bomb.* Worth any bullshit I gotta go through to protect it. Any questions?" He walked, no longer concerned about the dogs, as the old vampires just looked stunned. An international exterminator stepped forward.

It nodded at its squad, which nodded in return. "We follow your orders . . . Damn . . . You did that?" The exterminator fell back into formation, simply shaking its head.

Carlos gave a brief nod of recognition to the international team. He liked them already. Could hang like his old squad, and were so different from the domestic couriers that got on his nerves. Yeah. Recognize.

The chairman, slightly out of breath, held himself up using the table, glancing at the screeching, disoriented mass of domestic couriers and then the full council. "Give this man *whatever* it takes to contain this cargo! Whatever is required!" He was breathing hard as he tried to make his way back to his throne. "She was doing 'the righteous light acts' before Rivera infected her, now look at her in just ten nights."

Quiet fell over the group as another disruption sent the bats screeching again. The chairman had tears of appreciation in his eyes. His voice was a mere whisper as he stared at Carlos in awe.

"In *just* ten nights, Rivera . . ."

The six-vampire squad simply appeared in the center of the concert throng that was mesmerized by the performance. There was no need to even be smooth. The few people standing nearby started, but obviously assumed that Carlos and his bodyguards had advanced from behind them in the crush of the crowd.

He glanced at his messengers who were immediately hit with the adrenaline rush. "You're showing fangs, and it ain't cool. Chill, blend in, and remember what I said. Not here. We all need to fan out. Give me some space. *Vamanos!*"

Damali's voice was ripping him apart, but he scanned the terrain as his messengers dissolved into nothingness. The adrenaline level of the audience, the sweat, the blood, was making him shaky. It was clear that if Damali performed like this during a ripening, he'd have to kill five guards and take out council. *Shit.* Get-high was everywhere, too. Nearly buzzed, Carlos tried to keep his focus on his only target. Damali.

He'd purposely surfaced deep enough in the crowd that she wouldn't be able to see him because of the angle of the lights. He was pretty sure that she wouldn't be able to sense him, either, if he could just be cool. Chill. Father Patrick was right. He was getting stronger. The old man was also right about another thing, too. The pull to power like this was hard to ignore. Almost as hard to ignore as Damali up there.

The only thing he could hope was that she'd be so engrossed in the performance that she'd be too distracted to pick him up. The scents and vibrations were so intense all around him that, even as a master vampire, with superior tracking capability, he was having a hard time. She would, too. Then, she lifted her head and looked in his direction, again moving to the front of the stage. He let his breath out when she then walked to the other side of it. Yeah, for a moment she'd detected something, but had done a smooth, theatrical recovery.

But girlfriend was wearing that red dress and her voice was like a magnet. However, he was not about to get any closer. Wasn't advisable. Over here, the Covenant's prayer line wasn't a ground wire to keep him anchored. Over here, Damali's compound fortress wasn't a prayer beacon reminder. Over here, there was no distance between him and the call that was kicking his ass. He was going to have to eat soon. Ever since he'd embarrassed himself and had flipped out on her in the woods, he was not going near her. Not like that. Definitely not in front of his squad. He had to conquer that shit, first.

The smell of perspiration-soaked concertgoers perfumed the air and was almost asking too much of his restraint. With that strong vibe coming from the crowd, plus watching Damali holler up onstage, anything could jump off. He just hoped his exterminators could be cool. He sensed for them. They were. Odd. It was as though their transmissions were blocked. Council? Something wasn't right. He then looked back at the stage. Damn, one woman creating all this havoc.

That's right, he had to remember that he was angry with her, too. She'd had some other man all up in her face. Not that he could necessarily blame the brother. However, it was a matter of principle.

Carlos glanced around the audience which was in a state of near hysteria. On the other hand, what was he going to do, off fifty thousand, who all had the same thing running through their minds even while their women and other females swayed to the music beside them? Crazy. He just would not look at the stage, is all. He could hang. But the whiff of Neteru she was sending his way was murder. Yet, it didn't make sense. Damali wasn't ripening, wasn't due for seven more years.

He fought it at first, but then gave in to a deep inhale. The sensation of her scent filled his nostrils, coating his tongue, his throat, and slid down his insides like some sweet, forbidden fruit. He ran his hand over his jaw and ran his tongue over his teeth, holding himself in check. Damali never smelled that thick, that dark, that positively . . .

A female hand traced up his back and touched his shoulder. Startled, he turned abruptly and looked into a pair of dark brown eyes that flickered green. The beauty standing before him was almost his height, and her well-toned arm had the muscular structure of a female bodybuilder. Her skin was flawless, like highly polished mahogany, and her hair was in a hundred jet-black braids that hung down her back. *La vampira*, if he'd ever seen one.

She smiled a half smile of recognition, showing a little fang. Carlos's eyes traveled down her stacked body. All she had on was a crocheted black bra, her coffee-bean-brown, hard nipples peeking at him through sections of it. A sheer black sarong, and what appeared to be a thong under that, covered her from the waist down. He could feel her entering his thoughts, dredging current vocabulary from it. Okay, cool, she was a foreign vamp chick. If she needed vocab to communicate with him, with a body like hers, no problem—even though he didn't generally deal with other females, being hooked up with Damali and all.

Then again, there was something a little primal about her, if not were-demon. It was in the green flicker in her eyes and in the shape of her jaw, which was slightly wider at the chin where lower incisors would be. Always a dead giveaway. But her top incisors were awesome. Vamp all the way.

He studied her ears, which came to a very subtle point and laid back against her skull. If he didn't know better . . . But he wasn't registering anything demon, and his squad hadn't bristled. Nah, she wasn't a were. What she was, was fine as shit. If she had a thing for the were-shapes, that was cool. The old vamps had to stop being so prejudiced. Needed to embrace a few personal choice differences. Not all were-demon forms were disgusting, especially packaged in a vamp body like that.

Conflicted, he hesitated. What was he saying? Was he on crack, or some shit? Vampires *didn't* deal with demons, were-demons, or any other variety. Yet she smelled so fucking good—no demon tracer at all. She smiled and he struggled to remember that . . . he already had a woman . . . the one onstage that had called him up from Hell. So who was this one who was all up in his grille?

Despite his resolve to distance himself from possible trouble, he took his time to enjoy the stranger's ample, firm, melon shaped breasts, and the way her tight waist sported a gold hoop in her sunken navel. Right under it was a silky trail of flat, wispy black hair that dipped under her low-slung sarong. His mouth went dry. The knot in the side of the skirt's fabric exposed a well-curved, well-toned hip. She opened her thigh a bit, and he noted that her equally toned perfect legs were longer than his. Dayumm, she was fine. He studied her face, admiring how her feline, almond-shaped eyes blazed over high, chiseled cheekbones, and her jaw was squared to a strong chin. She arched an eyebrow, and an electric current passed through him, just imagining the bite she could probably deliver.

"Is it later, yet?" she asked in a seductive tone that he could hear despite the ear-splitting decibels of the music.

He'd watched her lush mouth work with the words, and saw the glistening gold ball that pierced her tongue. Damn, it was *her*—the voice that had been in his head, cracking his skull for over a month. Her hand went to his chest. He now had his back completely to the stage. Her palm burned him, sending a scorching heat down his abdomen toward his groin. Face to face, this was definitely some strong vibe. Wasn't shit here to block it. Calling upon his last reserves of discipline, he grabbed her wrist.

"Do I know you?" He'd meant the question to come out with more threat in it, but damn, just look at her.

"Do you have to know me?"

Okay. A player. He could dig it, but now was not the time, if ever.

"Need to know a little somethin', somethin'. I don't just roll like that."

"Oh . . ." she clucked her tongue, coming in closer, and making the ball on it bounce. "I thought your kind was notorious for being down for whatever. Certainly not monogamous."

The statement backed him up. His mind had to adjust. He could hear Damali behind him, crooning her song . . . but he was single, after all. And she had had some guy up in her face. He had never been monogamous in his life, or accused of such slander. This fine woman had just challenged him and called him a punk—knowing he was a master vamp. Was she mad?

She laughed. "My bad," she whispered, her other hand dipping low, stroking the part of him that was rock hard.

"What are you?" he asked, allowing her to touch him for a moment. Then he collected himself enough to halt her stroking. He used his energy to push a small opening in the heaving crowd so he could claim some space and get his head together.

She stepped in closer, and the scent of her was disorienting. Carlos shook his head to clear it. He glanced briefly over his shoulder at the stage. He was smelling Neteru everywhere, and it was making him high. In fact, he was tripping so badly at the moment that he swore he'd caught a whiff of fully ripened Neteru again.

"I'm something you've needed for a long time," she murmured. "And much better than what's up there begging for you with no pride . . . us older women don't go there." She backed up, cocked her head and smiled wider. "Have fun with the little girl for now, but let me know in a couple of nights—or I'll find you again. Don't make me have to look for you. That won't be pleasant."

"Hold up," Carlos said, starting to get pissed off. Nobody told him some shit like that and then walked, fine or not. Plus, he didn't like the disrespect toward Damali. She needed to check herself. "If I'm interested, I'll let you know."

"Whatever," she said coolly. "But when you're done with the young girl, come find a real woman." She sauntered back over to him. "The double plunge I've got will knock your head back." Her voice dropped an octave and her scent thickened around him. "Remember, baby, she can't even bear fangs." She licked his throat before he could stop her, and was gone.

Stunned, he stood there for a moment just looking at where she'd been. This was no ordinary vamp, or average lower-level vapor move. This was some smooth, almost master vampire level shit . . . But she smelled like Neteru? *Ripe Neteru*—that had drugged him out of his mind for a few seconds . . . Enough to make him turn his attention away from Damali? Oh, hell no. This was real crazy. Female master vamp? At council-level strength . . . was there such a thing? No.

Wasn't a female vamp at that rank, yet—no record of anything like that in the territories, especially not in his.

Nuit would have never made one, and he damned sure wouldn't have with Damali near. Council wouldn't make one either, knowing a female Neteru was on the planet. Why, so a master female vamp could off their daywalker vessel? Would never happen. Carlos glanced at the stage. It had to be a second-level vamp. But how in the hell did she get that strong?

Now the shit was really bothering him, because the truth was, she could have telepathically given him a run for his money. Might have taken him, simply because he'd underestimated her as a basic territory female.

He stood there for a moment, becoming outraged. Then he was through—totally outdone. He could not believe that arrogant, fine-assed vamp! Part of him was enraged because the lick had indeed knocked his head back, and left him wobbling, in public, in the middle of a concert stadium. The other half of him was angry with himself for not just brushing her off from the get-go . . . but there was something so slayer about her that it messed him up. But that was impossible. And it pissed him off to no end that she'd made him crave what could never happen . . . a double plunge with Damali.

Carlos tried to shake the image that had replayed itself in his brain too many times. He closed his eyes to try to ward off the sensation, but that only made matters worse. He could almost feel it rock him where he stood. A hot body beneath him, torched with near-climax fever, Neteru in his nose, a beautiful pair of glistening fangs plunging his throat at the same time his scored hers . . . right at the moment of truth . . . a high-velocity rush of blood exchange sending recycled pleasure through both of them at once; two parallel, excruciating pleasure lines burning up atmosphere, dissolving matter till those sensations crossed and atomically fused in one central explosion—*the vanishing point.*

He opened his eyes, mad at himself, mad at the world, angry that he even thought about it, much less fantasized about it. Impossible. He could only take Damali there after she turned . . . What? Uh, uh. Now he was really mad, because he was definitely tripping. She could never turn, and not just because she was council's vessel. It wasn't even about that—not with her.

And, fuck it, he had more willpower than that. So what if a vamp female could go there; he was committed. That's right. He was committed, he reminded himself repeatedly as he regulated his breathing. So what that he'd seen that shit when he sat in a throne seat. Yeah, the thrones had good video, all the knowledge of the line. But he could hang. Just keep that as an intellectual experience. He didn't have to go there and step out on D. He could wait seventy or eighty years till his baby passed away to try it. A shudder rippled through him as the image faded away.

Shit, what was he going to do? Live almost a century as a master being a virgin to *that* experience? Yeah, he could hang, he told himself again firmly. Besides, he'd die in seven if he went with the priests' deal. Carlos tried to make himself laugh it off. Death in seven would be a release from this temptation bullshit, not just his soul's salvation. Maybe in seven, just before Damali ripened, he'd go get a good run out, and give the clerics his head on a silver platter. That way, she wouldn't know, he could get his soul back, and could take his little transgression to the grave. They said if a man repented, all would be forgiven, right?

He looked toward the direction where the female vamp had vanished. He didn't even catch her name. If he found the fine female, and was really sorry after . . . He laughed. Oh, shit. He didn't want to think about any of it. But it was really getting on his nerves to have to deal with it. Damn choices! He didn't need variables like that in his life.

His annoyance turned itself to Damali. This was all her fault. If she had chilled, let him stay in LA, had kept her ass in the States, hadn't started a buncha shit with some guy over here. If she hadn't done this freaking concert! What's more, if she hadn't called him like that. By what right did she have to put their personal business in the streets, huh? He could feel himself getting whipped into a total tirade as she went down on her knees on the stage and the audience hit a new level of frenzy. Carlos closed his eyes.

She was too passionate. She was working on the wrong side of his brain. She was messing with his control factor. The crowd was too hyped. He had ripe Neteru in his system, musta been a contact high from the stage. He could feel his gums ripping he wanted her so much.

Unable to stop himself, he turned and looked at her. He shoved his hands in his pockets to keep from seeing them tremble. Man . . . when he got backstage, he was gonna tell her ass off!

Champagne bottles spilled their foam essence across the floor as Rider sloshed it, taking a laughing swig from one in each hand. The sound of all the corks going off was like the pop-pop of gunfire. Big Mike and Shabazz leveraged their weight against the door, closing off a hundred flashbulbs. The media had been shut out. Damali and Marlene slapped high fives, and Dan poured overflowing paper cups of semi-warm champagne for the group. Jose was rubbing JL's head and laughing, while JL play-boxed him within the stadium locker room.

"Did we take Brazil, people, or what?" Rider opened his arms wide and jumped up on a locker bench.

"We rocked da house, man!" Big Mike yelled, snatching a bottle from Rider.

"Y'all worked it," Damali said laughing.

"No, li'l sis, you *wurked* it. Daaaaayum," Shabazz said, getting a swig of Big Mike's bottle.

"No lie, D," Jose said, pounding Shabazz's fist. "Baby girl owned the stadium!"

"Right," Dan was yelling from his position by the lockers. "I can't wait to see the ink on this tomorrow. The media hype is gonna be crazy."

"Mad-crazy," Marlene agreed.

Damali watched them all, and laughed, but felt like a spectator as well. From a remote part of her mind, pure defeat claimed her. Marlene picked up on the vibe, but kept her smile bright, easing toward Damali.

"We were ridiculous, gang," Damali repeated, trying to convince herself.

But as the words came out of her mouth, the group went still. Swirling energy made papers fly, cups turn over, instruments fall, and a couple of bulbs in the makeup mirror blow. It was like a giant storm had been unleashed in the locker-dressing room, and it took a few seconds for her team to mentally switch gears and try to scramble to assemble weapons. Black smoke rose from the floor, and in the center of it Carlos appeared.

He didn't even take a breath as he began to pace. "I'll tell you what's fucking ridiculous, Damali, is to ever see my woman perform some, some—I don't know what you call it, but it reached Hell and back!"

The entire team stared at him, mouths agape.

"Yo, Carlos, uh—"

"Shut up, Rider! This is between me and her!"

Damali's hand found her hip. She looked him up and down. Had the nerve to be coming in here all fly, wearing a damned black linen Versace suit, serving a damned cranberry collarless raw silk shirt like he was out where he shouldn't have been . . . oh, she'd kick his ass. . . .

"Where have *you* been? Let's start there."

Carlos slapped the center of his chest, bearing full fangs, and walking in a wider circle. "Where have I been? Where have I been!"

"Is there an echo in the room? I said—"

"Where have *you* been? Huh? A couple of weeks, and I'm in my lair tasting the sweat of some other man after you've been off doing the Lambada! Are you insane? While I'm on parole, and shit—trying to stay away from a body count over here!"

A locker took the brunt of the blow, caving in as Carlos punched it while stalking past it. Black smoke still hung in the air, and Damali's eyes widened. Oh, shit. Not good. But she wasn't hearing no yang. "Where were you, then, so that I didn't have to call you like that?"

He walked away from her. The team started backing up, mumbling and looking for a quick exit. This was between her and Carlos. Marlene crossed her arms and folded them over her chest with a smirk. Yeah, yeah, yeah, he could be angry if he wanted to, but she wanted a response. Mar had told her to send a shock wave subterranean, and it got his attention. Good.

"I was worried sick about you, and you just vanished into the night. What was I supposed to do? Just sit back and—"

"You were supposed to respect what I told you, woman."

"What?" Both hands found her hips. "I don't know who you think you're talking to but—"

"I missed you so much that it didn't make sense. I had to go find my old lair in Beverly Hills to chill out, or the old guys in the cabin would have been toast! Shit, Damali, your ass is so stubborn!"

He paced away from her and the team's heads pivoted from Damali back to Carlos as though watching a tennis match. Marlene didn't help matters by grunting and nodding in agreement with her. Oh, so her mom was on her side, too. Women!

Damali let her breath out hard. "All right, Carlos. My bad."

"Damn straight, your bad. Do you know I had to bring international messengers with me—five, burly, WWF-looking, second-generation, *exterminator* vamps from outlying neutral territories to make it through the tunnels?"

Damali covered her mouth.

"That's right," he said pointing toward the door. "Five sons-abitches I have to keep on a short leash while I'm over here, lest we have a topside international incident! And I'm not all that stable myself . . . all 'cause I missed you so bad."

He stood there in front of her, taking in deep gulps of air, too ashamed by the admission, especially in front of the other men. He gave Rider a glare that warned him about the peril of his throat if a sarcastic comment came up from it. Big Mike was cool enough to look away, and Shabazz could dig it. The man started packing gear like nothing had happened. Jose started picking up cups from the floor with Dan, and JL just sat there in shock. *Whatever.*

"I'm going to go eat, and then I'm gonna crash, and then I'm going back to LA. I just came to be sure you were all right. Apparently you are, so I'm out." He turned to leave, but could feel Damali walk up behind him. Her hand touched his shoulder, and the tremor it sent through him was just as she'd said, ridiculous. But he felt her stiffen, and it made him look at her.

"Where have you been?" she asked, backing away from him.

The team went still. Shabazz discreetly found his gun and nodded at Big Mike. Carlos began backing up. All rage wilted.

"Baby, I was, right here, at the concert. You felt me, right?" His hands were out in front of him, but he glanced at the guys who were shaking their heads. All the brothers knew this stance. Marlene had folded her arms over her chest.

"You were at this concert, saw me on my knees in front of a crowd of a hundred thousand, and you ignored me?" Damali's comment had begun at a low, threatening timbre, issued from behind her teeth and rose to a full holler as she finished the sentence.

"No, no, I wasn't ignoring you," Carlos said fast. "I was trying to chill. I was trying to—"

"Push up on a demon! You're trailing sulfur! And it's female!" Damali's eyes narrowed as she turned on her heel and started grabbing up costumes, flinging her headpiece and then kicking a chair out of her way.

"She wasn't a demon, D. You know I don't roll like that. She was a second-generation vamp . . . just part of the territory females. Baby, for real—"

"Aw, man . . ." Big Mike murmured. "Brother . . ."

"Least you could have taken a shower first," Rider mumbled. "Young, dumb, and fulla—"

"It wasn't all that," Carlos argued, his glance going between the guardians and Damali. This was bullshit. He had to talk to her *and* her big brothers? He tried to get near her now that they'd lowered weapons, but she shrugged his hand off of her shoulder and spun on him.

"Don't you touch me! Don't even think about it. How could you?" She turned away and held her arms around herself. "All I did was go out dancing, but you—"

"I didn't. I swear, girl," he said in a gentle voice.

You thought about it real hard though, Damali thought, her anger building.

"Wait!" Marlene walked forward, between Damali and Carlos, and the team gathered around.

"Carlos," Marlene said in a steady voice. "What did this she-demon look like, and where was she when you saw her?"

He shrugged, and didn't feel like talking about this in front of the team. "I keep telling y'all, she was a vamp—and it wasn't what you think." He didn't have to answer to anybody there, not even Damali. Besides, they had it all twisted. She wasn't a demon. He started walking away. He and the exterminators could just go eat, and then jet back to the States before daybreak.

"Carlos," Marlene repeated in a firm voice. "Neteru is the only thing that would have gotten you so buzzed and Damali isn't in cycle. We need a description, so we can deal with it."

He looked at Marlene as Damali went to stand by her side.

"Men are so stupid," Damali whispered and shook her head. She turned away. "What did she look like?"

Carlos kept his eyes on Marlene, intermittently glancing over to Damali's back. How did one describe this other woman in front of his own woman and her family, to the degree that he needed to? What, he was supposed to just tell all in front of guardian brothers and a seer who wasn't having it? The point was moot, anyway. This was just a very fine vamp that had gotten him in a very sticky situation.

But the situation called for diplomacy, because he certainly didn't want Damali to bug any more than she was already. She was hurt, and all he wanted to do was privately apologize. Hurting her had never been his intention. But, they had a point. Girlfriend had showed up at the concert. And he wondered how she'd gotten past the lights and prayers. If this devious, jealous female vamp was stalking Damali and the team, they had a right to know.

"She's tall," Carlos said slowly. "Near my height." Damali didn't turn around and he was glad she didn't, or she would have seen the guys issue appreciative glances toward each other.

He could feel Damali attempting to pry his mind open, but on this one, it was black box, need-to-know basis only. He wasn't budging.

"Dark brown, green eyes—flicker yellow . . . yeah, they glow," he said, answering the unspoken group question. "Built," he added casually. "You know . . . uh, athletic. Long, black hair in braids down her back, high cheekbones. Aw'ight-looking woman," he added to minimize the sting.

Big Mike silently made brick-house proportions discreetly for Carlos who just nodded. Big Mike nodded. A silent understanding passed between them. Carlos closed his eyes. He and Mike shared the same taste in women. But this was humiliating.

"What else?" Mar said with a tone of disgust.

"Uh, she was wearing black. One of those bra things, and a sheer skirt—thong under it. Pierced navel, gold hoop."

Damali turned around. "You got close enough to see her navel, did you?"

Carlos swallowed as she slowly walked up to him.

"So where did you meet her, huh? I think it's really interesting how you couldn't even give me the courtesy of a call back but then show up in a big puff of smoke, outraged that I've been dancing with another man. Well, you need to check that and tell us what we need to know about this female."

He stared at her, seeing that heat in her eyes, and felt joy bloom inside him. The fact that she was so outraged, cared so much that he might have potentially been with somebody else, had actually claimed him as her one and only, did something to him. It was like he was watching her mouth move, but that's all he could focus on. The shape of it, the blaze in her eyes. The way her head went from side to side as her finger wagged with her complaint, one hand on her hip in the to-die-for dress. He smiled.

Damali's eyes narrowed.

"This shit ain't funny, Carlos! Answer the question!"

"Which one?" He was not being smart. For the life of him he couldn't remember what they were arguing about. He had a villa in the hills, fully stocked bar, Jacuzzi, all baby had to do was chill . . .

"Which one?"

He was just coming out of the trance when lightning struck his face and dazed him. She was standing there, breathing hard, about to cry. The team held their breaths. She'd slapped the taste out of his mouth. He didn't know what possessed him, but his hands went to the sides of her face, and he pulled her in close. His head tilted, and he kissed her as hard as he needed to. Right there, no pretense. No shame. Just like she'd crooned for him in front of an audience. Whatever. They were wasting time.

He let her go and she covered her heart with her hand for a moment.

"I wasn't with her like that. Can't you tell? She was tracking down sloppy seconds from the jones I had for you. She rolled up on me, not the other way around. She made an offer; I refused. Period. Drop it. Now you wanna get out of here, or what?"

"Carlos, listen," Marlene said fast. "Both of you listen—just for once. There's another entity out there that's possibly stronger than either one of you right now, and she's twisted. From what I can gather, she was at this concert site."

"Marlene, you're bugging. That female is fronting like she's a master vamp wannabe—and ain't hardly stronger than me. Damali can take her, too—"

"Not if she's been able to co-opt and reproduce the one thing that you have practically no immunity to. The scent."

Carlos glanced away from Marlene's probing eyes. "They only make one real Neteru every millennium, remember? Damali's it," Carlos said in a low timbre, staring at Damali who looked at him like he was dinner. "I can handle that situation. That's why I came up here with a squad. If Damali wants to go with me, I'll have her at the hotel before sunrise. Y'all just watch your backs. Second-level females are generally spiteful and have a bad temper when they don't get their way—girlfriend didn't get nothing, so she might have a case of the ass . . . real attitude."

The look Damali issued him was so intense, so desire-filled, yet so torn, that it made him go still. He could feel it through his skin the way she wanted to be with him. Something had definitely kicked up a notch. He wasn't sure if it was the song, seeing Damali openly, without shame, give him her all, or what, but Marlene's worries about some lower-level female that was supposed to have cornered some Neteru scent was bouncing off his eardrums and falling on the floor right about through here.

"Am I hearing you right, Rivera?" Rider asked slowly, quietly, no play in his tone. "You've got a team of five vampires on steroids, just up from Hell, supposedly going to watch our backs?" Rider walked toward him, suddenly grabbed his arm, and looked him in the eyes. "Are you fucking nuts?"

Carlos just looked at Rider's hand until he removed it. "They're my squad. They follow my orders. I told 'em no eating in town, and not to touch a hair on your heads. Even the priests are under the safety mark. My order."

"You hear yourself, man?" Shabazz stepped in near Rider. "You're high. You ain't making sense. Never in history has a guardian or a Covenant team gotten a mark of safety from the vampire nations."

"Never in history has a Neteru placed a call down to Hell, made the courier bats lose orbit in the Vampire Council's supreme chamber, or sent bass-line at a concert down to disturb our transport systems." His gaze was on Damali as he spoke to Shabazz, and he loved the fact that she'd smiled. "You walk a bad bass, brother. They heard it . . . just like they heard my baby wailing up here . . . messed the old boys up—slayed 'em. Just like she's killing me, right now. I'll bring her home before tomorrow morning. My word."

"Isn't there a soul in here concerned about the fact that we're dealing with an entity that is mirroring the most potent aspect of the Neteru defense system?" Marlene threw up her hands and began walking around the room. "Is it me, people?"

"She can't front Neteru," Carlos argued, still focused on Damali. "If female vamps could do that, they'd all conjure it. Besides, even if I wasn't hooked up with D, I wouldn't roll with girlfriend. She's got a freaky side, likes to live on the edge of danger—saw her hanging down in the badlands on level five in Hell . . . probably transformed into something and cast the illusion that she was in heat to keep 'em from killing her . . . mighta even done the unthinkable and got with a couple were-wolves or were-jags, who knows? The chick is nuts. That's where the sulfur probably came from. But if council catches her ass doing black-blood exchanges, shit. That ain't my problem. Her choice. If she did, though, and she's in my zones, I'll have to dust her myself."

He glanced at the men on the team. "Some shit is just unnatural, and at council level, a black-blood exchange with were-demons is a capital offense. Feel me?"

"You met her down there?" Damali was twirling the end of a lock around her finger, and looking at the floor when she spoke.

"Yeah. Wasn't no thing," Carlos said, moving closer to her. Damali's quiet tone and the sad look in her eyes had stopped the other guardians from asking more, and he was glad it did. He didn't want to talk to them; he wanted to talk to her. Privately. They needed to nip this argument in the bud, and squash it. But he knew he had to tell her something that would make her willing to go with him, and definitely needed to tell her people something so they wouldn't talk her out of it. Complex.

"Baby, I was checking out the levels," he said calmly, trying to sound rational as he explained. "I was doing some undercover work, trying to see if there was any link between the deaths in the news, and anything down sub, but she pushed up on me on level five. I declined. Came here to be sure my baby was safe. She must have tracked me here and tried me in the crowd; I blew her off. End of story. That's it. My boys can handle a vamp female, if she's that stupid to go after a guardian team . . . and after I brushed her off, I don't think she is. Only Neteru I got in my nose is you, baby."

"Oh, Lord have mercy," Marlene sighed, plopping down on a bench in defeat. "Gentlemen, get your weapons. Hopefully that's all it is . . . Carlos would know. He's the only one that can truly detect actual Neteru presence—and if the man swears that this is just a general female vamp, we have to go with it. For now." Marlene looked at him hard. "But if you are wrong, and you put Damali in harm's way, a possible were-jaguar demon is the last thing you'll have to worry about. In fact, the Vampire Council will have to send up a rescue-and-recovery team to find the body parts I will separate from you, understood, Carlos?"

"Yes, ma'am. And if she's not still angry at me," Carlos said with a sheepish grin, "I'll have Damali back at the hotel before it gets light." He looked at Damali who had a wide grin on her face. "You mad at me?"

She shook her head no.

"You miss me?"

She nodded. "You heard me all the way down there?"

He nodded.

"You miss me?"

He smiled.

Before she could say another word, he sent a burst of energy from within him. The air in the room swept lightweight objects into a tornado swirl, Damali was in his arms, and they were gone.

She landed on her feet still pressed against Carlos's chest. She stared at him, backed away a bit, and gaped at the environment. "You're stronger. I can feel a different kind of energy running through you. It's darker, Carlos . . . and I'm worried."

He nodded. "There's a lot of stuff I can do now, baby, that's gonna rock your world. You have no idea. I'm just coming into my own."

She glanced around the outrageously decadent villa he'd brought her to. The tone of his voice made her wary. Things were fine before. She wasn't sure she liked this new aspect of him.

"How far away from the stadium are we?"

This move, while romantic, was seriously disconcerting. He was definitely stronger, she kept repeating in her mind like a mantra. There was no safe house with prayer lines nearby. Her Isis blade was at the stadium. Things were going down in a foreign land, and she was separated from her team, her family. This man seemed a little close to the edge. He looked at her differently than he had before, way carnal. Way more passion in the vibration. Dark passion.

"About eight miles away," he murmured, "in the hillside of Jardim

Botanico. Driving, it's farther, because of the roads . . . but we're not that far from the hotel the way I can get you there."

He stalked toward her, watched her back up, looking hunted. He loved it. She was playing with his mind. She had no idea. If she had been ripening on him, she would have gotten pregnant tonight. Period. There was no decision.

"Uh, wow. Eight miles, huh? You couldn't project four between the safe house cabin and the compound not so long ago. Then, you were able to manifest objects like a car, and transform rooms. Seems like each night, you get more and more power, especially after you go subterranean." She was talking fast and walking around the room, glancing at furnishings, but not losing sight of his proximity to her. "This is so cool, beautiful breeze, the bed, the moon, candles, tile floors. This stuff looks permanent, not like the illusions you cast in the cleric's place. Grates must come down at dawn, huh, to cover the deck and windows? Like the fireplace," she said dodging to a fireplace poker. "Maybe we could start it?"

He snapped. The fireplace lit. He didn't say a word. She didn't put down the poker.

"Tell me about this chick."

He shook his head no. "I don't want to even think about that right now."

His eyes flickered then went solid red, and she walked further out of his reach, holding the poker as she passed gorgeous marble furnishing with slate tables, wrought-iron chairs with sumptuous velvet seats, and hopped over the inland stream that ended in the far corner of the room into a waterfall and sunken Jacuzzi. She was not so much interested in this potential female vamp threat as she was monitoring the change going on with him. Carlos seemed darker, less himself, and definitely more dangerous.

There were even more black spots in his mind that were sealed, old places she'd never been locked out of before. What was that about? And while she could actually feel his hands on her, sending excruciating pleasure through her, a part of her was on guard, yet she didn't know why. Plus he'd lied to her by omission and had tried to block her second sight to what was going on here. Maybe it was the way his eyes hunted her? He'd looked at her like that before in the woods that night. Yet, this was different. It made her uncomfortable. There was something about it that made her know he might just go all the way on her and flip this time.

"Are you hungry?" he murmured, his eyes half closed, his nostrils flaring ever so slightly as she walked around the edges of the room. "You need dinner . . . something to drink?"

She was gonna need all her strength tonight. No doubt. And if she lived till morning from what he was going to lay on her, then she'd definitely needed to eat . . . especially when he woke up—hungry.

She stalled. "Yeah. I'm starved."

He didn't immediately answer her. "Yeah. So am I." His voice was even. His tone lethal. His shaft was so hard it was sending spasms through his groin that she could feel across the room.

"Then maybe you should make a run, you know. I mean, before, we had the monks, the refrigerators, everything was—"

"Cool."

"Yeah. Everything was real cool."

He nodded. He tried to collect himself. This was Damali. He had to remember that. He loved her.

"Before I go make a run, what do you feel like eating?"

She shrugged. "I don't know. They use a lot of red meat here—" She stopped midsentence. "It's hard to get vegetarian stuff here, is what I'm saying."

"I know." He closed his eyes and breathed in deeply. "Tell me the dish, and I'll make it so." Why was she baiting him?

"Better yet," she said fast, monitoring his intensity, "you go eat, and after you're cool, I might have made up my mind."

"Good idea." His statement was issued from his throat, and in a blink he was air and gone.

Damali's shoulders dropped two inches. Her hands were shaking. What was that shit? He'd looked at her like he'd turn her into a vamp—just outright flat-line her. She walked back and forth within the cliff lair. No way down, no way out, no roads for miles, only option was to try to climb a cliff at night in a red concert dress and heels? It was like an eagle's nest! *This was insane.* She should have never called him to Brazil. She shouldn't have called him here like that. There was too much stimulation. He was high . . . Oh Lord.

She neared the edge of the bed. How long could they keep this mess going on, anyway? Vampires were renowned for their constant need for sex—seduction was their middle name. Plus, if he was getting stronger, pretty soon, docile deer in the States, or picking off a cow from a rancher from time to time was not going to work. The monks' blood wasn't working, obviously. Boss hadn't even come with a supply, and was freelancing, *in Rio?*

Seven years of this? What was she talking about, seven years? There was no guarantee that she'd make it, he'd make it, or what would happen after that. Homeboy might turn to dust, for all she knew. Not even the old Templar knew. This crap had never been done before.

The entire inside of her skull was splitting. She finally sat down on the edge of the huge futon bed that had an indoor, pristine stream running around it. She gazed at it with both awe and profound grief. It was decadently set so that one could easily roll right off of the mattress into the turquoise pool that was as wide as the bed. If they wanted to, they could make love all the way toward the waterfall in the room, slip over that and land in a hot tub. She had to hand it to the vamps; when it came to pleasure, they went all out.

Marlene had tried to warn her before she and Carlos ever took that first plunge. Their eyes glowed red because it was the primal center of the chakra system covering the reproductive organs . . . just like the gold tone ruled the stomach and gall center. Red for passion and anger, deep gold for hunger and indignation. Lighter gold as you moved up the torso. Green ruled the heart—either love or the green-eyed monsters, which were jealous-hearted creatures. The demon realms didn't produce eye colors that went above the middle chakra, the heart chakra, where the spiritual side of the soul took over.

Mar said it, said it, said it. She wished she had Madame Isis, and could see the jewels in the handle of her blade. Oh, man, Carlos hadn't flickered gold tonight. Brother went pure red. She peered down at her dress—and she'd called him from the Vampire Council table, to Rio, of all freaking places in the world, in a red dress? Damali just shook her head. Got him to the point were he went *there* to get an escort? Didn't trust himself around the Covenant that saved him? Had studied Shabazz and Big Mike for a minute in the locker room, already having tasted their blood? Was she crazy?

These creatures were truly organized, too. International transport?

Borrowed lairs like freakin' timeshares? Armed couriers? Probably stocked fridge—but Carlos didn't want what was in it. Needed a hit of adrenaline. What was he going to do, stampede a herd of buffalo out there or something? Crazy. Suddenly she wanted to cry.

CHAPTER SIXTEEN

MUCH BETTER than venison. Chasing down a herd and cornering a huge beast that fought hard to live was so much better than the deer begging him with their eyes not to attack before bolting. He loved the primal feel, the power behind his capability to shape shift. Though he wouldn't do it in front of Damali anymore, since it bugged her out.

Damn, he hadn't even gone all the way, and she'd freaked. That was cool. Some things she didn't need to see. There were plenty of other pleasures he could expose her to that he hadn't even draped on her yet, guaranteed to blow her mind. He chuckled just thinking about a few options. She'd liked that mist thing, though . . . touching everywhere at once, turning the entire surface of her skin into one aching erogenous zone, then materializing inside her on a hard thrust. She'd definitely liked that. He shook his head.

Still, there was nothing like the big cats. A part of him could understand the female vamp's proclivity for it, although hanging on level five was a little over the top. But that realm did have some fantastic shit to draw from. Yeah, he liked panther.

Wolves were cool, too. He'd tried that shape once or twice. But he was more of a panther kind of guy. They rolled solo. But if her team ever came into such power as to be able to transform, he imagined Damali's guardians more as wolf types, a group, a pack. Cool people. Hung tight as a strategic unit. He liked them, and respected that about them.

But his baby was definitely all panther. Not because of the way she hung tight with family; that was not a panther trait. It was the way she moved that gave him a jungle-cat image of her . . . feline, agile. A huntress. No, not a panther, but rather a lioness. Fought with ferocity. Was loyal. *Loved* pleasure, could give it and take it all night. Regal. Yeah. A young queen. That's what his Leo baby was. Golden colored.

Sexy as hell . . . Damn, if she could bear fangs . . . He immediately banished the thought.

It was dangerous to even go there, thinking of any of them as an extension of his vampire life. It had to be the environment, and the simple fact that he'd never turned a single soul into a vampire. Maybe one night? No. He was serving time and on a mission to reclaim his soul. That would not be forgiven. An affair, maybe they'd turn a blind eye . . . but if he jacked a human, all bets were off.

Decisions, decisions, and forbidden knowledge dangling before him that was so tempting. He smiled, thinking of Eve. Had he been in the Garden, he mighta had to take a bite of apple, too. Wasn't all her fault. Shit, if Adam couldn't hang, what was the sister supposed to do? All she wanted was learn from a master, and the guy who came to teach her was the best in the business. Girlfriend got a bad rap.

Carlos sighed and looked up at the full moon. Knowledge acquisition was in his nature as a vampire. What did they want from him? At the base of all power was extreme knowledge. At the core of every vampire was a hunger for power, which rivaled their thirst for blood, and their razor-sharp minds siphoned and absorbed new information like a sponge. That was what they were, as an entity—siphons, Carlos reasoned. Even their language, *Dananu,* meant "to be strong." Its roots were in ancient Babylonian, the true first language of his kind—pure decadence, and it morphed and updated every time a new master was added to the lines, bringing knowledge to the collective body at council, which then drank it all in like fresh blood.

To not know, through experience, what a double plunge felt like . . . or what pleasure a turn bite could explode within him, was torture. And he'd come to a dangerous place in a very dangerous frame of mind, loving the complexity of living on the edge, while also hating it—not good. But the polarities of his life drew a tension line through it that was highly erotic.

Yeah, Brazil was dangerous because of her polarities. It was an erotic epicenter of tensions held in check by a fragile, taunt thread. Just like him. The very ground throbbed with a different type of energy. Sensual energy. Passionate battles. Rich, black earth. Crime, poverty, and wealth living in extremes side by side. Horrible pollution and factory encroachment. Wilderness still uninhabited—virgin. Like him in so many ways . . . unexplored regions in his own darkness. The Amazon running through it like a serpent . . . rain forests that provided a third of the world's air supply.

He breathed in the wondrous, unpolluted air, licked the remains of blood off his paw, flexed his claws, stopped, smelled the air again, and turned his head to the side.

"Save me any?" a husky female voice purred, loping in his direction, her green-gold eyes glistening in the night.

Carlos remained very, very still. She circled him, edging toward his kill. He snarled, she purred deeper. Her black coat glistened with moonlight shards of blue.

"Mind if I have some of your leftovers . . . since, like you commanded, I'll have to take sloppy seconds these days?" Her voice was low and sultry, inviting.

His eyes narrowed, and he loped away from her. This bitch was in his head, blocking Damali. He could feel it as she was speaking to him. Probably why he'd been close to the edge earlier, too. No wonder D was acting so weird when they got to the lair. His baby was walking the perimeter of the room like he'd attack her or something. Perhaps she had sensed the presence of something trying to take hold of him, enter and bend his will to deliver a turn bite, but couldn't place her finger on it—especially coming from him. Carlos snarled.

"Couldn't hang, could she?" the female said, edging closer to him than was advisable.

He snarled again, swatted at the female vamp to back her up, then got a whiff of her and pinned her under all fours, his jaws over her throat, warning her. He could taste Neteru on the back of his tongue, along with a slight hint of sulfur that made him release his jaws. The combination was disorienting. Half of him tensed, ready for a were-demon taken down, the other side of him was ready to begin a full-fledged vamp-on-vamp seduction. Hard core. He let her go and just glared at her, but still kept her pinned beneath, deciding.

She laughed, catching him off guard, and transforming into a naked woman right under him. He couldn't move, and felt his shape slowly shifting into man.

"Listen, I got somebody, okay?"

"Don't we all?"

She touched his chest, and he was surprised to find that it was bare. The sensation she sent through him lowered his incisors.

"She burned you, baby. You've suffered a lot for her, and she doesn't appreciate it. Made you miss your chance to rule the world, and has you in agony every moment of your existence . . . I can give you hot daylight like you've never imagined." She traced a searing line around the outer edges of his scar with her tongue. "Take me to the vanishing point, lover, and I promise you, you won't ever look back."

His arms were trembling under his own weight, but he knew it wasn't from the push-up. It started when she arched, dropped fang, and the moonlight glinted off them.

"Seven more years before she'll grow up. Think about it."

"How'd you conjure Neteru?" he murmured, knowing that he should just roll off her, but at the moment was transfixed.

"I'll tell you, later," she whispered hoarsely, then nipped his shoulder, sending a mild shudder through him. "You like it?"

"Yeah," he said on a deep inhale. "But that's not the point."

She allowed her hand to trail down his abdomen as she tangled her legs around his. "Isn't the prime directive of all master vampires . . . pure . . . pleasure?"

He swallowed hard. There was no arguing that. He pushed her braids over her shoulder as she closed her eyes and offered him her throat. Immediately, the urge to sink into her sopping valley was almost as great as his thirst for the blood in her jugular. It was the false scent she emitted. But how did she collect and transmit it? Not even council-level master vamps could corner and hold the fragrance. And certainly no mere second-level female vamp had ever been able to. His scar tingled. She opened her eyes.

"Talk to me," he whispered. "Where did you come from? What makes you think you can push up on a master vampire after he's told you no, and not lose your throat?"

It annoyed him that he was breathing hard and she was smiling. When she gripped him tightly in her hand, he drew a sharp gasp and closed his eyes. Yeah, he was gonna have to repent.

"I come from here," she murmured. "But that's ancient history, and you know the last thing you feel like doing right now is talking to me."

He nodded, that was no lie. But the thin thread that held him back from entering her was the need for knowledge. Information was power, and if a female vamp in his territory had figured out how to conjure ripened Neteru, *that* was *absolute* power in his realm. He kissed her shoulder, buying time, ignoring her moan. It meant he'd have a substance that not even council could manufacture without killing their vessel.

His mind attacked the puzzle, coming away with an opportunity in its grasp. He nipped down on her collarbone and then looked at her hard, his gaze traveling down her voluptuous body. If this babe had a stash of Neteru, and she was a female in his territory obliged to follow his orders, then just before Damali ripened there was a chance to set up a decoy. Very interesting, and very powerful. Didn't she know that power was the most potent aphrodisiac among vampire men? Finding out the answer to her secret would be a discovery more satisfying than cuming. He rolled off her and took several deep inhalations.

"What's wrong?" she asked in a breathless murmur.

He smiled. Damn she was fine, but she had something more important that he needed. "You never answered my question."

She smiled. "Curiosity killed the cat." Her hand slid down her belly and disappeared between her legs. Her eyes held his then slowly closed as she let out a quiet gasp.

He chuckled. She was pulling out all the stops. Had gone succubus on him. She had filled his shaft and made pre-cum ooze. He loved the challenge of it. Master-to-strong-female in a mental duel of seduction. Brand new shit that he'd never tried . . . never had to go this extreme. It was so thoroughly titillating to his most sensitive erogenous zone—his mind. Damali didn't require that of him, their bond was different, pure passion. This was a power struggle of the most erotic kind. He'd never allow a female vamp to best him at the foundation of his vampiric skill set.

"Oh, but, baby," he said in a deep resonating tone designed to run all through her. "Satisfaction brought him back." He sent a hard phantom thrust into her, then pulled it out real slow, making her arch and look at him with hunger. Shit, this was *his* game—and he was master of it.

She rolled over and pushed herself up on all fours, and glanced over her shoulder at him with a sly smile. Her pendulous breasts swayed and the moonlight struck her back and covered her ass like a glistening splatter of pale blue paint. She was breathing through her mouth and he could see the little gold ball on her tongue bounce with each inhale. "You know . . ." she purred, allowing her voice to emanate from her chest like a cat's, "she can't take a panther love bite."

Okay, now it was on. She'd made him stop breathing for a second.

"Vampires can only heal the normal puncture wound and maybe the bruises around it in humans," she said, low and throaty as she dipped her spine and crouched closer to the ground. "But if you get rough, and accidentally get carried away, you could break her shoulder with the impact from your jaws." She licked her lips and then whispered. "I can regenerate, baby. She can't. Go for it. You know you want it."

He would not allow her to see him swallow hard. That she'd used Damali's phrase pissed him off to no end, but he let it slide to trap her with her own drama.

"I know," he said, licking her with sensation from where he sat. "That's why I'm here with you. Just show me how you make Neteru. I won't tell." He opened her with his tongue, and traced her sphincter with it. "Come on, baby . . . why you making us suffer like this?"

Then he looked at the moon and made the sensation instantly go away. "You ever been with a master that's hyped on Neteru?" He glanced at her and mentally captured her hips with both hands as he studied his nails, allowing the sensation to trace each ample cheek as he dragged his palms down them and opened them hard. "It's an experience. Trust me. And girlfriend could hang."

"It's not important where it's made, as long as I wear it for you, right?" she said on a ragged breath, looking at him eagerly, but then closed her eyes as he mentally came to her and bit her. "I'll show you . . . after . . . just . . ."

"I want to know now," he said, then shape-shifted and growled low in his throat and began stalking her. It was with no small measure of satisfaction that her voice caught and she shape-shifted for him with tears of desire in her eyes.

In two fast lunges, he'd pounced her, pinned her, and had bitten her shoulder without breaking the skin. The sound that came up from her insides almost messed him up, and had almost made him stop playing with her. He shook off the shudder, licked her throat hard, and raked her side with a claw, then let her go. "Talk to me."

He stood up and walked away transformed and put on a pair of leather pants—just to help him focus. He blocked out the sound of her short pants, and flattened her on her back, forcing her to shape-shift back into a woman. In his mind he envisioned her navel ring and sucked it.

"All right. Shit." She sat up and wrapped her arms around her knees.

For a moment neither of them said a word. The atmosphere was thick with their scents, but her Neteru fragrance was giving way to a definite hint of sulfur. He could feel her tensing behind him while trying to come down from the duel. He had to admit that he was glad she gave in when she did. A couple more rounds, and he might have had to concede.

"Why do you always have a hint of sulfur trailing you?" he asked, honing in on the scent that stripped his desire for her. "If I didn't know better . . ."

"No," she said, standing. "It's not what you think."

He stared at her hard, no amusement in his eyes. If he'd been going one on one with some fucking were-demon . . .

"Okay. I go to level five a lot," she said quietly. "I felt you when you passed through." She looked up at him, but kept her distance. "All-male, knocked my head back, made me come out to investigate what new master had come down from topside."

She was pissing him off. Stroking his ego would work about as good as stroking his dick at this point.

"What's a fine female like you doing down on five in the were-realms?" He crossed his arms, becoming outraged at the thought of it. "From my fucking territory, too. Total disrespect. I ought not even consider—"

"Baby, listen," she said fast. "Okay . . . I know it's not done. But, I'm a second-generation, two-hundred-year-old vampire. There is not much in the world that easily rocks my boat. What haven't I seen or heard or done? The council forbids many things but we lower gens have to find our amusement somewhere . . . as well as our power."

She looked down. "The last thing on most masters' and certainly the council members' mind is the amusement of their lower gens—that is, as long as they don't find out about them." She shrugged. "Besides, I was made by Nuit, so I guess I am a little . . . twisted."

He unfolded his arms and raked his fingers through his hair, and then let his breath out hard. What could he say to that? Nuit had a lot of strange shit going on topside, and his bites had demon hybrid all in them. Foul motherfucker . . . and turned a woman this fine into a serious freak? He halfway felt sorry for her. Carlos shoved his hands in his pockets and just stared at her.

"Aw'ight," he said, finally relaxing. "But how do you keep the weres from attacking you? That shit is dangerous, and also way out of order—not sanctioned. You know they hate our kind, and even as fine as you are, I can't figure out how—"

"For the same reason they don't attack you," she said, her tone growing tense with repressed anger.

He looked at her and took a step toward her. "What did you say to me?"

She scooted up. "You know how this works," she said, defiance in her eyes as she lifted her chin. "Your soul gets shredded and divided on the levels you died in. Mine, like yours, had a visit down on three—with the revenge Amanthras, and bottomed out on five—rage, with the weres, before vamps claimed it." She tossed her braids over her shoulders. "That's why you can't keep yourself away from going panther every now and then, any more than I can, because you're just as angry as me." Her eyes held his, searching for compassion, and her tone became gentler. "That's why I was looking for you so hard . . . we're such a good match in every way."

Carlos walked away from her. Those eyes were too intense, her argument was too logical, and she was too damn fine to be out in the dark talking to him like this. "All right. I'll buy that—for a brief visit. But hanging out there, the weres should have eaten and digested your ass by now."

"That's not what they want to do with my ass when I go there," she said, her tone holding indignation. When he turned to look at her hard, there was no apology in her eyes. "You know in your marrow that because of where your soul slid and bottomed out before the vamps got to it, you love to go panther. Don't you?"

The muscles in his jaw pulsed. He couldn't immediately answer that charge.

"When I enter that realm," she said, her voice seductive, "I come in at their mating dens and immediately go into heat."

He looked away. He was not hearing it.

"The were-realms are separated into hierarchies, based upon animal dominance in the filas above . . . so below," she said, her voice a warm balm against his neck even though she hadn't moved.

He could feel her stalking him as she raked his mind with new information—information that even council didn't have. He shut his eyes as her hand slid up his back and she spoke wisdom into his shoulder.

"The big cats are at the top of the food chain, then wolfen, then the others, based on predatory skill, strength, mobility. Each of the levels within level five has feeding grounds . . . the bones at the outer edge of that realm are dumped there and are from thousands of years of feedings."

Her hand caressed his ass through his pants, making him clench it to stave off an obvious shudder of pleasure. Her voice became a throaty whisper punctuated by a cat hiss. "The mating dens are like you would not believe." She laughed and sent him images of her travels. "There's more than one way to skin a cat, and more than one way to dog a dog."

Immediately, dark cave terrains entered his mind. Heavy vines and dense jungle foliage covered the entrances. Human body remains were piled deep before them . . . love offerings, dinner after, he knew what it was as soon as he saw it. He heard the brutal, grunting sounds of mating, low cat rumblings of exquisite satisfaction, deep hisses and snarls that set his teeth on edge and sent a shiver down his spine that shamed him. He tried to wrest his brain away, gathering up his curiosity and hurling it far from him. Oh, no, he did not need to see that.

But she was steadfast and adamant as the terrain changed and mentally took him up a level to the wolfen realms of dark forests. The howls almost spilt his eardrums, and the panting made him hold up his hand to signal her to stop.

"I'm a vampire, sis. I don't roll like that. You oughta know better." He walked away, offended, shaking his head, and wondering how in

the hell he was gonna look at Damali in the eye ever again. He'd almost taken her there . . . oh shit . . .

"Naw," he said firmly, not caring that this stray female was laughing at him. "Uh-uh. That shit is so damned unsmooth—no style, no
fucking finesse. Just flat out nasty, woman."

The more she laughed, the angrier he became. It was too fresh a
wound, and he'd come too close to losing his vampire ethos when this
siren's call had hit him. Around his woman, too. Oh, no! He wasn't
having it.

"Don't call me again for that shit. Don't even dangle the thought
my way, ever. They don't even have a damned, clean-running blood
source down there—the shit is primitive! Fucking dead meat and old
blood everywhere. Just living like animals! Rolling in caves and
bondage dens, and shit, without the comforts of a fly lair. Motherfuckers don't know what silk is. *Repugnante!*" he yelled, and then
hocked and spit on the ground. "Never. I forbid it in my territory."

He closed his eyes and folded his arms over his chest, summoning
calm. He was not going to allow this shit to piss him off to this degree. A near miss wasn't a total disaster, and that would just get folded
away in his dark mental closet with a lot of other shit he didn't want
to think about.

"Don't knock it till you've tried it, Carlos. You don't know how
good it feels to just let all your vampire inhibitions go and take a walk
on the were-demon side. I'll take you there, and won't tell anybody, if
you just promise to do me while we're down there."

"What part of what I said didn't you hear?"

Silence settled between them for a moment as her offer hung in the
balance.

He opened his eyes. Reality snapped back, and he turned around
and looked at her hard. "A master vampire, caught down in level-five
mating dens, with a female vamp fronting like a jaguar in heat?" He
laughed. "Are you insane? You got a death wish?" He walked away
from her when she didn't blink. "Sis, I don't know that much about
the were-realms, but I know what male vamps are like in-lair with females in a state . . . I might be all that, but if twenty or more amped-
up motherfuckers smell a master vamp in their mating dens—" he
held up his hands as she began to near him. "Don't even go there. I'm
just trying to keep were-demons out of my territory topside."

"But that's where the Neteru scent is, lover." She smiled and shook her head.

"What? How?" He put his hands on his hips. "Bullshit!"

"Only male vampires have this thing for Neteru. The were-demons are impervious to it. Since their borders were strong—"

"How'd they get the shit?"

"Simple," she said with a wave of her hand. "They took down a Neteru five hundred years ago."

He just stared at her.

"They killed her, Carlos. Neterus can heal from any realm's turn bites, but she's still mortal. They bit her while she was sick from a human disease to mark her for their zones, and took the body when she died. Her soul ascended because she never gave in to the realm's pull, but they had the essence of her from her carcass . . . it's their secret weapon against male vampires, especially masters. And, there's not much left of it—her body was injured and disease-decayed when they got it and the potion is so old . . . they keep the remainder of her flesh in a special container in their Jaguar Senate sector."

"Damn . . ." He rubbed his jaw and nodded. Girlfriend was dropping serious science and about to make him run a fool's errand behind it. "All right, then," he said, beginning to pace. "Coupla questions. One, how did you find out, and two, how did you gain access to it?"

She smiled and flashed him full fang. "I fucked a were-wolf good, and made him howl at the moon. He told me about the rumor that was an intra-level lower down with the big cats. I shape-shifted, and found a senator who wanted to know what a double plunge was all about."

"Shit!" Carlos backed up and put his hands over his ears and closed his eyes. "That's a capital offense, and you never told me! I never heard it. Cool?" He looked at her hard and dropped his hands and grabbed her by both arms. "You know how dangerous that shit is? You took that motherfucker to the vanishing point?"

"Curiosity killed the cat." She laughed and stepped closer to him. "Well, actually the hunger for power killed the cat. He thought that if he was the one who came out of the V-point then he would possess my vampire powers and the weres would still hold the Neteru scent. Not a temptation to resist easily. Besides, I'm the one left standing."

He shoved her away hard. "Listen, sister. I'm not going to report it, only because . . . well . . . shit, because you were on a mission to find out something that could rock the vamp empire. Neteru is volatile substance—like a damned nuclear bomb. It would have every male turn on each other and wipe each other out, even at council level. I'm talking major implosion and unrest."

"I know," she murmured, unfazed. "That's why Neterus primarily hunt vampires—the most advanced level of the dark realms. And that's why they always cremate their bodies on hallowed ground when they die. Poor thing . . . she died in the jungle before her team could get to her."

"But to take him to *the vanishing point,* you had to double plunge a top-ranking—which means, a black blood transfer," he whispered in horror. "When y'all came out of the fusion point, it was a fifty-fifty chance that you would have vanished, been sucked into his body, and could have given a strong were-demon all the powers of our vampire level."

Carlos started pacing again as he wiped his brow. "You could have given a were-demon the potential to turn their victims in three days, instead of having to wait a whole lunar cycle until the moon went full again. You would have sped up their breeding process."

"That's why he was so anxious to try it. Only vampires know how to go to the vanishing point, baby. Were-demons can't produce the euphoria rush, or do the velocity . . . they need a good engine to get their thing off." She dropped her voice to a sensual purr. "I'm rocket fuel."

He spun on her as the magnitude of the offense swept through him, and pointed at her, his arm outstretched so taunt that his hand shook. "You could have given him *unlimited* mobility like us. He wouldn't have been bound to hunt in the region where he was first made—he could travel without boundaries like we can. He wouldn't have to wait till the full moon to feed and come topside. That's why it's a capital offense! If one of them got that juice from you, baby, and then they did blood exchanges with each other—"

"Uhmmm-hmmm," she said, running her hands through her hair. "It was a risk, but it was worth it—since I came out of the fusion, and he didn't."

For a moment, all he could do was stare at her.

"But you're missing the point," Carlos said cautiously. "It could have gone down way differently, and their side could have become our greatest nemesis, beyond what they already are."

"No, *you're* missing the point," she said, her voice very quiet but firm. "I came out with everything he had." She paused to let the information sink in. "I can do daylight."

CHAPTER SEVENTEEN

CARLOS STARED at the outrageous female before him, forgetting how to breathe. She *had* to be lying.

"I can come up during the day while here in Brazil—*full equatorial UV blast*. But, alas, I'm bound to this region because he was. Small issue. But at night—and I don't have to wait for the full moon—I can come up anytime, like our kind. Unfortunately, like the were-race that's trapped by the grounds they were felled on, I do have to stay here . . . unless you can give me a boost out."

"That's what I'm talking about. Unsanctioned mess backfires all the time, and isn't stable. That's why council doesn't allow it on level six. That's the behavior of demons—and vampire intellect knows when to step off some outrageous nonsense. We've seen where this kinda stuff leads. It's mad-scientist type shit. And you lost your mobility behind it. Serves you right."

She lifted her chin higher. "All right, I may have lost my mobility, but I gained a whole lot beyond the sun, which should have been enough to convince you. When I shape-shift, it's no vampire parlor trick. Trust me. The were-demons *own* that form. That's their foundation. It's primal, it's stronger, it's faster, it hunts better, and brings down kill more effectively than a vampire just amusing himself by trying on different shapes!"

She strutted away a few feet, leaving Carlos speechless, and then smiled. "He, like most men, was so anxious to try it for the power rush as much as for the pussy." She shrugged. "Their ranks were thinning out because of the were-animal militias that have been hunting them down during their limited topside access time . . . and with nowhere to run, because their territories are so gated . . . and with master vampires setting them in fits, what can I say? He was down to take a risk for the Big Cat Nation, if he could expand his borders and increase their rate of turns. For sunlight, I was ready to take a risk, too.

So, we struck a deal; a hit of Neteru, for a shot at the vanishing point. Fair exchange. Winner takes all, and like most men, he assumed he'd best me. But I also knew where his stash was."

Then she laughed, and to Carlos's horror her incisors came down—two up top, two ripping up from the bottom . . . just like a panther's.

"Oh, shit . . . Baby, look at you!"

"Yeah, well," she sighed. "The fellas on level five like it."

Carlos instantly bulked to battle stance. His voice dropped and he circled her. "Did you take any were-demon males there afterward? It's a matter of empire security, and you need to answer me fast."

She backed up, walking counterclockwise to him, but didn't seem afraid. "No. I took one gamble and came up holding aces. Why would I allow some lower-level were demon to put me at risk to take all this back?"

He stopped stalking her but had not normalized.

"I saved it for the master vampire in my territory, who I hear is about to be made council."

"Do any other vampires know about this? Is this info out?"

"No. Well, the bats gossip about my treks down there . . . and the Amanthas are snooping around—maybe that's why they didn't attack you because they knew you'd be running into me, sooner or later. And the weres think I'm pretty valuable . . . you should hear the offers their top brass is throwing my way for just a chance to check me out. But it's all idle speculation and not even council can tell. All I have to do is consume a little human flesh to help me normalize, and go topside during the day to burn off the Neteru. But four-fangs, regardless, I would be very alluring to a power-hungry topside vamp male."

"But you haven't shared this with *anybody* else?" He dredged her mind so brutally that her nose began to bleed.

"No," she said, sniffing back blood and wiping her nose with the back of her hand.

He normalized.

"That's right," she said, thoroughly offended. "If two vampires go to the vanishing point, I can transfer all this to you. When we go there, since we're not two different species, both of us drop out of it breathless—but that's about it. I didn't inform the were-jag of the total risks, believe me." She shook her head, disgusted.

He didn't know what to say. This variable was scaring him, and the package it came in was too lovely for words.

"It's like, if you could go there with a regular human, our primary form—their soul weight would ensure they dropped out afterward and wouldn't be consumed into the dominant form." She chuckled. "They just can't do it. They don't have the phenomenal blood siphon and transfusion mechanism like we do," she said, now coming to him.

"We can't take a human to the vanishing point, and you know that. Just like a were-demon can't make me take him there. Vamp males lower than second-level can't do it, only masters can—so it's not like I can just go turn some guy then drop this on him. And you can sense that no other vampire males have crossed your borders, and I can't go out. There are no second-levels in the province; council wiped them out because they sensed some kind of threat. So why are you so angry?"

"I should have been informed." That was all he could say. Women could be so damned treacherous it was scary.

"That's why I was calling you so hard for over a month, as soon as this opportunity presented itself. But, if you ever want to taste daylight, or what it really feels like to hit the edge of the universe in raw were-panther form . . . with all that incredible, primal jaguar power under your hood . . . burning up ground like a high-velocity drag race—"

She stopped. Her eyes got wide and her fangs retracted, then she covered her mouth and laughed. "Oh no!"

He walked away. She'd gotten into his mind and found the race, plus a few things he definitely didn't want her to know. His head had been a damned open door seeking knowledge about this twisted shit so hard that he'd left the back bolt off. Fuck it. He was out. He slammed his mind shut.

"Wait a minute," she said, trying not to laugh. "But, you're *a master*. You have two continents under your belt, baby, and are on your way to a throne. Don't you want to rule the world? You mean to stand here and tell me, you haven't actually taken anybody for a ride like that? As awesome as you are?" She looked him up and down, her gaze lingering over his body like a sweet caress, undressing him with her eyes. "We need to rectify that immediately . . . *that's* unnatural, at your age."

He was gonna serve her vapor and be invisible so fast that the air would suck out of her lungs and turn them inside out! This humiliation was beyond his personal limit. But he had to salvage his dignity. He also had to keep this chick contained. If another master got to her first . . .

"I had my reasons," he grumbled, not looking at her. "The moment I got made, there was ripe Neteru topside, and I had a primary mission—protect the vessel from rebels. After that, I've been focused on one thing—protecting the vessel from damage. Chasing stray tail and losing cargo valuable to the empire was not on my agenda." He turned and pointed at her, his eyes narrowing. "That shit will never happen on my watch. Especially not for some mad science. There's only one sure way to make daywalkers, and that's through a Neteru, not this convoluted shit!"

She ignored his outburst and passively slipped her hand within his. The submissive way she did it began to de-escalate his rage. She led him back to a small clearing. Why he was following this woman, he wasn't quite sure. If knowledge was indeed power, he had just gotten his mind blown. Maybe that's why he didn't resist when she leaned into him and kissed him tenderly and pulled back to look into his eyes.

"You're right. Maybe I shouldn't have done it. But I'm not all that bad," she whispered. "No different from you. I was trapped, and wanted a way out. I lost patience. Nuit had botched the job, then you lost her and nobody could find you—not even council for a bit. You fellas were fucking up opportunities, big time, and I got tired of waiting. That's the truth and I'm sorry."

She kissed him again and let her hand run down his chest. "But I will tell you," she admitted softly, "the Neteru I took has . . . it has side effects that aren't pleasant. Maybe it's because I'm a female vamp, or it was so old?"

"Talk to me," he said in a quiet voice, no longer angry, just weary.

"It gives you flashbacks, like a conscience at times. It's scary . . . and I'm only telling you because I don't want you to get upset if you experience certain things, after we hit the point. Maybe it won't affect you that way. Perhaps because you're stronger as a master, I don't know. Maybe you can go into my head and get rid of the nightmares that I got from the tainted product? You used to distribute illegal substances when you were alive," she said gently. "With your new power . . . tell me you have something that will bring me down."

She embraced him and laid her head on his shoulder. It was reflex that made his hand stroke her hair. He looked up at the stars, knowing that there was no running from a conscience once you had one. Neteru would give you that—flashbacks and a conscience. He oughta know. His was kicking his ass right now for several reasons. The things he did in his old life was just one of them.

He kissed her temple and let his breath out hard. "Open your mind for me, and let me see if I can pull the poison out. But, I don't know if I can." Hell, he didn't know if he should. Probably the best thing to do would be to dust her and put her out of her misery, as well as take a volatile temptation variable off the game table for the empire and for himself.

He closed his eyes as she looked up at him, trusting, searching for his help. Her hand touched his cheek.

"I see why she's so crazy about you, even though her job is to hunt you," she murmured, and waited for him to open his eyes and look at her. "Thank you."

Tears of relief filled her eyes, and she brought her mouth close to his. "I can't be in your mind, unless you're also in mine. It is the way of the Neteru, too. See for yourself."

Terrible images shook him. Children, women running, screaming, a full-scale massacre in progress. Men fighting with inferior arms. Then he saw *her*, hair rising on the wind, her warriors behind her. Heard her war cry. Gorgeous, natural beauty in the heat of sudden battle. She was trying to fight gunboats, cannons, men who had no mercy. He saw her people bound and shackled, women raped. Horrible disease-ridden bodies with priests splashing anointment on them, unknowingly passing their diseases with their robes and blankets.

This mysterious female vampire stood before him, her hands trembling on his shoulders. A sob caught in her throat, but he heard her swallow it away. He stared up at the moon and could not bear the images that marched across it. He saw a Neteru team in her mind die off, one by one, until the Amazon Neteru was alone—an Isis sword raised. He nuzzled her temple and cradled her cheek as hot tears fell against his palm, and her tears sent shards of pain through his fingers. And before his will could consult his brain, he allowed her to see his life echo back at her, making her cover her mouth and nod. She understood . . . just like he did.

"When did she fall? When did her people lose their Neteru?" he murmured, no longer out of control, or in need of being sated by any woman. This was just too intense—all of it. Carlos brought his hands up to his temples, trying to sort it all out.

"She fought as long as she could, but they came . . . so many of them. They weren't vampires, or demons—but they acted like them. The Neteru perished. Her people were tired, had never endured such atrocities. They contracted the invaders' diseases. Their weapons never felled her, but she became sick."

She covered her face with her hands. "But how could she keep the human invaders at bay and pestilence from the very air?" Her voice ragged, she turned to him, her eyes filled with anguish. Her visions were staggering and it made Carlos release her. She spoke like a person having a nervous breakdown, or a schizophrenic. He stood there, totally stunned, watching this female vampire vacillate between knowing what was real and not understanding what was just a vision, illusion. It was the most frightening thing he'd witnessed in a while.

"When the Neteru became ill, her mother-seer could see that she was lost to them, that they had lost. And she grieved. Oh, how she grieved, Carlos. She made a pact with the were-demons tied to this region. She allowed them to give her and the guardian team the turn bite and then take the Neteru's body down to level five. The Neteru's soul ascended, but her body was taken down to level five. They boiled it down and captured the Neteru essence. It was such a small portion, but it was enough to be a weapon that could tip the scales in their favor in the oncoming Final War."

"And what did the mother-seer get out of this?" Carlos asked horrified. "What could she have possibly gained by allowing her Neteru to be desecrated?"

"A chance at revenge," she said, her breathing ragged. "She allowed herself to be turned so that she could rise again, consume the Neteru's essence, destroy those who had destroyed them, and forever guard the lands of their beloved Neteru."

"Seems like a job for the Amanthras to me," Carlos said, folding his arms across his chest. "They're the revenge demons. Why didn't she summon them?"

She gave a shaky smile. "You're right, but Amanthras are limited topside. They must either possess a body or attach themselves to a building of some kind. Allying themselves with Nuit gave them more power than they had ever experienced as a species, but that *only* came as a result of the alliance. The mother-seer needed far more mobility and power to exact revenge on the scale she wanted." She smiled. "You must also remember that she was a guardian, and though broken she still thought like one. Were-demons are mortal enemies of vampires and she planned to continue fighting against the vampires. What better way to do that than as a were-demon possessing the scent of the Neteru?"

"So what happened? We would have heard of a were-demon trailing the Neteru's scent long before this. The Vampire Council would have taken her out."

She looked away. "The senates betrayed her. They didn't want to waste the small portion of Neteru scent on one grieving woman's wish for revenge. They wanted to hold on to it, to use it as their own personal weapon in the upcoming Final War." She took a deep breath. "She and her guardian team tried to take it from them. They didn't succeed and were confined on level five." She looked at Carlos. "Nuit's portals allowed them to escape, but by then the Neteru essence was gone." She gave another small shaky smile. "See, I had happened. But they didn't know that and the first killings that went down had been done out of anger . . . and of course, out of the need to feed. Were-demons must consume human flesh in order to survive." She tilted her head to the side. "And then something interesting happened."

Carlos watched her warily. "What?"

"They found me . . . and knelt at my feet." She smiled again, showing her upper and lower incisors. "Apparently, they believe that somehow their wish has been fulfilled, the Neteru's essence lives on and is topside again. Only it has been done through me."

Carlos stared at her in disbelief. "They think you are their leader." It was a statement, not a question.

She nodded. "Oh, yes." She moved up close to him. "Do you realize how powerful I am? I am a vampire who can walk in daylight, I hold the Neteru's scent, and I have a guardian team at my command. That is why I have been calling you so hard." She leaned in close as if she were going to kiss him. Her breath was coming in soft pants, her excitement at being near him clear on her face, in the way she molded her body to his. "The memories of the Neteru and the memories of the seer-mother, because they were so linked, sear my brain. I know what was done to their people. The humans who destroyed this land weren't so different from our kind. They came as explorers. They came as starving, humble men in need of refuge—and the indigenous people had great kindness, mercy, and took them in. Then they sent more ships and returned with plunderers. Conquistadors. This time around, we will be the ones. It's always been about power; the humans themselves have blood on their hands   so why protect them? Together—if you make the right decision tonight—we can conquer all that they have built." She lay her lips against his in a hot, gentle kiss, and then pulled back again. "Be my mate, Carlos Rivera, and make it happen."

Carlos stared at her, almost numb. He pushed her away from him, his expression hardening, his eyes narrowing shrewdly.

"Cut the bullshit and tell me what you'd really get out of hooking up with me. And don't even bother trying to stroke my ego. I'm a businessman, baby, and I can smell shit all over this sweet little deal you're offering."

She stepped back from him, glaring at him in annoyance. Carlos waited.

"I can't leave the region," she finally said. "When I took the were-demon to the vanishing point, I gained daylight, but I lost the ability to move about freely." She looked uncomfortable. "There have also been some other side effects. Sometimes, the were-jag qualities threaten to . . . take over. There are some nights it's difficult for me to turn back into my natural form." She stared up at him. "I can take you to the V-point and gift you with daylight, but I need you to flat-line me when you do so. It has to also be a total black blood exchange and it must be one with a master vampire." She licked her lips. "Please."

Carlos stared at the beautiful, twisted creature and knew he was going to have to dust her.

"If you want me to cast the illusion of the current Neteru for the task, to make it easier for you—"

"No!" Carlos stepped back from her. "Are you crazy?"

"Are you?" She moved closer and stared at him hard. "I offer you the chance of an unending lifetime. Through me, and only through me, you can have everything you want—a Neteru, an empire, light invincibility . . ." She outstretched her arm, motioning toward the horizon. "The world, in daylight, Carlos. Me, at your side, forever—we could rule, and no other master vampire could ever rival you, no human could vanquish us, and I—"

"Enough! Shut up! Don't even go there." He paced away from her, the temptation of what she'd just offered, along with the thick scent she was producing again, was all too dangerous, but too practical a solution to his many problems to consider.

"Tell me you don't want that, never considered having a Neteru by your side for eternity? Tell me that and I'll be gone."

For a moment, he couldn't answer, then found his voice. "Not like this. I didn't want it like this."

She shook her head.

Carlos shut his eyes tightly and walked farther from her and sat down hard on the grass. The images scrambling her brain were so terrible that his head dropped between his bent knees in the darkness. None of what she said was a lie, and he could hear a child's screams echoing on the night air. Could see a mother-seer guardian in abject pain, hidden in the bush, too much of a warrior to surrender to death . . . even at the piteous shrieks of her own child being repeatedly raped by conquistadors . . . her limp little body fed to crocodiles to draw the team out. A mother-seer so devastated because her Neteru didn't come at the ultimate cries of an innocent. But she stayed in the brush guarding the entry to the compound. For the cause. For the tribe. For her people. Protecting her Neteru at all costs, not knowing the Neteru had already been killed by disease.

She neared Carlos, but stood just out of his reach. "Don't judge me so harshly, Carlos Rivera. What I am now is *nothing* in comparison to the conquistadors! Don't even judge that guardian team. Her child, her mother, her sisters . . . her guardian sisters, each killed, bodies desecrated . . . Her mother-seer could bear no more. And for a warrior to fall to a disease that puts hideous bruises and sores on her face, stealing even her Neteru's dignity in death? From her mother-seer's perspective, she was already an ugly, dying creature with no honor, no people, and nothing to lose. What was a soul worth at that moment, if it could not right a wrong so great?"

"Smallpox," Carlos whispered. His mind wrapped around of all things, a prayer. Dear God in Heaven, men of the church did this? Yet, a man of the church had told him the kinds of things the demon realms sent to break a guardian or Neteru's spirit. Damali entered his mind as he looked at this crazy, yet beautiful, female vampire, wondering her age. But that information was so cloaked he couldn't even sense it. She looked Amazon, and he wondered where Nuit had found her.

He stared at this gorgeous but crazy female vampire near him. He owed her a lot, because she'd given him a sense of what the demon realms had planned. He immediately thought of Damali in contrast with the ancient Neteru. They had broken the ancient one's back, taken everything, and left her spirit to perish. Like Father Patrick had warned—first her mind, then her body, and ultimately her spirit. The screams of her people and her mother-seer's child ate away at her mind, the smallpox ate away at her body, and on her deathbed, this woman had given up hope and surrendered her spirit into the light— only to have a dark ritual desecrate her body . . . misguided hope for justice violating everything she stood for, and the atrocity was committed by one of her own . . . from within her ranks, one of her most trusted.

It was a warning, a sign. It gave him serious pause as he sat by this tortured creature that was his simply because of geography. She had shared so much knowledge. It had been a true gift, because it shed so much light on the Neteru he had to protect. How long would it be before the dark forces came after Damali, if they didn't think he had her on lock? The negative energies had already begun swirling around her, stripping away her protective layers one by one.

They sat on the grass together, quietly—him deciding, her waiting. There was much to consider on both sides of this equation.

He had been Damali's primary guardian; her destined life-mate, but had gone dark. It had almost ripped her heart out and stolen her hope. Marlene, her mother-seer, had almost been broken by the screams of her child being taken by a predator. Jose had been crushed emotionally by the loss of Dee Dee. Rider had lost Tara to a turn, but had never had the heart to kill her . . . that story was locked in his territory, he knew it the moment he did a roll call inventory of the available territory females while sitting on a monk's cot killing time. But that was also about a man loving a woman, so he'd just let Rider's personal business be.

The other guardians had had their trials, too. Shit, Big Mike almost took a turn in New Orleans—the female in that region was still messed up behind that. But mild panic washed through Carlos when he thought of how close he'd come to turning Damali on so many occasions . . . How different was he than that grieving, pain-riddled mother-seer who simply wanted her beloved Neteru to live forever? Not much. Love was complex, and could easily get twisted.

He glanced at the female beside him who was breathing hard and still shuddering from images. He put his arm around her and pulled her close, allowing her to lean against him and she closed her eyes. The quest for power had fucked her up good. *Judge not, lest ye be judged,* slipped into his mind. Were he in the same situation, would he have given in to the same temptation? Who knew?

He stood, slit his wrist, and offered it to her. Compassion tore at him as she hungrily siphoned the vein. He watched her close her eyes, take a sip, and grimace on the first swallow as a shudder ran through her, connecting them. She pulled away for a moment, breathing hard and grabbed her stomach as though she'd been punched. Total awe claimed him as she went back to the vein and pulled harder on it, sending more terrible images up his arm and into his mind. But it was so bizarre. Within those images were shock waves of dark pleasure as her saliva entered his bloodstream . . . violent, bestial, torrid images that almost swayed him where he stood.

"I am so sorry the product did this to you, baby." Carlos shook his head and looked up at the sky. "Rule the world. To what end? Damn."

She got up and began walking in an agitated circle around him, counterclockwise to his wary moves when he slowly matched her orbit . . . her entire being naked, pained, gorgeous. Begging him to side with her cause with her eyes. "Power needs no explanation. It is the purest substance in the universe!"

"Let me give you some more to bring you down," he said quietly, slitting his wrist again harder with his nail, and then pumped his fist.

"You can flat-line me, then you won't have to worry about it." She straightened and walked over to him slowly, the noise of the jungle, his blood dripping into the grass, and their breathing the only sounds to be heard.

As she neared him, he saw the image in her eyes and heard the threat to his life in his mind. She'd what? Rape him? If it wasn't so ridiculously off the wall, he might have laughed. But the dead-serious look she gave him almost made him bulk for battle. There was a maleness in her imagery of coming out of the vanishing point that disturbed him. It was definitely time to bring her down. This was why he never touched his own product . . . and after seeing this, not to mention gaining a conscience, he wasn't in the business anymore. After tonight, he was definitely out.

Carlos continued to let his blood splatter that ground to signal her, now or never. He was two seconds from sealing his vein and walking.

She dropped to her knees and it took everything in him not to kneel with her and stroke the pain away from her head. But there was something that registered caution within him. It was the underlying violent image she'd sent that kept him on guard, standing, and in a power position the way the throne dictated feeding lower generations.

He forced himself to watch her from a detached place in his mind as she took his wrist hungrily. He winced when she locked her lips around his flesh and began to suck so hard it was almost painful. Yet, he was also mesmerized as he watched her take from him, his ruby blood turning black on her mouth as it dribbled down her chin and mixed with the air. He'd never fed a naked vamp female from his wrist before. The process was deep. He had so many responsibilities to truly internalize in his role as a territory master. All he could do was watch as she siphoned him, looking up every few seconds, and then going back to the open vein. Seeing the wild look in her eyes was so horrifyingly erotic that he almost snatched back his arm, but he didn't have it in him to deny a creature so wounded.

Carlos was numb. He understood there was nothing he could say to a being so mentally twisted by a narcotic, so right, yet so wrong. She was on a real bad trip and was going to have to ride it out alone. There was nothing more he could do for her.

Father Patrick's words echoed in his skull as he slowly blocked this tortured beauty from further access to his mind. He had been her. There was only one difference . . . somebody with light in her soul had gotten to him first. Karma. He was looking at a female version of himself. Her rage was magnificent.

And, at the same time, he knew that Damali, safely stowed in his lair, was only safe for the moment. This female would go after Damali, when Damali came after her. It was in their nature.

"You have a great expanse in your heart," she said, finally standing with effort, wiping her mouth, and walking away.

Carlos cocked his head to the side. Her vocabulary had changed. The street slang she'd dredged from his mind was replaced by the syntax of her era.

"You would have been a good companion warrior in my time. But I will settle for you being a good one-time lover—it must be. We are equals. We understand each other." She sighed. "In one night, perhaps two, then there will be no choice. Get rid of the young huntress. She'll come for my territory and try to send me back from whence I came—and we cannot allow that to happen. Bring me the Isis, so that I know your word is your bond." Then the look in her eyes became deadly.

"You said 'we'?" Carlos stayed calm, trying to measure his words as her form got smaller. This was too serious, too dangerous. Now she was talking about killing D? Uh, uh . . . she'd better walk that fucking high off fast. Things had kicked up a level. Strip Damali of the Isis, and do her—or protect her life by taking this babe to the vanishing point? The only reason he didn't smoke this crazy bitch on the spot was because she had said "we."

She turned and looked at him squarely and then laughed. "You even have the conquistador's name and language upon you, Master Rivera. But I look in your eyes, and I see my people in them. You were stolen, oppressed, too. I will give you back to yourself. Freedom. Power. The sun. We." She paused. "Don't make me have to deal with her. There are a lot of females in this section of your territory that do not appreciate this new Neteru."

"On my orders—you and every female vampire in my territory—stay away from Damali, her guardians, that whole team! I will not have it—you hear me? You rush her, you die! The only reason I'm letting you walk is because you're high. Tomorrow night, we'll discuss this whole daylight bullshit. We clear?"

She blew him a kiss and vanished. He remained on the hillside, a dead water buffalo at his feet. The intoxicating scent of mature Neteru and sulfur wafting toward him from a black forest before him. Damali seemed so far away. Far away from his reality, and this older woman who had blown his mind. This lair queen knew what the bitter side of life tasted like. Shared his darkness. Stoked it. Made him wonder. Made him weigh the scales of right versus wrong. Took gray matter out of the equation. Had opened his nose, and gotten a fingernail beneath the edge of his heart, threatening to flip it. He'd wanted to weep for her because she was so utterly insane. Had made him want to take her in panther form, primal. Had let him know that under no uncertain terms, she'd wanted him.

She had made him an offer. Daylight—the ultimate gift. Could pace herself and be patient. Had power. Had self-control. Was mature. Had suffered the abominable. Was probably turned during the era of chaos she'd shown him. Had witnessed death and destruction that he'd only seen once dead. Was overtaken by the spirit of a Neteru at least five hundred years old, because she'd eaten tainted flesh. Had made semen spill from the tip of his quivering member just talking about going to the vanishing point with her. With Damali, that could never happen. With this queen, topside and subterranean were up for grabs, due to a fluke. A variable. And his blood had made her worse, not better.

Carlos closed his eyes and rubbed his hands over his face, and sealed his wrist wound. Oh . . . shit . . . his old guardian traits and a residual of a soul hanging in the balance had kicked this bullshit in her up a notch. He was the insider; the one that had tipped the balance with a misguided act of compassion that would hurt the living Neteru . . . for all the wrong reasons, at a *very* bad time.

The older female's logic was twisted. So was his. But was it? She had a just cause to return the lands to their rightful owners, but her methods . . . Vampires were not the rightful owners of this land. They'd colonized it, too.

She'd opened her legs for him, as well as her mind, and arched up to him to save her world as though she were a Neteru, and wanted to save the vamp empire in the same breath. She was so confused it made him shudder. She was right; they were both cut from the same cloth. He wanted to live in both worlds, too. She had made him think of things he was afraid to admit to himself. Had whispered of unparalleled power into his ear while stroking his chest with her hands. Had served indescribable options on a silver platter while nude. Had made him want to protect her, as much as he wanted to push her twisted being away and stake her . . . as much as he'd wanted to mount her and ride her hard.

He had a problem. A dilemma. Damali had a problem. A threat. He had a soul in the balance. The woman, who posed an offer, didn't have one to worry about. His was slipping into darkness fast as he walked slowly away from the dead carcass. He still wanted her, but knew he shouldn't. His body said one thing. His mind said something else. His intellect was torn. His heart was unsure. It didn't even beat—that, too, was dead, no wonder. He was a vampire. She was one, too. Damali was a human, Neteru notwithstanding. He had to make a decision and quickly. This mysterious older female had made him think about his future, and hope for it, while fearing it.

And yet, he still didn't even know her name.

CHAPTER EIGHTEEN

DREAD WAS a constant companion as Damali got up from the bed and walked over the little indoor footbridge at the base of the futon. She peered at the stream that separated the room into two sides, knowing that she, too, was stuck in the middle. What more was she than a small bridge between desire and the solid material worlds on the other side of a stream that beckoned? What more had she been to Carlos?

From her raised vantage point above the blue water, she could see out to the stars and the full moon past the deck. Sheer white curtains floated toward her like ghosts. Maybe they were no more than her memories, caught on the night air, hopelessly flailing against the wind. She was caught between the supernatural and natural, fighting against the wind, too. How did you fight nature, basic instinct?

Under any other circumstances this place would have been paradise. The calls of night birds and insects, sounds of the cycle of life, filled the sweet night air, blowing into the cliff lair on the breeze. She breathed in deeply, willing away the grief. Her best friend was no longer her best friend, he had dark secrets. Her lover was no longer her lover; she feared him. Hope was dying like the embers in the fireplace. You cannot bring something back from the dead. It is beyond mortal control.

Yet ten glorious nights of forgetting that harsh fact wrapped around her, just as she wrapped her arms about herself. The way he'd made her feel . . . Damali briefly shut her eyes as a familiar ache for him claimed her. How was she ever going to forget what they shared? How was she going to let go of this place he'd owned in her heart? She opened her eyes. She had to do what she had to do. If he wound up on the wrong side of the bridge, she'd put his soul to rest with tears in her eyes. She'd do it with love, she'd do it with honor, but she'd do it.

Her free hand reached out, while her other hand clutched at the poker that she'd never put down, trying to sense him. She swept the room again in futile hope that there would be anything of use as a weapon in a vampire's lair. Foolish. Every piece of wrought-iron furniture was woven into ornate curlicues. Nothing had a sharp point. The slate tabletops were too heavy for even her to lift. From a round, iron ring in the high ceiling, sheer drapes formed a tent over the futon. The bed was a sumptuous soft mattress of goose down covered in white silk with twenty lush pillows spilling over it. Oh, yeah, right, smother him to death. She sighed.

The torches that lit the room were immovable iron holders soldered to the stone walls. Six-foot tall, white candles stood on the floor without any base. The one wrought-iron holder that had smaller candles in it was built into the slate-and-tile floor. The greatest weapon she had was a brass fireplace poker—which had no effect on a vampire. Hand-to-hand combat, with practically nothing in her hand? This was definitely being assed out.

With two hours till dawn, she had few options. Sunlight would be her only defense. But it was hard enough to perform onstage for more than two hours, let alone try to walk the perimeter of tight confines, stalling with what? Witty conversation. Yeah, for a fully fed, master vampire, that was coming back all messed up in his mind, horny as hell, and not very patient . . . if he hadn't lied about abstaining for two weeks.

He'd been gone an awful long time, too. He was close, but she couldn't sense him at all. Either his new strength blocked her, or he'd placed a steel cage over his emotions. Either possibility was not good. What it was that she was afraid of in him now, she couldn't put her finger on. In truth, he hadn't done anything that should have made her distrust him like this. She was acting like he was going to kill her, or something. That was crazy. But, then, why was the hair standing up on the back of her neck and arms?

If all Carlos wanted was a serious rock-the-house, that shouldn't have made her feel like this. If anything, she could go back to the hotel all smiles. But every fiber in her was on red alert. Her instincts were coiled just as tight as the muscles in her body. Damali's gaze swept the room slowly, detecting. She tilted her head. The cicadas had gone still. No night sounds were outside. She glanced around the room looking for cover. Under a table would be a trap. Not an option.

The air moved. A whooshing sound registered and her hand reached up before her eyes could see what was coming, and she snatched at the air. An arrow burned her palm as she caught it. She glanced at it quickly. The metal tip looked like the point of her Isis blade and had come in the open sliding doors to the deck. She ducked as a second arrow whizzed by her shoulder and stuck into the stone wall.

"Shit . . ." she whispered. If it went through solid stone, then the archer had one helluva arm. Instantly crouching low, she knew she had to get off the bridge, and take cover. But as soon as she bent, a large, green-eyed crocodile materialized in the water beneath her. Somersaulting off the footbridge, she landed on the other side by the fireplace as the beast took a chunk out of the flimsy wooden structure, casting aside boards as it shook its massive head and leaped out of the stream.

With an Isis-tipped arrow and a brass fireplace poker, Damali backed up. The beast let out a low rumble of warning. She kept her eyes locked with the glowing green orbs that narrowed on her, then suddenly back-flipped from in front of the open hearth, put both weapons in one hand, and grabbed a heavy chair, toppling it before her as a shield. The animal was on her in seconds, and she sought the tabletop, which it immediately flipped with its nose, hurling her across the room in the direction of the futon.

Damali reached out, breaking her fall with the tent of sheers that surrounded the bed, using them as they crumpled under her weight to scramble up toward the iron ring in the ceiling. Her two weapons were on the floor, and sharp, saliva-dripping jaws opened beneath her. Occasionally the beast would jump and snap at her dangling legs. A shoe dropped and the thing ate it whole. Her damp palms were betraying her as she held on for dear life. It was hard to get body leverage in a damnable gown. From the corner of her eye she saw the surface of the hot tub slither, and fixed her gaze on the new threat that could probably reach her.

A huge black-and-green anaconda lifted its head from the Jacuzzi. Its eyes glowed green and the crocodile calmed down, simply staring up as the serpent slowly inched its muscular body up the side of the wall. It worked against the stones in a lazy, threatening zigzag pattern. A seductive, sultry dance of motion, it slithered toward the wide deck drape rods, and Damali watched the creature thread itself through so that it would have reach from that point to the ring in the middle of the ceiling.

She tightened her grip as the thing's jaws unhinged and its neck dipped into a U, swaying its head in a hypnotic pre-strike dance. Ten-inch fangs dripped yellowish ooze that made the floor below sizzle and burn away. The crocodile backed up and opened its jaws, waiting, its ragged, gleaming teeth readied for the snap.

As the serpent reared its head back to deliver a forceful stroke, Damali swung forward, then back, returning with a powerful kick when the creature missed on the first attempt. The heel of her other shoe snapped off and fell. Her blow stunned it, made it back up for a second, dazed, but its eyes quickly narrowed. Instinctively she knew she'd really pissed this snake off now. The thing hissed, drew way back, and was coming in for a sure strike, but a loud growl from below stopped the snake.

Damali tightened her sliding grip as a third predator entered the room. The crocodile was backing up, snapping, but on the defensive and keeping its distance. The snake was retreating, uncoiling, and soon it dropped onto the floor and slid over the edge of the deck, disappearing in the cliffs. But what circled below her was just as bad. This thing could reach her. This thing had jaws worse than what she'd just faced.

Glowing red orbs narrowed, the beast snarled, and circled beneath her. Her heart was beating a hole out of her chest. The huge panther stood four feet at the shoulders, and looked like nothing she'd ever seen in a zoo. Its fangs hung out of its mouth at saber-tooth proportions, and the muscles in its back met in the center, kneading as it circled and snarled. Its chest was a deep barrel of pure strength, and its forearms and haunches were a thicket of sinew beneath a velvety, blue-black coat.

This thing was fucking with her big time, just circling, now purring. Jesus! Her two paltry weapons were on the floor, and even if she could drop fast enough to grab them, which was doubtful given the lightning agility of a creature like this, to what end? Its claws were humongous. As it walked it left deep grooves in the freaking slate floor! Its reach had to be double hers, so even if she had the Isis, the length would still put her at a disadvantage. This thing would snap brass or an arrow with one swipe, taking her arm with it. She wasn't supposed to die like this, Lord. Not in a vampire lair at twenty-one!

But if she was going down, then she was going out swinging. She gave the thing beneath her an evil grin. "Come on, you bastard!" she yelled in frustration. If she was gonna die, she wanted it to be swift. That's all she asked.

The thing sat back on its haunches, looked up, retracted its claws, and licked a paw casually. Then it stood, snorted, and transformed into Carlos.

Damali didn't even blink; she just hung from her crouched position, stunned, her bare feet against the ceiling, gazing down over her shoulder. Her body was such a tight ball of knots pressed against the ceiling that her muscles had locked.

"Come down. I won't bite," Carlos said quietly.

Was he out of his fucking mind? *Come down?* She just looked at him, unable to move.

"The coast is clear, you can let go."

Her mind was hearing the words, but they made no sense. He could turn into something like that, and she was supposed to let go of the only safe place in the room?

"Damali, baby . . . let go, I'll catch you."

This motherfucker had claws two seconds ago . . . Catch her?

"Honey, I know this has been deep, and I know you're pretty freaked out right now, but, you have to come down." His voice was smooth, controlled, even.

Been deep? *Been deep?*

"Damali, I don't want to have to come up there and pry your fingers off the ring. As tight as you're holding on, I could break a finger, and—"

"Don't come near me!" she yelled. "Just don't come near me!"

"It's me, Carlos. Remember?" He opened his arms under her. "Baby—"

"Baby?" She scrunched herself up tighter, practically flattening herself to nothingness against the stucco.

"It's going to be light soon, and I need to get you back to the hotel while I still have enough energy. I'm not going to hurt you. My word."

His word didn't mean squat! She couldn't read him, couldn't tell if it was him, or one of the things that attacked her.

"I know what you're thinking, but—"

"No, you don't," she said in short pants. "You have no idea what I'm thinking."

"That's fair," he said on a long, patient exhale and sat down on the bed, glancing around at the battle-ravaged room. "Some night, huh?" He shook his head and collected the arrow and the fireplace poker, extending it up toward her as a peace offering. "Here," he said with disdain. "Arm yourself, but do come down. I'll go to the other side of the room. Drop on the bed, and we'll talk."

She studied him hard, and released her hold just enough to snatch the outstretched weapons he held with one hand. She put the thin shafts of spears between her teeth and returned her grasp. Her arms and back and buttocks hurt from the exertion. Every muscle was trembling with the need to release its tense hold, and she eyed him as he moved across the room. Saliva ran down her cheeks as she bit down hard on the brass and wood. She dropped, landed on her feet, and immediately took a fighter's stance. She broke the arrow over her knee. Wood. That's right, fucking wood. The arrow tip was now a dagger. The fireplace poker was a spear. The back half of the arrow was a stake. She now possessed three weapons, and felt much improved.

But her hands would not stop shaking as she looked across the room at the vampire who casually righted a chair and sat down heavily in it, raking his fingers through his hair. He didn't even watch her as she put more distance between them.

"Watch your back," he murmured. "You've got it toward the open deck, and I have no idea what they'll try to pull."

"They! Who's they?"

"A strong second-level and her girls."

"What?"

"She's whack, D, with a serious hit of old Neteru in her from a nasty potion. I don't know all the details about what's in it or how they actually made it, but you can't go fucking with this chick. You hear me?" He looked at her squarely, his gaze unwavering. "For once in your life, I want you to listen to what I've gotta say."

Damali waited, and put her back against one of the stone walls.

"She's in a lot of pain, baby. Twisted." His voice trailed off and he stood and glanced away.

His sudden motion made Damali's muscles tense and move counterclockwise as Carlos walked. He kept his back to her, but she was fully aware of how fast he could spin and strike, if he were of a mind to do so. Pure survival instinct bubbled within her. She sensed something within him that was borderline. She picked up a threat from him, not sure why, but didn't really care. As long as he was talking, not getting close, keeping a relaxed posture, his back toward her, she could deal—a little. However, the fact that his mind was sealed was possibly the worst part of it all.

"You don't want to see what I have in my head," he said quietly, not facing her.

"Why not? You always shared with me before—we didn't have secrets. Then you kept critical info from me about all this shit going down in Brazil. I don't like it."

"I know. Neither do I." He stopped moving and leaned on the mantel of the hearth. "Some things about me you don't need to see . . . like that transformation. It scared the shit out of you. I never wanted you to see me out of human form. Mist is one thing, but as animal—that's something else." He glanced over his shoulder. "Yeah, I can see it in your eyes. And if you thought that was a mindblower, you should see me in a full hunt when I bring down my prey." His gaze slipped away from her again. "Tried to tell you what I am."

Her stance relaxed. The truth in his words eased her fist out of a clench, but the tightness of her hands went to the muscles around her heart. His form began to blur as she fought back tears. She wiped her face.

"Damali, go home. Get on the next thing smoking. Get your team out of harm's way. Some things you can't fight."

"So, I'm supposed to just leave here with a crazy second-level female vamp on the loose, killing innocent people?"

He turned and stared at her. "In a word, yes. I'll handle it."

She returned the glare. "How long do you think it will be before she comes to find me, and—"

"Months." He looked away.

"Months?"

"That will give you time to get out of Dodge, move the compound, and she won't be concerned with—"

"Move the compound? Are you crazy? I didn't even run from the vamp empire in Hell!"

"You need to run from this, D. Call it defensive measures, if it will help your ego." He walked away, kicked the overturned table, and leaned on the wall with both hands.

"My ego?"

"Yeah, your ego!" he shouted. "Let this go, D, before you have to deal with something that's gonna kick your ass and crush your heart!" He spun and stared at her hard.

The brimming tears had long burned away from her eyes, and what glittered in them was pure defiance. He shook his head.

"This isn't ego. I am the Neteru. I don't run." She sniffed the air. "Sulfur." Her gaze narrowed. "You were with it, weren't you? What kind of demon is it?"

He didn't answer her immediately. "I keep telling you that she's not a demon. She's a female—"

"I don't care what it was. Why didn't you smoke it, if you knew it might double back and come for me?"

He looked away. "Baby . . . It got confusing out there. It was in a lot of pain. I was trying to—"

"You hesitated." She looked at him hard, her glare boring into his back until he faced her. "You told me that I was the one who was blind. You came into my compound and demonstrated for me what a lapse in judgment could cost me. Right?"

He couldn't respond.

"You came into my house and showed me the deal. Now I'm standing here in yours telling you the same thing. That was no female vampire. It's a demon!" She swallowed hard and looked beyond the deck. "What hurts me so bad, Carlos, is that I don't trust you anymore." She returned her gaze to him, trying to keep the emotion out of her voice as he looked at one of the torches on the wall. "If what came in here is part of her squad, and they came in animal form, then she's a were-demon—and *you'd* better not get it twisted."

Carlos shook his head. "No," he said quietly. "She's just an older female that took some shit that—"

"Listen to yourself!" she shouted, her voice catching in her throat. "I don't care what she is, she came up from Hell!" Damali took in two deep breaths trying to stabilize her voice. She pointed at him with the fireplace poker. "My job as a Neteru is to exterminate anything that comes up from underground." Their eyes met. *"Anything,"* she said evenly, her gaze locking with his. "And I, as you recently told me, have *not* been handling my business."

"We both haven't," he said quietly. There was no anger in his tone, not even defensiveness. "And here we are again, like old times, at philosophical odds." He sighed and looked beyond the deck. "You're supposed to be planting that wood in your hand in my chest, right about through here—and I'm supposed to be fully compromising you and anything human around you . . . for the cause. Your people against my people. But that is not what we've been doing during those ten nights." He chuckled sadly. "You've gone against every thing your people told you about me, and I've been lying and ducking and dodging trying to keep mine at bay just to be with you. I got weary of the struggle tonight."

He pushed himself off the mantel and went to stand in the opening of the deck, just looking out at the moon, and allowing the breeze to capture him. He could feel a spike of anxiety shoot through her system. It wasn't normal fight-or-flight hormone; it was fear, but not terror. It was so dense and heavy that it practically colored the air gray.

"She's more to you than just some . . . You were gone a long time—and you didn't dust her."

He heard her swallow, and heard the response to his possible betrayal in her tense whisper. She'd been right. He didn't dust a threat to her. At the moment, he wasn't sure why. And that potential threat had sent in a posse to hunt his baby, against his direct command. Crazy thing was, he didn't attack them, just made them go away. He'd found himself rationalizing the whole episode, giving the offenders pardon in his mind, telling himself that the only reason the mysterious female had disobeyed him was because she was blitzed—like that should have mattered.

And it deeply disturbed him that he was trying to protect two females at once, for some unfathomable reason . . . his main woman, Damali, and this new, exciting, captivating thing that had temporarily blown his mind. Nothing he could say at this juncture would make this sound right, because it wasn't. There was nothing to draw from to mask this, to convert it into a pretty picture. Even as a master of illusion, he didn't have a quick line that could make this be all right.

"She's one of your lair whores, now . . . is that it?"

"She's something more deadly than that," he stated evenly and turned to face her. If he couldn't give Damali anything else, at least she deserved the truth. She needed to know, by what was said and unsaid, the depth of the thing that he'd been in denial about for the ten nights he'd spent with her. It was only a matter of time before his will gave out. It had frayed so badly out in the wilderness that there was no sense in playing with himself or her about it. He could still taste this mystery woman in the back of his throat, she was in his nose, on his skin, and he knew as sure as sunset that he'd set her up in his main villa in Brazil . . . and would visit her often. Might even bring her fresh kill.

"I'm a master vampire. From this, baby, you run." What else was there to say when she just stared at him battling tears and swallowing hard?

The look on her face couldn't have been worse if he'd driven a knife through her heart. Shock fused with hurt, becoming rage, turning into pain in a slow dawning. He'd never ever seen the fight knocked out of her, and it pained him to no end that he'd been the one to deliver the blow. It was all in her eyes, those beautiful, brown, pain-stricken eyes. But he also had to be real. If they had no future, not one he could live with for her sake, then now was the time to end things. Ending on the truth was the most honorable solution. He owed her at least that much.

Damali slowly lowered her weapons. There was no fear, no anger, just total defeat in her expression. She understood what he was saying. He let his breath out hard and looked away. All resistance had gone out of her body, and she was sipping air slowly. She shook her head in a painful rhythm of disbelief. He glanced back at her, unable to break the spell she always had on him. He absorbed her hurt as he watched the brass poker fall, then the arrow tip, and then the wooden stake made from it. The clatter against the hard surface pierced his ears. He saw her hand slowly sweep down her chest as though trying to restart her own heart, and he turned and continued to stand before the open deck doors, staring up at the moon.

In that moment, that inner part of him that still remembered what it was like to have a soul wept, though not a single tear fell. His insides were bleeding, but there was nothing he could do. She was so stubborn, yet deserved the truth. How could he promise her what he couldn't even promise himself? He had felt the primal pull of the beast within him, and the reaction he'd had toward the new female had been visceral. Lust and ambition drowned him, and was encoded within the deep lake of his loins, the need to procreate—turn humans to replace his territorial losses, create solid lieutenants, to build an empire, to mate with his own kind—the undead—but it wasn't love. She had to understand that. He wanted Damali safe, out of harm's way, but he also needed to do what he had to do. He heard her swallow again, hard, and knew no tears were flowing. She was sucking it up, and the river of pain in her was the tributary.

"I should get you back to the hotel," he said softly, not taking a step toward her.

She only nodded. He waited.

"You want her that much?" Damali was barely breathing when she finally spoke.

He didn't answer. She took the silence as his answer. Damali turned and looked him in the eye. She didn't use her gift, or any special powers. And that look, more than a wooden stake, more than a silver blade, stripped the air from his lungs and sent a hurt so deep into his core that he almost couldn't stand. But he also couldn't look away from that source of profound agony. The priests had told him to block the shot. He'd ripped out her heart, instead.

"I just have one question," she said in a quiet, defeated voice. Her gaze never wavered. Her chin lifted with dignity. Her bottom lip quivered as she breathed. Yet her stance was firm. "All that time, when you were with me . . . how much of it was me . . . and how much of it was your desire to conquer the Neteru?"

It must have stripped her bare to bring that question to her lips. The brutal honesty in it filleted him. Shame washed through him that she would even have to ask. He'd been wrong; there was no ego in this struggle. He couldn't breathe; much less answer her question. Didn't she know? He had loved her when he was a living man. Had loved her when they were kids. Had wanted her so badly some nights that he thought he'd lose his mind. She was the only woman in his life that had ever turned down all that he had, wasn't the least bit interested in material gain or what he could do for her, and had worried about him—the man, the vampire—had tried to protect something so ephemeral as his soul.

And for the same reasons then, that were repeating themselves now, he'd pushed her away to protect her. Conquer her? Never. He'd been the one who had surrendered. She was the embodiment of everything that had ever been good, and right, and real in his world. Nothing could replace that, but everything could take it away.

This attack sadly proved his theory. He had hoped he'd been wrong. But he also knew better than to hope for something so tenuous. He knew his kind, and how they operated. As above in the drug life, so below in the underworld. It was a warning for him to make a decision, and make it fast. By the time he'd reentered the lair, he had made his decision. He would take the offer he couldn't refuse and block the shot—and it had less to do about him than it did Damali's personal safety. He'd use his forces to protect her as long as he could, then those at higher levels in the upper realms would have to do their thing. He couldn't guard her forever, nor could he block the shot indefinitely. One day her heart would get broken, one way or another. He'd had time to ponder that truth. So, now, or seven years from now—which was such a short time anyway when one considered eternity—what difference did it make?

There would come a time when he was away, distracted, or couldn't get to her. Then what? He'd rather let her go than see her torn apart by the myriad of predators Hell could unleash. He'd rather give the Devil her due, and appease the beast, cut a deal, a compromise, than to ever draw Damali into the complex cesspool that surrounded him.

She nodded, but didn't understand his silence. "If I'm lucky, I'll get old one day." She chuckled quietly. It was the hard, hollow sound that came from bitter resignation. "You won't. My body will get flabby. My hair will gray. My eyes will dim. My blade hand will tremble with arthritis. My womb will remain empty. But I will look back and remember ten nights when I loved a man with my entire soul till I saw lights. If I have nothing else, even if it wasn't real to you, I will have known what it was like to be ready to die for someone."

Her admission in the wake of all she thought about him, all that she assumed, tore him apart. He sucked in a huge breath, trying to think of how to explain. "I loved you, too, baby," was all he could whisper.

She stared at him. "Loved. Past tense," she said. "I still love you, and I don't even know why." She collected the arrow tip, and stood facing him. "Please, take me back to my family." When he moved toward her, she held up her hand. "If you choose to walk this path, and you have, I will hunt you. Not out of revenge. Not out of spite. But if you go completely dark, take bodies, turn victims, or aid another vampire—male or female—in doing said same, I will hunt you down and kill you. We can end this tonight."

He saw the resignation not the defeat in her, and knew the next time they encountered each other it would be a fight to the death. How was he supposed to stand against that?

"If you win, all I ask is that you don't turn me. Let me go out with honor." She lifted her chin higher, her back straight. "Don't feed on me, or allow my body to be desecrated like that—you owe me that much." Her voice was calm, even, and controlled, but her eyes said it all. "And keep the same seal on my people, my family, the clerics. You owe us all that much. And, just for the record, don't you *ever* again not trust me to do my job, which is hunting vampires."

He backed away from her, appalled, shaking his head. "I could never do that," he whispered, sickened by what she proposed. "And they'll always have my seal." He shook his head. "How could I desecrate *you*?"

She nodded and rubbed a sudden chill from her arms. "In many ways, I suppose you already have."

CHAPTER NINETEEN

THE DEBATE raged on about what could possibly be lurking near Brazil, but Rider sat silently, just looking out of the limousine window. He hated not knowing the lay of the land, and felt handicapped by not having fluent knowledge of the language. He felt trapped, could feel the sensation rising within him fast, threatening to suffocate him. He studied the dark, mountain road. Mist surrounded the vehicle, and there was no other traffic. The limousine bounced along the uneven asphalt, and the moon shimmered overhead. They were going down another dark path that felt like one more blind alley. He had been down too many in his life, and this was the last one he was willing to explore.

"Let me out," he said, his voice low. The walls of the vehicle seemed like they were closing in on him.

The group stopped talking and looked at him.

"I have to get out," he said again softly. "Please let me out." He looked at the team's stunned expressions. "This is where I get off," he said, his voice beginning to become strained, rising as he spoke, each word becoming louder and louder. "I don't want to go see some fellow guardian team in the hills. I don't want to make another goddamned choice about shit. I'm exhausted—mentally wrung out. I do not care if it's demons or vampires or a fucking drug dealer, just as long as the bastards kill me quick!"

He drew a ragged breath and placed his hand on the door, and nodded toward the driver. "Tell that motherfucker to open the door before I shoot the window out!"

"Rider, man, be cool," Shabazz said, his voice low and comforting, but steady. "I know you're tired. We all are," he said, trying to reach some rational part of Rider's mind. "Marlene's been getting wild visions just from the land we're on. My reflexes have been hair-trigger, like I'm about to go off any minute, which ain't good in a foreign joint where there's no such thing as parole. Feel me? There's so much stimuli here that Mike is picking up everything and nothing at the same time. The young bucks are wigging, and are overextended after the concert. Your nose is off, 'cause you're exhausted."

"Right now, you could light a Cuban cigar next to me, and I wouldn't know it."

Shabazz kept his gaze on Rider's, waiting for him to remove his hand from the door. No one else spoke. All that could be heard was the drone of the motor. "Man, it's gonna be all right."

"It's not going to be all right!" Rider drew his Glock and pointed it toward his window. "She looked like Tara."

Big Mike exchanged a glance with Shabazz and Jose, then sent a warning glance around the team. No one said a word and Marlene swallowed hard.

"It's all right, man," Big Mike said slowly, his voice low and steady. "That was a gift."

"It was *not* a gift," Rider said, now looking at Big Mike, but his hand was no longer on the door handle. Angry tears shone in his eyes and his gun trembled as he lowered the weapon and pointed it toward the floor. He shook his head. "That chick in the club . . . she looked just like her." He breathed in a shaky inhale. "It was a curse that just brought it all back, Mike. I shouldn't have taken her back to the room."

Quiet enveloped the group as Rider's breathing steadied.

"There comes a point in a man's life where he reaches his limit," Rider said, his voice just above a murmur. "When you gotta let something go, no matter how much that shit hurts. Then you start over, and try not to look back." His gaze sought the window again, and he stared out past the blackened windows. "That's all Rivera is trying to say. I can dig it. Been there. This bullshit going down over here is part of his territory—let him handle it. Damali isn't in any danger from him, she's in danger from not letting go when she should."

Shabazz slowly reached out and put his hand on Rider's shoulder. "Gimme your gun, man. Let me hold it for you tonight . . . I wouldn't want you to get hurt."

"Yeah, man," Jose said, his voice dropping to a soothing octave. "Give 'Bazz the gun, me and you can talk this out . . . just like old times, just like we always do around this time of year. It's gonna be all right."

Rider chuckled. But the sound of it was distant as he lifted his Glock, ignored Shabazz's open hand and Jose's pleas, and put the weapon to his temple. "I wouldn't want anything else to happen to me, either," he said, his gaze never leaving the window. "There was only one person I'd take a bite from, and she's history."

"Rider," Marlene said, her voice quiet and strained. "Baby, listen. If we're dealing with demons, one just got to your head . . . remember I told you that you and Dan were more susceptible on this mission . . . Dan has German in his line, you've got European, and whatever's out there has an ax to grind. Put the gun down, honey. We love you. We've all got a past that haunts, and you're right. The past is hard to live with. Why don't we go home, figure this all out, huh? Let's just live through one more night, and when this child comes back to the hotel, she'll be baptized by the experience of a broken heart, too. And every one of us in here can testify, one by one . . . Carlos will be able to, as well."

"We'll let the man clean out his own territory," Big Mike said, reaching across Shabazz and putting a gentle but firm hand on Rider's biceps to lower the gun away from his skull. "There's a hundred and forty-four thousand guardians on the planet, brother. We're just one team of seven that happened to get the hard task of guarding a Neteru. We can let a couple of vamps get smoked by the other teams. And in those other teams, who knows . . . there might be somebody worth taking a bullet for. You understand, man?"

Rider nodded, swallowed hard, and put the safety back on his gun before putting it in his shoulder holster hard. "That's all I was saying," he whispered, and looked at the stricken expressions of the younger guardians. He could feel the muscles in his jaw pulse as he blinked back tears and they burned away. "Rivera is a good man," he said, his voice steadier as his gaze went back to the window. "Had a tough choice—one of his own, or one not like him . . . didn't matter where his heart was. He could do this quick and draw that knife out of the wound in one hard pull, or drag this shit out for seven years in fucked-up increments." He nodded again, just staring. "Quick is always better." Then he sat back and slung his arm over his eyes and took a deep breath.

No sooner than he'd sat back, the window shattered, the limousine swerved, and then hit a tree. The team tumbled out of their seats and scrambled to right themselves, their nervous gazes shooting around to see if anyone had been hurt. Rider yanked an arrow out of the upholstery by Marlene's head, his hand shaking. Two seconds earlier, if he hadn't sat back, it would have gone through his temple.

The fractured radiator hissed, and the entire front of the limo was an accordion of crumbled metal. The tree didn't even lean. The driver was slumped over the wheel.

"Incoming!" Rider hollered, as another arrow whizzed through the missing windshield and hit the empty front passenger seat.

Big Mike quickly looked at the driver through the partially broken separation window. He kicked out the remaining glass, reached over the seat, and forced the man back. He looked down and pulled a bloody arrow from the center of the driver's chest with a rip. "We got a major problem, people."

The limo rocked as something landed on the top of it. Mike adjusted his shoulder cannon, aimed at the ceiling, and fired, opening a large hole in the roof. "We've gotta get out, or we're sitting ducks in here."

Rider put his head up through the gaping hole, cocked his gun at the blackness, and ducked down again fast. "I didn't see anything," he said, breathless.

"You won't," Marlene told him in a flat tone. "Look at this arrowhead. Amazon. Shaped just like an Isis blade point. Just like you'd find on a guardian team's weapons."

"Oh, shit . . ." Rider was about to go up through the hole again when the vehicle rocked from sudden weight. A jaguar peered down through the blown-out steel, snarled, and vanished.

The group stared at the drip of saliva that was now sizzling a hole in the limousine floor carpet.

"I smell it now, if I didn't before—sulfur." Rider looked at his junior tracker partner for confirmation.

Jose concurred. "Demon with a heavy animal tracer. Gotta be a were."

"We've got one choice," Shabazz said. "We can sit here while they pick us off one by one, or get out and go down swinging."

"We swing, dude," Rider agreed. "On three?"

The team looked out the missing windshield through to where the divider used to be.

"We'd better swing hard, because I count several pairs of green glowing eyes dead ahead." JL glanced over his shoulder as six jaguars materialized out of the dense mist.

"There're too many of them to go out there," Dan whispered.

"Shit," Marlene whispered, clutching Damali's sword. "The only way we can—"

But her words failed her as a hand punched through the driver's-side window and yanked the dead driver out. Shabazz opened fire and missed the black hooded entity. It snarled, brandished a battle-ax, and leaped with five other hooded figures in front of the advancing row of jaguars.

"What the fuck?" Rider's voice trailed off and he knelt on the vehicle floor, facing the windshield with his gun pointing toward the missing pane. "Vamps, too? All in the same night?"

"I'm going over the seat!" Dan hollered. "C'mon, JL. I'll cover you. Try to see if we can start the engine!"

"Dan, sit your ass down! You're a target, like Rider. The engine and radiator are done. You see that front end?" Big Mike pointed with his shoulder cannon. "Everybody, conserve artillery, and only shoot at what comes near us. If they fight over us as dinner, maybe they'll thin their own numbers out. We pick off what's left."

"Sounds like a plan," Shabazz said, covering a back window as the limo rocked with weight again.

They were moving backward away from the tree. Shabazz squinted, trying to get a visual on what had them, in order to get off a solid shot. The team's attention darted between the standoff before them and the invisible force pulling the wrecked vehicle away from the tree trunk.

"Hold up," Marlene said fast. "I can see. Hold your fire."

"What?" Rider put his left hand under his right wrist to steady his weapon.

JL, Dan, and Jose had crossbows assembled and aimed.

"I said, hold your fire! It's our only way out of here!"

The back windshield peeled away like it was a piece of paper, and two red, glowing eyes stared back through it without a face. Massive incisors opened and a snarl emanated from the creature. Marlene's hand went to Rider's trembling arm, and she held up her other hand to keep Shabazz and the others steady.

"We will repair your engine and radiator. But you must be quick. The demons are upon you. Daylight comes soon—and makes our assistance limited."

But as the entity spoke, it suddenly burst into flames and disintegrated.

"I can fire now, huh, Mar?" Rider shouted, opening a round of gunfire with Big Mike and Shabazz.

A dart flew past him, lodging in the leather seat a millimeter from his upper arm. Dan released a crossbow stake, but it simply passed through thin air. Before them, the standoff broke into a free-for-all battle as the jaguars lunged at the hooded creatures. Horrible snarls and hisses echoed into the night air.

"Keep that back window covered!" Shabazz ordered, tumbling into the front seat with Dan.

"Shabazz, no!" Marlene yelled, another dart missing him by inches. "They use poison! Use the holy-water grenades, Dan. The crossbow arrows aren't fast enough. They don't work on the demons, and don't shoot the vamps. They're allies!"

A blue electric arc shattered the side window upon Marlene's words. Shabazz yelled, "Noooo!" his gun firing toward nothing, passing through the light that wracked Marlene's convulsing form. The arc was unbreakable. The front window was vulnerable as the team scrambled to help Marlene, unable to touch her as the current riddled her.

The energy that held her was as bright as lightning, and as her body shook from the jolt that paralyzed her, the team drew back, not knowing what to fire at. The energy receded, dropping Marlene in a smoldering heap, and an albino human female face lowered into the side window. Her light brown locks were woven with gold bands, and her eyes glowed green, her evil grin disfigured by fangs. She disappeared before Big Mike's shoulder cannon payload passed the horizon of the window.

Just beyond the side of a limousine another vampire guard was felled, disintegrated by a hail of silver-tipped arrows. Shabazz was over the seat, holding Marlene to his chest, one arm extended with his weapon, his body swinging wildly as he quickly aimed in different directions. A hooded creature jumped into the driver's seat that Shabazz had abandoned, and when Dan raised his crossbow, the vampire slapped it away, put his finger in the ignition, and the engine fired.

"Drive!" Then the creature was gone.

Dan slid over and took the wheel; Rider jumped in the front with him to cover their driver. Big Mike put one hand on Shabazz's shoulder, covering him as he tried to revive Marlene. Both JL and Jose stood up through the hole, using it like a machine gun turret, leveling crossbows at the misty night while Dan drove the vehicle down the street in reverse. Spinning fast, he wheeled the limo in a circle, threw it into drive, and stomped the pedal to the floor.

"You know where you're going? You can't see shit out here!"

"No," Dan yelled at Rider. "But anywhere is better than where we were. Fuck it. If we have to drive around like maniacs till dawn, what dif does it make?"

"Point taken," Rider admitted. "How's Mar?"

Rider peered over the seat. His eyes met Mike's. Big Mike shook his head. Shabazz brought Marlene's limp body closer against his, and rocked harder, saying nothing, nuzzling her cheek with his own.

"Son of a bitch!" Rider punched the dashboard and swallowed hard, blinking back the emotion.

Dan simply drove.

Sudden motion at the door brought Damali to her feet, crossbow raised, chin lowered, her sight on the target; anything that came through the door would be toast.

Big Mike barreled through the hotel-room door first, an Uzi leveled as he kicked it in, and Shabazz came in carrying Marlene in his arms, followed by Jose, JL, and Dan, Rider bringing up the rear— backing in, his gun toward the hall before shutting the door.

All weapons dropped, the team gathered around the bed, and Shabazz gently lowered Marlene and laid his head on her chest. The rest of the group backed up as they saw his fist slowly clench the covers around her. His shoulders shook. A sob caught in Damali's throat. Her crossbow fell to the floor. She stood there, stunned, not believing her eyes. Hot moisture made everything go hazy, and her voice came from her belly, as she screamed, "No!"

Fighting against the hands that grabbed for her, she pushed them away.

"Let me at her, Shabazz. Please, 'Bazz! I got this, trust me!"

Tears coursed down his dark, stricken face, but he sucked in a deep breath, stood, and stepped to the side. Damali pressed her face to Marlene's chest and closed her eyes. Then she took a deep breath and opened her mind. Her hands caressed the crown of Marlene's head, her fingers tangling in Marlene's dense thicket of silver locks. Frantic, Damali tried to still herself, tried to remember everything Marlene had taught her about healing, removing dark-arts magic, restoring wholeness, breaking horrible illusions. She breathed slowly, willing Marlene's soul to hear hers. Silent tears ran down the bridge of her nose, dripping onto Marlene's chest. The smell of sulfur sent a stench of raw skin and acid into the back of Damali's throat where the arc of negative energy had struck.

In her mind, she could see the electric blue light that was darkened by a black, writhing mass of adders that it carried, their green eyes glowing as they'd entered Marlene's chest, strangling her heart, trying to stop the flow of her life force. She covered their entry point on Marlene's chest with both hands, her eyes shut tight, as she mentally siphoned them to her with her younger, angrier, more vital energy. She could feel them enter her palms, slide up her arms, and enter her chest cavity.

Damali's chest began to sting, burn, and sear her cotton T-shirt to her as her lungs became filled with suffocating sulfur. Her chest felt tight, her innards moved, consumed by a slithering mass that snapped at her heart tissue and soft organs. She cried out. Big Mike rushed toward her, but Rider held him.

Shabazz began a silent prayer, his hands clasped, his eyes shut tight, now on his knees. Dan knelt beside him as Damali worked, joining in the prayer with Shabazz in Hebrew. Rider's hands went to Damali's shoulders and Big Mike added his with Jose's, sending energy, power, prayers, light to the fallen Marlene. Shabazz lowered his face to the bed covers, his body shaking with the effort to control his tears. The pain that went through Damali's chest felt like her heart was being stripped from it, but she would not stop. Dear God in Heaven, not Marlene!

Pain made her breaths come in short pants. Panic ripped at her mind. But she held on, sending love, light, and warmth. Images echoed in her skull. She saw the thing that had sent the horrible dark charge. Her eyes locked with its demonic stare. Damali sat up, trapped in the vision, holding Marlene's clothes in tight fists.

"You can't have her!" she said, her voice coming out almost in a growl. "It is *not* her time."

Damali yanked her hands away from Marlene's chest and made fists, holding a part of the evil within them. She stood and shrugged off the other guardians' touch for their safety. She knew it would concentrate, would try to pull back into one black mass. An eerie dark light swirled around Damali's clenched fists as she opened them and stepped away from the bed, then slapped her own chest hard, taking a small portion of what had attacked Marlene into her. "And you don't have that kind of power!"

Damali's body instantly arched as the black charge entered her, and she tried to draw the negative energy away from Marlene toward her. The air around both women crackled with dark current, and a volt snapped Damali with a hard jerk as a charred filament threaded out of Marlene and connected both women at the heart level chakra like a snakelike black cord.

"Toss me my blade, but don't touch me," Damali said, her voice strong through labored breaths. She didn't even open her eyes, just heard her weapon chime as a teammate threw it. She felt for it blindly as she reached out and caught it mid-air. With one swing, she broke the dark cord connection that was beginning to choke her, then leaped up on the bed, one foot on either side of Marlene's body.

She placed the Isis tip over Marlene's heart, and watched the dark filament attack it, leaving Marlene to creep up the blood grooves in the sword, cover her hand, and slide up her blade arm in a slow approach to her heart. *That's right, come to me. I'm younger, stronger, more vital, have a weapon. You want the group leader, the seer, female energy. Come for the Neteru.* Her mind screamed at the darkness, baiting it, drawing it, *Yes, come to me, she's old.* When the last of the black plasma had stopped coming from Marlene's chest, Damali raised the Isis and began a loud chant of Psalm Ninety-One—the psalm of protection during battle.

Immediately, the dark cord receded from her shoulder in a fast-moving, smoking, angry swirl back down her arm as though trying to escape the route it had traveled. The moment it hit the handle of the blade the black plasma sparked, ignited, and torched everything on the blade, leaving a green slimy residue that ran down the blood grooves when Damali lowered it over the side of the bed away from her and

Marlene. The group watched it burn, turn to ash, then disappear.

Blue electric current rippled across Marlene's shut lids as soon as the last of the ash had vanished. Marlene gasped and arched violently, then relaxed. She coughed, wheezed, and drew in a huge gulp of air, then vomited over the side of the bed.

Damali knelt and held Marlene's locks out of her face, while her body continued to empty itself. An open sob wracked Shabazz as he clutched Marlene's concert robe and buried his face in it. Damali touched Marlene's face.

"You learned good, baby," Marlene said, her voice a hoarse whisper. She wiped her mouth with the back of her hand. She caressed the top of Shabazz's head. He was breathing hard as he clasped her hand, but had recovered.

"Get her some water," he said, glancing up at Mike.

Rider went to get towels to clean up the mess by the bed, and the others helped as Shabazz just stayed by her side stroking her hair, dabbing perspiration off her forehead, and swallowing hard. Marlene sat up a little, took a sip of water, and spit it into the waste can Rider held for her. She took a bit of toothpaste from Damali's finger when Big Mike offered it, and swished her mouth out, then shook her head.

"Close one," she murmured, shutting her eyes and drinking a full glass of water.

Damali nodded, her hand went to her chest, and her voice fractured with rage. She was seeing red, little pinpoints of it wafting past her corneas, almost scorching them from the inside out. "Too close. This was over the top!" Damali picked up her sword and her grip tightened on Madame Isis. She looked around at her team, realizing that she had almost lost them.

"Everybody else is all right," Shabazz said, his voice hoarse as he stood slowly. "I've just never seen Marlene take a hit like that. We're all right. After this, I'm done."

"Shabazz," Marlene said quietly. "Guardians never run." She touched his face. "This thing is—"

"I'm going alone," Damali said, sitting down beside Marlene and taking up one of her hands. "I will cut this bitch's heart out. She went for my moms, my mother-seer—had my partner, Rider, almost shoot himself in the head? Got my man acting stupid? Oh, hell no!" Her gaze swept the group. "I understand 'Bazz's point—it is too dangerous for a lot of members on this team. But, you know what? I'm so fucking done, if I get one of them before I die, that's all right by me."

She looked at Shabazz, thoroughly understanding his position, and also could dig why her team was silently riding the fence, not trying to sway the decision to fight so that if something happened to Marlene again, their own consciences wouldn't kill them—if they lived. Both elder members would lay heavy on all their hearts, if the shit got any crazier than it already had. She kissed Marlene's forehead fast and stood and walked to the terrace doors and flung them open. "It's on now, you whore!" she yelled, then slammed the glass so hard it almost shattered.

Rider glanced at Damali and Shabazz, then cast his gaze around the room, allowing it to settle on Marlene. "I don't think Carlos knows what he's dealing with. He told us it was a female vamp. What attacked us were were-demons from this region. I was the first one ready to break camp and ready to go home, too. But my mind can't wrap around a piece of this puzzle." He rubbed his jaw and looked at Shabazz. "You should take Marlene home, man. Wouldn't nobody blame you . . . least of all, me."

"I hear you, but, we're okay, everything's gonna be fine. Gotta pick your battles, just wasn't ready for this one." Shabazz's voice sounded more like he was trying to convince himself than anyone else, but the group simply nodded. They could all dig it. The team was shook.

"Marlene, you were right all along—Carlos doesn't know shit. These are were-demons, girl. His ass is tripping, so don't factor in what he has to say. The two that came for me—one as a croc, the other as an anaconda . . . right in Carlos's fucking lair, his shit is so raggedy." She stood and began pacing. "I'm done."

"What?" Rider had stopped her from pacing by holding her elbow. "In a master vamp's lair? How the hell did they breach his—"

"He thought she was a female vamp, and obviously didn't bar her or her girls from his bedroom," Damali said quickly, cutting Rider off. "The point is, I was in there with no Isis, a freakin' brass fireplace poker, and a twelve-foot crocodile materialized in the stream in the bedroom—then a giant anaconda slithered out of the goddamned hot tub."

"I'm not going to ask about the appointments in these vamp lairs," Rider said slowly, "but, uh, where was lover-man when the shit was hitting the fan?" He folded his arms over his chest. "This ain't his style, D. Not the way he feels about you. And you are still valuable to the vamp empire. To them, you're precious cargo, and he wouldn't risk that; the man has two very compelling reasons to keep you out of harm's way. He couldn't have known about this."

"The first one would have been enough for Rivera," Jose said. "Trust me on that." He looked at Damali and his gaze slid from her toward the window. "He didn't sanction a hit."

"Nah," Big Mike said, looking at Rider. "Homeboy might have decided to take the vampires' offer, but I agree with Rider and Jose, and I *know* he wouldn't willingly put Damali in harm's way . . . and demons? C'mon, y'all. Something's up with that. He don't roll like that. Where was he when they breached his lair, baby?"

Marlene struggled to sit up and Shabazz helped her, as all eyes in the room went to Damali. She studied the blade in her hand.

"Out feeding," Damali said, humiliation coating her tongue as she said it. "Or, whatever."

"He was feeding, D," JL said quietly. "Don't go there."

Again, no one spoke for a moment, but Dan's soft voice of reason broke the silence.

"Well, it was Carlos's crew that bailed us out, D. Rivera kept his word."

Damali nodded. But a rage so deep, worse than she'd ever known, threatened to make her scream. The emotion was so close to the surface of her skin it was making her itch. A war cry trapped in her throat mixed with the tears of anguish she'd swallowed and threatened to choke her.

"If there's been some kind of new alliance between the vamp empire and the strongest demon forces out there, the weres, then we need to go to Bahia," Marlene said quietly. "We can't run from this, or allow how we individually feel to cloud the issue."

Her gaze went to Shabazz and she cupped his cheek, and she briefly closed her eyes as he kissed the center of her palm and took her hand. She looked at Damali until Damali turned to face her. "He came for you when you were blind . . . you've gotta come for him now." She hesitated as she watched the tears rising in Damali's eyes. "Regardless, you and I both know that we cannot have an alignment that might allow these two entities to share power."

Damali nodded. "Vamps have mobility to go wherever they want, demons have access to daylight." She let out a weary breath. "Yeah, Mar. I know."

"Then, we need to at least warn the crew in Bahia about what Marlene is talking about. Matter of fact, if they've seen something like this, maybe they'd have weapons for it, because we sure don't." JL's gaze swept the group. "That's freakin' courtesy, folks. Imagine how we'd feel if another team knew about the whole Nuit thing, and just ran?"

"That's what telephones and fax machines and the Internet is for, little brother. We can get word to 'em. No need for a guided tour." Shabazz's eyes remained on Marlene. "The more I'm thinking about it, the whole thing is just too risky and my heart can't take it—honest to God."

"I love you, too," Marlene said quietly. "But you know in your soul, we've gotta go."

Shabazz stood and walked to stand by the terrace doors that Damali had abandoned and raked his fingers through his locks. Damali watched Marlene lie back down and close her eyes. She studied Shabazz's back as he breathed slowly.

"I can go alone or with a partial team, since it's just a fact-finding mission," Damali said softly, her rage dulling as she watched Shabazz's struggle. "I respect where Shabazz is coming from, and if our elder brother has a bad vibe—"

"No," Shabazz said in a weary tone. "We don't split up the group under any circumstances, personal or otherwise, when there's a clear and present threat. That's always been the rule."

"You sure, man?" Rider said, going to him.

Shabazz nodded. "Everybody get four hours of sleep. We'll check out at eleven tomorrow, send our stuff to the States, and get us a flight to Bahia, like Mar said. But in the meantime we get some sleep."

Shabazz walked back to Marlene, climbed up on the bed next to her, and spooned her from behind. Big Mike took a position in a chair facing the busted door, his Uzi over his lap as he shut his eyes. JL slid down against a wall, his crossbow on his legs. He leaned his head back, shut his eyes, and let his breath out hard. Rider snatched the desk chair, turned it around backward and sat, dropping his head to the desk. But his hand never left his gun. Jose and Dan slowly found a position by JL, flanking him on the floor.

"We might not be going anywhere," Marlene said with her eyes closed. "The driver . . . an innocent man. There'll be questions."

Damali closed her eyes as she found a soft chair and curled up in it. Somehow, the anger had blocked her fear, but it also lowered the veil expanding her awareness. She could intuit without full sight. In connecting with Marlene, she'd felt wisdom enter her. While she still couldn't see Carlos, the expressions on her team's faces, their beat-up, fatigued bodies, sent adrenaline through her. "Carlos's crew will clean up the situation."

"The vampire CIA, huh?" Rider chuckled wearily. "Operating in foreign countries, shifting the balance of power like a huge game board."

"Yeah," Damali muttered. "Somethin' like that."

She kept her eyes shut. A gray filter of new sunlight was trying to peek through the sides of the shut drapes. The guardians were there not to protect her; they were there because they were afraid to sleep alone. The burden of the shift in roles sat heavily on her chest and shoulders. Marlene had always said one day things would change.

But she had expected a long, drawn-out coming into her own. Yet, with a snap of Fate's fingers, a roll of Fate's dice, she was the den mother, the group leader, the general leading the charge. She now understood why Marlene and the others had given her as much time to be a kid as they could afford. It had been a small blessing, one to be cherished that she didn't fully appreciate until now.

Yes, she had led many a street fight. Sure, she had gone into fights before with Marlene and the guys. But never had one of her inner circle been this close to being lost. The Dee Dee thing was different. That had hurt like hell, but still . . . Dee Dee hadn't been one of their inner circle. Never had one so close as Marlene, her seer-mother and friend, ever come so near to dying, or had needed her so much. What if she hadn't been able to save Marlene? What if it hadn't been black-magic energy that had dropped Mar; what if it had been an arrow or a bullet? She couldn't save her from that. What if fear paralyzed her and she wasn't able to save anyone? Then what?

This was so different, this new role in a strange, foreign land. Never had so much been siphoned from her soul in one night . . . a night when she needed to weep for a significant loss, but couldn't. Those days were over. She'd gone to sleep one night ago a girl and had woken up in a new land as a woman.

"Do you know where he is, baby?" Marlene's gentle question flitted across the room to Damali.

Damali didn't even open her eyes to answer as she drifted off to sleep. "No, Mar. It doesn't matter anymore, anyway. He's just another vampire."

Carlos stared at the remaining vampire from his international squad in disbelief. "What happened?"

The maimed transporter fell to his knees and hung his head before Carlos. Its hooded robe was in shreds, as was one of its arms. It had been stripped of its battle-axes, and one fang was missing. The eyes in its faceless expanse of blackness flickered dangerously, on the verge of going out.

"I need to feed," it heaved in a ragged whisper. "I cannot even transmit."

Begrudgingly, Carlos pushed back the sleeve of his suit and offered his wrist to the dying thing. Disgust filled him as the entity greedily accepted the offering, and immediately slit Carlos's vein and began to feed, making wet, sucking sounds.

"That's enough," Carlos snapped, pulling his arm away.

The entity stood slowly, humiliation flickering in its eyes. Shaking its head in a warning, its eyes were solid red and it pointed to them, telling Carlos without words to see for himself.

Carlos looked into the entity's eyes, nodded, and paced away from the creature. "It was beyond your control." He walked over to the hearth and slammed his fist into it. "Damn!"

"We protected the Neteru's people at all costs, as you ordered. But the toll was heavy, sir. Were-demons are formidable within their own power boundaries . . . even though it poaches your territory."

What could Carlos say? Their word had been their bond. He studied the creature and let his breath out with impatience. "Thank you," he muttered, but meaning it. He'd asked the impossible and these messengers had delivered. But demons against Damali's crew? Why? Her team was nowhere near where the bodies had dropped. Then a deeply disturbing reality hit him; if that whack female vamp had led them to the new Neteru so they could manufacture more essence . . . Carlos closed his eyes to gather calm. "Let council know what happened."

The entity sighed and nodded, seeming relieved. "I will transmit the situation to the Vampire Council. The Neteru is safe?"

"Yes," Carlos said, nodding with caution. "Go ahead and send."

He watched the red orbs disappear as his message was transmitted. The muscles in his back coiled with anticipation, as he waited for the messenger to reopen its eyes.

The chairman stood with his hands behind his back, his eyes closed, and his chin tilted toward the ceiling as he received the topside message. The Vampire Council sat silently, waiting, until the chairman opened his eyes.

"We have a disaster brewing topside," he said plainly, walking from behind the large pentagram-shaped table. Beyond belief, he shook his head as he spoke, his gaze roving over his council members, suspicion in his countenance. "See for yourself how we lost all but one of the international couriers we sent to protect Rivera's cargo. Pirated by level five were-demons? Impossible! A breach of this magnitude is an attempt to start another war—"

"While we are knowingly vulnerable," the counselor advised coolly.

Fury ripped through the chairman, but he remained outwardly calm. "Our world as we know it is changing. We were once a vast superpower, unmatched. But aggressive, weaker nations are utilizing terrorist tactics . . . they fight a very different war than we are used to."

"Do not underestimate their formidability, Mr. Chairman," the counselor said, his eyes never leaving the senior vampire. "We must get Rivera out of the hot zone, along with his cargo, before anything happens while they're there."

Another council member from the far end of the table spoke. "We must come to a decision, as dawn approaches, or adjourn. And we still have the matter of Rivera's missing soul. Our best man topside is in double jeopardy fighting unscrupulous forces such as these."

"I want his soul, or I want him out of there," the chairman said with a note of concern. "This courageous vampire is so—"

"We have the matter under control," the counselor interjected. "Mr. Chair—"

"No!" the chairman boomed. "Enough waiting!" Thick billows of black smoke surrounded his feet as he walked, rising in plumes around him as his robes swished against the marble floor. "You have sent soul searchers on rescue and recovery missions, and they have failed! *You* handle this personally, Mr. Counselor! Now!"

The international courier bristled, drawing Carlos to alert status. They both glanced at the horizon, knowing only a few minutes stood between them and certain incineration. Seeming confused, the now weaponless messenger stepped back. Carlos looked at him, hard. The messenger only offered one word.

"Incoming."

"The council? Near dawn?" Carlos studied the entity that only nodded. This was not good. He stepped back as a cavern opened within the center of the lair's slate floor and the requisite black plume of smoke screeched in a furious swirl, threatening to suck away the contents of the room with gale-force winds. Slowly, as the room came to a rest, the counselor stepped from the center of the abyss.

"Counselor Vlak?"

"Leave us," he said to the courier, ignoring Carlos's question. He stood staring out the deck opening until the entity disappeared, then he turned a sinister gaze on Carlos. He walked the perimeter of the room with his hands behind his back as he garnered enough restraint to speak.

"Your gates will come down in a few moments, so let us not mince words or play games." The counselor held Carlos's gaze in a lethal stare. "You and I both know your soul is not within the realms." When Carlos opened his mouth to form a protest, the counselor held up his hand. "You may fool that old, doddering idiot. He has become weak and senile with delusions of a return of the old way, but you are speaking to me now, not the chairman."

Counselor Vlak spit on the floor and wiped his mouth with the back of his hand. Carlos remained very, very still, ready for an attack.

"I thought about the options—the strategies available, as soon as my subterranean soul searchers came back with news that your soul could not be found. And that damnable prayer in your heart that you died with kept haunting me. So, we sent a our best searcher to the border of Purgatory as a last resort; a place we rarely go near as the dangers to our kind there are many." He laughed evilly, and shook his head. "Damali Richards's essence within your soul led our searcher right to it. We could not cross, but they were absolutely certain that there was one of ours behind the wall riddled with Neteru trail—and polluted by love. So I watched you . . . the refusal to traditionally feed on innocents, the refusal to take a life. All the signs, the *compassion* toward her team—*even clerics.*" He spat again and circled Carlos. "You even imperiled our best international couriers for her and her human guardians!"

"She's precious cargo to the Vampire Council," Carlos hedged, still not wanting to corroborate any evidence.

"My first impulse was to inform the council of your treachery and have them remand you to the Sea of Perpetual Agony," the counselor said, not the least bit fazed by the rebuttal. "But then, all my years as a Roman senator prevailed." He shook a bony finger in Carlos's face and smiled, his fangs lengthening. "A man so bold as to play three ends against the middle is a worthy competitor. And a man with something of value to lose, is a man who will cut a deal."

"What do you want?" Carlos whispered. For the first time since this entire travesty began, he felt cornered. He was cold-busted, and dangling by a thread over a precipice, and Damali was endangered from multiple realms.

"I want absolute power," the counselor said, calmly studying the lower echelon crest on his hooked finger.

"I don't have absolute power," Carlos said, no ruse in his reply. He opened his arms. "I'm a trapped and hunted man. What can I give you that you don't already have?"

"A trade," the counselor replied, looking up and holding him without blinking. "A discreet and quiet trade."

"Talk to me," Carlos said, glancing at the open deck doors. The iron lair seal had begun to lower.

"Fallon Nuit was a madman, but a brilliant one. His method of escape just needed refinement." The counselor threw his head back and laughed, sending a shrill echo through the lair. "There is nothing better than a double, double cross. He was let out by a variable, a woman who performed a ritual that released a demon above his incarceration lair. Nuit then formed an alliance with the Amanthra he was forced to cohabitate with."

"I know, I know," Carlos said, becoming nervous that he might be trapped in a lair all day with this lunatic. "But speak quickly."

"Yes. You are observant." The counselor let his breath out hard and pressed on. "But Nuit was arrogant, impatient, and I knew he would not be able to resist the Brazilian territory. This region is rich and has been one to fuel the demon empires with the atrocities of greed committed over this soil against innocents . . . and our history shows that the dark realms even claimed a guardian soul, the first and only in history, from here. But the were-demons had that soul in their possession—we had no access to it. We could learn no more about it, other than the fact that it fell from grace . . . until Nuit did one of his international concert locations here, an error in judgment. He opened a portal, and open portals allow for the passage of things in *and* out. Haste makes waste. Information is power—during the chaos in the demon realms, much of their information was at risk. My searchers, beholden to me under my council provinces, were able to spy and learn valuable secrets."

Slapping his hands together, he walked in a mad, gleeful circle, coming close to Carlos, sending his foul breath into Carlos's face.

"A coup . . . you'd overthrow the chairman?" Carlos now walked away from him in an agitated circle. He wasn't sure why all of this just didn't sit right with him, but it didn't.

"The old goat is past his prime," the counselor said quickly, his voice frantic with excitement. "He still holds onto the ways of chivalry and valor from the days up to the end of the Dracula era. He doesn't even believe in contracts to seal a deal. You were witness to that. I have been telling him for years that there are new technologies we can employ, and that the new breed of vampires knows nothing of the old ways, that he must update his methods."

The gate was half lowered, and panic was settling into Carlos's bones. "Then if there will be a coup, how can I, not even holding a confirmed council thro—"

"The old man doesn't know about the were-demon's small stash of Neteru. Just like he has no clue that your soul is in the wrong hands, safely stowed away in Purgatory—out of our reach. He thinks the demon realms have hijacked it, thus it's in the dark realms and obtainable."

The two men stared at each other for a moment. The counselor threw his head back and laughed. "Perfect, isn't it?"

"What do you want from me?" Carlos asked, now panicking.

"Take the female were-demon to the vanishing point." He smiled evilly. "She's beautiful, you've seen her."

"That was a female vamp!" Incredulous, Carlos walked back and forth, raking his fingers through his hair so hard his scalp nearly bled. "And to do that requires a black blood exchange with a were." He stopped and looked at the counselor. "That's illegal."

Counselor Vlak stared at him for a moment and then burst out laughing. "I do see why the old man tolerates you. They broke the mold when they made you." He shook his head. "That was a were-demon, young man. And you fed her from your veins. That, also, was not sanctioned." He continued to chuckle. "And I cannot believe that a man of your past is concerned about what is legal. Tell me your moral fiber is not—"

"She came at me like a vamp! I didn't know!"

"Older women can be intriguing, powerful, seductive . . . will lure you from where you should be into realms where you shouldn't go. Especially if they have a little black blood running through them to give them temporary powers of illusion to be all-vamp when they approach a very novice young male." He chuckled and studied his claws.

"You set me up . . ." Carlos felt himself about to bulk, but then thought better of it. Power for power and with dawn near, Vlak was an older entity that was not to be tried. "And she lied to me," he said, his voice unnaturally quiet as all of what he was learning sank in. The resistance to his territory, pushing contracts in his face, the counselor acting like he didn't want him to have South America, blocking his immediate access to a throne and calling for a vote later—all of it was bullshit to keep Vlak looking like the last entity who would collude with him. The game was deadly smooth.

"Of course she *lied* to you. She's a demon," he said, triumphant as awareness took hold within Carlos. "And *naturally* I set you up, that is my nature. Winner takes all. You didn't think I was going to allow you to descend that fast with such a vast territory, and to openly challenge me at council table in front of the others without a strategic response, did you?"

The two stared at each other for a moment, and then Vlak smiled.

"Good. We understand each other. The sun is coming, so let me say this quickly." Vlak shook his head. "There is always a variable, and black magic is powerful but unstable—that's why we prefer pure illusion, or moving existing matter. That crazy mother-seer were-demon is starting to have delusions that she is the Neteru . . . Her mind is easy to compromise." He arched his eyebrow. "One little sip of a dark guardian's blood and she was ready to make an overly compassionate master vampire her life-mate," he said then laughed. "Tragic."

Carlos rubbed his face with both palms as humiliation scored him, breathing into his hands as they slid past his eyes and over his nose, listening with horror, thinking of how twisted things could get when minds bent and snapped. He felt nauseous as he absorbed it all and as the counselor's voice became more urgent, more excited as he went on unraveling the sordid plot against the chairman.

"She escaped level five with the small portion of Neteru essence left, and trapped within the demon boundaries, tethered to the moon like the animal she'd become, she was desperate to escape before they found her again . . . and when one is desperate, one tends to make unwise, hasty decisions. It was perfect. My searcher brought me her proposal to give us access to daylight in the exchange for access to unlimited mobility, and I told her the truth wrapped around a lie; there was a new, very young, inexperienced master vampire with vast territory that shadowed hers—and that he, because he was younger, could take her to the V-point. I calmed her fears of the dangers, and told her that when it was done, however, she would not be consumed into you . . . I would ensure that for her, since I am, after all, council-level with powers that she couldn't fathom. Then, we struck a deal that with her daylight access, she would bring me the Neteru that we'd lost. I told her you were a small sacrifice and wouldn't be missed and performed the forbidden black blood exchange."

He laughed again and shook his head as Carlos simply stared at him. He glanced at the grate, which was now half lowered and still closing. "Foolish woman. She didn't know we already had the Neteru in our sights, and that with your soul weight, if you took her to the vanishing point, your dropout is guaranteed. And through you our empire would have access to daylight, plus a vessel that could produce daywalkers seven years from now." He paused and stared at Carlos. "I want that power."

"If *I* take her there, how would that help you? Through a throne transfer? You want me to rush the chairman?" Carlos asked, trying to remain calm.

Vlak smiled and made a little tsking sound of disapproval. "Silly boy, no. I will be there the moment you come out of the fusion point naked and shaking like a junkie. You'll be weak; will need to feed. You'll barely be able to lift your head. And if you do attempt to fight me, I can easily kill you, bleed myself out, and then drain you dry to recover. But it would be better for us to keep our dirty little secret until I can infect enough of my own army to storm the chambers. That crazy old bastard . . . He must be insane to believe that I would wait in line to receive the daywalker's bite! I will already be one, long before the Neteru is ready to give birth to them, and the chairman's throne, which goes back to the time of Paradise lost, will be mine."

He folded his hands behind his back, closed his eyes, and let his voice drop to a sinister whisper. "So, rather than make this messy and public, you'll come to my throat and I'll come to yours, double flat-line, total transfer." He looked at Carlos and tilted his head. "It will be enjoyable, trust me." He chuckled as the color drained from Carlos's face. "Ahhh . . . while alive, you never went to prison, did you? Shame, having missed so many different experiences. But this one foul act of willingly taking a were-demon to the vanishing point will most assuredly give us your soul. All will be well, and as it should be. Fair exchange, and I'm even allowing you to keep the Neteru."

Carlos's gaze narrowed on Vlak. Fury sent bile to his tongue as he remembered the subtle threat of violation that had threaded through his system as the demon siphoned his wrist. Yet Vlak's full-fanged smile contained cool confidence in a way that let him know the counselor had somehow trapped him.

"What if I just say, *fuck you?*"

"You catch on quick." Vlak smiled but returned a lethal stare. "It'll be my pleasure, but preferably after you do her and hijack daylight."

Instantly Carlos was in full battle bulk. He would take this mother-fucker's head off.

"I've got your insolent ass by the balls, Rivera." The counselor hadn't even matched Carlos's mortal combat challenge or backed up. He just continued to smile. "I have evidence that you did the black blood exchange with a were-demon, of which the council penalty is death. And if you're not around to protect the Neteru . . ."

Vlak's gaze went from red glowing orbs to black flickers. "Do you know how many ways we can torture her existence? We don't need her mind, won't care what plagues riddle her body, as long as her womb performs its function seven years from now. What we will do will make you puke. We can tap into her cellular structure in a way that we never could have had access to without you, until you bit her and carried her blood in your veins." He laughed cruelly as Carlos normalized. "That's right," he said with a nod, "you've got her DNA all in you—and trust me, I'll extract that from you drop by drop before you torch."

"You gave the demon blood, too, you lowlife sonofa—"

"With a searcher's testimony to back up my claims, whom do you think the old man will believe? He'll smell demon saliva in your system, and know that you did the exchange. You were so foolish to let her take from your wrist instead of from a goblet. There's no trace when you allow them to drink from a goblet." Vlak shook his head as he clucked his tongue. "You do know that I'm in charge of chamber inquisitions, *si?*"

He stared at Carlos hard when Carlos didn't immediately answer. "Take it or leave it. The offer is as I have described. If you refuse, I'll burn you—literally, by turning over evidence of your treason to the chairman."

"But the she-demon went after Damali already. If she goes near the Neteru to try to kill her, I'll have to smoke that crazy bitch." Carlos had meant his statement to come out as hard logic, a forceful slap of reality in Vlak's face. But instead it sounded more like an unsure question, holding the tone of near defeat in it.

"Oh, noooo," Vlak warned. "What she did was send you a message that she has lost patience, just like I have." His black gaze narrowed to a withering glare. "Fuck that bitch soon and be done with it! The longer you procrastinate, the more you put the daywalker breeder at risk. I need what you sire to come under my armies. Her heirs will pass the virus faster than through the black blood transfers, but will still be beholden to the case above them, mine."

He smiled and glanced at the grate that was three-quarters closed.

"What if the chairman gets hip, if he finds out like he found out about Nuit?" Carlos asked, his voice strained with panic. He felt like he was suffocating within his own lair.

"Nuit was sloppy and obvious. But more importantly, the chairman was your maker. That is why he favors you so, has such a blind, sickening, weak spot for you. He is too arrogant to concede that one of his own made vampires might deceive him. You can deceive him and go against him because of the little issue of your soul not belonging to the dark realms yet. A wonderful variable . . . that he knows nothing about. Make a choice—opportunities like this don't come often. So fuck that bitch for daylight, and that old man out of his throne, and be done with it!"

Carlos could feel the transport winds beginning to kick up, the smell of potent fumes and smoke gathering as the counselor began to dissolve away.

"Well who made you, then? How can *you* go against the chairman?" Carlos yelled, feeling the winds begin to go quiet, but his mind raging.

"Caligula Caesar!" the voice echoed up from the cavern. "Who else?"

CHAPTER TWENTY

HER GUARDIANS looked like a band of worn-out desperadoes. Each had on a variation of light-khaki army fatigues, heavy boots, safari hats, and sunglasses as they snoozed in the small charter plane waiting area. Tourists going on the more daring sight-seeing tours huddled nervously away from them, as though Damali's squad were drug-dealing hit men. People eyed the group's bulging duffle bags with suspicion in the oppressive heat.

The only reason that they'd been able to carry their artillery in such an open and flagrant display of firepower, despite the new era of heightened security everywhere in the world, was the fact that this tiny, puddle-jumper, flight school airstrip was off the beaten path— and no doubt, often used by the more unsavory element in the region. It seemed to Damali to be a place where a few dollars could get the local authorities to look the other way. Perhaps they had upon someone's word? She didn't even want to know what Marlene had done to transact their passage. But she was sure that, if it had been a more populated, commercial airport, they'd all be in a Brazilian jail somewhere by now.

Thank goodness Marlene had some contacts over here that could tell her where to go and with whom to do the travel arrangements. Otherwise, Damali knew she'd have to fight her own team to get them to part with their weapons, even in broad daylight. There would have been no way for her to get them to stash their gear in FX boxes disguised as stage equipment like they had to on the flight from the States. It was on, at this point. The fellas had rightly argued that under the circumstances, they wanted quick access to the heat they were packing. She could dig it. No one on the guardian team had really slept. They looked horrible.

Rider's jaw was covered with a thick five o'clock shadow, and he snored without shame under his scrunched-down hat. Sweat trickled down his temples and stained his back, chest, and underarms through his cotton T-shirt. Shabazz was practically gray, having kept one eye open all night just to be sure Marlene was still breathing. She was curled up in a fetal position in a chair with her head on Shabazz's lap, while he intermittently stroked her damp, silver locks. Dan was flushed, breathing with effort, and constantly wiping his drenched hair off his forehead. Big Mike just breathed slowly, and seemed to be the coolest of the bunch, but despite his warnings to be still, Jose and JL fanned themselves with a newspaper.

Frustration at the delay made Damali want to jump out of her skin. Everyone in Rio seemed to have a carefree, casual attitude about time. It had taken way longer than they expected, or in her opinion was necessary, to arrange for the shipment of their heavy band equipment and other items they no longer needed. Minivans were slow, airport personnel were slow, and the charter service was slow. No one moved with swift authority. Perhaps it was the oppressive heat. Perhaps it had something to do with the fact that the antique air conditioner needed Freon?

Damali dabbed the sweat from her brow and neck with a limp tissue as she tried to get comfortable in a hard plastic chair that stuck to her butt. The turquoise blue scooped seat was molding to her back, butt, and thighs, sealing her body to the suffocating surface.

Gnats and mosquitoes dive-bombed everyone in the room, oblivious to heavy coatings of insect repellent they all wore. The little pests were relentless, making people swat and slap themselves until the sheer volume of the attacks just made each person surrender to being bitten. Her only alternative was to spread her legs wide, lean her forearms on her knees, drop her head, and try to sleep like a soldier.

Finally, after two hours of waiting, their private flight was called. Damali didn't have the energy to stand, but understood why the guys were on their feet acting like they'd just hit lotto. Anything to be out of that dank waiting area was worth it.

But the group was also exceptionally quiet. Fatigue not only claimed them, so did fear of the unknown. In truth, this might be the last adventure they went on together, and she noted how considerate each teammate was being to one another.

Sure, they always operated as a crew, but they also bitched with each other the whole time they were performing a task. Rider would be fussing about everything in general, JL would be complaining about how sloppy everyone was with the technical equipment. Big Mike would be puffed up and close-mouthed about something smart Rider had said. Shabazz would get fed up and walk away with impatience, claiming not to have time for dumb shit. Jose and Dan would be steadily trying to keep the peace, while Marlene would get started, and make them go back over the entire process again.

Yet, as her guys filed out of the shack and down the tarmac to finally take their seats within the small twin-engine, the stronger ones were helping the guardians who possessed less bulk. Folks were giving up window seats, handing off fruit that could be peeled, passing snacks, and just chilling. Everyone was offering stuff to Marlene as she leaned against Shabazz. There was a community spirit happening, something going on that sealed the group's bond tighter than it had ever been. They were even sharing water with each other . . . would take a look at a partner and say, "Here, man, don't get dehydrated." Normally that was Marlene's roll—to check on everyone. Despite the perils of the journey, as Damali leaned back in her seat and looked down, one thought crossed her mind: it's all good.

Soon the jewel-green land beneath her became a blur as she dozed, her head bobbing, the drone of the plane's engines hypnotic. In her sleep-induced haze of semiconsciousness she felt like she, without the aid of the aircraft, was flying.

The sensation of freedom lifted her into cottony white clouds, the wind caressing her face as she soared. Her body dipped and rushed with the rivers, splashing cool, clear mountain water against her face. The smell of fresh grasses and wildflowers entered her nostrils, filling her nose and lungs with their sweet, pungent nectar. Her tongue could taste it as she took off running in a field, delighting in the textures of tall grasses that brushed her naked legs. Oh, but the forest, the dense tropical heat, and its sounds . . . a spectacular fusion of percussion and strings and flutes created by the natural chatter. Damali laughed in her sleep as a swirl of electric-blue butterflies took off as she approached. Parrots and wrens and creatures of flight in so many patterns and colors made her dizzy. Frogs and monkeys and tiny things that skittered coexisted with larger predators in each fila that only hunted what they needed—she watched.

Tears brimmed in her eyes as she sped past perfect harmony. Life balanced, natural. Beauty beyond comprehension, unfathomable danger. The magnificence of it all. Nothing wasted, everything designed and interwoven into the grand tapestry by grand design. Each blade of simple grass as awe-inspiring and necessary as the most complex creature. Remove one, and the tapestry is ruined, irrevocably altered. Like removing the bass, or keyboards, or guitar, or the single chime . . . once designed, once composed, it was what it was.

She felt the plane dip and returned to herself. Damali opened her eyes and peered around the cabin. Marlene lifted her head from Shabazz's chest and smiled. Damali wiped the tears from her face, stricken by the majesty she'd just witnessed. Marlene nodded again. Yeah, she thought, definitely a religious experience.

Although no one said a word as they deplaned and began walking down the tarmac, Damali's mind was racing at a thousand miles an hour. How could something from the darkness ever think it could go against the awesome power of the one who created all of this? She glanced around, incredulous. Pure genius, all-knowing, all power went into the creation of life itself—any life form came from the source, the one, the almighty. She'd known this before, had said it many, many times, but it hadn't registered at the profound soul level until now.

Immediately she became aware that her understanding had been intellectual, not emotional, it wasn't inside her; it was memorized like a school lesson, yet not inarguably known. But the sacredness and beauty of life was all around her as she allowed her gaze to pass the clutter of traffic and look out toward the jade-marbled hills beyond it. Then she looked up at the sun and shielded her eyes to its power. Whatever could create this, harness this, had dominion over this unparalleled power, was all.

Her mind flexed and the stars and moon filled it. The design . . . the design. It was all so rational, organized, planned. Who could not believe there were things greater, and that the side of what created it all in the first place would not triumph in the end? Damali covered her mouth with her hand, just looking out at nothing.

Near weeping as her team stood waiting on their ride, Marlene came to her side, took up Damali's hand and squeezed it.

"It finally hit you, huh, baby?"

She turned and stared at Marlene for a moment, not knowing how to respond.

"Finally felt it, didn't you? The connection."

Damali just nodded as Marlene kissed her cheek.

"You just hang onto that understanding, baby. No matter what happens, it doesn't matter. All good things are connected to the same source—only one side creates life, the other side destroys and creates death. They can't really kill you . . . or me, or the others, as long as our thread is connected to the right side. The side that goes on and creates, restores, and lives on."

"But, Mar, they almost killed you," Damali whispered.

"Almost killed my body," Marlene corrected gently. "As long as your spirit is right, you do not end. If my body had died, where do you think my soul would have gone?"

"Heaven, of course," Damali said quickly.

"And, which side do you think it would add to? This endless, nuclear combustion of turbine energy we are all connected to." Marlene smiled. "I would have fueled new life. Through spirit, you will learn in the hills, all matter is created. Life emerges from spirit, not the other way around. That is why souls are so valuable to both sides. One had an endless bounty of them; the other had none . . . the darkness covets what the light has in plentiful supply. They abuse the natural resource . . . but what they create is artificial, substandard, twisted, with no way to be efficiently, cleanly reabsorbed back into the spiritual ecosystem."

The guys had gathered near, making an intimate circle around Damali and Marlene to listen.

"Just like all of this greenery and the huge trees we see, all the plants and animals eventually die in the body, their remains get absorbed into fertile, rich soil, that later gives rise to something that reconstitutes into the growth of something new and beautiful. It is a perfect, efficient process. So, too, is a good soul. And as above, so below. But, man-made things cause pollutants, toxins, and cannot be reabsorbed, because those things, while manifest, were not created by the one."

"Mar, I just never understood the impact . . ." Damali leaned against Big Mike, needing to hold onto something tall and solid before her legs gave way.

"Whatever we are hunting, might be stronger in body, but is a spiritual pollutant, a toxin that the fragile ecosystem of the spirit world has no way to absorb. Thus, it is banished to the nether realm's dump site. Spiritual landfills are the best description of the dark side realms. They cannot create life—only twist and modify it. That's why Carlos's soul is so important to them and us . . . he's a great natural resource, like ore, that can either become steel beam for them that can never be absorbed, or important natural metallic infrastructure to our planet that is a part of the ecosystem. For us, he's gold."

"Deep," Rider said, shaking his head.

"You think she can beat this thing, Mar?" Shabazz stroked Marlene's back and stared at her with searching eyes.

"What they called up is stronger in body. Period. It can shape-shift, and is a more skilled warrior." Marlene put a hand on Damali's shoulder when Damali blanched. "But, you have a spirit. It doesn't. That's your strength and her vulnerability." Marlene smiled. "Have you seen the forces of nature destroy man-made stuff? Girl, dams have been washed away by natural floods, steel-beamed buildings have been rocked and felled by earthquakes, houses ripped apart by tornadoes. Forces of nature that even the nonsecular insurance industry, in *their* documents, call acts of God."

Marlene chuckled. "No, baby. They can fell a tree, they can strip-mine a mountain, and maybe temporarily harness some aspects of nature. But when it's all said and done, if that which is pure nature rears up and comes at 'em with sheer force—that, they ain't got nothing for."

Damali nodded as the team slapped fives, pounded fists, and grunted their agreement on the side of the road—pumped. However, Damali kept further reply to herself, not wanting to take away from Marlene's impassioned rah-rah speech. The fact was, Damali didn't want a single tree felled from her team, whether they would turn into spiritual essence, warrior angels, or whatever.

While all that Marlene had said was philosophically comforting, and intellectually stimulating, she wasn't trying to have none of her guys go out like that. Deep in her heart, each of her family members had their own irreplaceable and intrinsic value. She understood why Marlene had insisted they stop in Bahia to get spiritual fuel.

New dread overtook Damali. Marlene had come here to prepare her for the possibility that this battle would level casualties like no other before. Marlene obviously wanted her to be straight in her head if she had to watch one or many of her guys fall . . . even Marlene. Yeah, there were things she had to learn to figure out how to best this threat, but this side stop had as much to do with life after the team, as it did strategies to vanquish the enemy.

She glanced up at Big Mike, the big redwood, who was coddling her against him. Hell, no she didn't want this gentle, giant brother to fall. Nor did she want to see her mother-friend go up into the light . . . or JL, or Dan, or Jose's smiling faces laying on the rich, blood-covered earth to become a part of the cycle of life. If something happened to Rider, she would never recover, and God knows, if Shabazz went down, they'd have to sedate her.

Time crept in slow increments of perspiration. Forty-five minutes felt like four hours under the Salvador sun. Waiting on a bus in LA was very different than waiting on a minivan by a dusty road near the equator.

But it made perfect sense that a spiritual center would be near a port settled in 1549. One hundred and seventy-six churches, so much hallowed ground . . . yet sugar barons stole bodies from Africa and imported them to stolen lands. Settled? Nothing was settled in 1549, the drama had just begun, three years after the Amazon squad perished in '46. The numbers were the same as in the *Temt Tchaas,* everything coming full circle, just like her.

The scents of coriander, pepper spices, and roasted meats wafted from the vendors hawking fresh juices, cold coconut milk. Damali's stomach growled. African-based music was ever-present, as were the flies. Young vendors plied them with hand-woven bracelets that had three knots, brightly colored good luck charms that combined the African Candomble religion with Catholicism.

Damali chuckled, being a practitioner of neither sect, as a persistent boy just would not rest until she accepted one. He tied it in a knot around her wrist, eagerly accepting her coins, and smiling a brilliant white smile against ashy ebony skin, telling her quickly not to take it off, but to throw it in the sea when her wish came true. Was it that obvious she had a fervent wish? She laughed more to herself as they waited. Children and animals, the pure of heart, could always tell.

When Marlene abandoned a duffle-bag seat, and stood up with Shabazz's help, the entire team shielded their eyes and craned their necks in the direction of her gaze. A white, rusted-out van came to a lumbering stop, sending the roadside dust into a swirl around the team. A taller, browner, and more muscular version of Shabazz jumped out and raced toward Marlene. Damali cut her eyes at Shabazz from behind her sunglasses. Aw, shit . . .

The guy who swept Marlene up in a familiar embrace was all that and a bag of chips. Damali glanced at the faces of the team. No one's eyes could be seen behind their shades, but the tension in their bodies, and the way they ground out support for their brother with their clenched jaws said it all. Jose was nearly trembling, and she could see the veins standing in his temple. The brother from the van glanced at him briefly, smiled, and returned his focus to Marlene. What was that about?

This man had two inches in height on Shabazz, and Damali noted Shabazz trying to elongate his spine and puff up just a bit. The competitor for Marlene's affection had on a low-slung pair of jeans and no shirt. His chest was a dark set of perfect cinder blocks covered in a damp, glistening sheen of moisture. His torso was cut into six bricks that tapered into a slim waist. His locks were down his back, held by a thin leather strap. And judging by the power in his thick thighs, and his arms, he could take Shabazz if any drama kicked off. Damn. This was going to be a heck of a long visit in Bahia.

Sighing, and not totally sure why, Damali hoisted up her duffle. This brother was touching Marlene's cheek, staring into her eyes, and a private chuckle passed between them. Shabazz bristled, but didn't say a word, as Marlene turned to the group and formally introduced her mentor.

"Everybody, this is Kamal." Marlene's eyes sparkled behind her photo-gray round lenses. Her smile was as wide as a schoolgirl's. "Shabazz, Damali, Rider, Big Mike, JL, Jose, Dan—Kamal."

Each guardian muttered a half-civil hello. Shabazz had only nodded. Kamal chuckled, and went to the passenger's side of the van and opened the door, helping Marlene in first to sit beside him in the front. Shabazz just glared at the man, and grabbed his gear. But he was not fast enough to pick up Marlene's load. Kamal had swept it up in a deft, graceful motion, and all Damali could do was place a hand on Shabazz's shoulder. She would have sworn the man growled.

One by one, they piled into the cramped confines of the vehicle.

The thing sputtered and knocked, and looked like it was circa 1970s. But no one said a word.

"We gwan up to da mountains. It's late, and tonight the dances will show part of what you seek," Kamal shouted over his shoulder above the sputtering engine and loud African music that blared. "Safe ground, no? All protected by spiritual rings—no worries." Then he did the unspeakable. Turned to Marlene, smiled, and put his hand on her thigh. "Like old times, old gurl. Like da *ayahuasca* walk?"

Damali was rubbing Shabazz's back now, like he was a prizefighter sitting in a ring corner chair—just having been TKO'd by a former champion. She cast her gaze out the window. Lord, Lord, Lord please don't let no mess jump off with my already high-strung team. She sighed. The van was hot. Shabazz was smoldering. Big Mike and Rider were armed. This was supposed to be a spiritual enclave in the hills. Dang . . . she thought Marlene had been with monks and Templars all these years to gain insight, but it was obvious that Marlene had some other sources of information. Old times? She thought Marlene only dealt with the Covenant. Apparently so had Shabazz. Go figure.

Two hours later, and with a silent passenger section in the back, the van came to a stop. Kamal had pointed out all the sugar plantations, explained the politics of the region—the blend of African, Indian, and European peoples, and had given them a crash course in how the Candomble deities had been hidden within the Catholic religion by African slaves forced to give up their heritage.

Rather than focus on the private glances Kamal sent to Marlene, or the way Marlene swallowed away knowing smiles, Damali thought about Lemanja—the goddess of the river and waters he'd told them about. Maybe she would help? Damali chuckled. Going down the Amazon, assuming they made it that far, with the two elders of the group in a standoff, was not going to be good. *All right, Lemanja, this is your house over here . . . Dag, can you help a sister out?*

The group piled out of the van with a disgruntled series of grunts and stretches. People rubbed their shoulders, leaned forward to allow their spines to reset, and bent their knees. Even Rider, who normally complained about any minor inconvenience, didn't say a word.

But it was mercifully cooler in the mountains. The bush, as Kamal called it, was a rough-hewn version of forest with dense trees, wide palms, and tall grasses. He motioned toward what looked like a one-story, long, whitewashed shack. The paint on the clapboards was beginning to peel and Damali noted that there were no screens on any of the windows. There was no door to it, either. Obviously air-conditioning was missing in action, too. They were gonna get eaten alive by the bugs, and perhaps anything else that was out there at night.

"Put up your tings, then come to de riva. Marlene knows. Late afternoon, like early morning, we practice. Baths are in the natural riva. Insect repellent is from the bush, not de bottle." Kamal chuckled and a deep, resounding sound came from his full, sexy mouth. "You'll get the insects high."

Marlene offered him a wide smile and nodded. Then the man ran full-bolt through the woods and disappeared within it like he was a gazelle. Oh, boy . . .

No one said a word as they all marched up the steep incline to the guest house. The walk up the hill was enough to add muscles to one's legs, and this brother ran around the retreat grounds like it was downtown LA, not an obstacle underfoot or an incline in sight.

Climbing three shaky wooden flights up to the house porch, they filed through the door and just stared. Rickety metal cots with bare mattresses stared back at them. The water-stained blue-and-white ticking made it seem like the bedding was wearing convict's stripes. A thin layer of dust covered the floor and the one huge dresser in the room. They watched a fat beetle skittle by at the invasion. A single, bare bulb dangling from a metal chain served as the light. Spiderwebs and moth cocoons claimed the high corners of the ceiling. A carpenter wasp was busily working at a rain gutter.

Damali sighed, Marlene smiled, and Rider dropped his duffle bag with a thud.

"Ain't exactly the Copacabana Palace." Rider put his hands on his hips and glanced around.

"Man, don't start," Big Mike warned. "These folks are helping us out, and we all need to chill." But the fact that he'd shot a look in Shabazz's direction wasn't lost on a soul among them.

"It's all good," Damali said cheerfully, adding emphasis to the statement as she dropped her bag. "Let's go down and see what brother is up to by the river. Cool?"

"Yeah," Shabazz muttered. "Let's see what he's about."

It took her team fifteen minutes to pick their way through the thicket to a clearing. The heavy rhythm of drums and berimbau coming from the direction of the river fused with the chattering wildlife in the trees. Everything around them was alive.

Damali kept her lips sealed shut as Rider argued with Big Mike about the merits of having to use an outhouse versus indoor plumbing. She refused to get into the dispute when Rider started hollering about what might happen if he had to pee at night, and had to brave the unknown, alone, just to take a leak. The riotous conversation almost made her cover her mouth to keep from laughing out loud. But she dared not, lest Shabazz explode. He was so close to the edge that an electric current seemed to be going through his locks. She could dig it. There were no words when your competition was all that. Been there. Recently. Shoot, at least this guy Shabazz was worried about wasn't a demon from the depths of the Amazon.

But why did Marlene have to open her mouth to defend the spiritual hostel? If she had just been cool, hadn't said a word, then it could have remained smooth—but no.

"This is about spiritual expansion here. It's rustic because the emphasis is not on the physical—"

"Oh, that's good to know," Shabazz snapped. "Glad there was no emphasis on the physical!"

Marlene opened her mouth, then closed it with a smile and looked ahead as they made a path to the river.

On the other hand, it might have been better if the group just had a good old-fashioned, nonspiritual shouting match to clear the air before they got down there, because what they saw as they came to a halt, was gonna kill Shabazz.

Twenty-five hard, black bodies in thin, white loincloth strips moved like water on the flat sandy shore. Their fluid choreography was as breathtaking as their defined human structures. Burnt orange, late-afternoon sun reflected off onyx, sun-burnished skin. Kamal led the sultry *capoeira* fight dance that had the slow, controlled rhythms of Tai Chi combined with a mixture of kickboxing and karate. A guy as big as Mike worked out on the drums, and another slighter-built brother was funkin' out a berimbau. Yeah, Shabazz was going to have heart failure.

Damali glanced at him from the corner of her eye as the practicing brothers turned in unison, showing uncovered buns of steel as they bent their knees a millimeter from the sand, leaned back, their shoulders barely brushing the ground, and rose in a powerful, stable, slow limbo like a fighter avoiding the swipe of a broadsword. Kamal's long ponytail of locks gracefully swept the earth. A trickle of sweat ran down the center of his back, further defining the deep gorge of his spine that gave rise to thick walls of muscles on either side of it. And the brother was Marlene's age? Fifty something? Daaaayum . . . Okay, she had to talk to Shabazz. Later.

Marlene looked like her heart had stopped this time for real. Girlfriend was transfixed. Damali's gaze shot around the group nervously. Rider looked down at his own slight gut and shook his head. Dan had been so punked down that his shoulders slumped. Jose and JL had just leaned against a tree. Only Big Mike had the gumption to slap Shabazz on the back, obviously the only male on the team not feeling an ego singe.

"It's cool, brother. We good."

Shabazz only nodded, his jaw tense, his eyes unblinking, his gaze forward, his shoulders back—pissed.

She was not even going to ask Marlene how long she'd stayed here. She didn't want to know. True, these brothers looked like fighting machines. True, this center was probably where Marlene learned how to wield her walking stick. And, true, she might have learned divination and the process of calling down spirits, setting up protective prayer barriers, and cleansing baths, herbology, how to read the stars and all . . . but she also probably learned to appreciate some of the things that were *real hard* to walk away from. No wonder Marlene demonstrated such discipline. *This was you, girl?* Impressed, Damali mentally gave the older woman props. Ya just never could tell. Deep.

Blatant curiosity tugged at Damali until she couldn't help but monitor the expression on Marlene's face and glance at the control the *capoeira* master exhibited. He wasn't even breathing hard and was working his squad out like a champ. Marlene wasn't even breathing. Girlfriend was definitely going to have to give her some insight on how one walked away from something like that.

Damali could just picture it. Learning the stars from this master, under a flawless open sky? Bathing in the natural, in the river at dawn . . . walking in the woods to study nature, closing one's eyes to feel the energies enter you, making you one with the universe? Shit. Damali sat down on the ground, crossed her legs yoga style and leaned forward. This mess was reminding her of Carlos too much.

The hour passed as though it were a few minutes the same way it did in a club when the music is on and watching the people dancing holds your attention. As soon as the drums stopped, the freshly worked crew gave a slight bow of honor to their instructor and pandemonium broke out. They talked in a rapid patois-like language among themselves, and from what Damali could make out, they were joking with each other and commenting on their routine.

Kamal jogged ahead of the straggling fight-dancers and joined the guardian team. Still not breathing hard, he beamed at Marlene. Damali stood and dusted off her fatigues.

"Your squad is awesome," Damali said honestly, trying to play peacemaker.

"Thank you, pretty one," Kamal replied, bowing slightly. Then he turned and waved his crew to come meet the guardian group. "This is our brotherhood," he said with a proud wave of his hand.

Damali chuckled as the men in the group allowed their gazes to openly assess her and Marlene. Perfect white teeth set in dark skin so smooth it appeared to be marble flashed at her as though a hundred cameras had gone off at once. But the glances they gave Jose concerned her. It was a subtle thing, almost like a dog's bristle. They flexed a little, tilted their heads slightly, took a deep inhale, and then dismissed him with their eyes. Strange thing was, Jose had the same reaction to them.

"Abdul," one bolder brother said, stepping forward, immediately capturing Damali's hand, and kissing it like a gentle knight. His skin was the color of midnight, and his eyes blazed with mischief above high, chiseled cheekbones. His lush mouth relaxed into a sensual smile, and his voice dropped a purposeful octave. "Kamal said a team was coming to gain spiritual insight, but he *never* said we'd be visited by angels." He held her hand, stepping in closer.

Damali diplomatically extracted her hand with a smile, and raised her eyebrow.

"You are the Neteru?" another just as fine asked in awe. Before Damali could respond, he held up his hand. "Foolish question." The man laughed, outstretched his arms, and plunged an imaginary sword into the center of his chest. "Marry me. I am Ahmad."

All eyes were on her, curiosity mingling with awe as they bowed and held her gaze upon straightening their tall, proud backs. Yet she couldn't help notice how they occasionally glanced between their leader and Jose with confused expressions.

"Uh, this is my squad, fellas," Damali said, chuckling and flattered. "Marlene, and—"

"Marlene?" the huge drummer said, dropping his instrument and glancing at Kamal. *"The* Marlene?" The drummer immediately looked at Jose, then back to Kamal as though waiting for an explanation. "With *the Neteru* and him?"

Confused glances shot around the guardian team, but no one said anything. Kamal's people obviously had a problem with Jose, just like their man was having a silent problem with them. Shabazz hung back, his eyes a mystery behind dark glasses, not speaking, only issuing a nod when addressed. Later, Damali reminded herself. She'd do a sensory roll call with her group when they were alone. Now was not the time.

Kamal nodded, as though reading her mind and approving of her plan. He swallowed a smile, and sent his line of vision toward the bush. "Yes, brother. This is *Marlene*."

Marlene chuckled and studied the ground. The younger men in Kamal's group stood back, and then a flurry of indecipherable language exploded. One young brother just shook his head and slapped Kamal on the back. The drummer beamed at Marlene like she was the dinner he planned to feast on. A couple of the guys gave her bows of deference, and then glanced at Kamal with a too-wide grin.

"Enough," Kamal said after a moment. "Permit Damali to introduce the rest of her team."

"But, Marlene . . ." the drummer repeated, then let his breath out slowly.

"Uhmm . . . this is Shabazz, our *esteemed* Aikido master," Damali said very distinctly, issuing a long look to each bemused *capoeira* participant. "Big Mike, Rider, JL, Jose, and Dan," she said more quickly. "Each has a specialty and a gift," she added. "Shabazz is our tactile sensory, Marlene is our seer—they are our group's elders."

She had taken her time to be sure that she mentioned Marlene and

Shabazz twice as a unit—an inseparable one. Kamal was obviously a gentleman and deferred with grace, another bow in Shabazz's direction, his expression one of understanding, respect. But Kamal's team was not so ready to relent. Their own master being a source of adoration, one of the younger guys pressed on.

"Our Kamal is gifted with a trinity . . . the feeling, the nose, and sight—and is a worthy adversary in battle."

Seeming satisfied when Shabazz bristled, the young man stepped back into his group, his statement an open challenge. Damali cast a warning glance at Shabazz, who had visibly stiffened when told that Kamal had second sight. She understood that her martial arts master was too irate for words, but now was not the time to start no mess. Yeah, chill. Shabazz would get his ass kicked out here and really be embarrassed—which would mean her boys would have to jump in, and get theirs kicked, too. Then what? Shabazz was gonna have to get over the fact that this brother could do a mind lock with Mar and probably take her places in his head that Shabazz had only dreamed of. She felt his pain, but couldn't acknowledge it. She understood that, too . . . not being able to serve one's lover all that he desired.

The brief silence pulled everyone's nerves tight as both teams watched both masters. To diffuse the situation, Damali stepped forward with a smile. "I'm sure if Marlene brought us here, Kamal is all that. You gentlemen are top-notch as well. Thank you for your help."

With her words, Kamal's team seemed to acknowledge her peacekeeping gesture, and they took her compliment, one coming from the Neteru, with open satisfaction. They all relaxed their stances, and gave her slight bows of appreciation and backed up. *Finally*, she thought, *peace*.

"Your Aikido master is legendary," Kamal said in a respectful tone after a moment. "Marlene has communicated his honor in battle. We are pleased to have your entire guardian team as our guests. We eat by de riva, we divine what you need to know in an hour. Refresh yourselves."

Kamal's team nodded, but seemed totally disappointed that their master was going to stand down on the man-woman thing. Damali's squad almost let out an audible sigh of relief. Shabazz begrudgingly nodded, his chin still set hard like his shoulders, but at least his dignity was intact. Then again, she wondered if it was because the other master had *allowed* Shabazz to have his pride. It was a classy move, but it still denoted who had the option to back down, who didn't, whose yard this was, and who was in control.

Damali sized up the new spiritual master again, allowing her senses to inform her. Yeah, Shabazz was in trouble. This guy was not only stronger, but had the distinct advantage of three gifts—not just one, like Shabazz had. It was clear that her team had sensed this as well, or were at the very least unsure of the outcome should some bullshit kick off. Marlene was trying her best to act like nothing unusual had occurred, as though all the undercurrent was everyone's imagination. But a few things that were not her imagination: this guy had a scent that she couldn't describe. It was awesome, drew you, was earthy and rich. His skin was like sable, made you just want to reach out and touch it. And his voice, once relaxed, was almost like a purr. Okay, now she was trippin'.

Damali mulled these new dynamics over like worry beads as her team quietly trekked back up the hill.

Everything was changing. Or, was it that she was now seeing more clearly? She wasn't a kid anymore. She was stronger and getting an insider's view of the more private struggles of her elders, was granted a real seat at the invisible adult table. Stuff wasn't flying over her head, going unnoticed, just because she was preoccupied with her own adolescent needs and wants. She'd had some pain to wake her out of her stupor . . . she was seeing it all go down in quick glimpses, swallowed smiles, tensed jaws, a misplaced breath, the signals of body language that the uninitiated didn't catch. Things that got missed when you didn't know . . . or made the mistake of assuming that people older than you had never been down this road before.

Climbing the stairs, she watched all her warriors. They all had lives, a path. They all had been here, more than likely. Before this near-fiasco, she never thought about it much. She made a mental note to rely on some of those lessons. Instinct told her that she was fighting an older warrior on two fronts; the demon out there, as well as this thing about to blow up between Shabazz, Marlene, and this new guy's interest in Marlene. Maybe her old warriors might have some discreet knowledge to drop about how to diffuse something as volatile as this. She'd never dealt with any yang like this before, and wished she didn't have to, especially this far from home.

Damali found Marlene on the porch, gazing out at the trees. Wrapped up in their own desire to rest, the guys had each claimed a cot and dropped on it, even Shabazz.

"Hey," Damali murmured, keeping her voice low. "Can I ask you a question?"

"No," Marlene chuckled. "Not that one."

They both laughed quietly.

"Girlfriend, what'd you do up here?"

"Nuffin," Marlene said with a wink, teasing her. "Not a ting."

"Shabazz is having a coronary," Damali whispered.

"We have an open relationship . . . like he always wanted."

Damali went to the rail that appeared like it could barely hold the weight of a bird, and peered over the three-story drop. "He was really concerned when he thought we lost you, Mar. You need to ease up on the brother. And how you gonna bring him to *this place*? Dang, Mar, you're rough."

"I know he was concerned," Marlene said in a low, calm tone. "He and I are best friends. No problem with that. Much respect, much love. And the location couldn't be helped, given where we have to go. I wasn't trying to rub his nose in it." Then she giggled. "But there is this weird thing in the universe called karma. It just snaps back and kicks your ass when you least expect it." She covered her mouth and shook her head. "Damn. *Never in a million years* would I have thought I'd be back here with any of y'all."

Damali was covering her mouth, laughing harder, trying to remain quiet. The last thing she wanted was for Shabazz to overhear their giggling. They weren't laughing at him, but the girl-talk was too crazy not to laugh. She held Marlene's arm, stepped in close, and dropped her voice to a conspiratorial whisper. "What did you do to that man that has his whole squad tripping about *the* Marlene?"

"Oh, chile," Marlene murmured, closing her eyes, giggling intermittently, and wrapping her arms around herself. "That was a looong time ago, and I was young, okay? The man is a tactile . . ." Marlene breathed in and cleared her throat, opened her eyes, and almost fell over the banister as she leaned on it. "D, he's an olfactory like you just cannot understand—don't be too hard on Carlos for that attribute, okay honey? When a man has a nose, it's hard for him to shake a seductive scent. Ask me how I know." She leaned into Damali's right ear. "All I'ma say is, girl, the brother has the third-eye thing going on." Marlene shook her head and walked down the porch, found a step, and plopped down. "Whew."

Dumbstruck by Marlene's admission, the intensity of it, and the way the older woman's expression seemed to take her back in time, made Damali claim a seat next to her on the step. For a moment, neither of them spoke, and Damali wondered if this was what older women did with delicious memories—stored them away in a repository that they could pull out and savor, like a favorite old dress stored in an attic footlocker.

"Why'd you leave?"

Damali's question was a quest to understand how one pulled away from something that obviously had Marlene in a vise grip of passion at one time. Neither woman was giggling now, as their own thoughts eclipsed their mirth. This was some serious shit Marlene had walked away from. She needed to know how the sister did it. Needed the insight from Marlene about how one garnered the strength to break away from the man who had her so messed up. If Marlene would tell her, she'd use everything her mentor said to help break the grip Carlos had on her. Even out here, and after all she'd seen, she was still thinking about him.

"Maybe that's why I'm here now," Marlene said with a sad smile. "To tell you how I did." Marlene looked up at the sky and shook her head. "Y'all ask an *awful lot* of people sometimes."

She could tell by the way Marlene was taking her time to choose the words that opening this attic footlocker was going to bring out more than a sexy dress. But the question had been posed before the realization. Damali waited. There was nothing else to do as Marlene tried to fix her mouth to explain how one walked away from an apparent soul mate.

"Loved him," Marlene said so quietly that for a moment the cicadas went still. "Had to leave before I messed up."

"Messed up?" Wide-eyed, Damali just stared at her.

Marlene nodded with a knowing smile. "I came over here while I was still in training. We'd seen the premonition about Raven. I wasn't supposed to have children, remember?" Marlene sucked in a deep inhale. "Out here . . . shoot, girl . . . with him, I couldn't keep to no rhythm method."

Marlene closed her eyes. "Also couldn't keep myself from wanting to bear what he'd plant, and in this, the master had no control. Slipped up once, dodged a silver bullet by praying to the ancestors and fasting all month." She laughed so sadly that tears came to her eyes. "And then he drove me to town. I begged him to . . . before we really messed up, and his entire warrior team got massacred by the vamps looking for me, because they were looking for you—the only infant I was supposed to have in my arms. The vamps had been watching me for years, and tracking me. We all knew that it would only be a matter of time before they figured out a way to break Kamal's spiritual barriers to this compound. The demons were watching, too . . . looking for the Neteru to use your scent to battle the vamps. It wasn't worth risking what he'd built here, or what he was trying to do here. Wasn't worth a vamp or demon war against Kamal's people." Marlene sighed. "Then didn't I mess up and get pregnant by some other guy I didn't love anyway?"

When Damali just gaped at her, Marlene gave Damali a serious look. "Don't you tell Shabazz that mess, *ever*. He'll freak. It's already messing him up that he and Kamal share *a lot* of the same attributes. Would be okay if Shabazz was the original, and Kamal was the print, but girl . . . lemme just say, I done lived me some life out here, and it was *all good*." Marlene hesitated and allowed her gaze to slide away. "Kamal was the one. Then came Shabazz. It's complicated. I care for them both, love them both, and both of them are different and mean different things to me for different reasons. Shabazz is the one, now. But there was one before him. That's the part he won't be able to deal with—the fact that . . . Shit, I'm not even making sense to myself. There's a lot about this place that I couldn't tell him, or anybody in the group."

She looked at Damali, her eyes searching for acceptance. "Just trust me, no matter what kicks off that, you needed to come here to fight what we're facing, and that's paramount. The rest is history." She looked away and her voice became very distant. "If I didn't have to come back here, believe me, I wouldn't have. Too hard."

She didn't know what to say to Marlene as she watched the older guardian breathe deeply and her tears evaporate without falling. She'd sucked it up, took it like a woman, was gonna keep the peace, and chill. But how in the hell? Marlene's jaw was set hard, her gaze went to the horizon, and she blinked slowly, like packing away old still photos in a hidden album. But she could feel the current coming off Marlene. The old girl was jacked up. And the way Kamal had looked at her, like a battle-ax was in his chest, but was so fucking cool it didn't make sense.

"Much respect, Mar, and I'm so sorry you had to bring me here to open up a wound," she whispered, meaning it with all her heart. "But I don't think I'm there, yet, for real. To have the discipline." She held Marlene in her gaze. "Mar, I've seen some crazy, crazy, mad-crazy shit, right?"

Marlene nodded.

"The man told me some mess that made me stop breathing for a minute, okay?"

Marlene nodded.

"The entire world order is hanging in the balance, and I should be too done with him," Damali said in a quiet tone, her eyes searching Marlene's for answers.

Marlene smiled.

"I'm on my way out to possibly get all our asses kicked, and we might die."

"Yup."

"But Mar . . ." Damali whispered now, her hands clutching the hair on the crown of her head. "He's in my nose, in my mind, a part of my skin!"

"Yup," Marlene said standing. "Know whatcha mean."

"But . . ." Damali looked up, confused.

Marlene leaned down to keep the conversation from being overheard. "You will always feel that way about him. It will *never* go away. For you, it will burn like a never-ending fire, and for him it'll burn him like quicksilver would. It will always be fossil fuel. But when you get strong enough, you will walk away to avoid a disaster. That doesn't mean you'll stop smoldering, it just means that when you're not in the vicinity of the blaze, you won't go up in flames. Distance, darlin'. Time and distance. But don't drop a match near it—ever. No matter how much time has passed. Ask me how I know." Her smile was warm. "That's why nobody who was old enough to know better dropped a match near my situation today, or will speak on it. Take note."

Marlene smoothed the front of her T-shirt and looked up at the sky. "I'm cool. I'm cool y'all," she said, laughing. "Just one night, I can hang," she said, speaking to nothing and everything, especially herself. "Damn, the stars are dredging up all kinds of triangles." She looked at Damali, shook her head, and started walking. "Ain't *that* a bitch?"

CHAPTER TWENTY-ONE

THOUGH DAMALI'S hands were still sticky from the succulent mango juice that ran between her fingers, she was glad that she and Marlene were able to sneak down to the river for a quick bath and could change their clothes. She'd urged the guys to cool off, and was too grateful to Mar for rubbing the odd concoction of leaves on her that kept away the bugs. But the guys looked miserable.

Sweat had caked dirt lines at their necks; they were grubby as all get out. Streaks of smeared dust and perspiration marked their faces, and their fingernails were caked with two days' worth of travel and battle. Just looking at them made her feel yucky. And they were all supposed to bunk in the same room? Even the noses in the group didn't mind. Men. Damali sighed.

None of the team had shown any shame when a dripping array of fresh fruit was put before them along with the spicy dende-oil-seared kale blended with lime juice, garlic, and tomatoes, or the deep-fried bean cake with onion and pepper sauce, sans dried shrimp. Both Kamal and Marlene argued that the guardians needed their strength; meats sapped the energy field of the body, they said. It was all vegetarian fare tonight, and most of that consisted of uncooked foods. Fresh, cold coconut milk, papaya juice, mango juice, and flatbreads were inhaled without protest.

Time here was measured by the angle of the sun, the brightness of the stars, music, and activity. Kamal dropped back on his elbows on the gravelly riverbank, his billowing white pants reflecting the flickers of red and gold from the blaze of the campfire. Several of Damali's guardians yawned, sending a ripple of yawns and stretches throughout the group. Everyone relaxed except Marlene and Shabazz, and oddly, Jose. Damali was too full to immediately worry about it. The fire felt good, the breeze was soft and balmy. The sounds of the night were descending upon the river. The water made its own music. Brothers were laughing and talking among themselves, but Kamal's second in command, Abdul, made her chuckle.

"Marlene teach you about *mari ariri kero dohpa*?" He glanced at Kamal who only smiled as he came near Damali and sat down, trying to throw heavy rap.

"Our existence dreamlike appears," Damali said, knowing she was blowing his rap, but needing to set some boundaries. "Yeah, total opposite of western beliefs." From her peripheral vision she could see a few of the nearby brothers swallow away smiles, but they remain fixated on the verbal dance to see how their brother might recover.

He edged closer to her and gave a deferential nod in Marlene's direction, which seemed to make Kamal nod in appreciation. "Of course, you have a mother-seer who is renowned. She would have explained how the invisible, spiritual world is within the left brain, where fantastic artists like you draw from." His voice was low, sensual, and controlled as he ran his palm over his locks to demonstrate each side of the brain. "The right," he continued, "is the physical—what we call reality. But what is reality? Many things are illusion and yet they are so real."

Damali's smile broadened. Oh, now, see, brother was trying to get a metaphysical swerve on. She would not be baited as Abdul's finger trailed a lazy pattern in the sand and his intense, dark eyes glittered with open hunger. His vibe was so thick that she almost had to stand up and take a walk. Then he glanced up at the early moon that was competing to come out while the sun was setting, then over to Kamal, who only shook his head slowly in a quiet warning to be cool, then he returned his focus to her.

The glance he gave her was so hot it nearly burned her. She was so flustered by the bold approach that she looked down at the sand and began doodling in it with her finger. A part of her wanted to laugh . . . if Carlos were here to see Abdul's encroachment, or any of the pure animal magnetism exuded by the members of Kamal's team, shoot, it would be on. He'd turn the camp out, just like Shabazz probably wanted to now. And Carlos thought her dancing in a club was bad . . . Then just that fast her reality struck her. She and Carlos were done.

The moment the thought went through her mind, Abdul smiled.

"You are definitely left-brain oriented," he said, trying to flatter her, his smile brilliant. "That's the seat of moral authority, intuition, dreams, music." He leaned forward and reached for a peeled mango slice off a nearby platter and offered her a piece. The subtle action drew his team's full attention, and it made her guys briefly stop talking.

"Thank you," she said, taking the fruit. The translation was universal; if she'll take food from your hand, that's a sensual, intimate first step to seriously moving in for an encounter. She had to accept it, lest she embarrass the second in command in front of his boys. Then again, why not go for it? The brother was fine, she was single, he was a guardian, and, hey, if she was going to have to move on, had to begin to pick up the pieces of her life . . .

She smiled when Abdul moved closer, still deciding just how close she wanted him to be. She bit the mango slice and tried not to eat it too sensually, which was hard as the sweet juice of it dribbled down her chin and fingers. She could sense Abdul about to lean over and lick the juice from her chin, but then think better of it. He respectfully checked himself and sat back with a low laugh. Didn't Mar say there were a hundred and forty-four thousand guys like this she could choose from? Damn, this camp was loaded.

"I'm a tactical and a seer," he murmured. "That's why I'm interested in your mind, not just what you see, but what you feel." He reached for another piece of fruit, and ate it with blatant sensuality that made her look away and dab her chin.

She needed a fan.

Jose's jaw was locked so tightly that she was afraid he'd break it. The other guardians from her squad just ate nice and slow, watching the dynamic. But they had the same terrain-sweeping gaze that brothers issued in the clubs just before a bar fight was about to jump off. This was *not* good.

She glanced at Marlene for support and a bail out, noting that Marlene had stayed far away from Kamal while food was being passed, and that Shabazz was making it real clear whose territory she was within by holding the platter for her, refilling her drink. Wild. Yeah, Jose looked like he was going to go into apoplexy. He shot Abdul a lethal glare that made him slowly back up real slow, real cool, before returning his attention to her. Kamal's team reacted with a slow tilt of their heads and intermittent biceps flexes. Her guys glanced at each other and that's when Kamal sat up, seemingly annoyed at his younger team member. He gave Abdul a quick reprimand glance and then pirated Abdul's rap with a respectful tone and a platonic smile.

"What Abdul refers to means the sun-people dimension, dear Neteru. The left side is de older brother, and I know that Marlene has told you that in this side of da brain, the *emekori manhsa turi,* is where we interact with beings of the spiritual world and interpret the *bogari,* energy fields and transmissions from nature. The right side," he said, glancing at Abdul who was looking at the early moon with an expression of utter defeat, "the *mahsa turi,* is the younger brother. It is subservient to the left and rules practical knowledge. And while second in command, there are times where practical knowledge is important . . . to keep one's dreams in check."

Kamal smiled at her, and then at Abdul, before glancing at Marlene, who simply swallowed away a chuckle. "But the fissure between the halves, which we will explore tonight, is represented by a giant anaconda with stepping stones on its back . . . with a giant rock crystal shaped like a hexagon on its head. That's where we need to go to—"

"What did you say to Marlene?" Shabazz had turned from the river and his furious gaze locked with Kamal's.

The ripple of tension tore through both groups. Damali stiffened as she watched Marlene's tight expression. It was metaphysical info, true, but it was also suggestive as shit.

"I am talking about the hexagon. Two triangles make it. One half female, one half male. The nature energy runs through it. That's why it's primal, must be dealt with in a place like this to reach it." Kamal's voice was even, if not a bit patronizing, as he addressed Shabazz. He had not changed his relaxed position on the ground by the fire, nor did he seem concerned that Shabazz could rush him. "That's where we're going tonight. Good to tap into it after an awakening of certain energies."

"Brother, you know what—"

" 'Bazz," Marlene said quickly, "he's talking about triangles—"

Damali looked at Marlene, then Shabazz, and her stomach clenched when she heard Kamal let his breath out as though he were bored.

"Did you explain the *ayahuasca* walk to dis man so we can do the mind lock like we need to tonight without a problem?"

"First of all, you need to address me," Shabazz said walking forward, but Big Mike put a hand on his shoulder. "And second of all, yeah, I know about it." He looked at Marlene. "I just don't believe you were out here doing heavy hallucinogens with him, but that's a conversation for later. If you be cool, there won't be no problem."

Damali's eyes opened so wide she thought the corners of them would split. Oh, shit . . . Both teams were on standby now, but nobody moved.

"Shamanistic pharmaceuticals only taken with a real guide, during a ritual, and under monitored circumstances," Marlene said as calmly as she could. "The triangles are about the fact that the peoples of the Upper Rio Negro separate the male and female energies into the double triangle, the hexagon. It symbolizes both halves of the brain and there's a fusion of them shown as a windy, anaconda path between them."

She held Shabazz in a steady gaze that spoke volumes, namely, don't embarrass me out here. "Our Neteru has been dealing with triangles in planetary form since just before her twenty-first birthday—where two and one numerically make three—a trinity, a triangle. Right? She's faced three points of contention in her skills building, and has experienced this personally. We need to walk that fusion path, baby, to find out what's going on with this thing that attacked us. All three seers, me, Father Pat, and now, Kamal, feel a—"

"It is a real, erotic mental dance to get to fusion point and walk it—so you gwan hafta be cool, brother," Kamal said, his eyes glittering with something unreadable but akin to quiet rage. He narrowed his gaze as Shabazz flexed a fist. "And it's only something that can be done by a *real* guide."

Kamal was on his feet at the same time Shabazz broke free of Mike's hold. Damali had sensed the twig-snap of nerves before it happened, and was between both competitors in seconds.

"Listen, y'all. We've got this demon out here that's already attacked our team, and could attack yours." Both her arms were outstretched between the would-be combatants as she talked fast and used inscrutable logic as her weapon to keep them from squaring off.

"It somehow even masked itself to a master vampire, had him blitzed like he'd been exposed to ripened Neteru—he went for it, and didn't attack the demon. I saw it with my own eyes. We have three sides: vamps, demons, and us humans. Marlene is right. Some of this mess will be in the spirit realm of the supernatural; some of it resides on the practical side. And it is a combination of male and female energies, people. We have to work together to combat it." She looked at Kamal, begging him with her eyes to back down first. "You guys are were-demon specialists, right?"

Kamal nodded.

"Good, because we're vamp specialists. So let's do this thing and keep personal issues in the background." She looked at Shabazz. "We all have them going into this thing."

Shabazz nodded.

Both older warriors were sucking in hard inhales, nostrils flaring, battle stance readied, but oddly the rest of the team was watching this from a spectator's perspective. Marlene knew she was the fuse that could kick this whole thing off to another level, so she watched and didn't say a word.

"You actually saw him with some sort of false Neteru in his system?" Kamal finally asked, and relaxed his stance, which made Shabazz grudgingly follow suit.

"Yeah," Damali said, lowering her arms. "It was deep."

"And the vampire didn't attack you?"

She glanced at Marlene. She was not having this conversation in front of thirty or more men.

"No," Marlene said fast, coming to the rescue. "That's why we need to investigate."

Kamal nodded, no longer focused on Shabazz. He glanced around his team. "We'd heard about this substance that the were-demons created, but no one could get confirmation beyond rumor. We need to know about this as much as you do."

Progress. Damali walked away and sat down where she'd been. She noted that Abdul had moved to a respectable distance, and wasn't close enough to really push up on her. Everyone had come back to the fire except Shabazz, but she could understand it. Had someone not jumped in, it would have been on, and homeboy might have gotten his pride hurt for real. Her team fanned out, as did Kamal's. He went to where he'd been seated and leaned on his elbows looking at the sky.

"Need to get my focus back," Kamal said in what sounded like a near snarl. "Shit makes no sense."

"You fuckin' A-right, it don't," Shabazz muttered. "So do your shit and be done with it."

Kamal gave him a hard look and then focused on the fire, breathing hard, regaining his composure, and momentarily avoiding eye contact with Marlene.

It took a while for all the ruffled feathers to settle. The combatants had to save face, the teams had to deescalate, the storm had to pass. So everyone patiently waited, saying nothing but just doodling in the sand with a rock or a stick.

Kamal's eyes had gone half-mast as he meditated on the horizon. Once all the sudden adrenaline tension had left him, the way his locks swept the ground made him look like a large, sated lion. The setting sun fired his dark, bare chest with orange. Damali grabbed her knees, encircling them with her arms as she watched the invisible dance to restore order.

Mar kept her eyes on the dropping sun. Shabazz kept his eyes on the river. Damali's team studied the ground, pushing sand around with sticks. Kamal's team sprawled out on the grass and the shoreline, some watching the fire. Kamal closed his eyes, and kept his breathing steady. Damali watched.

"You ready, gurl?" Kamal murmured, after a while. "Sun's 'bout to set." He'd issued his comment on a languid breath, and sat up, shook his mane, and stretched.

Marlene nodded. Shabazz's line of vision remained fixed on the river.

"You know dis we dealin' wit is strong. I'm gwan hafta lock up wit cha, gurl. It's de only way."

Shabazz looked at him squarely, the threat implicit in his eyes, then he looked at Marlene.

"It's the only way, 'Bazz," Marlene said in a weary tone. "Both of us need to lock to get this done. Needs two seasoned seers with opposite gender energy to do this. We can't do stones or shells for this one."

Shabazz didn't nod or say a word, he just returned his gaze to the water. Big Mike looked away too, like his heart was breaking for Shabazz. JL and Dan just cast a glance into the fire. Rider was still doodling in the dirt with a stick with Jose.

Kamal reached into his pocket and pulled out several highly polished stones, opened his legs wide, making a circle between his legs that ended at his bare feet. With shells he made two triangles within it. One side for male energy, one side for female energy, which created a large hexagon shape on the shore. Seeming uncomfortable with the audience, Marlene took her time to stand and go to sit before Kamal. But when she did, he looked at her and smiled.

"Been long time," he murmured as her legs slipped over his and their hands joined.

Damali didn't move a muscle. Aw, shit . . . brother, *do not* strike a match. Shabazz's jaw muscles were jumping, as was the muscle in his upper right arm, his swing arm. Big Mike's hand landed on his shoulder once more. Shabazz looked away. Marlene didn't respond to the comment. But in a way she did, because she looked at the ground like she couldn't even bear to meet Kamal's eyes.

Kamal's half smile was barely visible, as he reached into his pocket again and pulled out a series of shells. "You're blocking, baby. You got to flow, or dis don't work. You know that. Flow wit me, and let me in."

Shabazz stood up and walked to the river's edge and back and sat down. Marlene nodded and closed her eyes, seeming unable to concentrate. The sun was a red-orange orb in a vast blue-gray carpet of clouds. Damali studied the vista. Hard.

Kamal released a sound from inside his chest, however, that made the group go still as their gazes shot to the divination. Even Kamal's guys were on their feet taking battle stances. The guttural, sensual timbre that came out of him, and the way Marlene's shoulders slumped, made every warrior in the house ready themselves for a showdown. It was on, now, no doubt. Shabazz was on his feet again, so was Damali, her hand in the center of his chest.

"I'm locked in with 'em, brother," she lied. "It's cool. It's, uh, part of the process."

Nobody relaxed, nobody moved. When Marlene let out a hard exhale and breathed in through her nose and trembled, Shabazz looked Damali dead in her eyes.

"You're locked in?"

"Yeah," she said quickly. "For real," and walked over to plop down near Marlene. *Girl, not here, not now, c'mon!*

"Fertility and restraint," Kamal murmured. "Yeah, I see it. I can feel it strong."

Damali let out a breath of relief, not caring that everyone around the fire heard it. Kamal's team squatted in a stand-down position. Shabazz turned his back, but listened.

"Orion, male energy. But also weaker male in the equation—dark. Two women. One stronger. Dark."

Perspiration had formed on Marlene's brow as Kamal clasped her hands tighter. Rider stood and came over to Damali, sitting down beside her.

"This part we know already, D. It's bullshit for Shabazz to have to deal with this," he whispered through his teeth.

"I know, I know, but this isn't like looking up an Internet file. It's a process, not an exact science. The seers have to get in sync first. Chill," she warned with a hissing whisper. "All these negative vibes are slowing it down. The faster it's over, the better."

Rider thrust his feet out before him and sighed. He closed his eyes.

"Oh, gurl, damn . . . I remember." Kamal had dropped his head back and was breathing through his mouth.

All teams shot to their feet. Big Mike was body-blocking Shabazz.

"Fuck all this! Damali, what the fuck is this bullshit?"

The two seers never even flinched. Kamal's men were cool, but amused—however, they were also ready. Damali's gaze shot between Shabazz, Big Mike, and Marlene. Shabazz was practically breathing fire. Big Mike was doing a two-step dance to keep him blocked. Rider looked like a defensive back, prepared for a tackle. The expressions on both Marlene and Kamal's faces sent a quiet ripple through Damali. She had never lied to Shabazz like that in her life, and God help her, she never wanted to hurt him—but what could she tell him? The ripple turned into a shudder within her. It was then that it became so clear.

"'Bazz . . . listen to me. Mar is not where you think." She approached him slowly, calmly, as if she were approaching a wounded animal.

"Then where the fuck is she, huh? Somebody answer me that shit, pronto!"

"She's where I've been," Damali said looking away, too humiliated to say more.

Immediately the struggle ceased. Big Mike dropped his hands, Rider sat back down, the teams fell into at-ease positions, Damali found Marlene's side again. Shabazz took a walk to the river's edge, returning after a moment and plopped down next to Mike.

"He's near," Kamal said in a husky voice. "No danger to us, but in pain . . . hurt. His chest. Heavy. Wants her bad."

"I know," Marlene said quietly. "Been that way for a long time."

Kamal threw his head back. "It's all through his system. The choice is killing him."

Marlene was drawing quick sips of air. "Her team . . ."

Suddenly Kamal stiffened, then he dropped Marlene's hands, stood up fast, and spun on Shabazz. "How you gwan let dis here woman almost die wit a gun in you hand! Bullshit!"

Everybody was on their feet now. Damali was between Shabazz and Big Mike. Rider was back up. JL, Jose, and Dan were holding a line between the teams. The two largest members of Kamal's team looked like they were ready to grab their master to avoid a brawl.

"It wasn't his fault," Marlene said, quickly standing.

"I don't need you to explain shit to this bastard about anything I did, or do!"

"You let a demon witch hit her wit dark current!"

"Yo, dude. None of us saw that coming," Rider said defensively.

Kamal was blowing hot snorts of pure rage out of his nose, and even his squad looked startled to see him lose his cool. "Dat's because your ass is fucking blind, mon! You had da gift—you would have known!"

"Motherfucker—"

Shabazz lunged. Big Mike lifted Shabazz off his feet and pulled him out of reach.

Kamal straightened his locks and turned to Marlene. "For dis, Marlene, you gwan need some serious help. No amateur."

Damali could see Marlene steadying herself, trying to maintain a calm voice as she carefully chose her words. "Kamal, what are we dealing with?"

Although Shabazz still bristled, the circle widened as the veteran seer went back to his circle and sat down. Bodies relaxed within the group. Marlene sat down again, but cast a warning glare to the team as the men one by one sat—Shabazz conceding last.

"Dis ting dat come up from de pit, lures him with ripe Neteru. Dis ting dat hunts the vampire is were-jaguar. Female hunter by day, transforms at night. She took down an entire guardian squad with her, all weres. He's torn, but isn't—you follow?"

Marlene nodded and took Kamal's hands again.

"Her seer is old, seasoned, like you, baby. I need to make you sometin' special. My mother, you know dat, was Tucanoan. I have their crystals. I'll make my baby an amulet, sometin' to keep—"

"Oh, fuck all dat," Shabazz said low in his throat. "All we need is some ammo, and—"

"You ain't take care of me woman enough to keep a witch from burning a hole in her chest!"

"First off, goddamn, she ain't your woman," Shabazz shot back, standing again, sending the group to their feet. "Second of all, for fifteen years, I protected her while your ass was hiding in the woods, okay? So don't tell me about ”

"Hidin' in de woods? What? I sent—"

"No!" Marlene yelled. "Everybody just amp down. We did not come here for this!"

Both Kamal and Shabazz backed away from each other. Damali looked from one group to the next and stepped up.

"Okay, look. Let's calm down. If Kamal has an amulet or a charm that will keep Marlene safe, then let's be rational."

"Thank you, gracious Neteru," Kamal said, still indignant. "It's a hexagon breastplate, white crystal, to keep her from getting her heart fried."

"All right, cool," Damali said quickly, glancing between both men. "Then what about the main one, the queen-demon I need to off?"

"You gwan hafta kill 'er wit love," Kamal said slowly. "Gwan hafta rip her heart out and then take her head off her shoulders so she can't tink about it. Kill da head, and de odders will die, too. But dis ting is like a hydra . . . many heads, many faces, only one though, makes the difference." He looked at Damali hard. "This demon wants the vampire in unnatural ways—will cause a breach if he succumbs to the scent."

Kamal began pacing and his team moved in closer, their faces strained. "If they become one, the vampire will have access to daylight."

Damali's hand slowly went to her mouth. "With the scent of ripe Neteru as the lure, and the promise of daylight, he'd made a choice too seductive to ignore. We have to get to her, first, then him."

Kamal's gaze became tender as he stared across the fire at Marlene.

His words were spoken so quietly, with so much pain laced through them, that his own team looked away, watching their master surrender.

"It'll keep coming back, gurl, if you don' *finish it*. And when you get near it, you will feel everyting it feels, know everyting it knows . . . and desire everyting it desires but cannot have. It's a female locked to a male, both trapped in their own realities—just hoping for a way to break free of them. It suffers, so be gentle wit it, though. When you kill it, kill it wit honor."

Marlene swallowed hard and looked away, then walked toward the river's edge. Shabazz headed for the guest house, and Kamal walked into the brush.

"You guys stay with her," Damali said to Rider, who only nodded. "I'm gonna go get 'Bazz," she added in Big Mike's direction.

Every man standing on the shore eventually one by one just ran their hands through their hair.

" 'Bazz, wait up," Damali called behind him, running to match his long strides. "Hold up," she urged, trying to keep up with his furious pace. "There's a message in this we gotta listen to."

Unexpectedly Shabazz stopped and whirled on her. "I heard the message, loud and clear. Didn't you?" He began walking again, yanking and kicking brush out of the way in the darkness.

For a while, she just walked by him in silence. Yeah, she heard both messages in Kamal's divination loud and clear. Saw it in Kamal's eyes, too. Saw it in the way it quietly broke Marlene's heart. This was really messed up. Her brother, mentor, friend was bleeding with a walking mortal wound. Her seer, mother-mentor was bleeding to death like a vein had been opened at the riverbank. And another master was somewhere in the bush eating his own heart out. This was screwed.

Shabazz punched the van as he passed it, kicked the post of the steps by the guest house, and paced back and forth like a caged bear. Moonlight and a dim floodlight washed over Shabazz's face, illuminating the silent anguish in it. His locks swung hard, slapping against his shoulders as he walked, having broken free of the band when Mike hurled him. Humiliation didn't even begin to describe the pain in his expression. It was far more complex, containing so much more than one thing.

"It was total disrespect, Damali. *Total* fucking disrespect!"

She didn't say a word. A match hadn't been lit; it was a torch—an old one. This forest fire it created in the bush had to burn. Yeah, it was disrespect, but a love jones will do that to ya, too. Yet as she watched the pain work its way out of Shabazz's system, enlightenment came with it. Damn, she'd just been there.

" 'Bazz," she said quietly, as his pacing slowed and he dropped to a step beside her. "She loves you, brother. Only you. I'm a seer, too. Remember?"

"I know what I felt, been feeling all day . . . and while I ain't no seer, I'm also not blind." Shabazz cast his gaze out toward the now-black bush, watching the campfire that was far away. "Fifteen years, D."

"Fifteen good ones, and plenty more."

Shabazz shook his head.

"Yeah, more good ones," Damali repeated, kicking a stone with her foot.

Shabazz released a hollow chuckle. "Met her in a freakin' alley." He continued to shake his head. "Can you believe it? Then lost her in a jungle. Go figure. Shit happens."

"Where did you meet her?" she asked in a soft voice, hoping to draw him out.

"I had just got out." Shabazz shrugged. "Shot my own boy by accident, so had to do some time." Shabazz looked away, his focus up at the now blue-black night and the stars.

"We was kids, you know. Out in the street, hustling. Waiting on a drop-off. My boy was behind me in the alley. Kept telling him to back up. He said he was. Every time I looked over my shoulder, he was ten paces back. But when I turned around to keep watch, I could feel him breathing down my neck. Then, he licked my throat."

Shabazz swallowed hard. "I was like, *what the fuck* . . . and when I turned around, somethin' I ain't never seen before was standing between me and my boy. I freaked. Unloaded a whole clip, and it went right through her into him. Then, it was gone, and my delivery came."

Shabazz stood, snapped his fingers. "Just like that. A life was gone, my life hung in the balance, and everything had changed. Damali, shit happens, but they never tell you that the shit happens fast . . . just like it did tonight."

She was sipping air quietly, as the pain of her eldest guardian brother's confession crushed the oxygen from her lungs. "Where did you meet Mar?" It was all she could think of to keep Shabazz talking, keep him purging his history so he could get his head right.

"While I was in, I kept feeling shit, sensing things. This cool brother helped me clean up—he watched my back so they ain't make me no bitch in there. First, I thought he was on me, you dig? But he was a seer. Said I had better things to do. So, he gave me an address in New Orleans—said there was this sister he once knew there who was a bad seer, who would know my path."

He stopped, looked at Damali, and sighed. "I ain't have *nuthin'* to lose, then, li'l sis. Nothin'. My whole posse was threatening me for shooting my boy, said I was claiming bullshit and trying to get off with an insanity rap, talking about vampires in an alley. Public defender got me a plea bargain. Had to finally admit to something I ain't do the way they said. My momma practically disowned me when I bargained—she didn't understand I wanted to see daylight before I died, then she up and died before I got out. Quick. Happens quick."

Damali nodded and kept her gaze level with Shabazz's.

"Went down there to the only address I had, but homegirl had moved. Went to a bar to figure out my next move. Got a drink. Left. Saw this sister in the alley out the corner of my eye, wielding a walking stick against three guys. Was deep. I stopped, was trying to stay out of bullshit—had just got out, didn't need no problems. But then the streetlight caught a fang, and I knew. Once you see it, you always know it, even at a distance. And I went in there with her—don't ask me why. Maybe I just wanted to connect with another living soul who had witnessed some shit like this. Had to help her, too, 'cause they were on her. Knew better than to pull my Glock." He laughed. "Yeah, I know, parole violation, but fuck it. I was goin' to New Orleans back in the day."

Damali smiled, watching Shabazz relive the past, watching his expression mellow, listening to his voice go gentle.

"She was beautiful, D. Poetry in motion. She kicked their asses. Knew my Aikido moves that I had learned under Haneef Shabazz. We didn't even have to look at each other, D. We were back-to-back, and stomped them vamps. *Together*. I kept them off her, she staked 'em.

We made a good team. Been with her ever since . . . shit . . . I didn't even go back to my motel room that night."

He laughed quietly, looked at the horizon. "Had done *ten years,* and hadn't been with nobody since I was eighteen. That first night out in the world, back in daylight, though . . . Spent it with Mar. Didn't even know her name—didn't care. Just wanted her." He nodded, and pushed away from the post. "Been that way ever since . . . but like I said, shit happens fast, and nothing lasts forever. Fuck it."

"You got your name from your mentor?" Damali avoided the obvious hurt, and backtracked the conversation to help keep Shabazz focused on that which was good.

"Yeah. Gave up my street name, and my family name . . . ain't had no family no more, so, whatever. Needed a new name and a new identity to keep myself from gettin' snuffed on the inside, and from my old posse when I got out. My boy's family didn't take it well that I was the one who'd put a bullet in him. Plus, Haneef had my back inside, literally. Was like a father to me. Gave the word, and it was so— I was off limits. His name was like a shield, and the man who'd had it had honor."

Shabazz let his breath out again on a quaky exhale, then recovered in moments. "I was hard, and all that . . . but I'ma tell you—five, ten, twenty to one and no weapon? Shcccit. Never been so scared in my damned life. Rather have a vamp snatch my heart out than live through some of what I saw inside. That's why some of this don't faze a brother, feel me? My mentor told me that until I could take ten to one, I'd always have fear in my eyes, which would draw 'em, the predators in the joint . . . and one day he might not be around. So, I listened, studied, and listened good. Feel me? Gotta be strategic. When you're weaker, gotta use your head to stay alive. Keep from getting jacked. Just like with the vamps."

She nodded and placed a hand on Shabazz's arm. "There's a lot worse things than dying."

"Right." He looked away.

"I listened to my mentors, and listened good . . . didn't I?"

Shabazz chuckled. "Sometimes."

She laughed with him. "But I was pretty good with healing Mar's heart, right?"

Shabazz nodded but kept his gaze on the stars. "You did good, baby girl—real good. Thank you." He looked at her and nodded. "Seriously." Then he swallowed hard and glanced away.

"I learned how to hear, see, feel, track, taste situations, right?"

Shabazz nodded. She made him look at her by brushing a lock over his shoulder.

"She ain't goin' nowhere. Yeah, there's history, but we all got a long story, 'Bazz . . . You just told me one. Kamal was just her mentor—she told me that, woman to woman. I felt her torn, trying to get info, trying to show you respect, and trying to be gentle with somebody who didn't do her no harm . . . who was trying to help our squad. Sis was between a rock and a hard place—like you were the other night in the club, before y'all left."

Shabazz laughed but let his gaze slip away. "You getting pretty good at this stuff we been teaching you to pick up on. Need to mind your business, though."

She chuckled and kissed his cheek. "She ain't goin nowhere, big brother. But she might need a protective escort down by the river all alone. Do what you want with it, but that's gospel." Damali walked up the steps and left Shabazz studying the moon. She wrapped her arms around herself and smiled as she heard him stroll back toward the bush.

CHAPTER TWENTY-TWO

JUST ONE night, she pleaded in prayer as she flopped down on a musty mattress. No more drama, just sleep. A camp of thirty-three warriors with the spiritual juice of a small army, who had enough amulets and circles and holy water lines drawn across sills and door jambs should allow a moment of peace—please, Father. Just another day. No screams in the night. No battle stations, no standoffs, nobody flare up, nobody get puffed up. Nobody break anybody else's heart or piss anybody else off. Please.

Damali threw her arm over her eyes, willing her body to relax. But her mind would not stop racing. Tomorrow might be the final showdown. Might be it. They'd have to hunt these things in the day while the Amazons were in human form, well before they transformed and got stronger. That much they'd figured out. These demons took human form by day, but at night, who knew the full extent of what they could become? Okay. Fine. But even as human female warriors, she had to admit, these bitches was bad.

"Cool," she said out loud to the empty room. Like Kamal said, warrior to warrior, and with honor. Hopefully he had a strong amulet, a little sometin', as he put it, for Mar. But damn, he was dancing on the edge of disrespect with 'Bazz. Love will make you stupid, step out of order, no matter how old.

Part of her really hurt for Kamal, though. It was crazy, but it had nothing to do with her rock-solid love for Shabazz, either. It was an oddly separate thing . . . compassion. That's what it was. She could feel that brother's deep-down soul wound. Knew what he was going through to want somebody so badly, but because of the realities of the situation, and the passage of time, had to let it go. But just to have to stand there and let it go and take it like a man. That was some deep and hard shit to do. For real discipline. Shabazz had that kind of control, too. She'd felt Kamal's desire for Marlene run all through her—not from second sight, but plain ole twenty-twenty vision. And she had felt Marlene's response. It was visceral. When Kamal locked into her, Marlene looked faint. Been there. Damali shook her head.

"Oh, Mar, sis, I been there," she murmured, repeating the thought. All out in public, in front of the team, wanting to crawl under a rock and die from the embarrassment. But can't do a thing to hide it because that lure is right in front of you and you're so hot you can't even play it off.

"Damn." At fifty-plus years old? Whew, shit. Memories would mess you up. There were no words. Now Marlene had to do the hardest thing in the world, kill part of her mind with honor. Had to act like she knows.

And what was that? Act like you know? When your brain was on fire? Lit by an old flame? Not to mention the other body parts that clear memory ignited. Shoooot.

Damali let her breath out hard, trying to fathom how any of this applied to the next day. This female were-jag demon wasn't going to run off in the bush from no love jones, or stalk away so there could be a confession followed by a meeting of the minds. This Amazon creature was coming for her, and was probably going to wield a battle-ax to try to lop off her fucking head! The situation did not apply, and they'd come all this way for only an amulet and some good food. Cool. Whateva.

If it gave Marlene a shield, then fine. But beyond that, it had probably been a waste of time—unless the guys could pull it together and work out some weapons strategies without arguing with Kamal's squad. This was Kamal and his boyz' house, their yard, just as much as the Amazon's. Maybe they'd just come here for discipline?

Her breaths started to come in slow, deep, drags of drifting sleep. Marlene and Kamal were supposed to know some people that knew some people who could get a boat with a full payload of automatics, silver dust and colloidal silver-filled shells, hallowed earth-packed bazookas—

"That'll help, but it won't work alone, baby," a familiar male voice whispered, inches from her face. "She moves too fast."

"Oh, shit! Don't do that!"

She sat up quickly, and jumped out of the bed. A collision of feel-ings swept through her. Anger, fear, invasion, remorse, relief, joy, de-sire . . . too many to catalog in her mind, or to prioritize.

"You learned a lot, tonight," the figure in the shadows murmured, low and seductive. "It was painful, but it was all good. You needed to see that. Sometimes shit ain't black and white."

"Carlos," she whispered furiously. "How the hell did you get in here?"

He chuckled, but the tone in his voice was sad. "I can get in, my squad and any other vamp can't. Guess a little bit of a soul, and a few prayers from the Covenant, work like a passport, baby."

"You need to get out of here. And I'm not sure how I feel about any of this mess between us, okay? You've obviously made your deci-sion. I told you, I made mine." The fact that he could move so easily through any barriers around her worried her.

He stepped in close enough for her to see him in the moonlight. The blue glow of it painted streaks down his black T-shirt, over his shoulder, and the bottom of his jaw. His eyes were dark, not flicker-ing. She was glad. But another part of her felt a pang because she no longer had that effect on him.

"I'm stronger, too, that's all," he murmured, stepping even closer now so their bellies touched. "You do have that effect on me, still. Al-ways will." He closed his eyes and smiled. "I'm just trying not to strike a match."

"You don't have the right to go into my head like that anymore," she said, pulling away. But she had to fold her arms to stop the shiver of want that rushed through her. She couldn't even watch the hunger in his eyes when he opened them. It wasn't gonna work this time. No.

"I didn't go into your head. All I had to do was listen to the night. I knew you wouldn't run, and were in trouble. Just like I know your team is in deep shit out here. That's why I came. You were yelling it in your mind, broadcasting it for me to hear." He chuckled, putting his hands on her shoulders and allowing them to deliciously slide down her arms. "You're powerful, honey. Your thoughts are stronger than you know. You also sent more than a regulation SOS to me. Af-ter what just went down between us, too . . . I don't have to go in to hear you. Never did."

"Look," she said with a swallow, stepping back. "My guys will be up here soon, this whole convo is bad form. Plus, this isn't even my people's place. It's a friend of Mar's—"

"You all need to watch your backs out here. They ain't what you think, baby. His squad has some deep shit with them. But they seem to be cool at the moment."

"They're trying to help us, no matter what you think you saw."

"So I gathered," he said softly against her neck as he moved in to seal the space she'd made between them. "Know exactly where the poor brother is. He's dying inside. But he had to make a decision."

"We both did."

She'd meant her voice to come out with more force, more anger. She also noticed that he had referred to Kamal, and not the incident with Abdul being in her face. Growth perhaps. Guilty conscience, most likely. But oddly, and as irrational as it was, the fact that the presence of another male competing for her attention hadn't even fazed him, stung.

"I know, baby," he said quietly after a moment. "This time I got myself really snagged between a rock and a hard place, but I wanted to see you just one more time. No disrespect to you, or your people intended."

His kissed her ear, and pulled it between his lips slowly, and let his breath out hard, then backed away. "I gotta go, but I just wanted you to know how I really felt, before some shit went down that's irreversible."

The sensation that began at her ear had traveled down her neck, past her shoulder, wound its way around her heart, and was sending a slow, deep charge of desire through her belly as it crept lower. She could barely speak, much less breathe, but she had to know. "You're gonna do this insane thing, aren't you? For power and glory? Try to hijack daylight? To what end?"

He shook his head and came in close to her again. Even though she stepped back, his finger traced her cheek. "Aw, baby, no. I'm doing it for you."

She closed her eyes at the sound of his voice, tender and gentle and reminding her with the touch the way he used to trace her face on the beach. "Don't do this, it's not fair."

"Life ain't fair," he said with a thick swallow. "I got busted. They found out I was playing both ends against the middle. The council called my bluff, the old counselor wants to cut a deal—your life, and your team's lives, for this one thing I gotta do for him. You're worth it."

"No, I'm not." She shook her head and reached up to stroke the nape of his neck. "Nobody is worth your soul. Why didn't you tell me before that they'd found you out?"

"My soul is probably not even on the table for negotiation, baby. That's long gone, now, no doubt. I'm scramblin' for crumbs at this juncture. When you do some shit and you plea-bargain, you gonna do some time. Shabazz told you as much. That's the law in all realms. So . . . I gotta go away for a little while. I didn't tell you earlier because I didn't want to break your heart. I knew you'd try to rush in and fix something that just couldn't be fixed."

Her hand slipped from his neck. Part of her registered something in him that gave her pause. He'd told her the truth but not all of it. He still had a window, a sliver of a chance, but had lost hope . . . was too afraid to gamble one more time. Why? And that information was securely locked away.

One palm rested on his shoulder as she held the side of his face, and her eyes sought his in the darkness. "Tell me why you have to do this. I can fight. We can get rid of this thing together."

"You won't give this up till I show you what you're up against, will you?"

"No, the deal is, *you* still don't get it." She stared at him, her body tense with renewed anger and frustration. "I'm a Neteru. This is what I do for a living . . . I'm not just *your woman,* or your ex-woman, whateva. What hurts more than you can know is that you have no respect for who I am, my capability, or my skill." She dropped her hands and folded her arms. "And it fucks me up, because, brother, I'm your damned equal. Yeah," she said, nodding slowly, her eyes never leaving his. "Different strengths, different skills, but just as worthy as yours— and don't you forget, I told your ass that this threat was serious— waaaay long before you had to come over here and find out. Do not patronize me, or treat me like some young girl who can't hold her own. Got it? Your info is late and corrupted. Female instinct. Neteru style."

He sighed and cradled her face in his hands and closed his eyes tight. Her speech, while noble, was way off the mark. She couldn't handle this bullshit coming down any better than he could, and she had no concept of how his world functioned . . . the lengths they would go.

"Damali, you have always been so stubborn, but I love you too much to watch you go out there without a strategy, just swinging wild tomorrow. This thing that hunts me is in so much pain, is so wounded, that it's gone insane. Yet, the glimmer of what she was, still remains—and they want to prostitute even that. Part of me feels sorry for her, strange as that may seem."

"Show me, then, and stop all the lies of omission and stop blocking my hunt," Damali whispered through her teeth. "Compassion is in the man I know, so it's not strange to me that you'd say that. But to never back down from a threat against the innocent, is in the woman before you. Give me and my team a fighting chance, Carlos. Lift the mental block on at least some of this and let me in . . . As crazy as it sounds, I'll be honest with you—even though you've lied to me, because I can stand up for my shit and put it in the light. That's a Neteru strength you need to respect. So, I won't lie, I miss being there . . . in your head with you, along with everything else we shared. One last gift. The truth, please, so I can turn it loose, and finish it."

Her words contained double meaning, and he nodded, acknowledging both issues. It was going to be hard to turn anything between them loose, or to finish it, and yet a mental lock was a final gift, as well as a final torture. So strange. So complex. His lungs expanded on a ragged inhale. He nodded.

She relaxed and touched his shoulders to make the connection more direct, but could tell he was gathering control over his emotions, just like she was. She could feel that through his hands, hear it in his breath, didn't need to do more than that. No extra-sensory perception required. She knew this man. He knew her.

Carlos's cool palms became warm against her face, and as their minds locked, a full blast of sensation hit her. Everything this man had kept away from her since it all began filled her, rushed through her, making them both fight not to make a sound in the charged night air. He suddenly held her to him hard, and she could feel him making love to her, right there, standing in the middle of the floor, neither of them moving, him clutching the back of her T-shirt, her holding his shoulder blades in a familiar embrace, phantom spasms claiming her, rocking her from memory. *No, that's not what I was asking you to share!* His eyes went solid red.

When he lowered his forehead to hers, the perspiration from his mingled with the sheen on hers. His damp cheek stuck to her cheek as his face slid to her throat. Her skin drank in his salty essence, making her knees buckle. He let out a hard pant and swallowed down a swift-moving moan that threatened to pass his lips, and turned his head from her.

This isn't fair . . .

I keep trying to tell you, none of this is fair. But you wanted everything in my head—this came before her, will be there after her. Respect that much truth from me.

Just the sensation of him repressing the spasm that was coursing through him made her gasp against her will. She pressed her breasts against his chest, unable to conquer the sting and ache, the need for him to touch her there. He lifted his head, and glanced at the bed. She immediately read the thought, and shook her head, even though he'd already banished the concept. Not here. Never anywhere.

He was talking to her in fits and starts of mentally stumbling words. Admonishing himself, trying to stick to the subject of the Amazon threat one moment, begging her for one more hard-down passionate time together in the next, his inner voice panicked. *After tonight . . . we won't ever again. Damn, just one more time.*

Instantly she could hear her shirt seams giving at the shoulders, and he flattened his palm against her back to keep from tearing the fabric. He dropped his hold on her, walking in a circle, going to the window to just be able to breathe.

"I know you already knew all this," he said, trying to steady himself. "But before you saw anything else, I wanted you to know how much you're in me, are a part of me. You needed to know that first."

"I don't understand? First?" She blinked back tears of fury. Oh, shit, it was already too late . . .

How could she comprehend any of his feelings if she went into the next level of his thoughts—the darker levels? Her understanding would get twisted, just like all things do when they sink into the abyss. It might ruin her. She didn't need knowledge like this.

Yet, the only thing he could hold onto was the hope that after what she'd just felt, she had to know beyond a shadow of a doubt just what she'd meant to him from the start. That total consumption, that brand, was right under the surface of his skin, damn near oozing out of it. She didn't have to venture deep to connect with it, and it had been a monster trying to hold her mind at bay. It was too hard, next to impossible, to keep it compartmentalized with the scent of her so close, her body heat sending infrared tracer toward him. The quick heartbeat in her chest was getting confused with the throb in his groin, was married to it now.

He was in so much distress, mentally, physically, emotionally, that for moments he couldn't answer her—new strength notwithstanding. He wasn't ever gonna be strong enough to pull out of her magnet. Her eyes. Her arms. Away from her mouth. Once he'd touched her, held her, it was all over. Kissed her, he was done. Remembered what it felt like to be inside her, history, her voice. Then he saw her onstage on her knees in her red dress, calling him hard like a siren . . . "Baby, don't make me do this . . ."

Tears glittered in her eyes. She didn't understand. Nothing he was about to do would ever change how he felt about her. But everything he was about to do would irrevocably change how she felt about him. And perhaps a selfish part of his mind, the part that knew he'd live an eternity like the old counselor, nursing the memories—he wanted a fresh videotape to play over and over again in his brain. She just didn't understand how much he needed to be with her just one more time before tomorrow night . . . just one more, long, sweet, pure, awesome, stop-the-hands-of-time till the sun came up before she'd never let him hold her like that again.

When she came to him and touched his back, her hands burned where they fell, and he thought for a moment that she might understand. He grabbed her so fast, and kissed her with such intensity that it brought new tears to her eyes as he sent his full spectrum of emotions for her without censure. He couldn't help it.

"Remember, please remember, no matter what," he whispered hard, panicked, kissing her face, her neck, her eyes, and finally her mouth, crushing it, making her scrabble at his back, yielding to the sway.

"You remember," she said on a shallow breath, breaking his seal. "This is how I've always felt about you . . . don't do this. Take me to a lair, somewhere, anywhere, just one more time . . . Carlos, please. If that's what you need to keep you from giving up your soul, then . . ."

Her fingernails dug into his scalp and through his hair as she pulled him down, standing on tiptoes, her body arching against him so hard that he had to break from her mouth to release the sound he could no longer swallow. The night creatures went still beyond the window. Near sobbing, he separated their bodies, and placed her hands at either side of his face, covering her wrists, holding her palms firm to his cheeks so she could read him deep.

"You're not safe in a lair with me, and I wouldn't be able to hear anything but you. I'm over the top. I've got two minutes and the whole camp squad will be up here. Look at it, baby, and weep. It's so ugly. Don't fight this thing on its home court. Go home."

He watched her struggle to remove her hands from beneath his, but he held her firmly. Tears ran down her face, and she began sobbing.

"Let me go!"

"No, you wanted to see it, and are determined to fight it. Then you have to know it." His voice was gentle, calm, her struggle maddening, ripping at his heart from the inside out.

He could hear a squadron rallying, running in their direction. Damali's shoulders were slumped, her head bent and resting against his chest. Repeatedly she wailed no. The sounds of heartbreak coming from low in her belly as she chanted, begged, saying no like a mere word could change his fate.

Bitter sobs threaded in the stanza. Her plea "No," had initially come out shrill, deepened, got bottom in it, was whispered, was harmonized with hiccupping tears, hysteria giving way to pleads, no, then lucid, calm, talking to his chest in a low murmur of reverence, speaking to it like it was a dark confessional, searching for an invisible priest within it to give her absolutions from the sin of still loving him. Trying to negotiate with the insane, trying to use one word to release the hostage, him, held behind high, dark walls.

Through the word no, he could still feel her loving him. Through the grisly visions trapped within the mind of a twisted entity, Damali loved him. Through the scenes of massacres he could feel her heart shattering for this thing that would take from her in much the same way. Even while she shut her eyes and sobbed until no more tears would come, she repeated the refrain, loving him so hard, refusing to turn it loose, even when her heart went into mild arrhythmia as she saw him lie down with another woman. That's when he couldn't hold on.

He pushed her away, the pain too great to endure. Looking at her once, he begged her in his head to remember who he was before she saw that, and was gone.

Frenzied yells for Damali bounced off the walls, echoed in her, scored her mind as she shut her eyes and sat down slowly on the side of a bed. Her hand remained over her chest as she sat without a word. Storm trooper–sounding footsteps slammed against the wood stairs, rocking the single-story guest house as thirty-two armed guardians tried to enter the bunker at once.

A chain yanked and a hundred watts slapped her tear-streaked face. A strong hand forced her chin to the side as three guardians appraised her neck and checked her for puncture wounds. Too late. It was in her heart, the gash. It was in her soul, the siphon. It was in her lungs, the silent scream. It was in her head, the unfathomable. And it ran all over her skin making it crawl.

Curiosity killed the cat; satisfaction of knowing wasn't even bringing her back. Every image was more horrible than the next, but the last one . . . no. The last one wasn't historical tragedy. The last one wasn't watching a war tear through a village, like a remote mental movie—a horrific but somewhat distant newsreel. It wasn't buffered by the double helix of memory passed from one entity, supplanted in the vision of another, with all the smells, sounds, textures, tastes removed from it in the transfer sanitized for her consumption. It wasn't like watching the sinister mob-like confession of the counselor, just a dirty deal. Angering, yes; heart stopping, no. Oh, no.

The last image was brought to her in Technicolor . . . just as her man had allowed it to take root in his desire, his bloodstream, then to harvest his mind.

She could feel the burn, the crave, took the hit of foreign Neteru that knocked his head back. Mature, ripened slayer. Felt the Amazon's skin, nuzzled her scent as her jaw grazed the inside of her thigh. Tangled her fingers in her long, dark braids, tasted her tart, blood-bitter mouth. Felt the power of her arch, heard her voice come from low in her throat, felt what he'd craved from the reverse point of view. Damali stared at the wall, staring a hole right through it as Shabazz knelt on one side of her, Kamal on the other, trying to reach her.

Wasn't nobody home to reach after the shit she just saw.

Damali closed her eyes slowly, willing the image to go away. But a permanent visual adhered to the inside of her lids. She could still feel Carlos, the tremble, the initial penetration, what it felt like to sink into aching, wet woman . . . the rip of incisors in a jaw as thrusts drew seed up from a tortured place beneath a shaft stroking pleasure, and the unrelenting need to deliver a bite at the same time. She was on her feet. The team backed up. She turned over a cot, wild in the eyes, driving that picture out of her head. Sad eyes met hers. Crossbows, arrows, walking sticks, automatic weapons were lowered.

"No!" She screamed again as the vision began to repeat in slow motion, Carlos's hand caressing a full, round hip—not hers, and knocking Big Mike to the floor when he came for her. "No, no, no, no no, no no, no no! I will not, oh, Father God, not, no no, shit no, oh no! I'm not seeing this!"

None of the team members said a word as Big Mike stood slowly, stunned at being toppled so easily, studying her with concern. But she could not stop walking, snorting the scent out of her nose, her lungs, her mind, spitting it out of the back of her throat, dry heaving, then dashing to the porch rail to give it away, mangoes and all. Wiping her mouth with the back of her hand, she brushed past Marlene.

"You're a seer—don't touch me. Not yet. This will ricochet through you." Damali kept walking, willing kinetic energy to be a blanket. She needed space, needed a magnet to erase the corrupted mental disk and get rid of the virus in her head.

"Oh, God," she whispered, new tears brimming, falling, having found the tapped reservoir refilled, the dam broke. But she would not let them touch her. All the faces in the room stared at her with concern, pity, whatever expressions she couldn't name.

If Madame Isis were in her hand, she would have cut them to keep them back from seeing this. She turned to Kamal, searching his eyes. "You *know*—tell them not to touch me!"

He nodded. "She's a vet now, too. Saw it all. Full-blast. Oh, sweet modder of God . . . Marlene, I held it back from even you, baby. No woman should see . . . Lord." Kamal walked away and punched the wall.

Shabazz and Rider glanced at Big Mike, confused. JL and Dan shrugged, not understanding. Jose ran his hands up his arms as Damali paced. Kamal's team looked like they were in shock, the question about what had happened poised on the edge of their lips, but their master had dared them to speak with a glare.

"You know how to fight her though, right?" Kamal said as Damali found a space against the wall, leaned against it, and shuddered.

"Oh," she whispered, not looking at anything, unable to meet any more eyes, "I know how to fight her. Cut her fucking heart out. Yeah, I know. Already planned."

"Go past de pain, and past de rage, and get still," Kamal said firmly.

Damali laughed. New tears sprung to her eyes and fell, and she laughed harder. It was the laughter of near-insanity from profound hurt.

"Get her some water, or something," Big Mike said in a raspy voice. "Slap her, I dunno. But don't let her go wherever she's going." He sucked in a shuddering breath and held it as Kamal shook his head.

"Water just run it all through her like a current right now. Better she deal here den out there in da heat of battle," Kamal replied, raking his hands through his locks, his line of vision on the floor. "Saw dis bullshit comin' when Mar called me. Blocked it from Mar, had to. Said, self, you gitting to be too ole for dese tings."

Shabazz nodded. "Word, man. What we need to do?"

Damali had stopped laughing, her gaze fixed, trying to shake the image of two panthers circling each other in a mating ritual out of her head.

"Make the panthers go away, Kamal. Brother . . . I just can't—" Her voice was a low, silent plea as she shut her eyes tightly and bent over, dry heaving again.

"I can't take it from you, gurl. Gotta run its course. You're all Neteru now, can see deeper than any of us—which is why you gotta guard your mind at all costs. I knew the dark lover would come . . . we didn't set a barrier for him, on account of who he was in dis triangle."

"What!" Rider had gotten up real close to Kamal's face, inadvisably close.

Kamal snarled. Rider backed away. Jose spun and went into a battle stance. Pure shock held Damali's other guardians momentarily still.

Kamal and every man on his team had upper and lower canines that were two inches long.

"What the fuck . . ." Shabazz whispered, as Damali and the team stared.

The room was divided in half. Kamal's team was on one side, the guardians on the other. Kamal's crew had bulked in size and had large canines now. Marlene sighed and walked between the lines.

"Tell 'em, Kamal." Marlene looked at Damali as she dry heaved, and glared at Jose. "Put it down, Jose. They're on our side."

"What the hell Mar?" Damali wheezed. "They don't need to be bulking now, and not on us!" She was in no condition to deal with this shit, too!

"Y'all got nicked? Oh shit . . ." Rider just shook his head. "Now we gotta deal with werewolves, too?"

"Were-humans," Kamal said more calmly, his jawline and his team's normalizing as Jose nervously lowered his weapon. Kamal cast a disparaging glance to his squad, and waited until they'd disarmed, appearing unfazed that the guardians hadn't followed suit. "That's why my crew had a problem with Jose. He's the weaker one I spoke of, got vamp in his line—"

"Get the fuck out of here!" Big Mike bellowed, noting that the other guardians stepped back from their own man, seriously confused.

"It was the Dee Dee tracer," Jose argued. "This is bull—"

"What?" Damali yelled, not knowing which side to go toward, if any.

"School her fast, Mar. I told you that this would come out—that you gwan hatfta tell your people 'bout dis." Kamal had yelled the command to Marlene in frustration, but the pain in Kamal's eyes kept all parties temporarily cool.

"Look, I doubt Jose has any vamp in him, but he got nicked, spiritually, by his old girlfriend—but he's healed, does daylight. That's what your men picked up. So, drop that," Marlene said calmly, quietly, as though speaking to people on the verge of nervous collapse. "Years ago, Kamal got bitten by a were-jag. Just nicked." She looked away from everyone and let her gaze go out the window. "When bitten by something from the were-realms, if the bite doesn't kill you, you're sorta trapped between here and there.

"That creates were-humans . . . and living weres have a chance, if they keep their karma straight, to ascend to the light when they die, unlike were-demons, which have no chance, unless deceived into the realm. Even those that die from a were-bite have a slim chance, as long as they make the right choice. That's because the choice always remains with the living, and with those who have died unwittingly as innocent victims. These guys still have souls. Everybody in Kamal's squad got nicked, and were brought here by their families for help. Upon their deaths, the were-attributes will flee. Their bodies and spirits normalize. Kamal set up this retreat, after his encounter, to help others sharing his same fate."

She glanced around. "They fight their impulses by eating nothing that contains blood or animal products. Their mission is to keep the demon elements from the were-realms at bay and away from humans. Their enemy is our enemy; their fight is our fight. They're our allies. They've got a militia that hunts the demons and tracks down human victims before they turn. They are the best of the best at what they do."

"I'm Kamal's second in command," Abdul said with pride. "I do rescue-and-recovery. Thirty days after a bite, a human victim has to make a choice—to eat flesh, human or otherwise, or refrain." He thrust his chin higher.

"We scout the hillside, villages, and find people to help them and to bring them to compounds like this. If they go demon, then they cannot come out until the full moon, their souls are damned, they are bound to a region, and they must live down in the pit of the were-realm. They eat human flesh when they come topside every thirty days to keep their human form from decomposing back to the date of their death. If the demons don't eat flesh, they have to stay in were-form, which means they cannot come out during daylight. They must be able to assume their nondecomposed form to blend in and scout for human victims they will feed on. They are dead; we are not. We are not demons. We are humans that have a compromised genetic structure. We live longer, age slower, but we're mortal and can die from injuries just like any of you."

His gaze softened on Damali. "We're faster, stronger, and have sharper senses than humans. It only gets a little intense during the full moon." He smiled and glanced away. "Then we do have to check our more primal side."

The tall brother that looked like Shabazz nodded. "Our urges are the same as the animal that bit us . . . it takes a *lot* of discipline to master and control that. That requires focus. We try to only partner with those like ourselves." He glanced at Abdul. "Because we might not be understood. There's a female encampment not too far away. A small sect of the Amazons used to be were-human, too. Their compound is marked by were-jaguar totems. They were guardians, like us. Used all the attributes of superior were-strength to fight evil, and were revered . . . among our clans and our colonies, they are legendary." He looked at Big Mike. "Brother, you know what I'm talking about. They're fine . . . tall, built like . . ." he sighed. "We generally stick to our clan."

"I hear you," Mike said with appreciation. "Think I pulled one in Rio." He rubbed his jaw, avoiding eye contact with the others. "I'm cool though, right, man?"

"As long as she didn't bite you. Maybe she was just from human Amazon lineage." He shook his head. "That's the thing . . . you just never know."

The two strong men on the teams looked at each other for a moment, then Big Mike smiled and glanced out the window as the guardians from Damali's team held their breaths.

"I'm cool," Big Mike muttered, and wiped his palm over his gleaming scalp. "But tell me this. If the small sect of Amazons were like you guys—were also guardians, then how did the demons get them? How'd they turn?"

"She polluted her own camp, that's another reason we have to be so careful among the were-human clans. The whole thing was a sad act of desperation." Abdul folded his arms over his chest and looked at Damali. "We always have two seers on our teams. An elder and an apprentice . . . that's why I was feeling your vibe so hard. Be wary when you go out there. She'll have a junior seer that can level dark arts, be careful of her. The older one that you're battling is twisted, thinks she's the Neteru now, but has probably taught her apprentice much."

"Yeah," Damali said quietly, looking at Marlene. "We experienced a little bit of what girlfriend's apprentice can do. But I had something for her."

Abdul paused, as though trying very hard to check himself, but lost the battle. "When, uh, I heard that you and your vampire were done, baby—"

Before Shabazz could respond, Kamal had walked a hot pace down the guardian lines toward Abdul, making his team part for him like the Red Sea.

"It wasn't all his fault," Damali said quickly, trying to avoid another disaster that could further splinter the teams or make them lose focus. "I was hurt and throwing vibe. Let's get back to the point." As tempers flared, she instantly became aware of the scent that had been haunting her—strong, primal, earthy, male pheromone, something stronger than human male, but not quite animal. There was too much going on before to put her finger on it, but now knowing what the other team was, she understood.

Abdul nodded and shot her a glance that said, *thank you*. "Look at the moon, man," he snapped toward their leader, as Kamal calmed down and walked away, trying to preserve his pride. "It was definitely no disrespect intended." He walked away and stood by the door with his arms folded, indignant at the rebuff. "Can't barely keep your own shit straight yourself, tonight. Don't worry 'bout me."

The obvious peacemaker in the group, Kamal's youngest man, Ahmad, immediately stepped between the possible combatants when Kamal whirled and snarled, backing Abdul up to stand nearly on the porch. All the Neteru guardian team could do was watch from the sidelines.

"While here, Neteru," Ahmad said with deference that seemed to slowly calm every male in the room, "we focus and hunt down the demons that made us. That focus is imperative—because each full moon, the demons will also seek a were-human, try to re-infect us anew, and try to get us to commit an atrocity that will allow them to trap our souls in their realms. They view us as infidels, literally, beings that have dodged a silver bullet—and we are mortal enemies with them. Vampires come for us, too, as they register us in their sensory awareness as were-demons. They make no distinction within our culture."

He glanced around the room. "They bite animals, too. Infect them, and turn them into familiars. The animal cannot take on human form, but the worst of its nature comes out, and it will do a demon's bidding, will bring information, and can be a disease carrier. So, if you see an animal that is larger and more aggressive than it should be, or that hunts humans almost exclusively, it's infected—an abomination of what the demons have altered. We hunt those, too, to put the were-creature out of its misery. Do not get the three categories confused; were-humans, were-creatures, and were-demons—each are different. We are not one and the same."

"And that's why you ain't got no real challenge from me," Kamal said in a hard tone, now looking at Shabazz. "She can't stay wit me, even if I wanted her to . . . or if she wanted to. There would be no future in it. One night, I'd level a bite. That's nature. Fuck it. I've said all that needs to be said."

Kamal glanced away, swallowed hard and went to stand in a far corner of the room. Damali's line of vision followed him, watching the shoulders of his team slump in defeat, as Shabazz seemed stunned by the man's sudden honest outburst.

Kamal nodded. "I run a clean operation here. I was a guardian, and hunted demons—still am, still do! I deserve respect for that, man. One got to me. Can happen to anybody. She came here before my encounter, my compound will remain a clean safe house, will be so until I die. That's why Mar had to leave here. In my early days, newly turned, I didn't have the restraint." He glared at Abdul. "In later years I learned *discipline*. It became evident dat one day I was gonna hurt her. So . . . we let it alone. I never passed this virus to her, hard though it was not to. But when she asked for my help, what could I say?" His gaze softened as it left Abdul and went to hold Marlene's. A sad understanding passed between them. "Vamps were following her, too. It was best."

The two looked at each other and glanced away, each considering a section of the barren wooden floor. Shabazz went to the window and let his breath out slowly.

"Like wit all tings, not just the vamps," Kamal said reverently, "it happens with us weres like dat, too. A nick that doesn't kill releases something powerful and can pass through generations. A vamp nick infects only the human that was bitten, but if they have children wit another human, it runs through the genes. Unlike the vamps, however, because I'm alive, I can directly sire. My children wit her woulda had some of me in them, been double vamp bait, and had to live this type of life."

He shot a glance to Shabazz, but it wasn't filled with rage, just defeat. The two guardians stared at each other. "So, we let it alone. So, you need to let the past between me and her rest. Me and her know what time it is—you ain't got nuttin' to do wit dat. I ain't no threat."

When Shabazz looked away, Kamal swallowed hard, his gaze seeking the sky. "If we don't kill, or never eat human flesh, then we are not doomed . . . but we have to keep our infection out of the generations. Every man on this team was nicked by the big cats of this region. The wolfen clans are indigenous to North America and Europe. Some of my men have come here as children 'cause of dat plague. Maybe that's why your man, Rivera, was so susceptible to his misfortunes? Maybe he had a little vamp in him already? Like me wit da were issue. Who knows? Dat isn't important. What is important is the fact dat he can track—because vamps and demons can smell each other immediately. Don' be hard on Mar. She didn't walk you into an ambush. She brought you to some people who can track demons and vamps better than anyone else on da planet . . . but also didn't fully inform you, because you would have freaked out and never agreed to come where you must."

Jose appeared faint from the new information that had just been draped on the group. Big Mike put his arm over Jose's shoulder in a quiet demonstration of emotional and physical support. "It's Dee Dee's tracer, man . . . you ain't vamp."

Kamal looked at Marlene's sad eyes and then over at Jose. "Yeah, man, that's probably what it is. But just in case me and my boys are right, and we're picking up a diluted strain of vamp, you need to watch da kind of women that you're attracted to. Understand? You gwan have a ting for sisters wit fangs and could find yourself turned one night. Dat boy definitely got a nose for da Neteru, and you don't hafta be a seer for dat—the odder vamp, the master one, gwan always have a problem wit his ass."

He looked at Big Mike, took a long sniff in his direction, and smiled. "You best school your young blood . . . you got nicked, but cleaned out, and know da deal. I can still smell it. That master vampire gwan take issue wit him, too, seven years from now being 'round your Neteru, living wit her in da compound, if we ain't wrong."

Big Mike's grip on Jose's shoulder tightened. "Our boy's cool.

This was just from something that went down in the States with his woman. You saw his ass roll up here in the sunlight, like Mar said. Don't trip, and stop messing with his head, brother. We all gotta keep our heads going into this fight."

"You're right." Kamal nodded, and his squad followed suit but seemed unconvinced.

"But you all let a goddamned master vampire up in here, too, in this twisted bullshit!" Shabazz suddenly began pacing back and forth before the window like a madman. "You have the nerve to talk to me about putting my woman at risk—and the Neteru? Fuck all this! You could have just told us what to do, then—"

"The dark lover had to *show* her dese tings, man. I had to get it in her head, let her feel it, so she had something to work wit. Will save her life. Couldn't just tell her, had to show her. Some tings you must experience to know in your soul, not just up in your head like from a book. You know dat as much as I do, brother. Dat's how your team been schoolin' her all along—demonstration . . . letting her taste life, den guiding the process. What about dis you don' understand? Huh? Because of Marlene, you can't tink straight?" Kamal sighed, weary patience laced in his breath. "You and me ain't dat different, same tribe. So, chill. Let ego go on dis, too. Just like I had to—way before she met you."

Shabazz bristled and stepped forward. "Nobody needed to come here for—"

"Bullshit!" Kamal yelled. "You blind? The Neteru needed to learn, see for herself, the kind of tough choices got to be made, sometime, for the good of the group." He pointed toward Damali, but his gaze was on Shabazz. "Can't speak out both sides of your mouth. Can't tell the young ones to do as I say, not as I do. Gotta show by example, and on dis one, Heaven asked a lot of *all* her instructors . . . even you. Can't put the whole squad in danger over your own personal shit; she had to learn dat! And, she needed to see that the master who was her lover was making a tough choice, too—pushed her away before what he is, or what was in his life, consumed her. That shit is beyond honorable; ask me how I know! Everybody in here bleeding. So, I'ma ask you again," he said, retracting his trembling arm, "You blind? You tink I wanted to reveal dis tough lesson in front of my own men? Fuck your ego. Hell yeah, I let her teacher come over our barriers to school her."

Kamal folded his arms over his chest and faced the wall, breathing hard. Shabazz just rubbed his jaw and went back to the window as both teams relaxed, sober defeat claiming all of them.

Rider backed up further, spat on the floor, and went to a wall to lean on it, nervously eyeing Kamal's crew. "Tell us something we can work with. Who cares who got nicked from what on these teams? The point is moot. We've all taken a hit from something by this age. It was just a bit of a mindblower to see it up close and personal, instead of theoretical, when you guys did the fang thing—but, hey, we all got issues." He shook his head in disbelief. "Mar, don't argue with me about drinking too much when, and if, we get home."

"Dis dark passion that you've seen has not happened yet, gurl," Kamal said carefully, his voice gentle as he spoke, not looking at Damali. "It was in his mind, a want, maybe a need. You got some visions to send her, too. Will draw her out. Make her use rage to battle you, not strategy. You got a soul dat can forgive, she don't. This one thinks she's the Neteru. This demon has ingested the essence, and it is corrupting her mind. Has polluted ripe Neteru scent to sway his judgment. She had an entire guardian squad trapped by a misguided—"

"I don't know anything anymore," Damali whispered.

"You do!" Kamal insisted and whirled on her. "It was the ancient Neteru's mother-seer that took her body and desecrated it, and chose to become a demon for vengeance and rage. If the portal is open, with those conflicts in her spirit, we might even have to battle Amanthras out there, who knows?"

"Her mother-seer?" Damali looked at Marlene horrified, finally hearing all the words that had been said around her.

"That's why you knew her magic, how to reverse it to save me. Baby, a Neteru went down, her mother-seer lost her mind, and did this terrible thing. Her team followed the seer into the pit, trying in vain to resurrect their Neteru, but what happened in the dark spell was the mother-seer took on everything she held dear about the Neteru. She's got the strength of a demon, but she will fight you like a Neteru warrior . . . and she wants Carlos to release her from regional and moon-based captivity. We've been over this, but your concentration has been scattered." Marlene looked at her with a gentle gaze. "In fact, she wants him as much as she wants the freedom . . . a dark guardian, an eternal mate. Baby, you've gotta fight this on a lot of levels."

Damali covered her face with her hands and breathed into them slowly to keep from hyperventilating. She finally understood what Carlos had said, and the profound pain that went with his crazy but honorable choice. Understood Marlene and Kamal's decision, and felt Shabazz's hurt like a knife to her skin. Everyone around her had done and was doing the right thing, but the shit hurt like hell, especially now that it was her turn to do said same.

"Now you got an image to put next to hers," Kamal said in a quiet voice. "Show her what it's like when a man wants to be there, versus when it's jus' somethin' to do, or he's forced. In dis case, it's somethin' he's being coerced to do—plantations did that to breed de oppressed, her own people. If she does dat to him, let her taste dat bitter wine."

Damali just lifted her head slowly and stared at Kamal, not even blinking.

"Oh shit, oh shit, oh shit!" Rider hollered, walking back and forth, losing a section of his sanity in the process. "Is that what that bastard came in here and showed her? Oh my God, no wonder she leveled Big Mike!"

"No lie, man . . . but if Damali did that, and you piss off that Amazon with the suggestion, Kamal, man . . ." Big Mike shook his head.

"Female strategy, done every day by wives to let an interloper know she's just a piece of tail. Show her how much he cared about you, wanted you, before you even had Neteru to knock his head back . . . let her see that shit raw. You were his choice; she was his option. There's a huge difference. Don't let her flip the script and mess with your head—you know who you are—his *first* love! That shit's stronger than Neteru. Claim your title. It will draw her out—" Marlene said coolly, "—will get her out in the open." Not a man spoke when Damali raised her head and stared at Marlene. "Baby, what else did you see?"

"How they did her people. Massacred them," Damali whispered.

"Show her how they did *your* people, which are also mixed with her people—making you both from the *same* people just a couple of continents in between," Marlene spat back. "*That's* what we both picked up, as seers, as soon as we set foot in the heart of Rio in the hotel lobby. So, show her a hundred twenty-five million in the Middle Passage," she added, waving her arms in the air. "If you wanna look in my eyes, I'll give you plenty of images from my folks down South, folks that raised me and taught me to see. Lynchings, rapes, burnings, all the same horrific shit—but your methods and her methods to correct oppression and injustice are real different, baby. Worlds apart, and ain't even the same. Just like what you and Carlos have is *very* different than her proposition."

"You gotta get to her fast and hard, den," Kamal said quietly. "Before the were-demon senates form an alliance with the weakened Amanthra empire—"

"What?" Rider was walking between Shabazz and Big Mike, shaking his head. "*They* have senates, plural, like the vampires have a council—"

"Don't be foolish," Kamal said with disdain, looking at Rider hard as his gaze scanned the group. "Every sector of the were-realm has a senate segregated by fila. Each of the Hell levels has some form of organized, governing body. There are *legions* of evil down below, brother, just like we got up here. Dat's why there are so many types of guardian teams on the planet. We may have deeper insight because of our circumstances, but we don' deal wit dem, thou'. Like I said, we are *not* demons—we are humans dat had da misfortune to get nicked. And we are very clear on what side of the line we're on." Satisfied when his entire were-human squad nodded, Kamal let his breath out hard and raked his fingers through his locks. "We got your back."

"Oh, I feel better," Rider said with a sneer of disgust.

Marlene walked away from Damali's side. "All respect for what that the female were-demon lost and endured, since she was once one of us—a Neteru guardian—but, yeah, you show her what you lost, first. You show her your history, too, honey. You've got one; believe me. Your past life was here, your DNA is tied to this region, and your people went through hell on earth, too. So, when you confront her in battle, you ask that twisted bitch if she's gonna pass out green cards for all the oppressed people of the world to keep them from becoming something her ancestors fought against! Ask her how she's gonna keep the same oppressed people, who've already had horrible things happen to them, from having to endure more—and ask her how she's going to keep the human power structures from nuking the joint, leaving a smoking, black hole topside," Marlene yelled. "And you ask her how she's going to justify going against you, *a Neteru*, a light-chosen warrior. If she has a sliver of a conscience left, even if only through ingesting the strength of character resident in a Neteru's cellular makeup, it might give her pause, might make her hesitate for a split second, and that's when you take her."

"Yeah, you think once the human superpowers find out, they won't detonate something, trying to stop a vamp-demon army that's come topside—not having a spiritual reference for how to deal with something like this? And you think they'll listen to us?" JL shook his head. "Can you see world leaders, or the United Nations convening a summit on this? They'll act like aliens had infested the planet, will shoot everything with all they've got, not realizing the firepower ain't what they need to fight this madness, and that this is a spiritual war."

"This crazy shit will kick off the Armageddon just from the fallout," Dan added with a shudder. "Maybe that's what this is? The prelude to the Armageddon?"

"Crazy motherfuckers with their fingers on the red button will probably go with the alien theory first—won't ask a church, temple, or mosque, and definitely ain't gonna come to no people down the way to get the answer. We're oppressed and ignorant, remember," Jose said, walking toward the porch.

"By the time they do, the war will be over," Rider snapped. "Just like that. All right. I'm down. This is big shit that transcends the drama, kiddo. We've gotta sync up with Kamal's team. We're talking potential world peace hanging in the balance. How many innocents do you think will die from a nuclear, human-sent blast?"

Marlene held Damali in a firm stare, sending confidence with it, trying to heal with a look. "You've got a long tale of woe that lasted the same four hundred years or more in the US. But you show her, also, the faces of the innocent people she murdered. Folks with children and partners, and parents, and what have you. Give her a dose of that while we're out there. She hit 'em with no warning, not like a warrior—and with no honor. Civilians. And they weren't even armed. You let her see it, taste it, breathe it, and ask her how it feels. Baby, you've gotta fight this one spiritually, psychologically, and with some serious artillery to back it up."

A grumble of agreement rippled through the room, fist pounds got exchanged, and suddenly the two teams became one.

"If she persists," Kamal said, rubbing his hands over his face, "den you twist her heart wit de last image you have, draw her out. Make her crazy, give it up—to da bone . . . till she don' care 'bout ambush, takin' cover, all she wants is your head on a pike, gurl. Den, you swing de Isis. Hear me? Show her you with Rivera, and what dat really means."

"Tell that bitch you're her daddy," Shabazz muttered. "Use what you saw, in any voice you need."

Shabazz and Kamal shared a glance, but this time it wasn't a look of hatred between ardent competitors. Their stare contained the silent agreement to disagree, for the good of the whole, for the safety of the squads, for the protection of the Neteru, for the love of Marlene, and with much respect for the position the other had to endure. The two masters nodded, then allowed their gazes to trap Marlene's for a moment before finding a neutral point in the room.

"She even wanted to take Madame Isis from me," Damali finally murmured. Steadier, more lucid, Damali nodded as the images receded. But the place inside her soul was raw. Stripped. Kamal looked at her, his eyes gentler now, and not blazing with conviction.

"Took a lot for him to show you what he showed you to save your life," Kamal murmured, sitting down on the side of a bed. "Felt da love. Dat's why I knew . . . let dat one through—set no barrier for the vampire wit half a soul in da balance. 'Cause de man would die for you. Dis makes one more time he did . . . 'cause he know, like any man in his right mind know—once a woman tink 'bout another lover wit him, let alone see it, part of dat love dies between you two."

"Baby," Marlene said gently, only looking at her, "you have immediate, recent, visceral memories of being with Carlos. It's a primary memory, not a secondary illusion of one . . . but stronger than even his fantasy of being with her, because you've lived it. Her images of the past don't have the texture of the present, because they were transferred to him—didn't come directly into your consciousness from experience. Just like what you show her of your history will have the depth of a textbook, or movie, because it's a fourth-generation down—my great-grandmother lived it, told my grandmother, who told my mother, who told me. What I show you, just like what Carlos showed you, is diluted. Only first-line feels it directly, the eyewitnesses. So, she won't smell the insides of the slave cargo ships, won't feel the lash. Unless she has a lot of compassion, and she doesn't, it won't move her."

When Damali nodded, Marlene pressed on, holding her in a stare to get through, to strip away some of the pain in the only way it can be purged at a time like this—by another supportive woman-friend's voice. "His fantasies of being with her are not grounded in the other senses all the way. Close, because he imagined it, but he still doesn't know because the act wasn't consummated. But you've got a nuclear bomb of recent memory grounded in every fiber of you. Hit the red button, baby. Use it. Blow her head up so we can take it off. Use the truth. And kill her with your love." She shook her head and closed her eyes. "That's what Father Pat had said. This scenario had to be fought with compassion and love, and he, as a cleric from an order with blood on his hands here, couldn't be there to witness it or help."

"You might feel like you're gonna die, and when you walk away from what you need to walk away from, part of you will," Rider said in an inordinately gentle tone, "but sometimes you have to opt to exist, even if it's not how you want to live. Y'all both might have to do that. Much as I hate to, I've gotta give Rivera credit for that. Welcome to being an adult. The shit sucks."

Kamal let his breath out slowly and rubbed his jaw and sent a silent message of thanks Rider's way for veering the way-too-personal subject away from him, Marlene, and Shabazz. He waited until Damali looked at him before he spoke.

"Granted, his fantasies were fucked up. But all I'ma say is, dis ain't happen yet, and nobody needta be judged on a fantasy, or we'd all go to Hell in a handbasket." Kamal's gaze swept the room, avoiding Marlene. "Ask any and all of your brothers, dey'll tell you. Don't let what *could* happen drive a wedge between you and him out dere. Deal wit what *did* happen, and if it's going to go down in a way you don' like, suck it up. That's life. You won't die of no broken heart—you will die, however, if you misjudge your opponent. Shit happens fast."

Shabazz looked at him. "Yeah it do, man. I'm real sorry it does, too."

The two old masters looked at each other again and nodded. Respect and silent understanding passed between them once more, sealing their pact to let their personal incident ride.

"Heal up your slayer's head, man. Baby girl took a hit of something she didn't need to see for years—if ever. Fucked-up, man . . . but in dis case it was de only way. Truth was da light. Bring da light."

"Word."

CHAPTER TWENTY-THREE

THIRTY-THREE VERY serious, fatigue-wearing warriors entered Belem, causing other pedestrians to cast fearful glances in the combined team's direction. Humid, thick air almost stole every breath while sweltering heat bore down on them. Waiting for Kamal to do the necessary weapons transaction with his unnamed contacts from places she was too weary to imagine, Damali absorbed the collage of tower blocks, crumbling Portuguese churches, and the dotting of Old World Mediterranean palaces in pastel hues. Cobblestones, hand-laid, brick by brick by slave labor met her footfalls. Every sense quickened, she was not about to miss anything that could be of importance to the group's safety.

Sitting, waiting, watching, sipping cool glasses of cupuacu juice on rickety wooden outdoor café chairs, the table umbrellas mild relief from the sun, she studied the terrain. A dog ran by and thirty-two pairs of eyes behind dark sunglasses, expressions masked, looked at the animal. Children and vendors plied their wares, but made no move toward her group this time. She hunted the environment with her sweeping gaze, roving over every aspect of it, taking mental snapshots of the borderline Belem presented between elegance and shabbiness. It was a gray zone, too.

She felt it. The Jesuits had aided in the destruction of the Indian populations here. Smallpox, dysentery, the lash for not adopting the conquering religion, cultural destruction as much as physical annihilation, people who had known freedom remanded to *aldeias*—reservations. Segregation. Lands snatched and plundered. Righteous anger lived here, just under the surface, crumbling the buildings as much as the weather and the insidious heat. They were getting closer to the Amazon. The question was, how to reach this agonized entity that wanted to unleash a demon army upon this land to wrest it back from modern invaders?

Damali looked up at the sun, not needing a watch now to tell the time. It was late. The travel had been yet again delayed, as things were always delayed in parts of the world that lived by the natural rhythms. She was still uncomfortable about Kamal's decision to go all the way with the group, since it was not the original plan. She was worried not because of Shabazz; a truce had been established. The elders forecast that the number thirty-three in a situation like this was a double trinity to deal with a triangular relationship; three issues within it— love, war, lessons. Two triangles made the hexagon balance. Three and three, the number thirty-three, half-were and half-human forces joined. Crazy. Yeah, they needed an army for this battle.

The triumvirate of Marlene and Kamal and Shabazz were cool. The men were cool; the teams had melded. But she looked at thirty-two innocent people possibly going to their final destination with her. The responsibility was enormous. She knew how her adversary felt. Damali had to respect that much about her. She respected the place from which the rage bubbled within the Amazon's soul. But the methods the Amazon used, and was about to deploy to redress the wrong, Damali could not abide.

"We're gwan fly into Santarem to refuel, den Manaus for de weapons," Kamal said in a low tone, returning to the table where Damali, Marlene, Shabazz, Rider, and Big Mike sat. "From dere, Jeeps take us to de boat. Once on de Amazon, look alive."

"Your people able to take that knot we gave you and convert it into some serious gear?" Shabazz had asked the question while studying his drink.

Kamal nodded.

"What we looking at, brother?" Big Mike said low, leaning in.

"Two bazookas wit crystal-packed shells. Semiautos for everybody; silver shards in de bullets. Hand grenades loaded wit crystal and silver shrapnel. Standard crossbows—but they're slow, and dese tings move fast. Ultraviolet light lanterns and floodlights, in case we get caught out dere after dark, which is not advisable. C-4 bricks coated in silver alloy. Other standards—holy water, hallowed-earth bombs, but crystal-tipped stakes. Food, bottled water, medical supplies, gasoline for the boat, regular guns for da caiman, de crocks, anaconda nets, tents— tings like dat, too."

The small group of generals nodded, satisfied.

"How'd you get all this arranged so fast, dude—not that I'm complaining, but damn?" Rider smiled and pounded Kamal's fist.

Kamal offered a lopsided smile in return, casting a sly look at Shabazz. "When you're *hiding* in de jungle for a couple decades, and have to ward off rebels, and whatever else come for ya, mon, ya learn to know some people who know some people."

Shabazz chuckled, his laughter an unspoken apology for the assumptions he'd made the night before. Kamal nodded, quietly accepting the apology with grace.

"But, if Shabazz is cool wit it . . . I have sometin' for Marlene." Kamal hesitated, stared at Shabazz for approval.

"Yeah," Shabazz murmured, nodding and taking a sip from his glass. "If you got something to protect her, cool."

Damali watched the transaction from a remote place in her mind, as Kamal went into the vest pocket of his fatigues and pulled out a magnificent hexagon-shaped quartz crystal the size of a small bread plate. It was dangling by a silver-and-gold chain, and the markings on it, except two overlapping triangles, were indecipherable. Kamal looked down at the amulet, rubbed the gleaming face of it with his thumb, and didn't take his eyes off it as he spoke.

"Was me modder's," he admitted quietly, taking a long breath before continuing. "Shoulda gave it to you a long time ago, to keep you safe while in de States." He nodded, in deep reflection, still not looking at Marlene. "But, no matter 'bout water under de bridge. Had solid protection wit you dere, anyway. Got good people around you, gurl. Just as well." He stood, glanced at Marlene, dismissed the past, and handed the amulet to Shabazz. "You take care of her heart now." Then Kamal stepped away from the table to go sit with his own men.

She watched Shabazz study the piece, look back at the man who had removed himself, then gaze at his prize, Marlene. Shabazz looped the amulet over Marlene's neck, stood, walked to Kamal, briefly rested a hand on his shoulder, then slipped inside the café. All the warriors in witness had lowered their eyes in reverence of the dignified act. Marlene's hands shook as she brought a glass of cool juice to her lips.

Damali stood and went to Kamal's table.

"Thank you," she said quietly, "for all your help. For everything." She appraised the three tables of young men, good men, fine men that were going off on a mission that wasn't necessarily theirs to fight.

"But none of you have to go the full distance with this. You've given us too much already."

A murmur of discontent rose from the tables. Kamal held up his hand.

"Dis ting ain't personal, gurl. Dis ting is 'bout everybody's way of life," he said, bidding her to sit in a chair that one of his men had abandoned for her. "Evil to walk da planet at will? Why you tink we live where we live, study what we study, give up what we give up? To hide when da hour comes? All my life," he said, motioning toward his men, "*all dey lives,* we knew we were summoned to a call . . . just didn't know when da call would come. It is now. We all go of free will. We all are prepared to do what we gotta do. Dis ain't on your shoulders, or Marlene's. If we die fighting for a good cause, we get released from dis half-life we've lived since nicked."

His gaze had slipped away from hers with the mention of Marlene, and she wondered how a person summoned such restraint. But she'd felt herself strengthen and her emotions harden in just one day. After last night, she now knew that she could take one helluva hit and still keep going. Kamal smiled.

"First time," he said with an empathetic grin, "is like a sucker punch. *Tink you gonna die.* But den, you don't. You surprise yourself, and you live. And just like you gotta break down da muscle, feel da burn, work through da pain to make your body stronger, you hafta remember, the heart is a muscle, too."

She nodded, smiled sadly, sighed, and stood. Kamal held her hand, stopping her.

"But, every warrior also knows dat it is foolish to suffer unnecessarily after you've worked a new muscle. Needs balm. Ointment. Care. Take care of everyting God gave you, including your heart, gurl. Sit down. Suffering for no reason is not courage, it's foolishness of youth. Proves no point."

Nervous, and not sure where the conversation was going, she sat slowly, her eyes steady on Kamal.

"You young bloods wear yourselves out, den don't do what is proper to heal and get stronger. That will only break you down, not build you up; will make you bitter. Dat's no good." He smiled, his eyes gentle, his voice tender as he traced her cheek the same way Carlos always had.

But it wasn't sexual; it was a touch of affection and admiration. Familial. She felt it enter her, and it calmed her while also shaming her that any glimmer of distrust remained in her about this man. She had so much to learn. And as she looked at this elder, this mentor, this guide, she thought about how odd life was. The man could pass for Shabazz's older brother. Who knows? Maybe they'd really shared the same ancestors, the same blood?

"I don't know how to heal after all this, assuming I'm still alive when it's over," she admitted.

"We don't know how dis gwan go down, right? But, say if God smiles on us, and you make it, den, I have a balm. Heal as much as you can before you take another blow, little sista. Before you work dat taxed muscle again. Dat's why time and attention heals wounds."

She squeezed his hand and chuckled. "Oh, Kamal . . ." She didn't know what to say. This man with his wisdom and wry sense of humor, his warmth; how did Marlene ever leave him, were-jag in his system, regardless?

"I'm gwan show you sometin', but I don't want you to tink I'm being fresh, all right?"

Damali swallowed away a smile with another tremor of guilt. She nodded.

Kamal opened his right hand wide and held it up to his shoulder level, splaying his fingers and closing his eyes. "You already know how to do dis," he murmured. "Nobody got to tell you. It's in your cells, gurl."

She watched him, stunned, as she raised her hand to hover a few inches from his. She could feel the electric current pass between their hands and knew he and Marlene had done this, too. And also understood that was why Marlene was so freaked when Carlos had called her like this from miles away. Carlos had opened his hand and mentally placed it on her compound window, and she'd responded in kind to feel his emotions across the distance, even through four inches of bulletproof glass.

The warmth in the center of her hand began to tingle. It was a very intimate gesture as they both sat in the late-afternoon sun breathing slowly.

"You do dis by de ocean, until your heartbeats match da waves," he murmured.

She wanted to weep, but didn't. Her tears had dried last night. "He doesn't have a heartbeat," she whispered.

"You're so wrong, gurl. Can't you feel it? His skin vibrates with your touch, his eyes, de way dey look at you. The breath he breathes in deep when you're in his arms. The way he catches your breath when you have him teeterin' on de edge of oblivion. All dis has a rhythm, a pulse, like music. Sync it up to da natural rhythm of da tide, and when your palm pulses to that rhythm, your heartbeat matches de pulse of the cosmos which is in the sea—sometin' unbroken since da dawn of time, place his hand over your heart, yours over his, and send him everytin' of love for him inside you. He will send it back, like da tide ebbs and flows, giving and receiving, da rocking motion of back and forth. It is how life is created, and it heals, gives birth to new tings, his heart will beat in your palm, and for your hand only."

Kamal lowered his palm and placed it on Damali's chest, and she was immediately filled from the inside out with indescribable peace, warmth, gentleness, solace, everything that Kamal wished for her that was good. She'd thought the tears were gone, but cleansing waters flushed her system of worry, doubt, fear, anger. She breathed hard and placed her hand over his chest in return, willing back his safety, his healing after finally losing Marlene, and when she opened her eyes she saw his eyes glittering with moist appreciation as he removed his hand from her chest.

"Thank you," he whispered. "Getting ole, and forgetting to put balm on myself from time to time."

No one said a word, but thirty-three veterans of spiritual wars simultaneously looked up from the barge, judging the low angle of the sun, concern in their eyes behind dark glasses. A low canopy of trees allowed in dappling sunlight. Insects hummed in loud passing whirrs and took potshots at human flesh. Dragonflies, water skeets, frogs, monkey chatter and birds reveled in their habitat, sending a chorus of busy jungle conversation to drift with the boat, unfazed.

This was their home. Mother Nature's domain. Lazy crocodiles sunned themselves on the shorelines; their huge jaws open, waiting, just in case something miscalculated a branch and fell from the trees. Sets of reptilian eyes slowly waded by the edges of the flat vessel, unconcerned by the gunmen who rested automatic weapons on their laps. Those eyes seemed to wink a warning that the armed men respected; sit too close to the edge, dangle a limb, and it's fair game.

The two-level boat pushed a V of disturbance through the brown water with a dull motor drone of its own. The flat, wide lower deck was a repository for three quarters of the team; the upper deck held the center core of warriors—Damali, Kamal, Shabazz, Marlene, Rider, Big Mike, and the dry ammo. Up high, if there was an ambush, the strongest would go first, but also had the most skill to survive a sudden attack. There was nothing to do but wait, move forward, endure the heat and humidity, and blend in with the rhythm of the Amazon. She could feel the jungle give strength to Kamal's group, and she monitored their vibrations, knowing somehow that his team hungered to hunt in a pack, called by the elements.

Finally, Kamal nodded. That slight motion was enough to bring the upper deck's inhabitants to attention.

He'd motioned toward two twelve-foot statues carved in black stone. The figures were almost obscured by the natural camouflage created by a heavy strangle of vines that wrapped around them. "From dis point," he said, his voice drawing the lower deck occupants' attention, "on guard."

All eyes carefully appraised what antiquity had left behind. The heads of the tall stone totems were of jaguars brandishing vicious fangs, eyes sunken. But the bodies bore human female breasts with hands crossed over them, fists clenching battle-axes, bows over their shoulders, quivers affixed to their hips, their bulging vulvas covered by loincloths, their calves wrapped in bootlegs, their feet hooked, jaguar claws.

"The heart of the old human were-jaguar territory is overrun by demons. We gwan hafta go three miles inland on foot to da caves. By day, dey sleep in their original female bodies. By night—"

"We have to get off this boat?" Rider wiped his brow and checked his weapon. "Thought we could serve this prom invitation long-distance, bazookas in hand."

"You know better than that, brother," Shabazz said as he checked his weapon. "Gotta take it to 'em, just like big-game vampire hunting in the day. Gotta catch 'em on the offense."

"Judging by the sun," Damali said, "we don't have much light left and we still have to drag all this ammo three miles inland toward their lairs, and get back to the boat before sundown."

"You hear how quiet it is all of a sudden?" Big Mike murmured.

Both decks of soldiers nodded and looked around.

"Dock it," Kamal ordered. "Don't have a lotta time to be worrying 'bout it."

Three annoyed crocodiles slipped into the water as the craft neared the shore. Even Big Mike took his time before jumping down from the vessel. The shore was pure mud, crocodiles moved fast—one false step, and it was over. But the big men got down first, and gave a nod of all clear.

Jumping down, the team disembarked, guns held high as Big Mike and Kamal's huge man, Drum, strained to draw the rope tight, mooring the boat to a nearby tree. Ammunition was loaded down next, also held high, handled with care to keep it dry and stable. Kamal began walking; nobody talked. Everybody listened and prayed.

All of a sudden Big Mike, on right flank, held up his hand. The group froze. He used his gun barrel to point at a massive coil that was silently unfurling under a wide spread of palm leaves on the ground.

"Anaconda," Kamal murmured. "It lives here. Don't bother her; she won't bother you. Rattlers will warn before dey strike, so open your ears and respect what you're being told." He began walking, then stopped and pointed up at another huge snake. "Emerald tree boa—dey blend in, look like sunlight coming through da trees, and drop heavy from them. Keep one eye up, one eye down, like de lizards out here do."

"Mike is right, though," Damali finally said. "It's too quiet." The group stopped walking. "The bird calls are too distant. They're moving away. Don't even hear insects." Damali sniffed, catching a foul whiff of something she couldn't immediately describe, and she glanced up at the waning sun. The dense thicket of trees made the light stop before it hit the jungle floor.

Rider sniffed with Kamal and Jose. Kamal's team seemed to be in sensory overload, as they cocked their heads and took in deep inhales to pick up a scent. Using the barrel of his automatic, Rider pointed toward a cluster of vines and broad leaves. Kamal nodded. Damali tightened her hold on her Isis blade, and Marlene gripped her fighting stick harder.

"Dead flesh," Kamal confirmed. Each of the teams' olfactory sensors just nodded.

Slowly advancing, Marlene held up her hand for the others to wait. In unison, they all looked at the same spot on the ground. Using the long ebony stick, she lifted the leaves and then quickly turned her head away. The corporeal remains of several rotting bodies writhed with insect larva, angry beetles, river rats, and small snakes all trying to continue the decomposition process that the sun had abandoned in the shade. "As many times as I see it, I can never get used to it," she said quietly.

Her stick trembling, Marlene motioned for the others to look at the dismembered arms, legs, heads, and still-slithering intestines. Talismans had been dropped over the remains. "Sorcery," she stated, and then covered her mouth and nose with her hand to help block the stench.

"We're near, but the markings are wrong. These decoys were only left to confuse our trackers. We could spend hours wandering around trying to find the right cave entrance." Damali shook her head. "By then, we'll be lost with no sense of how much remaining sunlight we had left. It's a trap. Take a whiff. Something stronger is coming from the other direction." She pivoted and headed off on a new trail for a few yards, then walked back.

Kamal smiled. Marlene smiled. Shabazz nodded, picked up a rock, and threw it a few yards toward the path where the entire team was previously headed. The slight vibration of the stone hitting the center of the trail sent a hail of arrows flying from both the left and right sides of the route that the team would have taken. The arrows whooshed and mounted in nearby foliage, sprung loose from a giant Venus flytrap catapult hidden under leaves. One of Kamal's squad raised a bow and arrow toward a high canopy of branches beyond that and fired. Heavy rocks and fetid dead bodies fell, blocking the same path.

The noses in the group dry heaved, but quickly collected themselves before they lost their lunch. Even without the gruesome discoveries, the terrain was brutal on all the five senses. Kamal's team seemed to be fairing better than her guys, having adapted to the jungle environment, but not by much. Human flesh was the most potent and disgustingly foul scent to the animal kingdom. To eat it was unnatural, especially among the wild. Most animals avoided it like the plague.

Damali nodded, forcing the foul air from her lungs. "Yup, folks. It's so quiet because we're so near. Let's move."

"Douse it," Marlene ordered, glancing at Dan. "Just like we do with prayers, black magic also sets up a perimeter. Drop some holy water on the talismans; don't worry about the sacrificed bodies in the traps—too dangerous. But where they've left markers, we can weaken their defense systems."

Dan complied, holding his nose and sidestepping toward the stinking morass on the ground under the leaves, one arm extended as he dropped an open vial and jumped back.

"Get back further than that," Marlene warned, not having to tell Dan twice as the pile of flesh smoldered, began to smoke, and released dense yellow sulfur.

"Definitely the work of demons," Marlene said.

"Okay. That was fun. Now can we please go? Us guys with the noses are catching it."

Rider held a bandanna over his face, and Jose's eyes were watering so badly it looked like he was crying. Kamal's skin had become ashen and seemed like he was about to wretch. Kamal's men were practically staggering. But oddly, even though Damali could taste it all in her throat, the putrid odor invading her nose, her stomach remained steady. Kamal looked at her, and pushed out an answer.

"You stronger, Neteru." Then he covered his face again and walked faster.

Suddenly the hair stood up on Damali's arms, and she stopped, making her way to the front of the line. "I need to walk point from here," she said, looking around, her Isis leveled. Spots moved ever so slightly, like sunlight dappling and shifting in the trees. "Shabazz, use a crossbow and stake, with a holy water tip, to light the trail. I don't want loud gunfire or bazookas going off before we get inside the caves." She pointed to the men behind her. "You guys in the rear, watch your backs, these things circle and pick off stragglers."

Shabazz nodded, sensing with his skin, catching the weapon JL threw toward him, but seeing nothing.

"Five o'clock, my right. A familiar, or one of her girls," Damali whispered. "Light it up, on my order. Soon as the blaze catches the trail, we advance, fast, before the map in the air disappears."

Damali waited and watched, Shabazz circling with her until she dropped her hand. He released the stake, thrusting back his shoulder, cutting through the branches and sinking into something soft that roared.

"Battle stations!"

A rush of leaves, crossbows leveled, two greenish-gold glowing eyes blinked. Then there was a loud hiss, a roar, and instant motion. A gunman from Kamal's team panicked and let out a round from his automatic weapon. The thing was only partially visible, as it lunged through the trees, its deep golden coat oozing black blood, spreading, closing the multiple black spots to cover it and turn the jaguar all midnight.

"Oh, shit . . ." Rider's section of the squad backed up. "We could use that shoulder cannon now, Big Mike!"

Big Mike fired, but the blast went past the entity as it moved in a lightning-fast, powerful dodge and was gone.

The shell hit with a loud boom and flash of bright yellow light and felled a tree. Spinning fast, the team whirled in all directions, hands sweaty, clenching weapons. Waiting for something to appear again so they could shoot it.

Using her sword as a pointer, Damali motioned to the air. "See why I just wanted to injure it and not kill it, fellas?" Her tone held annoyance. The rounds had probably echoed all through the lair caverns. Making the beast dodge a shoulder-cannon blast only stirred the air, disturbed the path of its retreat, and made the trail of sulfur it bled harder to track on foot. "Damn!"

Shoulders behind her sagged. She didn't look at the squads. She knew they didn't know, but if they were going in, they had to get something straight—if they didn't follow her lead, their asses were gonna die. She spun on the teams, her expression fierce.

"Look, something in me knows what's up out here. Don't ask me how. So let me guide you without giving me a lot of bullshit in return!"

"She's right," Marlene said. "She's the Neteru. She must be the one to lead us here."

Damali could feel her shoulders relax. Cool. Mar had her back. "We follow this trail, stay close, be strategic, and conserve artillery. That way, God willing, we all get back on that boat."

Damali waited. Heads slowly nodded in acceptance. Kamal and Shabazz pounded fists. Marlene gave her a thumbs-up.

"Cool. Follow the sulfur. We're going in."

CHAPTER TWENTY-FOUR

THE CLIMB to get into the demon's lair would be steep and treacherous. The footlocker of artillery was going to be a problem. The squads were breathing hard, bent over from the steady uphill trajectory. Even Kamal's guys looked winded, sweating, and several men were bent over, hands on knees, sucking in air. Marlene was holding onto a tree, her age beginning to tell on her. Just like there was no easy way to climb mountains with gear out in the wilderness, some things required endurance.

As they stood at the foot of the steep crag of pure rock incline, everyone on the squad shook their heads one by one. Her teams had their eyes on the ground-level mouth of the cave. However, vultures circled high above it. Damali watched the birds.

"There's an opening up there drawing the birds to the carcasses. If we go in from the bottom, there are traps for those coming in on foot. It's too far of a drop by rope, given the height of the trees. Girlfriend isn't stupid. She's very smart." Damali pointed up with her sword. "But, there's a hole up there. Bet she sleeps all day in the shade after eating, like all the big cats do."

"Don't they have to stay out of the light, though, to regenerate?" Rider had pulled off his hat to get more air.

"They have to *rest* in the day, they're weaker—but you just saw that thing that was spying on us, Rider. That was what they're like when they're weaker. But sunlight doesn't harm them like vamps."

"Duly noted," he conceded to Damali. "Now what? I'm not trying to leave the ammo behind."

"Normally, we've only seen the demons remain in human form by day," Kamal said, his voice tight. "If it held a were-shape in broad daylight, they're very strong."

"Yeah, I hear you," Damali muttered, her mind working. "This ain't the kind of place you go into with just a blade in your teeth."

"For real." Shabazz eyed the cave entrance. "Too easy."

"I agree," Kamal replied, glancing around.

They were stalled. The entire team was waiting for the order to move, but where did one go? Damali walked back from where they had come from for about ten feet and looked up the cliff. The desire to take off the Amazon-demon's head with Madame Isis was so strong it made her hands tremble. But they were losing sun.

"If we go up the side, we'd have to leave the heavy ammo, and with the way the cliffs are situated, and no mountain-climbing gear on us, a jag could take us easy. We'd die from the fall alone, and I've seen these things pull on their shape-shifting capacity to become huge snakes and crocks." She walked back to where the others stood and motioned toward the cave entrance. "We already know this is booby-trapped, but if we get into a jam, we can possibly force some of her own through it—in the heat of battle, in a flat-out retreat, disorientation is easy. Troops step on their own land mines all the time, if it gets hectic enough."

Kamal nodded. "De other entrances put us about a mile from her lair up top if we have to go through a more obscure opening. Then we have to hope dat we get up dere, zigzagging at an angle, before de sun drops and dey get even stronger." He glanced at Damali, and then at Shabazz and Marlene. "Unless . . ."

Tilting her head, Damali came near Kamal. "Brother, no disrespect, but time is of the essence."

"I know. But you gotta be strong. You gwan hafta speak out loud some tings to dis team to guide 'em . . . dat's gwan be hard."

"Oh, shit," Rider sighed.

"She don't have to go there, man," Big Mike argued. "We can do this like old times, you dig?"

"No. I'm cool," Damali said firmly. "Talk to me, Kamal."

He walked a pace away from her and stood with Marlene and Shabazz. "D, how does your man think?" Kamal asked gently.

"Oh, Lord, Kamal . . . don't make her go there," Marlene murmured.

"The Neteru got to tell it, Mar," Shabazz said, his voice unwavering. "You and I both know that. We got thirty-three lives on the line."

"Can't be no bullshit out here," Kamal added. "D, how he think?"

"I . . . I don't know what you mean, for real." Thoughts slammed and scattered within Damali's head. Two older male guardians were looking at her, searching her face, but she didn't know what part of the answer they were looking for. Carlos was shrewd. Intelligent. What did they want from her? "You need to be the ones that stop bullshitting out here," she snapped, feeling the pressure from their stares. "Say it plain. I'm no child!"

Shabazz and Kamal hesitated, obviously not expecting the indignant response. All team members straightened slowly and waited, watching.

"We're trying to hit were-demon mating dens, but if she's trying to snag a master vampire, you think he would go to her, or she would come to him?" Shabazz looked at Damali, an apology in his eyes. "From what we know of male vamps, during a seduction, they have to be the ones in control. Am I wrong?"

"If he gwan take her to mate her, where would he go?" The expression on Kamal's face looked so pained, like it was the last thing he'd wanted to ask—but through her lack of quick clarity, she'd forced him and Shabazz to go there.

Damali sucked in a deep breath, and tried not to allow her gaze to leave their faces. This shit hurt so bad that she almost couldn't talk.

"He's old-school," she said, her voice flat, confident, and devoid of emotion. She used her sword as a pointer. The edge of the blade disconnecting her emotions from her body, cutting them, hacking them away like useless vines that had barred her path. Yeah, the forest floor bled when she mentally cut away the part of herself that clung, but the vines would eventually grow back. They were in the way right now.

Damali massaged her temple with two fingertips. None of her men could look at her as she spoke. She studied the cave layout. "He wouldn't take her to the top if she's throwing scent like she's ripening . . . I should have known. She's up there now. But by sundown, she's coming in low, will come down to meet him, to bring him deeper into her lair."

"Why, when she has da strategic advantage of mobility out in the jungle, versus inside a cave?" Kamal asked, looking at the ground. "Or why wouldn't she stay at da top and wait for him? We just have to be sure the cave isn't a death trap for us. Dat's the only reason I'm picking at this fresh scab, baby."

"Carlos, in that state . . ." Damali steadied herself, leaning on the Isis. "In that state, the sun would come up on him. He wouldn't risk the rays, and he knows himself well enough to protect himself. Once he gets started, time stops for him."

"Damn . . ."

Rider's voice haunted her. She began walking, needing the motion of pacing to keep her mind from exploding.

"If he's being turned out, and she's giving off ripe Neteru, he'd take her to somewhere he knew no sunlight could harm him. Roll up on him while he's working, though, and you'll die."

The glances that the team exchanged made her want to impale herself on her own sword. But they needed to know what they were dealing with—how volatile a situation this was. "Once ripened Neteru hits his system, he'll be more dangerous to *any of us* than her eleven were-jags could ever be."

She looked up and made each member of the squads look at her, using sudden silence. "If you catch him with solid red in his eyes, do him without hesitation. He will even snap my neck in that state—if I get between him and her. I'm not ripe, and I'm the Neteru—a threat to his mate. He won't be rational. He won't be Carlos Rivera, he'll be Master Vampire Rivera, two extremely different entities."

Damali glanced up at the sky as the faces of the team blurred. "I've seen it . . . and once you see it, you never forget it. He was strong as shit and ripped a competitive male master's jaw off with one swipe, because there was a ripening slayer nearby." She swallowed and pointed to the top of the cliff. "She's no fool. By sundown, her crew won't even have to fight us, Rivera will. Why take the bullet when the male will? Law of the jungle, just like the streets.

"Let's move." Damali began walking again; her chest was getting tight as she spoke and they followed just listening. "Plus, she'll definitely need her strength to take the body blows and the siphon, especially if he doesn't love her. I was lucky that way, *then*. If we kill her early, and I happen to survive . . . he'll come for the next available female with the nearest scent that's driving him crazy—me. But he'll be very, very disappointed and angry, because I'm not ripening . . . so when he's done, what's left of me when he wakes up and needs to feed—"

Marlene's gasp behind her carved Damali's insides out. The fact that Big Mike had stopped walking for a minute hurt her through and through. Her biggest brother was shaking his head and repeating a mantra, "Oh, damn," low and quiet as he walked much slower. Kamal had so much pain in his stricken expression as he mouthed "I'm sorry," that Shabazz put a hand on his shoulder. Rider simply stopped, found a large bolder, and sat on it hard, crushing small stones with his foot. Dan had also stopped and was leaning against a tree like someone had punched him in the stomach, and Jose just looked off into the distance with JL, watching the vultures circle, not moving. But they had to know. More important, they had to keep walking. It was about survival.

"Gentlemen, let's move out," she ordered, and brought the team together in a forward progression once more, looking for potential lair entry points as she tried not to think too hard. But that battle was lost the closer they got to the base of the mountain. Her mind wouldn't let go of the thing that hurt her the most and it cut her deeply.

Kamal's team might act swiftly, having no prior knowledge of Carlos as anything but a vamp. They'd see him and do him. Point blank without blinking or stuttering. But her guys were in danger. Her guys would hesitate. Her guys would hold out for hope. Her guys would think of her heart. Her guys didn't understand what went through her hands the night before and terrorized her mind. And, before, she'd been the only Neteru in Carlos's nose. Her scent was dominant. Her cycle changes had been the only ones he followed like the natural phases of the moon.

When her guys saw him flip out, Carlos didn't have two competing priorities confusing him, enraging the beast within him. The Neteru guardians had been on Carlos's side before, the side that was protecting *his* interests—a ripening slayer. Now they'd be on opposing sides, as their squad attempted to get between a jacked up-male vamp and his cycle-ready female. Not good.

Their horror notwithstanding, her guys had to suck it up, and deal—or die. Like Kamal and Shabazz had both told her, "Shit happens fast."

"When Carlos wakes up, hungry and . . . When he wakes up. He'll take her to his place, or somewhere he can corner her and keep her till she goes out of phase, or her phony scent wears off. You won't be able to get to her then, because he won't even sleep in the daytime. As long as it's dark where he is . . ."

She stopped and looked up, sensing for a good entrance point and trying to think like a master vampire would. Damali's voice trailed off, needing a moment to say the words in her mind before she could form them on her lips and push them out of her mouth. The team stopped near her and hovered, their eyes hungry for understanding, but pure grief flickering within them.

"You can't even go into his lair during the day," she said plainly in a strong voice. "If she's in there, still in phase, he will be making love to her night and day as long as the lair stays dark. Do you follow?" She shot her glance around at the faces that just stared at her in disbelief. "He'll be ravenous."

"But, he's gotta feed," Marlene finally murmured. "Replenish his blood supply to regenerate."

"We've always gone after the vamps in their lairs during the day, right guys?" Rider glanced toward the others who nodded in confusion. "Damali, maybe because you're so caught up in this thing, you're exaggerating the—"

"No, Rider, everybody. I'm trying to tell you what I know from experience. You've only dusted lower generations in-lair, but this stuff is like PCP. Even the legendary vampire hunters don't have experience with this substance, because the masters they were hunting didn't have Neteru in their systems. But it will keep a master vamp up . . . you know what I mean."

She rubbed her hand over her face and sighed and began cutting away foliage. Each pair of available hands began clearing a path to the unknown, blindly following her. She'd tried to explain over breakfast that ripe Neteru would keep a master vamp awake, intermittently feeding and making love, until the object of his desire burned out of cycle or the phony scent evaporated. Then he'd drop.

The memory of how Carlos functioned stripped her just as brutally as she was slashing back the vines. It was simple. She'd told them, but in their hearts they just didn't want to believe what she knew. It was false hope. After that marathon, he'd seriously need to feed. Would eat whatever was within reach. Her team had to forget about hope. It was basic vampire instinct that they were trying to paint as a pretty picture. But the reality was ugly.

He'd keep whatever female was in his lair fed, just so she wouldn't die from the abuse—because he'd want her to live so she'd be able to respond under him. Damali hacked at the vines harder, needing to use up her rage on something. At night he'd hunt and drag the kill back to the lair, feed her, and start the process all over again. Jesus, don't make her explain this shit to them in more detail than she already had before . . .

Finally able to reach the cave wall, she walked ahead of her team around the base of the cave, unable to cope with her knowledge. He'd told her what to expect, but she hadn't understood until Carlos showed her with the images, let her feel them for herself. Firsthand experience. Completely primal. A hunger so profound that it was unfathomable. If what she'd seen was just a fantasy, then common sense extrapolated that vision into something real that was so much worse. She wanted to weep, but again could not. Her team was trudging behind her. The purging of information had left her hollow, and yet oddly unafraid. An Amazon arrow in the center of her chest wouldn't hurt as badly, and might put her out of her misery, she thought.

But she was not trying to endanger anyone else. Part of this was her personal battle, but most of it was a common battle for a common good. Her gaze narrowed, survival the singular goal.

"Found a portal," she said, flatly pointing to an opening that was low to the ground, and covered by a heap of dead human flesh.

"You have got to be kidding me." Rider glanced around and everyone shrugged. "Go through that disgusting pile on our hands and knees? Gimme a break."

"It's about four and a half feet high, but I put money on it that it opens higher a few hundred yards out."

They stared at Damali.

"This is not the normal vamp-lair, because this isn't your run of the mill, daytime smoke-a-vampire mission," she said with authority, not looking at the team, but keeping her eyes trained on the opening she was studying. She spoke to them, half thinking out loud and half processing the variables for herself.

"He's going after something in jag form, so he'll transform to match it. Male vamp, transformed into panther, is about four feet at the shoulders. Give him additional head space to lope at a full-speed run, in order to rush an attacker, he's gonna want a place were he can slow their exit to sunlight, and feed in a safe tunnel." Damali went to the heap, squatted, and poked in the gore with her sword and sniffed, getting a whiff of sulfur in the sickening mix. "Carlos didn't do this, though. She probably ordered this food left at his back door for him in preparation. Not his style. It's human. Woulda left her a buffalo carcass, something like that." She stood. "That much I still know about him."

Kamal sniffed and nodded. "It's were-demon marked. Damali is right."

She pulled herself up on a low-hanging branch and could make out a ledge about eight feet off the ground. She closed her eyes for a moment, feeling Carlos's presence had been there. "Found his front door." Damali looked down as her team assembled under her as she sheathed the Isis and began climbing.

"What are you doing?" Shabazz asked with a bewildered expression. "Didn't you just say—"

"He's not home yet," she shot back, grunting from the exertion of lifting herself. "Today, brother is getting his rest, probably ate real good last night, and at sundown, will shave, put on his rags, track a scent, and be out. So, we've gotta lay some booby traps in there now, and find the corridor that leads from her bedroom to his. Dig?"

"Damn . . ." Big Mike murmured, glancing at Shabazz, Rider, and Kamal. "Women are devious."

"Mike, you sure those detonators are good from this far away?" Damali glanced back at her team in the dank cavern.

"Yeah, we cool. Holy water set, C-4, right under the marble slab, li'l sis."

The lair was a cakewalk. If Damali's second sense was right, the Amazon's crew wasn't committed to guard it; their primary concern would be their queen. They were up top near her.

From what she'd gleaned from Carlos's mind, and the parts she filled in from common sense, since this was an unsanctioned vampire mission, there were no bats or messengers to contend with outside the master lair. One hundred yards into the cave from the ledge, it had gotten narrower and darker, until they had to fire lanterns to see.

But the heavy steel door wasn't bolted. From experience she knew they were bolted from the inside, and if nobody was home . . . Vampires didn't worry about break-ins. Human invasion was merely dinner dropping off at their door. While they were gone, all illusion disappeared and left what they'd found—a marble slab and sharp granite walls.

As the group moved forward, the cave widened again, and Damali halted them. The entire posse had been weaving their way past stalactites and stalagmites through the damp space, ducking at times where there were low spots, and avoiding small cave-dwelling rodents and insects underfoot along the path that she knew without knowing why she did.

"Ammonia," she whispered. "We got bats overhead."

"Here," Kamal said quietly, "we have natural vampire bats. As long as you move slowly, don't send them flying, dey shouldn't attack you—but dey do, at times, carry rabies."

"Oh, brother," Rider moaned as the group passed under a huge cavernous ceiling that wriggled and squeaked with the tightly packed, struggling vermin. "Why do we always have to go to the garden spots of the world, Damali? Geeze Louise," he fussed, pinching his nose as the bats indiscriminately plopped little globs of feces combined with urine-like leather-winged pigeons.

Dampness, sweat, and dread clung to their skins, and without ventilation in the caverns, it was insufferable. Albeit cooler in the cave than under the sun outside, the thick stillness of the air, along with the wafting bat odors and combined human team funk, was about to make everyone pass out. Water dripped in a steady rhythm from the multiple underground streams, and an echo resounded from it everywhere.

When Damali weaved, stopped, and leaned against the wall, the team took five gladly. She mopped her throat, forehead, and the back of her neck under her locks, holding her hair off her as she wiped away moisture with a bandanna in repetitive, futile strokes. The team's haggard breaths, and the echo of bottled-water seals breaking was the only sound to accompany the now far-off bat colony and the dripping water within the cave.

Damali lifted her head within the large expanse of cavern where they'd paused, listening past the team guzzling water, their breaths, the water of the drips . . . where was the drip . . . where was the drip? The bats weren't squeaking.

"Battle stations," she whispered. "Full metal jacket."

One by one the team passed the word, and each warrior slowly got his weapon readied, putting down his water carefully as though it were a bomb. Damali took a bottle cap from Shabazz and flipped it like a coin into the next tunnel opening, and immediately a hail of arrows was returned.

"Open fire!"

Ducking behind rocks and narrow ruts between boulders, her team sent rapid machine gunfire into the open tunnel where the arrows had been released. But soon she held up her hand, realizing that there was no return fire. Turning quickly to look behind them, the team froze, staring up at eleven low-crouched entities on cave ledges bearing fangs.

Green-gold eyes glistened in the darkness twenty feet above them. The lanterns exploded, putting the team in instant darkness. JL lit a flare, and it was summarily shot out of his hand by a blow dart. Then the eyes disappeared. The team drew in, standing back to back, aiming into the blackness, not knowing even if their own team members were before them.

Two eyes opened almost twenty-five feet out, a man yelled, his screams turning to shrieks, bones snapped, flesh ripped, the team fired. It became dead silent again.

Damali patted Mike for a grenade. "Light it up in here, Mike."

Hurling a series of holy-water bombs, the room flashed blue light, and then fast-rising plumes of yellow, fetid smoke gassed the team, choking them, blinding them, obscuring their vision. Kamal's men drew back.

Marlene shot a glance of concern and she dropped her voice to a tense whisper, close to a hiss. "Oh my God. They can't take the grenades, D. Kamal, you should have told us! They have an intolerance for what comes up from the demon pits, because of their human hybrid DNA that fights full turns. Get 'em out of here now! There's too much sulfur—"

"Do whatchu gotta do," Kamal yelled, still backing up and wheezing. "We normally fight them in the open, it's just da cave . . ."

"This is fucked up—we didn't know, man." Shabazz caught Kamal under his armpit as he stumbled and helped him to his feet. "But y'all ain't expendable. Get these men out of here."

"Just guard the Neteru," Kamal argued, clinging to Shabazz for support before he righted himself to lean against a wall. "We go all da way as one squad."

Damali glanced at Kamal's struggling team, and pushed herself off the wall. An adrenaline kick of pure frustration and rage jolted her forward through the sulfur, making her cut at nothing as she climbed on a high flat rock. Not another one of her men. Not one!

"You call yourself a warrior," she yelled, coughing and sputtering from the toxic fumes. "Then come out and fight!"

She had to get her now, well before sundown, well before things got crazier. The smoke was lifting, which meant they'd come in for another attack. All she could hope was that Kamal and his men had enough human-side to make them impervious to the demon sulfur that their other spiritual weapons would unleash. "Stand ready, guys!" The smoke was lifting, their barrier was burning off, and every warrior had to come out shooting and swinging.

As soon as Damali gave the order, a huge white jaguar parted the haze of smoke before her, lunging right at her. Damali dodged the lunge, getting a good slice in the shoulder section of the beast. It turned where it landed, let out a furious snarl, but it was positioned upon a jutting ledge in a way that would put Damali in the line of gunfire. Its angry glare swung from Damali to Marlene. From the corner of Damali's eye, she could see the other big cats had taken a position within tunnel openings overhead.

"This is your girl, Marlene," Damali said loudly, over her shoulder.

"I know," Marlene shot back, fast. She looked at the injured cat. "You wanna do this the hard way, or the easy way—seer-to-seer, *bitch?*"

The demon were-jag was off the ledge in the blink of an eye. Marlene backed up, circling with it, her prayer-reinforced stick in hand as she maneuvered herself and the stalking cat into a clear space. The jaguar hissed and swatted, tilting its head to get a good angle on Marlene's extremities, but Marlene was swift on her feet, her stick lethal.

"Stay with her, Mar," Shabazz called, frantically aiming and following Marlene's motion to cover her.

Kamal was crouching, moving, a semi in his hands and holding the creature in his sights, but he repeatedly called off fire, too, frustrated by the hazards of a deadly ricochet from solid rock. Damali was easing forward, the cats above on the ledges moving nearer to peer over it.

The white were-jaguar backed up, Marlene took a stance to prepare for a lunge, her stick a ready-made stake to spear the soft underbelly of the beast. Her team followed the moving forms, unable to get a clear shot that wouldn't imperil Marlene or Damali or cause a ricochet.

But unexpectedly, the thing circling stopped, transformed, and became human form. Marlene stopped, and remained in an Aikido stance.

"I should have finished you in the first ambush!" the albino warrior yelled, instantly sending a dark-blue electric current from her hand to Marlene's chest.

"No!" Shabazz hollered, but Kamal held him and Damali rushed to his side.

Marlene calmly closed her eyes and lowered her walking stick parallel to the ground as her crystal breastplate absorbed the energy. The current being sent into Marlene became weaker and weaker as the albino warrior screamed her discontent, fury drawing her fists into a ball. Marlene's eyes snapped open as the warrior rushed her. Marlene's knees bent, and the walking stick returned a bluish-white line of pure energy, knocking the albino on her back. Marlene was on her in seconds. It happened so quickly the creatures above couldn't lunge to save their comrade.

"Is that all you got?" Marlene said with disdain, immediately staking the creature before it could even sit up.

Struggling against the stake, a black-blood geyser spurted from the wound. Piercing shrieks of garbled warrior cries mixed with guttural were-demon howls filled the chamber as the thing at Marlene's feet bubbled and turned into green slime. Retrieving her stick, she joined the safety of the team crouched behind the rocks. Kamal slapped her five, Shabazz pounded her fist, and Damali hugged her fast.

"Mar, you took out their nerve center—they're blind, now. There's no top adviser. Plus, we wounded one outside. But we can't forget that the main one is a seer, too, unless she's totally gone into this Neteru wannabe bag." She looked at Kamal, trying to send her condolences through a firm squeeze on his arm. "Who did we lose? Your man, what was his name? I'm so sorry."

Kamal just shook his head. "Dominique . . . nineteen. No family. We were it. I'll bury whatever I find."

"I'll help you carry your man, if we get out," Shabazz murmured.

Damali moved forward when the eyes above disappeared. "They

wouldn't have pulled back unless they're using too much energy to fight us as jags in the daytime. We've got a short window. Like less than an hour. The primary nerve center is gone, we've wounded one, but we could do this all night—we're trading one for one. It's an even match." She sent her gaze around the team. "We're not losing any more of our men, especially with the sun dropping. We'll seal this joint with C-4 and blow this whole damned piece. Let it implode. Fuck it."

"Or, we can save the cave and all the innocent creatures in it," a smooth, female voice said from above, "and do this the old-fashioned way."

The team looked up fast, their gaze darting around the perimeter of the cave ledges above. Eleven stunning women with tall, proud carriages, skin hues that ranged from deep copper to highly polished black marble, stood above them with bows, battle-axes, blow darts and machetes in hand. One was badly wounded, her shoulder ragged and bleeding black blood. Had to be the one the crossbow snipe got. Yet, there was no other way to describe the magnificence of their presence, other than to admit they were awesome.

Each possessed a regal countenance. Their hair, eyes, skin—radiant. They glowered down at the huddled warriors with disdain and lifted their chins ever higher, their athletic carriages rippling with the readiness to strike.

"I don't want to blow the cave and jack with the ecosystem," Damali shouted, coming to the clear area and holding up her hand as her team protested with their eyes. "You took one of our men, rushed him, we had to do one of yours."

The queen stepped forward, her eyes flickering green and gold with controlled rage. "That was my mother-seer!" she yelled, pointing at the ground where only ooze remained.

This very, very was good. The delusion had set in. This horrifyingly beautiful demon actually thought she was the Neteru. Just like Carlos had shown her. Yeah, keep that crazy bitch in the fantasy. Make her fight on the terms of a Neteru, not a were-jag.

With her Isis, Damali motioned to Marlene. "That is *my* mother-seer. Yours went after her for no reason and began this conflict. You went after my moms, so now it's on!"

The Amazon nodded. Her warriors snarled and backed up. Damali could feel them ready to pounce, but then the injured one dropped. The Amazon ran to her fallen warrior's side, crushed her to her chest, dropped the body, and swallowed hard as it began to bubble.

"You owe me another body," the Amazon said through her teeth.

"All this bullshit over a man? What, are you crazy?" Damali asked, knowing that no female wanted to admit that she'd lost perspective or pride over a man, especially not a five-hundred-year-old warrior.

Damali glanced around at the warriors behind the older female demon who were exchanging gazes of confusion. "It didn't have to be all this," she yelled. "You could have come to me, told me who you were, then we coulda worked something out."

"You lie! You would never negotiate!"

"No, you lie! You're the one who lives in Hell, the zone of the silver-tongued devils. They already tricked you once. I'm a huntress, and a warrior, and do my shit out in the open. Now you're trying to front like you're something you're not—a Neteru!" She narrowed her gaze on the thing that was snarling. "Did you tell your demon girls that you were wearing Neteru, not to attract him so you could hunt and kill the master vamp in this territory blocking your feed zones, but that you'd plan to do him tonight . . . even left food at his lair door?"

The demon on the ledge screamed and raised a bow and arrow and pulled back hard, training it on Damali who didn't budge.

"Look at this shit. Punk bitch can't even come down here and take the Isis from me like a woman—'cause you know it's mine, by right!"

An arrow flew; Damali dodged it with a swift fake to the left, and caught it in her right hand. Her team bristled, but nobody opened fire. The group behind the Amazon narrowed their gazes, but Damali could feel an energy shift ever so slightly. Dissension was in the air. A memory of the old way was in the offing. She remembered what Shabazz had said, if you're weaker, be strategic. She remembered what Marlene had said, and watched the Amazon's eyes.

Damali folded her arms over her chest. "Your girls remember what it was like to protect a Neteru, don't they? By rights, you should be protecting me. I'm the real, living Neteru. But you've stolen the ancient Neteru's trademark, and you've tricked your own fellow guardians, too." She sent her glance to the Amazon's team. "She promised you your Neteru would resurrect, didn't she? Your seer-mother did some twisted shit and it didn't work." Then she smiled. "Or, maybe it did. Since I'm here five hundred years before my time—early, and have the Isis as proof I'm a Neteru."

Several demon eyes shared nervous glances up on the ledge, opening an opportunity for Damali to press her point.

"You and I share the same history, are of the same people . . . different eras. Believed in the same things. Then something happened to you, and you went south on us, literally. If you have nothing to hide, tell your girls to ask Carlos which Neteru *authentically* ripened first on his watch in this era—a master would know."

She could see them all hesitate, and the leader become concerned by their confusion, so Damali pressed on messing with their heads just like the best of mental seduction had taught her. She dropped her voice to a low, calm tone and looked at the weaker members of the group. "She's getting ready to cross realm boundaries and do a vamp because her potion didn't work. She led you to the pit, and left y'all hanging. Ask her."

The older warrior backed up, her gaze steady, but with her team not quite intact. "That is not true! We have never been from the same tribes. You come with your machines and filth that—"

"Take a look," Damali said, her pupils opening. "Marlene, Kamal, give a couple of her girls a view."

The two guardians stood by Damali, locking in with the ancient rogue guardian and her two top warriors that flanked her. Silent tears of memory streamed down the Amazons' faces. The one on the left turned away and breathed deeply, unable to take the images Marlene sent. The one on the right of the Amazon queen simply nodded and raised her hand to Kamal to request that he stop, and then conferred with the others behind her for a moment. Damali blinked, and took a deep breath, removing the Isis from the shallow plunge where she'd planted it into the rocky cave floor.

Holding up the Isis, Damali tilted her head. "Before you, Nzinga had this over in the Nubian Empire. What if she came back twisted during your Neteru's reign and tried to strip your huntress of her time? You wouldn't have it, would you? None of you who were guardians would have allowed it. It is in your code to protect a *living* Neteru, one from the light, not a dead one that's slithered up from the dark realms."

Murmurs echoed behind the angry queen. "Enough! I challenge you, then, to hold onto your reign. You have chosen a passive course for your era, instead of—"

"Instead of fucking up the world? Are you mad?" Damali was walking, no longer concerned about an arrow or being rushed by the demon were-jaguars. "You keep doing these unexplained ambushes on humans, they'll send in troops. They will nuke the Amazon looking for aliens and shit. Yes, you'll win, maybe, but they'll leave a smoking black hole for you to rule over! They have new shit up here topside these days. They have more than cannons and rifles."

She pointed her sword at the Amazon. "You shame our kind!" Damali glanced at the others. "Your girls died for you as the lead guardian once your Neteru fell, and followed you into the pit instead of Heaven, where they could have been reborn as warriors of light. They could have been fighting in spirit, swaying the balance, like the old way—which is not a passive move—it's *honorable*! But you let yourself and your other sister guardians go out like that."

Damali's breathing became ragged the angrier she became just thinking about it, but she reversed her strategy midway in her argument to throw her adversary off guard. Instead of outing the old mother-seer, she spoke to her as though she were the ancient Neteru. "You even put your mother-seer in jeopardy? Then you come back with a twisted plan? Look at them! These are the best of an era gone bad. Let them ascend!"

"There should be a fair challenge match, to end the Neteru feud," the warrior to the right of the queen said. "A true queen Amazon would never—"

It happened so fast both squadrons of fighters were left speechless. The Amazon ripped out the throat of her warrior in one lightning move. The stunned, lower-ranking were-jag fell slowly, looking confused, clutching the gaping black hole, gurgling black blood. The warriors on the ledge stepped back, casting nervous glances among them.

"If ever you challenge my authority—*ever!*"

"See, y'all. Your girl is over the top. Nobody else has to die, and mountains and shit don't have to blow up, if she'd just step outside and meet me woman-to-woman on a private matter we need to address. Damn . . ."

The warriors behind the Amazon backed up farther, nodded, transformed into feline form, then disappeared within the cavern.

"Deep," Shabazz murmured.

"See," Damali shouted, "some things ain't changed since the dawn of time!"

"At the top, me and you."

Damali and her team just stared at each other as the old Amazon backed away from the ledge and vanished.

CHAPTER TWENTY-FIVE

"ALL RIGHT," Damali said, talking fast. "We have like twenty minutes for me to get to the top, and do this thing while dissension is brewing in her ranks. I want these teams out of here, collect your man before something goes after the remains, and—"

"You are not going up there by yourself. Forget about it," Shabazz said, snatching her arm, making the team surround her with Kamal leading the pack.

"You're burning my daylight, big brother. She ain't taking my sword, trust me. So, I want the team on that boat, with Big Mike ready to blow the lair as soon as the sun hits the horizon, if I'm not back by the time you're ready to pull off. It doesn't have to be completely dark for Carlos to come at sundown, but I don't want him to have anywhere to hide out here. We need something to distract him, make him retreat for a few minutes to get himself a secure new base. Plus I meant what I said about not destroying the beauty of this—"

"No," Marlene snapped, walking away from her. "Absolutely not. I won't allow it."

The whole team shook their heads in unison.

Damali sighed with a hard rush of frustration. It was hopeless, and this team standoff was wasting valuable time.

"Then only take what you can carry. While I'm up there with her, nobody fires unless they are personally rushed. I don't care how close you think I am to biting it—you let me do this." She stared at her team hard. "It's more than about a Carlos thing, or even a demon problem."

When Kamal nodded, everybody went still, their eyes going between him and Damali.

Damali grabbed a crystal-tipped stake and thrust it in her pants back pocket. "He knows," she said with a half-smile, glancing at Kamal. "That's why dude is out here, and told me today . . . in the center of my chest. I saw it when the anger lifted and peace claimed me. That Amazon was *wronged,* people. She's crazy, but she was wronged. And there's only one way to rectify it now. Compassion enough to put her out of her misery."

Damali shook her head. "Even Carlos, in his messed-up state, felt for her. He sent that to me, too. Don't hate her. Hate what she's become, and what did this to her. *That,* I am going to deal with . . . the bastard that made her come back."

"Damali," Rider argued, his voice gentle, his eyes holding a combination of terror and confusion, "I know the code of a Neteru is supposed to have high ideals . . . but, baby . . ." He glanced at Big Mike and the rest for support, whose eyes all held the same expression of panic. "Please, D—"

"She's still an ancestral guardian, and there's a code," Damali said in a firm, quiet tone. "Because they came for her wrong, there's a hiccup in supernatural law—I want her back on our side. There's a tiny fragment of trapped light coming from the ascended Neteru in there that will sway the balance. They ingested the wrong thing . . . it'll give them a fragment of conscience, make them remember, and a second of hesitation will be my window. Eleven guardians might even ascend, if I take the head of the hydra. Means we get one hundred soul-weight to one, do the math . . . times eleven is an eleven-hundred soul-shift, with Neteru topspin in the equation. The Neteru that perished will have her old team back—righteous. Plus they're all warriors."

She pointed toward a tunnel that her heart told her led to the top. "You got it?"

Shabazz nodded. "Let's do this."

Army boots crushed bones and rotting animal carcasses as the guardians and Kamal's men passed; the stench of death and the hum of carrion-feeding insects got denser as the teams approached the apex of a narrow interior tunnel. Damali had the front, Big Mike and Drum had the back, with Marlene and all sensors in a closed-rank, single-file formation edging to the cliff top opening.

Vultures took flight; some dove and swooped at the human team to make their displeasure at an interrupted feeding known. Eight pairs of green, glowing eyes met the human squad from hidden shadows and small crags, but nothing moved.

All spectators gathered, a foul breeze blew, and Damali and the team's attention went to the cavernous location adjacent to them. Appearing out of the darkest corner, in full battle gear, the Amazon appeared.

Her polished gold breastplate, armbands, shin shields, and helmet glistened red in the setting sun. The brilliant white cloth of her battle robes seemed to absorb the colors of the sunset within each fold. Her hair was twisted high off her shoulders in an endless spiral of knotted braids, and her strong forearms flexed as her battle-ax lowered and she bent her knees prepared for war. She was indeed a queen.

The stalking dance began slowly without words or fanfare. Damali's sword was lowered, just like the Amazon's ax. Their movements were steady, controlled, and neither of them blinked. But time was not on Damali's side. A fight like this between two evenly matched opponents could take hours. She had less than a quarter hour. Without further hesitation, Damali locked in on her adversary, first sending her the message of respect. The woman was truly magnificent.

Seeming dazed, not expecting to sense that message, the Amazon widened the circle.

"They're going to use you," Damali said, resigned. "You know that, right?"

"You have minutes, young huntress. Pity. Because you, too, are magnificent. Your people have shared much with mine. I will give you that."

Damali nodded. "Don't you know that you won't come out of that vanishing point, the vampire will? You'll have been fucked over twice by power-hungry men."

"You lie because you love him," the Amazon replied, closing the gap. "You must accept defeat. Give me my sword. What I am after is freedom from all boundaries."

With the comment, Damali saw an in. A way to score her opponent's concentration, start the charge. "Yeah. I know all about that, too. Soon as the sun sets, you're coming for more than my Isis blade. But you can take the sword, you can take the body—but, girlfriend, you can never take my place."

Damali smiled to herself as she felt something prying into her brain for an explanation, the Amazon's telepathy feeling her out for assurance that the Amazon's evil plan wouldn't be derailed by a variable she'd overlooked. The Amazon was curious, suspicious. That was good.

And that was also when Damali sucker punched her with every bit of memory, sensation, and excruciating detail she could find. The Amazon lowered her weapon for just a fraction of a second, dazed, fury taking two seconds to boil over. Damali used those seconds to land a fly kick dead center in her opponent's stomach, shaking the Amazon's balance. But the agile senior warrior instantly flipped up from where she'd landed on the ground, and came back at Damali angrier than she was before the blow.

Two lightning-fast whooshes went down Damali's sides. She'd faked left, and the close heat of the missed ax-blade strike actually friction-burned the length of Damali's left arm. Anticipating the second swing, Damali had dodged right, narrowly avoiding the second pass of the deadly Amazon ax. The passes had been wielded within the span of two snaps of the fingers, but the Amazon was too near her to effectively stab at her with the Isis. She'd only slice her, and would lose momentum on the draw back. The were-demon was in close, enraged at what she saw and felt within Damali's mind. But the anger was making her sloppy. Damali landed a solid punch to her adversary's jaw when the ax came down again without precision aim, giving Damali time to back up for Isis range.

Using both hands, Damali put her full weight into the swing, but the Amazon bent back in a *capoeira* move, a limbo avoidance duck, and caught the Isis with the side of her ax. The vibration of the hard, clanging connection traveled up the Isis, through Damali's arm, nearly rattling her skeleton. Maybe Big Mike had been right—this bitch got stronger when she got angrier.

Momentarily winded from defending against the heavy, sword-connecting blow, Damali had to get out of the older warrior's swing range. She was strong as an ox, and angry as a bull. She'd lost two close guardian sisters and had killed one of her own; Damali had not. The Amazon was down three bodies on her team; Damali was down one. The Amazon had ingested her own Neteru, was tethered to that essence, was synced to the stolen fertility phases, was getting hyped from the waxing ripening cycle as the sun set; Damali's system was stabilized—save adrenaline. She'd been incarcerated in Hell for almost five hundred years; Damali had only visited to kick some ass and get out. She'd been in horrific human battles of biblical proportions; Damali definitely had never taken a human life. It was time to be strategic. Pure muscle was not gonna win this one.

Kamal's words entered Damali's head as both silent squads looked on; were-jaguar demons on one side, a combined team of Neteru guardians and were-humans on the other. Two spectator demons cast evil grins in the human seer's direction to warn Kamal to stay out of it. His words ebbed back as Damali avoided an ax landing in the center of her skull, propelling herself out of harm's way with a back flip.

She'd quickly tried to behead the Amazon as the ax weight of swing carried the ancient warrior forward to bend over, but the seasoned queen was too fast and was on her feet as Damali's sword was just rising.

The Isis was, for the first time in Damali's life, becoming a detriment. This older warrior used a skill that Damali hadn't seen before, and the Amazon was adept with the smaller, closer held, hand-to-hand combat weapons. The Isis dagger was too short-range for a stronger opponent like this one. Even if Damali had access to long-distance death carriers, like arrows or darts, those only worked in an ambush. If she had a Glock, she'd have to aim at something that moved like lightning. Even the sharpshooters hadn't been able to hit one of them good. Spraying an area with machine gunfire had been futile—these things vanished into thin air before the bullets struck. You had to catch them off guard, up close and personal while they charged.

A sudden blow to Damali's jaw from an unseen fist sent her hurling backward. The dropping sun was strengthening this enemy, giving the Amazon greater speed—which the ancient warrior didn't need to be effective. In slow motion Damali saw her opponent take a running leap, a shrill battle cry passing her lips as she went airborne, and Damali's boot connected with the center of her chest, flipping the Amazon over her.

The Amazon landed on her back and scrambled up. Damali jumped to her feet, too. Steel met steel in a sudden rage lunge. Every swing of the battle-ax caught on the sides of the Isis as Damali flipped the blade to match the blow. But the superior strength of the Amazon was literally walking Damali backward toward the edge of the cliff as the older warrior marched aggressively, swinging in strong matched strokes, constantly moving forward.

Marlene covered her mouth when Damali's boot met the edge of the high crevice. On the next raise of the ax, Damali head-butted the Amazon, ramming her stomach, knocking the wind out of her, but not before two sharp elbows came down hard on Damali's spine and a knee caught Damali right under her chin. Damali hit the ground and rolled away from an ax blade that became wedged in the dirt long enough for her to jump up and stand.

Jaw nearly cracked, lip bleeding, tongue cut from her mouth being slammed, her back bruised, Damali held her blade firm. Confidence was waning, as she also realized for the first time in her life, she was getting her ass kicked. Damn it was too early to be the end of an era. The thought had been isolated and dredged as soon as it slithered through Damali's mind. The Amazon smiled.

The two began the torturous process of circling again, but the thought Kamal had sent had already been working and taking root in Damali's brain. Slamming the older warrior, who was also breathing hard and showing mild signs of fatigue, Damali used the standoff to her advantage, hurling image after image of the Vampire Council and the counselor's deceit.

"No matter," the Amazon wheezed, sucking in huge inhales, trying to catch her breath.

"No matter?" Damali watched the glowing eyes, the twitching muscles. "Don't you know that in the midst of the act, they'll be a separation? You'll be vapor—Carlos still has soul weight!"

The Amazon straightened a little and backed up, quickly glancing at her squad that now began to move forward. Damali's squad raised weapons, but she held up her hand.

"Fool me once, shame on you. Fool me twice, shame on me." Damali nodded toward the sun that was touching the horizon, her chest heaving from the blows.

Damali's throat tightened, her mouth dry from exertion and emotion. "The old counselor, from the same tribes that overran your people, will hijack your daylight ability. You are just sunshine breeder-stock to them. You're mad, so you can't see it. He won't allow Carlos to reign with you; don't you get it? After Vlak bleeds the daylight out of him, Carlos is coming for me to make daywalkers. This is about absolute power. Vlak will suck him dry the moment you're vapor. That's how they roll down there. Then, in seven years, Vlak will probably double-cross Carlos again and be strong enough to come for me, too."

"Carlos would never submit himself to that abomination!" the older warrior shouted. "His people are my people. He's a dark warrior of honor! He's a master vampire and would never—"

"He still had a soul, that's why they can torture and compromise him!"

The Amazon stopped moving. Two sets of female eyes deadlocked. Both combatants were breathing hard, but remained still. Damali's irises were now totally eclipsed by her pupils, as the Amazon's green orbs peered into them.

"He's in Purgatory," Damali said through huffs of air. "He can come out before total sundown. He nearly wept for your loss, the atrocities that your people suffered. He told me to my face that you were majestic . . . but twisted, now. And what they didn't tell you was that you've got a slight chance, a fraction of an opportunity to stop this madness. The redemption clause—use it for you and your girls!"

The Amazon backed away in horror and disbelief as she stared into Damali's eyes and her own eyes went from solid green to flickering green-gold to deep, mahogany brown.

"They robbed you of your will to live, killing your child and bringing smallpox as their final weapon to your Neteru . . . knowing you would rather go to Hell than—as a warrior, in the middle of the worst scourge to come to your land—be forced to lay down and die without a fight. You couldn't do it. You were the mother-seer and thought you had failed. It warped your faith, stole your hope . . . the dark side got to someone your team could trust, someone from inside your camp—you. That's all you had left to believe in, after your Neteru fell, then the baby was killed."

Damali made the sign of the cross over her chest as she mentioned the infant, noting that the warrior's eyes filled with tears. "They seduced you with a deathbed offer when you got sick, too—your soul for a shot at revenge, right, sis? I can dig it, but it was a bad move, wasn't strategic on your part." Damali let her breath out in a rush. "Connect with me, guardian to Neteru, and tell me I'm wrong?"

Fists clenched tight at the Amazon's sides as she nodded. "Never would I surrender . . . you don't know what they did."

"Don't surrender," Damali told her. "Keep fighting—from the right side, though, my sister."

A flicker of green came back, the Amazon's eyes narrowed, and Damali tensed again.

"What hold do they have over him? What would a man who's tasted the sheer power of the sixth realm care that his soul was hostage? All souls are hostage to oppression, topside, as long as our people aren't free! His soul was in bondage by humans already!" The Amazon paced in an agitated line between her snarling were-jaguar demons behind her and a cavern tunnel. "Besides, if his soul is in Purgatory, it is untouchable even by the vampires! He would not care what Vlak said, if he had a redemption option. He could die with honor, then. You lie!"

The battle-ax left the Amazon's hand so fast, and with so much force as the sun dipped beneath the horizon that Damali couldn't even take a sip of air. The move she'd seen Kamal execute became one with Damali's consciousness. The response was not thought, it was cellular encryption that connected with her legs, bending her knees, dropping her a millimeter from the ground, flexing back her injured spine with a shard of pain to avoid the weapon that waddled in a blur past her breasts, chin, forehead, eyes and became lodged in the mountain wall.

Up fast, Damali spoke quickly to the unarmed, but seemingly more dangerous demon. "All that you say is true, but you forgot one variable."

"What?" The Amazon crouched low, like she would transform into a jaguar to even the odds of having lost her weapon.

"Me!" Damali shouted, her voice ringing in the mountainside cavern. In an act of frustration, foolish for battle, she opened her arms, almost like an act of surrender.

"Me, damn it," Damali repeated, losing her battle cool. "Me. Look and see for yourself. That's the only reason Vlak got to him. Me! That's the only reason he agreed. The only reason he fought to get out of the tunnels. Me. The man crawled across the desert and starved for three days, bitch, for me!"

The Amazon's entire were-jag team transformed into human form and studied Damali's eyes; all searching to be sure there was no fraud.

"Me!" Damali was now yelling, rage filtering through her, pumping adrenaline so hard her ears rang. "I branded him—me. The only reason he can see the edge of daylight is because of me! I've kept him on the edge of the light—me!" she exclaimed, slapping the center of her chest with one hand, leveling her sword with the other. "Don't tell me I'm a liar. Look in my eyes. You see for yourself. When you are down in that lair, the old bastard will be near to bleed the daylight access from the body that comes out of the point. *Carlos*. The only reason Carlos would allow some shit like that is because, to him, I'm worth it! The brother doesn't even care about his own soul! Get to that!"

Damali stepped closer. "Why would a master vampire submit to such rank humiliation? Why would he care to do his atonement? Huh! Me—because he loved me before he died, was turned with a prayer—*my prayer*—in his heart, and ya'll can't do shit with that, but dig it!"

Both sides became still. The Amazon stared at Damali for what seemed like a long time. "They won't rob me twice," she whispered, transformed, and took a running lunge at Damali before Damali could even raise her sword.

But the creature's leap and angle was just above Damali's shoulder. To avoid the contact, Damali went down hard on one knee, anticipating the leverage she'd need when the creature doubled back for the second lunge. The guardians were poised to protect against the other demons from entering the combat, but when the demons began stalking in Damali's direction, nobody fired.

Damali's gaze shot to her team, whose weapons weren't sounding, then toward the jaguars that passed her, as she spun quickly to see the position of the Amazon. She immediately jumped back, her heart skipping a beat, as she stared at the gruesome sight.

The Amazon's head had been severed by her own leap toward the entity she most wanted to destroy—Counselor Vlak. As he fully materialized, the were-jaguar had become enraged and airborne. Unwittingly he stood in front of the mountain cavern, blocking the blade, sidestepping the lunge, accidentally allowing the Amazon to take the impact.

"Stupid!" He was spitting and hissing, holding the head.

Timing was everything. Damali studied his countenance. He was definitely not trying to kill her. It was simply a matter of time and placement, where he'd materialized. Then again? She smiled. There were unseen forces on both sides shifting the balance, always. But where was Carlos?

"You foolish bitch!" he shrieked, walking in a trail of black smoke, talking to the decapitated head. "You've ruined everything!"

The other were-jaguars rumbled their complaint in low growls, stalking, circling, distracting the old vampire with snarls and hisses, but still not bold enough to rush one as old as Vlak.

Anoint da queen were-jag, quickly, Mar, Kamal whispered in thought to the other seer. *Weapons aren't firing because of the master vamp's psychic hold. But send the Amazon team to ascension with a prayer. Remember, you must cut off the head of the hydra. This one is anchored by a Neteru's essence and won't incinerate—so seal it with prayers to get da deceived Amazons to rest to go to the light. Take that ripe Neteru scent out of the air before the young male vampire shows up.*

Damali heard the thought transmission, and knew the old counselor would only be oblivious for a few seconds while he ranted about his lost cause, so she set up a distraction. "Too bad, but seven years from now, me and you? How about it?" Damali walked a wide circle, laughing as she glimpsed Marlene from the corner of her eye.

Counselor Vlak sneered at her. "You think that you have won this little escapade, but now I have no reason not to turn Rivera in and destroy him. In fact, if I call up a squadron of messengers right now, we could all end this in the jungle." The old creature made a tent with his fingers before his face and chuckled, shaking his head. "We can make your life a living Hell until we need you seven years from now."

"Possibly," Damali said, trying to remain cool. "But that's a lot of explaining to do, especially if the Vampire Council finds out about the Amazon."

She walked, holding Vlak's stare, showing him what she knew. "Mr. Counselor, honestly. Holding back on product from the Vampire Council—hiding ripened Neteru scent in a demon on level five, and in the Amazon?"

Damali clucked her tongue, enjoying torturing him as his beady red eyes narrowed. She could tell he was momentarily trapped; however, with an old master this shrewd, being caught in his own web of deception wouldn't last long. But more important than indulging in twisting the blade of her tongue in his temporary wound, she needed to stall long enough for Marlene to do her thing. He was also being disoriented by the demon's scent; she'd use that, too.

"And, you'd better not kill me—because then you'll have to wait *a thousand years* to get some, baby. Then, again, you think after this fiasco that the light is gonna make another Neteru anytime soon? Hmmm . . . Didn't you all have to wait like three thousand years, at one point in history? You know they work with the number three in Heaven—already sent her, Nzinga, and me way ahead of schedule . . ." She shot him a glare of pure contempt. "Ya blew your trinity, brother. They'll make your asses wait three thousand, my bet, for a shot at the title again." She paused for effect, watching the old vampire hesitate. "Hurt any of my people, I will literally fall on my sword . . . but not before I let the old boys know what you did." She watched the threat sink in.

"Kill yourself, and you won't ascend," he said, trying to recover, but his voice didn't have the same arrogant ring of authority in it.

"True . . . but I won't be on level six. I may be on level one as a disembodied spirit. Perhaps on level two and manifest as a poltergeist. I'll be a lost soul, some crazy Neteru chick who committed an unthinkable act and died of a broken heart. But rest assured I'll have a prayer in my heart when I go. And all I know is, you guys won't have me . . . and that will *really* piss off the chairman." She looked at him hard, no fraud in her tone. "Try me. Love will make you act stupid."

Marlene's lips continued to move and the head of the dead female were-jaguar began to smolder on the ground. The old vampire screeched, and sent a bolt of electrified fury toward Marlene, but the protective crystal breastplate she wore reflected it and sent it back to him. Seconds mattered. His semidisoriented state had been their salvation.

As the old master fell to the dirt beside the severed head, Big Mike tossed Damali a holy-water vile, and she caught it quickly. Vlak raised his hand to send a dark arc toward Damali, and as he moved, the were-jaguar demons nearby rushed him. Damali cast the vile hard, smashing it at the head of the creature next to Vlak.

Blue flames covered and spread from the incinerating head. Vlak's robes combusted on contact with the edge of the holy water's band of flame. Thick, black clouds plumed around him. But through the blackness, eleven white beams of energy immediately shot up—connecting to a single, wide amethyst beam of light that met them.

"The ancient Neteru collects her team . . ." Marlene's voice trailed off in awe.

Despite the majesty of the event, Damali didn't waste time while Vlak was deconstructing. His awful, screeching cries made the audio-sensitive guardians stoop and cover their ears.

It was not about leaving Vlak's end up to chance. Damali knew that with a vampire that old, one could never be too sure. Madame Isis raised, she looked Vlak dead in the eyes for just a second, added a smile, and plunged the Isis with her full weight behind it. "Rest in peace!"

She jumped back, hearing the high whine of energy gathering—then covered her head for the boom. The team was knocked off their feet from Vlak's body explosion, splattered with ash, and left coughing and sputtering as they stood up quickly.

"Blow the lair," she told Big Mike, snatching the Amazon's battle-ax out of the slit cavern wall. "Holy water this area down! Remove all traces of ripening Neteru in the air!"

Damali was running, helping people to their feet. "We gotta get out of here before they send up a search party—you don't just nuke a council-level vamp and not expect them to check it out! C'mon! And the level-five demons that were supposed to witness this ritual—to be sure their interests were protected, will come up through the lair breach . . . it's gotta be in their zone. We ain't outta the jungle yet! Let's move!"

"What are you saying?" The chairman screeched, leaning over the Vampire Council's table. "You and Counselor Vlak may have your differences, but he is still a ranking—"

"Look at me," Carlos said, breathing hard, his eyes set hard. "Do I look normal?"

A murmur went through the three seated council members.

"Where would I get a hit of ripened Neteru? I had international couriers with me! Look in my eyes—see for yourself!"

Three sets of cool, steely eyes gripped Carlos, and he could feel his stomach move and a sharp pain enter his intestines, dropping him to his knees before the council.

"Your charges are beyond sheer arrogance, it's pure hubris that has possessed you! I will rip out your gizzards and feed upon them myself," the old chairman warned. "If I sense duplicity . . ."

"Damali is out of phase, but you've got a level-five breach," he panted. "Our Neteru in a demon hot zone, and one senior council member about to turn a five-hundred-year-old, risen-demon, Amazon warrior, a trained Neteru guardian fighter, on her—then start a new empire with her."

"How can that be?" the chairman said, running his bony hand over his chin, but releasing Carlos from the painful hold. "There was no Neteru before Nzinga within the five-hundred-year range . . ."

The chairman's voice trailed off as he realized he gave Carlos too much information—highly guarded data only known at throne level. Carlos didn't blink, but the fact that it wasn't just an early sent Amazon Neteru, or Damali in the equation, another Neteru had been sent, too . . . all within a very short period of time. A trinity of them? And that info was so guarded that only old council seats knew? No wonder Nuit was so frantic to claim Damali. It was more than just daylight access, or even world domination. The last one bridged the millennium, and anything that created daylight capacities in the demon realms in this era was . . . they might try to rush even Heaven. These bastards were crazy. Oh, shit it was on. The Armageddon.

"All of this is speculation," the chairman said, coolly recovering. "Even if your claims about this demon are correct, her womb is dead."

Carlos nodded, standing with effort, using the seconds to work on his game. "She's got daylight—he's risking to do a black blood exchange—"

"Never . . ."

Carlos nodded. "Supernatural law; the demons tricked the Neteru's mother-seer, the mother-seer is doing time for the crime. But she wants out bad. She came to Vlak with a proposal after she became a were-demon, and Vlak saw an opening." He looked at the chairman hard. "You think he's out searching for my soul, don't you? Well, last night he came to see me just before dawn to strip my ass of pride and to get me to go against you. He's known where my soul is all along."

When the chairman didn't immediately answer, Carlos pressed on. "He sent his twisted demon bitch to my lair to pollute the perimeter with her hijacked scent during the day while he and I both slept. He's smart enough to stay away from it; is probably lying low and told her not to trail it into the mating dens . . . but when I woke up, it hit me. It leads a trail right to her dens, but probably not in it, where Vlak will be to ensure the exchange goes down right."

"Impossible. How did you break away from the trail?" the chairman said with fury in his eyes, but his tone not quite as sure as it had been. "If it was ripened Neteru . . ."

"The demon's batch is synthetic product, tainted, not as strong as the pure stuff. Its will-polluting effect is only temporary—like a quick rush . . . leaves you high, but not totally stupid-blitzed. That's what gave me a half-ounce of common sense to pull up from the trail and come here, first, to report in." Carlos opened his arms wide; the old men were wasting time and frustration was drilling a hole in his brain. "But you'd better kill me now if you think I'm not going back topside tonight."

The chairman's gaze narrowed. "I assure you we can accommodate your request here in chambers."

"What part about this don't you get?" he said louder than advisable. "Damali is *out of phase,* and you *know* that—which means I had to get this contraband from somewhere!" Carlos paused, trying to regain enough control to sound respectful—but if the old vamps didn't know for sure about the demon, had only heard rumors and only Vlak had solid proof . . . something happened at the borders of Purgatory . . . the forces of light had to be losing strength against evil on the planet. Now he understood the Covenant's haste and need to make every soul count, better understood his position in the equation, too. Very interesting . . .

"If I go back up and take another hit, Mr. Chairman, I could abort the whole mission by accidentally destroying our cargo because this is in my system. If the demon ain't around, I could hemorrhage Damali or kill her, if she gets in between me and whatever's trailing false Neteru, you know the outcome. The demon plans to double-cross Vlak and come out of the fusion then whack our vessel, or set me up to do it, so that she's the sole source of the daylight option. When I thought she was one of us, I did a mind lock with her, messing around . . . I went back in high—trust me, I'm much stronger than her under these conditions."

Renewed rage entered Carlos as the old men at the council table simply stared at him. The look of outright shock on the chairman's face helped Carlos build his case.

"Vlak is so stupid and so desperate for power that he doesn't see it! He not only betrayed us, but he's put our package in jeopardy, if his twisted plan fails." Carlos rubbed his face with both hands. "I need something to come down, man, before I go topside again." It was the stone-cold truth. His hands were shaking. "I've gotta get Damali out of harm's way for the empire. I need your help. Stop fucking with me and let me do my job."

The council ignored Carlos for a moment and conferred.

"Vlak would take such a risk, at his age?" the chairman asked evenly. "He would need insurance." His gaze narrowed on Carlos. "Wouldn't he?"

Nodding quickly, Carlos stepped forward, feeling the effects of Neteru rocking his concentration. Only the depth of his subterranean meeting was helping, but he knew it would be all over as soon as he hit topside—if they didn't gut him down here. "Vlak has been lying to us all. That stupid bastard allowed my soul to get dragged into Purgatory!" Carlos forced feigned rage, which wasn't hard to do with ripe Neteru in his system. "He lost mine! I'm doomed!"

A bolt of red, crackling current slammed into Carlos's chest. Were it not for the additional bulk from the ripened Neteru scent in his system and protective brand, his heart would be lying on the marble floor.

Bending over, his hands on his knees, Carlos sucked in huge inhales through his mouth. His eyes were shut tight as the fire of pain tore through his lungs, chest cavity, and began to ignite his liver.

The chairman had rounded the table with the others, which surrounded him. He snatched Carlos's chin up, making the sweat that ran down his face fling off it. "Tell me why, a man with such redemption options, would be standing in my sacred chambers telling me about a potential coup . . . one coming from a council seat, from a trusted adviser I have known for several thousand years!"

"Because I wanted the power." Carlos could feel his jaw crushing as the chairman's red glowing eyes went black. "But Vlak forgot a variable."

The two stared at each other and the chairman slowly released his grip. Carlos's chest heaved.

"I can't go against the vampire that made me . . . he told me who delivered the bite."

The chairman's hand lowered and he placed his hands behind his back.

"I didn't want to be in Purgatory, after having a chance to sit in Nuit's abandoned throne." What Carlos said was true but it could be taken in two ways. He knew which way the vampires before him would take it; they had a blind spot created by their evil perspective.

The chairman nodded, then rubbed his jaw. His fangs retracted, and he swept away toward the table, the others following him. Taking his time, he sat slowly, and after he did, the two others seated themselves at his left.

"I was willing to wait seven years for the chance to be made council. Ask your couriers; we all tried our best to keep your cargo out of harm's way. But Vlak put her in danger with his fucked-up plan, and was going to use my body—no self-respecting master would allow it. You know that."

The chairman nodded. "And, with my bite, you were strong enough to resist Vlak . . . were strong enough to drag yourself here even with ripe Neteru in your system. You also feared me more than him." He paused, his gaze raking Carlos. "Good," he finally said with a low hiss. "Wise choice."

The old vampire leveled his gaze on Carlos then looked away in the distance, thinking. "That I can believe, because you were made by the top of this empire." He nodded again. "Thank you. Your report has been most helpful. We will deal with Counselor Vlak in our own way. You may go. Bring me back my cargo."

Carlos shook his head, making the council go still. "I can't. That's what I've been trying to tell you," he said honestly, his gaze tearing between the council members. "Has it been so long since you've been topside?"

Their expressions held a lack of comprehension.

"I've got *ripe* Neteru in my system—but your cargo isn't ripe! Yeah, I can get her out of the Amazon, with some demon breach-sealers with me as backup, but I'll injure her. She'll hemorrhage internally. Don't you remem—"

"Yes," the chairman said, standing. "We'll have to send somebody else."

"But it's my mission!" Carlos was pacing in an agitated line. "Don't you have an antidote for this shit at your rank?"

The chairman looked at the others who shook their heads. "There's only one . . . and we have to destroy Vlak to do it. That will take time to locate him and corner him." The old vampire sighed and studied his claws. "The elixir from our table keeps us refined, balanced, and very strong while here—as our physical strength has ebbed over the years. But do not toy with our mental capacity, Carlos. Topside, you could have beaten Vlak. Why didn't you, especially with what courses through your system?"

"Because," Carlos said, combining the truth with the deception, "he also left me vulnerable when he lost my soul."

All the senior vampires looked at him, and Carlos saw that as his next in.

"Until you guys figure out a way to retrieve it, I have a weak spot for this Neteru. I would rather see her sire daywalkers willingly, to help our cause—even if I have to work on her for the duration of seven short years—than to see her emotions butchered by plagues." He took a deep breath, holding their gazes. "You have seen how effective I've been in swaying her to our side, haven't you? She's drawn to me *because* I have a piece of soul left—even I didn't understand that. She a Neteru, and could sense it. But I'm using it for the empire, and I'm patient, can wait for my opportunity . . . let's use it to work her. If you send somebody else, she'll fight to the death and may get injured or die—but she'll come to me, and only me!"

The chairman offered a lopsided smile and nodded.

"I've *proven* my loyalty by using my weakness to your advantage. For the dark realms, I was already marked. That's fact. I was turned during the commission of a crime—fact. I was supposed to be full-fledged, but was somehow robbed. I figured, fair exchange is no robbery . . . but I'm no fool. I wouldn't hurt the only chance we have to strengthen the empire. That's why I came here—home, first, and didn't go with Vlak, or try to follow the plan myself, using the Amazon."

The room went very, very still, save the screeches of the bats.

"When a council seat is lost, the throne runs black blood from that senior officer. The history of the event immediately burns into the arch of the seat. The only antidote for ripened Neteru is for a council member to be slain by a Neteru—and when the throne runs red blood, we can give the affected master a sip."

The chairman let out his breath hard and pointed to each throne. "Masters have been killed by a Neteru, that is the ongoing struggle . . . see for yourself in the high histories. But never has a slayer taken out one of our Vampire Council chairs. It would mean a search for a very crafty, and very old council member—and we'd have to allow her to kill him in order to remedy your condition."

The chairman chuckled. "Ah, the conundrum. While I have no problem in exterminating Counselor Vlak with my own bare hands, you would never be able to tolerate the wait while we found him, bound him, and brought her before the chair to kill him. We would have to exterminate you, just to get the act completed."

Leaning forward on the pentagram-shaped table, the chairman sighed, holding Carlos with an empathetic, but smug, stare. "My suggestion, then, is that you remain on the sixth level for a few evenings until our border patrols find and eliminate Vlak. We will perform the ceremony on the ancient Amazon ourselves, and will ensure the current Neteru's safety, but won't abduct her to cause her to fight us or sustain injury. We'll allow you to guard the younger vessel, as a reward for marvelous undercover work—once you have collected yourself. You're right; if she's with you willingly, then you're our safest long-term containment strategy—and your soul can stay where it is, until the seventh year . . . it's best to keep her confused . . . might even render her team and the Covenant off guard. But this is so very interesting . . . two available vessels, only seven years apart. Wonderful variable; unprecedented opportunity." He laughed deep and low in his throat. "Thank you, Mr. Rivera. You are amazing."

Carlos nodded. But pure defeat stripped every option away from his mind. Humiliated by his condition, and knowing that now they'd really do everything in their power to sway his soul just as Damali was ripening, made his shoulders slump. The word was out; his soul was hanging in the balance up in Purgatory. At least they still thought he was pissed off about that fact, and it being there made it impossible for them to read his mind at will.

The only small glimmer of hope within the travesty was the fact that they wouldn't hurt Damali, or her people. Greed was their imperative. They wouldn't jeopardize two shots at creating daywalkers, and that was the only thing he could hold onto.

There was nothing else to do but chill and suck it up. Still reeling from the effects of the intoxicant in his system, and slightly weakened by the council's initial angry beat-down, he knew he had to be hallucinating. Carlos laughed as he turned to walk away, wiping his nose with the back of his hand. Yeah, right, Vlak had gotten his heart cut out and his throne is running red. It wasn't even midnight. Boss would last more than a few hours topside, old and treacherous as he was. In his wildest dreams.

But sudden hisses and commotion behind Carlos made him turn around. He froze with the others, their eyes on Vlak's throne that had come to life in a red gurgling stream. The inscription within the arch of it flashed with a blue-white light that made them all cover their eyes. Then the light vanished, leaving a burning brand of a Neteru sword with a glowing date in the blade handle. Carlos stepped forward slowly as the glow of the date abated. Immediately a searing sound cracked into the throne's black marble, and a new etching began. A name was written.

Spellbound, the vampires stared at the inscription. The chairman dumped out the contents of his goblet and pressed the empty chalice against the bleeding arm of the throne, lifting it toward Carlos. They all understood. If Vlak was dead, so was the demon, so was the second option to make daywalkers—option one, Damali, was at risk.

"Give the man an army and strengthen Rivera's borders from every quadrant in the empire," the chairman said with controlled panic. "ASAP." His eyes narrowed. "This vessel is so much more than the millennium slayer, Carlos. She sways the Armageddon . . . was delivered five hundred years early, which is how we know the hour draws near. We did not even speak of it at the table before, because you were too new, and this was of such magnitude. However, with her squarely at risk in demon territory, you must be clear that no cost is too great to ensure her safe return. Now, do you understand? The precious nature of this cargo to our side is beyond measure."

He stared at the chairman. His instincts had been correct. The information slowly entered his mind, toppling one epiphany against the

next like mental dominoes falling. Yes, she was definitely precious beyond measure, and Vlak would have never given her up—even seven
years from now. Carlos knew in every fiber of his being now that
Vlak would have used him as a security guard to keep competitors
away while he was empire-building, then double-crossed him, killed
him, and added Damali to his stable, derailing anything she would
have accomplished during the big war.

For a fleeting moment, Carlos wondered if Damali even knew how
serious her role was. Then he shook the concept. Of course she had
to, Marlene and company had been schooling her for years. Pride for
her filled him instantly, as did the understanding of who she really
was. Respect . . . damn, she was the Neteru. It wasn't an intellectual
understanding anymore, clouded by passion, or the way he'd found
her in the streets all those years ago.

Carlos smiled, his voice a reverent whisper. "My baby's making
history."

The blast from Big Mike's charges flashed orange-red, and sent huge
chunks of dirt, rock, and foliage hurling into the jungle. The team
dropped, the ground beneath them unstable, as the explosion began a
rain of rock and dirt upon them from the side of the cliff. Frenzied
bats screeched and sought available escape paths. Righting themselves,
and racing toward the tunnels that brought them to the top, the team
scrambled to get out of the cave.

Damali shot out in front, leading the group through pitch blackness
from memory. There wasn't even enough light for her night vision to
be fully effective. But with what little she could sense, she got the
squad back to the center of the cavern where the were-jaguars had
ambushed them, the team feeling the walls blindly with their gun barrels angled down to avoid shooting a fellow teammate by accident.
When her foot struck something soft, Damali almost jumped out of
her skin. But then she remembered, and made the team come to a halt.

"I don't know if we can carry our man with us," she told the
group sadly, "even though we never leave our own."

They gathered around their dead man, but even Kamal shook his
head. They didn't have the manpower to carry Dominique as well as
the footlocker, and be alert.

"Anoint him here," Kamal said fast. "He was already were-human, and has been bitten again by were-demon—at least our man deserves to ascend."

Marlene hurried as the tunnel continued to rain rock.

"I'll carry him for you, brother," Big Mike boomed.

Drum put his hand on Mike's shoulder. "His body is jus' flesh and goes back to the earth. Long's we get his soul out, we, from our team, are cool with it. But, thank you."

Mike nodded, though Drum couldn't see the response. Damali glanced around in the darkness, seeing nothing, as Marlene quickly concluded, sensing where to drop a vial of holy water on Dominique's missing chest.

Just as she was about to tell the group to move, glowing green-and-gold eyes from every imaginable ledge appeared. Sulfur smoke filled the tunnel. Big Mike and Dan lobbed holy water grenades, and for three seconds of bright light amid horrible demon screeches, the team saw what they were up against. Pure Hell.

It was as though the entire demon world had evacuated the subterranean space they occupied and had descended on the cavern. Kamal's men were gagging, the grenades nearly felling them. It was clear that the ancient warrior had meant more to them than the vampire nation, and they had sent up serious representation to ensure no double-cross from Vlak.

Deformed animal shapes grotesquely fused with human forms stood poised for attack once the holy water rings began to burn off. Guardians quickly paired up with Kamal's men, trying to help their comrades, but also trying to keep themselves covered with weapons at the same time.

Acid-dripping fangs had flashed in the light, massive hooked claws had shielded hideous glowing eyes from the glare, greenish rotting skin befouled the air—this was the demon realm's warrior team.

In a unified thought, the human squadron opened fire, sending automatic-weapon magazine releases against demon targets that exploded, scrambled, and lunged again. It was like the things were splitting, multiplying as the guardian and were-human teams cut a path, backing into an open tunnel on the run, Mike and Drum hurling C-4 bricks and grenades behind them to seal off a path.

"Roll call!" Damali yelled, as they found a temporary shelter. "Anybody hurt?"

"No, we good!" Kamal hollered back. Rocks behind them made the group press forward, but as soon as they rounded the corner, Damali held out both hands. They were at the mouth of the booby-trapped tunnel. Behind them was half of Hell, before them was sudden death.

"Shit!"

"What's up, D—we gotta roll."

"Rider, this is the tunnel we were supposed to be sending the bad guys into."

"Oh, shit," Shabazz muttered.

"Send a crossbow stake through it—see how bad . . ."

Kamal's words tapered off as a low hissing sound filled their tunnel. It was coming from outside the cave, and in seconds a huge black snakehead eclipsed the moon. The thing's skull and jaws were the size of a Honda, and when its eyes flashed green, it unhinged its jaw to bear fangs as long as a tall man.

"I think we could use your shoulder cannons now, gentlemen," Damali whispered as the serpent slowly eased its way into the tunnel, viciously snapping in the process. "Let him get in good, so we don't miss . . . they move fast, I saw one in action."

Mike and Drum just nodded. The scratching at the blocked opening behind them had ceased, and the growls and screeches seemed to be moving, like the fight was going on outside now—probably to join this thing for dinner, Damali woefully thought.

But as the monster got fifty yards away from the team, a snap sounded, the beast looked up, and huge wooden spears impaled it. Furious, wounded, but not mortally so, it struggled against the spikes, slamming its head against the sides and ceiling of the tunnel, causing an avalanche from the commotion. Taking quick aim, Mike and Drum sent twin bazooka blasts at the creature, which blew it out of the tunnel, clearing the way.

The team was about to run forward, but Damali held up her hand, finding a rock, hurling it to the midsection of the tunnel, and the false floor gave way, revealing pikes. The problem was, however, pikes weren't the only things down there. The pit writhed and swelled with serpentine energy. Wet, slimy things half human and half snake unwound from the stakes and moved toward the group.

The team unleashed everything they had—automatics, crossbow

shots, holy water bombs, Damali taking swipes at things overhead with Madame Isis and the Amazon's battle-ax, dropping hissing heads as Marlene defended against them and batted them away with her stick. Artillery low, the things just kept coming, and then for no reason, retreated.

Huffing from exertion, the team stared at Damali—who stared at Kamal and his crew, then her gaze shot to Jose.

"Incoming," Jose said quietly, as the spent were-human team nodded, gagged, and looked like they would vomit from all the holy water smoke in tight confines.

Two of Kamal's men dropped, and neither their teammates nor members from Damali's guardian team could immediately help them up. She glanced at the fallen men with panic, as Drum weaved and Big Mike caught him under his arm.

"The sulfur. We've gotta get Kamal's men out, fast. So we're gonna have to creep along the sides while the enemy regroups. It's our only way out, but we have to leave the footlocker. It's too unstable, a man could fall, Kamal's men are getting sicker . . . plus, these things could snatch any of us down there at any second."

The team members murmured an uneasy agreement as Damali stepped forward, her boots crumbling rock and dirt along the edge. There was *nothing* to hold onto. The walls were slimy and slick, the soft edging was only four inches wide, and she was physically the lightest-weight member in the group. Big Mike and Drum would never make it. She glanced back, and returned to the squads, shaking her head.

"We're fucking trapped," Rider said quietly.

Growls made the group train its focus on the open, but inaccessible cave exit.

"We'll bring you over," a familiar voice said, materializing with a twenty-vampire squad.

The team just stared at Carlos, slowly raising weapons like Damali had told them to do. But the sheer size of him, as well as his squad that covered the entrance, gave the entire guardian and were-human team pause. Damali could not breathe. She was going to have to watch his beheading, if not do it herself. Her grip tightened on the Amazon's battle-ax, and Madame Isis. Several, if not all of her team members would die.

Carlos looked more pumped than he had in the tunnels before, when the entire team battled Nuit. His fangs were down at the ten-inch battle length; his eyes were solid red, his chest and shoulder enormous beneath black camouflage fatigues. His Green Beret–looking henchmen had no faces, just red glowing eyes within a black haze under hooded robes, and their arms were as thick as two of Big Mike's. Battle-axes in hand, they snarled and surrounded Carlos, who took a step forward, motioning for them to not enter the holy water smoked cavern with him.

"Steady, gentlemen," Damali murmured. "On my order—'cause you'd better not miss."

"What! Woman, are you crazy?" Carlos backed up, shook his head, and his henchmen growled. "We ain't got time for no theatrics! The gatekeeper Amanthra is down, we got a bunch of the weres, but you know in a minute, they'll be back at us—two levels of bullshit, D. This is a level-four and -five breach! So stop playing around!"

"I'm not playing, Carlos. You've got ripe Neteru—"

"I don't—"

"Then why do you look like that?" she shouted, her team holding, readied for the word.

"Because we been kickin' ass to give you a fucking chance to get out of here!"

"How'd you get the Neteru out your system, dude?" Rider shouted, unable to contain himself.

"Damali killed Vlak with the Isis, I was in chambers trying to raise a squad when the chair bled! Now, c'mon! We ain't got a lot of time!"

"Can you read him, D?" Shabazz said fast. "Get a bead on—"

"No! We don't have time for that!" Carlos was walking a hot line back and forth in front of the cave.

"Want us to extract the cargo, boss?" one of Carlos's entities asked with a glare. "We *can* go get her, if you want . . . as long as we don't get slashed, we can—"

"Oh, my God," she whispered, her gaze going to Marlene. "I'm cargo?"

"See, man! Shut up," Carlos fussed. "No. I'll go get her, because she'll start her team shooting and shit, and one of them might get fucked up if you guys go off."

"You damned straight dis joint'll be lit the fuck up, mon, you try en

grab de gurl. Not with ripe Neteru in your system. We go out moth-
erfuckin' swingin', boss—you know dat. You in our house out here!"

Shabazz pounded Kamal's fist, as the human squad held their
weapons tighter.

"Oh, shit . . ." Carlos began walking in a circle as his own team
growled. "Why, Damali, would you stand in front of an Amazon, tell
her all the shit you know about me is true, then be scared of what you
saw in a fantasy, huh? Damn, girl, you are pissing me off!"

"You heard what I said to her?" Damali cast a glance at her team,
which began to look confused.

"I was down there in council chambers getting my ass kicked,
okay? I was begging them to let me come up here and get you, told
them about Vlak's bullshit, and needed something, *anything,* to bring
me down so I could deal—and you are up here, yelling at the top of
your lungs about all the shit I did for you!"

He punched the cave wall, making part of it crumble. "Telling *all*
my fucking business, about the desert thing, and everything—and
now, you won't come with me so I can keep demons off your ass?" He
walked away. "I'm done. Just fuckin' done."

Carlos's henchmen cast nervous glances between the retreating
master vampire and the huddle of humans in the cave.

"Yo, boss," one of them hollered. "Whatchu want us to do with
the cargo, man?"

"Let the demons eat her and her squad! Half of 'em are were-
humans, anyway!" Carlos yelled back over his shoulder. "I can't take
anymore! This is the most *stubborn,* off-the-hook woman in the universe!"

Carlos spun on the confused henchmen, pointing a finger at them.
"Do you know, *this* is the woman who made a throne run red blood
in *council* chambers, first one in history to do a high-ranking council
member—her damned sword is branded in Vlak's throne—so don't
be crazy and go in there for her. Leave her. The demons want to wipe
out the vamp daywalker vessel, since theirs is gone. Her stubborn ass
will see when all the demons on levels four and five come up here. We
seal the level breaches, and I'm going to eat. I'm done." Carlos turned
his back to her and began walking while muttering. "Dusted almost
all my second-generations in my territory to keep her safe—for what?

Now I bring an army to save her, and she's arguing with me? Fuck it!"

Damali looked at her team, and they simply stared back at her, weapons lowering.

"Damn, gurl," Kamal murmured. "You hit a throne?"

"Yo, D, think you should ease up on your boy . . . seems to me like he's cool, and all . . . might get us out?" Big Mike shrugged and glanced at the others.

"Hey, let's not allow a little domestic difficulties to ruin the party," Rider quipped, glancing nervously toward Carlos. "Yo, man, she didn't mean it!" He looked back at Damali who bristled. "Did ya, hon?"

Begrudgingly, she sucked in a huge inhale and hollered Carlos's name, but he didn't answer.

"Aw, shit," Jose replied on a dejected note, as the henchmen started disappearing. "I think this time . . . ya know . . . I mean, even his brother and the rest of his posse was in that second-generation tier."

"I think our brother is straight, D," Marlene murmured. "That other stuff you saw, he didn't bring that right now."

Marlene was the only one that cut through her defenses. Damali let out her breath hard and folded her arms over her chest, a weapon in each fist. "Carlos," Damali yelled, "fine! Squash the other shit—we'll take that up later. Aw'ight, we could use a hand."

Carlos spun on her, stopping his retreating and confused squad. "No, you don't! You don't need me," he hollered back. He looked at his men, then at her trapped teams. "I saw you do some incredible shit." His voice mellowed. "I was so damned proud of you, I almost got smoked in council." He nodded to the messengers. "Say what you want, girlfriend is baaaad. Dusted a treasonous councilman, fucked up a rebel master—killed Nuit's ass with a prayer as she planted her sword. Did a drag race to protect my turf, rode shotgun with me . . . and kicked that bitch's ass up there, then served her a head trip like I ain't never seen. My boo is awesome."

He let his breath out hard, and studied her teams. "You all don't know what you've got on your side. Shit . . . I ain't messin' with her when she's like this. Naw, I ain't the one; I know better." He glared at Damali, but it softened as he looked at her. "You were right, my bad. I mean it, and I've even said it in front of your squad and mine. What else you want from me? I said I was sorry." He turned and walked away. "Plus, you've got a damned army in there, and can handle yourself without me."

Kamal moved from the middle of the huddle to stand by Damali and quietly spoke to her. "Call de man right, chile. I showed you— use da balm. Den apologize right, later. A man's pride is a terrible thing, and at the moment, his is beat down hard, and he needs it. That ain't changed since the beginning of time, and won't tonight, even in dis new millennium. You won. You the Neteru, that ain't changed neither—and nobody can take that from you . . . so don't cut off your nose to spite your face, proving what don't need ta be proved. Not out here."

She was about to fuss, but Kamal cut her off as Carlos and his men disappeared. "He got shit wit him, you got shit wit you . . . you right for wondering, he wrong for makin' you wonder . . . he right for coming when you needed him, you wrong for being ornery when he did—so squash the bullshit, and get our teams outta here."

Weary, Damali raised her hand and closed her eyes. She just wanted to go home. She just wanted to take a shower. She just wanted to sleep on clean sheets in an air-conditioned room with no bugs. She just wanted everybody to be all right. No more causalities, not even a hangnail. She just wanted poor Kamal to be able to bury his man in peace. She wanted to be off the fucking Amazon River and away from a foreign country . . . she didn't want to be dealing with demons. Her body hurt from almost getting her ass kicked, her man was bugging—

"You almost got your ass kicked?" Carlos was walking down the center of the tunnel, oblivious to the fact that it had no floor, and there were pikes below. He just strode across the expanse; his jaw set hard as Damali's team pointed gun barrels to the floor without blinking.

"She hit you in your face?" he asked, galled, turning Damali's cheek to the side gingerly with two fingers. "You know . . ." He shook his head, and called over his shoulder to his squad. "Clear that fucking exit and get my woman out of this insect-infested bullshit, would you!" He took Damali by the hand and began walking, but she hesitated.

Carlos let out his breath. "Girl, you oughta know me better than that."

"It ain't you, it's the ground, or the lack thereof," she said fast, her team peering over the edge of it with her.

"Like I said," he repeated with a hard snap of his fingers, making the cave floor solid and passable. "You oughta know me better than that."

Not even a cicada, mosquito, or water flea moved as the team got onto the barge with twenty-one extra passengers. Every human on the boat just took a very still corner of it, or sat on a box, but nobody was trying to say anything that could light a match.

Carlos materialized on the second level and walked up to Kamal. Nervous looks passed through the group, but again, no one said a word. "You the one who taught her how to refine her technique?"

"The balm," Kamal said cautiously.

Carlos nodded, glancing at Damali who was sitting on a crate, a battle-ax in one hand, a sword in the other, glowering at him. "Don't know whether to thank you, or rip your heart out, man."

Everybody bristled, even the vampire breach-sweepers that patrolled the decks for security.

"Was just jokin', man." Carlos chuckled. Kamal visibly relaxed. "Damn. Everybody's so jumpy."

"Like *nobody* has a reason to have their nerves fried after this fun adventure? A must-see for the guided Amazon tour brochures." Rider shook his head.

At first the flippant comment tensed the group to a danger level. The twenty security vampires on the decks stopped walking, and looked at Carlos as though not sure if a death reprimand was coming in Rider's direction. Every human muscle coiled, waiting for Rider to have gone too far this time. Rider simply spit in the water and leaned against the ammunitions crate. Carlos burst out laughing.

It was as though the echo had released the night sounds. The insects came back; crocks felt it was safe to slip back in the water. Owls took off from branches so they could go hunting again. The trees released their evening chorus-line show of bats. And one by one the laughter ignited, sending everyone into an unstoppable release of tension. Even Damali was laughing, and just gave up on being on guard.

"Oh, what the fuck . . . I'm so tired," she wheezed through the giggles. "Have you ever?"

"Y'all are cool," Carlos said, still chuckling. "Me and my boyz got everything locked down till dawn—by then, you'll be back in Manaus, can take your flights, and backtrack home. Damn, what a night." He glanced around one last time, letting his gaze settle on Damali for a minute. "Me and the boyz gotta go eat—we used up a lot of energy back there . . . but, you know, call me later, baby."

She smiled.

"Kamal gave you my pager number," Carlos said, chuckling deeper, moving toward her but not coming in close. "You already had my private cell digits."

She laughed. Kamal smiled.

"We'll see," she said, swallowing a smile and looking away toward the black water.

Carlos shrugged. "If you get tired of the bugs . . . want a hot shower . . . don't wanna wait in the airport lines . . . I might be able to find a good bottle of wine and a gourmet dinner—if a sister would act right."

"Damn, man, keep talking like that, and I'll go with you—a hot shower and no bugs?" Big Mike pounded Carlos's fist, then laughed. "Sheeit. Better act like you know."

She smiled, cocked her head to the side. "We'll see."

Carlos nodded, gave her a wide grin, and vanished with his team.

Marlene chuckled and folded her arms over her chest. "You gonna call him and take the short way home, or what, chile? Lemme know so we can figure out the passport problem."

"No worries," Kamal said with a sly smile, going down to the first deck. "I know some people who know some people if she needs a stamp to show she took the regular way home."

"Y'all putting me off the boat?" Damali shook her head, amused, but relieved, and yet too tired to think about any of it.

"Oh shit!" Drum's voice echoed in the night, bringing the entire squad to the front of the vessel.

Drum was peering down over the lifeless body of their fallen man, Dominique. His chest, face, and throat had been repaired, and it only appeared as though the young man was sleeping. The older warrior from Kamal's squad swallowed hard as he knelt beside the dead man and handed the note that was attached to Dominique's vest up to Kamal, who only nodded and closed his eyes.

"Class . . ." Kamal murmured. "Brother said to bury our own right."

"Damn," Shabazz whispered. "That's deep . . . was real cool of Rivera."

Marlene looked at Damali, and then glanced around at the faces that stood dumbfounded and a grin slowly captured her face. "Yeah, girl, we're putting you off this boat."

Damali nodded with a half smile. "That's cool. I got his new digits. But first, I'm calling my soul sister, Inez." Marlene gave her a knowing smile. "I've learned a little patience. The man can wait... Carlos Rivera ain't rushing me."

EPILOGUE

Three nights later . . .

"MARLENE SAID the Vlak hit and the Amazon soul recovery wrote itself into the *Neteru Temt Tchaas*—that book actually authors itself when stuff goes down," Damali murmured, looking over her glass of wine. She smiled and raised her eyebrow, gauging Carlos's suddenly poker-faced expression. "Her guardians are no longer scorched out of the book."

"Yeah," he said in a forced casual tone, sending his line of vision beyond the deck toward the ocean. He wondered what the text might write about him one day, or Damali? If Damali was here to sway the balance of the Armageddon, then what role would he play? He was a part of the drama somehow, too . . . or else he wouldn't be in her space. He was beginning to understand the clerics' interest in him more and more. He wondered if she thought about things like that?

But the problem was, he'd not only had a seat in Nuit's old throne, but had also taken *a sip* from a black throne. The power of that combination left little room for deniability; he was a dark guardian growing darker. Shit . . . he needed to be real; he was a master vampire, council-level now. And what Damali could never understand was the fact that now a little of Nuit and Vlak was in him, he was stronger than she could imagine, and his thirst for power had just been heightened by a jolt from the old Roman Empire. "That's cool," he said after a moment. "I never got the twisted one's name."

Damali chuckled. "Uhmmm-hmmm, I know," she said standing, not answering his unspoken question. She set down her glass, sashayed out toward the moonlight, and held onto the rail, giving him a mischievous glance over her shoulder. "I'll never tell you that, brother."

Coming up behind her, he laughed low next to her ear. "See, why you keep going there, woman?"

"Father Patrick said, 'Hi,' " she replied, chuckling deeper, avoiding the question and another caress. "The fellas are doing well, too. Kamal's crew is most excellent and said thanks again for what you did for them and Dominique. But poor Padre Lopez . . ." She winked at him and her smile widened.

"Is he all right?" Carlos asked, truly concerned. Guilt accosted him as he thought back on the images he'd sent the young priest.

"What did you do to him, Carlos?" She was smiling brightly with her head cocked to the side, pure mischief glittering in her eyes.

"*That,* I'll *never* tell you," he said, grinning despite his concern. "But is the man okay?"

"They wouldn't explain his issues, but said he's going into the Episcopal seminary since he really wants to get married, but still wants to be a man of the cloth." She made a little tsking sound with her tongue and giggled. "Carlos Rivera, you should be ashamed of yourself. Ten demerits and twenty-five Hail Mary's."

He laughed. "Well, at least I didn't bite him. And he's still on his own religious path . . . even if celibacy is gonna be a problem for him, now." Carlos sent his gaze out into the night and shook his head. This had been some mad-crazy drama.

She cast a sheepish glance in his direction, which he tried his best to ignore. "Oh, yeah," she said in a merry tone. "Kamal hooked up my passport—his peeps are good. Everybody is cool. And a little birdie told Berkfield that you had fled the country, so that poor man could rest. He was worried about you, too, Carlos, strange as that might sound. He was seriously relieved when he found out you weren't dead."

"He's cool people," Carlos replied in a distant voice, still thinking about all the human beings he'd affected one way or another. He wouldn't verbally address the fact that they all seemed to forget; he *was* dead. But the way she kept glancing at him with a teasing, playful expression made him reach for her.

She squealed and dodged his touch, hopping down the deck steps out onto a grassy clearing. She spun around under the moonlight, her arms wide, laughing, and intermittently running from his grasp, making him laugh, too.

"You need to stop messing with me, girl," he warned playfully, but loving every minute of the way she made him feel. There were moments with her that he actually felt free and alive. She was the only one that seemed to be able to make him laugh, really laugh, hard from way down in his soul.

"What's the matter?"

"Nothing," he said by rote, then forced himself to smile. He sat down on the grass and looked out at the stars, just listening to the ocean pound the cliffs and the shore.

The thought of his soul was sobering, and he eclipsed her view of what was truly on his mind. The reality of the future and his new appointment to a dark throne weighed heavily on his conscience. He was more than a master, he was a council level vampire with province over an army, had continents at his behest, and after Nuit's demise, there were only four other masters topside running Asia and Europe, Africa, and Australia. North and South America, plus the Caribbean, were his. It was a serious responsibility.

They now wanted him to rule from a cavern below, and to possibly make another master and to carve up some of his old turf for the Aussie, to cover what would then be his open territories in South America and North America. That would bring the world pentagram back into alignment. Council would have the six available continent and fertile holdings from each area, and level seven would go after the biblical city where it all began. They wanted him in the war room planning the Armageddon with them. Too crazy.

And how did one choose to take a life, drop a body, and turn it into something abominable, after all he'd seen and all he now knew? He'd have to find someone with hatred and power-lust in their soul, a willing person like that, and bring them into his fold, according to the council. Then he'd have to surround himself with a team of five made lieutenants, one from each territory that reported to a topside master, and that had once been like him—on a mission, jaded, and with no remorse. It would be a power trust of nearly invincible vampires wreaking havoc topside . . . and making second- and third-generation vamps to restore the broken ranks on every continent of the globe. Damali was supposed to combat that nexus of evil, and he was to protect her, as well as keep his soul ever elevating toward the light. Bullshit. How?

He glimpsed Damali's concerned expression as she came to him and sat down before him. He cast away her worries from his mental space as he continued to study the midnight-blue Heaven. She couldn't fix this. Nobody could. There was no sense in bringing her down. Time was not on his side, and soon there'd be no getting around the issue. If he didn't comply, the Vampire Council would figure out his duplicity, yet again. It wouldn't be long until they found out that he loved her so much that all their power didn't matter—that he'd been playing them, kicking game hard. He respected that they weren't stupid, only power drunk; there was a difference. But what if the shit got good to him? He wasn't above being seduced; he'd learned that much in Brazil. Even an old priest felt that coming . . . so did his woman.

Plus, the council already knew his weak spot—her. Already knew he had a soul caught between the upper and lower realms. They also had operatives everywhere. He couldn't play both ends against the middle forever. The only sliver of hope was what he'd told them about her; if she continued to sense he had a soul in Purgatory, she'd willingly stay at his side. But that would only buy seven years of temporary amnesty—maybe. After that . . .

Carlos sighed, his gaze set harder on the dark horizon. These three nights were only a military-type furlough for what the Vampire Council considered a job well done. He had twenty-seven more nights, and then his reality would permanently change. One month's leave to overindulge in the hedonistic pleasures of the earth—then they wanted him down on six, handling business from a power throne. A month. That was only a whisper in time when one considered eternity. A deep sadness filled him.

A part of him also grieved the loss of the Amazon—he could relate to her pain, her anger, and her righteous indignation . . . and even understand what had sent her down the wrong path. That much they shared in common; not knowing the full consequences of their actions before it was too late, then having no way to retreat from a very bad choice. Not to mention, all the people Damali had spoken of would be at extreme risk if he didn't somehow figure out a way to play this hand right. More important, she'd be at risk to his ever-darkening self.

"Seriously, baby. What's the matter?" Her voice was so tender it hurt to hear it.

"Nothing," he finally said in a far-off tone. "I just have a lot on my mind." That truth was as mirth-killing as the thought of what it would be like to, for once, hold her near and have her be able to listen to the sound of his heartbeat.

He watched the sudden joy in her vanish, stealing her playfulness away as the blue-white light of the moon glowed against her skin, making her appear to be an angel. Her bare feet against the damp grass, a sheath of white silk covering her . . . she was, in his mind, an angel. A wild, off-the-hook, sexy variable that had blessed him with her temporary company. But what was an angel doing with a dark entity like him?

"I'ma need to take you home, soon," he said quietly, as she leaned forward and touched his cheek with a worried look in her eyes.

"Why? *Pourquoi?* The night is young, and you've just spoiled me rotten with all that food in there . . . mangoes, and—"

"Because it's late," he said gently, touching her hair, lifting her locks over her shoulders and studying their soft beauty in his hands. "The Vampire Council knows my situation and probably how I feel about you, which they'll leverage against me soon. The Covenant will be looking for me. Right now, I'm only allowed this little bit of freedom because the Vampire Council knows you're safer with me than anyone or anything else topside at the moment. And, sooner or later, you've got work to do, too."

"And why is that a problem?" She tilted her head to the side, her eyes searching his. "If the Vampire Council thinks you're protecting their cargo, and the Covenant is happy with the eleven-hundred souls weight you just helped deliver, and all the recent demon conquests worked out fine, then—"

"Because I'm getting too used to this. One night I might not wanna let you go. That could be dangerous for us both."

She shrugged and kissed him gently. "I might not want to go one night when you should let me go, and I oughta leave. But that's a problem years away. Seven years away. I'm a big girl, and can handle myself. Learn to enjoy the moment, mon, every delicious beat in de music."

She smiled, even though it was tinged with sadness. She'd tried to make him laugh by badly mimicking Kamal's accent—but it wasn't working. Defeated, her shoulders sagged and she stroked his arm.

"Carlos, tomorrow, something else could happen, so . . . so flow with the beat while we have one."

He kissed her softly and took her hand, intent on ending what was becoming another serious addiction. "I can't feel certain beats, especially not the heart ones. Okay?"

She nodded, motioning toward the edge of the cliff with her chin. "Try something with me, and then I promise I'll go home." She stood and held out her hand to him.

He sighed, accepted her palm within his, and got up to follow her. She was so wonderfully exasperating at times, but she had no concept of what was going on behind the scenes, or how badly he wanted to make her live forever.

"Come over here, near the edge of this cliff so we can see the water. Then, sit down, and loop your legs over mine like this," she ordered, smoothing out the sheath of white silk nightgown over both their legs. "There's an old Ethiopian proverb: he who conceals his disease cannot be cured. Let me work on you with a little balm, okay?"

"All right, then what?" He smiled, despite his determination to remain somber. Even the contrast of what they had on said it all. Her white silk gown; his black silk pajama pants. Same fabric, but way different energies.

"Listen to the waves . . . and match your hand up with mine, but don't touch it. Just hold it close." She inhaled the salt air that rode on the breeze.

He complied, now intrigued. He knew Kamal and Marlene had taught her some new stuff, but to experience it was a curiosity that he couldn't resist. He could taste the salt in the air with her. That wasn't new, but in this context, it was working on his resolve to send her away. Yeah, he was definitely fascinated. Perhaps something more than that, as he watched her take slow breaths, and those wide brown irises of hers began to fade behind her pupils. In the moonlight, she was stunning.

"D, you know I can't do this, not with your eyes, and—"

"Shush," she whispered. "Listen to the waves. Relax. Concentrate. Breathe slowly and easy. Become one with the sound."

A slow heat formed in the center of his palm after a while, the sound of the surf pulsing in it. Her hand came nearer, only millimeters from his, and he could almost swear a mild current ran between both their splayed palms. But her eyes, just listing to the waves and searching the depths of them . . . hearing her heart, too, echo that same rhythm. He'd seen so much, but not this with her. Across the miles it was different, just a vibe, a thought transference. This was something so profound that he wasn't sure how to react to it. He knew of the balm technique, how to do it, how to send the feeling of platonic healing like he did with the were, or the sudden heat of seduction without direct touch, but had never experienced this calm bonding with her. Then she shut her eyes and moved her hand to the center of his bare chest and pressed against it slowly. Warmth radiated within him, sending peace, and love, and simple joy so sacred that he was forced to close his eyes to experience it. Reverence followed.

It felt like her hand was throbbing where it landed, but the sensation came from within the hollow cavity he owned. The internal muscles around where her hand lay constricted to the same steady cadence of a throb, like a pulse, like the ocean slamming against the cliffs, then receding. Startled, he opened his eyes, and laid his hand over her heart in response.

He could feel everything he'd ever dreamed that was good and right leave him and enter her, pick up her thudding heart rhythm, and reenter him. They sat that way for a long time, emotion welling in him to the point where moisture crept to his eyes. She'd shared her pulse. Her essence of life. His dreams and caring ran through her, passed through her aorta, and entered his, like a shared value, giving, receiving in a closed-loop exchange.

"See," she finally murmured. "It's all good. You have a heartbeat . . . you can feel things."

"It's in the palm of your hand," he whispered, awed.

"And in your skin," she said quietly.

"And in your thoughts."

She nodded. "In your touch."

He traced her jaw. "You still want to go home?"

She smiled. "That was what you wanted."

"Did I?"

She chuckled. "Uhmmm-hmmm."

"My bad." He looked at her, allowing his finger to trace her collarbone under the moonlight. She was right. His thoughts were hers and hers had become his in the sensual transfer, the sharing of her pulse. Now the throb burned somewhere else.

"See how synched up we are?"

He smiled, tracing her arm with the flat of his palm. "Want me to show you another way to synch up?"

"My wish came true," she murmured with a smile, breaking the three-knotted bracelet around her wrist that a child in Salvador had given her, then tossed it over the cliff into the sea.

He nodded. "Just local superstition, baby."

She looked at this man who'd been willing to give his soul for her, and twice she'd almost lost him to forces so dark that it made her shudder. She let her eyes leave his to trail down his chest and settle on the brand. No, he was hers, marked, and she wasn't about to let go of him without a fight. She would claim him for herself, as well as for her side . . . just like Marlene had said to, with authority.

"Yeah . . . might be a silly superstition, but it may be good luck, anyway. Who knows?" She looked up at him, captured by his intense, sensual stare. "You want me to leave you?"

He shook his head. "Naahhh, we've still got time."

Turn the page for a sneak peek at the next Vampire Huntress Legend novel

COMING IN JANUARY 2005

The Lair in St. Lucia . . .

"TELL ME your darkest fantasy," she murmured against his ear, gently pulling the lobe between her teeth.

Carlos smiled with his eyes still closed, too exhausted to do much else. Damali sounded so wickedly sexy, but why did women always go there searching for answers to questions they really didn't want to hear in bed? "I don't have any, except being with you."

"Tell me," she pleaded low and throaty, her voice so seductive that he'd swear she was all vamp.

No. He was not going to go there, no matter what. He was not going to stare into those big brown eyes of hers and get hypnotized by them. Dark fantasies. She had no idea what went through a master's mind. Despite himself, his smile broadened, although he was still not looking at her. The things he'd seen . . . *sheeit.* Had she any concept of the lifetimes of male vampire knowledge he'd acquired from Kemet through Rome and beyond, just by being offered a Council seat?

He stroked her still damp back, his fingers reveling in the tingling sensation her tattoo created as he touched the base of her spine, hoping she'd let his love be enough to satisfy her.

"You're my fantasy," he finally said to appease her when she became morbidly silent. But he'd also meant what he'd said, albeit skillfully avoiding the question she'd really asked. "You're this dead man's dream come true, baby."

Her response was a chuckle, followed by an expulsion of hot breath down the shaft of his ear canal. "Liar," she whispered, as she slid her body onto his. "I know where you want to go."

"D . . ." he murmured, too tired to argue with her, and much too compromised by her warmth to avoid being stirred by her butter softness. "C'mon, girl . . . stop playing."

His hand continued to stroke her back, finding the deep sway in it that gave rise to her firm, tight bottom. He allowed his fingers to leisurely play at the slit that separated its halves, enjoying the moistness that he knew he'd created there. Her immediate sigh made him shudder and seek her mouth to kiss her gently, half hoping to shut her up, half hoping to derail his own darkening thoughts. Without resistance, she deepened their kiss, rewarding his senses with a hint of mango, the merest trace of red wine, and her own sweetness fused with his salty aftermath as his tongue searched the soft interiors around it.

Damn, this woman was fine . . . five feet seven inches worth of buff curves packaged in flawless bronze skin, lush mouth, brunette locks that kissed her shoulders, and a shea oil scent that was working him. It always did. He breathed in the fragrances held by her still-damp scalp, vanilla, coconut oils, and then there was also the scent of heavy, pungent sex hanging in the air.

"You always smell *so* good," he murmured, kissing the edge of her jaw. He could still taste her on his mouth when he licked his lips, "Hmmm . . ." Sticky, sweet-salty, female. The way she breathed against his neck, and her head found the crook of his shoulder, she fit so perfectly, like a handmade blanket on him. Even exhausted, her slick wetness made him want to move just to maintain their friction, their pulse. Merely thinking about it made him hard again.

"I know you have to eat," she said in a husky tone against the sensitive part of his throat, her tongue trailing up his jugular vein, causing him to tighten his hold on her.

"Yeah, I do . . . in a few," he admitted quietly, now too distracted to go out hunting at the moment.

The way she tilted her hips forward, ever so slightly, a tease, an offering, just a contraction of the muscles beneath her bronze skin fought with the hunger and was winning. They'd been at it all night, and he glimpsed the moonlight that washed over her high behind through the deck opening. Silver blue hues shimmered on her smooth ass, and he touched the light with his fingers a millimeter above her skin. She shivered at the almost-touch. That was always her most powerful weapon; her reaction to whatever he was doing to her just blew him away. One more round and he'd have to go before dawn trapped and starved him.

"What's *your* darkest fantasy?" he said smiling, turning the question on her, and not caring that a little fang was beginning to show with his smile. He passed his tongue over his incisors, willing patience as he played the game that she seemed to be enjoying.

Damali brought her head up to stare into his eyes with a mischievous smirk. "My darkest fantasy is fulfilling yours."

He laughed low and deep and slow. "Yeah?" He raised an eyebrow in a challenge. "But I don't have any really dark fantasies . . . this is all I need."

"Liar," she said again, chuckling from within her throat and planting a wet kiss on his Adam's apple in a way that made him swallow hard. "I bet I know what it is, even if you won't tell me."

"This is working just fine," he murmured, tracing her sides and finding both of her breasts to gently cradle.

"But there's always more," she whispered, lowering her mouth to roughly suckle one of his nipples.

"Curiosity killed the cat," he told her arching, trying to penetrate her without success.

"But satisfaction brought her back." She lifted her head and stared at him hard, her smile strained with anticipation, her expression one of unmasked desire.

For a moment, neither of them spoke. The exchange was telepathic, electric, and he found her neck, kissed it hard, then her shoulder, licking a path down her collarbone. When she moaned, he almost lost it and bit her.

"Tell me what you want," he murmured hot against her breast, before pulling a taut nipple between his lips.

Her inhale was a deep hiss, a sound that traveled through his body, igniting his want for her that never seemed to disappear. Whatever she asked for, he'd give her one last time before dawn. Didn't she already know, *por ella seria capaz de cualquier cosa?* Yeah, he would do anything for her. "Tell me," he whispered, "and it's done."

"I've already told you," she said in a rasp, moving to allow him to slip inside her, then contracting around him before withdrawing.

"You have no idea . . . what you're doing to me." That was the pure truth. A scent that had been locked in the deep registers of his mind filtered into his awareness, gradually at first, and then stronger until it was all-consuming. Every inhalation now was riddled with the maddening aphrodisiac that he'd sworn he'd forget—had to—but it moved his body, banished a portion of his control. Master or not, Neteru was entering his system and slaying him.

Her skin had a sheen of perspiration on it, and she slid against him like water flowing over rocks, liquid fire motion, hips undulating in a slow, rolling current, with eddies that spontaneously spun, lurched, took him in to the hilt, then washed him ashore. His tightening grip would each time be enough to summon his return to her warm, wet center, only to be cast ashore by her fickle tide again and again, until he flipped her on her back and was done playing.

"Enough." There was no play in his tone. He was beyond games as he stared into her eyes; saw a glow of red reflected back from her dark brown irises, knowing it came from his. Her scent bathed him, made him shut his eyes tight as he breathed in deeply and entered her hard. "*This* is what I want."

His fingers tangled in her velvet spun locks, and her arches finally met him in a rhythm they both knew by heart—no stopping, no teasing, just hard down, uninterrupted returns until he felt his gums give way to the incisors he could no longer hold in check, no more than he could hold back the inevitable convulsion of pleasure that was about to rip through his groin.

Nuzzling his throat, her fingers wound through his hair, and he was surprised by the force of her pull, that her fingers had made a fist at the nape of his neck, and that one of her palms slid against his jaw to push his head back, her breath on his throat in the way he'd always imagined. Trembling with need, the sensation was so damned good . . . if only . . . she could . . . just once . . . *Oh, baby* . . .

Then she suddenly shifted her weight, her legs a leveraging vise, and rolled on top of him. Her strength came from nowhere. It happened so quickly. A sharp strike as fast as a cobra's tore at his throat, making him shut his eyes harder, his gasp fused with a groan that transformed into a wail, and the pull that siphoned his throat sent the convulsion of ecstasy throughout his system, emptied his scrotum until his body dry heaved, made his lashes flutter from the rapid seizure, where every pull from her lips erupted hot seed from him into her. Sheets gathered in knots within his fists before his hand again sought her skin, shards of color ricocheted behind his lids while he cradled her in his arms, stuttering through tears, *"Don't stop . . . take it all."*

His body went hot, then cold, minutes of unrelenting pleasure—her hold indomitable, a physical lock of sheer will, as she moved her hips in a lazy rhythm, ignoring his attempt to rush her with deep thrusts and staccato jerks, his voice foreign to him as it reverberated off the walls of the lair, echoed back, and taunted him . . . a master vampire . . . done for the first time, for real, by what could only be a female vamp. *A master female.* One conjured from his darkest fantasy, riding him with more than skill, precision, working his ass to the bone—slow torture that he couldn't stop, even if he'd wanted to.

Winded, siphoned, turned out, he could barely open his eyes but he had to. Which one of them had taken Damali's place, stolen her form? Daaayum, his territory had some shit with it . . . but never in his wildest dreams would he have imagined it to be like this. If Damali ever found out . . . and how did this female get in here? Where was D!

She smiled, looking down at him, and wiped her mouth with the back of her hand.

"Who made you, baby?" Dazed, that was all he could ask.

"You did," she said, chuckling low, and pressing an index finger over one of his streaming bite wounds to seal it. Then she slowly licked her finger and smiled before sealing the other so he wouldn't entirely bleed out.

Carlos blinked twice, staring. "Damali?" Two inches of fang glistened crimson in the moonlight within her lovely mouth, and a thin red line of blood had dribbled down her chin between her breasts. He resisted the urge to sit up and lick the dark trail up to her stained lips.

"Who else?" She shook her head, sat back with him still in her, and folded her arms over her chest. "Oh, so you had some other Jane on your mind while I was working?"

"No . . . oh . . . shit . . ."

He grabbed her by the hips, and extricated himself from her to stand, stumbling a bit, but he needed motion—fatigue and the siphon, notwithstanding. He had to break the physical contact with her. The pleasure wave of aftershocks were impairing his judgment, and if he bit her in this condition, he'd flat-line her for sure. Even standing away from her, he could still feel her hot seal. "No, no, no, no, no—this *cannot* be happening."

He could feel panic bubbling within him, and he had never been a brother to outright freak about anything. But this, of all the things he'd seen and been through so far, was scaring the shit out of him.

"No!" he said fast, walking in a circle, then going from the deck back to the side of the bed, gesturing with his hands in a naked frenzy. "Something went wrong. I have to get you back to the guardians—to Marlene, your Mom . . . baby, you're turning—"

"Turned," she sighed with a smile, "and I love it. Relax. What's done is done."

"Oh, my God, D—"

When she hissed and held both sides of her head and glared at him, he could feel hot tears begin to form in his eyes. He could call on the Almighty, but the Neteru couldn't? What the hell had he done?

Visit www.vampirehuntress.com for more.